ELEMENTS OF FICTION

ELEMENTS

OF FICTION

INTRODUCTION TO THE SHORT STORY

Jack Carpenter
Kansas State University

Peter Neumeyer
State University of New York at Stony Brook

WM. C. BROWN COMPANY PUBLISHERS
Dubuque, Iowa

Copyright © 1974 by Wm. C. Brown Company Publishers

Library of Congress Catalog Card Number: 73—93149

ISBN 0—697—03713—4

All rights reserved. No part of this publication may be reproduced, stored in a retrieval system, or transmitted, in any form or by any means, electronic, mechanical, photocopying, recording, or otherwise, without the prior written permission of the copyright owner.

Printed in the United States of America

*For Claire, Jessica, Zack,
Christopher, and Dan.*

Contents

PREFACE — ix

CHAPTER 1 / SUSPENSE AND TINGLES — 1

Edgar Allen Poe
    The Facts in the Case of M. Valdemar — 4
    Discussion and Questions, 11

Ambrose Bierce
    The Boarded Window — 14
    Discussion and Questions, 18

READING THE SHORT STORY — 18

Joyce Carol Oates
    Where Are You Going, Where Have You Been — 22
    Discussion and Questions, 36

CHAPTER 2 / PLOT — 38

Thomas Hardy
    The Three Strangers — 41
    Discussion, 59

STORIES WITHOUT PLOT — 63

Anton Chekhov
    Gusev — 65
    Discussion, 76

CHAPTER 3 / CHARACTERS — 78

James Joyce
    A Little Cloud — 84
    Discussion and Questions, 96

Doris Lessing
    The Black Madonna — 97
    Discussion and Questions, 109

CHAPTER 4 / SYMBOL — 112

W. S. Merwin
    The Medal of Disapproval — 116
        Discussion and Questions, 117

John Barth
    Night Sea Journey — 118
        Discussion and Questions, 125

Franz Kafka
    Jackals and Arabs — 127
        Discussion and Questions, 130

Nathaniel Hawthorne
    My Kinsman, Major Molineux — 133
        Discussion and Questions, 148

CHAPTER 5 / THEME AND TONE — 151

The Book of Ruth (from *the Bible*) — 153
    Discussion, 158

Yukio Mishima
    Patriotism — 159
        Discussion and Questions, 179

CHAPTER 6 / POINT OF VIEW — 181

James Baldwin
    Going to Meet the Man — 187
        Discussion and Questions, 201

Julio Cortázar
    End of the Game — 203
        Discussion and Questions, 212

Edouard Roditi
    The Vampires of Istanbul: A Study in Modern
    Communications Methods — 214
        Discussion and Questions, 230

CHAPTER 7 / ADDITIONAL STORIES — 232
Stephen Crane

Contents

The Snake	232
Ngugi wa Thiong'o	
A Meeting in the Dark	235
Flannery O'Connor	
Good Country People	247
Heinrich Böll	
The Balek Scales	264
D. H. Lawrence	
Tickets Please	271
Eudora Welty	
A Still Moment	282
E. M. Forster	
Mr Andrews	293
Ted Hughes	
Sunday	297
Michael Thelwell	
The Organizer	308
Peter Taylor	
Venus, Cupid, Folly and Time	331
William Faulkner	
Barn Burning	355
Guy de Maupassant	
Love: Three Pages from a Sportsman's Book	371
Nathaniel Hawthorne	
Wakefield	376
Nahid Rachlin	
Shadow Play	384
Alan Sillitoe	
The Loneliness of the Long-Distance Runner	389
Jorge Luis Borges	
The Unworthy Friend	420
Rudyard Kipling	
The Gardener	426

GLOSSARY OF LITERARY TERMS   **435**

Preface

This book develops from two closely related beliefs: first, that the chief purpose of art is to give pleasure; second, that as we increase our knowledge of an art, we increase the pleasure it gives us.

Love, sex, and marriage were not devised by the good God in order that there might be courses in "Family Living" in high schools and colleges. And similarly, no story worthy of the name was ever written or told so that it might be "learned" in a classroom. Stories are conceived to delight. They may delight by looking good, reading well, causing pleasant associations, or stimulating anticipations. They may delight too by increasing readers' understanding and appreciation—understanding and appreciation not only of the stories themselves, but of the reader's own life, love, surroundings, and experiences.

The stories in this volume were carefully selected for their capacity to delight readers, especially student readers. There are old stories here and new ones; stories by famous authors and by young writers just beginning their careers; there are stories by "teachable" old standbys such as Maupassant, Hawthorne, and Hardy, and challenging, rarer specimens by Ngugi wa Thiong'o, Cortázar, and Roditi; there are stories from Europe, Asia, Latin America, Africa, and the United States. This text offers a great variety of moods, themes, tones, techniques, thoughts, and characters, as well as a large and sufficiently diverse selection to please varying tastes. We are particularly pleased that despite the great diversity of stories, there are no "dogs" here; each story is good, and most, we think, are excellent

In making our selections we have also chosen stories with an eye to juxtaposition and to relationships. The stories in some measure shed light on each other; and the understanding and the insight given the reader by one story will at times cause an understanding, a realization, an insight, as regards another story. We suggest several stories for comparison in the text and in the teacher's manual, but the teacher will find many other possible combinations.

Finally, we have chosen stories that are worth teaching, stories that help the student increase his reading pleasure by helping him understand the techniques of fiction. One of the strengths of this book is that it directly confronts the task of teaching the inexperienced reader how to read and enjoy the modern "plotless" story, the kind of story about which students often remark, "I didn't like it. Nothing happened."

We want students to come to these stories fresh, their minds free from "accepted critical opinion," so that they may form their own critical judgments and arrive at their own insights. Our teaching experiences have convinced us that a textbook for undergraduates can be overburdened with apparatus, with learned comment that prejudices (and sometimes confuses) the inexperienced reader. So we have attempted, without being pushy or getting in the way, to provide students with just enough discussion and stimulating questions to assist them unobtrusively to enjoy what is there in a story, to perhaps help them catch what they just might have missed without a nudge from us. At the same time we have attempted to discuss the larger principles of story construction in general. The instructor may, of course, change the order of chapters if, for example, he or she prefers to discuss theme and tone before character or plot. Our only recommendation is that students read Chapter 1, "Suspense and Tingles," before going on to other stories because Chapter 1 serves as a general introduction to the entire volume.

We also believe that students need to have examples before them of how to write about fiction, how to apply a critical method; therefore, we have included several extended analyses of stories. At the same time we have reserved much of the critical commentary for the instructor's manual, leaving scope for the ingenuity and insight of the individual teacher.

Finally, and perhaps most important, we want to emphasize that literary analysis is not an arcane discipline known only to English teachers, but a commonsense way of looking at what we read. We show the student that the questions he asks about a life experience can profitably be asked about a reading experience. And the questions he or she learns to ask from the reading may, indeed, help the student cope more understandingly with the vagaries of life in general. In other words, "delight" in reading should have echoes in the larger context of life as it is lived.

Chapter 1

SUSPENSE AND TINGLES

"And what happened next?" That is our response when we are told about an exciting event—a robbery, a shipwreck, a romance. No one knows *why* human beings want to know what happened next, but they do. We are just plain curious. And not only do we want to know what happened in a robbery, a shipwreck or a romance; we want to know what happens next in stories about imaginary people doing imaginary things. Even very little children want to know "Did Mr. McGregor make rabbit stew out of Peter Rabbit?" "Did the man with the steam drill win the contest against John Henry and his sledge hammer?" "What happened next?" "Who won?" "Who dun'it?" So goes the refrain, and as long as people have asked such questions, someone has invented a tale to tell them. It is surely not an exaggeration to say that there is in human beings a basic urge to hear stories.

In addition to wanting to know what happened next, we also want stories to arouse us emotionally, to heighten our feelings. Children seated at night around a campfire or in a darkened room at a slumber party invariably tell ghost stories, the spookier the better. They seem to enjoy having their nerves jangled, teased, tensed, and exhausted. It is difficult to explain why anyone would want to be frightened—but sometimes we do, as attested by the number of "horror" movies at local theaters and "chiller" shows on TV. Fright is not the only emotion that people like to have aroused by stories and movies. How many readers have praised a story because it gave them "a good cry" or "made them feel good"? The point is, of course, that stories affect us, or to be more precise, stories create effects in us; they can make us feel intensely, and not just in obvious ways, but also in very subtle, complex ones.

But you don't need a book of instruction to teach you to ask "what happened next?" You don't need a teacher to teach you to feel curiosity, suspense, or horror. Either a story holds your attention or it doesn't. If stories gave only these simple pleasures, you would not need a class on the short story, or even this "introduction." You could read some stories merely for fun and not be bugged by teacherly questions and belabored by academic terms. Stories, however, do more than titillate us. They do more than give us happy endings and sympathetic heroes to please our private fantasies. Good stories challenge readers intellectually, emotionally, aesthetically, and morally. They require of readers a degree of thoughtful participation in the complex fictional worlds they represent. They make us feel—and *think*. They help us see what we have never seen before, and experience the familiar in new ways. A good story can jolt readers with all the impact and confusion of life itself.

Good stories also make demands on the reader, and in order to meet these demands, we need to learn to ask more than "what happened next?" We need to learn what stories do and how they do it, and we need to acquire a vocabulary that helps us to ask trenchant questions and make precise statements.

The poet John Ciardi once wrote an insightful and rather lengthy explanation of Robert Frost's seemingly simple poem, "Stopping by Woods on a Snowy Evening." Shortly thereafter he was inundated with letters telling him, in effect, that he was "murdering to dissect." "Get your big feet off my miracle," people wrote him. "You're spoiling a good thing by analyzing it." "I enjoyed the poem until you made a job of it." That was the spirit of the responses. Very wisely John Ciardi explained in reply that he wasn't murdering to dissect at all, but was analyzing in order to better understand and appreciate. Similarly, we all enjoy the soar and glide of a seagull, but the aeronautical engineer (who understands the principles of flight) may be in an even *better* position to see the beauty of that flight than is the layman. The aeronautical engineer knows the physical principles involved, and the miracle may seem to him even *more* miraculous than it does to others.

In a way, this same idea is the excuse for the present book. We may all enjoy a walk through the woods. But if we know something of the miraculous strength of seedlings pushing their way up to the light—well, then we have one more thing to enjoy. If we are alert to the chattering panic signals of the chipmunk and the squirrel, we have one more thing to hear. If we know the relationships among the various forest funguses and their hosts, we have one more thing to observe and to enrich our forest walk. Similarly, who can deny that a sailor alert to the interplay of

Suspense and Tingles

wind and waves has far more to watch, to see, to experience, than does his landlubber passenger. Each may be fully enjoying himself; but the man who knows what he is seeing is undoubtedly enjoying more things than his unknowing friend. The expert *sees* more because he *knows* more.

So, too, with literature—in our case, with stories. We all may enjoy a good yarn. But if, in addition, we have learned to recognize some of the virtuoso techniques of story telling, our enjoyment of the tale, far from being diminished, should be enhanced. It can even be argued that a better reader of stories is a better understander of human beings, and therefore may become a better human being. (The true test for this argument will be your own introspection after you have read many stories and perhaps been moved by some of them.)

In presenting a rather stringently abridged vocabulary for talking about literature, the editors are not giving you names to learn for learning's sake. It is our object to enhance your enjoyment of stories by bringing to the level of explicit consciousness some things you may be *feeling* about stories anyway, but for which you may not yet have words. You may sense a *mood,* a *tone,* even a *symbol;* and having acquired words for what you may be vaguely sensing, you may be better able to express to yourself your own feelings about a story that moves you.

Our objectives largely then are to give you more to enjoy, and to raise your level of awareness or of sensitivity when you do read stories, so that you will gain pleasure from things you might previously have bypassed. We want you to have two kinds of responses to the stories in this collection: first, the direct experience of reading for enjoyment; second, the conscious, analytical response based on the skills you acquire as you read more and more stories.

The first two stories in this collection are tales of horror and suspense, written by two masters of this type, Edgar Allen Poe and Ambrose Bierce. Both stories deal with the indispensable subject of horror tales—death; both build to surprise endings; both make only moderate demands on the reader. Neither is concerned with making profound statements about the human condition or with providing new knowledge about death. They are tales told purely for the delight of the reader; so the first time you read them, let the stories work on you, take you in. Then, on second reading, look for footprints the authors have left along the path to the surprise endings. Look for the techniques Poe uses to create the effects he seeks; try to figure out how Bierce manipulates the reader so that he is truly shocked at the story's conclusion.

The Facts in the Case of M. Valdemar

Edgar Allan Poe

Of course I shall not pretend to consider it any matter for wonder, that the extraordinary case of M. Valdemar has excited discussion. It would have been a miracle had it not—especially under the circumstances. Through the desire of all parties concerned, to keep the affair from the public, at least for the present, or until we had farther opportunities for investigation—through our endeavors to effect this—a garbled or exaggerated account made its way into society, and became the source of many unpleasant misrepresentations; and, very naturally, of a great deal of disbelief.

It is now rendered necessary that I give the facts—as far as I comprehend them myself. They are, succinctly, these:

My attention, for the last three years, had been repeatedly drawn to the subject of Mesmerism; and, about nine months ago, it occurred to me, quite suddenly, that in the series of experiments made hitherto, there had been a very remarkable and most unaccountable omission:—no person had as yet been mesmerized *in articulo mortis.* It remained to be seen, first, whether, in such condition, there existed in the patient any susceptibility to the magnetic influence; secondly, whether, if any existed, it was impaired or increased by the condition; thirdly, to what extent, or for how long a period, the encroachments of Death might be arrested by the process. There were other points to be ascertained, but these most ex-

From *The Works of Edgar Allen Poe,* vol. 2. New York: P. F. Collier and Sons, 1903.

cited my curiosity—the last in especial, from the immensely important character of its consequences.

In looking around me for some subject by whose means I might test these particulars, I was brought to think of my friend, M. Ernest Valdemar, the well-known compiler of the "Bibliotheca Forensica," and author (under the *nom de plume* of Issachar Marx) of the Polish versions of "Wallenstein" and "Gargantua." M. Valdemar, who has resided principally at Harlem, N. Y., since the year 1839, is (or was) particularly noticeable for the extreme spareness of his person—his lower limbs much resembling those of John Randolph; and, also, for the whiteness of his whiskers, in violent contrast to the blackness of his hair—the latter, in consequence, being very generally mistaken for a wig. His temperament was markedly nervous, and rendered him a good subject for mesmeric experiment. On two or three occasions I had put him to sleep with little difficulty, but was disappointed in other results which his peculiar constitution had naturally led me to anticipate. His will was at no period positively, or thoroughly, under my control, and in regard to *clairvoyance,* I could accomplish with him nothing to be relied upon. I always attributed my failure at these points to the disordered state of his health. For some months previous to my becoming acquainted with him, his physicians had declared him in a confirmed phthisis. It was his custom, indeed, to speak calmly of his approaching dissolution, as of a matter neither to be avoided nor regretted.

When the ideas to which I have alluded first occurred to me, it was of course very natural that I should think of M. Valdemar. I knew the steady philosophy of the man too well to apprehend any scruples from *him;* and he had no relatives in America who would be likely to interfere. I spoke to him frankly upon the subject; and, to my surprise, his interest seemed vividly excited. I say to my surprise; for, although he had always yielded his person freely to my experiments, he had never before given me any tokens of sympathy with what I did. His disease was of that character which would admit of exact calculation in respect to the epoch of its termination in death; and it was finally arranged between us that he would send for me about twenty-four hours before the period announced by his physicians as that of his decease.

It is now rather more than seven months since I received, from M. Valdemar himself, the subjoined note:

MY DEAR P——,
    You may as well come *now.* D—— and F—— are agreed that I cannot hold out beyond to-morrow midnight; and I think they have hit the time very nearly.
                                                                                            VALDEMAR.

I received this note within half an hour after it was written, and in fifteen minutes more I was in the dying man's chamber. I had not seen him for ten days, and was appalled by the fearful alteration which the brief interval had wrought in him. His face wore a leaden hue; the eyes were utterly lustreless; and the emaciation was so extreme, that the skin had been broken through by the cheekbones. His expectoration was excessive. The pulse was barely perceptible. He retained, nevertheless, in a very remarkable manner, both his mental power and a certain degree of physical strength. He spoke with distinctness—took some palliative medicines without aid—and, when I entered the room, was occupied in penciling memoranda in a pocket-book. He was propped up in the bed by pillows. Doctors D—— and F—— were in attendance.

After pressing Valdemar's hand, I took these gentlemen aside, and obtained from them a minute account of the patient's condition. The left lung had been for eighteen months in a semi-osseous or cartilaginous state, and was, of course, entirely useless for all purposes of vitality. The right, in its upper portion, was also partially, if not thoroughly, ossified, while the lower region was merely a mass of purulent tubercles, running one into another. Several extensive perforations existed; and, at one point, permanent adhesion to the ribs had taken place. These appearances in the right lobe were of comparatively recent date. The ossification had proceeded with very unusual rapidity; no sign of it had been discovered a month before, and the adhesion had only been observed during the three previous days. Independently of the phthisis, the patient was suspected of aneurysm of the aorta; but on this point the osseous symptoms rendered an exact diagnosis impossible. It was the opinion of both physicians that M. Valdemar would die about midnight on the morrow (Sunday). It was then seven o'clock on Saturday evening.

On quitting the invalid's bed-side to hold conversation with myself, Doctors D—— and F—— had bidden him a final farewell. It had not been their intention to return; but, at my request, they agreed to look in upon the patient about ten the next night.

When they had gone, I spoke freely with M. Valdemar on the subject of his approaching dissolution, as well as, more particularly, of the experiment proposed. He still professed himself quite willing and even anxious to have it made, and urged me to commence it at once. A male and a female nurse were in attendance; but I did not feel myself altogether at liberty to engage in a task of this character with no more reliable witnesses than these people, in case of sudden accident, might prove. I therefore postponed operations until about eight the next night, when the arrival of a medical student, with whom I had some acquaintance (Mr. Theodore L——l), relieved me from farther embarrassment. It had been my design, originally, to wait for the physicians; but I was induced to proceed, first by the urgent entreaties of M. Valdemar, and secondly, by my conviction that I had not a moment to lose, as he was evidently sinking fast.

Mr. L——l was so kind as to accede to my desire that he would take notes of all that occurred; and it is from his memoranda that what I now have to relate is, for the most part, either condensed or copied *verbatim.*

It wanted about five minutes of eight when, taking the patient's hand, I begged him to state, as distinctly as he could, to Mr. L——l, whether he (M. Valdemar) was entirely willing that I should make the experiment of mesmerizing him in his then condition.

He replied feebly, yet quite audibly, "Yes, I wish to be mesmerized" —adding immediately afterwards, "I fear you have deferred it too long."

While he spoke thus, I commenced the passes which I had already found most effectual in subduing him. He was evidently influenced with the first lateral stroke of my hand across his forehead; but although I exerted all my powers, no farther perceptible effect was induced until some minutes after ten o'clock, when Doctors D—— and F—— called, according to appointment. I explained to them, in a few words, what I designed, and as they opposed no objection, saying that the patient was already in the death agony, I proceeded without hesitation—exchanging, however, the lateral passes for downward ones, and directing my gaze entirely into the right eye of the sufferer.

By this time his pulse was imperceptible and his breathing was stertorous, and at intervals of half a minute.

This condition was nearly unaltered for a quarter of an hour. At the expiration of this period, however, a natural although a very deep sigh escaped the bosom of the dying man, and the stertorous breathing ceased —that is to say, its stertorousness was no longer apparent; the intervals were undiminished. The patient's extremities were of an icy coldness.

At five minutes before eleven, I perceived unequivocal signs of the mesmeric influence. The glassy roll of the eye was changed for that expression of uneasy *inward* examination which is never seen except in cases of sleep-waking, and which it is quite impossible to mistake. With a few rapid lateral passes I made the lids quiver, as in incipient sleep, and with a few more I closed them altogether. I was not satisfied, however, with this, but continued the manipulations vigorously, and with the fullest exertion of the will, until I had completely stiffened the limbs of the slumberer, after placing them in a seemingly easy position. The legs were at full length; the arms were nearly so, and reposed on the bed at a moderate distance from the loins. The head was very slightly elevated.

When I had accomplished this, it was fully midnight, and I requested the gentlemen present to examine M. Valdemar's condition. After a few experiments, they admitted him to be in an unusually perfect state of mesmeric trance. The curiosity of both the physicians was greatly excited. Dr. D—— resolved at once to remain with the patient all night, while Dr. F—— took leave with a promise to return at daybreak. Mr. L——l and the nurses remained.

We left M. Valdemar entirely undisturbed until about three o'clock in the morning, when I approached him and found him in precisely the same condition as when Dr. F—— went away—that is to say, he lay in the same position; the pulse was imperceptible; the breathing was gentle (scarcely noticeable, unless through the application of a mirror to the lips); the eyes were closed naturally; and the limbs were as rigid and as cold as marble. Still, the general appearance was certainly not that of death.

As I approached M. Valdemar I made a kind of half effort to influence his right arm into pursuit of my own, as I passed the latter gently to and fro above the person. In such experiments with this patient, I had never perfectly succeeded before, and assuredly I had little thought of succeeding now; but to my astonishment, his arm very readily, although feebly, followed every direction I assigned it with mine. I determined to hazard a few words of conversation.

"M. Valdemar," I said, "are you asleep?" He made no answer, but I perceived a tremor about the lips, and was thus induced to repeat the question, again and again. At its third repetition, his whole frame was agitated by a very slight shivering; the eyelids unclosed themselves so far as to display a white line of a ball; the lips moved sluggishly, and from between them, in a barely audible whisper, issued the words:

"Yes;—asleep now. Do not wake me!—let me die so!"

I here felt the limbs and found them as rigid as ever. The right arm, as before, obeyed the direction of my hand. I questioned the sleep-waker again:

"Do you still feel pain in the breast, M. Valdemar?"

The answer now was immediate, but even less audible than before:

"No pain—I am dying."

I did not think it advisable to disturb him farther just then, and nothing more was said or done until the arrival of Dr. F——, who came a little before sunrise, and expressed unbounded astonishment at finding the patient still alive. After feeling the pulse and applying a mirror to the lips, he requested me to speak to the sleep-waker again. I did so, saying:

"M. Valdemar, do you still sleep?"

As before, some minutes elapsed ere a reply was made; and during the interval the dying man seemed to be collecting his energies to speak. At my fourth repetition of the question, he said very faintly, almost inaudibly:

"Yes; still asleep—dying."

It was now the opinion, or rather the wish, of the physicians, that M. Valdemar should be suffered to remain undisturbed in his present apparently tranquil condition, until death should supervene—and this, it was generally agreed, must now take place within a few minutes. I concluded, however, to speak to him once more, and merely repeated my previous question.

While I spoke, there came a marked change over the countenance of the sleep-waker. The eyes rolled themselves slowly open, the pupils disappearing upwardly; the skin generally assumed a cadaverous hue, resembling not so much parchment as white paper; and the circular hectic spots which, hitherto, had been strongly defined in the centre of each cheek, *went out* at once. I use this expression, because the suddenness of their departure put me in mind of nothing so much as the extinguishment of a candle by a puff of the breath. The upper lip, at the same time, writhed itself away from the teeth, which it had previously covered completely; while the lower jaw fell with an audible jerk, leaving the mouth widely extended, and disclosing in full view the swollen and blackened tongue. I presume that no member of the party then present had been unaccustomed to death-bed horrors; but so hideous beyond conception was the appearance of M. Valdemar at this moment, that there was a general shrinking back from the region of the bed.

I now feel that I have reached a point of this narrative at which every reader will be startled into positive disbelief. It is my business, however, simply to proceed.

There was no longer the faintest sign of vitality in M. Valdemar; and concluding him to be dead, we were consigning him to the charge of the nurses, when a strong vibratory motion was observable in the tongue. This continued for perhaps a minute. At the expiration of this period, there issued from the distended and motionless jaw a voice—such as it would be madness in me to attempt describing. There are, indeed, two or three epithets which might be considered as applicable to it in part; I might say, for example, that the sound was harsh, and broken and hollow; but the hideous whole is indescribable, for the simple reason that no similar sounds have ever jarred upon the ear of humanity. There were two particulars, nevertheless, which I thought then, and still think, might fairly be stated as characteristic of the intonation—as well adapted to convey some idea of its unearthly peculiarity. In the first place, the voice seemed to reach our ears—at least mine—from a vast distance, or from some deep cavern within the earth. In the second place, it impressed me (I fear, indeed, that it will be impossible to make myself comprehended) as gelatinous or glutinous matters impress the sense of touch.

I have spoken both of "sound" and of "voice." I mean to say that the sound was one of distinct—of even wonderfully, thrillingly distinct—syllabification. M. Valdemar *spoke*—obviously in reply to the question I had propounded to him a few minutes before. I had asked him, it will be remembered, if he still slept. He now said:

"Yes;—no;—*I have been* sleeping—and now—now—*I am dead.*"

No person present even affected to deny, or attempted to repress, the unutterable, shuddering horror which these few words, thus uttered, were so well calculated to convey. Mr. L——l (the student) swooned. The nurses immediately left the chamber, and could not be induced to return. My own impressions I would not pretend to render intelligible to the reader. For nearly an hour, we busied ourselves, silently—without the utterance of a word—in endeavors to revive Mr. L——l. When he came to himself, we addressed ourselves again to an investigation of Valdemar's condition.

It remained in all respects as I have last described it, with the exception that the mirror no longer afforded evidence of respiration. An attempt to draw blood from the arm failed. I should mention, too, that this limb was no farther subject to my will. I endeavored in vain to make it follow the direction of my hand. The only real indication, indeed, of the mesmeric influence, was now found in the vibratory movement of the tongue, whenever I addressed M. Valdemar a question. He seemed to be making an effort to reply, but had no longer sufficient volition. To queries put to him by any other person than myself he seemed utterly insensible—although I endeavored to place each member of the company in mesmeric *rapport* with him. I believe that I have now related all that's necessary to an understanding of the sleep-waker's state at this epoch. Other nurses were procured; and at ten o'clock I left the house in company with the two physicians and Mr. L——l.

In the afternoon we all called again to see the patient. His condition remained precisely the same. We had now some discussion as to the propriety and feasibility of awakening him; but we had little difficulty in agreeing that no good purpose would be served by so doing. It was evident that, so far, death (or what is usually termed death) had been arrested by the mesmeric process. It seemed clear to us all that to awaken M. Valdemar would be merely to insure his instant, or at least his speedy dissolution.

From this period until the close of last week—*an interval of nearly seven months*—we continued to make daily calls at M. Valdermar's house, accompanied, now and then, by medical and other friends. All this time the sleep-waker remained *exactly* as I have last described him. The nurses' attentions were continual.

It was on Friday last that we finally resolved to make the experiment of awakening, or attempting to awaken him; and it is the (perhaps) unfortunate result of this latter experiment which has given rise to so much discussion in private circles—to so much of what I cannot help thinking unwarranted popular feeling.

For the purpose of relieving M. Valdemar from the mesmeric trance, I made use of the customary passes. These, for a time, were unsuccessful. The first indication of revival was afforded by a partial descent of the iris. It was observed, as especially remarkable, that this lowering of the pupil was accompanied by the profuse out-flowing of a yellowish ichor (from beneath the lids) of a pungent and highly offensive odor.

It was now suggested that I should attempt to influence the patient's arm, as heretofore. I made the attempt and failed. Dr. F—— then intimated a desire to have me put a question. I did so, as follows:

"M. Valdemar, can you explain to us what are your feelings or wishes now?"

There was an instant return of the hectic circles on the cheeks; the tongue quivered, or rather rolled violently in the mouth (although the jaws and lips remained rigid as before); and at length the same hideous voice which I have already described, broke forth:

"For God's sake!—quick!—quick!—put me to sleep—or, quick!—waken me!—quick!—*I say to you that I am dead!*"

I was thoroughly unnerved, and for an instant remained undecided what to do. At first I made an endeavor to re-compose the patient; but, failing in this through total abeyance of the will, I retraced my steps and as earnestly struggled to awaken him. In this attempt I soon saw that I should be successful—or at least I soon fancied that my success would be complete—and I am sure that all in the room were prepared to see the patient awaken.

For what really occurred, however, it is quite impossible that any human being could have been prepared.

As I rapidly made the mesmeric passes, amid ejaculations of "dead! dead!" absolutely *bursting* from the tongue and not from the lips of the sufferer, his whole frame at once—within the space of a single minute, or even less, shrunk—crumbled—absolutely rotted away beneath my hands. Upon the bed, before that whole company, there lay a nearly liquid mass of loathsome—of detestable putrescence.

■ DISCUSSION AND QUESTIONS

1. Writers of good horror tales are masterful psychologists: they know what frightens us, what makes us shudder; and they know that we are often morbidly attracted to the very things that frighten us most. In this story Poe exploits our fear of death and our curiosity about it by presenting in vivid de-

tails the death *and* decay of M. Valdemar. He also exploits our hope that "the encroachments of Death" can be delayed or that the soul exists beyond the final putrefaction of its bodily manifestation.

Are there subjects other than death that writers of horror stories and chiller movies can count on to both frighten and attract us? Why do so many people enjoy gruesome movies and terrifying tales?

2. Look closely at the language of the first paragraph of this story. Poe has filled this paragraph with words and phrases designed to tantalize the reader—"wonder," "extraordinary case," "excited discussions," "miracle," "especially under the circumstances," "disbelief"—without once revealing the nature of the "case" that has provoked so much excitement. In other words, Poe has carefully tried to draw the reader in, get him interested, without giving him any important "facts." Did this opening paragraph succeed in arousing your curiosity about what happened to Valdemar? What would have been the effect on the reader if Poe had revealed the awful truth about Valdemar's death at the beginning?

Imitating Poe's style, write an opening paragraph for this story in which you reveal the ending of the story right away. Perhaps something like this: "The death and decay of M. Valdemar, who was, prior to his demise, in a deep mesmeric state, has excited much discussion among a public possessed of few facts and agitated by many rumors. . . ."

3. "P—" claims he simply wants to give his readers a succinct account of the facts; in reality he does just the opposite. Instead of giving the facts succinctly, he has arranged them and withheld certain ones, in order to build his narrative toward a shocking climax. The fact is that Poe is cheating us, and we willingly accept his sleight of hand because his tricks please us. Notice how Poe's gamesmanship allows him to drop sneaky, teasing clues into the account of the facts. When first describing Valdemar, for instance, Poe says that he "is (or was) particularly noticeable for the extreme spareness of his person." The "is (or was)" is carefully planted to make the reader wonder, "which is it," because at this point in the story we don't know.

Newspaper articles, designed to be read quickly and easily, try to put the most important facts (Who? What? When? Where? Why?) in the opening sentence or paragraph. Write an obituary for your local campus or city newspaper announcing the death of M. Valdemar.

4. "My dear P—," writes Valdemar when he announces his impending death to the narrator of the story. "P—" obviously stands for Poe, but we should not think that the writer of this story and the fictional "teller" of it are identical. The "I" who relates the "facts" to us is himself a character in the story, a fictional "Poe" created specifically for this story. Describe "P—" and cite the words or phrases on which you base your description. What are his feelings toward his "friend" Valdemar? What were P—'s objectives in his experiment with Valdemar? How successful was he? What has prompted him to report the facts of the case?

5. Highly technical medical language can help keep a doctor emotionally detached from the personal suffering of the patient. Does the narrator of this story maintain a scientific and detached attitude through the events leading to the "detestable putrescence" that ends Valdemar's existence? What words does the narrator use to give the semblance of scientific detachment? Of course, the narrator is

telling this strange story after it happened, to set the record straight, so to speak. Has Valdemar's death meant anything to the narrator other than its being an "extraordinary case"?

6. Poe lingers over the description of Valdemar's cadaverous appearance. Is Poe's description effective? What details seem most vivid, most awful?

7. Why does the narrator so meticulously inform us of the timing of events? How much time passes between the onset of the hypnotic state and the final decay of the body? What is the effect on the reader of the information that *"an interval of nearly seven months"* has passed since the beginning of the hypnotic trance?

8. Does the reader empathize with Valdemar's personal suffering, feel strongly his last plea, "For God's sake —quick!—quick!—put me to sleep— or, quick! waken me!—quick!—*I say to you that I am dead"*? Do we feel the terror of being caught between life and death? How effective is the last image of the story?

The Boarded Window

Ambrose Bierce

In 1830, only a few miles away from what is now the great city of Cincinnati, lay an immense and almost unbroken forest. The whole region was sparsely settled by people of the frontier—restless souls who no sooner had hewn fairly habitable homes out of the wilderness and attained to that degree of prosperity which today we should call indigence than impelled by some mysterious impulse of their nature they abandoned all and pushed farther westward, to encounter new perils and privations in the effort to regain the meagre comforts which they had voluntarily renounced. Many of them had already forsaken that region for the remoter settlements, but among those remaining was one who had been of those first arriving. He lived alone in a house of logs surrounded on all sides by the great forest, of whose gloom and silence he seemed a part, for no one had ever known him to smile nor speak a needless word. His simple wants were supplied by the sale or barter of skins of wild animals in the river town, for not a thing did he grow upon the land which, if needful, he might have claimed by right of undisturbed possession. There were evidences of "improvement"—a few acres of ground immediately about the house had once been cleared of its trees, the decayed stumps of which were half concealed by the new growth that had been suffered to repair the ravage wrought by the ax. Apparently the man's zeal for agriculture had burned with a failing flame, expiring in penitential ashes.

From *The Collected Works of Ambrose Bierce,* vol. 2. New York: The Neale Publishing Company, 1909.

The Boarded Window

The little log house, with its chimney of sticks, its roof of warping clapboards weighted with traversing poles and its "chinking" of clay, had a single door and, directly opposite, a window. The latter, however, was boarded up—nobody could remember a time when it was not. And none knew why it was so closed; certainly not because of the occupant's dislike of light and air, for on those rare occasions when a hunter had passed that lonely spot the recluse had commonly been seen sunning himself on his doorstep if heaven had provided sunshine for his need. I fancy there are few persons living today who ever knew the secret of that window, but I am one, as you shall see.

The man's name was said to be Murlock. He was apparently seventy years old, actually about fifty. Something besides years had had a hand in his aging. His hair and long, full beard were white, his gray, lustreless eyes sunken, his face singularly seamed with wrinkles which appeared to belong to two intersecting systems. In figure he was tall and spare, with a stoop of the shoulders—a burden bearer. I never saw him; these particulars I learned from my grandfather, from whom also I got the man's story when I was a lad. He had known him when living nearby in that early day.

One day Murlock was found in his cabin, dead. It was not a time and place for coroners and newspapers, and I suppose it was agreed that he had died from natural causes or I should have been told, and should remember. I know only that with what was probably a sense of the fitness of things the body was buried near the cabin, alongside the grave of his wife, who had preceded him by so many years that local tradition had retained hardly a hint of her existence. That closes the final chapter of this true story—excepting, indeed, the circumstances that many years afterward, in company with an equally intrepid spirit, I penetrated to the place and ventured near enough to the ruined cabin to throw a stone against it, and ran away to avoid the ghost which every well-informed boy thereabout knew haunted the spot. But there is an earlier chapter—that supplied by my grandfather.

When Murlock built his cabin and began laying sturdily about with his ax to hew out a farm—the rifle, meanwhile, his means of support—he was young, strong, and full of hope. In that eastern country whence he came he had married, as was the fashion, a young woman in all ways worthy of his honest devotion, who shared the dangers and privations of his lot with a willing spirit and light heart. There is no known record of her name; of her charms of mind and person tradition is silent and the doubter is at liberty to entertain his doubt; but God forbid that I should share it! Of their affection and happiness there is abundant assurance in every added day of the man's widowed life; for what but the magnetism of a blessed memory could have chained that venturesome spirit to a lot like that?

One day Murlock returned from gunning in a distant part of the forest to find his wife prostrate with fever, and delirious. There was no physician within miles, no neighbor; nor was she in a condition to be left, to summon help. So he set about the tesk of nursing her back to health, but at the end of the third day she fell into unconsciousness and so passed away, apparently, with never a gleam of returning reason.

From what we know of a nature like his we may venture to sketch in some of the details of the outline picture drawn by my grandfather. When convinced that she was dead, Murlock had sense enough to remember that the dead must be prepared for burial. In performance of this sacred duty he blundered now and again, did certain things incorrectly, and others which he did correctly were done over and over. His occasional failures to accomplish some simple and ordinary act filled him with astonishment, like that of a drunken man who wonders at the suspension of familiar natural laws. He was surprised, too, that he did not weep—surprised and a little ashamed; surely it is unkind not to weep for the dead. "Tomorrow," he said aloud, "I shall have to make the coffin and dig the grave; and then I shall miss her, when she is no longer in sight; but now—she is dead, of course, but it is all right—it *must* be all right, somehow. Things cannot be so bad as they seem."

He stood over the body in the fading light, adjusting the hair and putting the finishing touches to the simple toilet, doing all mechanically, with soulless care. And still through his consciousness ran an undersense of conviction that all was right—that he should have her again as before, and everything explained. He had had no experience in grief; his capacity had not been enlarged by use. His heart could not contain it all, nor his imagination rightly conceive it. He did not know he was so hard struck; *that* knowledge would come later, and never go. Grief is an artist of powers as various as the instruments upon which he plays his dirges for the dead, evoking from some the sharpest, shrillest notes, from others the low, grave chords that throb recurrent like the slow beating of a distant drum. Some natures it startles; some it stupefies. To one it comes like the stroke of an arrow, stinging all the sensibilities to a keener life; to another as the blow of a bludgeon, which in crushing benumbs. We may conceive Murlock to have been that way affected, for (and here we are upon surer ground than that of conjecture) no sooner had he finished his pious work than, sinking into a chair by the side of the table upon which the body lay, and noting how white the profile showed in the deepening gloom, he laid his arms upon the table's edge, and dropped his face into them, tearless yet and unutterably weary. At that moment came in through the open window a long, wailing sound like the cry of a lost child in the far deeps of the darkening wood! But the man did not move. Again, and nearer than before, sounded that unearthly cry upon his failing sense.

The Boarded Window

Perhaps it was a wild beast; perhaps it was a dream. For Murlock was asleep.

Some hours later, as it afterward appeared, this unfaithful watcher awoke and lifting his head from his arms intently listened—he knew not why. There in the black darkness by the side of the dead, recalling all without a shock, he strained his eyes to see—he knew not what. His senses were all alert, his breath was suspended, his blood had stilled its tides as if to assist the silence. Who—what had waked him, and where was it?

Suddenly the table shook beneath his arms, and at the same moment he heard, or fancied that he heard, a light, soft step—another—sounds as of bare feet upon the floor!

He was terrified beyond the power to cry out or move. Perforce he waited—waited there in the darkness through seeming centuries of such dread as one may know, yet live to tell. He tried vainly to speak the dead woman's name, vainly to stretch forth his hand across the table to learn if she were there. His throat was powerless, his arms and hands were like lead. Then occurred something most frightful. Some heavy body seemed hurled against the table with an impetus that pushed it against his breast so sharply as nearly to overthrow him, and at the same instant he heard and felt the fall of something upon the floor with so violent a thump that the whole house was shaken by the impact. A scuffling ensued, and a confusion of sounds impossible to describe. Murlock had risen to his feet. Fear had by excess forfeited control of his faculties. He flung his hands upon the table. Nothing was there!

There is a point at which terror may turn to madness; and madness incites to action. With no definite intent, from no motive but the wayward impulse of a madman, Murlock sprang to the wall, with a little groping seized his loaded rifle, and without aim discharged it. By the flash which lit up the room with a vivid illumination, he saw an enormous panther dragging the dead woman toward the window, its teeth fixed in her throat! Then there were darkness blacker than before, and silence; and when he returned to consciousness the sun was high and the wood vocal with songs of birds.

The body lay near the window, where the beast had left it when frightened away by the flash and report of the rifle. The clothing was deranged, the long hair in disorder, the limbs lay anyhow. From the throat, dreadfully lacerated, had issued a pool of blood not yet entirely coagulated. The ribbon with which he had bound the wrists was broken; the hands were tightly clenched. Between the teeth was a fragment of the animal's ear.

■ DISCUSSION AND QUESTIONS

1. The first paragraph of Bierce's story describes how the American frontier pushed westward during the nineteenth century. This bit of history may seem unnecessary to the development of the tale. Bierce, however, wants to suggest in this opening that Murlock is different from other settlers; something has compelled him to remain in his house of logs with the boarded window. Bierce contrasts the zeal of the active frontierspeople with the gloom that surrounds Murlock and his run-down farm. What words does Bierce use to heighten this contrast? What does Murlock's "place" look like?

2. As we have said, horror stories depend for their effects on the writer's knowledge of what frightens us, what seems mysterious to us, what makes us shudder. Something about a falling down house with a boarded window appeals to our sense of mystery. Little children call such places "haunted houses." In fact, the narrator of this story tells us that as a boy he "penetrated to the place and ventured near enough to the ruined cabin to throw a stone against it, and ran away to avoid the ghost which every well-informed boy thereabout knew haunted the spot." What frightening devices, settings, noises, and symbols do writers of horror stories and directors of horror movies use again and again? At what precise point in the story does Bierce frighten us with something "that goes bump in the night"?

3. How concerned is he with developing his central character? Describe Murlock? How does his wife's apparent death and the panther's attack on her change him? What is Bierce's major concern in this story?

4. Who is telling this story? Who told it to him? And why?

READING THE SHORT STORY

Several reasons at least partially explain man's built-in love of stories, and people have told stories throughout history. The "short story" in the technical sense of the term is, however, a modern development in the history of tale telling. It is a literary genre or category with certain characteristics which distinguish it from sketches, parables, and novels. Yet because of its great variety it is almost impossible to define once and for all. Any definition must be elastic enough to stretch around stories as different as Poe's horror tale and John Barth's account of a sperm's voyage to love in "Night-Sea Journey."

Edgar Allen Poe helped formulate a definition of the modern short story when he wrote:

> A skillful artist has constructed a tale. He has not fashioned his thoughts to accommodate his incidents, but having deliberately conceived a certain *single effect* to be wrought, he then invents such incidents, he then combines such events, and discusses them in such tone as may best serve him in establishing this preconceived effect. If his very first sentence tends not to the outbringing of this effect, then

in his very first step has he committed a blunder. In the whole composition there should be no word written of which the tendency, direct or indirect, is not to the one preestablished design. And by such means, with such care and skill, a picture is at length painted which leaves in the mind of him who contemplates it with a kindred art, a sense of the fullest satisfaction. The idea of the tale, its thesis, has been presented unblemished, because undisturbed—an end absolutely demanded, yet, in the novel, altogether unattainable.[1]

The key here is Poe's insistence that the good "prose tale" (the term "short story" had not yet come into vogue) should strive for a unity of effect—a "single effect." In other words, it should be compressed and economical the way a poem is, free from digressions and irrelevancies, and marked by its intensity. Poe was most concerned for the story's sensational effect, usually achieved by a precise manipulation of plot. As you will discover while reading the stories in this book, modern writers have greatly expanded Poe's concept of "unity" or singleness of effect. But there is little disagreement that a short story must be complete in itself and that it must have unity, wholeness.

Tales and sketches do not present a single effect; they may digress, wander, add episode to episode with little unifying principle. The novel, with its large scope, can afford to present many effects and impressions, and in the novel there is more time and space for development of characters and situations. In order to achieve a compressed unity the short story generally limits its scope to a single event, a single emotion, a single impression, and a small number of characters. A story is meant to be read at one sitting; a novel may take days to read. So the story's effect must be sudden, powerful, revealing; whereas a novel can involve readers at a more leisurely pace, slowly illuminating complexities and nuances.

Unsophisticated readers, after a steady diet of fast-action fiction or sentimental romances ("packaged passion"), sometimes feel that nothing happens in the serious modern story. Perhaps they want stories to offer easy, vicarious alternatives to the subtle confusions and complexities of modern life. ("He held me, my heart pounding in rhythm with his powerful body.") The serious writer, however, seldom offers alternatives to confusion, he explores it; he doesn't avoid the complexities of modern life, he examines them. And in order to deal with these difficult subjects, a writer may have to use complex, even confusing, techniques. He may also write stories in which "little happens," little, that is, in the way of physical action—no pounding passions.

1. Excerpt taken from Poe's review of Hawthorne's *Twice-Told Tales. Graham's Magazine,* 1842.

Much of what happens in the modern story happens in the characters' minds, in the "interior world." Eudora Welty, one of America's most important short story writers, explains that she is largely concerned with the "mysteries" of the *inner life;* she tries to reveal what is secret, concealed in human character. Of course the secret, interior world of human consciousness is a strange, wonderful place, an attic filled with old pictures, bottles, broken toasters, highchairs, blueprints, trophies—all the symbols of human fears, dreams, desires, fantasies, and memories. Consciousness is often confused, disjointed, and illogical. Therefore, in attempting to reveal the drama of human consciousness, some modern writers have stopped stressing the orderly progression of plots, have played down external action, and have often abandoned photographic realism in favor of a more complex psychological realism.

Many of these attributes of the modern short story are discussed in detail in later sections of this book. The important thing to remember for now is that when we read modern stories we must read with focused attention; no detail should escape us. If a character in a story is shown "drinking a cup of spiced tea," instead of coffee or ordinary tea, we can bet that the author wants that detail to reveal something about the character. There is no room in the short story for irrelevant detail; as Chekhov put it, if a gun hangs on the wall at the beginning of a story, it had better be fired before the end of the story. In reading a novel the temptation is to skip over the descriptions, especially descriptions of setting. No such skipping can be done while reading a short story without losing some part of the story's meaning and effect. Description in stories does not exist merely to set the stage; it is a subjective index to characters, an enhancer of theme, or a creator of mood.

Thorough understanding of a story, then, depends on reading with focused attention, but it also depends on a knowledge of the elements and techniques of fiction. In this book we will talk about *plot, theme, character, tone, point of view,* and *symbol* as if these were the ingredients of a short story: take one cup *plot,* one cup *character,* a dash of *symbol,* put in *point of view* to taste, stir well, mix in some nice fresh language —the result, a short story. However, plot, character, or symbol are not "parts" of a story that exist alone. A story is not the result of following a recipe. So if we say that James Joyce's "A Little Cloud" is a story of character, we really mean to say that one facet of the work seems to us especially memorable—character. Character can be discussed separately, so can theme or symbol or point of view; but in the successful story they are thoroughly blended like the ingredients in a cake. We like a cake not because of the separate ingredients that went into it, but because of the way they have become the cake; conversely, if we truly like the cake, we want to know how it was made.

Analyzing stories is not an arcane activity or a riddle to which the teacher has the answer. Analyzing stories depends on common sense, intelligence, sensitivity, and the ability to ask the right questions. Simple questions such as:

   I. What is the *plot* of the story?
      A. What is the central conflict?
      B. Why did the author arrange the incidents in this order?

   II. Who are the *characters* doing the action?
      A. Why do they do what they do?
      B. What do the actions reveal about the characters?
      C. How do the actions follow from the natures of the characters?

   III. Where does the action take place *(setting)?*
      A. How does the setting influence the actions and the characters?
      B. Could these people exist and these incidents occur in a different setting?

   IV. Who is telling us about these people and incidents?
      A. How much does the teller *(narrator)* know about the situation?
      B. Does he tell us all he knows? Or more than he can know for sure?
      C. Can we trust the teller?

These questions should be kept in mind as you read the next story, Joyce Carol Oates's "Where Are You Going, Where Have You Been." Like the first two stories in this chapter, hers is suspenseful and, in its own way, a story about death. It provides a good example of how the contemporary writer can treat an old subject and yet be thoroughly modern. A comparison of her story with those of Poe and Bierce can reveal much about the changes in the short story over the past years. In the earlier stories the plot builds to a shocking climax, in both cases the realization that someone thought to be dead wasn't. But in "Where Are You Going, Where Have You Been" Oates seeks to do more than create the tingle of horror in her readers; she wants to reveal something about the nature of evil and about the character of a teenage girl confronting forces she little comprehends, forces that may destroy her. Connie, the main character in the Oates story, is destined for a kind of violent climax, but Oates does not show it; instead, she leaves that to the reader's imagination.

Where Are You Going, Where Have You Been?

Joyce Carol Oates
 (For Bob Dylan)

Her name was Connie. She was fifteen and she had a quick nervous giggling habit of craning her neck to glance into mirrors, or checking other people's faces to make sure her own was all right. Her mother, who noticed everything and knew everything and who hadn't much reason any longer to look at her own face, always scolded Connie about it. "Stop gawking at yourself, who are you? You think you're so pretty?" she would say. Connie would raise her eyebrows at these familiar complaints and look right through her mother, into a shadowy vision of herself as she was right at that moment: she knew she was pretty and that was everything. Her mother had been pretty once too, if you could believe those old snapshots in the album, but now her looks were gone and that was why she was always after Connie.

"Why don't you keep your room clean like your sister? How've you got your hair fixed—what the hell stinks? Hair spray? You don't see your sister using that junk."

Her sister June was twenty-four and still lived at home. She was a secretary in the high school Connie attended, and if that wasn't bad enough—with her in the same building—she was so plain and chunky and steady that Connie had to hear her praised all the time by her mother and her mother's sisters. June did this, June did that, she saved money and helped clean the house and cooked and Connie couldn't do a thing, her

Reprinted by permission of the author and Blanche C. Gregory, Inc. Copyright © 1966 Joyce Carol Oates.

mind was all filled with trashy daydreams. Their father was away at work most of the time and when he came home he wanted supper and he read the newspaper at supper and after supper he went to bed. He didn't bother talking much to them, but around his bent head Connie's mother kept picking at her until Connie wished her mother was dead and she herself was dead and it was all over. "She makes me want to throw up sometimes," she complained to her friends. She had a high, breathless, amused voice which made everything she said sound a little forced, whether it was sincere or not.

There was one good thing: June went places with girl friends of hers, girls who were just as plain and steady as she, and so when Connie wanted to do that her mother had no objections. The father of Connie's best girl friend drove the girls the three miles to town and left them off at a shopping plaza, so that they could walk through the stores or go to a movie, and when he came to pick them up again at eleven he never bothered to ask what they had done.

They must have been familiar sights, walking around that shopping plaza in their shorts and flat ballerina slippers that always scuffed the sidewalk, with charm bracelets jingling on their thin wrists; they would lean together to whisper and laugh secretly if someone passed by who amused or interested them. Connie had long dark blond hair that drew anyone's eye to it, and she wore part of it pulled up on her head and puffed out and the rest of it she let fall down her back. She wore a pull-over jersey blouse that looked one way when she was at home and another way when she was away from home. Everything about her had two sides to it, one for home and one for anywhere that was not home: her walk that could be childlike and bobbing, or languid enough to make anyone think she was hearing music in her head, her mouth which was pale and smirking most of the time, but bright and pink on these evenings out, her laugh which was cynical and drawling at home—"Ha, ha, very funny"—but high-pitched and nervous anywhere else, like the jingling of the charms on her bracelet.

Sometimes they did go shopping or to a movie, but sometimes they went across the highway, ducking fast across the busy road, to a drive-in restaurant where older kids hung out. The restaurant was shaped like a big bottle, though squatter than a real bottle, and on its cap was a revolving figure of a grinning boy who held a hamburger aloft. One night in mid-summer they ran across, breathless with daring, and right away someone leaned out a car window and invited them over, but it was just a boy from high school they didn't like. It made them feel good to be able to ignore him. They went up through the maze of parked and cruising cars to the bright-lit, fly-infested restaurant, their faces pleased and expectant as if they were entering a sacred building that loomed out of the night to give them what haven and what blessing they yearned for. They sat at the counter and crossed their legs at the ankles, their thin shoulders rigid with excitement, and listened to the music that made everything so good: the music was always in the background like music at a church service, it was something to depend upon.

A boy named Eddie came in to talk with them. He sat backwards on his stool, turning himself jerkily around in semi-circles and then stopping and turning again, and after a while he asked Connie if she would like something to eat. She said she did and so she tapped her friend's arm on her way out—her friend pulled her face up into a brave droll look—and Connie said she would meet her at eleven, across the way. "I just hate to leave her like that," Connie said earnestly, but the boy said that she wouldn't be alone for long. So they went out to his car and on the way Connie couldn't help but let her eyes wander over the windshields and faces all around her, her face gleaming with a joy that had nothing to do with Eddie or even this place; it might have been the music. She drew her shoulders up and sucked in her breath with the pure pleasure of being alive, and just at that moment she happened to glance at a face just a few feet from hers. It was a boy with shaggy black hair, in a convertible jalopy painted gold. He stared at her and then his lips widened into a grin. Connie slit her eyes at him and turned away, but she couldn't help glancing back and there he was still watching her. He wagged a finger and laughed and said, "Gonna get you, baby," and Connie turned away again without Eddie noticing anything.

She spent three hours with him, at the restaurant where they ate hamburgers and drank Cokes in wax cups that were always sweating, and then down an alley a mile or so away, and when he left her off at five to eleven only the movie house was still open at the plaza. Her girl friend was there, talking with a boy. When Connie came up the two girls smiled at each other and Connie said, "How was the movie?" and the girl said, *"You should know."* They rode off with the girl's father, sleepy and pleased, and Connie couldn't help but look at the darkened shopping plaza with its big empty parking lot and its signs that were faded and ghostly now, and over at the drive-in restaurant where cars were still circling tirelessly. She couldn't hear the music at this distance.

Next morning June asked her how the movie was and Connie said, "So-so."

She and that girl and occasionally another girl went out several times a week that way, and the rest of the time Connie spent around the house —it was summer vacation—getting in her mother's way and thinking, dreaming, about the boys she met. But all the boys fell back and dissolved into a single face that was not even a face, but an idea, a feeling, mixed up with the urgent insistent pounding of the music and the humid night air of July. Connie's mother kept dragging her back to the daylight by finding things for her to do or saying, suddenly, "What's this about the Pettinger girl?"

And Connie would say nervously, "Oh, her. That dope." She always drew thick clear lines between herself and such girls, and her mother was simple and kindly enough to believe her. Her mother was so simple, Connie thought, that it was maybe cruel to fool her so much. Her mother went scuffling around the house in old bedroom slippers and complained over the telephone to one sister about the other, then the other called up and the two of them complained about the third one. If June's name was mentioned her mother's tone was approving, and if Connie's name was mentioned it was disapproving. This did not really mean she disliked Connie and actually Connie thought that her mother preferred her to June because she was prettier, but the two of them kept up a pretense of exasperation, a sense that they were tugging and struggling over something of little value to either of them. Sometimes, over coffee, they were almost friends, but something would come up—some vexation that was like a fly buzzing suddenly around their heads—and their faces went hard with contempt.

One Sunday Connie got up at eleven—none of them bothered with church—and washed her hair so that it could dry all day long, in the sun. Her parents and sister were going to a barbecue at an aunt's house and Connie said no, she wasn't interested, rolling her eyes to let mother know just what she thought of it. "Stay home alone then," her mother said sharply. Connie sat out back in a lawn chair and watched them drive away, her father quiet and bald, hunched around so that he could back the car out, her mother with a look that was still angry and not at all softened through the windshield, and in the back seat poor old June all dressed up as if she didn't know what a barbecue was, with all the running yelling kids and the flies. Connie sat with her eyes closed in the sun, dreaming and dazed with the warmth about her as if this were a kind of love, the caresses of love, and her mind slipped over onto thoughts of the boy she had been with the night before and how nice he had been, how sweet it always was, not the way someone like June would suppose but sweet, gentle, the way it was in movies and promised in songs; and when she opened her eyes she hardly knew where she was, the backyard ran off into weeds and a fence-line of trees and behind it the sky was perfectly blue and still. The asbestos "ranch house" that was now three years old startled her—it looked small. She shook her head as if to get awake.

It was too hot. She went inside the house and turned on the radio to drown out the quiet. She sat on the edge of her bed, barefoot, and listened for an hour and a half to a program called XYZ Sunday Jamboree, record after record of hard, fast, shrieking songs she sang along with, interspersed by exclamations from "Bobby King": "An' look here you girls at Napoleon's—Son and Charley want you to pay real close attention to this song coming up!"

And Connie paid close attention herself, bathed in a glow of slow-pulsed joy that seemed to rise mysteriously out of the music itself and lay languidly about the airless little room, breathed in and breathed out with each gentle rise and fall of her chest.

After a while she heard a car coming up the drive. She sat up at once, startled, because it couldn't be her father so soon. The gravel kept crunching all the way in from the road—the driveway was long—and Connie ran to the window. It was a car she didn't know. It was an open jalopy, painted a bright gold that caught the sunlight opaquely. Her heart began to pound and her fingers snatched at her hair, checking it, and she whispered "Christ. Christ," wondering how bad she looked. The car came to a stop at the side door and the horn sounded four short taps as if this were a signal Connie knew.

She went into the kitchen and approached the door slowly, then hung out the screen door, her bare toes curling down off the step. There were two boys in the car and now she recognized the driver: he had shaggy, shabby black hair that looked crazy as a wig and he was grinning at her.

"I ain't late, am I?" he said.

"Who the hell do you think you are?" Connie said.

"Toldja I'd be out, didn't I?"

"I don't even know who you are."

She spoke sullenly, careful to show no interest or pleasure, and he spoke in a fast bright monotone. Connie looked past him to the other boy, taking her time. He had fair brown hair, with a lock that fell onto his forehead. His sideburns gave him a fierce, embarrassed look, but so far he hadn't even bothered to glance at her. Both boys wore sunglasses. The driver's glasses were metallic and mirrored everything in miniature.

"You wanta come for a ride?" he said.

Connie smirked and let her hair fall loose over one shoulder.

"Don'tcha like my car? New paint job," he said. "Hey."

"What?"

"You're cute."

She pretended to fidget, chasing flies away from the door.

"Don'tcha believe me, or what?" he said.

"Look, I don't even know who you are," Connie said in disgust.

"Hey, Ellie's got a radio, see. Mine's broke down." He lifted his friend's arm and showed her the little transistor the boy was holding, and now Connie began to hear the music. It was the same program that was playing inside the house.

"Bobby King?" she said.

"I listen to him all the time. I think he's great."

"He's kind of great," Connie said reluctantly.

"Listen, that guy's *great*. He knows where the action is."

Connie blushed a little, because the glasses made it impossible for her to see just what this boy was looking at. She couldn't decide if she liked him or if he was just a jerk, and so she dawdled in the doorway and wouldn't come down or go back inside. She said, "What's all that stuff painted on your car?"

"Can'tcha read it?" He opened the door very carefully, as if he was afraid it might fall off. He slid out just as carefully, planting his feet firmly on the ground, the tiny metallic world in his glasses slowing down like gelatine hardening and in the midst of it Connie's bright green blouse. "This here is my name, to begin with," he said. ARNOLD FRIEND was written in tar-like black letters on the side, with a drawing of a round grinning face that reminded Connie of a pumpkin, except it wore sunglasses. "I wanta introduce myself. I'm Arnold Friend and that's my real name and I'm gonna be your friend, honey, and inside the car's Ellie Oscar, he's kinda shy." Ellie brought his transistor radio up to his shoulder and balanced it there. "Now these numbers are a secret code, honey," Arnold Friend explained. He read off the numbers 33, 19, 17 and raised his eyebrows at her to see what she thought of that, but she didn't think much of it. The left rear fender had been smashed and around it was written, on the gleaming gold background: DONE BY CRAZY WOMAN DRIVER. Connie had to laugh at that. Arnold Friend was pleased at her laughter and looked up at her. "Around the other side's a lot more—you wanta come and see them?"

"No."

"Why not?"

"Why should I?"

"Don'tcha wanta see what's on the car? Don'tcha wanta go for a ride?"

"I don't know."

"Why not?"

"I got things to do."

"Like what?"

"Things."

He laughed as if she had said something funny. He slapped his thighs. He was standing in a strange way, leaning back against the car as if he were balancing himself. He wasn't tall, only an inch or so taller than she would be if she came down to him. Connie liked the way he was dressed, which was the way all of them dressed: tight faded jeans stuffed into black, scuffed boots, a belt that pulled his waist in and showed how lean he was, and a white pull-over shirt that was a little soiled and showed the hard small muscles of his arms and shoulders. He looked as if he probably did hard work, lifting and carrying things. Even his neck looked muscular. And his face was a familiar face, somehow: the jaw and chin and cheeks slightly darkened, because he hadn't shaved for a day or two, and the nose long and hawk-like, sniffing as if she were a treat he was going to gobble up and it was all a joke.

"Connie, you ain't telling the truth. This is your day set aside for a ride with me and you know it," he said, still laughing. The way he straightened and recovered from his fit of laughing showed that it had been all fake.

"How do you know what my name is?" she said suspiciously.

"It's Connie."

"Maybe and maybe not."

"I know my Connie," he said, wagging his finger. Now she remembered him even better, back at the restaurant, and her cheeks warmed at the thought of how she sucked in her breath just at the moment she passed him—how she must have looked to him. And he had remembered her. "Ellie and I come out here especially for you," he said. "Ellie can sit in back. How about it?"

"Where?"

"Where what?"

"Where're we going?"

He looked at her. He took off the sunglasses and she saw how pale the skin around his eyes was, like holes that were not in shadow but instead in light. His eyes were like chips of broken glass that catch the light in an amiable way. He smiled. It was as if the idea of going for a ride somewhere, to some place, was a new idea to him.

"Just for a ride, Connie sweetheart."

"I never said my name was Connie," she said.

"But I know what it is. I know your name and all about you, lots of things," Arnold Friend said. He had not moved yet but stood still leaning back against the side of his jalopy. "I took a special interest in you, such a pretty girl, and found out all about you like I know your parents and sister are gone somewheres and I know where and how long they're going to be gone, and I know who you were with last night, and your best girl friend's name is Betty. Right?"

He spoke in a simple lilting voice, exactly as if he were reciting the words to a song. His smile assured her that everything was fine. In the car Ellie turned up the volume on his radio and did not bother to look around at them.

"Ellie can sit in the back seat," Arnold Friend said. He indicated his friend with a casual jerk of his chin, as if Ellie did not count and she should not bother with him.

"How'd you find out all that stuff?" Connie said.

"Listen: Betty Schultz and Tony Fitch and Jimmy Pettinger and Nancy

Pettinger," he said, in a chant. "Raymond Stanley and Bob Hutter—"

"Do you know all those kids?"

"I know everybody."

"Look, you're kidding. You're not from around here."

"Sure."

"But—how come we never saw you before?"

"Sure you saw me before," he said. He looked down at his boots, as if he were a little offended. "You just don't remember."

"I guess I'd remember you," Connie said.

"Yeah?" He looked up at this, beaming. He was pleased. He began to mark time with the music from Ellie's radio, tapping his fists lightly together. Connie looked away from his smile to the car, which was painted so bright it almost hurt her eyes to look at it. She looked at that name, ARNOLD FRIEND. And up at the front fender was an expression that was familiar—MAN THE FLYING SAUCERS. It was an expression kids had used the year before, but didn't use this year. She looked at it for a while as if the words meant something to her that she did not yet know.

"What're you thinking about? Huh?" Arnold Friend demanded. "Not worried about your hair blowing around in the car, are you?"

"No."

"Think I maybe can't drive good?"

"How do I know?"

"You're a hard girl to handle. How come?" he said. "Don't you know I'm your friend? Didn't you see me put my sign in the air when you walked by?"

"What sign?"

"My sign." And he drew an X in the air, leaning out toward her. They were maybe ten feet apart. After his hand fell back to his side the X was still in the air, almost visible. Connie let the screen door close and stood perfectly still inside it, listening to the music from her radio and the boy's blend together. She stared at Arnold Friend. He stood there so stiffly relaxed, pretending to be relaxed, with one hand idly on the door handle as if he were keeping himself up that way and had no intention of ever moving again. She recognized most things about him, the tight jeans that showed his thighs and buttocks and the greasy leather boots and the tight shirt, and even that slippery friendly smile of his, that sleepy dreamy smile that all the boys used to get across ideas they didn't want to put into words. She recognized all this and also the singsong way he talked, slightly mocking, kidding, but serious and a little melancholy, and she recognized the way he tapped one fist against the other in homage to the perpetual music behind him. But all these things did not come together.

She said suddenly, "Hey, how old are you?"

His smile faded. She could see then that he wasn't a kid, he was much older—thirty, maybe more. At this knowledge her heart began to pound faster.

"That's a crazy thing to ask. Can'tcha see I'm your own age?"

"Like hell you are."

"Or maybe a coupla years older, I'm eighteen."

"Eighteen?" she said doubtfully.

He grinned to reassure her and lines appeared at the corners of his mouth. His teeth were big and white. He grinned so broadly his eyes became slits and she saw how thick the lashes were, thick and black as if painted with a black tar-like material. Then he seemed to become embarrassed, abruptly, and looked over his shoulder at Ellie. *"Him,* he's crazy," he said. "Ain't he a riot, he's a nut, a real character." Ellie was still listening to the music. His sunglasses told nothing about what he was thinking. He wore a bright orange shirt unbuttoned halfway to show his chest, which was a pale, bluish chest and not muscular like Arnold Friend's. His shirt collar was turned up all around and the very tips of the collar pointed out past his chin as if they were protecting him. He was pressing the transistor radio up against his ear and sat there in a kind of daze, right in the sun.

"He's kinda strange," Connie said.

"Hey, she says you're kinda strange! Kinda strange!" Arnold Friend cried. He pounded on the car to get Ellie's attention. Ellie turned for the first time and Connie saw with shock that he wasn't a kid either—he had a fair, hairless face, cheeks reddened slightly as if the veins grew too close to the surface of his skin, the face of a forty-year-old baby. Connie felt a wave of dizziness rise in her at this sight and she stared at him as if waiting for something to change the shock of the moment, make it all right again. Ellie's lips kept shaping words, mumbling along with the words blasting in his ear.

"Maybe you two better go away," Connie said faintly.

"What? How come?" Arnold Friend cried. "We come out here to take you for a ride. It's Sunday." He had the voice of the man on the radio now. It was the same voice, Connie thought. "Don'tcha know it's Sunday all day and honey, no matter who you were with last night today you're with Arnold Friend and don't you forget it!—Maybe you better step out here," He said, and this last was in a different voice. It was a little flatter, as if the heat was finally getting to him.

"No. I got things to do."

"Hey."

"You two better leave."

"We ain't leaving until you come with us."

"Like hell I am—"

"Connie, don't fool around with me. I mean, I mean, don't fool *around,*" he said, shaking his head. He laughed incredulously. He placed his sunglasses on top of his head, carefully, as if he were indeed wearing a wig, and brought the stems down behind his ears. Connie stared at him, another wave of dizziness and fear rising in her so that for a moment he wasn't even in focus but was just a blur, standing there against his gold car, and she had the idea that he had driven up the driveway all right but had come from nowhere before that and belonged nowhere and that everything about him and even about the music that was so familiar to her was only half real.

"If my father comes and sees you—"

"He ain't coming. He's at a barbecue."

"How do you know that?"

"Aunt Tillie's. Right now they're—uh—they're drinking. Sitting around," he said vaguely, squinting as if he were staring all the way to town and over to Aunt Tillie's backyard. Then the vision seemed to get clear and he nodded energetically. "Yeah. Sitting around. There's your sister in a blue dress, huh? And high heels, the poor sad bitch—nothing like you, sweetheart! And your mother's helping some fat woman with the corn, they're cleaning the corn—husking the corn—"

"What fat woman?" Connie cried.

"How do I know what fat woman. I don't know every goddam fat woman in the world!" Arnold Friend laughed.

"Oh, that's Mrs. Hornby.... Who invited her?" Connie said. She felt a little light-headed, Her breath was coming quickly.

"She's too fat. I don't like them fat. I like them the way you are, honey," he said, smiling sleepily at her. They stared at each other for a while, through the screen door. He said softly, "Now what you're going to do is this: you're going to come out that door. You're going to sit up front with me and Ellie's going to sit in the back, the hell with Ellie, right? This isn't Ellie's date. You're my date. I'm your lover, honey."

"What? You're crazy—"

"Yes, I'm your lover. You don't know what that is but you will," he said. "I know that too. I know all about you. But look: it's real nice and you couldn't ask for nobody better than me, or more polite. I always keep my word. I'll tell you how it is, I'm always nice at first, the first time. I'll hold you so tight you won't think you have to try to get away or pretend anything because you'll know you can't. And I'll come inside you where it's all secret and you'll give in to me and you'll love me—"

"Shut up! You're crazy!" Connie said. She backed away from the door. She put her hands against her ears as if she'd heard something terrible, something not meant for her. "People don't talk like that, you're crazy," she muttered. Her heart was almost too big now for her chest and its pumping made sweat break out all over her. She looked out to see Arnold Friend pause and then take a step toward the porch lurching. He almost fell. But, like a clever drunken man, he managed to catch his balance. He wobbled in his high boots and grabbed hold of one of the porch posts.

"Honey?" he said. "You still listening?"

"Get the hell out of here!"

"Be nice, honey. Listen."

"I'm going to call the police—"

He wobbled again and out of the side of his mouth came a fast spat curse, an aside not meant for her to hear. But even this "Christ!" sounded forced. Then he began to smile again. She watched this smile come, awkward as if he were smiling from inside a mask. His whole face was a mask, she thought wildly, tanned down onto his throat but then running out as if he had plastered make-up on his face but had forgotten about his throat.

"Honey—? Listen, here's how it is. I always tell the truth and I promise you this: I ain't coming in that house after you."

"You better not! I'm going to call the police if you—if you don't—"

"Honey," he said, talking right through her voice, "honey, I'm not coming in there but you are coming out here. You know why?"

She was panting. The kitchen looked like a place she had never seen before, some room she had run inside but which wasn't good enough, wasn't going to help her. The kitchen window had never had a curtain, after three years, and there were dishes in the sink for her to do—probably—and if you ran your hand across the table you'd probably feel something sticky there.

"You listening, honey? Hey?"

"—going to call the police—"

"Soon as you touch the phone I don't need to keep my promise and can come inside. You won't want that."

She rushed forward and tried to lock the door. Her fingers were shaking. "But why lock it," Arnold Friend said gently, talking right into her face. "It's just a screen door. It's just nothing." One of his boots was at a strange angle, as if his foot wasn't in it. It pointed out to the left, bent at the ankle. "I mean, anybody can break through a screen door and glass and wood and iron or anything else if he needs to, anybody at all and specially Arnold Friend. If the place got lit up with a fire honey you'd come running out into my arms, right into my arms and safe at home—like you knew I was your lover and stopped fooling around. I don't mind a nice shy girl but I don't like no fooling around." Part of those words were spoken with a slight rhythmic lilt, and Connie somehow recognized them—the echo of a song from last year, about a girl rushing into her boyfriend's arms and coming home again—

Connie stood barefoot on the linoleum floor, staring at him. "What do you want?" she whispered.

"I want you," he said.

"What?"

"Seen you that night and thought, that's the one, yes sir. I never needed to look any more."

"But my father's coming back. He's coming to get me. I had to wash my hair first—" She spoke in a dry, rapid voice, hardly raising it for him to hear.

"No, your daddy is not coming and yes, you had to wash your hair and you washed it for me. It's nice and shining and all for me. I thank you, sweetheart," he said, with a mock bow, but again he almost lost his balance. He had to bend and adjust his boots. Evidently his feet did not go all the way down; the boots must have been stuffed with something so that he would seem taller. Connie stared out at him and behind him Ellie in the car, who seemed to be looking off toward Connie's right, into nothing. This Ellie said, pulling the words out of the air one after another as if he were just discovering them, "You want me to pull out the phone?"

"Shut your mouth and keep it shut," Arnold Friend said, his face red from bending over or maybe from embarrassment because Connie had seen his boots. "This ain't none of your business."

"What—what are you doing? What do you want?" Connie said. "If I call the police they'll get you, they'll arrest you—"

"Promise was not to come in unless you touch that phone, and I'll keep that promise," he said. He resumed his erect position and tried to force his shoulders back. He sounded like a hero in a movie, declaring something important. He spoke too loudly and it was as if he were speaking to someone behind Connie. "I ain't made plans for coming in that house where I don't belong but just for you to come out to me, the way you should. Don't you know who I am?"

"You're crazy," she whispered. She backed away from the door but did not want to go into another part of the house, as if this would give him permission to come through the door. "What do you. . . . You're crazy, you . . ."

"Huh? What're you saying, honey?"

Her eyes darted everywhere in the kitchen. She could not remember what it was, this room.

"This is how it is, honey: you come out and we'll drive away, have a nice ride. But if you don't come out we're gonna wait till your people come home and then they're all going to get it."

"You want that telephone pulled out?" Ellie said. He held the radio away from his ear and grimaced, as if without the radio the air was too much for him.

"I toldja shut up, Ellie," Arnold Friend said, "you're deaf, get a hearing aid, right? Fix yourself up. This little girl's no trouble and's gonna be nice to me, so Ellie keep to yourself, this ain't your date—right? Don't hem in on me. Don't hog. Don't crush. Don't bird dog. Don't trail me," he said in a rapid meaningless voice, as if he were running through all the expressions he'd learned but was no longer sure which one of them was in style, then rushing on to new ones, making them up with his eyes closed, "Don't crawl under my fence, don't squeeze in my chipmunk hole, don't sniff my glue, suck my popsicle, keep your own greasy fingers on yourself!" He shaded his eyes and peered in at Connie, who was backed against the kitchen table. "Don't mind him honey he's just a creep. He's a dope. Right? I'm the boy for you and like I said you come out here nice like a lady and give me your hand, and nobody else gets hurt, I mean, your nice old bald-headed daddy and your mummy and your sister in her high heels. Because listen: why bring them in this?"

"Leave me alone," Connie whispered.

"Hey, you know that old woman down the road, the one with the chickens and stuff—you know her?"

"She's dead!"

"Dead? What? You know her?" Arnold Friend said.

"She's dead—"

"Don't you like her?"

"She's dead—she's—she isn't here any more—"

"But don't you like her, I mean, you got something against her? Some grudge or something?" Then his voice dipped as if he were conscious of a rudeness. He touched the sunglasses perched on top of his head as if to make sure they were still there. "Now you be a good girl."

"What are you going to do?"

"Just two things, or maybe three," Arnold Friend said. "But I promise it won't last long and you'll like me that way you get to like people you're close to. You will. It's all over for you here, so come on out. You don't want your people in any trouble, do you?"

She turned and bumped against a chair or something, hurting her leg, but she ran into the back room and picked up the telephone. Something roared in her ear, a tiny roaring, and she was so sick with fear that she could do nothing but listen to it—the telephone was clammy and very heavy and her fingers groped down to the dial but were too weak to touch it. She began to scream into the phone, into the roaring. She cried out, she cried for her mother, she felt her breath start jerking back and forth in her lungs as if it were something Arnold Friend were stabbing her with again and again with no tenderness. A noisy sorrowful wailing rose all about her and she was locked inside it the way she was locked inside this house.

After a while she could hear again. She was sitting on the floor with her wet back against the wall.

Arnold Friend was saying from the door, "That's a good girl. Put the phone back."

She kicked the phone away from her.

"No, honey. Pick it up. Put it back right."

She picked it up and put it back. The dial tone stopped.

"That's a good girl. Now you come outside."

She was hollow with what had been fear, but what was now just an emptiness. All that screaming had blasted it out of her. She sat, one leg cramped under her, and deep inside her brain was something like a pinpoint of light that kept going and would not let her relax. She thought, I'm not going to see my mother again. She thought, I'm not going to sleep in my bed again. Her bright green blouse was all wet.

Arnold Friend said, in a gentle-loud voice that was like a stage voice, "The place where you came from ain't there any more, and where you had in mind to go is cancelled out. This place you are now—inside your daddy's house—is nothing but a cardboard box I can knock down any time. You know that and always did know it. You hear me?"

She thought, I have got to think. I have to know what to do.

"We'll go out to a nice field, out in the country here where it smells so nice and it's sunny," Arnold Friend said. "I'll have my arms tight around you so you won't need to try to get away and I'll show you what love is like, what it does. The hell with this house! It looks solid all right," he said. He ran a fingernail down the screen and the noise did not make Connie shiver, as it would have the day before. "Now put your hand on your heart, honey. Feel that? That feels solid too but we know better, be nice to me, be sweet like you can because what else is there for a girl like you but to be sweet and pretty and give in?—and get away before her people come back?"

She felt her pounding heart. Her hand seemed to enclose it. She thought for the first time in her life that it was nothing that was hers, that belonged to her, but just a pounding, living thing inside this body that wasn't really hers either.

"You don't want them to get hurt," Arnold Friend went on. "Now get up, honey. Get up all by yourself."

She stood.

"Now turn this way. That's right. Come over here to me—Ellie, put that away, didn't I tell you? You dope. You miserable creepy dope," Arnold Friend said. His words were not angry but only part of an incantation. The incantation was kindly. "Now come out through the kitchen to me honey and let's see a smile, try it, you're a brave sweet little girl and now they're eating corn and hotdogs cooked to bursting over an outdoor fire and they don't know one thing about you and never did and honey you're better than them because not a one of them would have done this for you."

Connie felt the linoleum under her feet, it was cool. She brushed her hair back out of her eyes. Arnold Friend let go of the post tentatively and opened his arms for her, his elbows pointing in toward each other and his wrists limp, to show that this was an embarrassed embrace and a little mocking, he didn't want to make her self-conscious.

She put out her hand against the screen. She watched herself push the door slowly open as if she were safe back somewhere in the other doorway, watching this body and this head of long hair moving out into the sunlight where Arnold Friend waited.

"My sweet little blue-eyed girl," he said, in a half-sung sigh that had nothing to do with her brown eyes but was taken up just the same by the vast sunlit reaches of the land behind him and on all sides of him, so much land that Connie had never seen before and did not recognize except to know that she was going to it.

■ DISCUSSION AND QUESTIONS

1. Connie leads two lives: "Everything about her had two sides to it, one for home and one for anywhere that was not home...." Carefully delineate these two sides of Connie's personality, her home side and her not home side. What are Connie's attitudes toward her family? Toward her sister? Toward her girl friends?

2. Connie daydreams a lot about boys, yet her daydreams are never about a specific boy: "But all the boys fell back and dissolved into a single face that was not even a face, but an idea, a feeling, mixed up with the urgent insistent pounding of the music and the humid night air of July." She dreams of love that is "sweet, gentle." What are the sources of Connie's dreams? What are her feelings about Eddie and the other boys she meets at the drive-in restaurant?

3. Connie never consciously dreams about the kind of boy-girl relationship Arnold Friend demands—which is hardly "sweet, gentle." He looks at Connie "as if she were a treat he was going to gobble up and it was all a joke." Arnold says, "Yes, I'm your lover. You don't know what that is but you will." Why is his name ironic?

4. Arnold Friend has all the "right" words, the "right" clothes, the "right" mannerisms, but, as Connie notices, "All these things did not come together." She senses that there is something not quite right about him. Why, then, does she talk to him at all? Given Connie's personality, can she ever say "No!" to Arnold?

5. In an interview Joyce Carol Oates has said, "Arnold Friend is a fantastic figure: he is Death, he is the 'elf-knight' of the ballads, he is the Imagination, he is a Dream, he is a Lover, a Demon, *and all that.*" What evidence in the story supports Oates's statement? In other words, what clues

suggest that Arnold is Death or a Dream or a Demon?

6. If Arnold is an embodiment of some part of Connie's dreams, perhaps Oates is saying that Connie has two kinds of dreams—one derived from the images of love and romance in songs and movies; another that comes from deep within her, from a more primitive source, mysterious and unknown to her. We can see Arnold Friend as the terrifying realization of desires and dreams Connie has without being conscious of them; he is merely a mirror in which her secret desires are reflected.

If Connie were simply an innocent young girl, the story would be about the "rape of the innocent" by a nasty *older* man disguised as a youth. But Connie's character is complex. She lives two lives, as we noted earlier, and she is discovering her sexuality. Her failure to comprehend the full meaning and power of sex and the dangerous potentials inherent in her secret life lead inevitably to the fateful encounter with Arnold Friend.

7. How successfully has Oates created suspense and terror in this story? How does she achieve the effects she wants? What effect does the presence of Ellie and his transistor create? Describe Arnold Friend. What clothes does he wear? How old is he? Why are sunglasses sometimes frightening? Arnold seems to know everything about Connie and her family, and this knowledge scares Connie. Why? (Try putting yourself in Connie's place: feel what she feels; think what she must think.)

Chapter **2**

PLOT

Suspect appeared in doorway, saw officer of the law, and fled. Officer of the law determined that one man attending gathering was a constable. Officer of the law deputized others in gathering, and ordered constable, with those deputized, to pursue suspect. Suspect was pursued, but constable and deputies, due to nature of terrain and obscured vision, encountered difficulty during the pursuit. Suspect was finally apprehended and interrogated.

That is the way the police account of the chase and capture of a fugitive might read. It is the sequential narration of events as they happened. It may well be what Aristotle has called "the imitation of an action." Events are recorded, one after the other. The writer takes no liberties with the facts as they would have appeared to someone knowing nothing of the outcome. There are not even any assumptions about the alleged guilt of the "suspect." There is neither malice nor sympathy evident in the account. It is impersonal. Each sentence, we feel, might have been written down as the events described happened, without the author's having the slightest idea what the next sentence might be. It resembles a "case history." No wild hypotheses; no facts concealed or suppressed. Let us call such a sequential, open, "honest" account a *simple narrative account*—that is, the writer has not exaggerated, emphasized, or hidden anything.

A simple narrative account, then, is an "imitation," a rendering of external events, as they happened in time. The author of a simple narrative account, such as the police account above, has no motive other than to be "truthful."

A *plot* is not a "simple narrative account." A plot is constructed. A plot is composed. That is to say, the author of a plot has, in his mind, a "simple narrative account," but he does things with it. He may rearrange the events in time; he may tell the last event first and then relate how events led up to it; he may withhold essential facts in order that your puzzlement or your interest is sustained; he may be very prejudiced for or against one of the characters, and relate only that information which will support his prejudice, that will make you see the character in the light in which he wants you to see him. A plot is what an author does to the simple narrative account to make it a story, to give it a purpose. The impartial police report or a patient's case history does not have this purpose. In theory anyway, no one should know what the end result, or the effect of the whole, will be. It may turn out to be tragic for the suspect or the patient; it may be nothing at all. But not so a plotted story. The author of the plotted story knows precisely what the effect of each sentence, each word, each sequence, or each omission will be. A plot is not the mere sequence of action; it is what the artfully arranged combination of sequences of actions and the characters mean. A plot gives meaning to actions.

One of the most memorable distinctions between what we call simple narrative account and plot was made by the novelist E. M. Forster (who called "simple narrative account" simply "story"). Forster wrote " 'The king died and then the queen died' is a story. 'The king died, and then the queen died of grief' is a plot."[1] The author of Forster's plot had in mind a causality, a hypothesis, a point of view. He may have been right; he may very well have been wrong. It may in fact not be possible, medically speaking, to die of grief. But the author had a vision of the occasion, and he told it in accordance with his vision. He gave the simple sequence of events a meaning; and he therefore had the ingredients for a plot.

Forster might, with the same facts, have plotted quite a different story. For instance:

> One day the queen died. Physicians were called from all over the realm. In the post mortem, they examined her liver, her heart, her lungs. They saw nothing wrong. But searching through her papers, they found her diary. In it was an entry stating that in a dream her husband the king had appeared to her, telling her that, though it would be months before a courier could reach her with the news, he had been killed fighting the infidels. The queen, it was decided, had

[1] E. M. Forster, *Aspects of the Novel* (New York: Harcourt, Brace and Company, "A Harvest Book," 1954) p. 86.

died of grief. Three months later the news of the king's death was confirmed.

The teller of that story—using essentially the same facts—has withheld until the very end the crucial fact that the king died. The teller knew it from the beginning, but he did not let the reader in on his knowledge. Using storyteller craft, he artificially shaped a tale and formed a plot by arranging the incidents.

A plot, then, is a narrative account, artfully manipulated for artistic purpose, to give pleasure and to signify meaning.[2]

[2]The manner in which meaning is signified is more fully explored in the discussions of the Book of Ruth, and the stories by Mishima, Kafka, and Chekhov.

The Three Strangers

Thomas Hardy

Among the few features of agricultural England which retain an appearance but little modified by the lapse of centuries, may be reckoned the long, grassy and furzy downs, coombs, or ewe-leases, as they are called according to their kind, that fill a large area of certain counties in the south and south-west. If any mark of human occupation is met with hereon, it usually takes the form of the solitary cottage of some shepherd.

Fifty years ago such a lonely cottage stood on such a down, and may possibly be standing there now. In spite of its loneliness, however, the spot, by actual measurement, was not three miles from a county-town. Yet that affected it little. Three miles of irregular upland, during the long inimical seasons, with their sleets, snows, rains, and mists, afford withdrawing space enough to isolate a Timon or a Nebuchadnezzar; much less, in fair weather, to please that less repellent tribe, the poets, philosophers, artists, and others who "conceive and meditate of pleasant things."

Some old earthen camp or barrow, some clump of trees, at least some starved fragment of ancient hedge is usually taken advantage of in the erection of these forlorn dwellings. But, in the present case, such a kind of shelter had been disregarded. Higher Crowstairs, as the house was called, stood quite detached and undefended. The only reason for its precise situation seemed to be the crossing of two footpaths at right angles hard by, which may have crossed there and thus for a good five

From *Wessex Tales*. New York: Harper and Brothers Publishers, 1896.

hundred years. Hence the house was exposed to the elements on all sides. But, though the wind up here blew unmistakably when it did blow, and the rain hit hard whenever it fell, the various weathers of the winter season were not quite so formidable on the down as they were imagined to be by dwellers on low ground. The raw rimes were not so pernicious as in the hollows, and the frosts were scarcely so severe. When the shepherd and his family who tenanted the house were pitied for their sufferings from the exposure, they said that upon the whole they were less inconvenienced by "wuzzes and flames" (hoarses and phlegms) than when they had lived by the stream of a snug neighbouring valley.

The night of March 28, 182—, was precisely one of the nights that were wont to call forth these expressions of commiseration. The level rainstorm smote walls, slopes, and hedges like the clothyard shafts of Senlac and Crecy. Such sheep and outdoor animals as had no shelter stood with their buttocks to the winds; while the tails of little birds trying to roost on some scraggy thorn were blown inside-out like umbrellas. The gable-end of the cottage was stained with wet, and the evesdroppings flapped against the wall. Yet never was commiseration for the shepherd more misplaced. For that cheerful rustic was entertaining a large party in glorification of the christening of his second girl.

The guests had arrived before the rain began to fall, and they were all now assembled in the chief or living room of the dwelling. A glance into the apartment at eight o'clock on this eventful evening would have resulted in the opinion that it was as cosy and comfortable a nook as could be wished for in boisterous weather. The calling of its inhabitant was proclaimed by a number of highly-polished sheep-crooks without stems that were hung ornamentally over the fireplace, the curl of each shining crook varying from the antiquated type engraved in the patriarchal pictures of old family Bibles to the most approved fashion of the last local sheep-fair. The room was lighted by half-a-dozen candles, having wicks only a trifle smaller than the grease which enveloped them, in candlesticks that were never used but at high-days, holy-days, and family feasts. The lights were scattered about the room, two of them standing on the chimney-piece. This position of candles was in itself significant. Candles on the chimney-piece always meant a party.

On the hearth, in front of a back-brand to give substance, blazed a fire of thorns, that crackled "like the laughter of the fool."

Nineteen persons were gathered here. Of these, five women, wearing gowns of various bright hues, sat in chairs along the wall; girls shy and not shy filled the window-bench; four men, including Charley Jake the hedge-carpenter, Elijah New the parish-clerk, and John Pitcher, a neighbouring dairyman, the shepherd's father-in-law, lolled in the settle; a young man and maid, who were blushing over tentative *pourparlers* on

The Three Strangers 43

a life-companionship, sat beneath the corner-cupboard; and an elderly engaged man of fifty or upward moved restlessly about from spots where his betrothed was not to the spot where she was. Enjoyment was pretty general, and so much the more prevailed in being unhampered by conventional restrictions. Absolute confidence in each other's good opinion begat perfect serenity, was lent to the majority by the absence of any expression or trait denoting that they wished to get on in the world, enlarge their minds, or do any eclipsing thing whatever—which nowadays so generally nips the bloom and *bonhomie* of all except the two extremes of the social scale.

Shepherd Fennel had married well, his wife being a dairyman's daughter from a vale at a distance, who brought fifty guineas in her pocket—and kept them there, till they should be required for ministering to the needs of a coming family. This frugal woman had been somewhat exercised as to the character that should be given to the gathering. A sit-still party had its advantages; but an undisturbed position of ease in chairs and settles was apt to lead on the men to such an unconscionable deal of toping that they would sometimes fairly drink the house dry. A dancing-party was the alternative; but this, while avoiding the foregoing objection on the score of good drink, had a counterbalancing disadvantage in the matter of good victuals, the ravenous appetites engendered by the exercise causing immense havoc in the buttery. Sheperdess Fennel fell back upon the intermediate plan of mingling short dances with short periods of talk and singing, so as to hinder any ungovernable rage in either. But this scheme was entirely confined to her own gentle mind: the shepherd himself was in the mood to exhibit the most reckless phases of hospitality.

The fiddler was a boy of those parts, about twelve years of age, who had a wonderful dexterity in jigs and reels, though his fingers were so small and short as to necessitate a constant shifting for the high notes, from which he scrambled back to the first position with sounds not of unmixed purity of tone. At seven the shrill tweedle-dee of this youngster had begun, accompanied by a booming ground-bass from Elijah New, the parish-clerk, who had thoughtfully brought with him his favorite musical instrument, the serpent. Dancing was instantaneous, Mrs. Fennel privately enjoining the players on no account to let the dance exceed the length of a quarter of an hour.

But Elijah and the boy in the excitement of their position quite forgot the injunction. Moreover, Oliver Giles, a man of seventeen, one of the dancers, who was enamoured of his partner, a fair girl of thirty-three rolling years, had recklessly handed a new crown-piece to the musicians, as a bribe to keep going as long as they had muscle and wind. Mrs. Fennel, seeing the steam begin to generate on the countenances of her guests, crossed over and touched the fiddler's elbow and put her hand on the serpent's mouth. But they took no notice, and fearing she might lose her character of genial hostess if she were to interfere too markedly, she retired and sat down helpless. And so the dance whizzed on with cumulative fury, the performers moving in their planet-like courses, direct and retrograde, from apogee to perigee, till the hand of the well-kicked clock at the bottom of the room had travelled over the circumference of an hour.

While these cheerful events were in course of enactment within Fennel's pastoral dwelling an incident having considerable bearing on the party had occurred in the gloomy night without. Mrs. Fennel's concern about the growing fierceness of the dance corresponded in point of time with the ascent of a human figure to the solitary hill of Higher Crowstairs from the direction of the distant town. This personage strode on through the rain without a pause, following the little-worn path which, further on in its course, skirted the shepherd's cottage.

It was nearly the time of full moon, and on this account, though the sky was lined with a uniform sheet of dripping cloud, ordinary objects out of doors were readily visible. The sad wan light revealed the lonely pedestrian to be a man of supple frame; his gait suggested that he had somewhat passed the period of perfect and instinctive agility, though not so far as to be otherwise than rapid of motion when occasion required. At a rough guess, he might have been about forty years of age. He appeared tall, but a recruiting sergeant, or other person accustomed to the judging of men's heights by the eye, would have discerned that this was chiefly owing to his gauntness, and that he was not more than five-feet-eight or nine.

Notwithstanding the regularity of his tread there was caution in it, as in that of one who mentally feels his way; and despite the fact that it was not a black coat nor a dark garment of any sort that he wore, there was something about him which suggested that he naturally belonged to the black-coated tribes of men. His clothes were of fustian, and his boots hobnailed, yet in his progress he showed not the mud-accustomed bearing of hobnailed and fustianed peasantry.

By the time that he had arrived abreast of the shepherd's premises the rain came down, or rather came along, with yet more determined violence. The outskirts of the little settlement partially broke the force of wind and rain, and this induced him to stand still. The most salient of the shepherd's domestic erections was an empty sty at the forward corner of his hedgeless garden, for in these latitudes the principle of masking the homelier features of your establishment by a conventional frontage was unknown. The traveller's eye was attracted to this small building by the pallid shine of the wet slates that covered it. He turned aside, and, finding it empty, stood under the pent-roof for shelter.

While he stood the boom of the serpent within the adjacent house, and the lesser strains of the fiddler, reached the spot as an accompaniment to the surging hiss of the flying rain on the sod, its louder beating on the cabbage-leaves of the garden, on the straw hackles of eight or ten beehives just discernible by the path, and its dripping from the eaves into a row of buckets and pans that had been placed under the walls of the cottage. For at Higher Crowstairs, as at all such elevated domiciles, the grand difficulty of housekeeping was an insufficiency of water; and a casual rainfall was utilized by turning out, as catchers, every utensil that the house contained. Some queer stories might be told of the contrivances for economy in suds and dish-waters that are absolutely necessitated in upland habitations during the droughts of summer. But at this season there were no such exigencies; a mere acceptance of what the skies bestowed was sufficient for an abundant store.

At last the notes of the serpent ceased and the house was silent. This cessation of activity aroused the solitary pedestrian from the reverie into which he had lapsed, and, emerging from the shed, with an apparently new intention, he walked up the path to the house-door. Arrived here, his first act was to kneel down on a large stone beside the row of vessels, and to drink a copious draught from one of them. Having quenched his thirst he rose and lifted his hand to knock, but paused with his eye upon the panel. Since the dark surface of the wood revealed absolutely nothing, it was evident that he must be mentally looking through the door, as if he wished to measure thereby all the possibilities that a house of this sort might include, and how they might bear upon the question of his entry.

In his indecision he turned and surveyed the scene around. Not a soul was anywhere visible. The garden-path stretched downward from his feet, gleaming like the track of a snail; the roof of the little well (mostly dry), the well-cover, the top rail of the garden-gate, were varnished with the same dull liquid glaze; while, far away in the vale, a faint whiteness of more than usual extent showed that the rivers were high in the meads. Beyond all this winked a few bleared lamplights through the beating drops—lights that denoted the situation of the county-town from which he had appeared to come. The absence of all notes of life in that direction seemed to clinch his intentions, and he knocked at the door.

Within, a desultory chat had taken the place of movement and musical sound. The hedge-carpenter was suggesting a song to the company, which nobody just then was inclined to undertake, so that the knock afforded a not unwelcome diversion.

"Walk in!" said the shepherd promptly.

The latch clicked upward, and out of the night our pedestrian appeared upon the door-mat. The shepherd arose, snuffed two of the nearest candles, and turned to look at him.

Their light disclosed that the stranger was dark in complexion and not unprepossessing as to feature. His hat, which for a moment he did not remove, hung low over his eyes, without concealing that they were large, open, and determined, moving with a flash rather than a glance round the room. He seemed pleased with his survey, and, baring his shaggy head, said, in a rich deep voice, "The rain is so heavy, friends, that I ask leave to come in and rest awhile."

"To be sure, stranger," said the shepherd. "And faith, you've been lucky in choosing your time, for we are having a bit of a fling for a glad cause—though, to be sure, a man could hardly wish that glad cause to happen more than once a year."

"Nor less," spoke up a woman. "For 'tis best to get your family over and done with, as soon as you can, so as to be all the earlier out of the fag o't."

"And what may be this glad cause?" asked the stranger.

"A birth and christening," said the shepherd.

The stranger hoped his host might not be made unhappy either by too many or too few of such episodes, and being invited by a gesture to a pull at the mug, he readily acquiesced. His manner, which, before entering, had been so dubious, was now altogether that of a careless and candid man.

"Late to be traipsing athwart this coomb—hey?" said the engaged man of fifty.

"Late it is, master, as you say.—I'll take a seat in the chimney-corner, if you have nothing to urge against it, ma'am; for I am a little moist on the side that was next the rain."

Mrs. Shepherd Fennel assented, and made room for the self-invited comer, who, having got completely inside the chimney-corner, stretched out his legs and his arms with the expansiveness of a person quite at home.

"Yes, I am rather cracked in the vamp," he said freely, seeing that the eyes of the shepherd's wife fell upon his boots, "and I am not well fitted either. I have had some rough times lately, and have been forced to pick up what I can get in the way of wearing, but I must find a suit better fit for working-days when I reach home."

"One of hereabouts?" she inquired.

"Not quite that—further up the country."

"I thought so. And so be I; and by your tongue you come from my neighbourhood."

"But you would hardly have heard of me," he said quickly. "My time would be long before yours, ma'am, you see."

This testimony to the youthfulness of his hostess had the effect of stopping her cross-examination.

The Three Strangers

"There is only one thing more wanted to make me happy," continued the new-comer. "And that is a little baccy, which I am sorry to say I am out of."

"I'll fill your pipe," said the shepherd.

"I must ask you to lend me a pipe likewise."

"A smoker, and no pipe about'ee?"

"I have dropped it somewhere on the road."

The shepherd filled and handed him a new clay pipe, saying, as he did so, "Hand me your baccy-box—I'll fill that too, now I am about it."

The man went through the movement of searching his pockets.

"Lost that too?" said his entertainer, with some surprise.

"I am afraid so," said the man with some confusion. "Give it to me in a screw of paper." Lighting his pipe at the candle with a suction that drew the whole flame into the bowl, he resettled himself in the corner and bent his looks upon the faint steam from his damp legs, as if he wished to say no more.

Meanwhile the general body of guests had been taking little notice of this visitor by reason of an absorbing discussion in which they were engaged with the band about a tune for the next dance. The matter being settled, they were about to stand up when an interruption came in the shape of another knock at the door.

At sound of the same the man in the chimney-corner took up the poker and began stirring the brands as if doing it thoroughly were the one aim of his existence; and a second time the shepherd said, "Walk in!" In a moment another man stood upon the straw-woven doormat. He too was a stranger.

This individual was one of a type radically different from the first. There was more of the commonplace in his manner, and a certain jovial cosmopolitanism sat upon his features. He was several years older than the first arrival, his hair being slightly frosted, his eyebrows bristly, and his whiskers cut back from his cheeks. His face was rather full and flabby, and yet it was not altogether a face without power. A few grog-blossoms marked the neighbourhood of his nose. He flung back his long drab greatcoat, revealing that beneath it he wore a suit of cinder-gray shade throughout, large heavy seals, of some metal or other that would take a polish, dangling from his fob as his only personal ornament. Shaking the water-drops from his low-crowned glazed hat, he said, "I must ask for a few minutes' shelter, comrades, or I shall be wetted to my skin before I get to Casterbridge."

"Make yourself at home, master," said the sheperd, perhaps a trifle less heartily than on the first occasion. Not that Fennel had the least tinge of niggardliness in his composition; but the room was far from large, spare chairs were not numerous, and damp companions were not altogether desirable at close quarters for the women and girls in their bright-coloured gowns.

However, the second comer, after taking off his greatcoat, and hanging his hat on a nail in one of the ceiling-beams as if he had been specially invited to put it there, advanced and sat down at the table. This had been pushed so closely into the chimney-corner, to give all available room to the dancers, that its inner edge grazed the elbow of the man who had ensconced himself by the fire; and thus the two strangers were brought into close companionship. They nodded to each other by way of breaking the ice of unacquaintance, and the first stranger handed his neighbour the family mug—a huge vessel of brown ware, having its upper edge worn away like a threshold by the rub of whole generations of thirsty lips that had gone the way of all flesh, and bearing the following inscription burnt upon its rotund side in yellow letters:—

THERE IS NO FUN
UNTILL I CUM

The other man, nothing loth, raised the mug to his lips, and drank on, and on, and on—till a curious blueness overspread the countenance of the shepherd's wife, who had regarded with no little surprise the first stranger's free offer to the second of what did not belong to him to dispense.

"I knew it!" said the toper to the shepherd with much satisfaction. "When I walked up your garden before coming in, and saw the hives all of a row, I said to myself, 'Where there's bees there's honey, and where there's honey there's mead.' But mead of such a truly comfortable sort as this I really didn't expect to meet in my older days." He took yet another pull at the mug, till it assumed an ominous elevation.

"Glad you enjoy it!" said the shepherd warmly.

"It is goodish mead," assented Mrs. Fennel, with an absence of enthusiasm which seemed to say that it was possible to buy praise for one's cellar at too heavy a price. "It is trouble enough to make—and really I hardly think we shall make any more. For honey sells well, and we ourselves can make shift with a drop o' small mead and metheglin for common use from the comb-washings."

"O, but you'll never have the heart!" reproachfully cried the stranger in cinder-gray, after taking up the mug a third time and setting it down empty. "I love mead, when 'tis old like this, as I love to go to church o' Sundays or to relieve the needy any day of the week."

"Ha, ha, ha!" said the man in the chimney-corner, who, in spite of the taciturnity induced by the pipe of tobacco, could not or would not refrain from this slight testimony to his comrade's humour.

Now the old mead of those days, brewed of the purest first-year or maiden honey, four pounds to the gallon—with its due complement of white of eggs, cinnamon, ginger, cloves, mace, rosemary, yeast, and processes of working, bottling, and cellaring—tasted remarkably strong; but it did not taste so strong as it actually was. Hence, presently, the stranger in cinder-gray at the table, moved by its creeping influence, unbuttoned his waistcoat, threw himself back in his chair, spread his legs, and made his presence felt in various ways.

"Well, well, as I say," he resumed, "I am going to Casterbridge, and to Casterbridge I must go. I should have been almost there by this time; but the rain drove me into your dwelling, and I'm not sorry for it."

"You don't live in Casterbridge?" said the shepherd.

"Not as yet; though I shortly mean to move there."

"Going to set up in trade, perhaps?"

"No, no," said the shepherd's wife. "It is easy to see that the gentleman is rich, and don't want to work at anything."

The cinder-gray stranger paused, as if to consider whether he would accept that definition of himself. He presently rejected it by answering, "Rich is not quite the word for me, dame. I do work, and I must work. And even if I only get to Casterbridge by midnight I must begin work there at eight to-morrow morning. Yes, het or wet, blow or snow, famine or sword, my day's work to-morrow must be done."

"Poor man! Then, in spite o' seeming, you be worse off than we?" replied the shepherd's wife.

" 'Tis the nature of my trade, men and maidens. 'Tis the nature of my trade more than my poverty. . . . But really and truly I must up and off, or I shan't get a lodging in the town." However, the speaker did not move, and directly added, "There's time for one more draught of friendship before I go; and I'd perform it at once if the mug were not dry."

"Here's a mug o' small," said Mrs. Fennel. "Small, we call it, though to be sure 'tis only the first wash o' the combs."

"No," said the stranger disdainfully. "I won't spoil your first kindness by partaking o' your second."

"Certainly not," broke in Fennel. "We don't increase and multiply every day, and I'll fill the mug again." He went away to the dark place under the stairs where the barrel stood. The shepherdess followed him.

"Why should you do this?" she said reproachfully, as soon as they were alone. "He's emptied it once, though it held enough for ten people; and now he's not contented wi' the small, but must needs call for more o' the strong! And a stranger unbeknown to any of us. For my part, I don't like the look o' the man at all."

"But he's in the house, my honey; and 'tis a wet night, and a christening. Daze it, what's a cup of mead more or less? There'll be plenty more next bee-burning."

"Very well—this time, then," she answered, looking wistfully at the barrel. "But what is the man's calling, and where is he one of, that he should come in and join us like this?"

"I don't know. I'll ask him again."

The catastrophe of having the mug drained dry at one pull by the stranger in cinder-gray was effectually guarded against this time by Mrs. Fennel. She poured out his allowance in a small cup, keeping the large one at a discreet distance from him. When he had tossed off his portion the shepherd renewed his inquiry about the stranger's occupation.

The latter did not immediately reply, and the man in the chimney-corner, with sudden demonstrativeness, said, "Anybody may know my trade—I'm a wheelwright."

"A very good trade for these parts," said the shepherd.

"And anybody may know mine—if they've the sense to find it out," said the stranger in cinder-gray.

"You may generally tell what a man is by his claws," observed the hedge-carpenter, looking at his own hands. "My fingers be as full of thorns as an old pin-cushion is of pins."

The hands of the man in the chimney-corner instinctively sought the shade, and he gazed into the fire as he resumed his pipe. The man at the table took up the hedge-carpenter's remark, and added smartly, "True; but the oddity of my trade is that, instead of setting a mark upon me, it sets a mark upon my customers."

No observation being offered by anybody in elucidation of this enigma the shepherd's wife once more called for a song. The same obstacles presented themselves as at the former time—one had no voice, another had forgotten the first verse. The stranger at the table, whose soul had now risen to a good working temperature, relieved the difficulty by exclaiming that, to start the company, he would sing himself. Thrusting one thumb into the arm-hole of his waistcoat, he waved the other hand in the air, and, with an extemporizing gaze at the shining sheep-crooks above the mantelpiece, began:—

> O my trade it is the rarest one,
>   Simple shepherds all—
> My trade is a sight to see;
> For my customers I tie, and take them up on high,
>   And waft 'em to a far countree!

The room was silent when he had finished the verse—with one exception, that of the man in the chimney-corner, who, at the singer's word, "Chorus!" joined him in a deep bass voice of musical relish—

> And waft 'em to a far contree!

Oliver Giles, John Pitcher the dairyman, the parish-clerk, the engaged man of fifty, the row of young women against the wall, seemed lost in thought not of the gayest kind. The shepherd looked meditatively on the ground, the shepherdess gazed keenly at the singer, and with some suspicion; she was doubting whether this stranger were merely singing an old song from recollection, or was composing one there and then for the occasion. All were as perplexed at the obscure revelation as the guests at Belshazzar's Feast, except the man in the chimney-corner, who quietly said, "Second verse, stranger," and smoked on.

The singer thoroughly moistened himself from his lips inwards, and went on with the next stanza as requested:—

> My tools are but common ones,
>   Simple shepherds all—
> My tools are no sight to see:
> A little hempen string, and a post whereon to swing,
>   Are implements enough for me!

Shepherd Fennel glanced round. There was no longer any doubt that the stranger was answering his question rhythmically. The guests one and all started back with suppressed exclamations. The young woman engaged to the man of fifty fainted half-way, and would have proceeded, but finding him wanting in alacrity for catching her she sat down trembling.

"O, he's the—!" whispered the people in the background, mentioning the name of an onimous public officer. "He's come to do it! 'Tis to be at Casterbridge jail to-morrow—the man for sheep-stealing—the poor clockmaker we heard of, who used to live away at Shottsford and had no work to do—Timothy Summers, whose family were a-starving, and so he went out of Shottsford by the high-road, and took a sheep in open daylight, defying the farmer and the farmer's wife and the farmer's lad, and every man jack among 'em. He" (and they nodded towards the stranger of the deadly trade) "is come from up the country to do it because there's not enough to do in his own county-town, and he's got the place here now our own county man's dead; he's going to live in the same cottage under the prison wall."

The stranger in cinder-gray took no notice of this whispered string of observations, but again wetted his lips. Seeing that his friend in the chimney-corner was the only one who reciprocated his joviality in any way, he held out his cup towards that appreciative comrade, who also held out his own. They clinked together, the eyes of the rest of the room hanging upon the singer's actions. He parted his lips for the third verse; but at that moment another knock was audible upon the door. This time the knock was faint and hesitating.

The company seemed scared; the shepherd looked with consternation towards the entrance, and it was with some effort that he resisted his alarmed wife's deprecatory glance, and uttered for the third time the welcoming words, "Walk in!"

The door was gently opened, and another man stood upon the mat. He, like those who had preceded him, was a stranger. This time it was a short, small personage, of fair complexion, and dressed in a decent suit of dark clothes.

"Can you tell me the way to_____?" he began: when gazing round the room to observe the nature of the company amongst whom he had fallen, his lighted on the stranger in cinder-gray. It was just at the instant when the latter, who had thrown his mind into his song with such a will that he scarcely heeded the interruption, silenced all whispers and inquiries by bursting into his third verse:—

> To-morrow is my working day,
>   Simple shepherds all—
> To-morrow is a working day for me:
> For the farmer's sheep is slain, and the lad who did it ta'en,
>   And on his soul may God ha' merc-y!

The stranger in the chimney-corner, waving cups with the singer so heartily that his mead splashed over on the hearth, repeated in his bass voice as before:—

And on his soul may God ha' merc-y!

All this time the third stranger had been standing in the doorway. Finding now that he did not come forward or go on speaking, the guests particularly regarded him. They noticed to their surprise that he stood before them the picture of abject terror—his knees trembling, his hand shaking so violently that the door-latch by which he supported himself rattled audibly: his white lips were parted, and his eyes fixed on the merry officer of justice in the middle of the room. A moment more and he had turned, closed the door, and fled.

"What a man can it be?" said the shepherd.

The rest, between the awfulness of their late discovery and the odd conduct of this third visitor, looked as if they knew not what to think, and said nothing. Instinctively they withdrew further and further from the grim gentleman in their midst; whom some of them seemed to take for the Prince of Darkness himself, till they formed a remote circle, an empty space of floor being left between them and him—

> ... circulus, cujus centrum diabolus.

The room was so silent—though there were more than twenty people in it—that nothing could be heard but the patter of the rain against the window-shutters, accompanied by the occasional hiss of a stray drop that fell down the chimney into the fire, and the steady puffing of the man in the corner, who had now resumed his pipe of long clay.

The stillness was unexpectedly broken. The distant sound of a gun reverberated through the air—apparently from the direction of the county-town.

"Be jiggered!" cried the stranger who had sung the song, jumping up.

"What does that mean?" asked several.

"A prisoner escaped from the jail—that's what it means."

All listened. The sound was repeated, and none of them spoke but the man in the chimney-corner, who said quietly, "I've often been told that in this county they fire a gun at such times; but I never heard it till now."

"I wonder if it is *my* man?" murmured the personage in cinder-gray.

"Surely it is!" said the shepherd unvoluntarily. "And surely we've zeed him! That little man who looked in at the door by now, and quivered like a leaf when he zeed ye and heard your song!"

"His teeth chattered, and the breath went out of his body," said the dairyman.

"And his heart seemed to sink within him like a stone," said Oliver Giles.

"And he bolted as if he'd been shot at," said the hedge-carpenter.

"True—his teeth chattered, and his heart seemed to sink; and he bolted as if he'd been shot at," slowly summed up the man in the chimney-corner.

"I didn't notice it," remarked the hangman.

"We were all a-wondering what made him run off in such fright," faltered one of the women against the wall, "and now 'tis explained!"

The firing of the alarm-gun went on at intervals, low and sullenly, and their suspicions became a certainty. The sinister gentleman in cinder-gray roused himself. "Is there a constable here?" he asked, in thick tones. "If so, let him step forward."

The engaged man of fifty stepped quavering out from the wall, his betrothed beginning to sob on the back of the chair.

"You are a sworn constable?"

"I be, sir."

"Then pursue the criminal at once, with assistance, and bring him back here. He can't have gone far."

"I will, sir, I will—when I've got my staff. I'll go home and get it, and come sharp here, and start in a body."

"Staff!—never mind your staff; the man'll be gone!"

"But I can't do anything without my staff—can I, William, and John, and Charles Jake? No; for there's the king's royal crown a painted on en in yaller and gold, and the lion and the unicorn, so as when I raise en up and hit my prisoner, 'tis made a lawful blow thereby. I wouldn't 'tempt to take up a man without my staff—no, not I. If I hadn't the law to gie me courage, why, instead o' my taking up him he might take up me!"

"Now, I'm a king's man myself, and can give you authority enough for this," said the formidable officer in gray. "Now then, all of ye, be ready. Have ye any lanterns?"

"Yes—have ye any lanterns?—I demand it!" said the constable.

"And the rest of you able-bodied—"

"Able-bodied man—yes—the rest of ye!" said the constable.

"Have you some good stout staves and pitchforks—"

"Staves and pitchforks—in the name o' the law! And take 'em in yer hands and go in quest, and do as we in authority tell ye!"

Thus aroused, the men prepared to give chase. The evidence was, indeed, though circumstantial, so convincing, that but little argument was needed to show the shepherd's guests that after what they had seen it would look very much like connivance if they did not instantly pursue the unhappy third stranger, who could not as yet have gone more than a few yards over such uneven country.

A shepherd is always well provided with lanterns; and, lighting these hastily, and with hurdle-staves in their hands, they poured out of the door, taking a direction along the crest of the hill, away from the town, the rain having fortunately a little abated.

Disturbed by the noise, or possibly by unpleasant dreams of her baptism, the child who had been christened began to cry heart-brokenly in the room overhead. These notes of grief came down through the chinks of the floor to the ears of the women below, who jumped up one by one, and seemed glad of the excuse to ascend and comfort the baby, for the incidents of the last half-hour greatly oppressed them. Thus in the space of two or three minutes the room on the ground-floor was deserted quite.

But it was not for long. Hardly had the sound of footsteps died away when a man returned round the corner of the house from the direction the pursuers had taken. Peeping in at the door, and seeing nobody there, he entered leisurely. It was the stranger of the chimney-corner, who had gone out with the rest. The motive of his return was shown by his helping himself to a cut piece of skimmer-cake that lay on a ledge beside where he had sat, and which he had apparently forgotten to take with him. He also poured out half a cup more mead from the quantity that remained, ravenously eating and drinking these as he stood. He had not finished when another figure came in just as quietly—his friend in cinder-gray.

"O—you here?" said the latter, smiling. "I thought you had gone to help in the capture." And this speaker also revealed the object of his return by looking solicitously round for the fascinating mug of old mead.

"And I thought you had gone," said the other, continuing his skimmer-cake with some effort.

"Well, on second thoughts, I felt there were enough without me," said the first confidentially, "and such a night as it is, too. Besides, 'tis the business o' the Government to take care of its criminals—not mine."

"True; so it is. And I felt as you did, that there were enough without me."

"I don't want to break my limbs running over the humps and hollows of this wild country."

"Nor I neither, between you and me."

"These shepherd-people are used to it—simple-minded souls, you know, stirred up to anything in a moment. They'll have him ready for me before the morning, and no touble to me at all."

"They'll have him, and we shall have saved ourselves all labour in the matter."

"True, true. Well, my way is to Casterbridge; and 'tis as much as my legs will do to take me that far. Going the same way?"

"No, I am sorry to say! I have to get home over there" (he nodded indefinitely to the right), "and I feel as you do, that it is quite enough for my legs to do before bedtime."

The other had by this time finished the mead in the mug, after which, shaking hands heartily at the door, and wishing each other well, they went their several ways.

In the meantime the company of pursuers had reached the end of the hog's-back elevation which dominated this part of the down. They had decided on no particular plan of action; and, finding that the man of the baleful trade was no longer in their company, they seemed quite unable to form any such plan now. They descended in all directions down the hill, and straightway several of the party fell into the snare set by Nature for all misguided midnight ramblers over this part of the cretaceous formation. The "lanchets," or flint slopes, which belted the escarpment at intervals of a dozen yards, took the less cautious ones unawares, and losing their footing on the rubbly steep they slid sharply downwards, the lanterns rolling from their hands to the bottom, and there lying on their sides till the horn was scorched through.

When they had again gathered themselves together the shepherd, as the man who knew the country best, took the lead, and guided them round these treacherous inclines. The lanterns, which seemed rather to dazzle their eyes and warn the fugitive than to assist them in the exploration, were extinguished, due silence was observed; and in this more rational order they plunged into the vale. It was a grassy, briery, moist defile, affording some shelter to any person who had sought it; but the party perambulated it in vain, and ascended on the other side. Here they wandered apart, and after an interval closed together again to report progress. At the second time of closing in they found themselves near a lonely ash, the single tree on this part of the coomb, probably sown there by a passing bird some fifty years before. And here, standing a little to one side of the trunk, as motionless as the trunk itself, appeared the man they were in quest of, his outline being well defined against the sky beyond. The band noiselessly drew up and faced him.

"Your money or your life!" said the constable sternly to the still figure.

"No, no," whispered John Pitcher. " 'Tisn't our side ought to say that. That's the doctrine of vagabonds like him, and we be on the side of the law."

"Well, well," replied the constable impatiently; "I must say something, mustn't I? and if you had all the weight o' this undertaking upon your mind, perhaps you'd say the wrong thing too!—Prisoner at the bar, surrender, in the name of the Father—the Crown, I mane!"

The man under the tree seemed now to notice them for the first time, and, giving them no opportunity whatever for exhibiting their courage, he strolled slowly towards them. He was, indeed, the little man, the third stranger; but his trepidation had in a great measure gone.

"Well, travellers," he said, "did I hear ye speak to me?"

"You did: you've got to come and be our prisoner at once!" said the constable. "We arrest 'ee on the charge of not biding in Casterbridge jail in a decent proper manner to be hung to-morrow morning. Neighbours, do your duty, and seize the culpet!"

On hearing the charge the man seemed enlightened, and, saying not another word, resigned himself with preternatural civility to the search-party, who, with their staves in their hands, surrounded him on all sides, and marched him back towards the shepherd's cottage.

It was eleven o'clock by the time they arrived. The light shining from the open door, a sound of men's voices within, proclaimed to them as they approached the house that some new events had arisen in their absence. On entering they discovered the shepherd's living-room to be invaded by two officers from Casterbridge jail, and a well-known magistrate who lived at the nearest country-seat, intelligence of the escape having become generally circulated.

"Gentlemen," said the constable, "I have brought back your man—not without risk and danger; but every one must do his duty! He is inside this circle of able-bodied persons, who have lent me useful aid, considering their ignorance of Crown work. Men, bring forward your prisoner!" And the third stranger was led to the light.

"Who is this?" said one of the officials.

"The man," said the constable.

"Certainly not," said the turnkey; and the first corroborated his statement.

"But how can it be otherwise?" asked the constable.

"Or why was he so terrified at sight o' the singing instrument of the law who sat there?" Here he related the strange behaviour of the third stranger on entering the house during the hangman's song.

"Can't understand it," said the officer coolly. "All I know is that it is not the condemned man. He's quite a different character from this one; a gauntish fellow, with dark hair and eyes, rather good-looking, and with a musical bass voice that if you heard it once you'd never mistake as long as you lived."

"Why souls—'twas the man in the chimney-corner!"

"Hey—what?" said the magistrate, coming forward after inquiring particulars from the shepherd in the background. "Haven't you got the man after all?"

Well, sir," said the constable, "he's the man we were in search of, that's true; and yet he's not the man we were in search of. For the man we were in search of was not the man we wanted, sir, if you understand my every-day way; for 'twas the man in the chimney-corner!"

"A pretty kettle of fish altogether!" said the magistrate. "You had better start for the other man at once."

The prisoner now spoke for the first time. The mention of the man in the chimney-corner seemed to have moved him as nothing else could do. "Sir," he said, stepping forward to the magistrate, "take no more trouble about me. The time is come when I may as well speak. I have done nothing; my crime is that the condemned man is my brother. Early this afternoon I left home at Shottsford to tramp it all the way to Casterbridge jail to bid him farewell. I was benighted, and called here to rest and ask the way. When I opened the door I saw before me the very man, my brother, that I thought to see in the condemned cell at Casterbrige. He was in this chimney-corner; and jammed close to him, so that he would not have got out if he had tried, was the executioner who'd come to take his life, singing a song about it and not knowing that it was his victim who was close by, joining in to save appearances. My brother threw a glance of agony at me, and I knew he meant, 'Don't reveal what you see; my life depends on it.' I was so terror-struck that I could hardly stand, and not knowing what I did, I turned and hurried away."

The narrator's manner and tone had the stamp of truth, and his story made a great impression on all around.

"And do you know where your brother is at the present time?" asked the magistrate.

"I do not. I have never seen him since I closed this door."

"I can testify to that, for we've been between ye ever since," said the constable.

"Where does he think to fly to?—what is his occupation?"

"He's a watch-and-clock-maker, sir."

"A said 'a was a wheelwright—a wicked rogue," said the constible.

"The wheels of clocks and watches he meant, no doubt," said Shepherd Fennel. "I thought his hand were palish for's trade."

"Well, it appears to me that nothing can be gained by retaining this poor man in custody," said the magistrate; "your business lies with the other, unquestionably."

And so the little man was released off-hand; but he looked nothing the less sad on that account, it being beyond the power of magistrate or constable to raze out the written troubles in his brain, for they concerned another whom he regarded with more solicitude than himself. When this was done, and the man had gone his way, the night was found to be so far advanced that it was deemed useless to renew the search before the next morning.

Next day, accordingly, the quest for the clever sheep-stealer became general and keen, to all appearance at least. But the intended punishment was cruelly disproportioned to the transgression, and the sympathy of a great many country-folk in that district was strongly on the side of the fugitive. Moreover, his marvellous coolness and daring in hob-and-nobbling with the hangman, under the unprecedented circumstances of the shepherd's party won their admiration. So that it may be questioned if all those who ostensibly made themselves so busy in exploring woods and fields and lanes were quite so thorough when it came to the private examination of their own lofts and out-houses. Stories were afloat of a mysterious figure being occasionally seen in some old overgrown trackway or other, remote from turnpike roads; but when a search was instituted in any of these suspected quarters nobody was found. Thus the days and weeks passed without tidings.

In brief, the bass-voiced man of the chimney-corner was never recaptured. Some said that he went across the sea, others that he did not, but buried himself in the depths of a populous city. At any rate, the gentleman in cinder-gray never did his morning's work at Casterbridge, nor met anywhere at all, for business purposes, the genial comrade with whom he had passed an hour of relaxation in the lonely house on the slope of the coomb.

The grass has long been green on the graves of Shepherd Fennel and his frugal wife; the guests who made up the christening party have mainly followed their entertainers to the tomb; the baby in whose honour they all had met is a matron in the sere and yellow leaf. But the arrival of the three strangers at the shepherd's that night, and the details connected therewith, is a story as well known as ever in the country about Higher Crowstairs.

■ DISCUSSION

Look back at page 38 and the narrative account of the police case of a "suspect." You realize now, after reading "The Three Strangers" that, in point of fact, the author of the story knew much more about the nature of the "suspect" than is indicated in that ostensible "police account." Thomas Hardy knew, for example, that the second "suspect" was not really the sheep stealer. He was the innocent brother of the sheep stealer. Hardy knew that, even before he had the character first appear in the doorway, probably before he even sat down to write the story. So then the author did precisely what we have said must be done to a narrative account to make it a plot. By withholding information about the identity of the third stranger, Hardy artfully manipulated the straight narrative account. The reason he did this was solely to afford you, the reader, the pleasure that comes from being in suspense.

"The Three Strangers" could have been told this way:

> An escaped felon arrives at a lonely farmhouse, where a festival is under way. As it happens, the official hangman comes to the same farmhouse, imbibes with the felon, and talks with him. The firing of guns signals to the party that the news of the escaped felon has become known, but the felon continues not to be recognized. The hangman has no suspicion either. A third stranger, who is actually the brother of the escaped felon, comes to the door, sees his brother, takes fright, and flees. His sudden fear and flight make the group incorrectly assume that the brother is actually the criminal. They chase him over the dark countryside and eventually capture him. He then reveals himself to be, not the criminal, but the brother of the criminal, explaining that he fled because he was startled and frightened when he opened the door and saw his brother wedged in by the executioner, unable to escape. The crowd accepts this explanation, and they let the brother of the criminal go. After that, there is general public sympathy for the sheep stealer, and he is helped in maintaining his hiding from the law and is never found.

That's the way the narrative *might* have been given. How does this retelling differ from Hardy's version? In our retelling there is no *suspense.* You know from the outset that the first stranger is the fugitive criminal, and you know from the moment he is introduced that the third stranger is his brother. You are, it is fair to say, cheated of your pleasure in the story (which is why we could not have put the above narrative before the actual story in this book). You have not been allowed to guess, to wonder, to have the enjoyment of perhaps going up a blind alley. For in the real story, Hardy has greatly rearranged matters. The suspense he has allowed to develop in the reader (by withholding information) is a frequent ingredient of plot.

Suspense is built up in several ways. It can be built up by not telling you important facts, or by leading you up blind alleys, or by defeating your expectations. Hardy has let you think, at the beginning of the story, that the first stranger must be the fugitive; he then introduced the second stranger, whom you probably recognized as the executioner fairly quickly. Then Hardy shocks you once again by introducing the third stranger, who seems even more like the fugitive than does the first man, whom now presumably you are no longer sure of.

Suspense can, then, be aroused by the manipulation of events in order to frustrate your expectations, and to exercise your powers of reasoning. Suspense can also be aroused in some measure by the *setting* of the story. The story we are considering is set in a house placed alone, "detached and undefended" on a lonely down, far in the country, exposed to the elements. The night was cold and rainy, and animals sought shelter—though, inside, as we are told, all was cheerful. But lonely houses, set far from other habitation, and cold and rainy nights are ideal *settings* in which to begin a plot of suspense. Just as inclement weather is said to make arthritics feel pain, so, a wretched night in the setting of a tale gives the reader a shudder of anticipation.

Just as suspense can be furthered by the setting, it can also be furthered by the occurrence of *foreshadowing* elements in a tale. A foreshadowing is an intimation, a hint of something to come. The reader is flicked, teased, nudged by something that brings a thought to mind, faintly perhaps, but ominously. Our story, "The Three Strangers," avails itself of such foreshadowings. One occurs early on. The first stranger has arrived at the house of Shepherd Fennel. One thing only, he says, he needs now to make him happy sitting there by the chimney corner—tobacco. "I'll fill your pipe," said the shepherd. "I must ask you to lend me a pipe likewise," says the stranger, and sensibly the shepherd puzzles how it should happen that the smoker, out of tobacco, should also be wanting his pipe. Something is amiss, we must surely realize. This is no casual, leisurely wanderer in the lonely country. He must have been running from something, we rightly surmise.

A second foreshadowing occurs when Shepherd Fennel asks the first stranger what his occupation is. The stranger replies that he is a wheelwright. The carpenter in the crowd says you can always tell a man's trade by looking at his hands. Instantly, the stranger hides his hands, or, as Hardy put it, "they sought the shade." You are of course supposed to notice that. The author wants you to be suspicious of the stranger. He clearly wants you to see that the stranger has something to hide. All this foreshadowing exists in order to build up the suspense—which in this particular story is to be heightened by having you temporarily confused and having you question whether you were not perhaps very mistaken in ever having thought the first stranger guilty.

If you are beginning to feel that you are being played with, you are absolutely right. Story telling is a form of play. The skilled author does play with your emotions. He does not, as we have said before, tell you everything at the outset, but he hides facts from you; and he juxtaposes the telling of other facts in such a way that he will maximize your suspense, so that your interest and curiosity will be stretched to the limit. In "The Three Strangers" we are able to chart quite accurately the way in which Hardy has done this—the precise manner in which your interest and your curiosity are played, nursed along, played a little more, and finally satisfied as the story is "wrapped up."

The whole enterprise is not unlike playing in a fish. One must hook the fish first, that is, capture the interest of the reader. Then one reels him in—fish or reader—occasionally allowing him line, letting him have some runs, letting him follow his own ideas for awhile. But in the final reckoning, fisherman or storyteller is in control. The fish will be in the creel, and the storyteller knows that the reader will be, metaphorically speaking, in the palm of his hand. Let us see how this "playing in" works in "The Three Strangers."

The setting is given at the outset—the rainy night, the lonely cottage on the desolate down. But inside the cottage all is well: a cheerful party is celebrating a christening. Several pages are taken to tell you about the country folk, the jolliness of the gathering. Note that only a very slight ominous note has been sounded so far—the desolation of the scene outside. The author assumes that the reader has enough patience and enough self-restraint that, though perhaps his curiosity has been piqued by the intimation of the opening, he will be mannerly and patient while the simple country folk are described at their games. A poor reader, we might say right now, or an unexperienced one, like a little child, will demand instant gratification, will have none of the powers of self-control nor the ability to delay gratification that are called for by scenes of what Mark Twain called "weather"—that is, description, scene setting in which "nothing happens." But the more experienced the reader, the subtler the pleasures he can taste, the more he will find pleasures in the very delays, both in the "weather" descriptions themselves, and in the temporary frustration they give to the desire to know "what happens next."

After rather lengthy description of the country folks' festival we are introduced to a human figure on a "solitary hill." He has no name. He is a silhouette—a stranger—a shadow merely. Dramatically seen in the light of the moon, he comes on the scene, he enters the house. Our interest is being tickled. But Hardy gives us still more "weather," and we must be patient a while longer. Finally, however, the stranger is asked in, and in the light of the cottage we see more of him, we are allowed to notice that he is "dark in complexion and not unprepossessing as to feature." He is rendered with sufficient distinctiveness to set him off clearly from the crowd. Picture the scene on a stage. The stranger would stand out by lighting surely, by costume perhaps, and by his physique and restrained power in acting, if that were possible. Now we have a main character on whom we focus, around whom we can be sure much of the story will develop. The author has underlined this actor's authority and centrality for us by the manner in which he has made him appear on the scene: in the moonlight, alone on a solitary hill. He has told us directly that the man was "not unprepossessing," an understated way of saying he had something about him that commands our focus. He will be a main character, we can be sure. Another name for a main character is *protagonist*.

The protagonist, however, is only one of the main characters. Very frequently he is in conflict against a second character, originally called the *antagonist.* This second character (or antagonist) soon makes his appearance, being, fittingly for the pictorial impact of the scene, sharply distinguished from the first. He is older than the first; he is rounder, more jovial; his hair is graying, his eyebrows are bristly, and he has whiskers. He is, in fact, meant to be a contrast for the first, as in the TV western the black-hatted cowboy is opposed to the white-hatted cowboy. These are a dramatist's or storyteller's shorthand devices for distinguishing easily between the protagonist and the antagonist as they are pitted against each other in the conflict.

The *conflict* is what the plot revolves around. It is the hub or the keystone of the plot. It is what ties the plot together. Almost every plotted story has such a conflict. In our story the conflict is between the jolly, talkative second stranger, who, we soon learn, is the hangman, and the taciturn, self-contained first stranger, who, we have much reason to believe, must be the sheep stealer on whom the hangman has been summoned to work his trade. Here they are, so very close to each other, and the question, of course, is how long till the hangman recognizes the fugitive. We wonder about this question throughout the development, as they drink together and talk together, and as the second stranger reveals more and more of his trade, which at first no one was aware of. This *development* of the story—we could call it *rising action,* (thinking of our rising tension and suspense as we are caught up in it)—comes to a sort of *climax,* when (p. 51) the hangman, the "stranger in cinder-grey," holds out his cup and clinks glasses with the fugitive. Never had the two antagonists in the story been closer, nor will they be that close again. They touch for the first and only time in the story. It is the *high-point* of the unseen struggle between them, the climax.

Actually, it is more accurate to say, it is *a* climax, for "The Three Strangers" has a measure of complexity of plot that allows it to have not one, but two climaxes, and it would be difficult to determine which is the more intense. Just as the two men touch glasses, the third stranger enters. He takes one look, displays signs of extreme agitation, and runs away. Then the gun sounds, signalling a prisoner escaped from jail. Reasonably, the assembled people assume that the man who has just fled in such terror is the escaped convict. The reader's certainty that the first stranger, the man by the chimney corner, must have been the sheep stealer, is temporarily shaken.

Now we follow the crowd as they pursue the "fugitive." Such a chase scene is a further development of the plot, and its counterpart appears in thousands of stories—the sheriff chasing the bandit, the Indians chasing the cowboys, the Scotland Yard detective chasing either the villain or, perhaps, the hero whom he mistakes as the villain. As we read, or as we imagine, we can almost hear in our mind's ear the increasing tempo of the music, matching the increasing pace of the chase. Across the desert, over the bridge, along the outside of the moving train, faster, faster, faster, the music ever more furious, until finally, *he's caught*—*climax* number two! The "prisoner" is returned by the posse, and there waiting in the shepherd's living room are two officers from Casterbridge jail. "I have brought back your man. . . ." says the constable. "Who is this?" asks

Plot   63

one of the Casterbridge officials. "The man," says the constable. "Certainly not," says the Casterbridge official, and describes their escapee, who was obviously the first stranger, the man who had been sitting by the chimney corner. At this point the "prisoner" says he must explain, and explain he does. He unfolds the truth before us, unraveling the mysteries, the befuddlements, the confoundings of the plot. He gives us what is called a *dénouement*. A dénouement is, very simply, just this unravelling, this clearing up, this explanation of the difficulties and the intricacies that have been so painstakingly and artfully put together by the teller of the tale.

The dénouement of "The Three Strangers" reveals to us, of course, that we had been right all along. The first stranger *was* the escaped criminal. The second stranger was the hangman. The third stranger—whom Hardy from the outset, knew not to be the criminal—was thrown in as a false lead. We were *supposed* to be satisfied with our first interpretation, only to have our confidence shaken by the appearance and the immediate, suspicious-seeming reaction of the third stranger. Finally, after the rising action to the first climax—the glass clinking—and after the appearance of the third stranger, his chase, capture, and revelation of the "truth of the matter"—we are given one more explanation: that, indeed, there had been some truth in the riddle of the first stranger's saying he had been a wheelwright, since the "wheels" referred to meant the "wheels" and gears of clocks and watches.

This little cleverness, this little wordplay, brings out one last element in plot construction. From his first appearance, we were to feel some respect for the first stranger. He was "not unprepossessing"; he looked taller than he was; he had a certain athleticism to his stride; and, above all, his actions, his coolness in the face of great danger, were intended to arouse our sympathy and gain for him, sheep stealer though he was, a measure of admiration. In the greatest personal danger, he kept his nerve: he drank a toast with his hangman. There is something plucky, admirable, nervy about that. We would hate to see such a cool brave fellow—who even in a moment of peril can concoct a punning riddle about his job—utterly crushed and defeated. It's been a good fight, and there ought to be a reward, something in us whispers. The storyteller knows this feeling in his readers very well, and he will make his story more pleasing by satisfying that desire too. And so the plucky outlaw is never caught. It's not exactly that crime pays, but at least courage does have its rewards. He was never captured, though no one knows precisely what happened, whether he went across the sea, or hid himself in some great city at home. But the hangman lost his customer. It's an old tale of long ago, concludes Hardy. The baby in whose honor that christening was, is now an old lady "in the sere and yellow leaf." It's a story that they tell.

Stories Without Plot

We have been talking of plot, of artfully manipulated narrative with protagonist, antagonist, and a conflict to be resolved. Many stories are constructed just that way, and to the degree that they are resolved, that the strands of complication and the central conflict are clarified, to that degree they are satisfactory. "The Three Strangers" certainly is a story without loose ends. All actors are accounted for, no mystery is unexplained, and we are satisfied that matters have turned out about as they should. But by no means do all short stories work this way. As the writers Wallace and Mary Stegner have stated: "the short story as a distinctive form has turned away from plot, and has tended to become less a complication resolved than what Henry James was to call a 'situation revealed.' "[3]

"Situation revealed," that is the critical phrase.

For our example of a "situation revealed" we use a story by Chekhov, demonstrating that aesthetic pleasure may be evoked in ways more subtle than the manipulated narrative imitation of a conflict. The highest aesthetical satisfaction may well derive from the reader's growing recognition and his understanding of the characters and their situations. Such recognition and understanding does not require a plotted conflict and resolution at all. It needs merely the presentation of human beings, or of a human situation, and the revelation of the truth inherent in that human being or in that situation—a "gradual, slow illumination," as it has been called.

Whereas the "plotted" story derives its coherence from the fact that it is the exposition of one complication, the "unplotted" story derives its unity, its coherence, its "storyness," from the fact that it is one human being or one human moment that unfolds before us as the narrator gives us telling insights, sometimes directly, sometimes quite indirectly by nuance, suggestion, or even omission.

Chekhov's "Gusev" is an example of a story that does not rely primarily on plot. True there is the encounter, the exchange between the two very different characters, Pavel and Gusev. The former is verbal, ratiocinative, always outraged, always protesting, always lawyering away about life and its injustices; and the latter—Gusev—is gentle, ruminative, instinctive, uncomplaining, and above all, accepting. But this "conflict" is not an antagonist matter. Nothing really is at stake between the two characters. The story is named for Gusev; he is the main character without any question; and the story, using Gusev as mankind—everyman personified in him—is really, in its deepest reading, an expansion of the opening sentence: "It is already dark, it will soon be night." Read now the story of Gusev, and the story of the coming of the night.

---

[3]Wallace and Mary Stegner, eds., *Great American Short Stories* (New York: Dell Publishing Co., Inc., 1957) p. 15.

Gusev

Anton Chekhov

It is already dark, it will soon be night.

Gusev, a discharged private, half rises in his bunk and says in a low voice:

"Do you hear me, Pavel Ivanych? A soldier in Suchan was telling me: while they were sailing, their ship bumped into a big fish and smashed a hole in its bottom."

The individual of uncertain social status whom he is addressing, and whom everyone in the ship infirmary calls Pavel Ivanych, is silent as though he hasn't heard.

And again all is still. The wind is flirting with the rigging, the screw is throbbing, the waves are lashing, the bunks creak, but the ear has long since become used to these sounds, and everything around seems to slumber in silence. It is dull. The three invalids—two soldiers and a sailor—who were playing cards all day are dozing and talking deliriously.

The ship is apparently beginning to roll. The bunk slowly rises and falls under Gusev as though it were breathing, and this occurs once, twice, three times. . . . Something hits the floor with a clang: a jug must have dropped.

"The wind has broken loose from its chain," says Gusev, straining his ears.

This time Pavel Ivanych coughs and says irritably:

From *The Portable Chekhov,* edited and translated by Avrahm Yarmolinsky. Copyright © 1947 by The Viking Press, Inc. Reprinted by permission of the Viking Press, Inc.

"One minute a vessel bumps into a fish, the next the wind breaks loose from its chain. . . . Is the wind a beast that it breaks loose from its chain?"

"That's what Christian folks say."

"They are as ignorant as you. . . . They say all sorts of things. One must have one's head on one's shoulders and reason it out. You have no sense."

Pavel Ivanych is subject to seasickness. When the sea is rough he is usually out of sorts, and the merest trifle irritates him. In Gusev's opinion there is absolutely nothing to be irritated about. What is there that is strange or out of the way about that fish, for instance, or about the wind breaking loose from its chain? Suppose the fish were as big as the mountain and its back as hard as a sturgeon's, and supposing, too, that over yonder at the end of the world stood great stone walls and the fierce winds were chained up to the walls. If they haven't broken loose, why then do they rush all over the sea like madmen and strain like hounds tugging at their leash? If they are not chained up what becomes of them when it is calm?

Gusev ponders for a long time about fishes as big as a mountain and about stout, rusty chains. Then he begins to feel bored and falls to thinking about his home, to which he is returning after five years' service in the Far East. He pictures an immense pond covered with drifts. On one side of the pond is the brick-colored building of the pottery with a tall chimney and clouds of black smoke; on the other side is a village. His brother Alexey drives out of the fifth yard from the end in a sleigh; behind him sits his little son Vanka in big felt boots, and his little girl Akulka also wearing felt boots. Alexey has had a drop, Vanka is laughing, Akulka's face cannot be seen, she is muffled up.

"If he doesn't look out, he will have the children frostbitten," Gusev reflects. "Lord send them sense that they may honor their parents and not be any wiser than their father and mother."

"They need new soles," a delirious sailor says in a bass voice. "Yes, yes!"

Gusev's thoughts abruptly break off and suddenly without rhyme or reason the pond is replaced by a huge bull's head without eyes, and the horse and sleigh are no longer going straight ahead but are whirling round and round, wrapped in black smoke. But still he is glad he has had a glimpse of his people. In fact, he is breathless with joy, and his whole body, down to his fingertips, tingles with it. "Thanks be to God we have seen each other again," he mutters deliriously, but at once opens his eyes and looks for water in the dark.

He drinks and lies down, and again the sleigh is gliding along, then again there is the bull's head without eyes, smoke, clouds. . . . And so it goes till daybreak.

II

A blue circle is the first thing to become visible in the darkness—it is the porthole; then, little by little, Gusev makes out the man in the next bunk, Pavel Ivanych. The man sleeps sitting up, as he cannot breathe lying down. His face is gray, his nose long and sharp, his eyes look huge because he is terribly emaciated, his temples are sunken, his beard skimpy, his hair long. His face does not reveal his social status; you cannot tell whether he is a gentleman, a merchant, or a peasant. Judging from his expression and his long hair, he may be an assiduous churchgoer or a lay brother, but his manner of speaking does not seem to be that of a monk. He is utterly worn out by his cough, by the stifling heat, his illness, and he breathes with difficulty, moving his parched lips. Noticing that Gusev is looking at him he turns his face toward him and says:

"I begin to guess. . . . Yes, I understand it all perfectly now."

"What do you understand, Pavel Ivanych?"

"Here's how it is. . . . It has always seemed strange to me that terribly ill as you fellows are, you should be on a steamer where the stifling air, the heavy seas, in fact everything, threatens you with death; but now it is all clear to me. . . . Yes. . . . The doctors put you on the steamer to get rid of you. They got tired of bothering with you, cattle. . . . You don't pay them any money, you are a nuisance, and you spoil their statistics with your deaths. . . . So, of course, you are just cattle. And it's not hard to get rid of you. . . . All that's necessary is, in the first place, to have no conscience or humanity, and, secondly, to deceive the ship authorities. The first requirement need hardly be given a thought—in that respect we are virtuosos, and as for the second condition, it can always be fulfilled with a little practice. In a crowd of four hundred healthy soldiers and sailors, five sick ones are not conspicuous; well, they got you all onto the steamer, mixed you with the healthy ones, hurriedly counted you over, and in the confusion nothing untoward was noticed, and when the steamer was on the way, people discovered that there were paralytics and consumptives on their last legs lying about the deck. . . ."

Gusev does not understand Pavel Ivanych; thinking that he is being reprimanded, he says in self-justification:

"I lay on the deck because I was so sick; when we were being unloaded from the barge onto the steamer, I caught a bad chill."

"It's revolting," Pavel Ivanych continues. "The main thing is, they know perfectly well that you can't stand the long journey and yet they put you here. Suppose you last as far as the Indian Ocean, and then what? It's horrible to think of. . . . And that's the gratitude for your faithful, irreproachable service!"

Pavel Ivanych's eyes flash with anger. He frowns fastidiously and says, gasping for breath, "Those are the people who ought to be given a drubbing in the newspapers till the feathers fly in all directions."

The two sick soldiers and the sailor have waked up and are already playing cards. The sailor is half reclining in his bunk, the soldiers are sitting near by on the floor in most uncomfortable positions. One of the soldiers has his right arm bandaged and his wrist is heavily swathed in wrappings that look like a cap, so that he holds his cards under his right arm or in the crook of his elbow while he plays with his left. The ship is rolling heavily. It is impossible to stand up, or have tea, or take medicine.

"Were you an orderly?" Pavel Ivanych asks Gusev.

"Yes, sir, an orderly."

"My God, my God!" says Pavel Ivanych and shakes his head sadly. "To tear a man from his home, drag him a distance of ten thousand miles, then wear him out till he gets consumption and . . . and what is it all for, one asks? To turn him into an orderly for some Captain Kopeykin or Midshipman Dyrka! How reasonable!"

"It's not hard work, Pavel Ivanych. You get up in the morning and polish the boots, start the samovars going, tidy the rooms, and then you have nothing more to do. The lieutenant drafts plans all day, and if you like, you can say your prayers, or read a book or go out on the street. God grant everyone such a life."

"Yes, very good! The lieutenant drafts plans all day long, and you sit in the kitchen and long for home. . . . Plans, indeed! . . . It's not plans that matter but human life. You have only one life to live and it mustn't be wronged."

"Of course, Pavel Ivanych, a bad man gets no break anywhere, either at home or in the service, but if you live as you ought and obey orders, who will want to wrong you? The officers are educated gentlemen, they understand. . . . In five years I have never once been in the guard house, and I was struck, if I remember right, only once."

"What for?"

"For fighting. I have a heavy hand, Pavel Ivanych. Four Chinks came into our yard; they were bringing firewood or something, I forget. Well, I was bored and I knocked them about a bit, the nose of one of them, damn him, began bleeding. . . . The lieutenant saw it all through the window, got angry, and boxed me on the ear."

"You are a poor, foolish fellow. . . ." whispers Pavel Ivanych. "You don't understand anything."

He is utterly exhausted by the rolling of the ship and shuts his eyes; now his head drops back, now it sinks forward on his chest. Several times he tries to lie down but nothing comes of it: he finds it difficult to breathe.

"And what did you beat up the four Chinks for?" he asks after a while.

"Oh, just like that. They came into the yard and I hit them."

There is silence. . . . The card-players play for two hours, eagerly, swearing sometimes, but the rolling and pitching of the ship overcomes them, too; they throw aside the cards and lie down. Again Gusev has a vision: the big pond, the pottery, the village. . . . Once more the sleigh is gliding along, once more Vanka is laughing and Akulka, the silly thing, throws open her fur coat and thrusts out her feet, as much as to say: "Look, good people, my felt boots are not like Vanka's, they're new ones."

"Going on six, and she has no sense yet," Gusev mutters in his delirium. "Instead of showing off your boots you had better come and get your soldier uncle a drink. I'll give you a present."

And here is Andron with a flintlock on his shoulder, carrying a hare he has killed, and behind him is the decrepit old Jew Isaychik, who offers him a piece of soap in exchange for the hare; and here is the black calf in the entry, and Domna sewing a shirt and crying about something, and then again the bull's head without eyes, black smoke. . . .

Someone shouts overhead, several sailors run by; it seems that something bulky is being dragged over the deck, something falls with a crash. Again some people run by. . . . Has there been an accident? Gusev raises his head, listens, and sees that the two soldiers and the sailor are playing cards again; Pavel Ivanych is sitting up and moving his lips. It is stifling, you haven't the strength to breathe, you are thirsty, the water is warm, disgusting. The ship is still rolling and pitching.

Suddenly something strange happens to one of the soldiers playing cards. He calls hearts diamonds, gets muddled over his score, and drops his cards, then with a frightened, foolish smile looks round at all of them.

"I shan't be a minute, fellows. . . ." he says, and lies down on the floor.

Everybody is nonplussed. They call to him, he does not answer.

"Stepan, maybe you are feeling bad, eh?" the soldier with the bandaged arm asks him. "Perhaps we had better call the priest, eh?"

"Have a drink of water, Stepan. . . ." says the sailor. "Here, brother, drink."

"Why are you knocking the jug against his teeth?" says Gusev angrily. "Don't you see, you cabbage-head?"

"What?"

"What?" Gusev mimicks him. "There is no breath in him, he's dead! That's what! Such stupid people. Lord God!"

III

The ship has stopped rolling and Pavel Ivanych is cheerful. He is no longer cross. His face wears a boastful, challenging, mocking expression. It is as though he wants to say: "Yes, right away I'll tell you something that will make you burst with laughter." The round porthole is open and a soft breeze is blowing on Pavel Ivanych. There is a sound of voices, the splash of oars in the water. ... Just under the porthole someone is droning in a thin, disgusting voice; must be a Chinaman singing.

"Here we are in the harbor," says Pavel Ivanych with a mocking smile. "Only another month or so and we shall be in Russia. M'yes, messieurs of the armed forces! I'll arrive in Odessa and from there go straight to Kharkov. In Kharkov I have a friend, a man of letters. I'll go to him and say, 'Come, brother, put aside your vile subjects, women's amours and the beauties of Nature, and show up the two-legged vermin'. ... There's a subject for you."

For a while he reflects, then says:

"Gusev, do you know how I tricked them?"

"Tricked who, Pavel Ivanych?"

"Why, these people. ... You understand, on this steamer there is only a first class and a third class, and they only allow peasants, that is, the common herd, to go in the third. If you have got a jacket on and even at a distance look like a gentleman or a bourgeois, you have to go first class, if you please. You must fork out five hundred rubles if it kills you. 'Why do you have such a regulation?' I ask them. 'Do you mean to raise the prestige of the Russian intelligentsia thereby?' 'Not a bit of it. We don't let you simply because a decent person can't go third class; it is too horrible and disgusting there.' 'Yes, sir? Thank you for being so solicitous about decent people's welfare. But in any case, whether it's nasty there or nice, I haven't got five hundred rubles. I didn't loot the Treasury, I didn't exploit the natives, I didn't traffic in contraband, I flogged nobody to death, so judge for yourselves if I have the right to occupy a first class cabin and even to reckon myself among the Russian intelligentsia.' But logic means nothing to them. So I had to resort to fraud. I put on a peasant coat and high boots, I pulled a face so that I looked like a common drunk, and went to the agents: 'Give us a little ticket, your Excellency,' said I—"

"You're not of the gentry, are you?" asked the sailor.

"I come of a clerical family. My father was a priest, and an honest one; he always told the high and mighty the truth to their faces and, as a result, he suffered a great deal."

Pavel Ivanych is exhausted from talking and gasps for breath, but still continues:

"Yes, I always tell people the truth to their faces. I'm not afraid of anyone or anything. In this respect, there is a great difference between me and all of you, men. You are dark people, blind, crushed; you see nothing and what you do see, you don't understand. ... You are told that the wind breaks loose from its chain, that you are beasts, savages, and you believe it; someone gives it to you in the neck—you kiss his hand; some animal in a racoon coat robs you and then tosses you a fifteen-kopeck tip and you say: 'Let me kiss your hand, sir.' You are outcasts, pitiful wretches. I am different, my mind is clear. I see it all plainly like a hawk or an eagle when it hovers over the earth, and I understand everything. I am protest personified. I see tyranny—I protest. I see a hypocrite—I protest, I see a triumphant swine—I protest. And I cannot be put down, no Spanish Inquisition can silence me. No. Cut out my tongue and I will protest with gestures. Wall me up in a cellar—I will shout so that you will hear me half a mile away, or will starve myself to death, so that they may have another weight on their black consciences. Kill me and I will haunt them. All my acquaintances say to me: 'You are a most insufferable person, Pavel Ivanych.' I am proud of such a reputation. I served three years in the Far East and I shall be remembered there a hundred years. I had rows there with everybody. My friends wrote to me from Russia: 'Don't come back,' but here I am going back to spite them. . . . Yes. . . . That's life as I understand it. That's what one can call life."

Gusev is not listening; he is looking at the porthole. A junk, flooded with dazzling hot sunshine, is swaying on the transparent turquoise water. In it stand naked Chinamen, holding up cages with canaries in them and calling out: "It sings, it sings!"

Another boat knocks against it; a steam cutter glides past. Then there is another boat: a fat Chinaman sits in it, eating rice with chopsticks. The water sways lazily, white sea gulls languidly hover over it.

"Would be fine to give that fat fellow one in the neck," reflects Gusev, looking at the stout Chinaman and yawning.

He dozes off and it seems to him that all nature is dozing too. Time flies swiftly by. Imperceptibly the day passes. Imperceptibly darkness descends. . . . The streamer is no longer standing still but is on the move again.

IV

Two days pass. Pavel Ivanych no longer sits up but is lying down. His eyes are closed, his nose seems to have grown sharper.

"Pavel Ivanych," Gusev calls to him. "Hey, Pavel Ivanych."

Pavel Ivanych opens his eyes and moves his lips.

"Are you feeling bad?"

"No. . . . It's nothing. . . ." answers Pavel Ivanych gasping for breath. "Nothing, on the contrary. . . . I am better. . . . You see, I can lie down now. . . . I have improved. . . ."

"Well, thank God for that, Pavel Ivanych."

"When I compare myself to you, I am sorry for you, poor fellows. My lungs are healthy, mine is a stomach cough . . . I can stand hell, let alone the Red Sea. Besides, I take a critical attitude toward my illness and the medicines. While you—Your minds are dark. . . . It's hard on you, very, very hard!"

The ship is not rolling, it is quiet, but as hot and stifling as a Turkish bath; it is hard, not only to speak, but even to listen. Gusev hugs his knees, lays his head on them and thinks of his home. God, in this stifling heat, what a relief it is to think of snow and cold! You're driving in a sleigh; all of a sudden, the horses take fright at something and bolt. Careless of the road, the ditches, the gullies, they tear like mad things right through the village, across the pond, past the pottery, across the open fields. "Hold them!" the pottery hands and the peasants they meet shout at the top of their voices. "Hold them!" But why hold them? Let the keen cold wind beat in your face and bite your hands; let the lumps of snow, kicked up by the horses, slide down your collar, your neck, your chest; let the runners sing, and the traces and the whipple trees break, the devil take them. And what delight when the sleigh upsets and you go flying full tilt into a drift, face right in the snow, and then you get up, white all over with icicles on your mustache, no cap, no gloves, your belt undone. . . . People laugh, dogs bark. . . .

Pavel Ivanych half opens one eye, fixes Gusev with it and asks softly:

"Gusev, did your commanding officer steal?"

"Who can tell, Pavel Ivanych? We can't say, we didn't hear about it."

And after that, a long time passes in silence. Gusev broods, his mind wanders, and he keeps drinking water: it is hard for him to talk and hard for him to listen, and he is afraid of being talked to. An hour passes, a second, a third; evening comes, then night, but he doesn't notice it; he sits up and keeps dreaming of the frost.

There is a sound as though someone were coming into the infirmary, voices are heard, but five minutes pass and all is quiet again.

"The kingdom of Heaven be his and eternal peace," says the soldier with a bandaged arm. "He was an uneasy chap."

"What?" asks Gusev. "Who?"

"He died, they have just carried him up."

"Oh, well," mutters Gusev, yawning, "the kingdom of Heaven be his."

"What do you think, Gusev?" the soldier with the bandaged arm says after a while. "Will he be in the kingdom of Heaven or not?"

"Who do you mean?"

"Pavel Ivanych."

"He will. . . . He suffered so long. Then again, he belonged to the clergy and priests have a lot of relatives. Their prayers will get him there."

The soldier with the bandage sits down on Gusev's bunk and says in an undertone:

"You too, Gusev aren't long for this world. You will never get to Russia."

"Did the doctor or the nurse say so?" asks Gusev.

"It isn't that they said so, but one can see it. It's plain when a man will die soon. You don't eat, you don't drink, you've got so thin it's dreadful to look at you. It's consumption, in a word. I say it not to worry you, but because maybe you would like to receive the sacrament and extreme unction. And if you have any money, you had better turn it over to the senior officer."

"I haven't written home," Gusev sighs. "I shall die and they won't know."

"They will," the sick sailor says in a bass voice. "When you die, they will put it down in the ship's log, in Odessa they will send a copy of the entry to the army authorities, and they will notify your district board or something like that.

Such a conversation makes Gusev uneasy and a vague craving begins to torment him. He takes a drink—it isn't that; he drags himself to the porthole and breathes the hot, moist air—it isn't that; he tries to think of home, of the frost—it isn't that. . . . At last it seems to him that if he stays in the infirmary another minute, he will certainly choke to death.

"It's stifling, brother," he says, "I'll go on deck. Take me there, for Christ's sake."

"All right," the soldier with the bandage agrees. "You can't walk, I'll carry you. Hold on to my neck."

Gusev puts his arm around the soldier's neck, the latter places his uninjured arm round him and carries him up. On the deck, discharged soldiers and sailors are lying asleep side by side; there are so many of them it is difficult to pass.

"Get down on the floor," the soldier with the bandage says softly. "Follow me quietly, hold on to my shirt."

It is dark, there are no lights on deck or on the masts or anywhere on the sea around. On the prow the seaman on watch stands perfectly still like a statue, and it looks as though he, too, were asleep. The steamer seems to be left to its own devices and to be going where it pleases.

"Now they'll throw Pavel Ivanych into the sea," says the soldier with the bandage, "in a sack and then into the water."

"Yes, that's the regulation."

"At home, it's better to lie in the earth. Anyway, your mother will come to the grave and shed a tear."

"Sure."

There is a smell of dung and hay. With drooping heads, steers stand at the ship's rail. One, two, three—eight of them! And there's a pony. Gusev puts out his hand to stroke it, but it shakes its head, shows its teeth, and tries to bite his sleeve.

"Damn brute!" says Gusev crossly.

The two of them thread their way to the prow, then stand at the rail, peering. Overhead there is deep sky, bright stars, peace and quiet, exactly as at home in the village. But below there is darkness and disorder. Tall waves are making an uproar for no reason. Each one of them as you look at it is trying to rise higher than all the rest and to chase and crush its neighbor; it is thunderously attacked by a third wave that has a gleaming white mane and is just as ferocious and ugly.

The sea has neither sense nor pity. If the steamer had been smaller, not made of thick iron plates, the waves would have crushed it without the slightest remorse, and would have devoured all the people in it without distinguishing between saints and sinners. The steamer's expression was equally senseless and cruel. This beaked monster presses forward putting millions of waves in its path; it fears neither darkness nor the wind, nor space, nor solitude—it's all child's play for it, and if the ocean had its population, this monster would crush it, too, without distinguishing between saints and sinners.

"Where are we now?" asks Gusev.

"I don't know. Must be the ocean."

"You can't see land. . . ."

"No chance of it! They say we'll see it only in seven days."

The two men stare silently at the white phosphorescent foam and brood. Gusev is first to break the silence.

"There is nothing frightening here," he says. "Only you feel queer as if you were in a dark forest; but if, let's say, they lowered the boat this minute and an officer ordered me to go fifty miles across the sea to catch fish, I'll go. Or, let's say, if a Christian were to fall into the water right now, I'd jump in after him. A German or a Chink I wouldn't try to save, but I'd go in after a Christian."

"And are you afraid to die?"

"I am. I am sorry about the farm. My brother at home, you know, isn't steady; he drinks, he beats his wife for no reason, he doesn't honor his father and mother. Without me everything will go to rack and ruin, and before long it's my fear that my father and old mother will be begging their bread. But my legs won't hold me up, brother, and it's stifling here. Let's go to sleep."

V

Gusev goes back to the infirmary and gets into his bunk. He is again tormented by a vague desire and he can't make out what it is that he wants. There is a weight on his chest, a throbbing in his head, his mouth is so dry that it is difficult for him to move his tongue. He dozes and talks in his sleep and, worn out with nightmares, with coughing and the stifling heat, towards morning he falls into a heavy sleep. He dreams that they have just taken the bread out of the oven in the barracks and that he has climbed into the oven and is having a steam bath there, lashing himself with a besom of birch twigs. He sleeps for two days and on the third at noon two sailors come down and carry him out of the infirmary. He is sewn up in sailcloth and to make him heavier, they put two gridirons in with him. Sewn up in sailcloth, he looks like a carrot or a radish: broad at the head and narrow at the feet. Before sunset, they carry him on deck and put him on a plank. One end of the plank lies on the ship's rail, the other on a box placed on a stool. Round him stand the discharged soldiers and the crew with heads bared.

"Blessed is our God," the priest begins, "now, and ever, and unto ages of ages."

"Amen," three sailors chant.

The discharged men and the crew cross themselves and look off at the waves. It is strange that a man should be sewn up in sailcloth and should soon be flying into the sea. Is it possible that such a thing can happen to anyone?

The priest strews earth upon Gusev and makes obeisance to him. The men sing "Memory Eternal."

The seaman on watch duty raises the end of the plank, Gusev slides off it slowly and then flying, head foremost, turns over in the air and—plop! Foam covers him, and for a moment, he seems to be wrapped in lace, but the instant passes and he disappears in the waves.

He plunges rapidly downward. Will he reach the bottom? At this spot the ocean is said to be three miles deep. After sinking sixty or seventy feet, he begins to descend more and more slowly, swaying rhythmically as though in hesitation, and, carried along by the current, moves faster laterally than vertically.

And now he runs into a school of fish called pilot fish. Seeing the dark body, the little fish stop as though petrified and suddenly all turn round together and disappear. In less than a minute they rush back at Gusev, swift as arrows and begin zigzagging round him in the water. Then another dark body appears. It is a shark. With dignity and reluctance, seeming not to notice Gusev, as it were, it swims under him; then while he, moving downward, sinks upon its back, the shark turns, belly upward, basks in the warm transparent water and languidly opens its jaws with two rows of teeth. The pilot fish are in ecstasy; they stop to see what will happen next. After playing a little with the body, the shark nonchalantly puts his jaws under it, cautiously touches it with his teeth and the sailcloth is ripped the full length of the body, from head to foot; one of the gridirons falls out, frightens the pilot fish and striking the shark on the flank, sinks rapidly to the bottom.

Meanwhile, up above, in that part of the sky where the sun is about to set, clouds are massing, one resembling a triumphal arch, another a lion, a third a pair of scissors. A broad shaft of green light issues from the clouds and reaches to the middle of the sky; a while later, a violet beam appears alongside of it and then a golden one and a pink one ... The heavens turn a soft lilac tint. Looking at this magnificent enchanting sky, the ocean frowns at first, but soon it, too, takes on tender, joyous, passionate colors for which it is hard to find a name in the language of man.

■ DISCUSSION

"Gusev" is a story of revelation. All the details selected by the author were chosen with the single intention of illuminating the character of Gusev. The very fact that Gusev is such a simple soul, that without the probing and sensitive guidance of the author we might never have noticed him at all, serves merely to point out the nature of the storyteller's art—the very developed, advanced storyteller, who doesn't need a head-on clash between opposing forces to make a story, and who assumes that, with his guidance, the reader too will appreciate the beauty of the seemingly commonplace.

Between Pavel, the irritable, the man who seems to have knowledge of the affairs of the world, and the accepting Gusev, there is no direct conflict. Rather, Pavel's garrulous ill temper sets off even more strongly the acquiescence of Gusev. Pavel announces that he will allow no injustice to be done him. In fact, in the matter of not being charged for first-class passage, he does the worldly powers one better, cleverly obtaining for himself the cheaper third-class passage on the boat. Ironically, however, (and by "irony" we mean that we as readers can see the implications that the character himself cannot see) it may be precisely Pavel's own cleverness that defeated him, through the wretched conditions in the third-class passage that sealed his death. Be that as it may be, Pavel's jibbering protests make even more striking the manner in which Gusev lives with his fate, accepts himself in the order of nature, and acts without recriminations. "If you live as you ought and obey orders, who will want to wrong you?" asks Gusev. In five years, he was never in the guardhouse, he recalls, and was struck only once, for hitting a Chinese. Why did Gusev strike a Chinese? He was bored, he says. Gusev is no saint, implies Chekhov. When the pony on the deck shows its teeth and tries to bite Gusev's sleeve, Gusev responds naturally, humanly. "Damn brute!" he says.

More and more of Gusev is revealed to us as he embarks on his voyage to death, "fearing neither darkness nor the wind, nor space, nor solitude," as he sails on a sea that "has neither sense nor pity." "The voyage," as we explain elsewhere in this book, is one of the oldest and most natural metaphors or symbols for the short trip every man takes on this earth. And Gusev is a "typical" voyager—simple, homeloving, at times short-tempered. He is neither saint nor very great sinner. He is illuminated and revealed as simply a man engaged on the universal voyage into the night.

If that were all, "Gusev" would be an appealing tale. However, Chekhov has added one complication to the revealed picture. When the cantankerous Pavel, always out of harmony with everything human or natural, has been consigned to the deep, the sky overhead is bright with stars, peaceful, and quiet; but the ocean which has received his body is in an uproar, and "there is darkness and disorder." What happens when, shortly thereafter, the body of Gusev is sent to its burial in the sea? Looking like a "carrot or a radish" (poor mortal vegetable) sewn in his canvas, he slides into the water; foam covers him for a moment, and he appears wrapped in lace. Then he disappears from sight of those on the ship, though we the readers are allowed to follow the sack as it plunges first rapidly, then slowly, swaying rhythmically with the currents. First the little pilot fish nose the sack and dart away, bringing back the great, dark shark who dallies briefly and gently with the sack, and then, with his two great rows of teeth rips the sailcloth from head to foot—giving the final tone of mockery to the paltry ceremonials that human creatures perform in their attempts to deny oblivion. And so, shall we say, all is nothing? The ship, the ocean, the night carry saint and sinner alike into an inscrutable and endless darkness. Except—except for that last paragraph. The harmless Gusev is deposited into the unfeeling ocean, his radish body now presumably devoured by a shark—but overhead the heavens seem to give a sign. "The clouds are massing, one resembling a triumphal arch, another a lion, a third a pair of scissors" and great shafts of multicolored light stream from the heavens; the ocean, in sympathy with the celestial radiance, takes on a color too beautiful to be described by the languages of man.

Does, then, the story say that the last shall be first, the humblest shall be the mightiest? Are those clouds really symbols of an arch of triumph, a lion of royalty, and the scissors that in Greek and Norse mythology were the instruments that cut the delicate thread of the life of man? So the story has, on occasion, been interpreted, and reading it that way it is indeed an affirmation of the humble who shall see God. But we would argue vigorously otherwise, for clouds do not keep their shape; they drift and are gone. The ocean reflects the rays of the sun for an instant only. And, as Chekhov himself said at the outset, "It is already dark, it will soon be night." What do you think?

Chapter **3**

CHARACTERS

One of the great attractions of fiction, long or short, is its ability to depict imaginary people or *characters* whose lives and personalities interest us. These characters may seem as familiar as an old friend, or they may be strange creatures we would avoid in our daily lives (like Arnold Friend). Either way, something almost magical happens in the process of reading a good story: we begin to care about the characters, to feel that we know them well. Caring comes from knowing, and certainly in some senses we can know more about a character in a story than we can ever know about a living human being because stories are designed to illuminate personality by presenting characters in revealing situations and by illustrating their "inner" lives. The inner life of a real person remains something of a mystery no matter how "open" he or she is, and the most complex fictional characters can never be as complex as even a simple human being. This is not to say that stories cannot present complicated behavior and personality; it is merely to acknowledge the remarkable variety and mystery of human beings, and to state in another way the necessity of art to help us see into this mystery. Understanding fictional characters can give us insight into the wonders of human nature.

Analyzing fictional characters requires some of the same skills and sensitivity needed for understanding real people. Essentially both activities—character analysis and people analysis—require an interpretation of available clues or data. There are many clues to a person's motivations and personality, but we tend to rely largely on five: words, actions, appearances, backgrounds, and the opinions of others.

Words

Real and fictional people express their thoughts, hopes, beliefs, fears, and feelings in conversation or dialogue. But experience teaches us that we cannot simply listen to the words, *we must also interpret them,* deciding how much to believe as truth, how much to discredit. People may say more—or less—than they mean. Words can be used to reveal or conceal, and some people simply cannot use words confidently and effectively to make their meanings clear. In Doris Lessing's "The Black Madonna" Michele, the artist, can express his inner self in language, but Captain Stocker's regimented mind cannot easily open up to let his inner feelings and needs clarify themselves. When Stocker tries to communicate his troubles to Michele, saying, "what would you do if your wife . . . ," he doesn't finish the question; but we can infer the end of his thought and sense the pain behind it.

Actions

To some extent a person *is* what he *does.* Short stories focus on critical moments in characters' lives because these moments result in significant, revealing actions. In "The Black Madonna," for example, Captain Stocker, a stiff, professional soldier, risks his life to save his drunken Italian friend Michele. Michele is a free spirit, a painter whose life is antithetical to the military ideal. But friendship with Michele jeopardizes Stocker's career because it will not fit into the military mold the Captain has used to order his life. Therefore, he rejects Michele's friendship and the painting offered him as a gift of affection. These two actions —first, the willingness to sacrifice his life and then the rejection—reveal dramatically two incompatible sides of Stocker's personality.

"Actions speak louder than words," goes the old adage, meaning that a person can say one thing and do another. If he does so willfully, he is a hypocrite or a liar; if he does so unconsciously, he may be psychologically unable to act in accord with his ideals or his wishes. His actions may be compulsive, neurotic. He may lack insight into his own personality and motivations. The important thing for the reader is to be aware of discrepancies between words and deeds, and to be able to discern what both reveal about a character.

Appearance

Everything about the way a character looks—clothes, posture, makeup, hairstyle—contribute to our understanding of him. If a person wears only the latest fashions, this suggests something about his personality. It may suggest that he lacks individuality and can be victimized by trends in clothes, or by fads in ideas. Descriptions of appearance must not be slighted for they may contain valuable clues to the author's meaning. Clothes, for example, may have symbolic and thematic implications. In "A Little Cloud" James Joyce takes great care to describe Little Chandler's meticulous attention to his appearance: "He took the greatest care of his fair silken hair and moustache and used perfume discreetly on his handkerchief." As Chandler's personality unfolds, we see that his fastidious appearance provides clues to his inner needs and his vision of himself.

Backgrounds

Modern psychology and sociology have made us acutely aware of the cultural, religious, ethnic, racial, and family backgrounds that shape lives. A human being, these sciences tell us, does not exist apart from his environment, his "setting," anymore than a plant exists apart from the soil that surrounds its roots. If we truly want to know someone, then, we must understand how he is a product of the soil that nourished him. Captain Stocker is a good example of a character whose inner life is greatly determined by external circumstances: he is a product of a culture that believes in its supremacy over the dark peoples of the earth, that believes in a "work ethic," that cannot free itself emotionally from rules and regimented thinking.

Opinions of Others

In some stories, in most drama, and in life we learn much about a person or character from what others have to say about him. Shakespeare's *Antony and Cleopatra* opens with two Roman soldiers discussing how Antony, the greatest soldier in the world, has become a mere plaything of Cleopatra. In our evaluation of Antony we cannot overlook this condemnation of him by two soldiers who have served him faithfully in past combat. We weigh their opinions of Antony together with the opinions of him held by Cleopatra, Caesar, and Enobarbus. In each case we ask questions: Is this opinion valid? Is it complete? Is the holder of it trustworthy? Why does he feel this way? Do other characters share his views, or do they hold different ones? Then, from all these opinions, partial and biased, we form the total picture of this very complicated man, Antony.

II

A writer can present character in two ways—by telling or by showing. If he tells us about a character directly, his method of characterization is *expository*. If he allows his characters to be revealed indirectly through thought, dialogue, and action, his method is *dramatic*. Either method can be very effective, but the expository method used alone can rarely sustain the reader's attention throughout an entire story. Most writers use a combination of expository and dramatic presentations to bring their characters to life, the choice of method depending on the demands of plot and theme. At the beginning of "Where Are You Going, Where Have You Been," Joyce Carol Oates introduces her character directly: "Her name was Connie. She was fifteen and she had a quick nervous giggling habit of craning her neck to glance into mirrors, or checking other people's faces to make sure her own was all right" (p. 22). This exposition serves Ms. Oates's purposes very well, allowing her to sketch her central character quickly and clearly. Later in the story when Arnold Friend arrives at Connie's house, Oates dramatizes the scene, using less exposition and more dialogue and action to heighten the reader's involvement and anticipation.

Exposition can become direct editorial comment on the character—that is, instead of simply describing the character, as Ms. Oates does, the author may tell the reader what to think and feel about him. Ms. Oates could have said, "Connie was a vain, egotistical, shallow adolescent whose budding sexual drives got her into trouble." Far more effectively, Oates describes Connie's clothes, her vain mannerisms, her treatment of her parents in such a way that these details provide a vivid picture of a silly, naive girl whose secret life is potentially dangerous. Ms. Oates *shows* us what kind of person Connie is instead of *telling* us. She trusts us to form our own conclusions.

The more an author obviously manipulates the reader's judgment through assertions about a character, the less the reader participates in the imaginative creation of the fiction. Dramatic rendering of character invites or demands imaginative participation by the reader because he must infer what a character *is* from what the character *says* or *does*. Generally speaking, modern writers and experienced readers prefer dramatic presentation of character with little editorial comment. Modern readers resent having their feelings about fictional people forced upon them. If a writer insists on openly manipulating the feelings and judgments of the reader, we may suspect him of having a didactic or propagandistic purpose, of being inept—or of being cynical in the manner of hack writers.

Whatever way a writer chooses to present characters, he must decide how simple or complex, how *flat* or *round* to make them. Flat characters are one or two dimensional; they have one outstanding personality trait. We can usually summarize a flat character in a sentence or even a phrase —"hen-pecked husband," "Jewish mother," "old-maid librarian," "the faithful wife," "the prom queen." A round character, however, is complex, multifaceted, as difficult to label or categorize as a living human being. The actions of flat characters are generally quite predictable; the actions of round characters may be surprising and unexpected. Round characters are fascinating because they must deal with internal conflicts and contradictions in their lives just as we do.

Not all characters in a story need be presented as round and "lifelike." Writers need the flatest of characters—*stock characters, stereotypes, caricatures*—often to act as a contrast, or *foil,* to a round character, thus illuminating his personality. The important thing is that the character fulfill his role in the plot and theme of the story. Though Hamlet is surely one of the most complex figures in all of literature, some of the most delightful characters in the play—Rosencrantz, Guildenstern, and Osric—are flat, stock types. Despite their lack of complexity, they are absolutely essential to Shakespeare's purposes, because they help us to understand Hamlet.

Flat characters cannot change as a result of experience; they are *static.* A round character, however, can change his personality or outlook. If he does change he is said to be *dynamic.* The change may be slight, internal; in fact, if change is too radical, too sudden, we may not accept it as believable. Change must grow out of the character and the situation in which he finds himself. If Captain Stocker in "The Black Madonna" were suddenly to decide to give up his military position and become an artist, we would feel his conversion to be skin-deep and artificial. Nothing in his character or his background would justify such a radical change. The slight degree of understanding he gains about himself and Michele is all he is capable of, if his character is to be credible.

The essential ingredient for successful characterization is credibility. Fiction does not have to be a "slice of life," a documentary, in order to be plausible, to convey the impression that in the world of the story, these characters are credible. The whackiest characters can be made believable if the author can persuade the reader that *these* people would act *this* way in *these* circumstances. In *Gulliver's Travels* Swift creates a strange world inhabited by tiny Lilliputians and another world in which horses can talk. By first convincing the reader that the behavior of the Lilliputians or the talking horses is consistent within their worlds, he is also able to comment satirically on the vices and follies of real people.

Characters

As you read the stories by James Joyce and Doris Lessing keep these questions in mind:

> Do the characters' thoughts and actions result naturally from their personalities and the situations in which they find themselves? What details of the stories contribute to our understanding of the characters?

A Little Cloud

James Joyce

Eight years before he had seen his friend off at the North Wall and wished him godspeed. Gallaher had got on. You could tell that at once by his travelled air, his well-cut tweed suit, and fearless accent. Few fellows had talents like his and fewer still could remain unspoiled by such success. Gallaher's heart was in the right place and he had deserved to win. It was something to have a friend like that.

Little Chandler's thoughts ever since lunch-time had been of his meeting with Gallaher, of Gallaher's invitation and of the great city London where Gallaher lived. He was called Little Chandler because, though he was but slightly under the average stature, he gave one the idea of being a little man. His hands were white and small, his frame was fragile, his voice was quiet and his manners were refined. He took the greatest care of his fair silken hair and moustache and used perfume discreetly on his handkerchief. The half-moons of his nails were perfect and when he smiled you caught a glimpse of a row of childish white teeth.

As he sat at his desk in the King's Inns he thought what changes those eight years had brought. The friend whom he had known under a shabby and necessitous guise had become a brilliant figure on the London Press. He turned often from his tiresome writing to gaze out of the office window. The flow of a late autumn sunset covered the grass plots and

From *Dubliners* by James Joyce. Copyright © 1967 by the Estate of James Joyce. All rights reserved. Reprinted by permission of the Viking Press, Inc.

A Little Cloud

walks. It cast a shower of kindly golden dust on the untidy nurses and decrepit old men who drowsed on the benches; it flickered upon all the moving figures—on the children who ran screaming along the gravel paths and on everyone who passed through the gardens. He watched the scene and thought of life; and (as always happened when he thought of life) he became sad. A gentle melancholy took possession of him. He felt how useless it was to struggle against fortune, this being the burden of wisdom which the ages had bequeathed to him.

He remembered the books of poetry upon his shelves at home. He had bought them in his bachelor days and many an evening, as he sat in the little room off the hall, he had been tempted to take one down from the bookshelf and read out something to his wife. But shyness had always held him back; and so the books had remained on their shelves. At times he repeated lines to himself and this consoled him.

When his hour had struck he stood up and took leave of his desk and of his fellow-clerks punctiliously. He emerged from under the feudal arch of the King's Inns, a neat modest figure, and walked swiftly down Henrietta Street. The golden sunset was wanning and the air had grown sharp. A horde of grimy children populated the street. They stood or ran in the roadway or crawled up the steps before the gaping doors or squatted like mice upon the thresholds. Little Chandler gave them no thought. He picked his way deftly through all that minute vermin-like life and under the shadow of the gaunt spectral mansions in which the old nobility of Dublin had roystered. No memory of the past touched him, for his mind was full of a present joy.

He had never been in Corless's but he knew the value of the name. He knew that people went there after the theatre to eat oysters and drink liqueurs; and he had heard that the waiters there spoke French and German. Walking swiftly by at night he had seen cabs drawn up before the door and richly dressed ladies, escorted by cavaliers, alight and enter quickly. They wore noisy dresses and many wraps. Their faces were powdered and they caught up their dresses, when they touched earth, like alarmed Atalantas. He had always passed without turning his head to look. It was his habit to walk swiftly in the street even by day and whenever he found himself in the city late at night he hurried on his way apprehensively and excitedly. Sometimes, however, he courted the causes of his fear. He chose the darkest and narrowest streets and, as he walked boldy forward, the silence that was spread about his footsteps troubled him, the wandering, silent figures troubled him; and at times a sound of low fugitive laughter made him tremble like a leaf.

He turned to the right towards Capel Street. Ignatius Gallaher on the London Press! Who would have thought it possible eight years before? Still, now that he reviewed the past, Little Chandler could remember many signs of future greatness in his friend. People used to say that Ignatius was wild. Of course, he did mix with a rakish set of fellows at that time, drank freely and borrowed money on all sides. In the end he had got mixed up in some shady affair, some money transaction: at least, that was one version of his flight. But nobody denied him talent. There was always a certain ... something in Ignatius Gallaher that impressed you in spite of yourself. Even when he was out at elbows and at his wits' end for money he kept up a bold face. Little Chandler remembered (and the remembrance brought a slight flush of pride to his cheek) one of Ignatius Gallaher's sayings when he was in a tight corner:

"Half time now, boys," he used to say light-heartedly. "Where's my considering cap?"

That was Ignatius Gallaher all out; and, damn it, you couldn't but admire him for it.

Little Chandler quickened his pace. For the first time in his life he felt superior to the people he passed. For the first time his soul revolted against the dull inelegance of Capel Street. There was no doubt about it: if you wanted to succeed you had to go away. You could do nothing in Dublin. As he crossed Grattan Bridge he looked down the river towards the lower quays and pitied the poor stunted houses. They seemed to him a band of tramps, huddled together along the riverbanks, their old coats covered with dust and soot, stupefied by the panorama of sunset and waiting for the first chill of night to bid them arise, shake themselves and begone. He wondered whether he could write a poem to express his idea. Perhaps Gallaher might be able to get it into some London paper for him. Could he write something original? He was not sure what idea he wished to express but the thought that a poetic moment had touched him took life within him like an infant hope. He stepped onward bravely.

Every step brought him nearer to London, farther from his own sober inartistic life. A light began to tremble on the horizon of his mind. He was not so old—thirty-two. His temperament might be said to be just at the point of maturity. There were so many different moods and impressions that he wished to express in verse. He felt them within him. He tried to weigh his soul to see if it was a poet's soul. Melancholy was the dominant note of his temperament, he thought, but it was a melancholy tempered by recurrences of faith and resignation and simple joy. If he could give expression to it in a book of poems perhaps men would listen. He would

A Little Cloud 87

never be popular: he saw that. He could not sway the crowd but he might appeal to a little circle of kindred minds. The English critics, perhaps, would recognise him as one of the Celtic school by reason of the melancholy tone of his poems; besides that, he would put in allusions. He began to invent sentences and phrases from the notice which his book would get. *"Mr. Chandler has the gift of easy and graceful verse."* . . . *"A wistful sadness pervades these poems."* . . . *"The Celtic note."* It was a pity his name was not more Irish-looking. Perhaps it would be better to insert his mother's name before the surname: Thomas Malone Chandler, or better still: T. Malone Chandler. He would speak to Gallaher about it.

He pursued his revery so ardently that he passed his street and had to turn back. As he came near Corless's his former agitation began to overmaster him and he halted before the door in indecision. Finally he opened the door and entered.

The light and noise of the bar held him at the doorways for a few moments. He looked about him, but his sight was confused by the shining of many red and green wine-glasses. The bar seemed to him to be full of people and he felt that the people were observing him curiously. He glanced quickly to right and left (frowning slightly to make his errand appear serious), but when his sight cleared a little he saw that nobody had turned to look at him: and there, sure enough, was Ignatius Gallaher leaning with his back against the counter and his feet planted far apart.

"Hallo, Tommy, old hero, here you are! What is it to be? What will you have? I'm taking whisky: better stuff than we get across the water. Soda? Lithia? No mineral? I'm the same. Spoils the flavour. . . . Here, *garcon,* bring us two halves of malt whisky, like a good fellow. . . . Well, and how have you been pulling along since I saw you last? Dear God, how old we're getting! Do you see any signs of aging in me—eh, what? A little grey and thin on the top—what?"

Ignatius Gallaher took off his hat and displayed a large closely cropped head. His face was heavy, pale and clean-shaven. His eyes, which were of bluish slate-colour, relieved his unhealthy pallor and shone out plainly above the vivid orange tie he wore. Between these rival features the lips appeared very long and shapeless and colourless. He bent his head and felt with two sympathetic fingers the thin hair at the crown. Little Chandler shook his head as a denial. Ignatius Gallaher put on his hat again.

"It pulls you down," he said, "Press life. Always hurry and scurry, looking for copy and sometimes not finding it: and then, always to have something new in your stuff. Damn proofs and printers, I say, for a few days. I'm deuced glad, I can tell you, to get back to the old country. Does a fellow good, a bit of a holiday. I feel a ton better since I landed again in dear dirty Dublin. . . . Here you are, Tommy. Water? Say when."

Little Chandler allowed his whisky to be very much diluted.

"You don't know what's good for you, my boy," said Ignatius Gallaher. "I drink mine neat."

"I drink very little as a rule," said Little Chandler modestly. "An odd half-one or so when I meet any of the old crowd: that's all."

"Ah, well," said Ignatius Gallaher, cheerfully, "here's to us and to old times and old acquaintance."

They clinked glasses and drank the toast.

"I met some of the old gang today," said Ignatius Gallaher. "O'Hara seems to be in a bad way. What's he doing?"

"Nothing," said Little Chandler. "He's gone to the dogs."

"But Hogan has a good sit, hasn't he?"

"Yes; he's in the Land Commission."

"I met him one night in London and he seemed to be very flush. . . . Poor O'Hara! Boose, I suppose?"

"Other things, too," said Little Chandler shortly.

Ignatius Gallaher laughed.

"Tommy," he said, "I see you haven't changed an atom. You're the very same serious person that used to lecture me on Sunday mornings when I had a sore head and a fur on my tongue. You'd want to knock about a bit in the world. Have you never been anywhere even for a trip?"

"I've been to the Isle of Man," said Little Chandler.

Ignatius Gallaher laughed.

"The Isle of Man!" he said. "Go to London or Paris: Paris, for choice. That'd do you good."

"Have you seen Paris?"

"I should think I have! I've knocked about there a little."

"And is it really so beautiful as they say?" asked Little Chandler.

He sipped a little of his drink while Ignatius Gallaher finished his boldly.

"Beautiful?" sand Ignatius Gallaher, pausing on the word and on the flavour of his drink. "It's not so beautiful, you know. Of course, it is beautiful. . . . But it's the life of Paris; that's the thing. Ah, there's no city like Paris for gaiety, movement, excitement. . . ."

Little Chandler finished his whisky and, after some trouble, succeeded in catching the barman's eye. He ordered the same again.

I've been to the Moulin Rouge," Ignatius Gallaher continued when the barman had removed their glasses, "and I've been to all the Bohemian cafés. Hot stuff! Not for a pious chap like you, Tommy."

A Little Cloud

Little Chandler said nothing until the barman returned with two glasses: then he touched his friend's glass lightly and reciprocated the former toast. He was beginning to feel somewhat disillusioned. Gallaher's accent and way of expressing himself did not please him. There was something vulgar in his friend which he had not observed before. But perhaps it was only the result of living in London amid the bustle and competition of the Press. The old personal charm was still there under this new gaudy manner. And, after all, Gallaher had lived, he had seen the world. Little Chandler looked at his friend enviously.

"Everything in Paris is gay," said Ignatius Gallaher. "They believe in enjoying life—and don't you think they're right? If you want to enjoy yourself properly you must go to Paris. And, mind you, they've a great feeling for the Irish there. When they heard I was from Ireland they were ready to eat me, man."

Little Chandler took four or five sips from his glass.

"Tell me," he said, "is it true that Paris is so . . . immoral as they say?"

Ignatius Gallaher made a catholic gesture with his right arm.

"Every place is immoral," he said. "Of course you do find spicy bits in Paris. Go to one of the students' balls, for instance. That's lively, if you like, when the *cocottes* begin to let themselves loose. You know what they are, I suppose?"

"I've heard of them," said Little Chandler.

Ignatius Gallaher drank off his whisky and shook his head.

"Ah," he said, "you may say what you like. There's no woman like the Parisienne—for style, for go."

"Then it is an immoral city," said Little Chandler, with timid insistence —"I mean, compared with London or Dublin?"

"London!" said Ignatius Gallaher. "It's six of one and half-a-dozen of the other. You ask Hogan, my boy. I showed him a bit about London when he was over there. He'd open your eye. . . . I say, Tommy, don't make punch of that whisky: liquor up."

"No, really. . . ."

"O, come on, another one won't do you any harm. What is it? The same again, I suppose?"

"Well . . . all right."

"*François,* the same again. . . . Will you smoke Tommy?"

Ignatius Gallaher produced his cigar-case. The two friends lit their cigars and puffed at them in silence until their drinks were served.

"I'll tell you my opinion," said Ignatius Gallaher, emerging after some time from the clouds of smoke in which he had taken refuge, "it's a rum world. Talk of immorality! I've heard of cases—what am I saying?—I've known them: cases of ... immorality. ..."

Ignatius Gallaher puffed thoughtfully at his cigar and then, in a calm historian's tone, he proceeded to sketch for his friend some pictures of the corruption which was rife abroad. He summarised the vices of many capitals and seemed inclined to award the palm to Berlin. Some things he could not vouch for (his friends had told him), but of others he had had personal experience. He spared neither rank nor caste. He revealed many of the secrets of religious houses on the Continent and described some of the practices which were fashionable in high society and ending by telling, with details, a story about an English duchess—a story which he knew to be true. Little Chandler was astonished.

"Ah, well," said Ignatius Gallaher, "here we are in old jog-along Dublin where nothing is known of such things."

"How dull you must find it," said Little Chandler, "after all the other places you've seen!"

"Well," said Ignatius Gallaher, "it's a relaxation to come over here, you know. And, after all, it's the old country, as they say, isn't it? You can't help having a certain feeling for it. That's human nature. . . . But tell me something about yourself. Hogan told me you had . . . tasted the joys of connubial bliss. Two years ago, wasn't it?"

Little Chandler blushed and smiled.

"Yes," he said. "I was married last May twelve months."

"I hope it's not too late in the day to offer my best wishes," said Ignatius Gallaher. "I did't know your address or I'd have done so at the time."

He extended his hand, which Little Chandler took.

"Well, Tommy," he said, "I wish you and yours every joy in life, old chap, and tons of money, and may you never die till I shoot you. And that's the wish of a sincere friend, an old friend. You know that?"

"I know that," said Little Chandler.

"Any youngsters?" said Ignatius Gallaher.

Little Chandler blushed again.

"We have one child," he said.

"Son or daughter?"

"A little boy."

Ignatius Gallaher slapped his friend sonorously on the back.

"Bravo," he said, "I wouldn't doubt you, Tommy."

Little Chandler smiled, looked confusedly at his glass and bit his lower lip with three childishly white front teeth.

A Little Cloud

"I hope you'll spend an evening with us," he said, "before you go back. My wife will be delighted to meet you. We can have a little music and____"

"Thanks awfully, old chap," said Ignatius Gallaher, "I'm sorry we didn't meet earlier. But I must leave tomorrow night."

"Tonight, perhaps . . .?"

"I'm awfully sorry, old man. You see I'm over here with another fellow, clever young chap he is too, and we arranged to go to a little card-party. Only for that . . ."

"O, in that case . . ."

"But who knows?" said Ignatius Gallaher considerately. "Next year I may take a little skip over here now that I've broken the ice. It's only a pleasure deferred."

"Very well," said Little Chandler, "the next time you come we must have an evening together. That's agreed now, isn't it?"

"Yes, that's agreed," said Ignatius Gallaher. "Next year if I come, *parole d'honneur.*"

"And to clinch the bargain," said Little Chandler, "we'll just have one more now."

Ignatius Gallaher took out a large gold watch and looked at it.

"Is it to be the last?" he said. "Because you know, I have an a.p."

"O, yes, positively," said Little Chandler.

"Very well, then," said Ignatius Gallaher, "let us have another one as a *deoc an doruis*—that's good vernacular for a small whisky, I believe."

Little Chandler ordered the drinks. The blush which had risen to his face a few moments before was establishing itself. A trifle made him blush at any time: and now he felt warm and excited. Three small whiskies had gone to his head and Gallaher's strong cigar had confused his mind, for he was a delicate and abstinent person. The adventure of meeting Gallaher after eight years, of finding himself with Gallaher in Corless's surrounded by lights and noise, of listening to Gallaher's stories and of sharing for a brief space Gallaher's vagrant and triumphant life, upset the equipoise of his sensitive nature. He felt acutely the contrast between his own life and his friend's, and it seemed to him unjust. Gallaher was his inferior in birth and education. He was sure that he could do something better than his friend had ever done, or could ever do, something higher than mere tawdry journalism if he only got the chance. What was it that stood in his way? His unfortunate timidity! He wished to vindicate himself in some way, to assert his manhood. He saw behind Gallaher's refusal of his invitation. Gallaher was only patronising him by his friendliness just as he was patronising Ireland by his visit.

The barman brought their drinks. Little Chandler pushed one glass towards his friend and took up the other boldly.

"Who knows?" he said, as they lifted their glasses. "When you come next year I may have the pleasure of wishing long life and happiness to Mr. and Mrs. Ignatius Gallaher."

Ignatius Gallaher in the act of drinking closed one eye expressively over the rim of his glass. When he had drunk he smacked his lips decisively, set down his glass and said:

"No blooming fear of that, my boy. I'm going to have my fling first and see a bit of life and the world before I put my head in the sack—if I ever do."

"Some day you will," said Little Chandler calmly.

Ignatius Gallaher turned his orange tie and slate-blue eyes full upon his friend.

"You think so?" he said.

"You'll put your head in the sack," repeated Little Chandler stoutly, "like everyone else if you can find the girl."

He had slightly emphasised his tone and he was aware that he had betrayed himself; but, though the colour had heightened in his cheek, he did not flinch from his friend's gaze. Ignatius Gallaher watched him for a few moments and then said:

"If every it occurs, you may bet your bottom dollar there'll be no mooning and spooning about it. I mean to marry money. She'll have a good fat account at the bank or she won't do for me."

Little Chandler shook his head.

"Why, man alive," said Ignatius Gallaher, vehemently, "do you know what it is? I've only to say the word and tomorrow I can have the woman and the cash. You don't believe it? Well, I know it. There are hundreds—what am I saying?—thousands of rich Germans and Jews, rotten with money, that'd only be too glad. . . . You wait a while, my boy. See if I don't play my cards properly. When I go about a thing I mean business, I tell you. You just wait."

He tossed his glass to his mouth, finished his drink and laughed loudly. Then he looked thoughtfully before him and said in a calmer tone:

"But I'm in no hurry. They can wait. I don't fancy tying myself up to one woman, you know."

He imitated with his mouth the act of tasting and made a wry face.

"Must get a bit stale, I should think," he said.

Little Chandler sat in the room of the hall, holding a child in his arms. To save money they kept no servant but Annie's young sister Monica came for an hour or so in the morning and an hour or so in the evening to help. But Monica had gone home long ago. It was a quarter to nine. Little Chandler had come home late for tea and, moreover, he had forgotten to bring Annie home the parcel of coffee from Bewley's. Of course she was in a bad humour and gave him short answers. She said she would do without any tea but when it came near the time at which the shop at the corner closed she decided to go out herself for a quarter of a pound of tea and two pounds of sugar. She put the sleeping child deftly in his arms and said:

"Here. Don't waken him."

A little lamp with a white china shade stood upon the table and its light fell over a photograph which was enclosed in a frame of crumpled horn. It was Annie's photograph. Little Chandler looked at it, pausing at the thin tight lips. She wore the pale blue summer blouse which he had brought her home as a present one Saturday. It had cost him ten and elevenpence; but what an agony of nervousness it had cost him! How he had suffered that day, waiting at the shop door until the shop was empty, standing at the counter and trying to appear at his ease while the girl piled ladies' blouses before him, paying at the desk and forgetting to take up the odd penny of his change, being called back by the cashier, and finally, striving to hide his blushes as he left the shop by examining the parcel to see if it was securely tied. When he brought the blouse home Annie kissed him and said it was very pretty and stylish; but when she heard the price she threw the blouse on the table and said it was a regular swindle to charge ten and elevenpence for it. At first she wanted to take it back but when she tried it on she was delighted with it, especially with the make of the sleeves, and kissed him and said he was very good to think of her.

Hm! . . .

He looked coldly into the eyes of the photograph and they answered coldly. Certainly they were pretty and the face itself was pretty. But he found something mean in it. Why was it so unconscious and ladylike? The composure of the eyes irritated him. They repelled him and defied him: there was no passion in them, no rapture. He thought of what Gallaher had said about rich Jewesses. Those dark Oriental eyes, he thought, how full they are of passion, of voluptuous longing! . . . Why had he married the eyes in the photograph?

He caught himself up at the question and glanced nervously round the room. He found something mean in the pretty furniture which he had bought for his house on the hire system. Annie had chosen it herself and it reminded him of her. It too was prim and pretty. A dull resentment against his life awoke within him. Could he not escape from his little house? Was it too late for him to try to live bravely like Gallaher? Could he go to London? There was the furniture still to be paid for. If he could only write a book and get it published, that might open the way for him.

A volume of Byron's poems lay before him on the table. He opened it cautiously with his left hand lest he should waken the child and began to read the first poem in the book:

> Hushed are the winds and still the evening gloom,
>   Not e'en a Zephyr wanders through the grove,
> Whilst I return to view my Margaret's tomb
>   And scatter flowers on the dust I love.

He paused. He felt the rhythm of the verse about him in the room. How melancholy it was! Could he, too, write like that, express the melancholy of his soul in verse? There were so many things he wanted to describe: his sensation of a few hours before on Grattan Bridge, for example. If he could get back again into that mood. . . .

The child awoke and began to cry. He turned from the page and tried to hush it: but it would not be hushed. He began to rock it to and fro in his arms but its wailing cry grew keener. He rocked it faster while his eyes began to read the second stanza:

> Within this narrow cell reclines her clay,
>   That clay where once . . .

It was useless. He couldn't read. He couldn't do anything. The wailing of the child pierced the drum of his ear. It was useless, useless! He was a prisoner for life. His arms trembled with anger and suddenly bending to the child's face he shouted:

"Stop!"

The child stopped for an instant, had a spasm of fright and began to scream. He jumped up from his chair and walked hastily up and down the room with the child in his arms. It began to sob piteously, losing its breath for four or five seconds, and then bursting out anew. The thin walls of the room echoed the sound. He tried to soothe it but it sobbed more convulsively. He looked at the contracted and quivering face of the child and began to be alarmed. He counted seven sobs without a break between them and caught the child to his breast in fright. If it died! . . .

The door was burst open and a young woman ran in, panting.

"What is it? What is it?" she cried.

The child, hearing its mother's voice, broke out into a paroxysm of sobbing.

"It's nothing, Annie . . . it's nothing. . . . He began to cry. . . ."

She flung her parcels on the floor and snatched the child from him. "What have you done to him?" she cried, glaring into his face.

Little Chandler sustained for one moment the gaze of her eyes and his heart closed together as he met the hatred in them. He began to stammer:

"It's nothing.... He ... he began to cry.... I couldn't ... I didn't do anything.... What?"

Giving no heed to him she began to walk up and down the room, clasping the child tightly in her arms and murmuring:

"My little man! My little mannie! Was 'ou frightened, love? ... There now, love! There now! ... Lambabaun! Mamma's little lamb of the world! ... There now!"

Little Chandler felt his cheeks suffused with shame and he stood back out of the lamplight. He listened while the paroxysm of the child's sobbing grew less and less; and tears of remorse started to his eyes.

■ DISCUSSION AND QUESTIONS

1. Little Chandler is not terribly small physically, being "but slightly under the average stature." Is he a little man spiritually? What is his philosophy of life, which he calls the "wisdom of the ages"? In contrast, what is Chandler's view of his life? What is his job? What are his dreams and ambitions? How successfully has he realized his dreams? How old is he?

2. What do the references to poetry reveal about Little Chandler? What kind of poetry does he write?

3. An effective method of illuminating a character is to contrast him with a *foil*, another character with a different kind of personality. Gallaher is a perfect foil for Chandler. As Chandler remembers Gallaher he is almost a symbol of the little man's romantic dreams. Gallaher is a man of the world, a "brilliant" figure in the London press, a bold, boisterous man, a traveler —everything Chandler is not, including being a bachelor. Chandler feels weighted down with the dull routines of domesticity, a dull job, a dull city, "a sober inartistic life," life without romance. Whereas many people live quite happily without romance, Chandler has enough intelligence and sensitivity to be offended by the disparity between his dreams and his reality. He doesn't want to live a life of quiet conformity and defeat. How does Little Chandler's life differ from his friend Gallaher's?

4. How does the detailed description of his apartment reveal and define Chandler? What are Chandler's thoughts as he examines the photograph of his wife Annie? Why do her eyes irritate him? In what ways does their furniture remind him of Annie?

5. As he examines his "little house," he feels a "dull resentment" against his life and a desire to escape, to "live bravely like Gallaher." Why can't he escape?

It is important to visualize this scene: while thinking of a brave escape, this little man is rocking a baby in his arms and trying to read a Byron poem. What is the significance of these lines from the poem: "Within this narrow cell reclines her clay,/That clay where once ..."?

6. Chandler's only spontaneous, authentic action occurs when, trembling with rage, he yells "Stop!" at his child. What are the consequences of this action? What are Annie's responses to the baby and to Chandler? How artistically effective is this scene in showing Chandler's ineffectualness?

7. Explain Little Chandler's "tears of remorse" at the end of the story.

8. How does Chandler perceive his failure? What, in his view, has caused him to be defeated by life? Does the reader share his explanation?

The Black Madonna

Doris Lessing

There are some countries in which the arts, let alone Art, cannot be said to flourish. Why this should be so it is hard to say, although of course we all have our theories about it. For sometimes it is the most barren soil that sends up gardens of those flowers which we all agree are the crown and justification of life, and it is this fact which makes it hard to say, finally, why the soil of Zambesia should produce such reluctant plants.

Zambesia is a tough, sunburnt, virile, positive country contemptuous of subtleties and sensibility: yet there have been States with these qualities which have produced art, though perhaps with the left hand. Zambesia is, to put it mildly, unsympathetic to those ideas so long taken for granted in other parts of the world, to do with liberty, fraternity and the rest. Yet there are those, and some of the finest souls among them, who maintain that art is impossible without a minority whose leisure is guaranteed by a hard-working majority. And whatever Zambesia's comfortable minority may lack, it is not leisure.

Zambesia—but enough; out of respect for ourselves and for scientific accuracy, we should refrain from jumping to conclusions. Particularly when one remembers the almost wistful respect Zambesians show when an artist does appear in their midst.

Consider, for instance, the case of Michele.

Copyright © 1951, 1953, 1954, 1957, 1958, 1962, 1963, 1964, 1965 by Doris Lessing. Reprinted by permission of Simon & Schuster, Inc. and John Cushman Associates.

He came out of the internment camp at the time when Italy was made a sort of honorary ally, during the Second World War. It was a time of strain for the authorities, because it is one thing to be responsible for thousands of prisoners of war whom one must treat according to certain recognized standards; it is another to be faced, and from one day to the next, with these same thousands transformed by some international legerdemain into comrades in arms. Some of the thousands stayed where they were in the camps; they were fed and housed there at least. Others went as farm labourers, though not many; for while the farmers were as always short of labour, they did not know how to handle farm labourers who were also white men: such a phenomenon had never happened in Zambesia before. Some did odd jobs around the towns, keeping a sharp eye out for the trade unions, who would neither admit them as members nor agree to their working.

Hard, hard, the lot of these men, but fortunately not for long, for soon the war ended and they were able to go home.

Hard, too, the lot of the authorities, as has been pointed out; and for that reason they were doubly willing to take what advantages they could from the situation; and that Michele was such an advantage there could be no doubt.

His talents were first discovered when he was still a prisoner of war. A church was built in the camp, and Michele decorated its interior. It became a show-place, that little tin-roofed church in the prisoners' camp, with its whitewashed walls covered all over with frescoes depicting swarthy peasants gathering grapes for the vintage, beautiful Italian girls dancing, plump dark-eyed children. Amid crowded scenes of Italian life, appeared the Virgin and her Child, smiling and beneficent, happy to move familiarly among her people.

Culture-loving ladies who had bribed the authorities to be taken inside the camp would say, "Poor thing, how homesick he must be." And they would beg to be allowed to leave half a crown for the artist. Some were indignant. He was a prisoner, after all, captured in the very act of fighting against justice and democracy, and what right had he to protest?—for they felt these paintings as a sort of protest. What was there in Italy that we did not have right here in Westonville, which was the capital and hub of Zambesia? Were there not sunshine and mountains and fat babies and pretty girls here? Did we not grow—if not grapes, at least lemons and oranges and flowers in plenty?

People were upset—the desperation of nostalgia came from the painted white walls of that simple church, and affected everyone according to his temperament.

But when Michele was free, his talent was remembered. He was spoken of as "that Italian artist." As a matter of fact, he was a bricklayer. And the virtues of those frescoes might very well have been exaggerated. It is possible they would have been overlooked altogether in a country where picture-covered walls were more common.

When one of the visiting ladies came rushing out to the camp in her own car, to ask him to paint her children, he said he was not qualified to do so. But at last he agreed. He took a room in the town and made some nice likenesses of the children. Then he painted the children of a great number of the first lady's friends. He charged ten shillings a time. Then one of the ladies wanted a portrait of herself. He asked ten pounds for it; it had taken him a month to do. She was annoyed, but paid.

And Michele went off to his room with a friend and stayed there drinking red wine from the Cape and talking about home. While the money lasted he could not be persuaded to do any more portraits.

There was a good deal of talk among the ladies about the dignity of labour, a subject in which they were well versed; and one felt they might almost go so far as to compare a white man with a kaffir, who did not understand the dignity of labour either.

He was felt to lack gratitude. One of the ladies tracked him down, found him lying on a camp-bed under a tree with a bottle of wine, and spoke to him severely about the barbarity of Mussolini and the fecklessness of the Italian temperament. Then she demanded that he should instantly paint a picture of herself in her new evening dress. He refused, and she went home very angry.

It happened that she was the wife of one of our most important citizens, a General or something of that kind, who was at that time engaged in planning a military tattoo or show for the benefit of the civilian population. The whole of Westonville had been discussing this show for weeks. We were all bored to extinction by dances, fancy-dress balls, fairs, lotteries and other charitable entertainments. It is not too much to say that while some were dying for freedom, others were dancing for it. There comes a limit to everything. Though, of course, when the end of the war actually came and the thousands of troops stationed in the country had to go home—in short, when enjoying ourselves would no longer be a duty, many were heard to exclaim that life would never be the same again.

In the meantime, the tattoo would make a nice change for us all. The military gentlemen responsible for the idea did not think of it in these terms. They thought to improve morale by giving us some idea of what war was really like. Headlines in the newspaper were not enough. And in order to bring it all home to us, they planned to destroy a village by shell-fire before our very eyes.

First, the village had to be built.

It appears that the General and his subordinates stood around in the red dust of the parade-ground under a burning sun for the whole of one day, surrounded by building materials, while hordes of African labourers ran around with boards and nails, trying to make something that looked like a village. It became evident that they would have to build a proper village in order to destroy it; and this would cost more than was allowed for the whole entertainment. The General went home in a bad temper, and his wife said what they needed was an artist, they needed Michele. This was not because she wanted to do Michele a good turn; she could not endure the thought of him lying around singing while there was work to be done. She refused to undertake any delicate diplomatic missions when her husband said he would be damned if he would ask favours of any little Wop. She solved the problem for him in her own way: a certain Captain Stocker was sent out to fetch him.

The Captain found him on the same camp-bed under the same tree, in rolled-up trousers, and an uncollared shirt; unshaven, mildly drunk, with a bottle of wine standing beside him on the earth. He was singing an air so wild, so sad, that the Captain was uneasy. He stood at ten paces from the disreputable fellow and felt the indignities of his position. A year ago, this man had been a mortal enemy to be shot at sight. Six months ago, he had been an enemy prisoner. Now he lay with his knees up, in an untidy shirt that had certainly once been military. For the Captain, the situation crystallised in a desire that Michele should salute him.

"Piselli!" he said sharply.

Michele turned his head and looked at the Captain from the horizontal. "Good morning," he said affably.

"You are wanted," said the Captain.

"Who?" said Michele. He sat up, a fattish, olive-skinned little man. His eyes were resentful.

"The authorities."

"The war is over?"

The Captain, who was already stiff and shiny enough in his laundered khaki, jerked his head back frowning, chin out. He was a large man, blond, and wherever his flesh showed, it was brick-red. His eyes were small and blue and angry. His red hands, covered all over with fine yellow bristles, clenched by his side. Then he saw the disappointment in Michele's eyes, and the hands unclenched. "No, it is not over," he said. "Your assistance is required."

"For the war?"

"For the war effort. I take it you are interested in defeating the Germans?"

Michele looked at the Captain. The little dark-eyed artisan looked at the great blond officer with his cold blue eyes, his narrow mouth, his hands like bristle-covered steaks. He looked and said: "I am very interested in the end of the war."

"Well?" said the Captain between his teeth.

"The pay?" said Michele.

"You will be paid."

Michele stood up. He lifted the bottle against the sun, then took a gulp. He rinsed his mouth out with wine and spat. Then he poured what was left on the red earth, where it made a bubbling purple stain.

"I am ready," he said. He went with the Captain to the waiting lorry, where he climbed in beside the driver's seat and not, as the Captain had expected, into the back of the lorry. When they had arrived at the parade-ground the officers had left a message that the Captain would be personally responsible for Michele and for the village. Also for the hundred or so labourers who were sitting around on the grass verges waiting for orders.

The Captain explained what was wanted. Michele nodded. Then he waved his hand at the Africans. "I do not want these," he said.

"You will do it yourself—a village?"

"Yes."

"With no help?"

Michele smiled for the first time. "I will do it."

The Captain hesitated. He disapproved on principle of white men doing heavy manual labour. He said: "I will keep six to do the heavy work."

Michele shrugged; and the Captain went over and dismissed all but six of the Africans. He came back with them to Michele.

"It is hot," said Michele.

"Very," said the Captain. They were standing in the middle of the parade-ground. Around its edge trees, grass, gulfs of shadow. Here, nothing but reddish dust, drifting and lifting in a low hot breeze.

"I am thirsty," said Michele. He grinned. The Captain felt his stiff lips loosen unwillingly in reply. The two pairs of eyes met. It was a moment of understanding. For the Captain, the little Italian had suddenly become human. "I will arrange it," he said, and went off down-town. By the time he had explained the position to the right people, filled in forms and made arrangements, it was late afternoon. He returned to the parade-ground with a case of Cape brandy, to find Michele and the six black men seated together under a tree. Michele was singing an Italian song to them, and they were harmonizing with him. The sight affected the Captain like an attack of nausea. He came up, and the Africans stood to attention. Michele continued to sit.

"You said you would do the work yourself?"

"Yes, I said so."

The Captain then dismissed the Africans. They departed, with friendly looks towards Michele, who waved at them. The Captain was beef-red with anger. "You have not started yet?"

"How long have I?"

"Three weeks."

"Then there is plenty of time," said Michele, looking at the bottle of brandy in the Captain's hand. In the other were two glasses. "It is evening," he pointed out. The Captain stood frowning for a moment. Then he sat down on the grass, and poured out two brandies.

"Ciao," said Michele.

"Cheers," said the Captain. Three weeks, he was thinking. Three weeks with this damned little Itie! He drained his glass and refilled it, and set it in the grass. The grass was cool and soft. A tree was flowering somewhere close—hot waves of perfume came on the breeze.

"It is nice here," said Michele. "We will have a good time together. Even in a war, there are times of happiness. And of friendship. I drink to the end of the war."

Next day, the Captain did not arrive at the parade-ground until after lunch. He found Michele under the trees with a bottle. Sheets of ceiling board had been erected at one end of the parade-ground in such a way that they formed two walls and a part of a third, and a slant of steep roof supported on struts.

"What's that?" said the Captain, furious.

"The church," said Michele.

"Wha-at?"

"You will see. Later. It is very hot." He looked at the brandy bottle that lay on its side on the ground. The Captain went to the lorry and returned with the case of brandy. They drank. Time passed. It was a long time since the Captain had sat on grass under a tree. It was a long time, for that matter, since he had drunk so much. He always drank a great deal, but it was regulated to the times and seasons. He was a disciplined man. Here, sitting on the grass beside this little man whom he still could not help thinking of as an enemy, it was not that he let his self-discipline go, but that he felt himself to be something different: he was temporarily set outside his normal behaviour. Michele did not count. He listened to Michele talking about Italy, and it seemed to him he was listening to a savage speaking: as if he heard tales from the mythical South Sea islands where a man like himself might very well go just once in his life. He found himself saying he would like to make a trip to Italy after the war. Actually, he was attracted only by the North and by Northern people. He had visited Germany, under Hitler, and though it was not the time to say so, had found it very satisfactory. Then Michele sang him some Italian songs. He sang Michele some English songs. Then Michele took out photographs of his wife and children, who lived in a village in the mountains

The Black Madonna 103

of North Italy. He asked the Captain if he were married. The Captain never spoke about his private affairs.

He had spent all his life in one or other of the African colonies as a policeman, magistrate, native commissioner, or in some other useful capacity. When the war started, military life came easily to him. But he hated city life, and had his own reasons for wishing the war over. Mostly, he had been in bush-stations with one or two other white men, or by himself, far from the rigours of civilisation. He had relations with native women; and from time to time visited the city where his wife lived with her parents and the children. He was always tormented by the idea that she was unfaithful to him. Recently he had even appointed a private detective to watch her; he was convinced the detective was inefficient. Army friends coming from L_____ where his wife was, spoke of her at parties, enjoying herself. When the war ended, she would not find it so easy to have a good time. And why did he not simply live with her and be done with it? The fact was, he could not. And his long exile to remote bush-stations was because he needed the excuse not to. He could not bear to think of his wife for too long; she was that part of his life he had never been able, so to speak, to bring to heel.

Yet he spoke of her now to Michele, and of his favourite bush-wife, Nadya. He told Michele the story of his life, until he realized that the shadows from the trees they sat under had stretched right across the parade-ground to the grandstand. He got unsteadily to his feet, and said: "There is work to be done. You are being paid to work."

"I will show you my church when the light goes."

The sun dropped, darkness fell, and Michele made the Captain drive his lorry on to the parade-ground a couple of hundred yards away and switch on his lights. Instantly, a white church sprang up from the shapes and shadows of the bits of board.

"Tomorrow, some houses," said Michele cheerfully.

At the end of a week, the space at the end of the parade-ground had crazy gawky construction of lath and board over it, that looked in the sunlight like nothing on this earth. Privately, it upset the Captain; it was like a nightmare that these skeleton-like shapes should be able to persuade him, with the illusions of light and dark, that they were a village. At night, the Captain drove up his lorry, switched on the lights, and there it was, the village, solid and real against a background of full green trees. Then, in the morning sunlight, there was nothing there, just bits of board stuck in the sand.

"It is finished," said Michele.

"You were engaged for three weeks," said the Captain. He did not want it to end, this holiday for himself.

Michele shrugged. "The army is rich," he said. Now, to avoid curious eyes, they sat inside the shade of the church, with the case of brandy between them. The Captain talked, talked endlessly, about his wife, about women. He could not stop talking.

Michele listened. Once he said: "When I go home—when I go home—I shall open my arms . . ." He opened them, wide. He closed his eyes. Tears ran down his cheeks. "I shall take my wife in my arms, and I shall ask nothing, nothing. I do not care. It is enough to be together. That is what the war has taught me. It is enough, it is enough. I shall ask no questions and I shall be happy."

The Captain stared before him, suffering. He thought how he dreaded his wife. She was a scornful creature, gray and hard, who laughed at him. She had been laughing at him ever since they married. Since the war, she had taken to calling him names like Little Hitler, and Storm-trooper. "Go ahead, my little Hitler," she had cried last time they met. "Go ahead, my Storm-trooper. If you want to waste your money on private detectives, go ahead. But don't think I don't know what *you* do when you're in the bush. I don't care what you do, but remember that I know it . . ."

The Captain remembered her saying it. And there sat Michele on his packing-case, saying: "It's a pleasure for the rich, my friend, detectives and the law. Even jealousy is a pleasure I don't want any more. Ah, my friend, to be together with my wife again, and the children, that is all I ask of life. That and wine and food and singing in the evenings." And the tears wetted his cheeks and splashed on to his shirt.

That a man should cry, good lord! thought the Captain. And without shame! He seized the bottle and drank.

Three days before the great occasion, some high-ranking officers came strolling through the dust, and found Michele and Captain sitting together on the packing-case, singing. The Captain's shirt was open down the front, and there were stains on it.

The Captain stood to attention with the bottle in his hand, and Michele stood to attention too, out of sympathy with his friend. Then the officers drew the Captain aside—they were all cronies of his—and said, what the hell did he think he was doing? And why wasn't the village finished?

Then they went away.

"Tell them it is finished," said Michele. "Tell them I want to go."

"No," said the Captain. "No. Michele, what would you do if your wife . . ."

"This world is a good place. We should be happy—that is all."

"Michele . . ."

"I want to go. There is nothing to do. They paid me yesterday."

"Sit down, Michele. Three more days, and then it's finished."

"Then I shall paint the inside of the church as I painted the one in the camp."

The Captain laid himself down on some boards and went to sleep. When he woke, Michele was surrounded by the pots of paint he had used on the outside of the village. Just in front of the Captain was a picture of a black girl. She was young and plump. She wore a patterned blue dress and her shoulders came soft and bare out of it. On her back was a baby slung in a band of red stuff. Her face was turned towards the Captain and she was smiling.

"That's Nadya," said the Captain. "Nadya . . ." He groaned loudly. He looked at the black child and shut his eyes. He opened them, and mother and child were still there. Michele was very carefully drawing thin yellow circles around the heads of the black girl and her child.

"Good God," said the Captain, "you can't do that."

"Why not?"

"You can't have a black Madonna."

"She was a peasant. This is a peasant. Black peasant Madonna for black country."

This is a German village," said the Captain.

"This is my Madonna," said Michele angrily. "Your German village and my Madonna. I paint this picture as an offering to the Madonna. She is pleased—I feel it."

The Captain lay down again. He was feeling ill. He went back to sleep. When he woke for the second time it was dark. Michele had brought in a flaring paraffin lamp, and by its light was working on the long wall. A bottle of brandy stood beside him. He painted until long after midnight, and the Captain lay on his side and watched, as passive as a man suffering a dream. Then they both went to sleep on the boards. The whole of the next day Michele stood painting black Madonnas, black saints, black angels. Outside, troops were practising in the sunlight, bands were blaring and motorcyclists roared up and down. But Michele painted on, drunk and oblivious. The Captain lay on his back, drinking and muttering about his wife.

Then he would say "Nadya, Nadya," and burst into sobs.

Towards nightfall the troops went away. The officers came back, and the Captain went off with them to show how the village sprang into being when the great lights at the end of the parade-ground were switched on. They all looked at the village in silence. They switched the lights off, and there were only the tall angular boards leaning like gravestones in the moonlight. On went the lights—and there was the village. They were silent, as if suspicious. Like the Captain, they seemed to feel it was not right. Uncanny it certainly was, but *that* was not it. Unfair—that was the word. It was cheating. And profoundly disturbing.

"Clever chap, that Italian of yours," said the General.

The Captain, who had been woodenly correct until this moment, suddenly came rocking up to the General, and steadied himself by laying his hand on the august shoulder. "Bloody Wops," he said. "Bloody kaffirs. Bloody . . . Tell you what, though, there's one Itie that's some good. Yes, there is. I'm telling you. He's a friend of mine, actually."

The General looked at him. Then he nodded at his underlings. The Captain was taken away for disciplinary purposes. It was decided, however, that he must be ill, nothing else could account for such behaviour. He was put to bed in his own room with a nurse to watch him.

He woke twenty-four hours later, sober for the first time in weeks. He slowly remembered what had happened. Then he sprang out of bed and rushed into his clothes. The nurse was just in time to see him run down the path and leap into his lorry.

He drove at top speed to the parade-ground, which was flooded with light in such a way that the village did not exist. Everything was in full swing. The cars were three deep around the square, with people on the running-boards and even the roofs. The grandstand was packed. Women dressed up as gypsies, country girls, Elizabethan court dames, and so on, wandered about with trays of ginger beer and sausage-rolls and programmes at five shillings each in aid of the war effort. On the square, troops deployed, obsolete machine-guns were being dragged up and down, bands played, and motorcyclists roared through flames.

As the Captain parked the lorry, all this activity ceased, and the lights went out. The Captain began running around the outside of the square to reach the place where the guns were hidden in a mess of net and branches. He was sobbing with the effort. He was a big man, and unused to exercise, and sodden with brandy. He had only one idea in his mind —to stop the guns firing, to stop them at all costs.

Luckily, there seemed to be a hitch. The lights were still out. The unearthly graveyard at the end of the square glittered white in the moonlight. Then the lights briefly switched on, and the village sprang into existence for just long enough to show large red crosses all over a white building beside the church. Then moonlight flooded everything again, and the crosses vanished.

"Oh, the bloody fool!" sobbed the Captain, running, running as if for his life. He was no longer trying to reach the guns. He was cutting across a corner of the square direct to the church. He could hear some officers cursing behind him: "Who put those red crosses there? Who? We can't fire on the Red Cross."

The Captain reached the church as the searchlights burst on. Inside, Michele was kneeling on the earth looking at his first Madonna. "They are going to kill my Madonna," he said miserably.

"Come away, Michele, come away."

The Black Madonna

"They're going to . . ."

The Captain grabbed his arm and pulled. Michele wrenched himself free and grabbed a saw. He began hacking at the ceiling board. There was a dead silence outside. They heard a voice booming through the loudspeakers: "The village that is about to be shelled is an English village, not as represented on the programme, a German village. Repeat, the village that is about to be shelled is . . ."

Michele had cut through two sides of a square around the Madonna.

"Michele," sobbed the Captain, *"get out of here."*

Michelle dropped the saw, took hold of the raw edges of the board and tugged. As he did so, the church began to quiver and lean. An irregular patch of board ripped out and Michele staggered back into the Captain's arms. There was a roar. The church seemed to dissolve around them into flame. Then they were running away from it, the Captain holding Michele tight by the arm. "Get down," he shouted suddenly, and threw Michele to the earth. He flung himself down beside him. Looking from under the crook of his arm, he heard the explosion, saw a great pillar of smoke and flame, and the village disintegrated in a flying mass of debris. Michele was on his knees gazing at his Madonna in the light from the flames. She was unrecognizable, blotted out with dust. He looked horrible, quite white, and a trickle of blood soaked from his hair down one cheek.

"They shelled my Madonna," he said.

"Oh, damn it, you can paint another one," said the Captain. His own voice seemed to him strange, like a dream voice. He was certainly crazy, as mad as Michele himself . . . He got up, pulled Michele to his feet, and marched him towards the edge of the field. There they were met by the ambulance people. Michele was taken off to hospital, and the Captain was sent back to bed.

A week passed. The Captain was in a darkened room. That he was having some kind of a breakdown was clear, and two nurses stood guard over him. Sometimes he lay quiet. Sometimes he muttered to himself. Sometimes he sang in a thick clumsy voice bits out of opera, fragments from Italian songs, and—over and over again—"There's a Long Long Trail." He was not thinking of anything at all. He shied away from the thought of Michele as if it were dangerous. When, therefore, a cheerful female voice announced that a friend had come to cheer him up, and it would do him good to have some company, and he saw a white bandage moving towards him in the gloom, he turned sharp over on to his side, face to the wall.

"Go away," he said. "Go away, Michele."

"I have come to see you," said Michele. "I have brought you a present."

The Captain slowly turned over. There was Michele, a cheerful ghost in the dark room. "You fool," he said. "You messed everything up. What did you paint those crosses for?"

"It was a hospital," said Michele. "In a village there is a hospital, and on the hospital the Red Cross, the beautiful Red Cross—no?"

"I was nearly court-martialed."

"It was my fault," said Michele. "I was drunk."

"I was responsible."

"How could you be responsible when I did it? But it is all over. Are you better?"

"Well, I suppose those crosses saved your life."

"I did not think," said Michele. "I was remembering the kindness of the Red Cross people when we were prisoners."

"Oh shut up, shut up, shut up."

"I have brought you a present."

The Captain peered through the dark. Michele was holding up a picture. It was of a native woman with a baby on her back smiling sideways out of the frame.

Michele said: "You did not like the haloes. So this time, no haloes. For the Captain—no Madonna." He laughed. "You like it? It is for you. I painted it for you."

"God damn you!" said the Captain.

"You do not like it?" said Michele, very hurt.

The Captain closed his eyes. "What are you going to do next?" he asked tiredly.

Michele laughed again. "Mrs. Pannerhurst, the lady of the General, she wants me to paint her picture in her white dress. So I paint it."

"You should be proud to."

"Silly bitch. She thinks I am good. They know nothing—savages. Barbarians. Not you, Captain, you are my friend. But these people they know nothing."

The Captain lay quiet. Fury was gathering in him. He thought of the General's wife. He disliked her, but he had known her well enough.

"These people," said Michele. "They do not know a good picture from a bad picture. I paint, I paint, this way, that way. There is the picture—I look at it and laugh inside myself." Michele laughed out loud. "They say, he is a Michelangelo, this one, and try to cheat me out of my price. Michele—Michelangelo—that is a joke, no?"

The Captain said nothing.

"But for you I painted this picture to remind you of our good times with the village. You are my friend. I will always remember you."

The Captain turned his eyes sideways in his head and stared at the black girl. Her smile at him was half innocence, half malice.

"Get out," he said suddenly.

Michele came closer and bent to see the Captain's face. "You wish me to go?" He sounded unhappy. "You saved my life, I was a fool that night. But I was thinking of my offering to the Madonna—I was a fool, I say it myself. I was drunk, we are fools when we are drunk."

"Get out of here," said the Captain again.

For a moment the white bandage remained motionless. Then it swept downwards in a bow.

Michele turned towards the door.

"And take that bloody picture with you."

Silence. Then, in the dim light, the Captain saw Michele reach out for the picture, his white head bowed in profound obeisance. He straightened himself and stood to attention, holding the picture with one hand, and keeping the other stiff down his side. Then he saluted the Captain.

"Yes, *sir,*" he said, and he turned and went out of the door with the picture.

The Captain lay still. He felt—what did he feel? There was a pain under his ribs. It hurt to breathe. He realized he was unhappy. Yes, a terrible unhappiness was filling him, slowly, slowly. He was unhappy because Michele had gone. Nothing had ever hurt the Captain in all his life as much as the mocking *Yes, sir.* Nothing. He turned his face to the wall and wept. But silently. Not a sound escaped him, for the fear the nurses might hear.

■ DISCUSSION AND QUESTIONS

1. Lessing begins her story with a discussion of Art and the circumstances in which it flourishes. Do the first three paragraphs of the story prepare the reader for the events that follow? Are they really necessary to the story? What do we learn from these paragraphs about Zambesia and its two populations? Who are the leisured "minority" and the "hard-working majority" she refers to? What circumstances, in your opinion, do produce art?

2. What reactions do the people of Westonville have to Michele and his painting? What is his attitude toward his paintings and toward the patrons who commission him to do their portraits?

3. Michele made his reputation as an artist by decorating the interior of the church in the military camp. What subjects did he depict in his "religious" frescoes? What do these subjects reveal about Michele's personality?

4. Verbal irony is a mode of speech which allows the speaker to imply attitudes or judgments that are different from those literally expressed. Simply put, verbal irony is saying one thing and meaning another.

The narrator of this story is a member of the Westonville white community, but she seems to view her neighbors, especially the "culture-loving ladies," ironically. What do these ladies know about culture? Is the name "culture-loving ladies" ironic?

The narrator knows that Michele is not a great artist and tells us that he was, in fact, a bricklayer, not a painter. "It is possible," she says, that his paintings "would have been overlooked altogether in a country where picture-covered walls were more common." This is an ironic "put down" of the ladies who cannot distinguish Art from "nice likenesses." (What is the difference?) Here is another instance of the ironic tone of the narrator: "There was a good deal of talk among the ladies about the dignity of labour, a subject in which they were well versed. . . ." (p. 99). Why is this statement ironic? Can you find other examples of the narrator's use of verbal irony?

5. Has Ms. Lessing reduced Michele to a stereotype Italian like the ones in ethnic jokes? In what ways has she made him a "typical" Italian? Is he a round or a flat character?

6. When Captain Stocker first meets Michele, the contrast between the two men is striking. Stocker, of course, is wearing his uniform. How is Michele dressed? What is he doing? Why does Stocker "desire that Michele should salute him"? (Notice at the end of the story that it is Michele's salute that causes Stocker so much pain.)

After Michele consents to build the village, he talks Stocker into going after something to drink. When Stocker returns with the brandy, he finds Michele and the six black men singing an Italian song. What does Stocker feel when he sees this harmonious septet? Why?

7. Look closely at the scene in which Stocker and Michele first drink brandy together (p.102). When they sit down on the grass, Stocker thinks of Michele as the "enemy." How do his thoughts about Michele change as they drink more and more, and Michele talks more and more? Who are the "Northern people" Stocker has always been attracted to? Why would he have found Germany "very satisfactory"? (Note: his wife calls him "little Hitler.") Why do Michele's tales about Italy make Stocker feel he is listening to a "savage," as if he were hearing stories about "mythical South Sea islands"?

8. The narrator never tells us what Michele thinks or feels. We have to infer this from his actions and words. What can we infer about his motivations, his longings, his feelings? Is he merely a fun-loving, slightly degenerate fellow who loves a bottle of wine, a song, and his wife?

9. Michele, irresponsible though he may be, is nonetheless a remarkably likeable fellow. How does Lessing make the reader like him?

10. Lessing sketches in many details of Captain Stocker's life. We learn of his wife and children, of his relations with bush women, of the private detective he hires to watch his wife. How do Stocker's feelings for his wife differ from Michele's for his? What does Stocker feel for Nadya? What do these feelings for his wife and Nadya reveal about his personality?

11. What is Michele's definition of happiness? What does he want out of life? What does Stocker want?

12. Michele communicates his inner self through words, songs, and paintings. How much of his inner self can Stocker communicate to others?

Why? What changes occur in Stocker when he gets drunk? What does the last line of the story mean?

13. A forceful way of making the reader respond favorably to a character is to contrast him with another character who is unattractive or unlikeable. In what specific ways is Michele contrasted with Stocker? Is Stocker likeable? What is Michele's attitude toward the native Africans? How do the British officers and ladies feel toward them?

Chapter 4

SYMBOL

Jonathan Swift, the author of *Gulliver's Travels,* invented in that book a race of people able to talk only about objects which they could carry with them. They were burdened by carrying enormous packs, and their conversations were limited by what they could point to. We are of course not limited in that way. We are able to talk of all sorts of things, sensations, moods, ideas, for which there are no physical objects to point to. Not only are we capable of forming concepts for which there are no physical objects to point to, but it is possible for us to have moods, feelings, and simultaneous and complicated combinations of feelings for which we do not even have precise words. That's where *symbols* come in.

Whereas it is usually the case that words stand for specific things—chair, spoon, journey, laurel wreath, scissors—sometimes these same words must be used to mean more than they do on the surface. Then these words or phrases become *symbols.* Symbols are words that suggest much more than they mean on the surface and are necessary to help us express complex ideas. A flag, a cross, a star of David—these are symbols. A flag is not the geographical boundaries of a country—it is the idea of a country. To put that idea into words would take volumes, and still the topic would not be exhausted. We would still have feelings left over that would not have been described. So the flag acts as an evoker of all those notions we have of a country. Some of the notions are expressible in words, others may not be. But they are all called to mind by the symbol, the flag. A symbol is, then, by its nature, open-ended. It has many expressible meanings; and it has many meanings which may not be expressible at all. Similar to the flag are the religious symbols, the cross or the star of David. Those simple signs evoke a host of complicated and interrelated feelings.

A *symbol,* then, is a word or phrase or image (sign) that stands for a larger idea.

It is convenient to classify symbols into three categories: *natural symbols, conventional symbols, private symbols.*

Natural symbols are words or images that suggest their larger meanings to the reader without the reader having to be instructed in those meanings. They seem to have an inherent "rightness" about them; readers anywhere will probably offer similar interpretations of natural symbols. For example, it somehow seems right that the span of a person's life should be symbolized by a journey. We even have expressions in our American language that suggest the similarity—"what *path in life* will you take," "that's *the road* I will follow," etc. We need not inform our hearers that we don't really mean *path* and *road.* We can almost surely assume they will not take us literally, but will understand us to mean "what are you going to do in your life?" or "this is what I expect to do in life." It is almost as though the power to interpret "path," "road," "voyage" is part of our genetic equipment.[1]

A *conventional symbol* is an image that has, by tradition and by certain people in the course of time and in a limited place, been assigned a meaning beyond itself. A round metal disc dangling from a piece of ribbon does not, in itself, have any characteristics that say "we think you are a wonderful person." Yet among many people over the course of hundreds of years a metal disc on a piece of ribbon has been the award given by a ruler, a government, or some other arbiter of merit, to show an individual that his actions have been approved of. The "medal," as it is called, is by convention given to the person of whom you approve (it is not worn by the person who is doing the approving, nor is it given to the person of whom you disapprove). It is a symbol—a conventional symbol—of approval.

You may not know what a wreath made of laurel (bay tree) leaves means. In ancient times such a wreath was given to emperors, victorious generals, great athletes, great poets. It might as easily have been the leaves of an oak tree. But by tradition, by convention, the laurel has been

---

[1]The very interesting question of whether similar interpretation of such basic natural symbols would hold true for people in very different cultures and very different times has not been conclusively settled. Some psychologists and anthropologists who have explored this matter say yes, certain symbols—for example, water, or the notion of the importance of grouping elements of a story in threes, three sisters, three strangers, three attempts, etc. —are indeed universal for the human race.

used. In England a poet laureate is still chosen every so often—a poet worthy of the laurel wreath, who becomes the "official" poet of the kingdom. The laurel wreath is a conventional symbol that goes to the victor, to the person most honored. Frequently the conventional symbol, the laurel wreath, is pictured on the conventional symbol, the medal on a ribbon. What do you think a medal with a laurel wreath on it must mean?

A *private symbol* is one that one author, or perhaps a small group of writers or artists, has made his own conventional symbol. Holden Caulfield, the young hero of the novel *The Catcher in the Rye,* wears a baseball cap. In moments of stress he turns the cap around on his head so that the visor is in the back, the way catchers in baseball games wear their caps. Frequently this action by Holden means that he would like to catch somebody, to rescue them, to save them. This particular meaning of being a catcher has specific significance within the world of this novel only—and nowhere else. Since it is such a private symbol for this one author in this one novel, the author has had his young hero explain precisely and explicitly what he means when he thinks that he is a catcher in a field of rye.

Scissors are not a universal symbol. They do not, in themselves, bring to mind anything specific. They are neither a natural symbol, nor a conventional one. In Franz Kafka's story, "Jackals and Arabs," however, they have considerable significance, they point to something else. The rusty pair of sewing scissors which the jackals give to the narrator to slit the throats of the Arabs "goes wandering through the desert and will wander with us to the end of our days," says the Arab to the narrator. "Every European is offered it for the great work," he says.

These scissors, then, are invested with great, but elusive, symbolic significance. They are the age-old instrument for the performing of some portentous and also symbolic action. They have existed presumably almost since the beginning of history, and they make their appearance every time a European is approached by the jackals to murder their primal enemies, the Arabs. What, precisely, these scissors are, we don't know. We don't even know what the Europeans, the jackals, and the Arabs are, precisely, in this strange story. They are more than *merely* Europeans, jackals, and Arabs; for if they were only Europeans, jackals, and Arabs, the story would have only a very narrow topical interest. They are groups, obviously, that are enemies since time immemorial. We receive the strong suggestion that these Europeans, jackals, and Arabs are types of, or stand for, all factions that have been natural enemies for all time—perhaps men and beasts, perhaps great divisions of the populations of mankind. The only thing we know for sure is that the author was not writing an account merely of Europeans, jackals, and Arabs.

Symbol

But let us return to the scissors. They are like other great symbols, the flag or the grail—objects invested with enormous significance, of highest import to an entire population. The only difference is that these scissors are *not* a flag or a grail, the signification of which millions of people would feel instantly. They are simple, rusty, sewing scissors, invented by Franz Kafka and put into a dramatic situation in a story, a situation in which they are talked of as though they were a flag or a grail. By perceiving these scissors within the context of the story, we see *how* they are meant to express meanings beyond themselves. We understand that they are objects invested with historical and sacred importance, treasured as though they were sacramental objects. They are in a sense sacramental because the jackals forever hope that these instruments will be used in some great ritual action—killing the Arabs. So then, the scissors are a *private symbol*—a symbol invented by this author for this purpose in this story only—and also a symbol that does not need explicit explanation (as does the catcher in the rye), since the explanation becomes sufficiently clear in the context of the story.

Symbol, Theme, Story

A symbol, we have noted, signifies something beyond itself. A good story also signifies something beyond itself, something intricately tied in with its theme. A theme is, according to Flannery O'Connor, what is "embodied" or "made concrete" by the story. In fact, the theme is, in large measure, the significance which resonates beyond the mere tale itself. (For further explanation of *theme* see pp.151-52.) Now you can readily see that if a symbol is the concrete expression of ideas beyond itself, and if a story is also the concrete expression of something (a "meaning," a theme) beyond itself, story and symbol share important characteristics in common. In fact, we can truthfully say that, though symbols are not stories, very many good stories are symbols. Stories are embodiments or concretizations of ideas (themes) beyond themselves, and they are worth having because their precise meaning "can't be said in any other way." Every word in the story will count toward the sum total of that story's significance—as we shall explore more carefully when we discuss some specific words in "Jackals and Arabs."

The Medal of Disapproval

W. S. Merwin

> We have spoken of medals that are given as awards for heroism or for great acts. Assume that you are designing a medal that will be used for *shameful* acts. What design would you put on such a medal? Think of one or several items for each side of the medal, and explain why you think they are suitable.

It has, of course, two sides.

There is the side without a face. On this side the symbols are arranged like objects in the nest of a rat—fixed, neatly interrelated, but so far from their original backgrounds and purposes that it is often hard to say what they are. On the other hand it is obvious that they bespeak immeasurable age, and an authority that is on intimate terms with the order of the cosmos itself. Indeed they may be interpreted as being an extension of that order. Sometimes there is a laurel crown. Empty. Occasionally there is a lamp. Often, in fact almost always, there are numbers. This side is clearly abstract and there is no appeal to it. It is the side that is presented, in due course, to the person disapproved of.

Then there is the other side called the face. And in fact it has a head on it. The head of a ruler, a hero of some kind, a forbear. But whatever motto surrounds him, his face is turned away. It is turned away forever. There is no appeal to this side, either. It too is abstract. This is the side that is worn facing outward, by the disapproving. Then the other side is worn facing inward.

From *The Miner's Pale Children* by W. S. Merwin. Copyright © 1969, 1970 by W. S. Merwin. Reprinted by permission of Atheneum Publishers.

Symbol

■ DISCUSSION AND QUESTIONS

W. S. Merwin has done precisely what you were asked to do before you read the story: he has designed a "medal of disapproval."

1. Who is to wear the medal of disapproval—the person disapproved of, the disapprover, or both?

2. What items does Merwin picture on his medal of disapproval? What do you think the items on the medal signify? Why is the laurel crown "empty"? Why are there numbers on the medal, and why do you think Merwin does not bother to tell you what the numbers are? Does it matter that we don't know whose head is on the medal, or what motto is on the medal?

Note that the author tells you explicitly, in the third sentence, that the objects pictured on the medal are symbols. Are they natural, conventional, or private symbols, or are they some combination of these?

3. This little story—it is really more of a sketch—would be too trivial to include in this collection if it did not have meaning beyond itself. By means of the symbols he employs, however, the author is telling us something about the nature of being disapproved of, and also about the nature of being someone who disapproves. Every image, every symbol in the story contributes to that notion, and again, "it can't be said in any other way." Nonetheless, attempt to explain some of the ideas that the story expresses about what it is like (a) to be disapproved of, and (b) to be someone who disapproves. What is meant by the fact that the disapprover wears the medal with the image of a head of "a ruler, a hero of some kind, a forbear,"—but that this head is turned away? What significance is there in the fact that the head is turned away "forever"?

Night-Sea Journey

John Barth

"One way or another, no matter which theory of our journey is correct, it's myself I address; to whom I rehearse as to a stranger our history and condition, and will disclose my secret hope though I sink for it.

"Is the journey my invention? Do the night, the sea, exist at all, I ask myself, apart from my experience of them? Do I myself exist, or is this a dream? Sometimes I wonder. And if I am, who am I? The Heritage I supposedly transport? But how can I be both vessel and contents? Such are the questions that beset my intervals of rest.

"My trouble is, I lack conviction. Many accounts of our situation seem plausible to me—where and what we are, why we swim and whither. But implausible ones as well, perhaps especially those, I must admit as possibly correct. Even likely. If at times, in certain humors—stroking in unison, say, with my neighbors and chanting with them 'Onward! Upward!'—I have supposed that we have after all a common Maker, Whose nature and motives we may not know, but Who engendered us in some mysterious wise and launched us forth toward some end known but to Him—if (for a moodslength only) I have been able to entertain such notions, very popular in certain quarters, it is because our night-sea journey partakes of their absurdity. One might even say: I can believe them *because* they are absurd.

"Night-Sea Journey" copyright © 1966 by John Barth from the book *Lost in the Funhouse* by John Barth. Reprinted by permission of Doubleday and Company, Inc.

"Has that been said before?

"Another paradox: it appears to be these recesses from swimming that sustain me in the swim. Two measures onward and upward, flailing with the rest, then I float exhausted and dispirited, brood upon the night, the sea, the journey, while the flood bears me a measure back and down: slow progress, but I live, I live, and make my way, aye, past many a drowned comrade in the end, stronger, worthier than I, victims of their unremitting *joie de nager*. I have seen the best swimmers of my generation go under. Numberless the number of the dead! Thousands drown as I think this thought, millions as I rest before returning to the swim. And scores, hundreds of millions have expired since we surged forth, brave in our innocence, upon our dreadful way. 'Love! Love!' we sang then, a quarter-billion strong, and churned the warm sea white with joy of swimming! Now all are gone down—the buoyant, the sodden, leaders and followers, all gone under, while wretched I swim on. Yet these same reflective intervals that keep me afloat have led me into wonder, doubt, despair—strange emotions for a swimmer!—have led me, even, to suspect . . . that our night-sea journey is without meaning.

"Indeed, if I have yet to join the hosts of the suicides, it is because (fatigue apart) I find it no meaningfuller to drown myself than to go on swimming.

"I know that there are those who seem actually to enjoy the night-sea; who claim to love swimming for its own sake, or sincerely believe that 'reaching the Shore,' 'transmitting the Heritage' (*Whose* Heritage, I'd like to know? And to whom?) is worth the staggering cost. I do not. Swimming itself I find at best not actively unpleasant, more often tiresome, not infrequently a torment. Arguments from function and design don't impress me: granted that we can and do swim, that in a manner of speaking our long tails and streamlined heads are 'meant for' swimming; it by no means follows—for me, at least—that we *should* swim, or otherwise endeavor to 'fulfill our destiny.' Which is to say, Someone Else's destiny, since ours, so far as I can see, is merely to perish, one way or another, soon or late. The heartless zeal of our (departed) leaders, like the blind ambition and good cheer of my own youth, appalls me now; for the death of my comrades I am inconsolable. If the night-sea journey has justification, it is not for us swimmers ever to discover it.

"Oh, to be sure, 'Love!' one heard on every side: 'Love it is that drives and sustains us!' I translate: we don't know *what* drives and sustains us, only that we are most miserably driven and, imperfectly, sustained. *Love* is how we call our ignorance of what whips us. 'To reach the Shore,' then: but what if the Shore exists in the fancies of us swimmers merely, who dream it to account for the dreadful fact that we swim, have always and only swum, and continue swimming without respite (myself excepted) until we die? Supposing even that there *were* a Shore—that, as a cynical companion of mine once imagined, we rise from the drowned to discover all those vulgar superstitions and exalted metaphors to be literal truth: the giant Maker of us all, the Shores of Light beyond our night-sea journey!—whatever would a swimmer do there? The fact is, when we imagine the Shore, what comes to mind is just the opposite of our condition: no more night, no more sea, no more journeying. In short, the blissful estate of the drowned.

" 'Ours not to stop and think; ours but to swim and sink. . . .' Because a moment's thought reveals the pointlessness of swimming. 'No matter,' I've heard some say, even as they gulped their last: 'The night-sea journey may be absurd, but here we swim, will-we nill-we, against the flood, onward and upward, toward a Shore that may not exist and couldn't be reached if it did.' The thoughtful swimmer's choices, then, they say, are two: give over thrashing and go under for good, or embrace the absurdity; affirm in and for itself the night-sea journey; swim on with neither motive nor destination, for the sake of swimming, and compassionate moreover with your fellow swimmer, we being all at sea and equally in the dark. I find neither course acceptable. If not even the hypothetical Shore can justify a sea-full of drowned comrades, to speak of the swim-in-itself as somehow doing so strikes me as obscene. I continue to swim—but only because blind habit, blind instinct, blind fear of drowning are still more strong than the horror of our journey. And if on occasion I have assisted a fellow-thrasher, joined in the cheers and songs, even passed along to others strokes of genius from the drowned great, it's that I shrink by temperament from making myself conspicuous. To paddle off in one's own direction, assert one's independent right-of-way, overrun one's fellows without compunction, or dedicate oneself entirely to pleasures and diversions without regard for conscience—I can't finally condemn those who journey in this wise; in half my moods I envy them and despise the weak vitality that keeps me from following their example. But in reasonabler moments I remind myself that it's their very freedom and self-responsibility I reject, as more dramatically absurd, in our senseless circumstances, than tailing along in conventional fashion. Suicides, rebels, affirmers of the paradox—nay-sayers and yea-sayers alike to our fatal journey—I finally shake my head at them. And splash sighing past their corpses, one by one, as past a hundred sorts of others: friends, enemies, brothers; fools, sages, brutes—and nobodies, million upon million. I envy them all.

"A poor irony: that I, who find abhorrent and tautological the doctrine of survival of the fittest (*fitness* meaning, in my experience, nothing more than survival-ability, a talent whose only demonstration is the fact of survival, but whose chief ingredients seem to be strength, guile, callousness), may be the sole remaining swimmer! But the doctrine is false as well as repellent: Chance drowns the worthy with the unworthy, bears up the unfit with the fit by whatever definition, and makes the night-sea journey essentially *haphazard* as well as murderous and unjustified.

" 'You only swim once.' Why bother, then?

" 'Except ye drown, ye shall not reach the Shore of Life.' Poppycock.

"One of my late companions—that same cynic with the curious fancy, among the first to drown—entertained us with odd conjectures while we waited to begin our journey. A favorite theory of his was that the Father does exist, and did indeed make us and the sea we swim—but not a-purpose or even consciously; He made us, as it were, despite Himself, as we make waves with every tail-thrash, and may be unaware of our existence. Another was that He knows we're here but doesn't care what happens to us, inasmuch as He creates (voluntarily or not) other seas and swimmers at more or less regular intervals. In bitterer moments, such as just before he drowned, my friend even supposed that our Maker wished us unmade; there was indeed a Shore, he'd argue, which could save at least some of us from drowning and toward which it was our function to struggle—but for reasons unknowable to us He wanted desperately to prevent our reaching that happy place and fulfilling our destiny. Our 'Father,' in short, was our adversary and would-be killer! No less outrageous, and offensive to traditional opinion, were the fellow's speculations on the nature of our Maker: that He might well be no swimmer Himself at all, but some sort of monstrosity, perhaps even tailless; that He might be stupid, malicious, insensible, perverse, or asleep and dreaming; that the end for which He created and launched us forth, and which we flagellate ourselves to fathom, was perhaps immoral, even obscene. Et cetera, et cetera: there was no end to the chap's conjectures, or the impoliteness of his fancy; I have reason to suspect that his early demise, whether planned by 'our Maker' or not, was expedited by certain fellow-swimmers indignant at his blasphemies.

"In other moods, however (he was as given to moods as I), his theorizing would become half-serious, so it seemed to me, especially upon the subjects of Fate and Immortality, to which our youthful conversations often turned. Then his harangues, if no less fantastical, grew solemn and obscure, and if he was still baiting us, his passion undid the joke. His objection to popular opinions of the hereafter, he would declare, was their claim to general validity. Why need believers hold that *all* the drowned rise to be judged at journey's end, and nonbelievers that drowning is final without exception? In *his* opinion (so he'd vow at least), nearly everyone's fate was permanent death; indeed he took a sour pleasure in supposing that every 'Maker' made thousands of separate seas in His creative life-time, each populated like ours with millions of swimmers, and that in almost every instance both sea and swimmers were utterly annihilated, whether accidentally or by malevolent design. (Nothing if not pluralistical, he imagined there might be millions and billions of 'Fathers,' perhaps in some 'night-sea' of their own!) However—and here he turned infidels against him with the faithful—he professed to believe that in possibly a single night-sea per thousand, say, one of its quarter-billion swimmers (that is, one swimmer in two hundred fifty billions) achieved a qualified immortality. In some cases the rate might be slightly higher; in others it was vastly lower, for just as there are swimmers of every degree of proficiency, including some who drown before the journey starts, unable to swim at all, and others created drowned, as it were, so he imagined what can only be termed impotent Creators, Makers unable to Make, as well as uncommonly fertile ones and all grades between. And it pleased him to deny any necessary relation between a Maker's productivity and His other virtues—including, even, the quality of His creatures.

"I could go on (*he* surely did) with his elaboration of these mad notions—such as that swimmers in other night-seas needn't be of our kind; that Makers themselves might belong to different *species,* so to speak; that our particular Maker mightn't Himself be immortal, or that we might be not only His emissaries but His 'immortality,' continuing His life and our own, transmogrified, beyond our individual deaths. Even this modified immortality (meaningless to me) he conceived as relative and contingent, subject to accidental or deliberate termination: his pet hypothesis was that Makers and swimmers *each generate the other*—against all odds, their number being so great—and that any given 'immortality-chain' could terminate after any number of cycles, so that what was 'immortal' (still speaking relatively) was only the cyclic process of incarnation, which itself might have a beginning and an end. Alternatively he liked to imagine cycles within cycles, either finite or infinite: for example, the 'night-sea,' as it were, in which Makers 'swam' and created night-seas and swimmers like ourselves, might be the creation of a larger Maker, Himself one of many, Who in turn et cetera. Time itself he regarded as relative to our experience, like magnitude: who knew but what, with each thrash of our tails, minuscule seas and swimmers, whole eternities, came to pass—as ours, perhaps, and our Maker's Maker's, was elapsing between the strokes of some supertail, in a slower order of time?

"Naturally I hooted with the others at this nonsense. We were young then, and had only the dimmest notion of what lay ahead; in our ignorance we imagined night-sea journeying to be a positively heroic enterprise. Its meaning and value we never questioned; to be sure, some must go down by the way, a pity no doubt, but to win a race requires that others lose, and like all my fellows I took for granted that I would be the winner.

We milled and swarmed, impatient to be off, never mind where or why, only to try our youth against the realities of night and sea; if we indulged the skeptic at all, it was a droll, half-contemptible mascot. When he died in the initial slaughter, no one cared.

"And even now I don't subscribe to all his views—but I no longer scoff. The horror of our history has purged me of opinions, as of vanity, confidence, spirit, charity, hope, vitality, everything—except dull dread and a kind of melancholy, stunned persistence. What leads me to recall his fancies is my growing suspicion that I, of all swimmers, may be the sole survivor of this fell journey, tale-bearer of a generation. This suspicion, together with the recent sea-change, suggests to me now that nothing is impossible, not even my late companion's wildest visions, and brings me to a certain desperate resolve, the point of my chronicling.

"Very likely I have lost my senses. The carnage at our setting out; our decimation by whirlpool, poisoned cataract, sea-convulsion; the panic stampedes, mutinies, slaughters, mass suicides; the mounting evidence that none will survive the journey—add to these anguish and fatigue; it were a miracle if sanity stayed afloat. Thus I admit, with the other possibilities, that the present sweetening and calming of the sea, and what seems to be a kind of vasty presence, song, or summons from the near upstream, may be hallucinations of disordered sensibility. . . .

"Perhaps, even, I am drowned already. Surely I was never meant for the rough-and-tumble of the swim; not impossibly I perished at the outset and have only imaged the night-sea journey from some final deep. In any case, I'm no longer young, and it is we spent old swimmers, disabused of every illusion, who are most vulnerable to dreams.

"Sometimes I think I am my drowned friend.

"Out with it: I've begun to believe, not only that *She* exists, but that She lies not far ahead, and stills the sea, and draws me Herward! Aghast, I recollect his maddest notion: that our destination (which existed, mind, in but one night-sea out of hundreds and thousands) was no Shore, as commonly conceived, but a mysterious being, indescribable except by paradox and vaguest figure: wholly different from us swimmers, yet our complement; the death of us, yet our salvation and resurrection; simultaneously our journey's end, mid-point, and commencement; not membered and thrashing like us, but a motionless or hugely gliding sphere of unimaginable dimension; self-contained, yet dependent absolutely, in some wise, upon the chance (always monstrously improbable) that one of us will survive the night-sea journey and reach . . . Her! *Her,* he called it, or *She,* which is to say, Other-than-a-he. I shake my head; the thing is too preposterous; it is myself I talk to, to keep my reason in this awful darkness. There is no She! There is no You! I rave to myself; it's Death alone that hears and summons. To the drowned, all seas are calm. . . .

"Listen: my friend maintained that in every order of creation there are two sorts of creators, contrary yet complementary, one of which gives rise to seas and swimmers, the other to the Night-which-contains-the-sea and to What-waits-at-the-journey's-end: the former, in short, to destiny, the latter to destination (and both profligately, involuntarily, perhaps indifferently or unwittingly). The 'purpose' of the night-sea journey—but not necessarily of the journeyer or of either Maker!—my friend could describe only in abstractions: *consummation, transfiguration, union, contraries, transcension of categories.* When we laughed, he would shrug and admit that he understood the business no better than we, and thought it ridiculous, dreary, possibly obscene. 'But one of you,' he'd add with his wry smile, 'may be the Hero destined to complete the night-sea journey and be one with Her. Chances are, of course, you won't make it.' He himself, he declared, was not even going to try; the whole idea repelled him; if we chose to dismiss it as an ugly fiction, so much the better for us; thrash, splash, and be merry, we were soon enough drowned. But there it was, he could not say how he knew or why he bothered to tell us, any more than he could say what would happen after She and Hero, Shore and Swimmer, 'merged identities' to become something both and neither. He quite agreed with me that if the issue of that magical union had no memory of the night-sea journey, for example, it enjoyed a poor sort of immortality; even poorer if, as he rather imagined, a swimmer-hero plus a She equaled or became merely another Maker of future night-seas and the rest, at such incredible expense of life. This being the case—he was persuaded it was—the merciful thing to do was refuse to participate; the genuine heroes, in his opinion, were the suicides, and the hero of heroes would be the swimmer who, in the very presence of the Order, refused Her proffered 'immortality' and thus put an end to at least one cycle of catastrophes.

"How we mocked him! Our moment came, we hurtled forth, pretending to glory in the adventure, thrashing, singing, cursing, strangling, rationalizing, rescuing, killing, inventing rules and stories and relationships, giving up, struggling on, but dying all, and still in darkness, until only a battered remnant was left to croak 'Onward, upward,' like a bitter echo. Then they too fell silent—victims, I can only presume, of the last frightful wave—and the moment came when I also, utterly desolate and spent, thrashed my last and gave myself over to the current, to sink or float as might be, but swim no more. Whereupon, marvelous to tell, in an instant the sea grew still! Then warmly, gently, the great tide turned, began to bear me, as it does now, onward and upward will-I nill-I, like a flood of joy—and I recalled with dismay my dead friend's teaching.

"I am not deceived. This new emotion is Her doing; the desire that possesses me is Her bewitchment. Lucidity passes from me; in a moment

Night-Sea Journey

I'll cry 'Love!' bury myself in Her side, and be 'transfigured!' Which is to say, I died already; this fellow transported by passion is not I; *I am he who abjures and rejects the night-sea journey!* I. . . .

"I am all love. 'Come!' She whispers, and I have no will.

"You who I may be about to become, whatever You are: with the last twitch of my real self I beg You to listen. It is *not* love that sustains me! No; though Her magic makes me burn to sing the contrary, and though I drown even now for the blasphemy, I will say truth. What has fetched me across this dreadful sea is a single hope, gift of my poor dead comrade: that You may be stronger-willed than I, and that by sheer force of concentration I may transmit to You, along with Your official Heritage, a private legacy of awful recollection and negative resolve. Mad as it may be, my dream is that some unimaginable embodiment of myself (or myself plus Her if that's how it must be) will come to find itself expressing, in however garbled or radical a translation, some reflection of these reflections. If against all odds this comes to pass, may You to whom, through whom I speak, do what I cannot: terminate this aimless, brutal business! Stop Your hearing against Her song! Hate love!

"Still alive, afloat, afire. Farewell then my penultimate hope: that one may be sunk for direst blasphemy on the very shore of the Shore. Can it be (my old friend would smile) that only utterest nay-sayers survive the night? But even that were Sense, and there is no sense, only senseless love, senseless death. Whoever echoes these reflections: be more courageous than their author! An end to night-sea journeys! Make no more! And forswear me when I shall forswear myself, deny myself, plunge into Her who summons, singing. . . .

" 'Love! Love! Love!' "

■ DISCUSSION AND QUESTIONS:

1. An *allegory* is a story that uses symbols in a fairly clear and systematic way. The subjects of the story can almost be "translated" into other entities, often religious or philosophical, and they will keep those meanings throughout the story. The subjects of the story are concrete equivalents for abstractions. John Barth's story, "Night-Sea Journey" comes very close to being allegory.

In the introduction to this section on "symbol" we have already discussed the *natural symbol*, the journey. Note that we now have such a journey. Why is the journey in a "night-sea"? Specifically, why "night" rather than "day"? And why "sea" rather than "pond"? Why not "swimming pool"? What characteristics does a "sea" have that a "swimming pool" does not have?

2. You should observe that the story begins with quotation marks and ends with quotation marks. Each paragraph, as well, opens with quotation marks, though there are none at the

end of the paragraphs. What does that mean?

3. On page 121 we find the following:
"*'You only swim once.' Why bother, then?*" What do the double quotation marks mean? Does the expression "You only swim once" remind you of any other commonly heard expressions? What? So, if we "translate" the allegorical-symbolic language, what does "You only swim once" mean?

4. John Barth speaks of "the father." He is, of course, not speaking of our biological father, but using the term as it is used in very many religions. The term, Father, is a *metaphor*. We understand that whomever Barth is speaking of partakes of many of the characteristics of a father, even though he is not a biological father. He is a father, however, whose name we capitalize—Father—and to whom we refer, even in the pronominal form, with an initial capital—Himself. One of the primary ways in which He is understood to be like a father is that He "made" us. The teller of the story says that his friend had a theory that perhaps the Father made us without even being aware He made us ("as we make waves with every tail-thrash"), and is not even now aware of our existence. What are some other theories that are put forth in the story about the relationship of the Father to the creatures He has made?

Does the teller of the story firmly believe there is a Father?

5. Why do you think, John Barth has the narrator of "Night-Sea Journey" attribute theories of the origin and the meaning of the night-sea journey to a fictitious "friend" whom we don't even meet in the story, rather than giving those theories to the narrator who tells the story? (And what happened to the "friend"?)

6. Up to a certain point, Barth's allegory is very transparent. That is to say, it is easy to translate. You should have had no trouble interpreting Who the Father is, who the swimming creatures exemplified by the narrator are, what the journey is, and what the night-sea is. Those symbols are so close to being natural symbols that we have little difficulty in interpreting them. However, on p.123 a new symbol, a new idea, is brought into the story—a She, a certain mysterious female, or female concept. There is no absolutely precise translation of what She is. However, from the context in the story, you can form many conclusions about some of the attributes of *She*. What are some of the characteristics of *She*? Do you think *She* has the power to save the narrator? (To answer that you must read the last three paragraphs several times with the very greatest care.)

7. Assume the proposition that the universe is senseless, pointless, and without reason. Assume that there is no point nor purpose to the life of man on earth, and that there is no rational explanation why one man succeeds, why another dies, why one man prospers and another suffers. Assume that even those who say "all is irrational" are wrong, because to say "all is irrational" is to make a rational statement—and there is not even that much reason in the universe. You might attempt to picture that philosophical notion by making a story of swimmers in a sea at night, aimlessly striving to go somewhere, anywhere, and randomly drowning in the dark waters. Can you think of *other* terms, other images in which you can make the same philosophical point? Do not use "swimmers" and do not use a dark sea.

Jackals and Arabs

Franz Kafka

> The story that follows is, ostensibly, about jackals who hate Arabs, and who approach a "European" narrator with a pair of rusty sewing scissors, begging him to slit the Arabs' throats. But since we know that jackals can't talk, and could hardly seek to exterminate a population with a pair of sewing scissors, it is reasonable for us to think further about the meaning of the story. What, precisely, Kafka had in mind has been much debated and is extremely difficult to specify. However, there do exist techniques in reading a story which will help us come closer to the meaning of the story. One of these techniques is to distinguish what characteristics the author has given his main characters. What words are used to describe them? What are the main characters compared to? Read the story once to get the general drift of it. Then read it a second time, listing on a piece of paper some of the words that are used to describe either the beings or actions of (a) Arabs, (b) jackals, (c) the desert.

We were camping in the oasis. My companions were asleep. The tall, white figure of an Arab passed by; he had been seeing to the camels and was on his way to his own sleeping place.

I threw myself on my back in the grass; I tried to fall asleep; I could not; a jackal howled in the distance; I sat up again. And what had been so far away was all at once quite near. Jackals were swarming round me,

Reprinted by permission of Schocken Books, Inc. from *The Penal Colony* by Franz Kafka. Copyright © 1948 by Schocken Books, Inc.

eyes gleaming dull gold and vanishing again, lithe bodies moving nimbly and rhythmically, as if at the crack of a whip.

One jackal came from behind me, nudging right under my arm, pressing against me, as if he needed my warmth, and then stood before me and spoke to me almost eye to eye.

"I am the oldest jackal far and wide. I am delighted to have met you here at last. I had almost given up hope, since we have been waiting endless years for you; my mother waited for you, and her mother, and all our fore-mothers right back to the first mother of all the jackals. It is true, believe me!"

"That is surprising," said I, forgetting to kindle the pile of firewood which lay ready to smoke away jackals, "that is very surprising for me to hear. It is by pure chance that I have come here from the far North, and I am making only a short tour of your country. What do you jackals want, then?"

As if emboldened by this perhaps too friendly inquiry the ring of jackals closed in on me; all were panting and openmouthed.

"We know," began the eldest, "that you have come from the North; that is just what we base our hopes on. You Northerners have the kind of intelligence that is not to be found among Arabs. Not a spark of intelligence, let me tell you, can be struck from their cold arrogance. They kill animals for food, and carrion they despise."

"Not so loud," said I, "there are Arabs sleeping near by."

"You are indeed a stranger here," said the jackal, "or you would know that never in the history of the world has any jackal been afraid of an Arab. Why should we fear them? Is it not misfortune enough for us to be exiled among such creatures?"

"Maybe, maybe," said I, "matters so far outside my province I am not competent to judge; it seems to me a very old quarrel; I suppose it's in the blood, and perhaps will only end with it."

"You are very clever," said the old jackal; and they all began to pant more quickly; the air pumped out of their lungs although they were standing still; a rank smell which at times I had to set my teeth to endure streamed from their open jaws, "you are very clever; what you have just said agrees with our old tradition. So we shall draw blood from them and the quarrel will be over."

"Oh!" said I, more vehemently than I intended, "they'll defend themselves; they'll shoot you down in dozens with their muskets."

"You misunderstand us," said he, "a human failing which persists apparently even in the far North. We're not proposing to kill them. All the water in the Nile couldn't cleanse us of that. Why, the mere sight of their living flesh makes us turn tail and flee into cleaner air, into the desert, which for that very reason is our home."

Jackals and Arabs

And all the jackals around, including many newcomers from farther away, dropped their muzzles between their forelegs and wiped them with their paws; it was as if they were trying to conceal a disgust so overpowering that I felt like leaping over their heads to get away.

"Then what are you proposing to do?" I asked, trying to rise to my feet; but I could not get up; two young beasts behind me had locked their teeth through my coat and shirt; I had to go on sitting. "These are your trainbearers," explained the old jackal, quite seriously, "a mark of honor." "They must let go!" I cried, turning now to the old jackal, now to the youngsters. "They will, of course," said the old one, "if that is your wish. But it will take a little time, for they have got their teeth well in, as is our custom, and must first loosen their jaws bit by bit. Meanwhile, give ear to our petition." "Your conduct hasn't exactly inclined me to grant it," said I. "Don't hold it against us that we are clumsy," said he, and now for the first time had recourse to the natural plaintiveness of his voice, "we are poor creatures, we have nothing but our teeth; whatever we want to do, good or bad, we can tackle it only with our teeth." "Well, what do you want?" I asked, not much mollified.

"Sir," he cried, and all the jackals howled together; very remotely it seemed to resemble a melody. "Sir, we want you to end this quarrel that divides the world. You are exactly the man whom our ancestors foretold as born to do it. We want to be troubled no more by Arabs; room to breathe; a skyline cleansed of them; no more bleating of sheep knifed by an Arab; every beast to die a natural death; no interference till we have drained the carcass empty and picked its bones clean. Cleanliness, nothing but cleanliness is what we want"—and now they were all lamenting and sobbing—"how can you bear to live in such a world, O noble heart and kindly bowels? Filth is their white; filth is their black; their beards are a horror; the very sight of their eye sockets makes one want to spit; and when they lift an arm, the murk of hell yawns in the armpit. And so, sir, and so, dear sir, by means of your all-powerful hands slit their throats through with these scissors!" And in answer to a jerk of his head a jackal came trotting up with a small pair of sewing scissors, covered with ancient rust, dangling from an eyetooth.

"Well, here's the scissors at last, and high time to stop!" cried the Arab leader of our caravan who had crept upwind towards us and now cracked his great whip.

The jackals fled in haste, but at some little distance rallied in a close huddle, all the brutes so tightly packed and rigid that they looked as if penned in a small fold girt by flickering will-o'-the-wisps.

"So you've been treated to this entertainment too, sir," said the Arab, laughing as gaily as the reserve of his race permitted. "You know, then, what the brutes are after?" I asked. "Of course," said he, "it's common knowledge; so long as Arabs exist, that pair of scissors goes wandering through the desert and will wander with us to the end of our days. Every European is offered it for the great work; every European is just the man that Fate has chosen for them. They have the most lunatic hopes, these beasts; they're just fools, utter fools. That's why we like them; they are our dogs; finer dogs than any of yours. Watch this, now, a camel died last night and I have had it brought here.

Four men came up with the heavy carcass and threw it down before us. It had hardly touched the ground before the jackals lifted up their voices. As if irresistibly drawn by cords each of them began to waver forward, crawling on his belly. They had forgotten the Arabs, forgotten their hatred, the all-obliterating immediate presence of the stinking carrion bewitched them. One was already at the camel's throat, sinking his teeth straight into an artery. Like a vehement small pump endeavoring with as much determination as hopefulness to extinguish some raging fire, every muscle in his body twitched and labored at the task. In a trice they were all on top of the carcass, laboring in common, piled mountain-high.

And now the caravan leader lashed his cutting whip crisscross over their backs. They lifted their heads; half swooning in ecstasy; saw the Arabs standing before them; felt the sting of the whip on their muzzles; leaped and ran backwards a stretch. But the camel's blood was already lying in pools, reeking to heaven, the carcass was torn wide open in many places. They could not resist it; they were back again; once more the leader lifted his whip; I stayed his arm.

"You are right, sir," said he, "we'll leave them to their business; besides, it's time to break camp. Well, you've seen them. Marvelous creatures, aren't they? And how they hate us!"

■ DISCUSSION AND QUESTIONS:

1. Four paragraphs from the end, the Arab tells the European that the jackals "are our dogs." Now there are dogs in the world, and there are dogs. What are some characteristics of "dogs"? There are "old, faithful, loyal, loving, brave, trusty, watchful dogs," and there are dogs that "cringe, slink, crawl with tail between legs, that empty garbage pails, and howl in wretchedness." When the Arab says of the jackals "they are our dogs," which kind of dog is he talking about? When the hero in a melodrama says to the villain, "you cursed dog," what dog characteristics does he imply that the villain has?

2. Consult your list of jackal, Arab, and desert characteristics? Did you notice the following:

The narrator cannot sleep. A jackal *howls* in the distance. Then the jackals *swarm* around him. He begins talking with the jackals and forgets to kindle the fire which lies ready *to smoke away* the jackals. What kind of creatures does one *smoke out?* When the jackals pant, a *rank smell* emanates from their *open jaws.* In fact, very many things the narrator says about the jackals have to do with jaws and teeth. Notice all the passages in which the jackals' teeth, or their bite is commented on. At one point the narrator cannot get up because two of the beasts "had locked their teeth" through his coat and shirt. When a camel dies, the jackals drain the carcass of blood, and they pick the bones clean. These jackals, compared by the Arab to dogs, crawl on their bellies, and they hate—though they forget their hatred and almost swoon in ecstasy when they have a stinking camel carrion to chew on, sinking their teeth in the artery. Only the greed for putrid meat seems to calm the "raging fire" within them—fire of what, of hatred, of gluttony? Only leeches or perhaps the worst nightmare we can have of ravening dogs (and it is a slander on dogs to think of them that way) can match the picture the author has painted of the twitching, jerking mass of blood-hungry beasts piled high on top of each other in mindless savagery of hunger. So, then, what kind of creatures have we in these jackals?

3. How do these jackals address the "Europeans?" "You Northerners have the kind of intelligence that is not to be found among Arabs." "You are very clever...." What does the verb, "to fawn" mean?

4. Just as you have begun to establish a composite picture of the jackals (a) by looking at the words used to describe them or their actions, and (b) considering what they are compared to, and (c) looking at the words they, themselves, use and the manner in which they speak, so you can also attempt to form a composite picture of the other main characters—the Arabs, the narrator, even the desert itself, at least the way it is spoken of by the jackals. How is the desert spoken of by the jackals?

5. The mere sight of Arabs, says the jackal, makes the jackals flee into the "cleaner air, into the desert." The jackals want to be troubled no more by Arabs; they want "room to breathe; a skyline cleansed" of Arabs. The jackals do not want beasts slaughtered by Arabs. They want all animals to die "a natural death." They want to drain "the carcass empty," and "pick the bones clean."

Shall we change our picture of the jackals now? Are they not so bad after all? At first they are likened to mindless, ravening, fawning, cringing, bloodthirsty dogs. But what they *really* want, it seems, is a world cleansed of humans, or at least of Arabs, in whose armpits, as the jackals tell it, all Hell yawns wide and dark. Get rid of the filth of humanity, these creatures of the desert say, and the world will be cleansed, animals will die naturally, and nature shall take its course. It is human beings, then, that are the corrupters of the onetime uncorrupted world.

But is that really true? Remember who is saying it. These cringing, fawning, flattering (lying) beasts say it. And then comes the showdown, the Arab laughs gaily and lashes "his cutting whip crisscross over their backs." An "entertainment," the Arab calls the spectacle we have witnessed between the European and the jackals. He has seen it often before. It's an age-old diversion; it's time to break camp now and "leave them to their business," he says grandly. He delights in the fact that the jackals hate the Arabs; however, we are quite sure he does not often deign to honor them by remembering the hatred. It was merely a diversion for him. For the jackals, of course, it is a way of life.

What are we to make of this strange story? What of the Northerner who comes to the jackals like a Messiah ("we have been waiting endless years for you; my mother waited for you, and her mother, and all our fore-mothers right back to the first mother of all the jackals.")? The Arab implies the jackals tell that story to everyone that comes along. And those strangely sacramental "sewing scissors, covered with ancient rust," scissors that go "wandering through the desert" for all time —what of them?

Here now we learn an important lesson in the reading of a symbolic story. We must understand clearly that, though in an allegory it is possible to translate symbols into reality, one for one, in many of the very best symbolic stories that is absolutely impossible. There is no *one-for-one translation possible.* That the Arab lashes the jackals crisscross across their backs with the whip *may* have reference to the Christian symbol of the cross. If we know that the author of the story invested many of his stories with religious symbols (see Kafka's story "In the Penal Colony"), and if we realize that our story is set in a biblical land, we may be inclined to interpret the crisscross whiplash as a religious symbol. But then again, we might not. The only rule that can be given to a reader is:

> *Find out all you can about the author and the story, and then use your good sense. Informed good sense is, finally, the best guide in interpreting a story.*

We can ask what the "Jackals mean," what the "Arabs mean," and what the "scissors mean." We can attempt to translate these symbolic manifestations. We may say that, in this story, a "savior" has come to a servile race which is under the control of a masterful, superior, yet cruel, race; that the "savior" is offered a perhaps preposterous sacramental instrument by which to effect the salvation of the servile race; and that the masters, at the end, show their contempt in addition to their superiority and cruelty. But it does not follow that, once we have decided on a meaning for the characters and items in a story, we have unlocked *the* one single meaning for the story. The story may mean—and if it is a good one, does mean—far more than the sum of its parts. If a one-to-one translation were possible, the author could have said what he meant the first time, and we would not need the story. But a good story has echoes and ramifications; its meanings reverberate. Only those stories that lend themselves to continually challenging interpretations are worth rereading. Those are the great stories.

My Kinsman, Major Molineux

Nathaniel Hawthorne

> A journey, we have pointed out before, is one of the most basic of natural symbols. What are the characteristics of the young man taking the journey in the story that follows? What does he know at the end of his journey that he did not know at the beginning?

After the kings of Great Britain had assumed the right of appointing the colonial governors, the measures of the latter seldom met with the ready and general approbation which had been paid to those of their predecessors, under the original charters. The people looked with most jealous scrutiny to the exercise of power which did not emanate from themselves, and they usually rewarded their rulers with slender gratitude for the compliances by which, in softening their instructions from beyond the sea, they had incurred the reprehension of those who gave them. The annals of Massachusetts Bay will inform us, that of six governors in the space of about forty years from the surrender of the old charter, under James II, two were imprisoned by a popular insurrection; a third, as Hutchinson inclines to believe, was driven from the province by the whizzing of a musket-ball; a fourth, in the opinion of the same historian, was hastened to his grave by continual bickerings with the House of Representatives; and the remaining two, as well as their successors, till the Revolution, were favored with few and brief intervals of peaceful sway. The inferior members of the court party, in times of high political excitement, led scarcely a more desirable life. These remarks may serve as a preface to the following adventures, which chanced upon a summer night, not far from a hundred years ago. The reader, in order to avoid a long and dry detail of colonial affairs, is requested to dispense with an account of the train of circumstances that had caused much temporary inflammation of the popular mind.

From *The Snow Image,* published in 1852.

It was near nine o'clock of a moonlight evening, when a boat crossed the ferry with a single passenger, who had obtained his conveyance at that unusual hour by the promise of an extra fare. While he stood on the landing-place, searching in either pocket for the means of fulfilling his agreement, the ferryman lifted a lantern, by the aid of which, and the newly risen moon, he took a very accurate survey of the stranger's figure. He was a youth of barely eighteen years, evidently country-bred, and now, as it should seem, upon his first visit to town. He was clad in a coarse gray coat, well worn, but in excellent repair; his under garments were durably constructed of leather, and fitted tight to a pair of serviceable and well-shaped limbs; his stockings of blue yarn were the incontrovertible work of a mother or a sister; and on his head was a three-cornered hat, which in its better days had perhaps sheltered the graver brow of the lad's father. Under his left arm was a heavy cudgel formed of an oak sapling, and retaining a part of the hardened root; and his equipment was completed by a wallet, not so abundantly stocked as to incommode the vigorous shoulders on which it hung. Brown, curly hair, well-shaped features, and bright, cheerful eyes were nature's gifts, and worth all that art could have done for his adornment.

The youth, one of whose names was Robin, finally drew from his pocket the half of a little province bill of five shillings, which, in the depreciation in that sort of currency, did but satisfy the ferryman's demand, with the surplus of a sexangular piece of parchment, valued at three pence. He then walked forward into the town, with as light a step as if his day's journey had not already exceeded thirty miles, and with as eager an eye as if he were entering London city, instead of the little metropolis of a New England colony. Before Robin had proceeded far, however, it occurred to him that he knew not whither to direct his steps; so he paused, and looked up and down the narrow street, scrutinizing the small and mean wooden buildings that were scattered on either side.

"This low hovel cannot be my kinsman's dwelling," thought he, "nor yonder old house, where the moonlight enters at the broken casement; and truly I see none hereabouts that might be worthy of him. It would have been wise to inquire my way of the ferryman, and doubtless he would have gone with me, and earned a shilling from the Major for his pains. But the next man I meet will do as well."

He resumed his walk, and was glad to perceive that the street now became wider, and the houses more respectable in their appearance. He soon discerned a figure moving on moderately in advance, and hastened his steps to overtake it. As Robin drew nigh, he saw that the passenger was a man in years, with a full periwig of gray hair, a wide-skirted coat of dark cloth, and silk stockings rolled above his knees. He carried a long and polished cane, which he struck down perpendicularly before him at every step; and at regular intervals he uttered two successive hems, of a peculiarly solemn and sepulchral intonation. Having made these observations, Robin laid hold of the skirt of the old man's coat, just when the light from the open door and windows of a barber's shop fell upon both their figures.

"Good evening to you, honored sir," said he, making a low bow, and still retaining his hold of the skirt. "I pray you tell me whereabouts is the dwelling of my kinsman, Major Molineux."

The youth's question was uttered very loudly; and one of the barbers, whose razor was descending on a well-soaped chin, and another who was dressing a Ramillies wig, left their occupations, and came to the door. The citizen, in the mean time, turned a long-favored countenance upon Robin, and answered him in a tone of excessive anger and annoyance. His two sepulchral hems, however, broke into the very centre of his rebuke, with most singular effect, like a thought of the cold grave obtruding among wrathful passions.

"Let go my garment, fellow! I tell you, I know not the man you speak of. What! I have authority, I have—hem, hem—authority; and if this be the respect you show for your betters, your feet shall be brought acquainted with the stocks by daylight, tomorrow morning!"

Robin released the old man's skirt, and hastened away, pursued by an ill-mannered roar of laughter from the barber's shop. He was at first considerably surprised by the result of his question, but, being a shrewd youth, soon thought himself able to account for the mystery.

"This is some country representative," was his conclusion, "who has never seen the inside of my kinsman's door, and lacks the breeding to answer a stranger civilly. The man is old, or verily—I might be tempted to turn back and smite him on the nose. Ah, Robin, Robin! even the barber's boys laugh at you for choosing such a guide! You will be wiser in time, friend Robin."

He now became entangled in a succession of crooked and narrow streets, which crossed each other, and meandered at no great distance from the water-side. The smell of tar was obvious to his nostrils, the masts of vessels pierced the moonlight above the tops of the buildings, and the numerous signs, which Robin paused to read, informed him that he was near the centre of business. But the streets were empty, the shops were closed, and lights were visible only in the second stories of a few dwelling-houses. At length, on the corner of a narrow lane, through which he was passing, he beheld the broad countenance of a British hero swinging before the door of an inn, whence proceeded the voices of many guests. The casement of one of the lower windows was thrown back, and a very thin curtain permitted Robin to distinguish a party at supper, round a well-furnished table. The fragrance of the good cheer steamed forth into the outer air, and the youth could not fail to recollect that the last remnant of his travelling stock of provision had yielded to his morning appetite, and that noon had found and left him dinnerless.

"Oh, that a parchment three-penny might give me a right to sit down at yonder table!" said Robin, with a sigh. "But the Major will make me welcome to the best of his victuals; so I will even step boldly in, and inquire my way to his dwelling."

He entered the tavern, and was guided by the murmur of voices and the fumes of tobacco to the public-room. It was a long and low apartment, with oaken walls, grown dark in the continual smoke, and a floor which was thickly sanded, but of no immaculate purity. A number of persons—the larger part of whom appeared to be mariners, or in some way connected with the sea—occupied the wooden benches, or leather-bottomed chairs, conversing on various matters, and occasionally lending their attention to some topic of general interest. Three or four little groups were draining as many bowls of punch, which the West India trade had long since made a familiar drink in the colony. Others, who had the appearance of men who lived by regular and laborious handicraft, preferred the insulated bliss of an unshared potation, and became more taciturn under its influence. Nearly all, in short, evinced a predilection for the Good Creature in some of its various shapes, for this is a vice to which, as Fast Day sermons of a hundred years ago will testify, we have a long hereditary claim. The only guests to whom Robin's sympathies inclined him were two or three sheepish countrymen, who were using the inn somewhat after the fashion of a Turkish caravansary; they had gotten themselves into the darkest corner of the room, and heedless of the Nicotian atmosphere, were supping on the bread of their own ovens, and the bacon cured in their own chimney-smoke. But though Robin felt a sort of brotherhood with these strangers, his eyes were attracted from them to a person who stood near the door, holding whispered conversation with a group of ill-dressed associates. His features were separately striking almost to grotesqueness, and the whole face left a deep impression on the memory. The forehead bulged out into a double prominence, with a vale between; the nose came boldly forth in an irregular curve, and its bridge was of more than a finger's breadth; the eyebrows were deep and shaggy, and the eyes glowed beneath them like fire in a cave.

While Robin deliberated of whom to inquire respecting his kinsman's dwelling, he was accosted by the innkeeper, a little man in a stained white apron, who had come to pay his professional welcome to the stranger. Being in the second generation from a French Protestant, he seemed to have inherited the courtesy of his parent nation; but no variety of circumstances was ever known to change his voice from the one shrill note in which he now addressed Robin.

"From the country, I presume, sir?" said he, with a profound bow. "Beg leave to congratulate you on your arrival, and trust you intend a long stay with us. Fine town here, sir, beautiful buildings, and much that may interest a stranger. May I hope for the honor of your commands in respect to supper?"

"The man sees a family likeness! the rogue has guessed that I am related to the Major!" thought Robin, who had hitherto experienced little superfluous civility.

All eyes were now turned on the country lad, standing at the door, in his worn three-cornered hat, gray coat, leather breeches, and blue yarn stockings, leaning on an oaken cudgel, and bearing a wallet on his back.

Robin replied to the courteous innkeeper, with such an assumption of confidence as befitted the Major's relative. "My honest friend," he said, "I shall make it a point to patronize your house on some occasion, when" —here he could not help lowering his voice—"when I may have more than a parchment three-pence in my pocket. My present business," continued he, speaking with lofty confidence, "is merely to inquire my way to the dwelling of my kinsman, Major Molineux."

There was a sudden and general movement in the room, which Robin interpreted as expressing the eagerness of each individual to become his guide. But the innkeeper turned his eyes to a written paper on the wall, which he read, or seemed to read, with occasional recurrences to the young man's figure.

"What have we here?" said he, breaking his speech into little dry fragments. " 'Left the house of the subscriber, bounden servant, Hezekiah Mudge,—had on, when he went away, gray coat, leather breeches, master's third-best hat. One pound currency reward to whosoever shall lodge him in any jail of the province.' Better trudge, boy; better trudge!"

Robin had begun to draw his hand towards the lighter end of the oak cudgel, but a strange hostility in every countenance induced him to relinquish his purpose of breaking the courteous innkeeper's head. As he turned to leave the room, he encountered a sneering glance from the bold-featured personage whom he had before noticed; and no sooner was he beyond the door, than he heard a general laugh, in which the innkeeper's voice might be distinguished, like the dropping of small stones into a kettle.

"Now, is it not strange," thought Robin, with his usual shrewdness,— "is it not strange that the confession of an empty pocket should outweigh the name of my kinsman, Major Molineux? Oh, if I had one of those grinning rascals in the woods, where I and my oak sapling grew up together, I would teach him that my arm is heavy though my purse be light!"

On turning the corner of the narrow lane, Robin found himself in a spacious street, with an unbroken line of lofty houses on each side, and a steepled building at the upper end, whence the ringing of a bell announced the hour of nine. The light of the moon, and the lamps from the numerous shop-windows, discovered people promenading on the pavement, and amongst them Robin hoped to recognize his hitherto inscrutable relative. The result of his former inquiries made him unwilling to hazard another, in a scene of such publicity, and he determined to walk slowly and silently up the street, thrusting his face close to that of every elderly gentleman, in search of the Major's lineaments. In his progress, Robin encountered many gay and gallant figures. Embroidered garments of showy colors, enormous periwigs, gold-laced hats, and silver-hilted swords glided past him and dazzled his optics. Travelled youths, imitators of the European fine gentlemen of the period, trod jauntily along, half dancing to the fashionable tunes which they hummed, and making poor Robin ashamed of his quiet and natural gait. At length, after many pauses to examine the gorgeous display of goods in the shop-windows, and after suffering some rebukes for the impertinence of his scrutiny into people's faces, the Major's kinsman found himself near the steepled building, still unsuccessful in his search. As yet, however, he had seen only one side of the thronged street; so Robin crossed, and continued the same sort of inquisition down the opposite pavement, with stronger hopes than the philosopher seeking an honest man, but with no better fortune. He had arrived about midway towards the lower end, from which his course began, when he overheard the approach of some one who struck down a cane on the flag-stones at every step, uttering, at regular intervals, two sepulchral hems.

"Mercy on us!" quoth Robin, recognizing the sound.

Turning a corner, which chanced to be close at his right hand, he hastened to pursue his researches in some other part of the town. His patience now was wearing low, and he seemed to feel more fatigue from his rambles since he crossed the ferry, than from his journey of several days on the other side. Hunger also pleaded loudly within him, and Robin began to balance the propriety of demanding, violently, and with lifted cudgel, the necessary guidance from the first solitary passenger whom he should meet. While a resolution to this effect was gaining strength, he entered a street of mean appearance, on either side of which a row of ill-built houses was straggling towards the harbor. The moonlight fell upon no passenger along the whole extent, but in the third domicile which Robin passed there was a half-opened door, and his keen glance detected a woman's garment within.

"My luck may be better here," said he to himself.

Accordingly, he approached the door, and beheld it shut closer as he did so; yet an open space remained, sufficing for the fair occupant to observe the stranger, without a corresponding display on her part. All that Robin could discern was a strip of scarlet petticoat, and the occasional sparkle of an eye, as if the moonbeams were trembling on some bright thing.

"Pretty mistress," for I may call her so with a good conscience, thought the shrewd youth, since I know nothing to the contrary,—"my sweet pretty mistress, will you be kind enough to tell me whereabouts I must seek the dwelling of my kinsman, Major Molineux?"

Robin's voice was plaintive and winning, and the female, seeing nothing to be shunned in the handsome country youth, thrust open the door, and came forth into the moonlight. She was a dainty little figure, with a white neck, round arms, and a slender waist, at the extremity of which her scarlet petticoat jutted out over a hoop, as if she were standing in a balloon. Moreover, her face was oval and pretty, her hair dark beneath the little cap, and her bright eyes possessed a sly freedom, which triumphed over those of Robin.

"Major Molineux dwells here," said this fair woman.

Now, her voice was the sweetest Robin had heard that night, the airy counterpart of a stream of melted silver; yet he could not help doubting whether that sweet voice spoke Gospel truth. He looked up and down the mean street, and then surveyed the house before which they stood. It was a small, dark edifice of two stories, the second of which projected over the lower floor, and the front apartment had the aspect of a shop for petty commodities.

"Now, truly, I am in luck," replied Robin, cunningly, "and so indeed is my kinsman, the Major, in having so pretty a housekeeper. But I prithee trouble him to step to the door; I will deliver him a message from his friends in the country, and then go back to my lodgings at the inn."

"Nay, the Major has been abed this hour or more," said the lady of the scarlet petticoat; "and it would be to little purpose to disturb him tonight, seeing his evening draught was of the strongest. But he is a kind-hearted man, and it would be as much as my life's worth to let a kinsman of his turn away from the door. You are the good old gentleman's very picture, and I could swear that was his rainy-weather hat. Also he has garments very much resembling those leather small-clothes. But come in, I pray, for I bid you hearty welcome in his name."

So saying, the fair and hospitable dame took our hero by the hand; and the touch was light, and the force was gentleness, and though Robin read in her eyes what he did not hear in her words, yet the slender-waisted woman in the scarlet petticoat proved stronger than the athletic country youth. She had drawn his half-willing footsteps nearly to the threshold, when the opening of a door in the neighborhood startled the Major's housekeeper, and, leaving the Major's kinsman, she vanished speedily into her own domicile. A heavy yawn preceded the appearance of a man, who, like the Moonshine of Pyramus and Thisbe, carried a lantern, needlessly aiding his sister luminary in the heavens. As he walked sleepily up the street, he turned his broad, dull face on Robin, and displayed a long staff, spiked at the end.

"Home, vagabond, home!" said the watchman, in accents that seemed to fall asleep as soon as they were uttered. "Home, or we'll set you in the stocks by peep of day."

"This is the second hint of the kind," thought Robin. "I wish they would end my difficulties, by setting me there to-night."

Nevertheless, the youth felt an instinctive antipathy towards the guardian of midnight order, which at first prevented him from asking his usual question. But just when the man was about to vanish behind the corner, Robin resolved not to lose the opportunity, and shouted lustily after him,—

"I say, friend! will you guide me to the house of my kinsman, Major Molineux?"

The watchman made no reply, but turned the corner and was gone; yet Robin seemed to hear the sound of drowsy laughter stealing along the solitary street. At that moment, also, a pleasant titter saluted him from the open window above his head; he looked up, and caught the sparkle of a saucy eye; a round arm beckoned to him, and next he heard light footsteps descending the staircase within. But Robin, being of the household of a New England clergyman, was a good youth, as well as a shrewd one; so he resisted temptation, and fled away.

He now roamed desperately, and at random, through the town, almost ready to believe that a spell was on him, like that by which a wizard of his country had once kept three pursuers wandering, a whole winter night, within twenty paces of the cottage which they sought. The streets lay before him, strange and desolate, and the lights were extinguished in almost every house. Twice, however, little parties of men, among whom Robin distinguished individuals in outlandish attire, came hurrying along; but, though on both occasions they paused to address him, such intercourse did not at all enlighten his perplexity. They did but utter a few words in some language of which Robin knew nothing, and perceiving his inability to answer, bestowed a curse upon him in plain English and hastened away. Finally, the lad determined to knock at the door of every mansion that might appear worthy to be occupied by his kinsman, trusting that perserverance would overcome the fatality that had hitherto thwarted him. Firm in this resolve, he was passing beneath the walls of a church, which formed the corner of two streets, when, as he turned into the shade of its steeple, he encountered a bulky stranger, muffled in a cloak. The man was proceeding with the speed of earnest business, but Robin planted himself full before him, holding the oak cudgel with both hands across his body as a bar to further passage.

"Halt, honest man, and answer me a question," said he, very resolutely. "Tell me, this instant, whereabouts is the dwelling of my kinsman, Major Molineux!"

"Keep your tongue between your teeth, fool, and let me pass!" said a deep, gruff voice, which Robin partly remembered. "Let me pass, I say, or I'll strike you to the earth!"

"No, no, neighbor!" cried Robin, flourishing his cudgel, and then thrusting its larger end close to the man's muffled face. "No, no, I'm not the fool you take me for, nor do you pass till I have an answer to my question. Whereabouts is the dwelling of my kinsman, Major Molineux?"

The stranger, instead of attempting to force his passage, stepped back into the moonlight, unmuffled his face, and stared full into that of Robin.

"Watch here an hour, and Major Molineux will pass by," said he.

Robin gazed with dismay and astonishment on the unprecedented physiognomy of the speaker. The forehead with its double prominence, the broad hooked nose, the shaggy eyebrows, and fiery eyes were those which he had noticed at the inn, but the man's complexion had undergone a singular, or, more properly, a twofold change. One side of the face blazed an intense red, while the other was black as midnight, the division line X being in the broad bridge of the nose; and a mouth which seemed to extend from ear to ear was black or red, in contrast to the color of the cheek. The effect was as if two individual devils, a fiend of fire and a fiend of darkness, had united themselves to form this infernal visage. The stranger grinned in Robin's face, muffled his party-colored features, and was out of sight in a moment.

"Strange things we travellers see!" ejaculated Robin.

He seated himself, however, upon the steps of the church-door, resolving to wait the appointed time for his kinsman. A few moments were consumed in philosophical speculations upon the species of man who had just left him; but having settled this point shrewdly, rationally, and satisfactorily, he was compelled to look elsewhere for his amusement. And first he threw his eyes along the street. It was of more respectable appearance than most of those into which he had wandered; and the moon, creating, like the imaginative power, a beautiful strangeness in familiar objects, gave something of romance to a scene that might not have possessed it in the light of day. The irregular and often quaint architecture of the houses, some of whose roofs were broken into numerous little peaks, while others ascended, steep and narrow, into a single point, and others again were square; the pure snow-white of some of their complexions, the aged darkness of others, and the thousand sparklings, reflected from bright substances in the walls of many; these matters engaged Robin's attention for a while, and then began to grow wearisome. Next he endeavored to define the forms of distant objects, starting away, with almost ghostly indistinctness, just as his eye appeared to grasp them; and finally he took a minute survey of an edifice which stood on the opposite side of the street, directly in front of the church-door, where he was stationed. It was a large, square mansion, distinguished from its neighbors by a balcony, which rested on tall pillars, and by an elaborate Gothic window, communicating therewith.

"Perhaps this is the very house I have been seeking," thought Robin.

Then he strove to speed away the time, by listening to a murmur which swept continually along the street, yet was scarcely audible, except to an unaccustomed ear like his; it was a low, dull, dreamy sound, compounded of many noises, each of which was at too great a distance to be separately heard. Robin marvelled at this snore of a sleeping town, and marvelled more whenever its continuity was broken by now and then a distant shout, apparently loud where it originated. But altogether it was a sleep-inspiring sound, and, to shake off its drowsy influence, Robin arose, and climbed a windowframe, that he might view the interior of the church. There the moonbeams came trembling in, and fell down upon the deserted pews, and extended along the quiet aisles. A fainter yet more awful radiance was hovering around the pulpit, and one solitary ray had dared to rest upon the open page of the great Bible. Had nature, in that deep hour, become a worshipper in the house which man had built? Or was that heavenly light the visible sanctity of the place,—visible because no earthly and impure feet were within the walls? The scene made Robin's heart shiver with a sensation of loneliness stronger than he had ever felt in the remotest depths of his native woods; so he turned away and sat down again before the door. There were graves around the church, and now an uneasy thought obtruded into Robin's breast. What if the object of his search, which had been so often and so strangely thwarted, were all the time mouldering in his shroud? What if his kinsman should glide through yonder gate, and nod and smile to him in dimly passing by?

"Oh that any breathing thing were here with me!" said Robin.

Recalling his thoughts from this uncomfortable track, he sent them over forest, hill, and stream, and attempted to imagine how that evening of ambiguity and weariness had been spent by his father's household. He pictured them assembled at the door, beneath the tree, the great old tree, which had been spared for its huge twisted trunk and venerable shade, when a thousand leafy brethren fell. There, at the going down of the summer sun, it was his father's custom to perform domestic worship, that the neighbors might come and join with him like brothers of the family, and that the wayfaring man might pause to drink at that fountain, and keep his heart pure by freshening the memory of home. Robin distinguished the seat of every individual of the little audience; he saw the good man in the midst, holding the Scriptures in the golden light that fell from the western clouds; he beheld him close the book and all rise up to pray. He heard the old thanksgivings for daily mercies, the old supplications for their continuance, to which he had so often listened in weariness, but which were now among his dear remembrances. He perceived the slight inequality of his father's voice when he came to speak of the absent one; he noted how his mother turned her face to the broad and knotted trunk; how his elder brother scorned, because the beard was rough upon his upper lip, to permit his features to be moved; how the younger sister drew down a low hanging branch before her eyes; and how the little one of all, whose sports had hitherto broken the decorum of the scene, understood the prayer for her playmate, and burst into clamorous grief. Then he saw them go in at the door; and when Robin would have entered also, the latch tinkled into its place, and he was excluded from his home.

"Am I here, or there?" cried Robin, starting; for all at once, when his thoughts had become visible and audible in a dream, the long, wide, solitary street shone out before him.

He aroused himself, and endeavored to fix his attention steadily upon the large edifice which he had surveyed before. But still his mind kept vibrating between fancy and reality; by turns, the pillars of the balcony lengthened into the tall, bare stems of pines, dwindled down to human figures, settled again into their true shape and size, and then commenced a new succession of changes. For a single moment, when he deemed himself awake, he could have sworn that a visage—one which he seemed to remember, yet could not absolutely name as his kinsman's—was looking towards him from the Gothic window. A deeper sleep wrestled with and nearly overcame him, but fled at the sound of footsteps along the opposite pavement. Robin rubbed his eyes, discerned a man passing at the foot of the balcony, and addressed him in a loud, peevish, and lamentable cry.

"Hallo, friend! must I wait here all night for my kinsman, Major Molineux?"

The sleeping echoes awoke, and answered the voice; and the passenger, barely able to discern a figure sitting in the oblique shade of the steeple, traversed the street to obtain a nearer view. He was himself a gentleman in his prime, of open, intelligent, cheerful, and altogether prepossessing countenance. Perceiving a country youth, apparently homeless and without friends, he accosted him in a tone of real kindness, which had become strange to Robin's ears.

"Well, my good lad, who are you sitting here?" inquired he. "Can I be of service to you in any way?"

"I am afraid not, sir," replied Robin, despondingly; "yet I shall take it kindly, if you'll answer me a single question. I've been searching, half the night, for one Major Molineux; now, sir, is there really such a person in these parts, or am I dreaming?"

"Major Molineux! The name is not altogether strange to me," said the gentleman, smiling. "Have you any objection to telling me the nature of your business with him?"

Then Robin briefly related that his father was a clergyman, settled on a small salary, at a long distance back in the country, and that he and Major Molineux were brothers' children. The Major, having inherited riches, and acquired civil and military rank, had visited his cousin, in great pomp, a year or two before; had manifested much interest in Robin and an elder brother, and, being childless himself, had thrown out hints respecting the future establishment of one of them in life. The elder brother was destined to succeed to the farm which his father cultivated in the interval of sacred duties; it was therefore determined that Robin should profit by his kinsman's generous intentions, especially as he seemed to be rather the favorite, and was thought to possess other necessary endowments.

"For I have the name of being a shrewd youth," observed Robin, in this part of his story.

"I doubt not you deserve it," replied his new friend, good-naturedly; "but pray proceed."

"Well, sir, being nearly eighteen years old, and well grown, as you see," continued Robin, drawing himself up to his full height, "I thought it high time to begin the world. So my mother and sister put me in handsome trim, and my father gave me half the remnant of his last year's salary, and five days ago I started for this place, to pay the Major a visit. But, would you believe it, sir! I crossed the ferry a little after dark, and have yet found nobody that would show me the way to his dwelling; only, an hour or two since, I was told to wait here, and Major Molineux would pass by."

"Can you describe the man who told you this?" inquired the gentleman.

"Oh, he was a very ill-favored fellow, sir," replied Robin, "with two great bumps on his forehead, a hook nose, fiery eyes; and, what struck me as the strangest, his face was of two different colors. Do you happen to know such a man, sir?"

"Not intimately," answered the stranger, "but I chanced to meet him a little time previous to your stopping me. I believe you may trust his word, and that the Major will very shortly pass through this street. In the mean time, as I have a singular curiosity to witness your meeting, I will sit down here upon the steps and bear you company."

He seated himself accordingly, and soon engaged his companion in animated discourse. It was but of brief continuance, however, for a noise of shouting, which had long been remotely audible, drew so much nearer that Robin inquired its cause.

"What may be the meaning of this uproar?" asked he. "Truly, if your town be always as noisy, I shall find little sleep while I am an inhabitant."

"Why, indeed, friend Robin, there do appear to be three or four riotous fellows abroad to-night," replied the gentleman. "You must not expect all the stillness of your native woods here in our streets. But the watch will shortly be at the heels of these lads and"—

"Ay, and set them in the stocks by peep of day," interrupted Robin, recollecting his own encounter with the drowsy lantern-bearer. "But, dear sir, if I may trust my ears, an army of watchmen would never make head against such a multitude of rioters. There were at least a thousand voices went up to make that one shout."

"May not a man have several voices, Robin, as well as two complexions?" said his friend.

"Perhaps a man may; but Heaven forbid that a woman should!" responded the shrewd youth, thinking of the seductive tones of the Major's housekeeper.

The sounds of a trumpet in some neighboring street now became so evident and continual, that Robin's curiosity was strongly excited. In addition to the shouts, he heard frequent bursts from many instruments of discord, and a wild and confused laughter filled up the intervals. Robin rose from the steps, and looked wistfully towards a point whither people seemed to be hastening.

"Surely some prodigious merry-making is going on," exclaimed he. "I have laughed very little since I left home, sir, and should be sorry to lose an opportunity. Shall we step round the corner by that darkish house, and take our share of the fun?"

"Sit down again, sit down, good Robin," replied the gentleman, laying his hand on the skirt of the gray coat. "You forget that we must wait here for your kinsman; and there is reason to believe that he will pass by, in the course of a very few moments."

The near approach of the uproar had now disturbed the neighborhood; windows flew open on all sides; and many heads, in the attire of the pillow, and confused by sleep suddenly broken, were protruded to the gaze of whoever had leisure to observe them. Eager voices hailed each other from house to house, all demanding the explanation, which not a soul could give. Half-dressed men hurried towards the unknown commotion, stumbling as they went over the stone steps that thrust themselves into the narrow foot-walk. The shouts, the laughter, and the tuneless bray, the antipodes of music, came onwards with increasing din, till scattered individuals, and then denser bodies, began to appear round a corner at the distance of a hundred yards.

"Will you recognize your kinsman, if he passes in this crowd?" inquired the gentleman.

"Indeed, I can't warrant it, sir; but I'll take my stand here, and keep a bright lookout," answered Robin, descending to the outer edge of the pavement.

A mighty stream of people now emptied into the street, and came rolling slowly towards the church. A single horseman wheeled the corner in the midst of them, and close behind him came a band of fearful wind-instruments, sending forth a fresher discord now that no intervening buildings kept it from the ear. Then a redder light disturbed the moonbeams, and a dense multitude of torches shone along the street, concealing, by their glare, whatever object they illuminated. The single horseman, clad in a military dress, and bearing a drawn sword, rode onward as the leader, and, by his fierce and variegated countenance, appeared like war personified; the red of one cheek was an emblem of fire and sword; the blackness of the other betokened the mourning that attends them. In his train were wild figures in the Indian dress, and many fantastic shapes without a model, giving the whole march a visionary air, as if a dream had broken forth from some feverish brain, and were sweeping visibly through the midnight streets. A mass of people, inactive, except as applauding spectators, hemmed the procession in; and several women ran along the sidewalk, piercing the confusion of heavier sounds with their shrill voices of mirth or terror.

"The double-faced fellow has his eye upon me," muttered Robin, with an indefinite but an uncomfortable idea that he was himself to bear a part in the pageantry.

The leader turned himself in the saddle, and fixed his glance full upon the country youth, as the steed went slowly by. When Robin had freed his eyes from those fiery ones, the musicians were passing before him, and the torches were close at hand; but the unsteady brightness of the latter formed a veil which he could not penetrate. The rattling of wheels over the stones sometimes found its way to his ear, and confused traces of a human form appeared at intervals, and then melted into the vivid light. A moment more, and the leader thundered a command to halt: the trumpets vomited a horrid breath, and then held their peace; the shouts and laughter of the people died away, and there remained only a universal hum, allied to silence. Right before Robin's eyes was an uncovered cart. There the torches blazed the brightest, there the moon shone out like day, and there, in tar-and-feathery dignity, sat his kinsman, Major Molineux!

He was an elderly man, of large and majestic person, and strong, square features, betokening a steady soul; but steady as it was, his enemies had found means to shake it. His face was pale as death, and far more ghastly; the broad forehead was contracted in his agony, so that his eyebrows formed one grizzled line; his eyes were red and wild, and the foam hung white upon his quivering lip. His whole frame was agitated by a quick and continual tremor, which his pride strove to quell, even in those circumstances of overwhelming humiliation. But perhaps the bitterest pang of all was when his eyes met those of Robin; for he evidently knew him on the instant, as the youth stood witnessing the foul disgrace of a head grown gray in honor. They stared at each other in silence, and Robin's knees shook, and his hair bristled, with a mixture of pity and terror. Soon, however, a bewildering excitement began to seize upon his mind; the preceding adventures of the night, the unexpected appearance of the crowd, the torches, the confused din and the hush that followed, the spectre of his kinsman reviled by that great multitude,—all this, and, more than all, a perception of tremendous ridicule in the whole scene, affected him with a sort of mental inebriety. At that moment a voice of sluggish merriment saluted Robin's ears; he turned instinctively, and just behind the corner of the church stood the lantern-bearer, rubbing his eyes, and drowsily enjoying the lad's amazement. Then he heard a peal of laughter like the ringing of silvery bells; a woman twitched his arm, a saucy eye met his, and he saw the lady of the scarlet petticoat. A sharp, dry cachinnation appealed to his memory, and, standing on tiptoe in the crowd, with his white apron over his head, he beheld the courteous little innkeeper. And lastly, there sailed over the heads of the multitude a great, broad laugh, broken in the midst by two sepulchral hems; thus, "Haw, haw, haw,—hem, hem,—haw, haw, haw, haw!"

The sound proceeded from the balcony of the opposite edifice, and thither Robin turned his eyes. In front of the gothic window stood the old citizen, wrapped in a wide gown, his gray periwig exchanged for a nightcap, which was thrust back from his forehead, and his silk stockings hanging about his legs. He supported himself on his polished cane in a fit of convulsive merriment, which manfested itself on his solemn old features like a funny inscription on a tombstone. Then Robin seemed to hear the voices of the barbers, of the guests of the inn, and of all who had made sport of him that night. The contagion was spreading among the multitude, when all at once, it seized upon Robin, and he sent forth a shout of laughter that echoed through the street,—every man shook his sides, every man emptied his lungs, but Robin's shout was the loudest there. The cloud-spirits peeped from their silvery islands, as the congregated mirth went roaring up the sky! The Man in the Moon heard the far bellow. "Oho," quoth he, "the old earth is frolicsome to-night!"

When there was a momentary calm in the tempestuous sea of sound, the leader gave the sign, the procession resumed its march. On they went, like fiends that throng in mockery around some dead potentate, mighty no more, but majestic still in his agony. On they went, in counterfeited pomp, in senseless uproar, in frenzied merriment, trampling all on an old man's heart. On swept the tumult, and left a silent street behind.

"Well, Robin, are you dreaming?" inquired the gentleman, laying his hand on the youth's shoulder.

Robin started, and withdrew his arm from the stone post to which he had instinctively clung, as the living stream rolled by him. His cheek was somewhat pale, and his eye not quite as lively as in the earlier part of the evening.

"Will you be kind enough to show me the way to the ferry?" said he, after a moment's pause.

"You have, then, adopted a new subject of inquiry?" observed his companion, with a smile.

"Why, yes, sir," replied Robin, rather dryly. "Thanks to you, and to my other friends, I have at last met my kinsman, and he will scarce desire to see my face again. I begin to grow weary of a town life, sir. Will you show me the way to the ferry?"

"No, my good friend Robin,—not to-night, at least," said the gentleman. "Some few days hence, if you wish it, I will speed you on your journey. Or, if you prefer to remain with us, perhaps, as you are a shrewd youth, you may rise in the world without the help of your kinsman, Major Molineux."

■ DISCUSSION AND QUESTIONS

1. When finally we have encountered Major Molineux, in his dire circumstances, we are told that he was of "strong, square features, betokening a steady soul." That description is typical of the symbolic method at the simplest level. The outside is said to "betoken" (reflect, or signify) inner meaning. Thus, in the church Robin visits, a faint radiance hovered around the pulpit, "and one solitary ray had dared rest upon the open page of the great Bible." The sanctity of the Bible is illuminated, quite literally, by a divine shaft of light. So holiness is demarked. Similarly, Robin meets a horrible stranger with a "broad hooked nose ... shaggy eyebrows ... fiery eyes," whose forehead has a "double prominence," and whose face is divided down the middle, half "blazed an intense red ... the other ... black as midnight." In case you missed the point, the author tells you in the next sentence that "the effect was as if two individual devils, a fiend of fire and a

Symbol

fiend of darkness, had united themselves. ..."

Thus, on the most surface level, Hawthorne is patently a symbolic writer. Exteriors betoken meanings. However, the story must be read for meanings deeper than the obvious ones. It is not, in short, a simple tale of colonial New England. We have already pointed out that we deal with a journey, and we have asked what you know about the journeyer. Let us point out that the name "Robin" is a diminutive of the name Robert. We have, then, the suggestion of a very young fellow embarking on this journey. At the outset he must cross a river, the same river he wants to recross to escape at the end, but which he is told he cannot go across for some days. You might recall that in classical mythology access to the Underworld was likewise across a river, the river Acheron. Robin is a youth "of barely eighteen years," "country-bred," and carrying for protection "a heavy cudgel formed of an oak sapling." Youths from the country, young men in their prime, have been for all recorded time the protagonists of stories about journeys, quests, and searches. Think of all the tales of pure-hearted and brave knights setting out on their adventures and voyages through lands of temptations and pitfalls, armed only with their innocence, their pureness of heart, and their sturdy lances. What connection do you see between them and young Robin? How good a defense will his "heavy cudgel formed of an oak sapling" be against the types of dangers Robin encounters?

2. Just as life is often seen symbolically as a voyage or a journey, so the assimilated actions and eruptions of mankind are often spoken of (also symbolically) as a parade, a pageant, a "passing show." Consider the paragraph beginning "A mighty stream of people," in which Robin again sees the man with the fierce, two-colored countenance. This is a paragraph describing a parade, a pageant, a show that passes before young Robin. Wind instruments usually are described as whistling sweet tunes. What sort of wind instruments does Robin hear? What are the lights like in which he views the scene? What would they look like if you were making a painting? Make a list of words in this paragraph that describe appeals to the senses. What sounds does Robin hear? What colors does he see?

3. With the biblical story of Adam and Eve we are given a concept that has been called "the fortunate fall." The idea of "the fortunate fall" is meant to suggest that, though Adam and Eve were perfectly happy in Paradise, something was lacking there. There was no challenge, no real test of their *human* (as opposed to purely instinctive, animal) capabilities. But with their expulsion from Paradise, though Evil entered the experience of man, so too did the possibility for free—albeit often difficult—moral choice and the potential for *human* greatness. As long as everything is provided for man without his exerting himself, we cannot really say he has been tested, has been good, has done something great. But once man has entered the world of experience, once he has grown free, independent of amniotic security, then we may begin to speak of great and human achievements accomplished by a free and purposeful being.

Do you think that Robin's voyage can be considered as one from Innocence to Experience, from the infantile and womblike security of unknowing, to open encounter with the world of Good and Evil, with all the exhilaration and depression that such encounter entails?

If Robin's journey is one from Innocence to Experience, what, precisely, do you think Robin has learned?

Do you think that he will ever be able to get the ferry back? Why, or why not?

Chapter **5**

THEME AND TONE

Theme is the controlling idea that informs a literary work. It is not the moral. It is not precisely the "meaning," though it is very close to meaning. Flannery O'Connor, one of the great masters of the short story form, has written of theme and meaning:

> People talk about the theme of a story as if the theme were like a string that a sack of chicken feed is tied with. They think that if you can pick out the theme, the way you pick the right thread in the chicken-feed sack, you can rip the story open and feed the chickens. But this is not the way meaning works in fiction.... The meaning of a story has to be embodied in it, has to be made concrete in it. A story is a way to say something that can't be said in any other way, and it takes every word in the story to say what the meaning is.[1]

Theme is cousin to meaning, and it helps define the meaning (which, to repeat, is *not* the "moral").

Consider the story of Ruth in the Bible. The tale concerns a homeless refugee who meets and marries a well-to-do landowner. That is the simple narrative line, but it is not the theme. The theme is what this meeting and marriage between the two lonely people means, and what the marked courtesy, decency, and mannerliness between all the people in this little tale means. The theme is not "it's good to be nice to people." That would

---

1. Flannery O'Connor. "Writing Short Stories." In *Mystery and Manners*. New York: Farrar, Straus, and Giroux, 1969.

be a moral. Stories with explicit morals exist too—and they are usually called *fables*. For example, the story of the fox who attempted to reach the high-growing bunch of grapes, but could not, and who walked off in disgust, saying "they're probably sour anyway," is a fable, and its moral is that it is an unattractive characteristic to criticize something one cannot attain. The story of Ruth really has no such moral. It does not say "it's good to be kind and thoughtful." It simply—very simply—presents a picture, gentled and made soft, like a photograph taken through a mist, of people who are good and kind. You may draw your own conclusion.

Ruth

A Story of Olden Time

Now it came to pass in the days when the judges ruled, that there was a famine in the land. And a certain man of Bethlehemjudah went to sojourn in the country of Moab, he, and his wife, and his two sons. And the name of the man *was* Elimelech, and name of his wife Naomi, and the name of his two sons Mahlon and Chilion, Ephrathites of Bethlehemjudah. And they came into the country of Moab, and continued there. And Elimelech Naomi's husband died; and she was left, and her two sons. And they took them wives of the women of Moab; the name of the one *was* Orpah, and the name of the other Ruth: and they dwelt there about ten years. And Mahlon and Chilion died also both of them; and the woman was left of her two sons and her husband.

Then she arose with her daughters-in-law, that she might return from the country of Moab: for she had heard in the country of Moab how that the Lord had visited his people in giving them bread. Wherefore she went forth out of the place where she was, and her two daughters-in-law with her; and they went on the way to return unto the land of Judah. And Naomi said unto her two daughters-in-law, Go, return each to her mother's house: the Lord deal kindly with you, as ye have dealt with the dead, and with me. The Lord grant you that ye may find rest, each *of you* in the house of her husband. Then she kissed them; and they lifted up their voice, and wept. And they said unto her, Surely we will return with thee unto thy people. And Naomi said, Turn again, my daughters: why will ye go with me? *are* there yet *any more* sons in my womb, that they may be your husbands? Turn again, my daughters, go *your way;* for I am too old to have a husband. If I should say, I have hope, *if* I should have a husband also to-night, and should also bear sons; Would ye tarry for them till they were grown? would ye stay for them from having husbands? nay, my daughters; for it grieveth me much for your sakes that the hand of the Lord is gone out against me. And they lifted up their voice, and wept again: and Orpah kissed her mother-in-law, but Ruth clave into her.

And she said, Behold, thy sister-in-law is gone back unto her people, and unto her gods: return thou after thy sister-in-law. And Ruth said, Entreat me not to leave thee, *or* to return from following after thee: for whither thou goest, I will go; and where thou lodgest, I will lodge: thy people *shall be* my people, and thy God my God: Where thou diest, will I die, and there will I be buried: the Lord do so to me, and more also, *if aught* but death part thee and me. When she saw that she was steadfastly minded to go with her, then she left speaking unto her.

So they two went until they came to Bethlehem. And it came to pass, when they were come to Bethlehem, that all the city was moved about them, and they said, *Is* this Naomi? And she said unto them, Call me not Naomi, call me Mara: for the Almighty hath dealt very bitterly with me. I went out full, and the Lord hath brought me home again empty: why *then* call ye me Naomi, seeing the Lord hath testified against me, and the Almighty hath afflicted me? So Naomi returned, and Ruth the Moabitess, her daughter-in-law, with her, which returned out of the country of Moab: and they came to Bethlehem in the beginning of barley harvest.

And Naomi had a kinsman of her husband's, a mighty man of wealth, of the family of Elimelech; and his name *was* Boaz. And Ruth the Moabitess said unto Naomi, Let me now go to the field, and glean ears of corn after *him* in whose sight I shall find grace. And she said unto her, Go, my daughter. And she went, and came, and gleaned in the field after the reapers: and her hap was to light on a part of the field *belonging* unto Boaz, who *was* of the kindred of Elimelech. And, behold, Boaz came from Bethlehem, and said unto the reapers, The Lord *be* with you. And they answered him, The Lord bless thee. Then said Boaz unto his servant that was set over the reapers, Whose Damsel *is* this? And the servant that was set over the reapers answered and said, It *is* the Moabitish damsel that came back with Naomi out of the country of Moab: And she said, I pray you, let me glean and gather after the reapers among the sheaves: so she came, and hath continued even from the morning until now, that she tarried a little in the house.

Then said Boaz unto Ruth, Hearest thou not, my daughter? Go not to glean in another field, neither go from hence, but abide here fast by my maidens: *Let* thine eyes *be* on the field that they do reap, and go thou after them: have I not charged the young men that they shall not touch thee? and when thou art athirst, go unto the vessels, and drink of *that* which the young men have drawn. Then she fell on her face, and bowed herself to the ground, and said unto him, Why have I found grace in thine eyes, that thou shouldest take knowledge of me, seeing I *am* a stranger? And Boaz answered and said unto her, It hath fully been showed me, all that thou hast done unto thy mother-in-law since the death of thine husband; and *how* thou hast left thy father and thy mother, and the land of thy nativity, and art come unto a people which thou knewest not heretofore. The LORD recompense thy work, and a full reward be given thee of the LORD GOD of Israel, under whose wings thou art come to trust. Then she said, Let me find favor in thy sight, my lord; for that thou hast comforted me, and for that thou hast spoken friendly unto thine handmaid, though I be not like unto one of thine handmaidens. And Boaz said unto her, At mealtime come thou hither, and eat of the bread, and dip thy morsel in the vinegar. And she sat beside the reapers: and he reached her parched *corn,* and she did eat, and was sufficed, and left. And when she was risen up to glean, Boaz commanded his young men, saying, Let her glean even among the sheaves, and reproach her not: And let fall also *some* of the handfuls of purpose for her, and leave *them,* that she may glean *them,* and rebuke her not.

So she gleaned in the field until even, and beat out that she had gleaned: and it was about an ephah of barley. And she took *it* up, and went into the city; and her mother-in-law saw what she had gleaned: and she brought forth, and gave to her that she had reserved after she was sufficed. And her mother-in-law said unto her, Where hast thou gleaned to-day? and where wroughtest thou? blessed be he that did take knowledge of thee. And she showed her mother-in-law with whom she had wrought, and said, The man's name with whom I wrought to-day *is* Boaz. And Naomi said unto her daughter-in-law, Blessed *be* he of the LORD, who hath not left off his kindness to the living and to the dead. And Naomi said unto her, The man *is* near of kin unto us, one of our next kinsmen. And Ruth the Moabitess said, He said unto me also, Thou shalt keep fast by my young men, until they have ended all my harvest. And Naomi said unto Ruth her daughter-in-law, *It is* good, my daughter, that thou go out with his maidens, that they meet thee not in any other field. So she kept fast by the maidens of Boaz to glean unto the end of barley harvest and of wheat harvest; and dwelt with her mother-in-law.

Then Naomi her mother-in-law said unto her, My daughter, shall I not seek rest for thee, that it may be well of thee? And now *is* not Boaz of our kindred, with whose maidens thou wast? Behold, he winnoweth barley to-night in the threshingfloor. Wash thyself therefore, and anoint thee, and put thy raiment upon thee, and get thee down to the floor: *but* make not thyself known unto the man, until he shall have done eating and drinking. And it shall be, when he lieth down, that thou shalt mark the place where he shall lie, and thou shalt go in, and uncover his feet, and lay thee down; and he will tell thee what thou shalt do. And she said unto her, All that thou sayest unto me I will do.

And she went down unto the floor, and did according to all that her mother-in-law bade her. And when Boaz had eaten and drunk, and his heart was merry, he went to lie down at the end of the heap of corn: and she came softly, and uncovered his feet, and laid her down. And it came to pass at midnight, that the man was afraid, and turned himself: and, behold, a woman lay at his feet. And he said, Who *art* thou? And she answered, I *am* Ruth thine handmaid: spread therefore thy skirt over thine handmaid; for thou *art* a near kinsman. And he said, Blessed *be* thou of the Lord, my daughter; for thou hast showed me more kindness in the latter end than at the beginning, inasmuch as thou followedst not young men, whether poor or rich. And now, my daughter; fear not; I will do to thee all that thou requirest: for all the city of my people doth know that thou *art* a virtuous woman. And now it is true that I *am thy* near kinsman: howbeit there is a kinsman nearer than I. Tarry this night, and it shall be in the morning, *that* if he will perform unto thee the part of a kinsman, well; let him do the kinsman's part: but if he will not do the part of a kinsman to thee, then will I do the part of a kinsman to thee, *as* the Lord liveth: lie down until the morning.

And she lay at his feet until the morning: and she rose up before one could know another. And he said, Let it not be known that a woman came unto the floor. Also he said, Bring the veil that *thou hast* upon thee, and hold it. And when she held it, he measured six *measures* of barley, and laid *it* on her: and she went into the city. And when she came to her mother-in-law, she said, Who *art* thou, my daughter? And she told her all that the man had done to her. And she said, These six *measures* of barley gave he me; for he said to me, Go not empty unto thy mother-in-law. Then said she, Sit still, my daughter, until thou know how the matter will fall: for the man will not be in rest, until he have finished the thing this day.

Then went Boaz up to the gate, and sat him down there: and, behold, the kinsman of whom Boaz spake came by; unto whom he said, Ho, such a one! turn aside, sit down here. And he turned aside, and sat down. And he took ten men of the elders of the city, and said, Sit ye down here. And they sat down. And he said unto the kinsman, Naomi, that is come again out of the country of Moab, selleth a parcel of land which *was* our brother Elimelech's: And I thought to advertise thee, saying, Buy *it* before the inhabitants, and before the elders of my people. If thou wilt redeem *it*, redeem *it:* but if thou wilt not redeem *it, then* tell me, that I may know: for *there is* none to redeem *it* besides thee; and I *am* after thee. And he said, I will redeem *it.* Then said Boaz, What day thou buyest the field of the hand of Naomi, thou must buy *it* also of Ruth the Moabitess, the wife of the dead, to raise up the name of the dead upon his inheritance. And the kinsman said, I cannot redeem *it* for myself, lest I mar mine own inheritance: redeem thou my right to thyself; for I cannot redeem *it.*

Now this *was the manner* in former time in Israel concerning redeeming and concerning changing, for to confirm all things; a man plucked off his shoe, and gave *it* to his neighbor: and this *was* a testimony in Israel. Therefore the kinsman said unto Boaz, Buy *it* for thee. So he drew off his shoe. And Boaz said unto the elders, and *unto* all the people, Ye *are* witnesses this day, that I have bought all that *was* Elimelech's, and all that *was* Chilion's and Mahlon's, of the hand of Naomi. Moreover Ruth the Moabitess, the wife of Mahlon, have I purchased to be my wife, to raise up the name of the dead upon his inheritance, that the name of the dead be not cut off from among his brethren, and from the gate of this place: ye *are* witnesses this day. And all the people that *were* in the gate, and the elders, said, *We are* witnesses. The LORD make the woman that is come into thine house like Rachel and like Leah, which two did build the house of Israel: and do thou worthily in Ephratah, and be famous in Bethlehem: And let thy house be like the house of Pharez, whom Tamar bare unto Judah, of the seed which the LORD shall give thee of this young woman.

So Boaz took Ruth, and she was his wife: and when he went in unto her, the LORD gave her conception, and she bare a son. And the women said unto Naomi, Blessed *be* the LORD, which hath not left thee this day without a kinsman, that his name may be famous in Israel. And he shall be unto thee a restorer of *thy* life, and a nourisher of thine old age: for thy daughter-in-law, which loveth thee, which is better to thee than seven sons, hath borne him. And Naomi took the child, and laid it in her bosom, and became nurse unto it. And the women her neighbors gave it a name, saying, There is a son born to Naomi; and they called him Obed: he *is* the father of Jesse, the father of David.

Now these *are* the generations of Pharez: Pharez begat Hezron, And Hezron begat Ram, and Ram begat Amminadab, And Amminadab begat Nahshon, and Nahshon begat Salmon, And Salmon begat Boaz, and Boaz begat Obed, And Obed begat Jesse, and Jesse begat David.

■ DISCUSSION

Relationships between people in this simple tale are civilized and decorous. People look out for each other, are thoughtful of each other, and kind. Courtesy and civilized, kindly relationships—something like that is the theme. Very related to theme, and helping facilitate the theme, is the *tone*.

Tone refers to the author's *attitude toward* his subject or toward his audience. The attitude can be shown in several ways—by the words the author chooses to use, by the incidents he chooses to tell (and the ones he chooses to omit), and by the manner (for example, the sequence) in which he chooses to tell them.

The teller of the Book of Ruth could have emphasized the horrors of the famine which Ruth and Naomi sought to escape, or he might have explored the physical, sexual cravings of lonely people. But he didn't. Rather, he described those moments in which one person listens to another, is loyal to another, is respectful, and heeds traditions and formalities. Out of the myriad events of everyday, the author has chosen just those events which make us feel the story's relatively coherent singleness of effect: its tone of civilized consideration for the feelings of others. This tone, in turn, helps us perceive the theme of lovingness and of decorum in human relations.

Patriotism

Yukio Mishima

> Yukio Mishima's "Patriotism" is also, in many ways, a story of love, and of customs, traditions, and loyalty. It examines aspects of human relationships that are explored in The Book of Ruth too. It's title might have been "Love," as easily as "Patriotism"—though for Western readers that title would perhaps have taken on an irony that it would not suggest to an Oriental reader.

On the twenty-eighth of February, 1936 (on the third day, that is, of the February 26 Incident), Lieutenant Shinji Takeyama of the Konoe Transport Battalion—profoundly disturbed by the knowledge that his closest colleagues had been with the mutineers from the beginning, and indignant at the imminent prospect of Imperial troops attacking Imperial troops—took his officer's sword and ceremonially disemboweled himself in the eight-mat room of his private residence in the sixth block of Aoba-cho, in Yotsuya Ward. His wife, Reiko, followed him, stabbing herself to death. The lieutenant's farewell note consisted of one sentence: "Long live the Imperial Forces." His wife's, after apologies for her unfilial conduct in thus preceding her parents to the grave, concluded: "The day which, for a soldier's wife, had to come, has come. . . ." The last moments of this heroic and dedicated couple were such as to make the gods themselves weep. The lieutenant's age, it should be noted, was thirty-one, his

Yukio Mishima, *Death in Midsummer and Other Stories*, translated by Geoffrey Sargent. Copyright © 1966 by New Directions Publishing Corporation. Reprinted by permission of New Directions Publishing Corporation.

wife's twenty-three; and it was not half a year since the celebration of their marriage.

II

Those who saw the bride and bridegroom in the commemorative photograph—perhaps no less than those actually present at the lieutenant's wedding—had exclaimed in wonder at the bearing of this handsome couple. The lieutenant, majestic in military uniform, stood protectively beside his bride, his right hand resting upon his sword, his officer's cap held at his left side. His expression was severe, and his dark brows and wide-gazing eyes well conveyed the clear integrity of youth. For the beauty of the bride in her white over-robe no comparisons were adequate. In the eyes, round beneath soft brows, in the slender, finely shaped nose, and in the full lips, there was both sensuousness and refinement. One hand, emerging shyly from a sleeve of the over-robe, held a fan, and the tips of the fingers, clustering delicately, were like the bud of a moonflower.

After the suicide, people would take out this photograph and examine it, and sadly reflect that too often there was a curse on these seemingly flawless unions. Perhaps it was no more than imagination, but looking at the picture after the tragedy it almost seemed as if the two young people before the gold-lacquered screen were gazing, each with equal clarity, at the deaths which lay before them.

Thanks to the good offices of their go-between, Lieutenant General Ozeki, they had been able to set themselves up in a new home at Aoba-chō in Yotsuya. "New home" is perhaps misleading. It was an old three-room rented house backing onto a small garden. As neither the six- nor the four-and-a-half-mat room downstairs was favored by the sun, they used the upstairs eight-mat room as both bedroom and guest room. There was no maid, so Reiko was left alone to guard the house in her husband's absence.

The honeymoon trip was dispensed with on the grounds that these were times of national emergency. The two of them had spent the first night of their marriage at this house. Before going to bed, Shinji, sitting erect on the floor with his sword laid before him, had bestowed upon his wife a soldierly lecture. A woman who had become the wife of a soldier should know and resolutely accept that her husband's death might come at any moment. It could be tomorrow. It could be the day after. But, no matter when it came—he asked—was she steadfast in her resolve to accept it? Reiko rose to her feet, pulled open a drawer of the cabinet, and took out what was the most prized of her new possessions, the dagger her mother had given her. Returning to her place, she laid the dagger without a word on the mat before her, just as her husband had laid his sword. A

Patriotism

silent understanding was achieved at once, and the lieutenant never again sought to test his wife's resolve.

In the first few months of her marriage Reiko's beauty grew daily more radiant, shining serene like the moon after rain.

As both were possessed of young, vigorous bodies, their relationship was passionate. Nor was this merely a matter of the night. On more than one occasion, returning home straight from maneuvers, and begrudging even the time it took to remove his mud-splashed uniform, the lieutenant had pushed his wife to the floor almost as soon as he had entered the house. Reiko was equally ardent in her response. For a little more or a little less than a month, from the first night of their marriage Reiko knew happiness, and the lieutenant, seeing this, was happy too.

Reiko's body was white and pure, and her swelling breasts conveyed a firm and chaste refusal; but, upon consent, those breasts were lavish with their intimate, welcoming warmth. Even in bed these two were frighteningly and awesomely serious. In the very midst of wild, intoxicating passions, their hearts were sober and serious.

By day the lieutenant would think of his wife in the brief rest periods between training; and all day long, at home, Reiko would recall the image of her husband. Even when apart, however, they had only to look at the wedding photograph for their happiness to be once more confirmed. Reiko felt not the slightest surprise that a man who had been a complete stranger until a few months ago should now have become the sun about which her whole world revolved.

All these things had a moral basis, and were in accordance with the Education Rescript's injunction that "husband and wife should be harmonious." Not once did Reiko contradict her husband, nor did the lieutenant ever find reason to scold his wife. On the god shelf below the stairway, alongside the tablet from the Great Ise Shrine, were set photographs of their Imperial Majesties, and regularly every morning, before leaving for duty, the lieutenant would stand with his wife at this hallowed place and together they would bow their heads low. The offering water was renewed each morning, and the sacred sprig of *sasaki* was always green and fresh. Their lives were lived beneath the solemn protection of the gods and were filled with an intense happiness which set every fiber in their bodies trembling.

III

Although Lord Privy Seal Saito's house was in their neighborhood, neither of them heard any noise of gunfire on the morning of February 26. It was a bugle, sounding muster in the dim, snowy dawn, when the ten-minute tragedy had already ended, which first disrupted the lieutenant's slumbers. Leaping at once from his bed, and without speaking a word, the lieutenant donned his uniform, buckled on the sword held ready for him by his wife, and hurried swiftly out into the snow-covered streets of the still darkened morning. He did not return until the evening of the twenty-eighth.

Later, from the radio news, Reiko learned the full extent of this sudden eruption of violence. Her life throughout the subsequent two days was lived alone, in complete tranquillity, and behind locked doors.

In the lieutenant's face, as he hurried silently out into the snowy morning, Reiko had read the determination to die. If her husband did not return, her own decision was made: she too would die. Quietly she attended to the disposition of her personal possessions. She chose her sets of visiting kimonos as keepsakes for friends of her schooldays, and she wrote a name and address on the stiff paper wrapping in which each was folded. Constantly admonished by her husband never to think of the morrow, Reiko had not even kept a diary and was now denied the pleasure of assiduously rereading her record of the happiness of the past few months and consigning each page to the fire as she did so. Ranged across the top of the radio were a small china dog, a rabbit, a squirrel, a bear, and a fox. There were also a small vase and a water pitcher. These comprised Reiko's one and only collection. But it would hardly do, she imagined, to give such things as keepsakes. Nor again would it be quite proper to ask specifically for them to be included in the coffin. It seemed to Reiko, as these thoughts passed through her mind, that the expressions on the small animals' faces grew even more lost and forlorn.

Reiko took the squirrel in her hand and looked at it. And then, her thoughts turning to a realm far beyond these childlike affections, she gazed up into the distance at the great sunlike principle which her husband embodied. She was ready, and happy, to be hurtled along to her destruction in that gleaming sun chariot—but now, for these few moments of solitude, she allowed herself to luxuriate in this innocent attachment to trifles. The time when she had genuinely loved these things, however, was long past. Now she merely loved the memory of having once loved them, and their place in her heart had been filled by more intense passions, by a more frenzied happiness. . . .For Reiko had never, even to herself, thought of these soaring joys of the flesh as a mere pleasure. The February cold, and the icy touch of the china squirrel, had numbed Reiko's slender fingers; yet, even so, in her lower limbs, beneath the ordered repetition of the pattern which crossed the skirt of her trim *meisen* kimono, she could feel now, as she thought of the lieutenant's powerful arms reaching out toward her, a hot moistness of the flesh which defied the snows.

She was not in the least afraid of the death hovering in her mind. Waiting alone at home, Reiko firmly believed that everything her hus-

Patriotism

band was feeling or thinking now, his anguish and distress, was leading her—just as surely as the power in his flesh—to a welcome death. She felt as if her body could melt away with ease and be transformed to the merest fraction of her husband's thought.

Listening to the frequent announcements on the radio, she heard the names of several of her husband's colleagues mentioned among those of the insurgents. This was news of death. She followed the developments closely, wondering anxiously, as the situation became daily more irrevocable, why no Imperial ordinance was sent down, and watching what had at first been taken as a movement to restore the nation's honor come gradually to be branded with the infamous name of mutiny. There was no communication from the regiment. At any moment, it seemed, fighting might commence in the city streets, where the remains of the snow still lay.

Toward sundown on the twenty-eighth Reiko was startled by a furious pounding on the front door. She hurried downstairs. As she pulled with fumbling fingers at the bolt, the shape dimly outlined beyond the frosted-glass panel made no sound, but she knew it was her husband. Reiko had never known the bolt on the sliding door to be so stiff. Still it resisted. The door just would not open.

In a moment, almost before she knew she had succeeded, the lieutenant was standing before her on the cement floor inside the porch, muffled in a khaki greatcoat, his top boots heavy with slush from the street. Closing the door behind him, he returned the bolt once more to its socket. With what significance, Reiko did not understand.

"Welcome home."

Reiko bowed deeply, but her husband made no response. As he had already unfastened his sword and was about to remove his greatcoat, Reiko moved around behind to assist. The coat, which was cold and damp and had lost the odor of horse dung it normally exuded when exposed to the sun, weighed heavily upon her arm. Draping it across a hanger, and cradling the sword and leather belt in her sleeves, she waited while her husband removed his top boots and then followed behind him into the "living room." This was the six-mat room downstairs.

Seen in the clear light from the lamp, her husband's face, covered with a heavy growth of bristle, was almost unrecognizably wasted and thin. The cheeks were hollow, their luster and resilience gone. In his normal good spirits he would have changed into old clothes as soon as he was home and have pressed her to get supper at once, but now he sat before the table still in his uniform, his head drooping dejectedly. Reiko refrained from asking whether she should prepare the supper.

After an interval the lieutenant spoke.

"I knew nothing. They hadn't asked me to join. Perhaps out of consideration, because I was newly married. Kano, and Homma too, and Yamaguchi."

Reiko recalled momentarily the faces of high-spirited young officers, friends of her husband, who had come to the house occasionally as guests.

"There may be an Imperial ordinance sent down tomorrow. They'll be posted as rebels, I imagine. I shall be in command of a unit with orders to attack them.... I can't do it. It's impossible to do a thing like that."

He spoke again.

"They've taken me off guard duty, and I have permission to return home for one night. Tomorrow morning, without question, I must leave to join the attack. I can't do it, Reiko."

Reiko sat erect with lowered eyes. She understood clearly that her husband had spoken of his death. The lieutenant was resolved. Each word, being rooted in death, emerged sharply and with powerful significance against this dark, unmovable background. Although the lieutenant was speaking of his dilemma, already there was no room in his mind for vacillation.

However, there was a clarity, like the clarity of a stream fed from melting snows, in the silence which rested between them. Sitting in his own home after the long two-day ordeal, and looking across at the face of his beautiful wife, the lieutenant was for the first time experiencing true peace of mind. For he had at once known, though she said nothing, that his wife divined the resolve which lay beneath his words.

"Well, then..." The lieutenant's eyes opened wide. Despite his exhaustion they were strong and clear, and now for the first time they looked straight into the eyes of his wife. "Tonight I shall cut my stomach."

Reiko did not flinch.

Her round eyes showed tension, as taut as the clang of a bell.

"I am ready," she said. "I ask permission to accompany you."

The lieutenant felt almost mesmerized by the strength in those eyes. His words flowed swiftly and easily, like the utterances of a man in delirium, and it was beyond his understanding how permission in a matter of such weight could be expressed so casually.

"Good. We'll go together. But I want you as a witness, first, for my own suicide. Agreed?"

When this was said a sudden release of abundant happiness welled up in both their hearts. Reiko was deeply affected by the greatness of her husband's trust in her. It was vital for the lieutenant, whatever else might happen, that there should be no irregularity in his death. For that reason there had to be a witness. The fact that he had chosen his wife for this was the first mark of his trust. The second, and even greater mark, was that though he had pledged that they should die together he did not intend to kill his wife first—he had deferred her death to a time when he would no longer be there to verify it. If the lieutenant had been a suspicious husband, he would doubtless, as in the usual suicide pact, have chosen to kill his wife first.

When Reiko said, "I ask permission to accompany you," the lieutenant felt these words to be the final fruit of the education which he had himself given his wife, starting on the first night of their marriage, and which had schooled her, when the moment came, to say what had to be said without a shadow of hesitation. This flattered the lieutenant's opinion of himself as a self-reliant man. He was not so romantic or conceited as to imagine that the words were spoken spontaneously, out of love for her husband.

With happiness welling almost too abundantly in their hearts, they could not help smiling at each other. Reiko felt as if she had returned to her wedding night.

Before her eyes was neither pain nor death. She seemed to see only a free and limitless expanse opening out into vast distances.

"The water is hot. Will you take your bath now?"

"Ah yes, of course."

"And supper . . .?"

The words were delivered in such level, domestic tones that the lieutenant came near to thinking, for the fraction of a second, that everything had been a hallucination.

"I don't think we'll need supper. But perhaps you could warm some sake?"

"As you wish."

As Reiko rose and took a *tanzen* gown from the cabinet for after the bath, she purposely directed her husband's attention to the opened drawer. The lieutenant rose, crossed to the cabinet, and looked inside. From the ordered array of paper wrappings he read, one by one, the addresses of the keepsakes. There was no grief in the lieutenant's response to this demonstration of heroic resolve. His heart was filled with tenderness. Like a husband who is proudly shown the childish purchases of a young wife, the lieutenant, overwhelmed by affection, lovingly embraced his wife from behind and implanted a kiss upon her neck.

Reiko felt the roughness of the lieutenant's unshaven skin against her neck. This sensation, more than being just a thing of this world, was for Reiko almost the world itself, but now—with the feeling that it was soon to be lost forever—it had freshness beyond all her experience. Each moment had its own vital strength, and the senses in every corner of her body were reawakened. Accepting her husband's caresses from behind, Reiko raised herself on the tips of her toes, letting the vitality seep through her entire body.

"First the bath, and then, after some sake . . . lay out the bedding upstairs, will you?"

The lieutenant whispered the words into his wife's ear. Reiko silently nodded.

Flinging off his uniform, the lieutenant went to the bath. To faint background noises of slopping water Reiko tended the charcoal brazier in the living room and began the preparations for warming the sake.

Taking the *tanzen*, a sash, and some underclothes, she went to the bathroom to ask how the water was. In the midst of a coiling cloud of steam the lieutenant was sitting cross-legged on the floor, shaving, and she could dimly discern the rippling movements of the muscles on his damp, powerful back as they responded to the movement of his arms.

There was nothing to suggest a time of any special significance. Reiko, going busily about her tasks, was preparing side dishes from odds and ends in stock. Her hands did not tremble. If anything, she managed even more efficiently and smoothly than usual. From time to time, it is true, there was a strange throbbing deep within her breast. Like distant lightning, it had a moment of sharp intensity and then vanished without trace. Apart from that, nothing was in any way out of the ordinary.

The lieutenant, shaving in the bathroom, felt his warmed body miraculously healed at last of the desperate tiredness of the days of indecision and filled—in spite of the death which lay ahead—with pleasurable anticipation. The sound of his wife going about her work came to him faintly. A healthy physical craving, submerged for two days, reasserted itself.

The lieutenant was confident there had been no impurity in that joy they had experienced when resolving upon death. They had both sensed at that moment—though not, of course, in any clear and conscious way —that those permissible pleasures which they shared in private were once more beneath the protection of Righteousness and Divine Power, and of a complete and unassailable morality. On looking into each other's eyes and discovering there an honorable death, they had felt themselves safe once more behind steel walls which none could destroy, encased in an impenetrable armor of Beauty and Truth. Thus, so far from seeing any inconsistency or conflict between the urges of his flesh and the sincerity of his patriotism, the lieutenant was even able to regard the two as parts of the same thing.

Thrusting his face close to the dark, cracked, misted wall mirror, the lieutenant shaved himself with great care. This would be his death face. There must be no unsightly blemishes. The cleanshaven face gleamed once more with a youthful luster, seeming to brighten the darkness of the mirror. There was a certain elegance, he even felt, in the association of death with this radiantly healthy face.

Just as it looked now, this would become his death face! Already, in fact, it had half departed from the lieutenant's personal possession and had become the bust above a dead soldier's memorial. As an experiment he closed his eyes tight. Everything was wrapped in blackness, and he was no longer a living, seeing creature.

Returning from the bath, the traces of the shave glowing faintly blue beneath his smooth cheeks, he seated himself beside the now well-kindled charcoal brazier. Busy though Reiko was, he noticed, she had found time lightly to touch up her face. Her cheeks were gay and her lips moist. There was no shadow of sadness to be seen. Truly, the lieutenant felt, as he saw this mark of his young wife's passionate nature, he had chosen the wife he ought to have chosen.

As soon as the lieutenant had drained his sake cup he offered it to Reiko. Reiko had never before tasted sake, but she accepted without hesitation and sipped timidly.

"Come here," the lieutenant said.

Reiko moved to her husband's side and was embraced as she leaned backward across his lap. Her breast was in violent commotion, as if sadness, joy, and the potent sake were mingling and reacting within her. The lieutenant looked down into his wife's face. It was the last face he would see in this world, the last face he would see of his wife. The lieutenant scrutinized the face minutely, with the eyes of a traveler bidding farewell to splendid vistas which he will never revisit. It was a face he could not tire of looking at—the features regular yet not cold, the lips lightly closed with a soft strength. The lieutenant kissed those lips, unthinkingly. And suddenly, though there was not the slightest distortion of the face into the unsightliness of sobbing, he noticed that tears were welling slowly from beneath the long lashes of the closed eyes and brimming over into a glistening stream.

When, a little later, the lieutenant urged that they should move to the upstairs bedroom, his wife replied that she would follow after taking a bath. Climbing the stairs alone to the bedroom, where the air was already warmed by the gas heater, the lieutenant lay down on the bedding with arms outstretched and legs apart. Even the time at which he lay waiting for his wife to join him was no later and no earlier than usual.

He folded his hands beneath his head and gazed at the dark boards of the ceiling in the dimness beyond the range of the standard lamp. Was it death he was now waiting for? Or a wild ecstasy of the senses? The two seemed to overlap, almost as if the object of this bodily desire was death itself. But, however that might be, it was certain that never before had the lieutenant tasted such total freedom.

There was the sound of a car outside the window. He could hear the screech of its tires skidding in the snow piled at the side of the street. The sound of its horn re-echoed from near-by walls. . . . Listening to these noises he had the feeling that this house rose like a solitary island in the ocean of a society going as restlessly about its business as ever. All around, vastly and untidily, stretched the country for which he grieved. He was to give his life for it. But would that great country, with which he was prepared to remonstrate to the extent of destroying himself, take the slightest heed of his death? He did not know; and it did not matter. His was a battlefield without glory, a battlefield where none could display deeds of valor: it was the front line of the spirit.

Reiko's footsteps sounded on the stairway. The steep stairs in this old house creaked badly. There were fond memories in that creaking, and many a time, while waiting in bed, the lieutenant had listened to its welcome sound. At the thought that he would hear it no more he listened with intense concentration, striving for every corner of every moment of this precious time to be filled with the sound of those soft footfalls on the creaking stairway. The moments seemed transformed to jewels, sparkling with inner light.

Reiko wore a Nagoya sash about the waist of her *yukata,* but as the lieutenant reached toward it, its redness sobered by the dimness of the light, Reiko's hand moved to his assistance and the sash fell away, slithering swiftly to the floor. As she stood before him, still in her *yukata,* the lieutenant inserted his hands through the side slits beneath each sleeve, intending to embrace her as she was; but at the touch of his finger tips upon the warm naked flesh, and as the armpits closed gently about his hands, his whole body was suddenly aflame.

In a few moments the two lay naked before the glowing gas heater.

Neither spoke the thought, but their hearts, their bodies, and their pounding breasts blazed with the knowledge that this was the very last time. It was as if the words "The Last Time" were spelled out, in invisible brushstrokes, across every inch of their bodies.

The lieutenant drew his wife close and kissed her vehemently. As their tongues explored each other's mouths, reaching out into the smooth, moist interior, they felt as if the still unknown agonies of death had tempered their senses to the keenness of red-hot steel. The agonies they could not yet feel, the distant pains of death, had refined their awareness of pleasure.

"This is the last time I shall see your body," said the lieutenant. "Let me look at it closely." And, tilting the shade on the lampstand to one side, he directed the rays along the full length of Reiko's outstretched form.

Reiko lay still with her eyes closed. The light from the low lamp clearly revealed the majestic sweep of her white flesh. The lieutenant, not without a touch of egocentricity, rejoiced that he would never see this beauty crumble in death.

Patriotism 169

At his leisure, the lieutenant allowed the unforgettable spectacle to engrave itself upon his mind. With one hand he fondled the hair, with the other he softly stroked the magnificent face, implanting kisses here and there where his eyes lingered. The quiet coldness of the high, tapering forehead, the closed eyes with their long lashes beneath faintly etched brows, the set of the finely shaped nose, the gleam of teeth glimpsed between full, regular lips, the soft cheeks and the small, wise chin . . . these things conjured up in the lieutenant's mind the vision of a truly radiant death face, and again and again he pressed his lips tight against the white throat—where Reiko's own hand was soon to strike—and the throat reddened faintly beneath his kisses. Returning to the mouth he laid his lips against it with the gentlest of pressures, and moved them rhythmically over Reiko's with the light rolling motion of a small boat. If he closed his eyes, the world became a rocking cradle.

Wherever the lieutenant's eyes moved his lips faithfully followed. The high, swelling breasts, surmounted by nipples like the buds of a wild cherry, hardened as the lieutenant's lips closed about them. The arms flowed smoothly downward from each side of the breast, tapering toward the wrists, yet losing nothing of their roundness or symmetry, and at their tips were those delicate fingers which had held the fan at the wedding ceremony. One by one, as the lieutenant kissed them, the fingers withdrew behind their neighbor as if in shame. . . . The natural hollow curving between the bosom and the stomach carried in its lines a suggestion not only of softness but of resilient strength, and while it gave forewarning of the rich curves spreading outward from here to the hips it had, in itself, an appearance only of restraint and proper discipline. The whiteness and richness of the stomach and hips was like milk brimming in a great bowl, and the sharply shadowed dip of the navel could have been the fresh impress of a raindrop, fallen there that very moment. Where the shadows gathered more thickly, hair clustered, gentle and sensitive, and as the agitation mounted in the now no longer passive body there hung over this region a scent like the smoldering of fragrant blossoms, growing steadily more pervasive.

At length, in a tremulous voice, Reiko spoke.

"Show me. . . . Let me look too, for the last time."

Never before had he heard from his wife's lips so strong and unequivocal a request. It was as if something which her modesty had wished to keep hidden to the end had suddenly burst its bonds of constraint. The lieutenant obediently lay back and surrendered himself to his wife. Lithely she raised her white, trembling body, and—burning with an innocent desire to return to her husband what he had done for her—placed two white fingers on the lieutenant's eyes, which gazed fixedly up at her, and gently stroked them shut.

Suddenly overwhelmed by tenderness, her cheeks flushed by a dizzying uprush of emotion, Reiko threw her arms about the lieutenant's close cropped head. The bristly hairs rubbed painfully against her breast, the prominent nose was cold as it dug into her flesh, and his breath was hot. Relaxing her embrace, she gazed down at her husband's masculine face. The severe brows, the closed eyes, the splendid bridge of the nose, the shapely lips drawn firmly together . . . the blue, cleanshaven cheeks reflecting the light and gleaming smoothly. Reiko kissed each of these. She kissed the broad nape of the neck, the strong, erect shoulders, the powerful chest with its twin circles like shields and its russet nipples. In the armpits, deeply shadowed by the ample flesh of the shoulders and chest, a sweet and melancholy odor emanated from the growth of hair, and in the sweetness of this odor was contained, somehow, the essence of young death. The lieutenant's naked skin glowed like a field of barley, and everywhere the muscles showed in sharp relief, converging on the lower abdomen about the small, unassuming navel. Gazing at the youthful, firm stomach, modestly covered by a vigorous growth of hair, Reiko thought of it as it was soon to be, cruelly cut by the sword, and she laid her head upon it, sobbing in pity, and bathed it with kisses.

At the touch of his wife's tears upon his stomach the lieutenant felt ready to endure with courage the cruelest agonies of his suicide.

What ecstasies they experienced after these tender exchanges may well be imagined. The lieutenant raised himself and enfolded his wife in a powerful embrace, her body now limp with exhaustion after her grief and tears. Passionately they held their faces close, rubbing cheek against cheek. Reiko's body was trembling. Their breasts, moist with sweat, were tightly joined, and every inch of the young and beautiful bodies had become so much one with the other that it seemed impossible there should ever again be a separation. Reiko cried out. From the heights they plunged into the abyss, and from the abyss they took wing and soared once more to dizzying heights. The lieutenant panted like the regimental standard-bearer on a route march. . . . As one cycle ended, almost immediately a new wave of passion would be generated, and together—with no trace of fatigue—they would climb again in a single breathless movement to the very summit.

IV

When the lieutenant at last turned away, it was not from weariness. For one thing, he was anxious not to undermine the considerable strength he would need in carrying out his suicide. For another, he would have been sorry to mar the sweetness of these last memories by overindulgence.

Since the lieutenant had clearly desisted, Reiko too, with her usual compliance, followed his example. The two lay naked on their backs, with fingers interlaced, staring fixedly at the dark ceiling. The room was warm from the heater, and even when the sweat had ceased to pour from their bodies they felt no cold. Outside, in the hushed night, the sounds of passing traffic had ceased. Even the noises of the trains and streetcars around Yotsuya station did not penetrate this far. After echoing through the region bounded by the moat, they were lost in the heavily wooded park fronting the broad driveway before Akasaka Palace. It was hard to believe in the tension gripping this whole quarter, where the two factions of the bitterly divided Imperial Army now confronted each other, poised for battle.

Savoring the warmth flowing within themselves, they lay still and recalled the ecstasies they had just known. Each moment of the experience was relived. They remembered the taste of kisses which had never wearied, the touch of naked flesh, episode after episode of dizzying bliss. But already, from the dark boards of the ceiling, the face of death was peering down. These joys had been final, and their bodies would never know them again. Not that joy of this intensity—and the same thought had occurred to them both—was ever likely to be re-experienced, even if they should live on to old age.

The feel of their fingers intertwined—this too would soon be lost. Even the wood-grain patterns they now gazed at on the dark ceiling boards would be taken from them. They could feel death edging in, nearer and nearer. There could be no hesitation now. They must have the courage to reach out to death themselves, and to seize it.

"Well, let's make our preparations," said the lieutenant. The note of determination in the words was unmistakable, but at the same time Reiko had never heard her husband's voice so warm and tender.

After they had risen, a variety of tasks awaited them.

The lieutenant, who had never once before helped with the bedding, now cheerfully slid back the door of the closet, lifted the mattress across the room by himself, and stowed it away inside.

Reiko turned off the gas heater and put away the lamp standard. During the lieutenant's absence she had arranged this room carefully, sweeping and dusting it to a fresh cleanness, and now—if one overlooked the rosewood table drawn into one corner—the eight-mat room gave all the appearance of a reception room ready to welcome an important guest.

"We've seen some drinking here, haven't we? With Kan and Homma and Noguchi . . ."

"Yes, they were great drinkers, all of them."

"We'll be meeting them before long, in the other world. They'll tease us, I imagine, when they find I've brought you with me."

Descending the stairs, the lieutenant turned to look back into this calm, clean room, now brightly illuminated by the ceiling lamp. There floated across his mind the faces of the young officers who had drunk there, and laughed, and innocently bragged. He had never dreamed then that he would one day cut open his stomach in this room.

In the two rooms downstairs husband and wife busied themselves smoothly and serenely with their respective preparations. The lieutenant went to the toilet, and then to the bathroom to wash. Meanwhile Reiko folded away her husband's padded robe, placed his uniform tunic, his trousers, and a newly cut bleached loincloth in the bathroom, and set out sheets of paper on the living-room table for the farewell notes. Then she removed the lid from the writing box and began rubbing ink from the ink tablet. She had already decided upon the wording of her own note.

Reiko's fingers pressed hard upon the cold gilt letters of the ink tablet, and the water in the shallow well at once darkened, as if a black cloud had spread across it. She stopped thinking that this repeated action, this pressure from her fingers, this rise and fall of faint sound, was all and solely for death. It was a routine domestic task, a simple paring away of time until death should finally stand before her. But somehow, in the increasingly smooth motion of the tablet rubbing on the stone, and in the scent from the thickening ink, there was unspeakable darkness.

Neat in his uniform, which he now wore next to his skin, the lieutenant emerged from the bathroom. Without a word he seated himself at the table, bolt upright, took a brush in his hand, and stared undecidedly at the paper before him.

Reiko took a white silk kimono with her and entered the bathroom. When she reappeared in the living room, clad in the white kimono and with her face lightly made up, the farewell note lay completed on the table beneath the lamp. The thick black brushstrokes said simply:

"Long Live the Imperial Forces—Army Lieutenant Takeyama Shinji."

While Reiko sat opposite him writing her own note, the lieutenant gazed in silence, intensely serious, at the controlled movement of his wife's pale fingers as they manipulated the brush.

With their respective notes in their hands—the lieutenant's sword strapped to his side, Reiko's small dagger thrust into the sash of her white kimono—the two of them stood before the god shelf and silently prayed. Then they put out all the downstairs lights. As he mounted the stairs the lieutenant turned his head and gazed back at the striking, white-clad figure of his wife, climbing behind him, with lowered eyes, from the darkness beneath.

The farewell notes were laid side by side in the alcove of the upstairs room. They wondered whether they ought not to remove the hanging scroll, but since it had been written by their go-between, Lieutenant General Ozeki, and consisted, moreover, of two Chinese characters signifying "Sincerity," they left it where it was. Even if it were to become stained with splashes of blood, they felt that the lieutenant general would understand.

The lieutenant, sitting erect with his back to the alcove, laid his sword on the floor before him.

Reiko sat facing him, a mat's width away. With the rest of her so severly white the touch of rouge on her lips seemed remarkably seductive.

Across the dividing mat they gazed intently into each other's eyes. The lieutenant's sword lay before his knees. Seeing it, Reiko recalled their first night and was overwhelmed with sadness. The lieutenant spoke, in a hoarse voice:

"As I have no second to help me I shall cut deep. It may look unpleasant, but please do not panic. Death of any sort if a fearful thing to watch. You must not be discouraged by what you see. Is that all right?"

"Yes."

Reiko nodded deeply.

Looking at the slender white figure of his wife the lieutenant experienced a bizarre excitement. What he was about to perform was an act in his public capacity as a soldier, something he had never previously shown his wife. It called for a resolution equal to the courage to enter battle; it was a death of no less degree and quality than death in the front line. It was his conduct on the battlefield that he was now to display.

Momentarily the thought led the lieutenant to a strange fantasy. A lonely death on the battlefield, a death beneath the eyes of his beautiful wife . . . in the sensation that he was now to die in these two dimensions, realizing an impossible union of them both, there was sweetness beyond words. This must be the very pinnacle of good fortune, he thought. To have every moment of his death observed by those beautiful eyes—it was like being borne to death on a gentle, fragrant breeze. There was some special favor here. He did not understand precisely what it was, but it was a domain unknown to others: a dispensation granted to no one else had been permitted to himself. In the radiant, bridelike figure of his white-robed wife the lieutenant seemed to see a vision of all those things he had loved and for which he was to lay down his life—the Imperial Household, the Nation, the Army Flag. All these, no less than the wife who sat before him, were presences observing him closely with clear and never-faltering eyes.

Reiko too was gazing intently at her husband, so soon to die, and she thought that never in this world had she seen anything so beautiful. The lieutenant always looked well in uniform, but now, as he contemplated death with severe brows and firmly closed lips, he revealed what was perhaps masculine beauty at its most superb.

"It's time to go," the lieutenant said at last.

Reiko bent her body low to the mat in a deep bow. She could not raise her face. She did not wish to spoil her make-up with tears, but the tears could not be held back.

When at length she looked up she saw hazily through the tears that her husband had wound a white bandage around the blade of his now unsheathed sword, leaving five or six inches of naked steel showing at the point.

Resting the sword in its cloth wrapping on the mat before him, the lieutenant rose from his knees, resettled himself cross-legged, and unfastened the hooks of his uniform collar. His eyes no longer saw his wife. Slowly, one by one, he undid the flat brass buttons. The dusky brown chest was revealed, and then the stomach. He unclasped his belt and undid the buttons of his trousers. The pure whiteness of the thickly coiled loincloth showed itself. The lieutenant pushed the cloth down with both hands, further to ease his stomach, and then reached for the white-bandaged blade of his sword. With his left hand he massaged his abdomen, glancing downward as he did so.

To reassure himself on the sharpness of his sword's cutting edge the lieutenant folded back the left trouser flap, exposing a little of his thigh, and lightly drew the blade across the skin. Blood welled up in the wound at once, and several streaks of red trickled downward, glistening in the strong light.

It was the first time Reiko had ever seen her husband's blood, and she felt a violent throbbing in her chest. She looked at her husband's face. The lieutenant was looking at the blood with calm appraisal. For a moment—though thinking at the same time that it was hollow comfort—Reiko experienced a sense of relief.

The lieutenant's eyes fixed his wife with an intense, hawk-like stare. Moving the sword around to his front, he raised himself slightly on his hips and let the upper half of his body lean over the sword point. That he was mustering his whole strength was apparent from the angry tension of the uniform at his shoulders. The lieutenant aimed to strike deep into the left of his stomach. His sharp cry pierced the silence of the room.

Despite the effort he had himself put into the blow, the lieutenant had the impression that someone else had struck the side of his stomach agonizingly with a thick rod of iron. For a second or so his head reeled and he had no idea what had happened. The five or six inches of naked point had vanished completely into his flesh, and the white bandage, gripped in his clenched fist, pressed directly against his stomach.

He returned to consciousness. The blade had certainly pierced the wall of the stomach, he thought. His breathing was difficult, his chest thumped violently, and in some far deep region, which he could hardly believe was a part of himself, a fearful and excruciating pain came welling up as if the ground had split open to disgorge a boiling stream of molten rock. The pain came suddenly nearer, with terrifying speed. The lieutenant bit his lower lip and stifled an instinctive moan.

Was this *seppuku?*—he was thinking. It was a sensation of utter chaos, as if the sky had fallen on his head and the world was reeling drunkenly. His will power and courage, which had seemed so robust before he made the incision, had now dwindled to something like a single hairlike thread of steel, and he was assailed by the uneasy feeling that he must advance along this thread, clinging to it with desperation. His clenched fist had grown moist. Looking down, he saw that both his hand and the cloth about the blade were drenched in blood. His loincloth too was dyed a deep red. It struck him as incredible that, amidst this terrible agony, things which could be seen could still be seen, and existing things existed still.

The moment the lieutenant thrust the sword into his left side and she saw the deathly pallor fall across his face, like an abruptly lowered curtain, Reiko had to struggle to prevent herself from rushing to his side. Whatever happened, she must watch. She must be a witness. That was the duty her husband had laid upon her. Opposite her, a mat's space away, she could clearly see her husband biting his lip to stifle the pain. The pain was there, with absolute certainty, before her eyes. And Reiko had no means of rescuing him from it.

The sweat glistened on her husband's forehead. The lieutenant closed his eyes, and then opened them again, as if experimenting. The eyes had lost their luster, and seemed innocent and empty like the eyes of a small animal.

The agony before Reiko's eyes burned as strong as the summer sun, utterly remote from the grief which seemed to be tearing herself apart within. The pain grew steadily in stature, stretching upward. Reiko felt that her husband had already become a man in a separate world, a man whose whole being had been resolved into pain, a prisoner in a cage of pain where no hand could reach out to him. But Reiko felt no pain at all. Her grief was not pain. As she thought about this, Reiko began to feel as if someone had raised a cruel wall of glass high between herself and her husband.

Ever since her marriage her husband's existence had been her own existence, and every breath of his had been a breath drawn by herself. But now, while her husband's existence in pain was a vivid reality, Reiko could find in this grief of hers no certain proof at all of her own existence.

With only his right hand on the sword the lieutenant began to cut sideways across his stomach. But as the blade became entangled with the entrails it was pushed constantly outward by their soft resilience; and the lieutenant realized that it would be necessary, as he cut, to use both hands to keep the point pressed deep into his stomach. He pulled the blade across. It did not cut as easily as he had expected. He directed the strength of his whole body into his right hand and pulled again. There was a cut of three or four inches.

The pain spread slowly outward from the inner depths until the whole stomach reverberated. It was like the wild clanging of a bell. Or like a thousand bells which jangled simultaneously at every breath he breathed and every throb of his pulse, rocking his whole being. The lieutenant could no longer stop himself from moaning. But by now the blade had cut its way through to below the navel, and when he noticed this he felt a sense of satisfaction, and a renewal of courage.

The volume of blood had steadily increased, and now it spurted from the wound as if propelled by the beat of the pulse. The mat before the lieutenant was drenched red with splattered blood, and more blood overflowed onto it from pools which gathered in the folds of the lieutenant's khaki trousers. A spot, like a bird, came flying across to Reiko and settled on the lap of her white silk kimono.

By the time the lieutenant had at last drawn the sword across to the right side of his stomach, the blade was already cutting shallow and had revealed its naked tip, slippery with blood and grease. But, suddenly stricken by a fit of vomiting, the lieutenant cried out hoarsely. The vomiting made the fierce pain fiercer still, and the stomach, which had thus far remained firm and compact, now abruptly heaved, opening wide its wound, and the entrails burst through, as if the wound too were vomiting. Seemingly ignorant of their master's suffering, the entrails gave an impression of robust health and almost disagreeable vitality as they slipped smoothly out and spilled over into the crotch. The lieutenant's head drooped, his shoulders heaved, his eyes opened to narrow slits, and a thin trickle of saliva dribbled from his mouth. The gold markings on his epaulettes caught the light and glinted.

Blood was scattered everywhere. The lieutenant was soaked in it to his knees, and he sat now in a crumpled and listless posture, one hand on the floor. A raw smell filled the room. The lieutenant, his head drooping, retched repeatedly, and the movement showed vividly in his shoulders. The blade of the sword, now pushed back by the entrails and exposed to its tip, was still in the lieutenant's right hand.

It would be difficult to imagine a more heroic sight than that of the lieutenant at this moment, as he mustered his strength and flung back his head. The movement was performed with sudden violence, and the back of his head struck with a sharp crack against the alcove pillar. Reiko had been sitting until now with her face lowered, gazing in fascination at the tide of blood advancing toward her knees, but the sound took her by surprise and she looked up.

The lieutenant's face was not the face of a living man. The eyes were hollow, the skin parched, the once so lustrous cheeks and lips the color of dried mud. The right hand alone was moving. Laboriously gripping the sword, it hovered shakily in the air like the hand of a marionette and strove to direct the point at the base of the lieutenant's throat. Reiko watched her husband make this last, most heart-rending, futile exertion. Glistening with blood and grease, the point was thrust at the throat again and again. And each time it missed its aim. The strength to guide it was no longer there. The straying point struck the collar and the collar badges. Although its hooks had been unfastened, the stiff military collar had closed together again and was protecting the throat.

Reiko could bear the sight no longer. She tried to go to her husband's help, but she could not stand. She moved through the blood on her knees, and her white skirts grew deep red. Moving to the rear of her husband, she helped no more than by loosening the collar. The quivering blade at last contacted the naked flesh of the throat. At that moment Reiko's impression was that she herself had propelled her husband forward: but that was not the case. It was a movement planned by the lieutenant himself, his last exertion of strength. Abruptly he threw his body at the blade, and the blade pierced his neck, emerging at the nape. There was a tremendous spurt of blood and the lieutenant lay still, cold blue-tinged steel protruding from his neck at the back.

V

Slowly, her socks slippery with blood, Reiko descended the stairway. The upstairs room was now completely still.

Switching on the ground-floor lights, she checked the gas jet and the main gas plug and poured water over the smoldering, half-buried charcoal in the brazier. She stood before the upright mirror in the four-and-a-half-mat room and held up her skirts. The bloodstains made it seem as if a bold, vivid pattern was printed across the lower half of her white kimono. When she sat down before the mirror, she was conscious of the dampness and coldness of her husband's blood in the region of her thighs, and she shivered. Then, for a long while, she lingered over her toilet preparations. She applied the rouge generously to her cheeks, and her lips too she painted heavily. This was no longer make-up to please her husband. It was make-up for the world which she would leave behind, and there was a touch of the magnificent and the spectacular in her brushwork. When she rose, the mat before the mirror was wet with blood. Reiko was not concerned about this.

Returning from the toilet, Reiko stood finally on the cement floor of the porchway. When her husband had bolted the door here last night it had been in preparation for death. For a while she stood immersed in the consideration of a simple problem. Should she now leave the bolt drawn? If she were to lock the door, it could be that the neighbors might not notice their suicide for several days. Reiko did not relish the thought of their two corpses putrefying before discovery. After all, it seemed, it would be best to leave it open. . . . She released the bolt, and also drew open the frosted-glass door a fraction. . . . At once a chill wind blew in. There was no sign of anyone in the midnight streets, and stars glittered ice-cold through the trees in the large house opposite.

Leaving the door as it was, Reiko mounted the stairs. She had walked here and there for some time and her socks were no longer slippery. About halfway up, her nostrils were already assailed by a peculiar smell.

The lieutenant was lying on his face in a sea of blood. The point protruding from his neck seemed to have grown even more prominent than before. Reiko walked heedlessly across the blood. Sitting beside the lieutenant's corpse, she stared intently at the face, which lay on one cheek on the mat. The eyes were opened wide, as if the lieutenant's attention had been attracted by something. She raised the head, folding it in her sleeve, wiped the blood from the lips, and bestowed a last kiss.

Then she rose and took from the closet a new white blanket and a waist cord. To prevent any derangement of her skirts, she wrapped the blanket about her waist and bound it there firmly with the cord.

Reiko sat herself on a spot about one foot distant from the lieutenant's body. Drawing the dagger from her sash, she examined its dully gleaming blade intently, and held it to her tongue. The taste of the polished steel was slightly sweet.

Reiko did not linger. When she thought how the pain which had previously opened such a gulf between herself and her dying husband was now to become a part of her own experience, she saw before her only the joy of herself entering a realm her husband had already made his own. In her husband's agonized face there had been something inexplicable which she was seeing for the first time. Now she would solve that riddle. Reiko sensed that at last she too would be able to taste the true bitterness and sweetness of that great moral principle in which her husband believed. What had until now been tasted only faintly through her husband's example she was about to savor directly with her own tongue.

Reiko rested the point of the blade against the base of her throat. She thrust hard. The wound was only shallow. Her head blazed, and her hands shook uncontrollably. She gave the blade a strong pull sideways. A warm substance flooded into her mouth, and everything before her eyes reddened, in a vision of spouting blood. She gathered her strength and plunged the point of the blade deep into her throat.

Theme and Tone 179

■ DISCUSSION AND QUESTIONS

To Western eyes, the double suicide of Lieutenant Takeyama and his lovely young wife Reiko may appear bizarre and grotesque. We must remember, however, that to the Japanese, at least as late as the second World War, the Emperor was divine. ("On the god shelf below the stairway, alongside the tablet from the Great Ise Shrine, were set photographs of their Imperial Majesties, and regularly every morning, before leaving for duty, the lieutenant would stand with his wife at this hallowed place and together they would bow their heads low.") Thus, when his closest friends, who were "Imperial Troops," attacked the remaining, loyal Imperial troops, they were not only mutineers, but desecrators and defilers of divinity and of the moral order (as Mishima writes in the story, "All these things had a moral basis, . . ."). Still, they were Takeyama's closest friends too, and friendship ties its own bonds. In consequence, Takeyama is in a dilemma, torn between two loyalties, and his last note, "Long live the Imperial Forces," can be taken to refer to either group, thus verbalizing the dilemma. Such a dilemma, the condition of being torn between loyalties, is the stuff of tragedy. Antigone, in Sophocles' play of that name, is torn between loving loyalty to her slain brother, whose body she feels compelled to bury, and the king's command that the corpse of a traitor to the kingdom is to remain unburied, to be eaten by the dogs.

The theme of our story, however, is not the dilemma, for that is quickly solved by the protagonists. There is no question about which way lies duty, and the emphasis falls on the chilling, relentless, inevitable, but perhaps above all orderly, traditional, formalized manner in which first Takeyama, and then Reiko, carry out all that is fitting in the context of their tradition and their culture. Their bloody suicide is in the highest sense precisely what is demanded by both their most sacred religion and their equally sacred and elevated love. So, different as it may seem on the surface, the *theme* of the story "Patriotism" is really quite akin to that of the Book of Ruth: tradition, loyalty, decorum, and—yes, strange as it may seem on first thought—Love.

Can you itemize six actions performed by the Lieutenant and by Reiko that examplify the fact that their actions are not acts of chaotic passion, but rather manifestations of order, protocol, and sacred tradition?

Now, *tone* may be more subtle to define in "Patriotism." We have stressed the orderliness and the decorum that are attached to the ritual suicide. At the same time, however, there is another aspect worth noting. While there is, indeed, a celebration of the physical reality, an appreciation of the arrangement of the house, of the dark boards of the ceiling, of the dress, and above all, of the beautiful, youthful bodies of the protagonists, there is also quite clearly a current of hysteria, an extravagant exhilaration in the contemplation of pain and death. "Please do not panic, . . ." Takeyama may say to his wife before disemboweling himself, but we, the readers, may well feel that Mishima, by the meticulousness of his description, say of the spilling out of entrails, or by the way he carries us so long at such a measured pace to the bloody climax, wants to have us walk a tightwire precisely on the very brink of panic. Doubtlessly the story is in firm control, but one slip, one faltering on the part of the teller (or even the translator), we feel, and we would be plunged into an adventure of wild and bloody chaos.

Such risk-taking by the author is surely on purpose, for wild madness and bloody hysteria have long been recognized as lurking behind the seemingly placid facades of controlled and autocratic states (and families) and repressed and inhibited individuals. There is in human beings a delirium, a bloody and primal madness, it seems, that is generally restrained by society, or rechannelled into work and art. But it is there. And it wants out! So a great part of the strength of Mishima's story comes from the tautness, the tension we sense (whether we can explain it or not) as we read this tale in which the universal daemonic seethes just below the surface, kept in check by the iron discipline of the very attractive, human, and vulnerable young lieutenant.

Chapter **6**

POINT OF VIEW

Almost everyone has told a child a story, either a familiar fairy tale or a yarn invented for the occasion. When we amuse a child with the one about the three bears, we generally begin with the age-old "Once upon a time...." Then we go on to narrate the story, knowing exactly how it is going to turn out, what baby bear will say about his porridge, and how Goldilocks simply loves the little bed. When we tell a story this way, we are using the *third person omniscient* point of view. The teller knows all; he is outside the story looking in, not a participant in it. An omniscient teller is like a pilot observing and describing the terrain below.

But suppose Goldilocks told her own story, perhaps beginning with, "It was such a nice, sunny day and the woods smelled so good that I decided to go for a walk," and ending with, "When I woke up there were these three awful, giant bears trying to eat me, so I ran and ran as fast as I could and tore my new dress when I jumped out of the window. I'll never go into the woods alone again." From this point of view, the *first person point of view,* the story every child knows so well is different in theme and effect from the traditional tale. Goldilocks cannot know what the bears think about her unmannerly intrusion into their home. She can know only what she thinks and feels; it is her story and she is at the center of it. The first person point of view, however, does not have to be that of the central character of the story; it can be that of a minor or secondary character who observes the scenes around him.

It is quite clear that the omniscient point of view provides the writer (or teller) with the greatest liberties in narrating his story. He can move freely over his materials, revealing to the reader the contents of any character's mind, interpreting actions, analyzing motives. He may explain the theme or significance of the story. He may even evaluate the characters, as in this passage from an often reprinted version of "The Three Bears":

> And while they [the bears] were away a little girl called Goldilocks, who lived at the other side of the wood and had been sent on an errand by her mother, passed by the house, and looked in at the window. And then she peeped in at the keyhole, for *she was not at all a well-brought-up little girl.* Then seeing nobody in the house, she lifted the latch. The door was not fastened, because *the Bears were good Bears, who did nobody any harm,* and never suspected that anybody would harm them. So Goldilocks opened the door and went in; and well-pleased was she when she saw the porridge on the table. If *she had been a well-brought-up little girl,* she would have waited till the Bears came home, and then, perhaps, they would have asked her to breakfast; for *they were good* Bears—a little rough or so, as the manner of Bears is, but for all that *very good-natured and hospitable.* But *she was an impudent, rude little girl,* and so she set about helping herself. (Emphasis added.)

It is unlikely that a sophisticated writer today would so blatantly editorialize about his characters. He would probably aim for a more objective point of view by presenting his characters dramatically, thus forcing the reader to make his own evaluations. (See the chapter on "Character".) The writer who says, "If she had been a well-brought-up little girl" wants to emphasize a *moral* for his readers or listeners—good little girls stay out of strange beds, or something like that. Stories for mature readers eschew "moral" messages and simple plots with good/bad characters. Instead, these stories examine themes. Only a silly reader of "Where Are You Going, Where Have You Been" would say that its moral is "good little girls stay out of strange beds."

The author may set limits on his omniscience, on how much he knows and can report. He may reveal the thoughts of only one character and not the thoughts of all characters. In "Going to Meet the Man" James Baldwin tells the story of a white Southern deputy sheriff from a *limited omniscient point of view.* Baldwin gets inside the mind of this bigot and reveals the source of his fears and hatred. The writer shows only the thoughts of Jesse, not the thoughts of his wife or his father. We can learn what his father thinks only if Jesse infers it. The limits that Baldwin sets on himself insure a tightly unified story; the reader's attention remains fixed on Jesse throughout.

Baldwin could have allowed Jesse to tell his own story, using the first person point of view. Our job of literary understanding is to determine

Point of View

why Baldwin chose to use the limited third person point of view. In other words, what does Baldwin gain by this choice?

Either point of view insures that the story will be tightly unified, the reader's attention fixed on Jesse throughout his night of terror. But Baldwin's choice allows him to present Jesse from inside so that the reader knows what Jesse thinks and feels and from outside so the reader knows what Jesse's thoughts and feelings reveal. The reader knows much more about Jesse's motives than Jesse can comprehend. In Jesse's eyes, for example, he is "a good man, a God-fearing man." But as Baldwin records Jesse's thoughts on his moral goodness, he also makes clear that Jesse sees no incongruity between being a good, God-fearing man and being a racist/rapist who considers Negroes as animals. If Jesse narrates his own story, we might identify and sympathize with him because we would see everything through his eyes and through his twisted sense of right and wrong. But since we have a more complete view of Jesse—a view from inside and outside—our sympathy is limited.

If Jesse told his own story the language would have to be his language —crude, imprecise, vague. The language Baldwin uses to expose Jesse's thought is Baldwin's—exact, controlled, calculated. It is Baldwin who, explaining what Jesse feels lying in the dark beside his wife Grace, says, "He lay there, one hand between his legs, staring at the frail sanctuary of his wife." The diction is important—but it is not Jesse's diction. With the words "frail sanctuary" Baldwin has implicitly stated one of his themes in this story: white men regard Black women as pleasure animals and their white wives as sacred, fragile creatures devoid of lust and passion.

There are times when a writer wants the reader to identify to some degree with his central character and to hear the story in the character's own language. Here are the opening sentences of two great novels about young people:

> You don't know about me without you have read a book by the name of *The Adventures of Tom Sawyer*. That book was made by Mr. Mark Twain, and he told the truth, mainly. There was things which he stretched, but mainly he told the truth. That is nothing. I never seen anybody but lied one time or another, without it was Aunt Polly, or the widow, or maybe Mary. (Mark Twain. *The Adventures of Huckleberry Finn*. New York: Holt, Rinehart, Winston, 1957.)

> "What's it going to be then, eh?"
> There was me, that is Alex, and my three droogs, that is Pete, Georgie, and Dim, Dim being really dim, and we sat in the Korova Milkbar making up our rassoodocks what to do with the evening, a flip dark chill winter bastard though dry. The Korova Milkbar was a milk-plus

mesto, and you may, O my brothers, have forgotten what these mestos were like, things changing so skorry these days and everybody very quick to forget, newspapers not being read much neither. (Anthony Burgess. *A Clockwork Orange.* New York: W. W. Norton and Co., 1963.)

In each case the author wanted to show the world through the eyes and words of a boy, to present that unique view of life each boy has. Huck, and Alex talk directly to us, just as if we were all sitting around having a beer and swapping true stories. They address us as "you," and Alex even confides in us as if we were his "brothers." As we listen to these fellows talk to us about their adventures, mishaps, problems, we feel very close to them, almost sharing their lives. We float on the raft with Huck instead of observing from the shore; we stand right beside Alex as he slashes Dim with his knife.

The first person point of view, then, adds credibility, immediacy, and "lifelikeness" to the story. The author seems to disappear, leaving the reader in the hands of the narrator. There is little distance between us and Huck or Alex; and we experience their stories almost as if they were happening to us. The effect is that the reader may be so close to the action that he begins to share the character's perception of the world, even when, as in *A Clockwork Orange,* that perception is grossly distorted. Unless he is wary, the reader may so completely identify with the narrator's vision that he abandons his critical intelligence and escapes into the character's life.

Clearly, many readers become, in their fantasies, Mike Hammer or Travis McGee as these super studs narrate their violent and erotic adventures in Mickey Spillane and John D. MacDonald novels. Readers who share vicariously Mike Hammer's gut delight in bashing a broad with a gun, are too close to the action to step back and evaluate Mike Hammer and his beliefs. Mickey Spillane's success depends on his skill in making the reader accept Mike Hammer's personal moral code—a code distilled in such titles as *Vengeance is Mine* and *I, The Jury.**

The inexperienced reader may assume that the first person narrator and the author *always* share similar moral perspectives, when in fact the narrator may be radically different from his creator. A narrator's perceptions of an experience may be confused, limited; he may even be designed to purposefully deceive the reader. Furthermore, the reader may simply know much more about the significance of the narrator's actions and

---

*There is little doubt that Spillane himself shares Hammer's cruel, crude beliefs or that Hammer is the author's ego ideal. Spillane played the role of Mike Hammer in a movie version of one of the novels; and more recently, Spillane's wife posed for the salacious cover of a paperback edition.

thoughts than does the narrator himself. A first person narrator is, after all, a character in the story, not simply a spokesman for the author.

In summary, then, analyzing point of view means asking: Who is telling the story? What is his/her angle of vision and relationship to the events? Is he/she detached or involved? Is his/her view of the experience trustworthy? Is the narrator's view of the experience complete, or is it limited? Is the narrator presented ironically? How does the point of view help the writer organize his materials?

It is more important to answer these questions carefully than merely to categorize a narrator as "omniscient" or "first person." The answers to these questions lead to the very heart of the story, its meaning.

Discussion and Writing Assignment

Suppose you're a writer. You've got this dynamic idea for a story about a young girl with golden curls who meets three bears in the woods. Having made certain strategic decisions about what the bears eat, what they sit on, and where they sleep, you're ready to write the first sentence. Now you are confronted with a tough, but interesting problem: Who will tell the story? You know exactly how the story is going to come out, what baby bear feels when he sees his broken chair, which bed Goldilocks (that's what, in a burst of inspiration, you've decided to call her) prefers. Since you are omniscient, why not tell the story yourself? If you narrate it, you can be a kind of god who has peopled a world which you know *everything* about. So you begin: "Once upon a time there were three bears, who lived together in a house of their own, in a wood." Sounds okay, a little familiar, but it's a beginning.

Perhaps you ought to reach for something fresher, say letting one of the bears—the big bear will do—tell his own story. There might be advantages to this strategy. First, the bear storyteller could explain how badly he and the other bears felt about finding an expensive chair broken and an empty porridge bowl after returning from their nature walk. If the bears explain how disturbed they were by their discovery, the reader might believe it, because, after all, it did happen to the bears—not to you, the writer. If a bear tells the story, however, there is no way for him to report Goldilocks' feelings. If you, the all-knowing author, tell the story, you can tell every thought she has; but big bear (whose real name is Harold) cannot; his knowledge is limited to what he sees, hears, and thinks.

What does Goldilocks think and feel? Perhaps curiosity at first about the little house? Then hunger, satisfied with a "just right" bowl of porridge, then drowsiness. Then FEAR! Suppose you decide to play up the fear angle. In that case maybe it's best to have Goldilocks tell the story because it's through her eyes that the bears look menacing, not through a bear's eyes. You could make the reader feel fear because Goldilocks is both the narrator and the central character in the story.

But being a careful beginner at story writing, you work through other possible points of view or angles of vision on your story before you settle on one that works best for the story and theme. Perhaps a passing woodsman saw the whole thing. . . . Or perhaps Goldilocks' great granddaughter is telling the story to her daughter as a warning about going out at night into the streets of the City. Or. . . .

The point is, of course, that if there is a tale, there must be a teller. But for any story there are many possible tellers. Take a few minutes off from your reading at this point and write three beginnings for your story, "The Three Bears," telling the story through three different narrators. Read your openings aloud to the class for discussion. What are the advantages and disadvantages of each *point of view?*

Going to Meet the Man

James Baldwin

"What's the matter?" she asked.

"I don't know," he said, trying to laugh. "I guess I'm tired."

"You've been working too hard," she said. "I keep telling you."

"Well, goddammit, woman," he said, "it's not my fault!" He tried again; he wretchedly failed again. Then he just lay there, silent, angry, and helpless. Excitement filled him just like a toothache, but it refused to enter his flesh. He stroked her breast. This was his wife. He could not ask her to do just a little thing for him, just to help him out, just for a little while, the way he could ask a nigger girl to do it. He lay there, and he sighed. The image of a black girl caused a distant excitement in him, like a far-away light; but, again, the excitement was more like pain; instead of forcing him to act, it made action impossible.

"Go to sleep," she said, gently, "you got a hard day tomorrow."

"Yeah," he said, and rolled over on his side, facing her, one hand still on one breast. "Goddamn the niggers. The black stinking coons. You'd think they'd learn. Wouldn't you think they'd learn? I mean, *wouldn't you?*"

"They're going to be out there tomorrow," she said, and took his hand away, "get some sleep."

He lay there, one hand between his legs, staring at the frail sanctuary of his wife. A faint light came from the shutters; the moon was full. Two

Copyright © 1965 by James Baldwin. From *Going to Meet the Man* by James Baldwin. Reprinted by permission of the publisher, The Dial Press.

dogs, far away, were barking at each other, back and forth, insistently, as though they were agreeing to make an appointment. He heard a car coming north on the road and he half sat up, his hand reaching for his holster, which was on a chair near the bed, on top of his pants. The lights hit the shutters and seemed to travel across the room and then went out. The sound of the car slipped away, he heard it hit gravel, then heard it no more. Some liver-lipped students, probably, heading back to that college—but coming from where? His watch said it was two in the morning. They could be coming from anywhere, from out of state most likely, and they would be at the court house tomorrow. The niggers were getting ready. Well, they would be ready, too.

He moaned. He wanted to let whatever was in him out; but it wouldn't come out. Goddamn! he said aloud, and turned again, on his side, away from Grace, staring at the shutters. He was a big, healthy man and he had never had any trouble sleeping. And he wasn't old enough yet to have any trouble getting it up—he was only forty-two. And he was a good man, a God-fearing man, he had tried to do his duty all his life, and he had been a deputy sheriff for several years. Nothing had ever bothered him before, certainly not getting it up. Sometimes, sure, like any other man, he knew that he wanted a little more spice than Grace could give him and he would drive over yonder and pick up a black piece or arrest her, it came to the same thing, but he couldn't do that now, no more. There was no telling what might happen once your ass was in the air. And they were low enough to kill a man then, too, everyone of them, or the girl herself might do it, right while she was making believe you made her feel so good. The niggers. What had the good Lord Almighty had in mind when he made the niggers? Well. They were pretty good at that, all right. Damn. Damn. Goddamn.

This wasn't helping him to sleep. He turned again, toward Grace again, and moved close to her warm body. He felt something he had never felt before. He felt that he would like to hold her, hold her, hold her, and be buried in her like a child and never have to get up in the morning again and go downtown to face those faces, good Christ, they were ugly! and never have to enter that jail house again and smell that smell and hear that singing; never again feel that filthy, kinky, greasy hair under his hand, never again watch those black breasts leap against the leaping cattle prod, never hear those moans again or watch that blood run down or the fat lips split or the sealed eyes struggle open. They were animals, they were no better than animals, what could be done with people like that? Here they had been in a civilized country for years and they still lived like animals. Their houses were dark, with oil cloth or cardboard in the windows, the smell was enough to make you puke your guts out, and there they sat, a whole tribe, pumping out kids, it looked like, every damn five minutes, and laughing and talking and playing music like they didn't have a care in the world, and he reckoned they didn't, neither, and coming to the door, into the sunlight, just standing there, just looking foolish, not thinking of anything but just getting back to what they were doing, saying, Yes suh, Mr. Jesse. I surely will, Mr. Jesse. Fine weather, Mr. Jesse. Why, I thank you, Mr. Jesse. He had worked for a mail-order house for a while and it had been his job to collect the payments for the stuff they bought. They were too dumb to know that they were being cheated blind, but that was no skin off his ass—he was just supposed to do his job. They would be late—they didn't have the sense to put money aside; but it was easy to scare them, and he never really had any trouble. Hell, they all liked him, the kids used to smile when he came to the door. He gave them candy, sometimes, or chewing gum, and rubbed their rough bullet heads—maybe the candy should have been poisoned. Those kids were grown now. He had had trouble with one of them today.

"There was this nigger today," he said; and stopped; his voice sounded peculiar. He touched Grace. "You awake?" he asked. She mumbled something, impatiently, she was probably telling him to go to sleep. It was all right. He knew that he was not alone.

"What a funny time," he said, "to be thinking about a thing like that —you listening?" She mumbled something again. He rolled over on his back. "This nigger's one of the ringleaders. We had trouble with him before. We must have had him out there at the work farm three or four times. Well, Big Jim C. and some of the boys really had to whip that nigger's ass today." He looked over at Grace; he could not tell whether she was listening or not; and he was afraid to ask again. "They had this line you know, to register"—he laughed, but she did not—"and they wouldn't stay where Big Jim C. wanted them, no, they had to start blocking traffic all around the court house so couldn't nothing or nobody get through, and Big Jim C. told them to disperse and they wouldn't move, they just kept up that singing, and Big Jim C. figured that the others would move if this nigger would move, him being the ringleader, but he wouldn't move and he wouldn't let the others move, so they had to beat him and a couple of the others and they threw them in the wagon—but *I* didn't see this nigger till I got to the jail. They were still singing and I was supposed to make them stop. Well, I couldn't make them stop for me but I knew he could make them stop. He was lying on the ground jerking and moaning, they had threw him in a cell by himself, and blood was coming out his ears from where Big Jim C. and his boys had whipped him. Wouldn't you think they'd learn? I put the prod to him and he jerked some more and he kind of screamed—but he didn't have much voice left. "You make them stop that singing," I said to him, "you hear me? You make them stop that singing." He acted like he didn't hear me and I put it to him again, under his arms, and he just rolled around on the floor and blood started coming from his mouth. He'd pissed his pants already." He paused. His mouth felt dry and his throat was as rough as sandpaper; as he talked, he began to hurt all over with that peculiar excitement which refused to be released. "You all are going to stop your singing, I said to him, and you are going to stop coming down to the court house and disrupting traffic and molesting the people and keeping us from our duties and keeping doctors from getting to sick white women and getting all them Northerners in this town to give our town a bad name —!" As he said this, he kept prodding the boy, sweat pouring from beneath the helmet he had not yet taken off. The boy rolled around in his own dirt and water and blood and tried to scream again as the prod hit his testicles, but the scream did not come out, only a kind of rattle and a moan. He stopped. He was not supposed to kill the nigger. The cell was filled with a terrible odor. The boy was still. "You hear me?" he called. "You had enough?" The singing went on. "You had enough?" His foot leapt out, he had not known it was going to, and caught the boy flush on the jaw. *Jesus,* he thought, *this ain't no nigger, this is a goddamn bull,* and he screamed again, "You had enough? You going to make them stop that singing now?"

But the boy was out. And now he was shaking worse than the boy had been shaking. He was glad no one could see him. At the same time, he felt very close to a very peculiar, particular joy; something deep in him and deep in his memory was stirred, but whatever was in his memory eluded him. He took off his helmet. He walked to the cell door.

"White man," said the boy, from the floor, behind him.

He stopped. For some reason, he grabbed his privates.

"You remember Old Julia?"

The boy said, from the floor, with his mouth full of blood, and one eye, barely open, glaring like the eye of a cat in the dark, "My grandmother's name was Mrs. Julia Blossom. *Mrs.* Julia Blossom. You going to call our women by their right names yet.—And those kids ain't going to stop singing. We going to keep on singing until every one of you miserable white mothers go stark raving out of your minds." Then he closed the one eye; he spat blood; his head fell back against the floor.

He looked down at the boy, whom he had been seeing, off and on, for more than a year, and suddenly remembered him: Old Julia had been one of his mail-order customers, a nice old woman. He had not seen her for years, he supposed that she must be dead.

He had walked into the yard, the boy had been sitting in a swing. He had smiled at the boy, and asked, "Old Julia home?"

The boy looked at him for a long time before he answered. "Don't no Old Julia live here."

"This is her house. I know her. She's lived here for years."

The boy shook his head. "You might know a Old Julia someplace else, white man. But don't nobody by that name live here."

He watched the boy; the boy watched him. The boy certainly wasn't more than ten. *White man.* He didn't have time to be fooling around with some crazy kid. He yelled, "Hey! Old Julia!"

But only silence answered him. The expression on the boy's face did not change. The sun beat down on them both, still and silent; he had the feeling that he had been caught up in a nightmare, a nightmare dreamed by a child; perhaps one of the nightmares he himself had dreamed as a child. It had that feeling—everything familiar, without undergoing any other change, had been subtly and hideously displaced: the trees, the sun, the patches of grass in the yard, the leaning porch and the weary porch steps and the cardboard in the windows and the black hole of the door which looked like the entrance to a cave, and the eyes of the pickaninny, all, all, were charged with malevolence. *White man.* He looked at the boy. "She's gone out?"

The boy said nothing.

"Well," he said, "tell her I passed by and I'll pass by next week." He started to go; he stopped. "You want some chewing gum?"

The boy got down from the swing and started for the house. He said, "I don't want nothing you got, white man." He walked into the house and closed the door behind him.

Now the boy looked as though he were dead. Jesse wanted to go over to him and pick him up and pistol whip him until the boy's head burst open like a melon. He began to tremble with what he believed was rage; sweat, both cold and hot, raced down his body, the singing filled him as though it were a weird, uncontrollable, monstrous howling rumbling up from the depths of his own belly, he felt an icy fear rise in him and raise him up, and he shouted, he howled, "You lucky we *pump* some white blood into you every once in a while—your women! Here's what I got for all the black bitches in the world—!" Then he was, abruptly, almost too weak to stand; to his bewilderment, his horror, beneath his own fingers, he felt himself violently stiffen—with no warning at all; he dropped his hands and he stared at the boy and he left the cell.

"All that singing they do," he said. "All that singing." He could not remember the first time he had heard it; he had been hearing it all his life. It was the sound with which he was most familiar—though it was also the sound of which he had been least conscious—and it had always contained an obscure comfort. They were singing to God. They were singing for mercy and they hoped to go to heaven, and he had even sometimes felt, when looking into the eyes of some of the old women, a few of the very old men, that they were singing for mercy for his soul, too.

Of course he had never thought of their heaven or of what God was, or could be, for them; God was the same for everyone, he supposed, and heaven was where good people went—he supposed. He had never thought much about what it meant to be a good person. He tried to be a good person and treat everybody right: it wasn't his fault if the niggers had taken it into their heads to fight against God and go against the rules laid down in the Bible for everyone to read! Any preacher would tell you that. He was only doing his duty: protecting white people from the niggers and the niggers from themselves. And there were still lots of good niggers around—he had to remember that; they weren't all like that boy this afternoon; and the good niggers must be mighty sad to see what was happening to their people. They would thank him when this was over. In that way they had, the best of them, not quite looking him in the eye, in a low voice, with a little smile: We surely thanks you, Mr. Jesse. From the bottom of our hearts, we thanks you. He smiled. They hadn't all gone crazy. This trouble would pass.—He knew that the young people had changed some of the words to the songs. He had scarcely listened to the words before and he did not listen to them now; but he knew that the words were different; he could hear that much. He did not know if the faces were different, he had never, before this trouble began, watched them as they sang, but he certainly did not like what he saw now. They hated him, and this hatred was blacker than their hearts, blacker than their skins, redder than their blood, and harder, by far, than his club. Each day, each night, he felt worn out, aching, with their smell in his nostrils and filling his lungs, as though he were drowning—drowning in niggers; and it was all to be done again when he awoke. It would never end. It would never end. Perhaps this was what the singing had meant all along. They had not been singing black folks into heaven, they had been singing white folks into hell.

Everyone felt this black suspicion in many ways, but no one knew how to express it. Men much older than he, who had been responsible for law and order much longer than he, were now much quieter than they had been, and the tone of their jokes, in a way that he could not quite put his finger on, had changed. These men were his models, they had been friends to his father, and they had taught him what it meant to be a man. He looked to them for courage now. It wasn't that he didn't know that what he was doing was right—he knew that, nobody had to tell him that; it was only that he missed the ease of former years. But they didn't have much time to hang out with each other these days. They tended to stay close to their families every free minute because nobody knew what might happen next. Explosions rocked the night of their tranquil town. Each time each man wondered silently if perhaps this time the dynamite had not fallen into the wrong hands. They thought that they knew where all the guns were; but they could not possibly know every move that was made in that secret place where the darkies lived. From time to time it was suggested that they form a posse and search the home of every nigger, but they hadn't done it yet. For one thing, this might have brought the bastards from the North down on their backs; for another, although the niggers were scattered throughout the town—down in the hollow near the railroad tracks, way west near the mills, up on the hill, the well-off ones, and some out near the college—nothing seemed to happen in one part of town without the niggers immediately knowing it in the other. This meant that they could not take them by surprise. They rarely mentioned it, but they *knew* that some of the niggers had guns. It stood to reason, as they said, since, after all, some of them had been in the Army. There were niggers in the Army right now and God knows they wouldn't have had any trouble stealing this half-assed government blind —the whole world was doing it, look at the European countries and all those countries in Africa. They made jokes about it—bitter jokes; and they cursed the government in Washington, which had betrayed them, but they had not yet formed a posse. Now, if their town had been laid out like some towns in the North, where all the niggers lived together in one locality, they could have gone down and set fire to the houses and brought about peace that way. If the niggers had all lived in one place, they could have kept the fire in one place. But the way this town was laid out, the fire could hardly be controlled. It would spread all over town— and the niggers would probably be helping it to spread. Still, from time to time, they spoke of doing it, anyway; so that now there was a real fear among them that somebody might go crazy and light the match.

They rarely mentioned anything not directly related to the war that they were fighting, but this had failed to establish between them the unspoken communication of soldiers during a war. Each man, in the thrilling silence which sped outward from their exchanges, their laughter, and their anecdotes, seemed wrestling, in various degrees of darkness, with a secret which he could not articulate to himself, and which, however directly it related to the war, related yet more surely to his privacy and his past. They could no longer be sure, after all, that they had all done the same things. They had never dreamed that their privacy could contain any element of terror, could threaten, that is, to reveal itself, to the scrutiny of a judgment day, while remaining unreadable and inaccessible to themselves; nor had they dreamed that the past, while certainly refusing to be forgotten, could yet so stubbornly refuse to be remembered. They felt themselves mysteriously set at naught, as no longer entering into the real concerns of other people—while here they were, outnumbered, fighting to save the civilized world. They had thought that people would care—people didn't care; not enough, anyway, to help them. It would have been a help, really, or at least a relief, even to have been forced to surrender. Thus they had lost, probably forever, their old and easy connection with each other. They were forced to depend on each other more and, at the same time, to trust each other less. Who could tell when one of them might not betray them all, for money, or for the ease of confession? But no one dared imagine what there might be to confess. They were soldiers fighting a war, but their relationship to each other was that of accomplices in a crime. They all had to keep their mouths shut.

I stepped in the river at Jordan.

Out of the darkness of the room, out of nowhere, the line came flying up at him, with the melody and the beat. He turned wordlessly toward his sleeping wife.

I stepped in the river at Jordan.

Where had he heard that song?
"Grace," he whispered. "You awake?"
She did not answer. If she was awake, she wanted him to sleep. Her breathing was slow and easy, her body slowly rose and fell.

I stepped in the river at Jordan.
The water came to my knees.

He began to sweat. He felt an overwhelming fear, which yet contained a curious and dreadful pleasure.

I stepped in the river at Jordan.
The Water came to my waist.

It had been night, as it was now, he was in the car between his mother and his father, sleepy, his head in his mother's lap, sleepy, and yet full of excitement. The singing came from far away, across the dark fields. There were no lights anywhere. They had said good-bye to all the others and turned off on this dark dirt road. They were almost home.

I stepped in the river at Jordan,
The water came over my head,
I looked way over to the other side,
He was making up my dying bed!

"I guess they singing for him," his father said, seeming very weary and subdued now. "Even when they're sad, they sound like they just about to go and tear off a piece." He yawned and leaned across the boy and slapped his wife lightly on the shoulder, allowing his hand to rest there for a moment. "Don't they?"

"Don't talk that way," she said.

"Well, that's what we going to do," he said, "you can make up your mind to that." He started whistling. "You see? When I begin to feel it, I gets kind of musical, too."

Oh, Lord! Come on and ease my troubling mind!

He had a black friend, his age, eight, who lived nearby. His name was Otis. They wrestled together in the dirt. Now the thought of Otis made him sick. He began to shiver. His mother put her arm around him.

"He's tired," she said.

"We'll be home soon," said his father. He began to whistle again.

"We didn't see Otis this morning," Jesse said. He did not know why he said this. His voice, in the darkness of the car, sounded small and accusing.

"You haven't seen Otis for a couple of mornings," his mother said.

That was true. But he was only concerned about *this* morning.

"No," said his father, "I reckon Otis's folks was afraid to let him show himself this morning."

"But Otis didn't do nothing!" Now his voice sounded questioning.

"Otis *can't* do nothing," said his father, "he's too little." The car lights picked up their wooden house, which now solemnly approached them, the lights falling around it like yellow dust. Their dog, chained to a tree, began to bark.

"We just want to make sure Otis *don't* do nothing," said his father, and stopped the car. He looked down at Jesse. "And you tell him what your Daddy said, you hear?"

"Yes sir," he said.

His father switched off the lights. The dog moaned and pranced, but they ignored him and went inside. He could not sleep. He lay awake, hearing the night sounds, the dog yawning and moaning outside, the sawing of the crickets, the cry of the owl, dogs barking far away, then no sounds at all, just the heavy, endless buzzing of the night. The darkness pressed on his eyelids like a scratchy blanket. He turned, he turned again. He wanted to call his mother, but he knew his father would not like this. He was terribly afraid. Then he heard his father's voice in the other room, low, with a joke in it; but this did not help him, it frightened him more, he knew what was going to happen. He put his head under the blanket, then pushed his head out again, for fear, staring at the dark window. He heard his mother's moan, his father's sigh; he gritted his teeth. Then their bed began to rock. His father's breathing seemed to fill the world.

That morning, before the sun had gathered all its strength, men and women, some flushed and some pale with excitement, came with news.

Jesse's father seemed to know what the news was before the first jalopy stopped in the yard, and he ran out, crying, "They got him, then? They got him?"

The first jalopy held eight people, three men and two women and three children. The children were sitting on the laps of the grown-ups. Jesse knew two of them, the two boys; they shyly and uncomfortably greeted each other. He did not know the girl.

"Yes, they got him," said one of the women, the older one, who wore a wide hat and a fancy, faded blue dress. "They found him early this morning."

"How far had he got?" Jesse's father asked.

"He hadn't got no further than Harkness," one of the men said. "Look like he got lost up there in all them trees—or maybe he just got so scared he couldn't move." They all laughed.

"Yes, and you know it's near a graveyard, too," said the younger woman, and they laughed again.

"Is that where they got him now?" asked Jesse's father.

By this time there were three cars piled behind the first one, with everyone looking excited and shining, and Jesse noticed that they were carrying food. It was like a Fourth of July picnic.

"Yeah, that's where he is," said one of the men, "declare, Jesse, you going to keep us here all day long, answering your damn fool questions. Come on, we ain't got no time to waste."

"Don't bother putting up no food," cried a woman from one of the other cars, "we got enough. Just come on."

"Why, thank you," said Jesse's father, "we be right along, then."

"I better get a sweater for the boy," said the mother, "in case it turns cold."

Jesse watched his mother's thin legs cross the yard. He knew that she also wanted to comb her hair a little and maybe put on a better dress, the dress she wore to church. His father guessed this, too, for he yelled behind her, "Now don't you go trying to turn yourself into no movie star. You just come on." But he laughed as he said this, and winked at the men; his wife was younger and prettier than most of the other women. He clapped Jesse on the head and started pulling him toward the car. "You all go on," he said, "I'll be right behind you. Jesse, you go tie up that there dog while I get this car started."

The cars sputtered and coughed and shook; the caravan began to move; bright dust filled the air. As soon as he was tied up, the dog began to bark. Jesse's mother came out of the house, carrying a jacket for his father and a sweater for Jesse. She had put a ribbon in her hair and had an old shawl around her shoulders.

"Put these in the car, son," she said, and handed everything to him. She bent down and stroked the dog, looked to see if there was water in his bowl, then went back up the three porch steps and closed the door.

"Come on," said his father, "ain't nothing in there for nobody to steal." He was sitting in the car, which trembled and belched. The last car of the caravan had disappeared but the sound of singing floated behind them.

Jesse got into the car, sitting close to his father, loving the smell of the car, and the trembling, and the bright day, and the sense of going on a great and unexpected journey. His mother got in and closed the door and the car began to move. Not until then did he ask, "Where are we going? Are we going on a picnic?"

He had a feeling that he knew where they were going, but he was not sure.

"That's right," his father said, "we're going on a picnic. You won't ever forget *this* picnic—!"

"Are we," he asked, after a moment, "going to see the bad nigger— the one that knocked down old Miss Standish?"

"Well, I reckon," said his mother, "that we *might* see him."

He started to ask, *Will a lot of niggers be there? Will Otis be there?* —but he did not ask his question, to which, in a strange and uncomfortable way, he already knew the answer. Their friends, in the other cars, stretched up the road as far as he could see; other cars had joined them; there were cars behind them. They were singing. The sun seemed, suddenly very hot, and he was, at once very happy and a little afraid. He did not quite understand what was happening, and he did not know what to ask—he had no one to ask. He had grown accustomed, for the solution of such mysteries, to go to Otis. He felt that Otis knew everything. But he could not ask Otis about this. Anyway, he had not seen Otis for two days; he had not seen a black face anywhere for more than two days; and he now realized, as they began chugging up the long hill which eventually led to Harkness, that there were no black faces on the road this morning, no black people anywhere. From the houses in which they lived, all along the road, no smoke curled, no life stirred—maybe one or two chickens were to be seen, that was all. There was no one at the windows, no one in the yard, no one sitting on the porches, and the doors were closed. He had come this road many a time and seen women washing in the yard (there were no clothes on the clotheslines) men working in the fields, children playing in the dust; black men passed them on the road other mornings, other days, on foot, or in wagons, sometimes in cars, tipping their hats, smiling, joking, their teeth a solid white against their skin, their eyes as warm as the sun, the blackness of their skin like dull fire against the white of the blue or the grey of their torn clothes. They passed the nigger church—dead-white, desolate, locked up; and the graveyard, where no one knelt or walked, and he saw no flowers. He wanted to ask, *Where are they? Where are they all?* But he did not dare. As the hill grew steeper, the sun grew colder. He looked at his mother and his father. They looked straight ahead, seeming to be listening to the singing which echoed and echoed in this graveyard silence. They were strangers to him now. They were looking at something he could not see. His father's lips had a strange, cruel curve, he wet his lips from time to time, and swallowed. He was terribly aware of his father's tongue, it was as though he had never seen it before. And his father's body suddenly seemed immense, bigger than a mountain. His eyes, which were grey-green, looked yellow in the sunlight; or at least there was a light in them which he had never seen before. His mother patted her hair and adjusted the ribbon, leaning forward to look into the car mirror. "You look all right," said his father, and laughed. "When that nigger looks at you, he's going to swear he throwed his life away for nothing. Wouldn't be surprised if he don't come back to haunt you." And he laughed again.

The singing now slowly began to cease; and he realized that they were nearing their destination. They had reached a straight, narrow, pebbly road, with trees on either side. The sunlight filtered down on them from a great height, as though they were underwater; and the branches of the trees scraped against the cars with a tearing sound. To the right of them, and beneath them, invisible now, lay the town; and to the left, miles of trees which led to the high mountain range which his ancestors had crossed in order to settle in this valley. Now, all was silent, except for the bumping of the tires against the rocky road, the sputtering of motors, and the sound of a crying child. And they seemed to move more slowly. They were beginning to climb again. He watched the cars ahead as they toiled patiently upward, disappearing into the sunlight of the clearing. Presently, he felt their vehicle also rise, heard his father's changed breathing, the sunlight hit his face, the trees moved away from them, and they were there. As their car crossed the clearing, he looked around. There seemed to be millions, there were certainly hundreds of people in the clearing, staring toward something he could not see. There was a fire. He could not see the flames, but he smelled the smoke. They were on the other side of the clearing, among the trees again. His father drove off the road and parked the car behind a great many other cars. He looked down at Jesse.

"You all right?" he asked.

"Yes, sir," he said.

"Well, come on, then," his father said. He reached over and opened the door on his mother's side. His mother stepped out first. They followed her into the clearing. At first he was aware only of confusion, of

Going to Meet the Man   199

his mother and father greeting and being greeted, himself being handled, hugged, and patted, and told how much he had grown. The wind blew the smoke from the fire across the clearing into his eyes and nose. He could not see over the backs of the people in front of him. The sounds of laughing and cursing and wrath—and something else—rolled in waves from the front of the mob to the back. Those in front expressed their delight at what they saw, and this delight rolled backward, wave upon wave, across the clearing, more acrid than the smoke. His father reached down suddenly and sat Jesse on his shoulders.

Now he saw the fire—of twigs and boxes, piled high; flames made pale orange and yellow and thin as a veil under the steadier light of the sun; grey-blue smoke rolled upward and poured over their heads. Beyond the shifting curtain of fire and smoke, he made out first only a length of gleaming chain, attached to a great limb of the tree; then he saw that this chain bound two black hands together at the wrist, dirty yellow palm facing dirty yellow palm. The smoke poured up; the hands dropped out of sight; a cry went up from the crowd. Then the hands slowly came into view again, pulled upward by the chain. This time he saw the kinky, sweating, bloody head—he had never before seen a head with so much hair on it, hair so black and so tangled that it seemed like another jungle. The head was hanging. He saw the forehead, flat and high, with a kind of arrow of hair in the center, like he had, like his father had; they called it a widow's peak; and the mangled eyebrows, the wide nose, the closed eyes, and the glinting eye lashes and the hanging lips, all streaming with blood and sweat. His hands were straight above his head. All his weight pulled downward from his hands; and he was a big man, a bigger man than his father, and black as an African jungle cat, and naked. Jesse pulled upward; his father's hands held him firmly by the ankles. He wanted to say something, he did not know what, but nothing he said could have been heard, for now the crowd roared again as a man stepped forward and put more wood on the fire. The flames leapt up. He thought he heard the hanging man scream, but he was not sure. Sweat was pouring from the hair in his armpits, poured down his sides, over his chest, into his navel and his groin. He was lowered again; he was raised again. Now Jesse knew that he heard him scream. The head went back, the mouth wide open, blood bubbling from the mouth; the veins of the neck jumped out; Jesse clung to his father's neck in terror as the cry rolled over the crowd. The cry of all the people rose to answer the dying man's cry. He wanted death to come quickly. They wanted to make death wait: and it was they who held death, now, on a leash which they lengthened little by little. *What did he do?* Jesse wondered. *What did the man do? What did he do?* —but he could not ask his father. He was seated on his father's shoulders, but his father was far away. There were two older men, friends of his father's, raising and lowering the chain; everyone, indiscriminately, seemed to be responsible for the fire. There was no hair left on the nigger's privates, and the eyes, now, were wide open, as white as the eyes of a clown or a doll. The smoke now carried a terrible odor across the clearing, the odor of something burning which was both sweet and rotten.

He turned his head a little and saw the field of faces. He watched his mother's face. Her eyes were very bright, her mouth was open: she was more beautiful than he had ever seen her, and more strange. He began to feel a joy he had never felt before. He watched the hanging, gleaming body, the most beautiful and terrible object he had ever seen till then. One of his father's friends reached up and in his hands he held a knife: and Jesse wished that he had been that man. It was a long, bright knife and the sun seemed to catch it, to play with it, to caress it—it was brighter than the fire. And a wave of laughter swept the crowd. Jesse felt his father's hands on his ankles slip and tighten. The man with the knife walked toward the crowd, smiling slightly; as though this were a signal, silence fell; he heard his mother cough. Then the man with the knife walked up to the hanging body. He turned and smiled again. Now there was a silence all over the field. The hanging head looked up. It seemed fully conscious now, as though the fire had burned out terror and pain. The man with the knife took the nigger's privates in his hand, one hand, still smiling, as though he were weighing them. In the cradle of the one white hand, the nigger's privates seemed as remote as meat being weighed in the scales; but seemed heavier, too, much heavier, and Jesse felt his scrotum tighten; and huge, huge, much bigger than his father's, flaccid, hairless, the largest thing he had ever seen till then, and the blackest. The white hand streched them, cradled them, caressed them. Then the dying man's eyes looked straight into Jesse's eyes—it could not have been as long as a second, but it seemed longer than a year. Then Jesse screamed, and the crowd screamed as the knife flashed, first up, then down, cutting the dreadful thing away, and the blood came roaring down. Then the crowd rushed forward, tearing at the body with their hands, with knives, with rocks, with stones, howling and cursing. Jesse's head, of its own weight, fell downward toward his father's head. Someone stepped forward and drenched the body with kerosene. Where the man had been, a great sheet of flame appeared. Jesse's father lowered him to the ground.

"Well, I told you," said his father, "you wasn't never going to forget *this* picnic." His father's face was full of sweat, his eyes were very peaceful. At that moment Jesse loved his father more than he had ever loved him. He felt that his father had carried him through a mighty test, had revealed to him a great secret which would be the key to his life forever.

"I reckon," he said. "I reckon."

Going to Meet the Man 201

Jesse's father took him by the hand and, with his mother a little behind them, talking and laughing with the other women, they walked through the crowd, across the clearing. The black body was on the ground, the chain which had held it was being rolled up by one of his father's friends. Whatever the fire had left undone, the hands and the knives and the stones of the people had accomplished. The head was caved in, one eye was torn out, one ear was hanging. But one had to look carefully to realize this, for it was, now, merely, a black charred object on the black, charred ground. He lay spread-eagled with what had been a wound between what had been his legs.

"They going to leave him here, then?" Jesse whispered.

"Yeah," said his father, "they'll come and get him by and by. I reckon we better get over there and get some of that food before it's all gone."

"I reckon," he muttered now to himself, "I reckon." Grace stirred and touched him on the thigh: the moonlight covered her like glory. Something bubbled up in him, his nature again returned to him. He thought of the boy in the cell; he thought of the man in the fire; he thought of the knife and grabbed himself and stroked himself and a terrible sound, something between a high laugh and a howl, came out of him and dragged his sleeping wife up on one elbow. She stared at him in a moonlight which had now grown cold as ice. He thought of the morning and grabbed her, laughing and crying, crying and laughing, and he whispered, as he stroked her, as he took her, "Come on, sugar, I'm going to do you like a nigger, just like a nigger, come on, sugar, and love me just like you'd love a nigger." He thought of the morning as he labored and she moaned, thought of morning as he labored harder than he ever had before, and before his labors had ended, he heard the first cock crow and the dogs begin to bark, and the sound of tires on the gravel road.

■ DISCUSSION AND QUESTIONS

1. In this story Baldwin goes inside the mind of a white Southern deputy sheriff to show how this man's hatred of "niggers" began and how it gnaws away at his manhood, his very sense of who he is. Baldwin, of course, could have told a story about the Black victims of this man's evil, but instead he chose to try to explain or understand Jesse's behavior—explain, not forgive. Is it possible that Baldwin used this limited omniscient point of view in order to keep the lid on his own emotions so they wouldn't boil over as he wrote a story about the stupidity and evil of a lynch-mob mentality? In other words, doesn't his aesthetic choice help him restrain his moral fury? And doesn't it prove the "humanity" of Baldwin as well?

2. The story takes place one night —for Jesse a night of fear and impo-

tence. How much insight does Jesse have into his fear, hatred, and impotence?

3. As Jesse lies in the dark, frightened by the sounds of tires on the gravel, we are reminded that other men, Black men, have lain in the dark, their eyes and ears straining to sense the presence of someone out to get them. The victimizer has become the victim. What is the relationship of fear and potency?

4. How much does Jesse understand about the political actions of the Blacks or about the needs and deprivations that lead to violent confrontations?

5. As Jesse lies waiting, he remembers a family trip to a lynching which became for the boy a kind of initiation. Baldwin says, "He [Jesse] felt that his father had carried him through a mighty test, had revealed to him a great secret which would be the key to his life forever" (p.200). How are Jesse's father and mother affected by the lynching? How is young Jesse changed by witnessing this macabre celebration?

6. "He thought of the boy in the cell; he thought of the man in the fire; he thought of the knife and grabbed himself and stroked himself and a terrible sound, something between a high laugh and a howl, came out of him and dragged his sleeping wife up on one elbow." After he recalls the lynching and specifically the way the Black victim's "privates" were cut off with a knife, Jesse's "nature" returns to him and he can "take" his wife. What does this sequence of events indicate about the source of Jesse's potency? About the sexual strength of victimizers?

7. Compare Jesse's feelings about Black women with his feelings about his wife. What is the meaning of Jesse's whisper to his wife at the end of the story, "Come on, sugar, I'm going to do you like a nigger, just like a nigger, come on, sugar, and love me just like you'd love a nigger"?

8. How does the fact that we know so much about what goes on in Jesse's mind—his doubts, his anger, his fears —influence our judgment of him? Has Baldwin chosen a point of view that allows us to feel some sympathy or compassion for Jesse, or perhaps a combination of sympathy and loathing?

9. Is Jesse also a victim of racism? Of his parents' racism?

End of the Game

Julio Cortázar

Letitia, Holanda and I used to play by the Argentine Central tracks during the hot weather, hoping that Mama and Aunt Ruth would go up to their siesta so that we could get out past the white gate. After washing the dishes, Mama and Aunt Ruth were always tired, especially when Holanda and I were drying, because it was then that there were arguments, spoons on the floor, secret words that only we understood, and in general, an atmosphere in which the smell of grease, José's yowling, and the dimness of the kitchen would end up in an incredible fight and the subsequent commotion. Holanda specialized in rigging this sort of brawl, for example, letting an already clean glass slip into the pan of dirty water, or casually dropping a remark to the effect that the Loza house had two maids to do all the work. I had other systems: I liked to suggest to Aunt Ruth that she was going to get an allergy rash on her hands if she kept scrubbing the pots instead of doing the cups and plates once in a while, which were exactly what Mama liked to wash, and over which they would confront one another soundlessly in a war of advantage to get the easy item. The heroic expedient, in case the bits of advice and the drawn-out family recollections began to bore us, was to upset some boiling water on the cat's back. Now that's a big lie about a scalded cat, it really is, except that you have to take the reference to cold water literally; because

From *End of the Game and Other Stories,* by Julio Cortázar, translated by Paul Blackburn. Copyright © 1967, 1963 by Random House, Inc. Reprinted by permission of Pantheon Books, a Division of Random House, Inc.

José never backed away from hot water, almost insinuating himself under it, poor animal, when we spilled a half-cup of it somewhere around 220° F, or less, a good deal less, probably, because his hair never fell out. The whole point was to get Troy burning, and in the confusion, crowned by a splendid G-flat from Aunt Ruth and Mama's sprint for the whipstick, Holanda and I would take no time at all to get lost in the long porch, toward the empty rooms off the back, where Letitia would be waiting for us, reading Ponson de Terrail, or some other equally inexplicable book.

Normally, Mama chased us a good part of the way, but her desire to bust in our skulls evaporated soon enough, and finally (we had barred the door and were begging for mercy in emotion-filled and very theatrical voices), she got tired and went off, repeating the same sentence: "Those ruffians'll end up on the street."

Where we ended up was by the Argentine Central tracks, when the house had settled down and was silent, and we saw the cat stretched out under the lemon tree to take its siesta also, a rest buzzing with fragrances and wasps. We'd open the white gate slowly, and when we shut it again with a slam like a blast of wind, it was a freedom which took us by the hands, seized the whole of our bodies and tumbled us out. Then we ran, trying to get the speed to scramble up the low embankment of the right-of-way, and there spread out upon the world, we silently surveyed our kingdom.

Our kingdom was this: a long curve of the tracks ended its bend just opposite the back section of the house. There was just the gravel incline, the crossties, and the double line of track; some dumb sparse grass among the rubble where mica, quartz and feldspar—the components of granite—sparkled like real diamonds in the two o'clock afternoon sun. When we stooped down to touch the rails (not wasting time because it would have been dangerous to spend much time there, not so much from the trains as for fear of being seen from the house), the heat off the stone roadbed flushed our faces, and facing into the wind from the river there was a damp heat against our cheeks and ears. We liked to bend our legs and squat down, rise, squat again, move from one kind of hot zone to the other, watching each other's faces to measure the perspiration—a minute or two later we would be sopping with it. And we were always quiet, looking down the track into the distance, or at the river on the other side, that stretch of coffee-and-cream river.

After this first inspection of the kingdom, we'd scramble down the bank and flop in the meager shadow of the willows next the wall enclosing the house where the white gate was. This was the capital city of the kingdom, the wilderness city and the headquarters of our game. Letitia was the first to start the game; she was the luckiest and the most privileged of the three of us. Letitia didn't have to dry dishes or make the beds, she could laze

End of the Game 205

away the day reading or pasting up pictures, and at night they let her stay up later if she asked to, not counting having a room to herself, special hot broth when she wanted it, and all kinds of other advantages. Little by little she had taken more and more advantage of these privileges, and had been presiding over the game since the summer before, I think really she was presiding over the whole kingdom; in any case she was quicker at saying things, and Holanda and I accepted them without protest, happy almost. It's likely that Mama's long lectures on how we ought to behave toward Letitia had had their effect, or simply that we loved her enough and it didn't bother us that she was boss. A pity that she didn't have the looks for the boss, she was the shortest of the three of us and very skinny. Holanda was skinny, and I never weighed over 110, but Letitia was scragglier than we were, and even worse, that kind of skinniness you can see from a distance in the neck and ears. Maybe it was the stiffness of her back that made her look so thin, for instance she could hardly move her head from side to side, she was like a folded-up ironing board, one of those kind they had in the Loza house, with a cover of white material. Like an ironing board with the wide part up, leaning closed against the wall. And she led us.

The best satisfaction was to imagine that someday Mama or Aunt Ruth would find out about the game. If they managed to find out about the game there would be an unbelievable mess. The G-flat and fainting fits, incredible protests of devotion and sacrifice ill-rewarded, and a string of words threatening the more celebrated punishments, closing the bid with a dire prediction of our fates, which consisted of the three of us ending up on the street. This final prediction always left us somewhat perplexed, because to end up in the street always seemed fairly normal to us.

First Letitia had us draw lots. We used to use pebbles hidden in the hand, count to twenty-one, any way at all. If we used the count-to-twenty-one system, we would pretend two or three more girls and include them in the counting to prevent cheating. If one of them came out 21, we dropped her from the group and started drawing again, until one of us won. Then Holanda and I lifted the stone and we got out the ornament-box. Suppose Holanda had won, Letitia and I chose the ornaments. The game took two forms: Statues and Attitudes. Attitudes did not require ornaments but an awful lot of expressiveness, for Envy you could show your teeth, make fists and hold them in a position so as to seem cringing. For Charity the ideal was an angelic face, eyes turned up to the sky, while the hands offered something—a rag, a ball, a branch of willow—to a poor invisible orphan. Shame and Fear were easy to do; Spite and Jealousy required a more conscientious study. The Statues were determined, almost all of them, by the choice of ornaments, and here absolute liberty reigned. So that a statue would come out of it, one had to think carefully of every detail in the costume. It was a rule of the game that the one chosen could not take part in the selection; the two remaining argued out the business at hand and then fitted the ornaments on. The winner had to invent her statue taking into account what they'd dressed her in, and in this way the game was much more complicated and exciting because sometimes there were counterplots, and the victim would find herself rigged out in adornments which were completely hopeless; so it was up to her to be quick then in composing a good statue. Usually when the game called for Attitudes, the winner came up pretty well outfitted, but there were times when the Statues were horrible failures.

Well, the story I'm telling, lord knows when it began, but things changed the day the first note fell from the train. Naturally the Attitudes and Statues were not for our own consumption, we'd have gotten bored immediately. The rules were that the winner had to station herself at the foot of the embankment, leaving the shade of the willow trees, and wait for the train from Tigre that passed at 2:08. At that height above Palermo the trains went by pretty fast and we weren't bashful doing the Statue or the Attitude. We hardly saw the people in the train windows, but with time, we got a bit more expert, and we knew that some of the passengers were expecting to see us. One man with white hair and tortoise-shell glasses used to stick his head out of the window and wave at the Statue or the Attitude with a handkerchief. Boys sitting on the steps of the coaches on their way back from school shouted things as the train went by, but some of them remained serious and watching us. In actual fact, the Statue or the Attitude saw nothing at all, because she had to concentrate so hard on holding herself stock-still, but the other two under the willows would analyze in excruciating detail the great success produced, or the audience indifference. It was a Wednesday when the note dropped as the second coach went by. It fell very near Holanda (she did Malicious Gossip that day) and ricocheted toward me. The small piece of paper was tightly folded up and had been shoved through a metal nut. In a man's handwriting, and pretty bad too, it said: "The Statues very pretty. I ride in the third window of the second coach. Ariel B." For all the trouble of stuffing it through the nut and tossing it, it seemed to us a little dry, but it delighted us. We chose lots to see who would keep it, and I won. The next day nobody wanted to play because we all wanted to see what Ariel B. was like, but we were afraid he would misinterpret our interruption, so finally we chose lots and Letitia won. Holanda and I were very happy because Letitia did Statues very well, poor thing. The paralysis wasn't noticeable when she was still, and she was capable of gestures of enormous nobility. With Attitudes she always chose Generosity, Piety, Sacrifice and Renunciation. With Statues she tried for the style of the Venus in the parlor which Aunt Ruth called the Venus de Milo. For that reason we chose ornaments especially so that Ariel would be very impressed. We hung a piece of green velvet on her like a tunic, and a crown of willow on her hair. As we were wearing short sleeves, the Greek effect was terrific. Letitia practiced a little in the shade, and we decided that we'd show ourselves also and wave at Ariel, discreetly, but very friendly.

Letitia was magnificent, when the train came she didn't budge a finger. Since she couldn't turn her head, she threw it backward, bringing her arms against her body almost as though she were missing them; except for the green tunic, it was like looking at the Venus de Milo. In the third window we saw a boy with blond curly hair and light eyes, who smiled brightly when he saw that Holanda and I were waving at him. The train was gone in a second, but it was 4:30 and we were still discussing whether he was wearing a dark suit, a red tie, and if he were really nice or a creep. On Thursday I did an Attitude, Dejection, and we got another note which read: "The three of you I like very much. Ariel." Now he stuck his head and one arm out the window and laughed and waved at us. We figured him to be eighteen (we were sure he was no older than sixteen), and we decided that he was coming back every day from some English school, we couldn't stand the idea of any of the regular peanut factories. You could see that Ariel was super.

As it happened, Holanda had the terrific luck to win three days running. She surpassed herself, doing the attitudes Reproach and Robbery, and a very difficult Statue of The Ballerina, balancing on one foot from the time the train hit the curve. The next day I won, and the day after that too; when I was doing Horror, a note from Ariel almost caught me on the nose; at first we didn't understand it: "The prettiest is the laziest." Letitia was the last to understand it; we saw that she blushed and went off by herself, and Holanda and I looked at each other, just a little furious. The first judicial opinion it occurred to us to hand down was that Ariel was an idiot, but we couldn't tell Letitia that, poor angel, with the disadvantage she had to put up with. She said nothing, but it seemed to be understood that the paper was hers, and she kept it. We were sort of quiet going back to the house that day, and didn't get together that night. Letitia was very happy at the supper table, her eyes shining, and Mama looked at Aunt Ruth a couple of times as evidence of her own high spirits. In those days they were trying out a new strengthening treatment for Letitia, and considering how she looked, it was miraculous how well she was feeling.

Before we went to sleep, Holanda and I talked about the business. The note from Ariel didn't bother us so much, thrown from a train going its own way, that's how it is, but it seemed to us that Letitia from her privileged position was taking too much advantage of us. She knew we weren't going to say anything to her, and in a household where there's someone with some physical defect and a lot of pride, everyone pretends to ignore it starting with the one who's sick, or better yet, they pretend they don't know that the other one knows. But you don't have to exaggerate it either, and the way Letitia was acting at the table, or the way she kept the note, was just too much. That night I went back to having nightmares about trains, it was morning and I was walking on enormous railroad beaches covered with rails filled with switches, seeing in the distance the red glows of locomotives approaching, anxiously trying to calculate if the train was going to pass to my left and threatened at the same time by the arrival of an express back of me or—what was even worse—that one of the trains would switch off onto one of the sidings and run directly over me. But I forgot it by morning because Letitia was all full of aches and we had to help her get dressed. It seemed to us that she was a little sorry for the business yesterday and we were very nice to her, telling her that's what happens with walking too much and that maybe it would be better for her to stay in her room reading. She said nothing but came to the table for breakfast, and when Mama asked, she said she was fine and her back hardly hurt at all. She stated it firmly and looked at us.

That afternoon I won, but at that moment, I don't know what came over me, I told Letitia that I'd give her my place, naturally without telling her why. That this guy clearly preferred her and would look at her until his eyes fell out. The game drew to Statues, and we selected simple items so as not to complicate life, and she invented a sort of Chinese Princess, with a shy air, looking at the ground, and the hands placed together as Chinese princesses are wont to do. When the train passed, Holanda was lying on her back under the willows, but I watched and saw that Ariel had eyes only for Letitia. He kept looking at her until the train disappeared around the curve, and Letitia stood there motionless and didn't know that he had just looked at her that way. But when it came to resting under the trees again, we saw that she knew all right, and that she'd have been pleased to keep the costume on all afternoon and all night.

Wednesday we drew between Holanda and me, because Letitia said it was only fair she be left out. Holanda won, darn her luck, but Ariel's letter fell next to me. When I picked it up I had the impulse to give it to Letitia who didn't say a word, but I thought, then, that neither was it a matter of catering to everybody's wishes, and I opened it slowly. Ariel announced that the next day he was going to get off at the nearby station and that he would come by the embankment to chat for a while. It was all terribly written, but the final phrase was handsomely put: "Warmest regards to the three Statues." The signature looked like a scrawl though we remarked on its personality.

While we were taking the ornaments off Holanda, Letitia looked at me once or twice. I'd read them the message and no one had made any comments, which was very upsetting because finally, at last, Ariel was going to come and one had to think about this new development and come to some decision. If they found out about it at the house, or if by accident one of the Loza girls, those envious little runts, came to spy on us, there was going to be one incredible mess. Furthermore, it was extremely unlike us to remain silent over a thing like this; we hardly looked at one another, putting the ornaments away and going back through the white gate to the house.

Aunt Ruth asked Holanda and me to wash the cat, and she took Letitia off for the evening treatment and finally we could get our feelings off our chests. It seemed super that Ariel was going to come, we'd never had a friend like that, our cousin Tito we didn't count, a dumbbell who cut out paper dolls and believed in first communion. We were extremely nervous in our expectation and José, poor angel, got the short end of it. Holanda was the braver of the two and brought up the subject of Letitia. I didn't know what to think, on the one hand it seemed ghastly to me that Ariel should find out, but also it was only fair that things clear themselves up, no one had to out-and-out put herself on the line for someone else. What I really would have wanted was that Letitia not suffer; she had enough to put up with and now the new treatment and all those things.

That night Mama was amazed to see us so quiet and said what a miracle, and had the cat got our tongues, then looked at Aunt Ruth and both of them thought for sure we'd been raising hell of some kind and were conscience-stricken. Letitia ate very little and said that she hurt and would they let her go to her room to read Rocambole. Though she didn't much want to, Holanda gave her a hand, and I sat down and started some knitting, something I do only when I'm nervous. Twice I thought to go down to Letitia's room, I couldn't figure out what the two of them were doing there alone, but then Holanda came back with a mysterious air of importance and sat next to me not saying a word until Mama and Aunt Ruth cleared the table. "She doesn't want to go tomorrow. She wrote a letter and said that if he asks a lot of questions we should give it to him." Half-opening the pocket of her blouse she showed me the lilac-tinted envelope. Then they called us in to dry the dishes, and that night we fell asleep almost immediately, exhausted by all the high-pitched emotion and from washing José.

The next day it was my turn to do the marketing and I didn't see Letitia all morning, she stayed in her room. Before they called us to lunch I went in for a moment and found her sitting at the window with a pile of pillows and a new Rocambole novel. You could see she felt terrible, but she started to laugh and told me about a bee that couldn't find its way out and about a funny dream she had had. I said it was a pity she wasn't coming out to the willows, but I found it difficult to put it nicely. "If you want, we can explain to Ariel that you feel upset," I suggested, but she said no and shut up like a clam. I insisted for a little while, really, that she should come, and finally got terribly gushy and told her she shouldn't be afraid, giving as an example that true affection knows no barriers and other fat ideas we'd gotten from *The Treasure of Youth,* but it got harder and harder to say anything to her because she was looking out the window and looked as if she were going to cry. Finally I left, saying that Mama needed me. Lunch lasted for days, and Holanda got a slap from Aunt Ruth for having spattered some tomato sauce from the spaghetti onto the tablecloth. I don't even remember doing the dishes, right away we were out under the willows hugging one another, very happy, and not jealous of one another in the slightest. Holanda explained to me everything we had to say about our studies so that Ariel would be impressed, because high school students despised girls who'd only been through grade school and studied just home ec and knew how to do raised needlework. When the train went past at 2:08, Ariel waved his arms enthusiastically, and we waved a welcome to him with our embossed handkerchiefs. Some twenty minutes later we saw him arrive by the embankment; he was taller than we had thought and dressed all in grey.

    I don't even remember what we talked about at first; he was somewhat shy in spite of having come and the notes and everything, and said a lot of considerate things. Almost immediately he praised our Statues and Attitudes and asked our names, and why had the third one not come. Holanda explained that Letitia had not been able to come, and he said that that was a pity and that he thought Letitia was an exquisite name. Then he told us stuff about the Industrial High School, it was not the English school, unhappily, and wanted to know if we would show him the ornaments. Holanda lifted the stone and we let him see the things. He seemed to be very interested in them, and at different times he would take one of the ornaments and say, "Letitia wore this one day," or "This was for the Oriental statue," what he meant was the Chinese Princess. We sat in the shade under a willow and he was happy but distracted, and you could see that he was only being polite. Holanda looked at me two or three times when the conversation lapsed into silence, and that made both of us feel awful, made us want to get out of it, or wish that Ariel had never come at all. He asked again if Letitia were ill and Holanda looked at me and I thought she was going to tell him, but instead she answered that Letitia had not been able to come. Ariel drew geometric figures in the dust with a stick and occasionally looked at the white gate and we knew what he was thinking, and because of that Holanda was right to pull out the lilac envelope and hand it up to him, and he stood there surprised with the envelope in his hand; then he blushed while we explained to him that Letitia had sent it to him, and he put the letter in an inside jacket

pocket, not wanting to read it in front of us. Almost immediately he said that it had been a great pleasure for him and that he was delighted to have come, but his hand was soft and unpleasant in a way it'd have been better for the interview to end right away, although later we could only think of his grey eyes and the sad way he had of smiling. We also agreed on how he had said good-bye: "Until always," a form we'd never heard at home and which seemed to us so godlike and poetic. We told all this to Letitia who was waiting for us under the lemon tree in the patio, and I would have liked to have asked her what she had said in the letter, but I don't know because she'd sealed the envelope before giving it to Holanda, so I didn't say anything about that and only told her what Ariel was like and how many times he'd asked for her. This was not at all an easy thing to do because it was a nice thing and a terrible thing at the same time; we noticed that Letitia was feeling very happy and at the same time she was almost crying, and we found ourselves saying that Aunt Ruth wanted us now and we left her looking at the wasps in the lemon tree.

When we were going to sleep that night, Holanda said to me, "The game's finished from tomorrow on, you'll see." But she was wrong though not by much, and the next day Letitia gave us the regular signal when dessert came around. We went out to wash the dishes somewhat astonished, and a bit sore, because that was sheer sauciness on Letitia's part and not the right thing to do. She was waiting for us at the gate, and we almost died of fright when we got to the willows for she brought out of her pocket Mama's pearl collar and all her rings, even Aunt Ruth's big one with the ruby. If the Loza girls were spying on us and saw us with the jewels, sure as anything Mama would learn about it right away and kill us, the nasty little creeps. But Letitia wasn't scared and said if anything happened she was the only one responsible. "I would like you to leave it to me today," she added without looking at us. We got the ornaments out right away, all of a sudden we wanted to be very kind to Letitia and give her all the pleasure, although at the bottom of everything we were still feeling a little spiteful. The game came out Statues, and we chose lovely things that would go well with the jewels, lots of peacock feathers to set in the hair, and a fur that from a distance looked like silver fox, and a pink veil that she put on like a turban. We saw that she was thinking, trying the Statue out, but without moving, and when the train appeared on the curve she placed herself at the foot of the incline with all the jewels sparkling in the sun. She lifted her arms as if she were going to do an Attitude instead of a Statue, her hands pointed at the sky with her head thrown back (the only direction she could, poor thing) and bent her body backwards so far it scared us. To us it seemed terrific, the most regal statue she'd ever done; then we saw Ariel looking at her, hung halfway out the window he looked just at her, turning his head and looking at her without seeing us, until the train carried him out of sight all at once. I don't know why, the two of us started running at the same time to catch Letitia who was standing there, still with her eyes closed and enormous tears all down her face. She pushed us back, not angrily, but we helped her stuff the jewels in her pocket, and she went back to the house alone while we put the ornaments away in their box for the last time. We knew almost what was going to happen, but just the same we went out to the willows the next day, just the two of us, after Aunt Ruth imposed absolute silence so as not to disturb Letitia who hurt and who wanted to sleep. When the train came by, it was no surprise to see the third window empty, and while we were grinning at one another, somewhere between relief and being furious, we imagined Ariel riding on the other side of the coach, not moving in his seat, looking off toward the river with his grey eyes.

■ DISCUSSION AND QUESTIONS

1. Julio Cortazar is a man, yet he chooses to have a woman tell this story about girls growing up. Sex, age, color of skin impose no restrictions on the imaginative writer's choice of a point of view for his/her stories. Consider other possible ways of narrating this story. What changes would result if Ariel were the narrator? Or Letitia?

2. The mystery of this story is the wonderful, strange love that develops between Ariel and Letitia and builds to the climatic moment when Letitia, bedecked in *real* jewels for a change, assumes the last "regal" pose of the game. Even the narrator has not penetrated to the heart of this mystery. She cannot know what goes on in Letitia's mind, what her feelings are about Ariel, or how painful the crippled back is. The narrator cannot tell the reader why Letitia assumes the painful pose for Ariel and then holds it until tears flow down her face. The narrator cannot tell why Ariel stops coming on the train or why the game ends, nor does she know the contents of Letitia's letter. Instead the reader is invited to infer answers to these questions from the actions of the story. If Letitia had told the story, she could have made quite clear how she felt about Ariel, about her possibilities for love, about her secret desires and fears, about the physical and emotional pain of being crippled.

3. We can infer that "the game" means different things to Letitia than to the healthy girls. The narrator cannot tell us the differences because she cannot know them. Does the reader know more than the narrator about what the game means for Letitia? What does it mean for her? Why does she take her mother's and her aunt's jewels for the last statue? What did Letitia tell Ariel in the letter?

4. Characterize the narrator. What are her attitudes toward the game? How many years after the end of the

game is she telling the story? What are her attitudes toward Letitia?

5. The game is a kind of theatrical event—young women in costumes holding poses for passengers on a train. All the passengers mentioned are male; all the members of the family are female. The narrator recalls her nightmares, and her description of these dreams seem blatantly sexual, the dreams of a pubescent girl.

Is the game itself a symbol? Why Statues and Attitudes?

6. Why must the game end?

The Vampires of Istanbul:
A Study in Modern Communications Methods

Edouard Roditi

Yeni Aksham, Istanbul, 7 February 1960, front page:

Our readers will be justifiably shocked to hear that cases of vampirism can still occur in the heart of a modern metropolis like Istanbul. Yesterday morning, the police of our city was suddenly called upon to investigate such a case and promptly arrested the chief culprit, Mahmut Osmanoglu, a carter, 48 years old, a native of Edirne, living in Fener at Küchük Gülhane Djaddesi 37.

While giving her ten-year-old son Hasan his weekly bath, Füreya Öztürk, a mother of five children living at Küchük Gülhane Djaddesi 11, noticed yesterday a suspicious scar on the child's upper arm. She recognized it at once as the mark left by the needle of a hypodermic syringe and began to question the boy. He then admitted that he and two of his companions had been accosted in the street the day before by an older man who promised to give them sweetmeats if they accompanied him to his room. The three boys agreed, in their innocence, and found themselves offered by the carter to two other vampires who had been waiting for him there while he went out to recruit their victims.

Hasan described to his mother in great detail the orgy of vampirism which then took place. The three men produced hypodermic syringes with which each one extracted blood from the upper arm of his chosen

Copyright © 1972 by New Directions Publishing Corporation.

victim, after which they drank this blood from ordinary tea glasses with great relish while the boys were given cordials and sweetmeats to help them recover from their fright.

Accompanied by her son, Füreya Öztürk went immediately to the nearest police station in the Fener district of our city, where she is well known as a respectable housewife, the pensioned widow of a Turkish war hero who was killed in Korea while fighting the Communists. To the sympathetic local police captain, she repeated her atrocious story. Quite understandably, the poor woman was in tears, as the police captain subsequently told our reporter. Two policemen, Muzafer Tavukdjuoglu and Ali Hamit, were sent out at once to investigate the case. Fortunately, the boy could still remember the house where he had been a victim of this disgusting orgy of vampirism. He was able to lead the police upstairs to the door of the very room which had been the scene of the crime. But the door was locked and the police found nobody there. Enquiries in the neighborhood revealed that the carter Mahmut Osmanoglu was probably still at work but could be found at home later in the evening.

The police waited till seven o'clock and then came again and found the carter alone in the lodging where he generally lives with his mother. He had just returned from work and, faced with an account of his crime, denied it. He admitted, however, that he and his two companions had practiced unnatural vices with the three boys and recompensed them as usual with sweetmeats. The three boys, he claimed, were regular visitors to his room, where they seemed to take pleasure in his company and in that of his friends. Mahmut Osmanoglu was then arrested on the charge of vampirism and the case is being investigated.

Yeni Aksham, 8 February 1960, p. 3, local news.

Mahmut Osmanoglu, the Vampire of Fener, has been unable or unwilling to identify for the police the two other vampires who perpetrated with him the disgusting crimes which we reported yesterday. After several hours of interrogation at the local police station and later at police headquarters, he finally alleged that he knew only one of the other two vampires, a member of our city's police force who visits him quite often in his room in the evening, often bringing an anonymous companion and threatening to arrest the carter for some past crime if he refuses to go out and recruit young vicitms for their orgies of blood-drinking. Police headquarters deny the validity of the carter's story, pointing out that it is an obvious attempt to discourage any further move on their part to uncover what now appears to be a secret network of vampires operating in this city.

Yeni Aksham, 10 February 1960, p. 3.

A second case of vampirism has been reported from Langna, where two young mothers saw an unknown old woman approach their little daughters in the street and offer sweetmeats to the children. The old woman was attacked and beaten by the indignant mothers and was already lying unconscious in the street when the police reached the scene of the incident and intervened. As it was impossible to question her on account of her condition, the woman was taken to hospital, pending further investigation of the matter. She has meanwhile been identified as Meriam Terzibashjian, 72 years of age, a native of Elazig and a widow, presently employed as a cleaning woman in the kitchens of the Armenian hospital in Psamatia.

Yeni Aksham 12 February 1960, p. 1 of the Weekly Literary and Scientific Supplement.

We have pleasure in offering to our readers today a scientific study on vampirism by Professor Reshat Allalemdji, the well-known authority whose recent proposals for solving Instanbul's traffic problems, by reducing the frequency of accident-proneness through psychoanalysis of all convicted violators of traffic regulations, caused so much comment when we published them here a few weeks ago. Professor Allalemdji studied medicine at Leipzig University, where a special course on vampirism is an integral part of the training of all medical students in the neuropsychiatric clinic of this world-famous university.—THE EDITORS

Though fortunately rare as a vice or as what we scientists who are not moralists prefer to call a mental disease, vampirism is one of those evils that have continued to plague mankind since the very dawn of civilization. There exist among us a number of unfortunate men and women whose physical health requires that they absorb regularly certain quantities of fresh human blood. If deprived of this diet, they die within a few days of a rare kind of pernicious anemia for which no adequate cure has yet been discovered. Whether their dread disease is hereditary or not, we may never be able to ascertain, cases of vampirism being fortunately so rare that it has so far proven impossible to compare and investigate them scientifically. Besides, most vampies, when caught and questioned, remain extremely reticent about their ghoulish habits.

For many centuries, our knowledge of vampirism was thus founded almost exclusively on a few legendary cases that had so shocked popular imagination that they had been committed to memory in ballads, fairy tales and other forms of folklore. The well-known story of Little Red Ridinghood and the Wolf is thus but a disguised account of a legendary French case of vampirism. The famous German poet Goethe also refers to a case of vampirism, probably of German origin, in his poem entitled *Der Erlkönig*.

Modern anthropology has revealed, however, that "where there is smoke there must also be fire," and that folklore and legends are the repository of truths which have survived from prehistoric times when man was not yet able to record in writing the facts that he had observed. Subsequent generations gradually distorted or embellished these facts with the inevitable inaccuracies of oral tradition. Legendary tales of vampirism are therefore being investigated scientifically by modern anthropologists in order to find out whether we have to deal here with a mental or physical disease, or perhaps with the clandestine practices of some secret cannibalistic religious cult. The present case of the vampires of Fener may thus offer Turkish scientists a rare opportunity to study in real life and at first hand what they all too often know only from the very secondary sources of folklore and legend.

Fortunately, history has already recorded two famous cases of vampirism which led to sensational trials in periods which have left us reliable firsthand documents. The first of these cases is that of Gilles de Rais (1404–1440), a man who was a Marshal of France and the companion in arms of Joan of Arc. After her trial and execution on a false accusation of witchcraft, he appears to have become, in spite of his distinguished military past and the responsibilities of his position, involved in the most disgusting practices of sorcery. At the time of his arrest and trial in Nantes, it was proven beyond dispute that he had already tortured and murdered at least eight hundred male adolescents. Though it was alleged by the prosecution that he had sacrificed them to the Devil in the course of criminal Black Masses, it is now generally agreed that he was a vampire and that the elaborate ceremonies that he conducted served only as a setting for obscene sacraments in the course of which he drank the blood of his young victims.

The second case, that of Countess Elizabeth Batthyani (1580–1640), occurred in Hungary. At the time of her trial, it was proven that she had enticed over six hundred attractive peasant girls into her castle, from which not one of them had even been seen to return alive. Witnesses at her trial testified that, whenever she saw a beautiful young girl, her mouth literally watered, so that the saliva could be seen dripping from her chin. Ever since the horrible revelations of her trial, human vampires have been believed to exist in quite large numbers in certain rural areas of Hungary, where cases of vampirism have again and again been denounced to the authorities, especially in those disputed frontier provinces, such as Transylvania and the Banat, where the feudal landowners were Hungarian nobles who ruthlessly exploited their Slavic or Rumanian serfs.

The Turkish vampires whose shocking practices have recently been revealed may thus prove, on further investigation, to be descendants of Hungarian vampires who came and settled in Istanbul when Hungary was still a province of our glorious Ottoman Empire, which might then add grist to the mills of those scientists who believe vampirism to be a hereditary disease. In any case, vampirism appears to be something utterly alien to our national character, since we find no mention of it in our native Turkish or Turanian folklore.

Professor Fakir Allalemdji
Psychiatrist,
Bakirköy Mental Hospital

Yeni Aksham 14 February 1960, p. 3.

The police continue to investigate the case of the vampires of Fener, diligently seeking to identify the two unknown accomplices who participated with the carter Mahmut Osmanoglu in the scenes of vampirism which he organized for them in his room. Yesterday, the three boys who had been victims of the orgy of drinking human blood that we had reported were brought face to face with the carter. Two of the boys failed to recognize him, declaring that they had never seen him before, which seems scarcely likely as they happen to be his neighbors, living in the same street where everyone knows everyone else, at least by sight. But these two boys also refuse to admit ever having been victims of any orgy of vampirism.

Only Hasan Öztürk continues to assert that he and his two companions had accompanied the carter to his room and met two other men there, after which the three older men took blood from the boys with hypodermic syringes and drank it fresh in tea glasses. Pressed by the police for a more detailed description of these two other men, Hasan Öztürk, who had already recognized and identified the carter Mahmut Osmanoglu as the man who first accosted him and his two companions in the street and organized in his room the whole orgy, now gave the following description of the two other unidentified culprits. One of them is tall and dark, about twenty-five years of age, wears a mustache and looks like a goalkeeper of the Fenerbahtche football team. The other is some ten years older and looks like the German film star Curd Jurgens. Police enquiries reveal, however, that Hamdi Kotcha, the well-known goalkeeper of the Fenerbahtche football team, was absent from Istanbul on the day of the crime, having accompanied his team to Izmir where they won a match against a team from Marash. Nor is the German film star Curd Jurgens recorded by our passport controls to have entered the country within the last two years, so that it is presumed that this may be a case of mistaken identities.

Yeni Aksham, Istanbul, 19 February 1960, Letter to the Editor, p. 3 of the Weekly Literary and Scientific Supplement.

Dear Sir,

I have been a faithful reader of *Yeni Aksham* for the past twenty years and have nearly always found myself warmly applauding its courageous and enlightened stand on all national issues. I was therefore all the more shocked when I read, in your issue of 12 February last, Dr. Allalemdji's deliberately obscurantist article on vampirism. Surely, such a sop thrown to the senile believers in the positivist historical science of fifty or more years ago was unworthy of a progressive newspaper.

I will take issue only on three points raised by Dr. Allalemdji in his article:

Firstly, all serious and objective students of medieval history now know, from the documents which have survived, what vested interests in religious prejudice and in reactionary feudalism were at work to conceal the real issues at stake in the trial of Gilles de Rais so as to avoid discrediting an outstanding member of the nobility in the eyes of its enemies. Gilles de Rais never practiced vampirism but was accused of it in order to cover up his other crimes. A homosexual debauchee, he had abducted countless young serfs from their modest peasant homes to serve him in his disgraceful orgies. But he soon tired of each one of them in turn and, instead of then allowing them to return to their villages and spread there the report of his debaucheries, preferred to castrate them and sell them as eunuchs to the Arab princes of the Maghreb. The Catholic Church, of course, could not tolerate the idea that Christians were thus being sold, beneath its very nose, by a Christian noble to more enlightened and less cruel Moslem masters, so that the truth was hushed up and a less politically dangerous accusation of vampirism formulated.

Secondly, reliable scholars have recently discovered in Hungary some of the documents of the trial of the infamous Countess Elizabeth Batthyani. From these it appears clearly that she was a paid agent of the Ottoman court, recruiting Hungarian peasant girls, famous for their milk, as wet nurses for unwanted Christian children who had been saved from dying of exposure when their parents had abandoned them. These children were being charitably brought up in Moslem orphanages to serve later as Janissaries in our Imperial regiments of converts to Islam. Here again, the Catholic Church and its feudal supporters refused to admit that such a clandestine trade existed in provinces that it claimed to control; again, it preferred to trump up a charge of vampirism, though the countess was known to suck milk from her victims and never blood, since she insisted on testing each one of them herself and had even acquired a somewhat infantile taste for human milk, which also explains why her mouth is reported to have watered at the mere sight of an opulent bosom.

On both these points, I am prepared to quote, should Dr. Allalemdji desire, all the relevant bibliographical sources in recent French or Hungarian scholarly publications. My third point is one of principle rather than of historical scholarship. Dr. Allalemdji quotes us cases of vampirism in which six hundred and even eight hundred victims were alleged to have been killed. In the recent Fener case, not a single victim has yet been reported to be missing or can be presumed to have been killed. Can the Fener case be compared in any way with these classical if somewhat unreliable cases of vampirism?
Sincerely yours,
Turgut Ekmekdjioglu
Professor of European History
Istanbul University

Yeni Aksham, 19 February 1960, Letter to the Editor, same page as the preceding one.

Dear Sir,
For many years I have deplored, like other devout patriots, the Godless policies of the successive governments of our unfortunate Republic. The present Fener case of vampirism proves how right I have been.

Had our nation remained faithful to its Moslem traditions, Turks of today would not have acquired as they have a taste for the red meat of animals which have not been slaughtered according to the strict rules of our religion. One sin leads to another and guzzling underdone steaks like the Infidels at the Istanbul Hilton Hotel or elsewhere in our increasingly degenerate cities has now led some of our more decadent compatriots to acquire a taste for human blood too. No restaurant in Turkey should be allowed to serve European-style steaks, especially that typically Infidel dish that is so blasphemously called Steak Tartare, as if our Moslem Tartar brethren could be suspected of ever having made a practice of eating anything as monstrously unclean.
Sincerely yours,
Hodja Ibrahim Hadjikaraosmanoglu

Yeni Aksham, Istanbul, 26 February 1960, Letter to the Editor, same page as the preceding letter.

Dear Sir,
I have read with great interest Dr. Allalemdji's article and the curious correspondence that it has provoked in your columns. All this reveals how ignorant most Turks have become of Turcology in general and, in particular, of the ancient customs and beliefs of our Turanian ancestors.

Let me assure you and your readers, as a professor of Turanian and Turkish folklore, that vampirism is an ancient and honorable Turkish and Turanian custom, originally a form of medicine once practiced in Central Asia by Shamanistic priests before our ancestors were converted to Islam. By sucking the sick blood out of their patients, these Shamanistic priests cured them of their diseases, all illnesses being, according to their doctrine, diseases of the blood.
Sincerely yours,
Turhan Tashkent
Professor of Turcology
University of Ankara

Yeni Aksham, 4 March 1960, Letter to the Editor, p. 3 of the Weekly Literary and Scientific Supplement.

Dear Sir,
Professor Tashkent is perfectly right. I come of a family that has for countless generations earned an honest livelihood, even after its conversion to Islam, by practicing Shamanistic medicinal vampirism in the Vilayet of Afyon Karahissar. When I was still a boy, long before my parents moved to Istanbul where my father subsequently became a well-known pedicure, I used to see hundreds of sick people brought to our house by their family and friends for treatment at the hands of my grandfather. He was generally content to accept modest fees and had specialized in the treatment of obesity. Our home had thus become a kind of clinic where my grandfather's cures of vampirism saved many a high Ottoman dignitary from becoming an ungainly old man and the laughing-stock of his inferiors. When Turks of the more privileged classes began to go abroad for more expensive and often less effective cures in well-publicized European watering places, my father solved the problem of our dwindling family practice by moving to Istanbul and setting himself up as a pedicure in the Passage in Beyoglu, where he still cured many a badly infected toe, however, by merely sucking it. I am sure that a number of your older readers will still remember having been treated by him.
Sincerely yours,
Boghatsch Hakimoglu

Yeni Aksham, Istanbul, 4 March 1960, same page as preceding letter.

Dear Sir,
As President of the Pan-Turanian Association of Shamanistic Vampires, I have been authorized by a quorum of our National Board to applaud and corroborate on its behalf every word of Professor Tashkent's remarkably objective letter. All our members have graduated from the last existing schools of ancient Shamanistic medicine. In Turkey, the last

of these schools is now situated in Urfa, in Anatolia; in recent years, we have no longer received any correspondence from the schools which still existed in the Russian Turkestan before the Soviet Revolution, so that we are not able to report on the present state of our science in Soviet Russia, where it may have been suppressed as a manifestation of Pan-Turanian nationalism in the course of the Stalinist persecutions which decimated the Moslem intelligentsia of the Central-Asian Soviet Republics.

Our school in Urfa had first been founded and endowed in the thirteenth century by Korkhut Seljuk, one of the last of the ruling princes of the Oghuz Beylik. Though our faculty still graduates a few selected Shamanistic physicians every year, these are now trained only in the theory of their science, without any practical experience of the treatment of human patients, if only to avoid all possible conflicts with existing Turkish laws regulating the practice of medicine. As an association, we therefore limit our activities to the organization of campaigns to promote a more enlightened appreciation of the value of our science and thus hope soon to obtain public support for changes in our legislation in order to prevent our venerable and valuable science from becoming extinct.
Yours sincerely,
Tchinghiz Hulaghuouglu

Yeni Aksham, Istanbul, 4 March 1960, same page as preceding letter.

Dear Sir,

I hope other readers of *Yeni Aksham* have realized as I did at once that all these countless cases of shameless vampirism which now disgrace our once beautiful and peaceful city in the eyes of the civilized world are the work of a small but well organized band of fanatical Armenians. It has long been known that Armenians require the blood of Moslem children to prepare the meat pies that they eat at their annual Easter celebrations. All too often, they have relied in the past on corrupt Turkish or Kurdish accomplices to procure them their victims. My point is proven by the fact that an Armenian hag who works in the kitchens of the Armenian hospital has also been arrested in the present campaign to eradicate this wave of terrorism which, as always, is seasonal. Though Turks, the other vampires were surely employed as her agents.
Sincerely yours,
Atilla Bayraktutan

Yeni Aksham, Istanbul, 4 March 1960, same page as preceding letter.

Dear Sir,

I'm a hospital nurse and midwife. In all these stories about vampires, one thing worries me. How could the mother of one of the three victims recognize immediately the mark on her son's arm as having been left

there by a hypodermic syringe? Unless she had special training as a nurse, how could she distinguish it from a mere scratch or a fleabite?
Respectfully yours,
Fazilet Bashkurt

Yeni Aksham, Istanbul, 4 March 1960, same page as preceding letter.

Dear Sir,
  My kind Turkish neighbor is writing this letter for me because I never attended a Turkish school and learned to write only Italian in the old days. Because I am a Christian, some Turkish vampires think they can steal my cats with impunity but we all worship one and the same God and there is justice now in our glorious Republic for all its citizens, regardless of race or religion. My cats are very beautiful and well fed and in the past ten years three of them have disappeared. I know that they have been victims of vampires and now my good Turkish neighbor shares my suspicion but we don't know what we should do about it. Isn't it illegal to steal cats and drink their blood like the blood of a human being? Are they the same vampires who drink the blood of both or are there two kinds of vampires, those who drink human blood and those who drink the blood of cats? Perhaps Professor Allalemdji can answer my questions.
Sincerely yours,
Daria Genovesi

Yeni Aksham, Istanbul, 6 March 1960, p. 3, local news.

The case of the vampires of Fener is still being diligently investigated by the police. Prompted by the interest which so many of our readers have displayed, our reporter went yesterday to police headquarters to find out what progress has been made in solving this remarkable mystery. As we had previously reported, Hamdi Kotcha, the well-known goalkeeper of the Fenerbahtche football team, was able to supply a satisfactory alibi when Hasan Öztürk, one of the victims of the vampires, described him as one of the three men who had participated in this orgy of drinking human blood. Hamdi Kotcha happened on that day to be with his team in Izmir, playing a match against a team from Marash. Through Interpol, our police has now been able to ascertain that the German film star Curd Jurgens happened that day to be working in a Hollywood studio, so that he too has now submitted a satisfactory alibi.
  The boy Hasan Öztürk remains the only witness of the actual orgies of vampirism which his mother, on the basis of his reports, denounced to the police. The other two boys whom he named as witnesses and co-victims continue to deny that the alleged vampires drank their blood. For lack of sufficiently conclusive evidence, the public prosecutor may therefore be obliged to drop the case against the carter Mahmut Osmanoglu,

the only vampire who has so far been identified and who is now under arrest. Though Mahmut Osmanoglu has meanwhile admitted having practiced unnatural vices with the three boys, the latter and their parents hotly deny any such degenerate tendencies in their families. For lack of a complaint, the public prosecutor cannot prosecute Mahmut Osmanoglu for the only crime that he has so far confessed.

As for the other vampire, the Armenian cleaning woman Meriam Terzibashjian who had been suspected of attempted vampirism in Langna, we regret to report that she died yesterday in the Armenian Hospital without having sufficiently recovered from her injuries, since February 10th, to be questioned by the police. Though all these investigations have so far proven to be somewhat confusing, it is believed at police headquarters that we may soon expect sensational revelations concerning the wave of vampirism that has swept our city.

Yeni Aksham, Istanbul, 11 March 1960, Letter to the Editor, p. 3 of the Weekly Literary and Scientific Supplement.

Dear Sir,

I am an unmarried mother and support myself, my little girl and my invalid mother on my earnings as a *tchivtiteli* dancer. I used to earn high fees in the most expensive night clubs in Beyoglu and many of your readers will remember the film in which I starred, *The Girl with the Golden Belly.* It told the story of my life and was elected as the most popular Turkish film of the year for the Berlin Film Festival. Unfortunately, a jury of foreigners in Berlin was unable to understand the significance of *The Girl with the Golden Belly* as an artistic milestone in the history of the emancipation of Turkish womanhood, so it failed to get a prize.

But this was not my only misfortune in that year when my stars gave me every indication that I should stay at home and never expose myself unnecessarily to alien forces and influences. One winter night, as I was walking home from work, I slipped on the ice of the frozen Beyoglu sidewalk and fell and injured my hip. My left buttock soon began to swell and is now much larger than my right buttock. I have tried every medical treatment available, but modern science has been of no assistance. My professional life is now ruined. When I dance the *tchivtiteli,* men only laugh at me and I'm lucky if I find work in a low water-front café in Tophane instead of the better Beyoglu night clubs. Can you recommend me a reliable Shamanistic vampire whose treatments might solve my problem?
Sincerely yours,
Djevrieh Holivutlu

Yeni Aksham, Istanbul, 11 March 1960, p. 3 of the Weekly Literary and Scientific Supplement.

Dear Sir,

I'm a devout Moslem and was shocked to read your Christian correspondent's suggestion that Turks could kill and eat cats. After all the years that she has lived in Turkey, Daria Genovesi, who appears to be a Turkish citizen, should really know that our Prophet taught us to respect cats above all other animals. No devout Turk, for instance, will ever drown a kitten, as the Infidels so frequently do. If there exist Turkish vampires that live on the blood of cats, they must surely be Kurdish Yazids who worship fire and the Devil. But with the constant influx of ignorant Anatolian villagers who seek work in our city, I would not be surprised to hear that Istanbul now harbors a secret community of Kurdish Yazids.

Another explanation for the disappearance of your correspondent's three cats might be that they were not really cats but cannibalistic weremice, in fact mice that adopt the appearance of cats only during the daytime and resume their natural form as mice at night. It is a scientific fact that when mice become too numerous for their own convenience they regulate their population by means of cannibalistic massacres. Some of the survivors then become weremice and continue to prey on other mice. But it sometimes happens that weremice also get attacked and killed by real cats. I witnessed a case once with my own eyes. I was living in Cairo in a house that was infested by mice, in an old building in Mousky. I acquired a cat, but she could not cope with the situation. All she ever did was eat, sleep and purr. One day, I bought some poison and placed pieces of poisoned cheese at strategic points on the floor in the kitchen. When I came home late that night from the movies, I found a dead mouse on the floor near the kitchen sink. Instead of picking it up and throwing it at once into the garbage can, I left it there and went to bed. The next morning, in the middle of the kitchen floor where I had seen the dead mouse, I found the corpse of my cat. It was perhaps a weremouse which, while it had been a mouse again at night, had eaten the poison and died; but at dawn its body had then assumed the form of a cat. Or had it died from eating a poisoned mouse? Weremice are very rare, however, and your correspondent's story of her vanished cats would constitute the first recorded case of a cat-lover being afflicted with three weremice. May I ask your correspondent if her three lost cats happened to be of the same family? It would be interesting to know whether this phenomenon is hereditary.

Sincerely yours,

Yilmaz Arslan, author of

Cats and their Ghosts,
(Istanbul, Kirmizi Gül Kitapevi, 1954.)

Yeni Aksham, Istanbul, 18 March 1960, Letter to the Editor, p. 3, of the Weekly Literary and Scientific Supplement.

Dear Sir,
   One of the oldest and most honorable members of our association of Shamanistic medical vampires has been authorized by us to treat your correspondent Miss Djevrieh Holivutlu as a charity patient and solely in order to demonstrate the usefulness and efficacity of our art. But she must first sign a notarized statement to the effect that she is willingly allowing herself to be used as a test case for scientific purposes and will make no claims on us should the experiment fail to give the desired results.
Sincerely yours,
Tchinghiz Hulaghuoglu

Yeni Aksham, Istanbul, 25 March 1960, Letter to the Editor, p. 3, of the Weekly Literary and Scientific Supplement.

Dear Sir,
   You sent me a disgusting old fraud who claimed to be a member in good standing of the National Schamanistic Order of Pan-Turanian Vampires. I am now writing to warn your readers against him. Not only was his treatment painful, humiliating and quite useless, but I now have a scar that is recognizably that of a vicious human bite further disfiguring my already swollen buttock. Instead of curing me, his treatment leaves me worse off than I was before.
Sincerely yours,
Djevrieh Holivutlu

Yeni Aksham, Istanbul, 1 April 1960, Letter to the Editor, p. 3 of the Weekly Literary and Scientific Supplement.

Dear Sir,
   As President of the Pan-Turanian Association of Shamanistic Vampires I must protest against your irresponsible publication of Miss Djevrieh Holivutlu's absurd and vicious allegations.
   She had previously signed a notarized statement, as requested, to the effect that she willingly allowed herself to be used as a test case in a scientific experiment and would make no claims if it failed to produce the desired results. As an eyewitness, I must now state that she did not behave, during the experiment, with the proper scientific objectivity. Instead of keeping her composure, she giggled, wriggled and squealed, so that it was almost impossible for our distinguished member to draw

blood from the affected buttock. After the experiment, she even had the effrontery to demand a fee, thus revealing that she believed she was engaging in some curious form of prostitution. Finally, if anyone now has a right to complain, it would surely be our distinguished member who, in his devotion to our venerable science, lost a tooth while trying to treat, free of charge, a silly and immoral woman who refused, as requested, to keep still while he was treating her. Throughout the experiment, she indeed behaved as if she were merely displaying her charms to her customary water-front audience in a low Tophane café.
Sincerely yours,
Tchinghiz Hulaghuoglu

Yeni Aksham, Istanbul, 1 April 1960, Letter to the Editor, same page as the preceding one.

Dear Sir,
My wife and I are much disturbed by the articles and letters you have published about the Fener vampires and about the plague of vampirism that threatens our children. As parents of five growing boys, we feel that everything should be done to protect the health and morals of those on whose shoulders rests the future of our nation. As for me, if I should ever chance to meet one of these vile and subversive vampires, I would tear him or her apart, regardless of age or sex, limb from limb with my own unarmed hands, then gladly lap up the blood and chew the liver of such a satanic creature. Any other fate would be too good for one of these monsters and I'm sure all other patriotic Turkish parents will agree with me. Long live our glorious Republic,
Alp Karagöz

Yeni Aksham, Istanbul, 1 April 1960, Letter to the Editor, same page as the preceding one.

Dear Sir,
I appeal to your kindness and to the mercy of your readers. Because I have never learned to read or write, I paid the writer in our neighborhood market in Fener to write this letter to all of you, from the widowed mother of the carter Mahmut Osmanoglu who was arrested over a month ago and accused of being a vampire. All my neighbors in Fener know what a good son he has always been, a devout Moslem and kind to all boys and cats in our neighborhood. People have read to me articles and letters you print and I can swear to you on all the Holy Writings of Our Prophet that my son has never stolen and eaten any cats nor does he drink the blood of any boys.
My husband was killed fighting rebel Kurds in the army. A few months later my son was born and never knew his father. We were starving in

Edirne and I came to Istanbul with my baby to find work. Many years, I worked all day and half the night in a laundry till I thought I would break my back. Then my boy grew up and went to work and he is a good boy and let me stay at home and said to me: Mother, you have worked long enough. After that he worked and we both lived on his pay.

Like many other sons who have never known their father my boy is devoted to his mother and has little use for the silly girls of today who think only of movies and gossip. But he has a good heart and would be a wonderful father. All the boys in our neighborhood know him. In summer he takes them to the beach on Sundays and teaches them to swim. In winter he teaches them useful things like how to mend a leaking roof or how to mend their own shoes.

This whole vampire business started when I was away visiting my sister in Edirne. A silly mother in our neighborhood then accused my son of drinking her son's blood. The truth of it is that this evil boy and his two companions are vampires. They came to our lodgings while I was away and threatened to denounce my son to the police if he didn't give them all his week's pay. They said he had taught them to smoke hashish with him in the vacant lot behind the ruins of the old Koranic school in the next street but that isn't true because my son never smokes hashish or even tobacco. After my son was arrested these three boys could no longer agree among themselves what they had accused my son of doing with them. One of them still says he is a vampire and drank their blood but the other boys say nothing. But these three boys are real vampires and you need only see my son now to know that they have been sucking his blood.

Yesterday I was allowed to visit my son for the first time in prison. Every day the police beat him and he now looks like a ghost. Believe me the real vampires are these lying boys and of course the police too. I'm only an old woman but I know a vampire when I see one and they don't suck blood, they drive good men like my son to despair and to their death. What we need now in Turkey is a caliph like King Solomon to render justice to the poor from his emerald and ruby throne. May God bless you if you print my letter,
Fatima Osmanoglu

Yeni Aksham, Istanbul, 1 April 1960, Letter to the Editor, same page as the preceding one.

Dear Sir,

Vampires, schmampires. Each time I read your newspaper I'm more ashamed of being a Turk. For well over a month, you have now been feeding us hair-raising stories about vampires attacking our children of both sexes. Then you published yesterday a front-page editorial describing how the deputies of the Government party, in our National Parliament in Ankara, had attacked the deputies of the Opposition in a violent free-for-all in the course of which they tore the furniture of the House of Representatives apart and beat each other with the remains of their seats. Such behavior disgraces our national politicians in the eyes of the civilized world. The only vampires that we have in Turkey are our politicians of both parties.

As long as you could recognize the Jews, the Armenians, the Greeks or the Shiah Moslems in our midst by their headdresses, we used to have massacres whenever our tempers rose to boiling point. Now we all wear more or less the same hats and massacre each other at random. The only solution to this problem of Turkish national unity would be to allow only two kinds of hats in Turkey: one hat for the sadists and another hat for the masochists, and no hat at all for the majority of neutrals. Tit for tat and hit for hat, everybody would then be happy, the sadists beating up the masochists and the masochists being merrily beaten up by the sadists with no complaints later, while the rest of us would go about our daily business in peace or sit back and applaud the massacre like a football match in the Beziktash Stadium.

Perhaps we need to be psychoanalyzed as a nation. We're all too bloodthirsty, all of us vampires at heart. It may be useful to be bloodthirsty in times of war, but we're a failure in peacetime as a democratic nation. As for me, I've made my choice and have become a vegetarian. If all Turks could only shift their attention from blood to chlorophyll, we might become a civilized nation within a couple of generations. Boys and girls would then be safe in our midst, but God protect a cabbage when I'm around! Vegetables already tremble when they see me approach them.
Sincerely yours,
Harun Pezevenkoglu

Yeni Aksham, Istanbul, 4 September 1960, p. 3 local news.

Our readers will remember that, six months ago, *Yeni Aksham* was the only daily newspaper in Istanbul to denounce as nonsense, from the very start, the absurd panic caused in our city by entirely unfounded rumors of vampirism. Thanks to our enlightened campaign, the innocent victim of this malicious gossip was finally proven to be no vampire and was released from prison.

But the press of other nations appears to be more credulous than ours. Foreign news agencies thus distributed to American newspapers distorted versions of our published reports of the investigation of the case of the alleged vampires of Fener. Thanks to our courageous press campaign, the carter Mahmut Osmanoglu, the only alleged vampire who had been arrested, has now been a free man again for many months. He was working peacefully at his old job as a carter, willing to forgive and forget, when he suddenly received two weeks ago a letter from America. After reading in the American press its somewhat sensational reports of alleged Turkish vampirism, an American research institute was offering Mahmut Osmanoglu a generous grant to come to America and cooperate there with a group of scientists on an important project to determine the physical and psychological causes of both hereditary and environmental vampirism. Yesterday morning, Mahmut Osmanoglu, accompanied by his aged mother, left Yesilköy airport for Chicago, where he will henceforth work as a kind of piece of human litmus paper to detect, by his reactions, who is a potential vampire and who is not.

Our reporter interveiwed Mahmut Osmanoglu at the airport, a few minutes before he boarded the plane. A man of few words, he declared only that he plans to spend much of his spare time in Chicago as a voluntary missionary to convert Americans to Islam. "I've been told," he declared, "that most of them live on a diet of pork and whiskey, though they would actually prefer to suck the blood of Communists. Every once in a while, however, they are obliged to send some of their more bloodthirsty vampires on raids to Cuba, San Domingo or Vietnam to suck the blood of Communists as they no longer have enough of them at home. It was high time I went to America to wean them away from their unclean diet and their propensity for political cannibalism."

Mahmut Osmanoglu's mission to America can thus be interpreted as Turkey's first attempt at technical assistance to an overdeveloped nation. We may soon expect other such idealistic Turkish pioneers to leave our country on similar UNESCO-sponsored projects to solve the problems of France, Western Germany, Sweden, Switzerland and the United Kingdom, nations which are equally infested, it seems, with the kind of vampirism that develops all too easily in an economy of leisure and plenty.

■ DISCUSSION AND QUESTIONS

1. This is a brilliant study in points of view. The author has disappeared from the tale, leaving readers in the hands of journalists and letter writers —each of whom writes with a distinct voice and a particular bias. In fact, one of the points or perhaps themes of the story is that no matter what the news event or phenomenon, each person sees it through his special pair of distorting lenses. In other words, perception is not objective. It is distorted or filtered through beliefs and attitudes.

We expect special interest groups to express their positions on an issue or event—for example, the Pan-Turanian Association of Shamanistic Vampires will fight tooth and nail to defend its beliefs in the medical value of its practices. But in case we didn't know already, Roditi shows in this clever satire that journalists, scholars,

Point of View

and scientists—all of whom claim great objectivity—also have their own axes to grind. If nothing else, newsmen want to sell newspapers. Notice, for instance, that the first sensational story of the "vampires" appeared on the front page of the *Yeni Aksham,* whereas the denunciation of the story and the announcement of the "alleged vampire's" release were printed seven months later on page three of the "local news" section, five months after the last letter to the editor on the subject had been printed. (Public figures such as politicians and entertainers often contend that scandalous allegations against them make headlines, while retractions and apologies appear in a two inch story on page 38.)

2. Identify clearly the point of view expressed in each segment of the story. Explain how each letter or news account is distorted by the writer's personal, subjective view of the event. An analysis of the original news story might, for instance, point to all the words, phrases, and facts (perhaps Mailer's word "factoid" is more accurate) that help slant the story and make it gruesomely titillating—such words as "orgy of vampirism," "disgusting orgy," "they drank this blood from ordinary tea glasses with great relish."

3. Write a fictional news story. Then write three letters from concerned citizens, each letter expressing a different point of view.

Chapter 7

ADDITIONAL STORIES

The Snake

Stephen Crane

Where the path wended across the ridge, the bushes of huckleberry and sweet fern swarmed at it in two curling waves until it was a mere winding line traced through a tangle. There was no interference by clouds, and as the rays of the sun fell full upon the ridge, they called into voice innumerable insects which chanted the heat of the summer day in steady, throbbing, unending chorus.

A man and a dog came from the laurel thickets of the valley where the white brook brawled with the rocks. They followed the deep line of the path across the ridge. The dog—a large lemon-and-white setter—walked, tranquilly meditative, at his master's heels.

Suddenly from some unknown and yet near place in advance there came a dry, shrill, whistling rattle that smote motion instantly from the limbs of the man and the dog. Like the fingers of a sudden death, this sound seemed to touch the man at the nape of the neck, at the top of the spine, and change him, as swift as thought, to a statue of listening horror, surprise, rage. The dog, too—the same icy hand was laid upon him, and he stood crouched and quivering, his jaw dropping, the froth of terror upon his lips, the light of hatred in his eyes.

Slowly the man moved his hands toward the bushes, but his glance did not turn from the place made sinister by the warning rattle. His fingers, unguided, sought for a stick of weight and strength. Presently they closed

From *The Pocket Magazine,* vol. 2, 1896. Also reprinted in *The Complete Stories and Sketches of Stephen Crane.* Garden City: Doubleday and Company.

about one that seemed adequate, and holding this weapon poised before him, the man moved slowly forward, glaring. The dog, with his nervous nostrils fairly fluttering, moved warily, one foot at a time, after his master.

But when the man came upon the snake, his body underwent a shock as if from a revelation, as if after all he had been ambushed. With a blanched face, he sprang forward, and his breath came in strained gasps, his chest heaving as if he were in the performance of an extraordinary muscular trial. His arm with the stick made a spasmodic, defensive gesture.

The snake had apparently been crossing the path in some mystic travel when to his sense there came the knowledge of the coming of his foes. The dull vibration perhaps informed him, and he flung his body to face the danger. He had no knowledge of paths; he had no wit to tell him to slink noiselessly into the bushes. He knew that his implacable enemies were approaching; no doubt they were seeking him, hunting him. And so he cried his cry, an incredibly swift jangle of tiny bells, as burdened with pathos as the hammering upon quaint cymbals by the Chinese at war— for, indeed, it was usually his death music.

"Beware! Beware! Beware!"

The man and the snake confronted each other. In the man's eyes were hatred and fear. In the snake's were hatred and fear. These enemies maneuvered, each preparing to kill. It was to be a battle without mercy. Neither knew of mercy for such a situation. In the man was all the wild strength of the terror of his ancestors, of his race, of his kind. A deadly repulsion had been handed from man to man through long dim centuries. This was another detail of a war that had begun evidently when first there were men and snakes. Individuals who do not participate in this strife incur the investigations of scientists. Once there was a man and a snake who were friends, and at the end, the man lay dead with the marks of the snake's caress just over his East Indian heart. In the formation of devices, hideous and horrible, Nature reached her supreme point in the making of the snake, so that priests who really paint hell well fill it with snakes instead of fire. These curving forms, these scintillant colorings create at once, upon sight, more relentless animosities than do shake barbaric tribes. To be born a snake is to be thrust into a place aswarm with formidable foes. To gain an appreciation of it, view hell as pictured by priests who are really skillful.

As for this snake in the pathway, there was a double curve some inches back of its head, which merely by the potency of its lines, made the man feel with tenfold eloquence the touch of the death-fingers at the nape of his neck. The reptile's head was waving slowly from side to side and its hot eyes flashed like little murder-lights. Always in the air was the dry, shrill whistling of the rattles.

"Beware! Beware! Beware!"

The man made a preliminary feint with his stick. Instantly the snake's heavy head and neck were bent back on the double curve and instantly the snake's body shot forward in a low, straight, hard spring. The man jumped with a convulsive chatter and swung his stick. The blind, sweeping blow fell upon the snake's head and hurled him so that steelcolored plates were for a moment uppermost. But he rallied swiftly, agilely, and again the head and neck bent back to the double curve, and the steaming, wide-open mouth made its desperate effort to reach its enemy. This attack, it could be seen, was despairing, but it was nevertheless impetuous, gallant, ferocious, of the same quality as the charge of the lone chief when the walls of white faces close upon him in the mountains. The stick swung unerringly again, and the snake, mutilated, torn, whirled himself into the last coil.

And now the man went sheer raving mad from the emotions of his forefathers and from his own. He came to close quarters. He gripped the stick with his two hands and made it speed like a flail. The snake, tumbling in the anguish of final despair, fought, bit, flung itself upon this stick which was taking its life.

At the end, the man clutched his stick and stood watching in silence. The dog came slowly, and with infinite caution stretched his nose forward, sniffing. The hair upon his neck and back moved and ruffled as if a sharp wind was blowing. The last muscular quivers of the snake were causing the rattles to still sound their treble cry, the shrill, ringing war chant and hymn of the grave of the thing that faces foes at once countless, implacable, and superior.

"Well, Rover," said the man, turning to the dog with a grin of victory, "we'll carry Mr. Snake home to show the girls."

His hands still trembled from the strain of the encounter, but he pried with his stick under the body of the snake and hoisted the limp thing upon it. He resumed his march along the path, and the dog walked, tranquilly meditative, at his master's heels.

A Meeting in the Dark

Ngugi wa Thiong'o

His mother used to tell him stories. "Once upon a time there was a young girl who lived with her father and mother in a lonely house that was hidden by a hill. The house was old but strong. When the rains came and the winds blew, the house remained firm. Her father and mother liked her, but they quarreled sometimes and she would cry. Otherwise, she was happy. Nobody knew of the house. So nobody came to see them. Then one day a stranger came. He was tall and handsome. He had milk-white teeth. Her mother gave him food. Then he told them of a beautiful country beyond the hill. The girl wanted to go there. Secretly, she followed the man. They had not gone very far when the stranger turned into an Irimu. He became ugly and he had another mouth at the back which was hidden by his long hair. Occasionally, the hair was blown by the wind. Flies were taken in and the mouth would be shut. The girl ran back. The bad Irimu followed her. She ran hard, hard, and the Irimu could not catch her. But he was getting nearer her all the time. When she came close to her home, she found the Irimu had stopped running. But the house was no longer there. She had no home to go to and she could not go forward to the beautiful land, to see all the good things, because the Irimu was on the way."

How did the story end? John wondered. He thought: "I wish I were young again in our old home, then I would ask my mother about it." But now he was not young; not young any more. And he was not a man yet!

From *African Short Stories.* New York: Collier Books, The Macmillan Co. 1970.

He stood at the door of the hut and saw his old, frail but energetic father coming along the village street, with a rather dirty bag made out of strong calico swinging by his side. His father always carried this bag. John knew what it contained: a Bible, a hymn book, and probably a notebook and a pen. His father was a preacher. It must have been he who had stopped his mother from telling him stories. His mother had stopped telling him stories long ago. She would say, "Now, don't ask for any more stories. Your father may come." So he feared his father. John went in and warned his mother of his father's coming. Then his father came in. John stood aside, then walked towards the door. He lingered there doubtfully, then he went out.

"John, hei, John!"

"Baba!"

"Come back."

He stood doubtfully in front of his father. His heart beat faster and an agitated voice within him seemed to ask: Does he know?

"Sit down. Where are you going?"

"For a walk, father," he answered evasively.

"To the village?"

"Well—yes—no. I mean nowhere in particular." John saw his father look at him hard, seeming to read his face. John sighed a very slow sigh. He did not like the way his father eyed him. He always looked at him as though John was a sinner, one who had to be watched all the time. "I am," his heart told him. John guiltily refused to meet the old man's gaze and looked past him and appealingly to his mother who was quietly peeling potatoes. But she seemed to be oblivious of everything around her.

"Why do you look away? What have you done?"

John shrank within himself with fear. But his face remained expressionless. However, he could hear the loud beats of his heart. It was like an engine pumping water. He felt no doubt his father knew all about it. He thought: "Why does he torture me? Why does he not at once say he knows?" Then another voice told him: "No, he doesn't know, otherwise he would have already jumped at you." A consolation. He faced his thoughtful father with courage.

"When is the journey?"

Again John thought—why does he ask? I have told him many times. Aloud, he said,

"Next week, Tuesday."

"Right. Tomorrow we go to the shops, hear?"

"Yes, Father."

"Then be prepared."

"Yes, Father."

"You can go."

"Thank you, Father." He began to move.

"John!"

"Yes?" John's heart almost stopped beating. That second, before his father's next words, was an age.

"You seem to be in hurry. I don't want to hear of you loitering in the village. I know you young men, going to show off just because you are going away! I don't want to hear of trouble in the village."

Much relieved, he went out. He could guess what his father meant by not wanting trouble in the village. How did the story end? Funny, but he could not remember how his mother had ended it. It had been so long ago. Her home was not there. Where did she go? What did she do?

"Why do you persecute the boy so much?" Susan spoke for the first time. Apparently she had carefully listened to the whole drama without a word. Now was her time to speak. She looked at her tough old preacher who had been a companion for life. She had married him a long time ago. She could not tell the number of years. They had been happy. Then the man became a convert. And everything in the home put on a religious tone. He even made her stop telling stories to the child. "Tell him of Jesus. Jesus died for you. Jesus died for the child. He must know the Lord." She too had been converted. But she was never blind to the moral torture he inflicted on the boy (that's what she always called John), so that the boy had grown up mortally afraid of him. She always wondered if it was love for the son. Or could it be a resentment because, well, they two had "sinned" before marriage? John had been the result of that sin. But that had not been John's fault. It was the boy who ought to complain. She often wondered if the boy had . . . but no. The boy had been very small when they left Fort Hall. She looked at her husband. He remained mute, though his left hand did, rather irritably, feel about his face.

"It is as if he was not your son. Or do you. . . ."

"Hm, sister." The voice was pleading. She was seeking a quarrel but he did not feel equal to one. Really, women could never understand. Women were women, whether saved or not. Their son had to be protected against all evil influences. He must be made to grow in the footsteps of the Lord. He looked at her, frowning a little. She had made him sin but that had been a long time ago. And he had been saved. John must not follow the same road.

"You ought to tell us to leave. You know I can go away. Go back to Fort Hall. And then everybody. . . ."

"Look, sister." He hastily interrupted. He always called her sister. Sister-in-the-Lord, in full. But he sometimes wondered if she had been truly saved. In his heart, he prayed: Lord, be with our sister Susan. Aloud, he continued, "You know I want the boy to grow in the Lord."

"But you torture him so! You make him fear you!"

"Why! He should not fear me. I have really nothing against him."

"It is you. You. You have always been cruel to him. . . ." She stood up. The peelings dropped from her frock and fell in a heap on the floor.

"Stanley!"

"Sister." He was startled by the vehemence in her voice. He had never seen her like this. Lord, take the devil out of her. Save her this minute. She did not say what she wanted to say. Stanley looked away from her. It was a surprise, but it seemed he feared his wife. If you had told people in the village about this, they would not have believed you. He took his Bible and began to read. On Sunday he would preach to a congregation of brethren and sisters.

Susan, a rather tall, thin woman, who had once been beautiful, sat down again and went on with her work. She did not know what was troubling her son. Was it the coming journey?

Outside, John strolled aimlessly along the path that led from his home. He stood near the wattle tree which was a little way from his father's house, and surveyed the whole village. They lay before his eyes—crammed—rows and rows of mud and grass huts, ending in sharp sticks that pointed to heaven. Smoke was coming out of various huts, an indication that many women had already come from the *shambas*. Night would soon fall. To the west, the sun was hurrying home behind the misty hills. Again, John looked at the crammed rows and rows of huts that formed Makeno Village, one of the new mushroom "towns" that grew up all over the country during the Mau Mau war. It looked so ugly. A pang of pain rose in his heart and he felt like crying—I hate you, I hate you. You trapped me alive. Away from you, it would never have happened. He did not shout. He just watched.

A woman was coming towards where he stood. A path into the village was just near there. She was carrying a big load of *kuni* which bent her into an Akamba-bow shape. She greeted him.

"Is it well with you, Njooni?"

"It is well with me, mother." There was no trace of bitterness in his voice. John was by nature polite. Everyone knew of this. He was quite unlike the other proud, educated sons of the tribe—sons who came back from the other side of the waters with white or Negro wives who spoke English. And they behaved just like Europeans! John was a favorite, a model of humility and moral perfection. Everyone knew that though a clergyman's son, John would never betray the tribe.

"When are you going to—to—"

"Makerere?"

"Makelele." She laughed. The way she pronounced the name was funny. And the way she laughed too. She enjoyed it. But John felt hurt. So everyone knew of this.

"Next week."
"I wish you well."
"Thank you, mother."

She said quietly—as if trying to pronounce it better—"Makelele." She laughed at herself again but she was tired. The load was heavy.

"Stay well, son."
"Go well and in peace, mother."

And the woman who all the time had stood, moved on, panting like a donkey, but obviously pleased with John's kindness.

John remained long looking at her. What made such a woman live on day to day, working hard, yet happy? Had she much faith in life? Or was her faith in the tribe? She and her kind, who had never been touched by ways of the white man, looked as though they had something to cling to. As he watched her disappear, he felt proud that they should think well of him. He felt proud that he had a place in their esteem. And then came the pang. *Father will know. They will know.* He did not know what he feared most; the action his father would take when he knew, or the loss of the little faith the simple villagers had placed in him, when they knew.

He went down to the small local teashop. He met many people who wished him well at the college. All of them knew that the Pastor's son had finished all the white man's learning in Kenya. He would now go to Uganda; they had read this in the *Baraza,* a Swahili weekly paper. John did not stay long at the shop. The sun had already gone to rest and now darkness was coming. The evening meal was ready. His tough father was still at the table reading his Bible. He did not look up when John entered. Strange silence settled in the hut.

"You look unhappy." His mother first broke the silence. John laughed. It was a nervous little laugh.

"No, mother," he hastily replied, nervously looking at his father. He secretly hoped that Wamuhu had not blabbed.

"Then I am glad."

She did not know. He ate his dinner and went out to his hut. A man's hut. Every young man had his own hut. John was never allowed to bring any girl visitor in there. He did not want "trouble." Even to be seen standing with one was a crime. His father could easily thrash him. He wished he had rebelled earlier like all the other young educated men. He lit the lantern. He took it in his hand. The yellow light flickered dangerously and then went out. He knew his hands were shaking. He lit it again and hurriedly took his big coat and a huge *Kofia* which were lying on the unmade bed. He left the lantern burning, so that his father would see it and think him in. John bit his lower lip spitefully. He hated himself for being so girlish. It was unnatural for a boy of his age.

Like a shadow, he stealthily crossed the courtyard and went onto the village street.

He met young men and women, lining the streets. They were laughing, talking, whispering. They were obviously enjoying themselves. John thought, they are more free than I am. He envied their exuberance. They clearly stood outside or above the strict morality that the educated ones had to be judged by. Would he have gladly changed places with them? He wondered. At last, he came to the hut. It stood at the very heart of the village. How well he knew it—to his sorrow. He wondered what he would do! Wait for her outside? What if her mother came out instead? He decided to enter.

"*Hodi!*"

"Enter. We are in."

John pulled down his hat before he entered. Indeed they were all there —all except she whom he wanted. The fire in the hearth was dying. Only a small flame from a lighted lantern vaguely illuminated the whole hut. The flame and the giant shadow created on the wall seemed to be mocking him. He prayed that Wamuhu's parents would not recognize him. He tried to be "thin," and to disguise his voice as he greeted them. They recognized him and made themselves busy on his account. To be visited by such an educated one who knew all about the white man's world and knowledge, and who would now go to another land beyond, was not such a frequent occurrence that it could be taken lightly. Who knew but he might be interested in their daughter? Stranger things had happened. After all, learning was not the only thing. Though Wamuhu had no learning, yet charms she had and she could be trusted to captivate any young man's heart with her looks and smiles.

"You will sit down. Take that stool."

"No!" He noticed with bitterness that he did not call her "mother."

"Where is Wamuhu?" The mother threw a triumphant glance at her husband. They exchanged a knowing look. John bit his lips again and felt like bolting. He controlled himself with difficulty.

"She has gone out to get some tea leaves. Please sit down. She will cook you some tea when she comes."

"I am afraid . . ." he muttered some inaudible words and went out. He almost collided with Wamuhu.

In the hut:

"Didn't I tell you? Trust a woman's eye!"

"You don't know these young men."

"But you see John is different. Everyone speaks well of him and he is a clergyman's son."

"Y-e-e-s! A clergyman's son? You forget your daughter is circumcised." The old man was remembering his own day. He had found for himself a good, virtuous woman, initiated in all the tribe's ways. And she had known no other man. He had married her. They were happy. Other men of his *Rika* had done the same. All their girls had been virgins, it being a taboo to touch a girl in that way, even if you slept in the same bed, as indeed so many young men and girls did. Then the white men had come, preaching a strange religion, strange ways, which all men followed. The tribe's code of behavior was broken. The new faith could not keep the tribe together. How could it? The men who followed the new faith would not let the girls be circumcised. And they would not let their sons marry circumcised girls. Puu! Look at what was happening. Their young men went away to the land of the white men. What did they bring? White women. Black women who spoke English. Aaa—bad. And the young men who were left just did not mind. They made unmarried girls their wives and then left them with fatherless children.

"What does it matter?" his wife was replying. "Is Wamuhu not as good as the best of them? Anyway, John is different."

"Different! Different! Puu! They are all alike. Those coated with the white clay of the white man's ways are the worst. They have nothing inside. Nothing—nothing here." He took a piece of wood and nervously poked the dying fire. A strange numbness came over him. He trembled. And he feared; he feared for the tribe. For now he said it was not only the educated men who were coated with strange ways, but the whole tribe. The tribe had followed a false *Irimu* like the girl in the story. For the old man trembled and cried inside, mourning for a tribe that had crumbled. The tribe had nowhere to go to. And it could not be what it was before. He stopped poking and looked hard at the ground.

"I wonder why he came. I wonder." Then he looked at his wife and said, "Have you seen strange behavior with your daughter?"

His wife did not answer. She was preoccupied with her own great hopes. . . .

John and Wamuhu walked on in silence. The intricate streets and turns were well known to them both. Wamuhu walked with quick light steps; John knew she was in a happy mood. His steps were heavy and he avoided people even though it was dark. But why should he feel ashamed? The girl was beautiful, probably the most beautiful girl in the whole of Limuru. Yet he feared being seen with her. It was all wrong. He knew that he could have loved her, even then he wondered if he did not love her. Perhaps it was hard to tell but had he been one of the young men he had met, he would not have hesitated in his answer.

Outside the village he stopped. She too stopped. Neither had spoken a word all through. Perhaps the silence spoke louder than words. Each was only too conscious of the other.

"Do they know?" Silence. Wamuhu was probably considering the question. "Don't keep me waiting. Please answer me," he implored. He felt weary, very weary. like an old man who had suddenly reached his journey's end.

"No. You told me to give you one more week. A week is over today."

"Yes. That's why I came!" John hoarsely whispered.

Wamuhu did not speak. John looked at her. Darkness was now between them. He was not really seeing her; before him was the image of his father —haughtily religious and dominating. Again he thought: I John, a priest's son, respected by all and going to college, will fall, fall to the ground. He did not want to contemplate the fall.

"It was your fault." He found himself accusing her. In his heart he knew he was lying.

"Why do you keep on telling me that? Don't you want to marry me?"

John sighed. He did not know what to do.

Once upon a time there was a young girl . . . she had no home to go to . . . she could not go forward to the beautiful land and see all the good things because the Irimu was on the way. . . .

"When will you tell them?"

"Tonight." He felt desperate. Next week he would go to the college. If he could persuade her to wait, he might be able to get away and come back when the storm and consternation had abated. But then the government might withdraw his bursary. He was frightened and there was a sad note of appeal as he turned to her and said:

"Look, Wamuhu, how long have you been pre— I mean like this?"

"I have told you over and over again. I have been pregnant for three months and mother is being suspicious. Only yesterday she said I breathed like a woman with a child."

"Do you think you could wait for three weeks more?" She laughed. Ah! the little witch! She knew his trick. Her laughter always aroused many emotions in him.

"All right. Give me just tomorrow. I'll think up something. Tomorrow I'll let you know all."

"I agree. Tomorrow. I cannot wait any more unless you mean to marry me."

Why not marry her? She is beautiful! Why not marry her? And do I or don't I love her?

She left. John felt as if she was deliberately blackmailing him. His knees were weak and lost strength. He could not move but sank on the ground in a heap. Sweat poured profusely down his cheeks, as if he had been running hard under a strong sun. But this was cold sweat. He lay on the grass; he did not want to think. Oh! No! He could not possibly face his father. Or his mother. Or Rev. Thomas Carstone who had had such faith

in him. John realized that he was not more secure than anybody else, in spite of his education. He was no better than Wamuhu. *Then why don't you marry her?* He did not know. John had grown up under a Calvinistic father and learnt under a Calvinistic headmaster—a missionary! John tried to pray. But to whom was he praying? To Carstone's God? It sounded false. It was as if he was blaspheming. Could he pray to the God of the tribe? His sense of guilt crushed him.

He woke up. Where was he? Then he understood. Wamuhu had left him. She had given him one day. He stood up; he felt good. Weakly, he began to walk back home. It was lucky that darkness blanketed the whole earth, and him in it. From the various huts, he could hear laughter, heated talks or quarrels. Little fires could be seen flickeringly red through the open doors. Village stars—John thought. He raised up his eyes. The heavenly stars, cold and distant, looked down on him, impersonally. Here and there, groups of boys and girls could be heard laughing and shouting. For them life seemed to go on as usual. John consoled himself by thinking that they too would come to face their day of trial.

John was shaky. Why! Why! Why could he not defy all expectations, all prospects of a future, and marry the girl? No. No. It was impossible. She was circumcised, and he knew that his father and the church would never consent to such a marriage. She had no learning, or rather she had not gone beyond Standard 4. Marrying her would probably ruin his chances of ever going to a University. . . .

He tried to move briskly. His strength had returned. His imagination and thought took flight. He was trying to explain his action before an accusing world—he had done so many times before, ever since he knew of this. He still wondered what he could have done. The girl had attracted him. She was graceful and her smile had been very bewitching. There was none who could equal her and no girl in the village had any pretence to any higher standard of education. Women's education was very low. Perhaps that was why so many Africans went "away" and came back married. He too wished he had gone with the others, especially in the last giant student airlift to America. If only Wamuhu had learning . . . and she was uncircumcised . . . then he might probably rebel. . . .

The light still shone in his mother's hut. John wondered if he should go in for the night prayers. But he thought against it; he might not be strong enough to face his parents. In his hut, the light had gone out. He hoped his father had not noticed it . . .

John woke up early. He was frightened. He was normally not superstitious but still he did not like the dreams of the night. He dreamt of circumcision; he had just been initiated in the tribal manner. Somebody —he could not tell his face—came and led him because he took pity on him. They went, went into a strange land. Somehow, he found himself alone. The somebody had vanished. A ghost came. He recognized it as the ghost of the home he had left. It pulled him back; then another ghost came. It was the ghost of the land he had come to. It pulled him from the front. The two contested. Then came other ghosts from all sides and pulled him from all sides so that his body began to fall into pieces. And the ghosts were unsubstantial. He could not cling to any. Only they were pulling him, and he was becoming nothing, nothing ... he was now standing a distance away. It had not been him. But he was looking at the girl, the girl in the story. She had nowhere to go. He thought he would go to help her; he would show her the way. But as he went to her, he lost his way ... he was all alone ... something destructive was coming towards him, coming, coming. ... He woke up. He was sweating all over —

Dreams about circumcision were no good. They portended death. He dismissed the dream with a laugh. He opened the window only to find the whole country clouded in mist. It was perfect July weather in Limuru. The hills, ridges, valleys and plains that surrounded the village were lost in the mist. It looked such a strange place. But there was almost a magic fascination in it. Limuru was a land of contrasts and evoked differing emotions, at different times. Once, John would be fascinated, and would yearn to touch the land, embrace it or just be on the grass. At another time he would feel repelled by the dust, the strong sun and the pot-holed roads. If only his struggle were just against the dust, the mist, the sun and the rain, he might feel content. Content to live here. At least he thought he would never like to die and be buried anywhere else but at Limuru. But there was the human element whose vices and betrayal of other men were embodied as the new ugly villages. The last night's incident rushed into his mind like a flood, making him weak again. He came out of his blankets and went out. Today he would go to the shops. He was uneasy. An odd feeling was coming to him, in fact had been coming, that his relationship with his father was perhaps unnatural. But he dismissed the thought. Tonight would be the "day of reckoning." He shuddered to think of it. It was unfortunate that this scar had come into his life at this time when he was going to Makerere and it would have brought him closer to his father.

They went to the shops. All day long, John remained quiet as they moved from shop to shop buying things from the lanky but wistful Indian traders. And all day long, John wondered why he feared his father so much. He had grown up fearing him, trembling whenever he spoke or gave commands. John was not alone in this.

Stanley was feared by all.

He preached with great vigor, defying the very gates of hell. Even during the Emergency, he had gone on preaching, scolding, judging and condemning. All those who were not saved were destined for hell. Above all, Stanley was known for his great moral observances—a bit too strict, rather pharisaical in nature. None noticed this; certainly not the sheep he shepherded. If an elder broke any of the rules, he was liable to be expelled, or excommunicated. Young men and women, seen standing together "in a manner prejudicial to church and God's morality" (they were one anyway), were liable to be excommunicated. And so, many young men tried to serve two masters, by seeing their girls at night and going to church by day. The alternative was to give up church-going altogether. . . .

Stanley took a fatherly attitude to all the people in the village. You must be strict with what is yours. And because of all this, he wanted his house to be a good example. That is why he wanted his son to grow up right. But motives behind many human actions may be mixed. He could never forget that he had also fallen before his marriage. Stanley was also a product of the disintegration of the tribe due to the new influences.

The shopping took a long time. His father strictly observed the silences between them and neither by word nor by hint did he refer to last night. They reached home and John was thinking that all was well when his father called him.

"John."

"Yes, father."

"Why did you not come for prayers last night?"

"I forgot—"

"Where were you?"

Why do you ask me? What right have you to know where I was? One day I am going to revolt against you. But immediately, John knew that this act of rebellion was something beyond him—not unless something happened to push him into it. It needed someone with something he lacked.

"I-I-I mean, I was—"

"You should not sleep so early before prayers. Remember to be there tonight."

"I will."

Something in the boy's voice made the father look up. John went away relieved. All was still well.

Evening came. John dressed like the night before and walked with faltering steps towards the fatal place. The night of reckoning had come. And he had not thought of anything. After this night all would know. Even Rev. Thomas Carstone would hear of it. He remembered Mr. Carstone and the last words of blessing he had spoken to him. No! he did not want to remember. It was no good remembering these things; and yet the words came. They were clearly written in the air, or in the darkness of his mind. "You are going into the world. The world is waiting even like a hungry lion, to swallow you, to devour you. Therefore, beware of the world. Jesus said, Hold fast unto. . . ." John felt a pain—a pain that wriggled through his flesh as he remembered these words. He contemplated the coming fall. Yes! He, John would fall from the Gates of Heaven down through the open waiting gates of Hell. Ah! He could see it all, and what people would say. Everybody would shun his company, would give him oblique looks that told so much. The trouble with John was that his imagination magnified the fall from the heights of "goodness" out of proportion. And fear of people and consequences ranked high in the things that made him contemplate the fall with so much horror.

John devised all sorts of punishment for himself. And when it came to thinking of a way out, only fantastic and impossible ways of escape came into his head. He simply could not make up his mind. And because he could not and he feared father and people, and he did not know his true attitude to the girl, he came to the agreed spot having nothing to tell the girl. Whatever he did looked fatal to him. Then suddenly he said—

"Look Wamuhu. Let me give you money. You might then say that someone else was responsible. Lots of girls have done this. Then that man may marry you. For me, it is impossible. You know that."

"No. I cannot do that. How can you, you—"

"I will give you two hundred shillings."

"No!"

"Three hundred!"

"No!" She was almost crying. It pained her to see him so.

"Four hundred, five hundred, six hundred!" John had begun calmly but now his voice was running high. He was excited. He was becoming more desperate. Did he know what he was talking about? He spoke quickly, breathlessly, as if he was in a hurry. The figure was rapidly rising —nine thousand, ten thousand, twenty thousand . . . He is mad. He is foaming. He is quickly moving towards the girl in the dark. He has laid his hands on her shoulders and is madly imploring her in a hoarse voice. Deep inside him, something horrid that assumes the threatening anger of his father and the village, seems to be pushing him. He is violently shaking Wamuhu, while his mind tells him that he is patting her gently. Yes. He is out of his mind. The figure has now reached fifty thousand shillings and is increasing. Wamuhu is afraid, extricates herself from him, the mad, educated son of a religious clergyman, and she runs. He runs after her and holds her, calling her by all sorts of endearing words. But he is shaking her, shake, shake, her, her—he tries to hug her by the neck, presses. . . . She lets out one horrible scream and then falls on the ground. And so all of a sudden, the struggle is over, the figures stop and John stands there trembling like the leaf of a tree on a windy day.

John, in the grip of fear, ran homeward. Soon everyone would know.

Good Country People

Flannery O'Connor

    Besides the neutral expression that she wore when she was alone, Mrs. Freeman had two others, forward and reverse, that she used for all her human dealings. Her forward expression was steady and driving like the advance of a heavy truck. Her eyes never swerved to left or right but turned as the story turned as if they followed a yellow line down the center of it. She seldom used the other expression because it was not often necessary for her to retract a statement, but when she did, her face came to a complete stop, there was an almost imperceptible movement of her black eyes, during which they seemed to be receding, and then the observer would see that Mrs. Freeman, though she might stand there as real as several grain sacks thrown on top of each other, was no longer there in spirit. As for getting anything across to her when this was the case, Mrs. Hopewell had given it up. She might talk her head off. Mrs. Freeman could never be brought to admit herself wrong on any point. She would stand there and if she could be brought to say anything, it was something like, "Well, I wouldn't of said it was and I wouldn't of said it wasn't," or letting her gaze range over the top kitchen shelf where there was an assortment of dusty bottles, she might remark, "I see you ain't ate many of them figs you put up last summer."
    They carried on their most important business in the kitchen at breakfast. Every morning Mrs. Hopewell got up at seven o'clock and lit her gas

From A Good Man Is Hard to Find, Copyright © 1965 by Flannery O'Connor. Reprinted by permission of Harcourt Brace Jovanovich, Inc.

heater and Joy's. Joy was her daughter, a large blonde girl who had an artificial leg. Mrs. Hopewell thought of her as a child though she was thirty-two years old and highly educated. Joy would get up while her mother was eating and lumber into the bathroom and slam the door, and before long, Mrs. Freeman would arrive at the back door. Joy would hear her mother call, "Come on in," and then they would talk for a while in low voices that were indistinguishable in the bathroom. By the time Joy came in, they had usually finished the weather report and were on one or the other of Mrs. Freeman's daughters, Glynese or Carramae. Joy called them Glycerin and Caramel. Glynese, a redhead, was eighteen and had many admirers; Carramae, a blonde, was only fifteen but already married and pregnant. She could not keep anything on her stomach. Every morning Mrs. Freeman told Mrs. Hopewell how many times she had vomited since the last report.

Mrs. Hopewell liked to tell people that Glynese and Carramae were two of the finest girls she knew and that Mrs. Freeman was a *lady* and that she was never ashamed to take her anywhere or introduce her to anybody they might meet. Then she would tell how she had happened to hire the Freemans in the first place and how they were a godsend to her and how she had had them four years. The reason for her keeping them so long was that they were not trash. They were good country people. She had telephoned the man whose name they had given as a reference and he had told her that Mr. Freeman was a good farmer but that his wife was the nosiest woman ever to walk the earth. "She's got to be into everything," the man said. "If she don't get there before the dust settles, you can bet she's dead, that's all. She'll want to know all your business. I can stand him real good," he had said, "but me nor my wife neither could have stood that woman one more minute on this place." That had put Mrs. Hopewell off for a few days.

She had hired them in the end because there were no other applicants but she had made up her mind beforehand exactly how she would handle the woman. Since she was the type who had to be into everything, then, Mrs. Hopewell had decided, she would not only let her be into everything, she would see to it that she was into everything—she would give her the responsibility of everything, she would put her in charge. Mrs. Hopewell had no bad qualities of her own but she was able to use other people's in such a constructive way that she never felt the lack. She had hired the Freemans and she had kept them four years.

Nothing is perfect. This was one of Mrs. Hopewell's favorite sayings. Another was: that is life! And still another, the most important, was: well, other people have their opinions too. She would make these statements, usually at the table, in a tone of gentle insistence as if no one held them but her, and the large hulking Joy, whose constant outrage had obliterated every expression from her face, would stare just a little to the side of her, her eyes icy blue, with the look of someone who has achieved blindness by an act of will and means to keep it.

When Mrs. Hopewell said to Mrs. Freeman that life was like that, Mrs. Freeman would say, "I always said so myself." Nothing had been arrived at by anyone that had not first been arrived at by her. She was quicker than Mr. Freeman. When Mrs. Hopewell said to her after they had been on the place a while, "You know, you're the wheel behind the wheel," and winked, Mrs. Freeman had said, "I know it. I've always been quick. It's some that are quicker than others."

"Everybody is different," Mrs. Hopewell said.

"Yes, most people is," Mrs. Freeman said.

"It takes all kinds to make the world,"

"I always said it did myself."

The girl was used to this kind of dialogue for breakfast and more of it for dinner; sometimes they had it for supper too. When they had no guest they ate in the kitchen because that was easier. Mrs. Freeman always managed to arrive at some point during the meal and to watch them finish it. She would stand in the doorway if it were summer but in the winter she would stand with one elbow on top of the refrigerator and look down on them, or she would stand by the gas heater, lifting the back of her skirt slightly. Occasionally she would stand against the wall and roll her head from side to side. At no time was she in any hurry to leave. All this was very trying on Mrs. Hopewell but she was a woman of great patience. She realized that nothing is perfect and that in the Freemans she had good country people and that if, in this day and age, you get good country people, you had better hang onto them.

She had had plenty of experience with trash. Before the Freemans she had averaged one tenant family a year. The wives of these farmers were not the kind you would want to be around you for very long. Mrs. Hopewell, who had divorced her husband long ago, needed someone to walk over the fields with her; and when Joy had to be impressed for services, her remarks were usually so ugly and her face so glum that Mrs. Hopewell would say, "If you can't come pleasantly, I don't want you at all." to which the girl, standing square and rigid-shouldered with her neck thrust slightly forward, would reply, "If you want me, here I am—LIKE I AM."

Mrs. Hopewell excused this attitude because of the leg (which had been shot off in a hunting accident when Joy was ten). It was hard for Mrs. Hopewell to realize that her child was thirty-two now and that for more than twenty years she had had only one leg. She thought of her still as a child because it tore her heart to think instead of the poor stout girl in her thirties who had never danced a step or had any *normal* good times. Her name was really Joy but as soon as she was twenty-one and away from home, she had had it legally changed. Mrs. Hopewell was certain that she had thought and thought until she had hit upon the ugliest name in any language. Then she had gone and had the beautiful name, Joy, changed without telling her mother until after she had done it. Her legal name was Hulga.

When Mrs. Hopewell thought the name, Hulga, she thought of the broad blank hull of a battleship. She would not use it. She continued to call her Joy to which the girl responded but in a purely mechanical way.

Hulga had learned to tolerate Mrs. Freeman who saved her from taking walks with her mother. Even Glynese and Carramae were useful when they occupied attention that might otherwise have been directed at her. At first she had thought she could not stand Mrs. Freeman for she had found that it was not possible to be rude to her. Mrs. Freeman would take on strange resentments and for days together she would be sullen but the source of her displeasure was always obscure; a direct attack, a positive leer, blatant ugliness to her face—these never touched her. And without warning one day, she began calling her Hulga.

She did not call her that in front of Mrs. Hopewell who would have been incensed but when she and the girl happened to be out of the house together, she would say something and add the name Hulga to the end of it, and the big spectacled Joy-Hulga would scowl and redden as if her privacy had been intruded upon. She considered the name her personal affair. She had arrived at it first purely on the basis of its ugly sound and then the full genius of its fitness had struck her. She had a vision of the name working like the ugly sweating Vulcan who stayed in the furnace and to whom, presumably, the goddess had to come when called. She saw it as the name of her highest creative act. One of her major triumphs was that her mother had not been able to turn her dust into Joy, but the greater one was that she had been able to turn it herself into Hulga. However, Mrs. Freeman's relish for using the name only irritated her. It was as if Mrs. Freeman's beady steel-pointed eyes had penetrated far enough behind her face to reach some secret fact. Something about her seemed to fascinate Mrs. Freeman and then one day Hulga realized that it was the artificial leg. Mrs. Freeman had a special fondness for the details of secret infections, hidden deformities, assaults upon children. Of diseases, she preferred the lingering or incurable. Hulga had heard Mrs. Hopewell give her the details of the hunting accident, how the leg had been literally blasted off, how she had never lost consciousness. Mrs. Freeman could listen to it any time as if it had happened an hour ago.

When Hulga stumped into the kitchen in the morning (she could walk without making the awful noise but she made it—Mrs. Hopewell was certain—because it was ugly-sounding), she glanced at them and did not speak. Mrs. Hopewell would be in her red kimono with her hair tied around her head in rags. She would be sitting at the table, finishing her breakfast and Mrs. Freeman would be hanging by her elbow outward from the refrigerator, looking down at the table. Hulga always put her eggs on the stove to boil and then stood over them with her arms folded, and Mrs. Hopewell would look at her—a kind of indirect gaze divided between her and Mrs. Freeman—and would think that if she would only keep herself up a little, she wouldn't be so bad looking. There was nothing wrong with her face that a pleasant expression wouldn't help. Mrs. Hopewell said that people who looked on the bright side of things would be beautiful even if they were not.

Whenever she looked at Joy this way, she could not help but feel that it would have been better if the child had not taken the Ph.D. It had certainly not brought her out any and now that she had it, there was no more excuse for her to go to school again. Mrs. Hopewell thought it was nice for girls to go to school to have a good time but Joy had "gone through." Anyhow, she would not have been strong enough to go again. The doctors had told Mrs. Hopewell that with the best of care, Joy might see forty-five. She had a weak heart. Joy had made it plain that if it had not been for this condition, she would be far from these red hills and good country people. She would be in a university lecturing to people who knew what she was talking about. And Mrs. Hopewell could very well picture her there, looking like a scarecrow and lecturing to more of the same. Here she went about all day in a six-year-old skirt and a yellow sweat shirt with a faded cowboy on a horse embossed on it. She thought this was funny; Mrs. Hopewell thought it was idiotic and showed simply that she was still a child. She was brilliant but she didn't have a grain of sense. It seemed to Mrs. Hopewell that every year she grew less like other people and more like herself—bloated, rude, and squint-eyed. And she said such strange things! To her own mother she had said—"Woman! do you ever look inside? Do you ever look inside and see what you are *not?* God!" she had cried sinking down again and staring at her plate, "Malebranche was right: we are not our own light. We are not our own light!" Mrs. Hopewell had no idea to this day what brought that on. She had only made the remark, hoping Joy would take it in, that a smile never hurt anyone.

The girl had taken the Ph.D. in philosophy and this left Mrs. Hopewell at a complete loss. You could say, "My daughter is a nurse," or "My daughter is a school teacher," or even, "My daughter is a chemical engineer." You could not say, "My daughter is a philosopher." That was something that had ended with the Greeks and Romans. All day Joy sat on her neck in a deep chair, reading. Sometimes she went for walks but she didn't like dogs or cats or birds or flowers or nature or nice young men. She looked at nice young men as if she could smell their stupidity.

One day Mrs. Hopewell had picked up one of the books the girl had just put down and opening it at random, she read, "Science, on the other hand, had to assert its soberness and seriousness afresh and declare that it is concerned solely with what-is. Nothing—how can it be for science anything but a horror and a phantasm? If science is right, then one thing stands firm: science wishes to know nothing of nothing. Such is after all the strictly scientific approach to Nothing. We know it by wishing to know nothing of Nothing." These words had been underlined with a blue pencil and they worked on Mrs. Hopewell like some evil incantation in gibberish. She shut the book quickly and went out of the room as if she were having a chill.

This morning when the girl came in, Mrs. Freeman was on Carramae. "She thrown up four times after supper," she said, "and was up twice in the night after three o'clock. Yesterday she didn't do nothing but ramble in the bureau drawer. All she did. Stand up there and see what she could run upon."

"She's got to eat," Mrs. Hopewell muttered, sipping her coffee, while she watched Joy's back at the stove. She was wondering what the child had said to the Bible Salesman. She could not imagine what kind of a conversation she could possibly have had with him.

He was a tall gaunt hatless youth who had called yesterday to sell them a Bible. He had appeared at the door, carrying a large black suitcase that weighted him so heavily on one side that he had to brace himself against the door facing. He seemed on the point of collapse but he said in a cheerful voice, "Good morning, Mrs. Cedars!" and set the suitcase down on the mat. He was not a bad-looking young man though he had on a bright blue suit and yellow socks that were not pulled up far enough. He had prominent face bones and a streak of sticky-looking brown hair falling across his forehead.

"I'm Mrs. Hopewell," she said.

"Oh!" he said, pretending to look puzzled but with his eyes sparkling, "I saw it said 'The Cedars,' on the mailbox so I thought you was Mrs. Cedars!" and he burst out in a pleasant laugh. He picked up the satchel and under cover of a pant, he fell forward into her hall. It was rather as if the suitcase had moved first, jerking him after it. "Mrs. Hopewell!" he said and grabbed her hand. "I hope you are well!" and he laughed again and then all at once his face sobered completely. He paused and gave her a straight earnest look and said, "Lady, I've come to speak of serious things."

"Well, come in," she muttered, none too pleased because her dinner was almost ready. He came into the parlor and sat down on the edge of a straight chair and put the suitcase between his feet and glanced around the room as if he were sizing her up by it. Her silver gleamed on the two sideboards; she decided he had never been in a room as elegant as this.

"Mrs. Hopewell," he began, using her name in a way that sounded almost intimate. "I know you believe in Chrustian service."

"Well yes," she murmured.

"I know," he said and paused, looking very wise with his head cocked on one side, "that you're a good woman. Friends have told me."

Mrs. Hopewell never liked to be taken for a fool. "What are you selling?" she asked.

"Bibles," the young man said and his eye raced around the room before he added, "I see you have no family Bible in your parlor, I see that is the one lack you got!"

Mrs. Hopewell could not say, "My daughter is an atheist and won't let me keep the Bible in the parlor." She said, stiffening slightly, "I keep my Bible by my bedside." This was not the truth. It was in the attic somewhere.

"Lady," he said, "the word of God ought to be in the parlor."

"Well, I think that's a matter of taste," she began. "I think . . ."

"Lady," he said, "for a Chrustian, the word of God ought to be in every room in the house besides in his heart. I know you're a Chrustian because I can see it in every line of your face."

She stood up and said. "Well, young man, I don't want to buy a Bible and I smell my dinner burning."

He didn't get up. He began to twist his hands and looking down at them, he said softly, "Well lady, I'll tell you the truth—not many people want to buy one nowadays and besides, I know I'm real simple. I don't know how to say a thing but to say it. I'm just a country boy." He glanced up into her unfriendly face. "People like you don't like to fool with country people like me!"

"Why!" she cried, "good country people are the salt of the earth! Besides, we all have different ways of doing, it takes all kinds to make the world go 'round. That's life!"

"You said a mouthful," he said.

"Why, I think there aren't enough good country people in the world!" she said, stirred. "I think that's what's wrong with it!"

His face had brightened. "I didn't inraduce myself," he said, "I'm Manley Pointer from out in the country around Willohobie, not even from a place, just from near a place."

"You wait a minute," she said. "I have to see about my dinner." She went out to the kitchen and found Joy standing near the door where she had been listening.

"Get rid of the salt of the earth," she said, "and let's eat."

Mrs. Hopewell gave her a pained look and turned the heat down under the vegetables. "*I* can't be rude to anybody," she murmured and went back into the parlor.

He had opened the suitcase and was sitting with a Bible on each knee.

"You might as well put those up," she told him. "I don't want one."

"I appreciate your honesty," he said. "You don't see any more real honest people unless you go way out in the country."

"I know," she said, "real genuine folks!" Through the crack in the door she heard a groan.

"I guess a lot of boys come telling you they're working their way through college," he said, "but I'm not going to tell you that. Somehow," he said, "I don't want to go to college. I want to devote my life to Chrustian service. See," he said, lowering his voice, "I got this heart condition. I may not live long. When you know it's something wrong with you and you may not live long, well then, lady . . ." He paused, with his mouth open, and stared at her.

He and Joy had the same condition! She knew that her eyes were filling with tears but she collected herself quickly and murmured, "Won't you stay for dinner? We'd love to have you!" and was sorry the instant she heard herself say it.

"Yes mam," he said in an abashed voice, "I would sher love to do that!"

Joy had given him one look on being introduced to him and then throughout the meal had not glanced at him again. He had addressed several remarks at her, which she had pretended not to hear. Mrs. Hopewell could not understand deliberate rudeness, although she lived with it, and she felt she had always to overflow with hospitality to make up for Joy's lack of courtesy. She urged him to talk about himself and he did. He said he was the seventh child of twelve and that his father had been crushed under a tree when he himself was eight years old. He had been crushed very badly, in fact, almost cut in two and was practically not recognizable. His mother had got along the best she could by hard working and she had always seen that her children went to Sunday School and that they read the Bible every evening. He was now nineteen years old and he had been selling Bibles for four months. In that time he had sold seventy-seven Bibles and had the promise of two more sales. He wanted to become a missionary because he thought that was the way you could do most for people. "He who losest his life shall find it," he said simply and he was so sincere, so genuine and earnest that Mrs. Hopewell would not for the world have smiled. He prevented his peas from sliding onto the table by blocking them with a piece of bread which he later cleaned his plate with. She could see Joy observing sidewise how he handled his knife and fork and she saw too that every few minutes, the boy would dart

Good Country People 255

a keen appraising glance at the girl as if he were trying to attract her attention.

After dinner Joy cleared the dishes off the table and disappeared and Mrs. Hopewell was left to talk with him. He told her again about his childhood and his father's accident and about various things that had happened to him. Every five minutes or so she would stifle a yawn. He sat for two hours until finally she told him she must go because she had an appointment in town. He packed his Bibles and thanked her and prepared to leave, but in the doorway he stopped and wrung her hand and said that not on any of his trips had he met a lady as nice as her and he asked if he could come again. She had said she would always be happy to see him.

Joy had been standing in the road, apparently looking at something in the distance, when he came down the steps toward her, bent to the side with his heavy valise. He stopped where she was standing and confronted her directly. Mrs. Hopewell could not hear what he said but she trembled to think what Joy would say to him. She could see that after a minute Joy said something and that then the boy began to speak again, making an excited gesture with his free hand. After a minute Joy said something else at which the boy began to speak once more. Then to her amazement, Mrs. Hopewell saw the two of them walk off together, toward the gate. Joy had walked all the way to the gate with him and Mrs. Hopewell could not imagine what they had said to each other, and she had not yet dared to ask.

Mrs. Freeman was insisting upon her attention. She had moved from the refrigerator to the heater so that Mrs. Hopewell had to turn and face her in order to seem to be listening. "Glynese gone out with Harvey Hill again last night," she said. "She had this sty."

"Hill," Mrs. Hopewell said absently, "is that the one who works in the garage?"

"Nome, he's the one that goes to chiropracter school," Mrs. Freeman said. "She has this sty. Been had it two days. So she says when he brought her in the other night he says, 'Lemme get rid of that sty for you,' and she says, 'How?' and he says, 'You just lay yourself down acrost the seat of that car and I'll show you.' So she done it and he popped her neck. Kept on a-popping it several times until she made him quit. This morning," Mrs. Freeman said, "she ain't got no sty. She ain't got no traces of a sty."

"I never heard of that before," Mrs. Hopewell said.

"He ast her to marry him before the Ordinary," Mrs. Freeman went on, "and she told him she wasn't going to be married in no *office*."

"Well, Glynese is a fine girl," Mrs. Hopewell said. "Glynese and Carramae are both fine girls."

"Carramae said when her and Lyman was married Lyman said it sure felt sacred to him. She said he said he wouldn't take five hundred dollars for being married by a preacher."

"How much would he take?" the girl asked from the stove.

"He said he wouldn't take five hundred dollars," Mrs. Freeman repeated.

"Well we all have work to do," Mrs. Hopewell said.

"Lyman said it just felt more sacred to him." Mrs. Freeman said. "The doctor wants Carramae to eat prunes. Says instead of medicine. Says them cramps is coming from pressure. You know where I think it is?"

"She'll be better in a few weeks," Mrs. Hopewell said.

"In the tube." Mrs. Freeman said. "Else she wouldn't be as sick as she is."

Hulga had cracked her two eggs into a saucer and was bringing them to the table along with a cup of coffee that she had filled too full. She sat down carefully and began to eat, meaning to keep Mrs. Freeman there by questions if for any reason she showed an inclination to leave. She could perceive her mother's eye on her. The first roundabout question would be about the Bible salesman and she did not wish to bring it on. "How did he pop her neck?" she asked.

Mrs. Freeman went into a description of how he had popped her neck. She said he owned a '55 Mercury but that Glynese said she would rather marry a man with only a '36 Plymouth who would be married by a preacher. The girl asked what if he had a '32 Plymouth and Mrs. Freeman said what Glynese had said was a '36 Plymouth.

Mrs. Hopewell said there were not many girls with Glynese's common sense. She said what she admired in those girls was their common sense. She said that reminded her that they had had a nice visitor yesterday, a young man selling Bibles. "Lord," she said, "he bored me to death but he was so sincere and genuine I couldn't be rude to him. He was just good country people, you know," she said, "—just the salt of the earth."

"I seen him walk up," Mrs. Freeman said, "and then later—I seen him walk off," and Hulga could feel the slight shift in her voice, the slight insinuation, that he had not walked off alone, had he? Her face remained expressionless but the color rose into her neck and she seemed to swallow it down with the next spoonful of egg. Mrs. Freeman was looking at her as if they had a secret together.

"Well, it takes all kinds of people to make the world go 'round," Mrs. Hopewell said. "It's very good we aren't all alike."

"Some people are more alike than others," Mrs. Freeman said.

Hulga got up and stumped, with about twice the noise that was necessary, into her room and locked the door. She was to meet the Bible salesman at ten o'clock at the gate.

Good Country People

She had thought about it half the night. She had started thinking of it as a great joke and then she had begun to see profound implications in it. She had lain in bed imagining dialogues for them that were insane on the surface but that reached below to depths that no Bible salesman would be aware of. Their conversation yesterday had been of this kind.

He had stopped in front of her and had simply stood there. His face was bony and sweaty and bright, with a little pointed nose in the center of it, and his look was different from what it had been at the dinner table. He was gazing at her with open curiosity, with fascination, like a child watching a new fantastic animal at the zoo, and he was breathing as if he had run a great distance to reach her. His gaze seemed somehow familiar but she could not think where she had been regarded with it before. For almost a minute he didn't say anything. Then on what seemed an insuck of breath, he whispered, "You ever ate a chicken that was two days old?"

The girl looked at him stonily. He might have just put this question up for consideration at the meeting of a philosophical association. "Yes," she presently replied as if she had considered it from all angles.

"It must have been mighty small!" he said triumphantly and shook all over with little nervous giggles, getting very red in the face, and subsiding finally into his gaze of complete admiration, while the girl's expression remained exactly the same.

"How old are you?" he asked softly.

She waited some time before she answered. Then in a flat voice she said, "Seventeen."

His smiles came in succession like waves breaking on the surface of a little lake. "I see you got a wooden leg," he said. "I think you're real brave. I think you're real sweet."

The girl stood blank and solid and silent.

"Walk to the gate with me," he said. "You're a brave sweet little thing and I liked you the minute I seen you walk in the door."

Hulga began to move forward.

"What's your name?" he asked, smiling down on the top of her head.

"Hulga," she said.

"Hulga," he murmured, "Hulga. Hulga. I never heard of anybody name Hulga before. You're shy, aren't you, Hulga?" he asked.

She nodded, watching his large red hand on the handle of the giant valise.

"I like girls that wear glasses," he said. "I think a lot. I'm not like these people that a serious thought don't ever enter their heads. It's because I may die."

"I may die too," she said suddenly and looked up at him. His eyes were very small and brown, glittering feverishly.

"Listen," he said, "don't you think some people was meant to meet on account of what all they got in common and all? Like they both think serious thoughts and all?" He shifted the valise to his other hand so that the hand nearest her was free. He caught hold of her elbow and shook it a little. "I don't work on Saturday," he said. "I like to walk in the woods and see what Mother Nature is wearing. O'er the hills and far away. Pic-nics and things. Couldn't we go on a pic-nic tomorrow? Say yes, Hulga," he said and gave her a dying look as if he felt his insides about to drop out of him. He had even seemed to sway slightly toward her.

During the night she had imagined that she seduced him. She imagined that the two of them walked on the place until they came to the storage barn beyond the two back fields and there, she imagined, that things came to such a pass that she very easily seduced him and that then, of course, she had to reckon with his remorse. True genius can get an idea across even to an inferior mind. She imagined that she took his remorse in hand and changed it into a deeper understanding of life. She took all his shame away and turned it into something useful.

She set off for the gate at exactly ten o'clock, escaping without drawing Mrs. Hopewell's attention. She didn't take anything to eat, forgetting that food is usually taken on a picnic. She wore a pair of slacks and a dirty white shirt, and as an afterthought, she had put some Vapex on the collar of it since she did not own any perfume. When she reached the gate no one was there.

She looked up and down the empty highway and had the furious feeling that she had been tricked, that he had only meant to make her walk to the gate after the idea of him. Then suddenly he stood up, very tall, from behind a bush on the opposite embankment. Smiling, he lifted his hat which was new and wide-brimmed. He had not worn it yesterday and she wondered if he had bought it for the occasion. It was toast-colored with a red and white band around it and was slightly too large for him. He stepped from behind the bush still carrying the black valise. He had on the same suit and the same yellow socks sucked down in his shoes from walking. He crossed the highway and said, "I knew you'd come!"

The girl wondered acidly how he had known this. She pointed to the valise and asked, "Why did you bring your Bibles?"

He took her elbow, smiling down on her as if he could not stop. "You can never tell when you'll need the word of God, Hulga," he said. She had a moment in which she doubted that this was actually happening and then they began to climb the embankment. They went down into the pasture toward the woods. The boy walked lightly by her side, bouncing on his toes. The valise did not seem to be heavy today; he even swung it. They crossed half the pasture without saying anything and then, putting his hand easily on the small of her back, he asked softly, "where does your wooden leg join on?"

Good Country People 259

She turned an ugly red and glared at him and for an instant the boy looked abashed. "I didn't mean you no harm," he said. "I only meant you're so brave and all. I guess God takes care of you."

"No," she said, looking forward and walking fast, "I don't even believe in God."

At this he stopped and whistled. "No!" he exclaimed as if he were too astonished to say anything else.

She walked on and in a second he was bouncing at her side, fanning with his hat. "That's very unusual for a girl," he remarked, watching her out of the corner of his eye. When they reached the edge of the wood, he put his hand on her back again and drew her against him without a word and kissed her heavily.

The kiss, which had more pressure than feeling behind it, produced that extra surge of adrenalin in the girl that enables one to carry a packed trunk out of a burning house, but in her, the power went at once to the brain. Even before he released her, her mind, clear and detached and ironic anyway, was regarding him from a great distance, with amusement but with pity. She had never been kissed before and she was pleased to discover that it was an unexceptional experience and all a matter of the mind's control. Some people might enjoy drain water if they were told it was vodka. When the boy, looking expectant but uncertain, pushed her gently away, she turned and walked on, saying nothing as if such business, for her, were common enough.

He came along panting at her side, trying to help her when he saw a root that she might trip over. He caught and held back the long swaying blades of thorn vine until she had passed beyond them. She led the way and he came breathing heavily behind her. Then they came out on a sunlit hillside, sloping softly into another one a little smaller. Beyond, they could see the rusted top of the old barn where the extra hay was stored.

The hill was sprinkled with small pink weeds. "Then you ain't saved?" he asked suddenly, stopping.

The girl smiled. It was the first time she had smiled at him at all. "In my economy," she said, "I'm saved and you are damned but I told you I didn't believe in God."

Nothing seemed to destroy the boy's look of admiration. He gazed at her now as if the fantastic animal at the zoo had put its paw through the bars and given him a loving poke. She thought he looked as if he wanted to kiss her again and she walked on before he had the chance.

"Ain't there somewheres we can sit down sometime?" he murmured, his voice softening toward the end of the sentence.

"In the barn," she said.

They made for it rapidly as if it might slide away like a train. It was a large two-story barn, cool and dark inside. The boy pointed up the ladder that led into the lift and said, "It's too bad we can't go up there."

"Why can't we?" she asked.

"Yer leg," he said reverently.

The girl gave him a contemptuous look and putting both hands on the ladder, she climbed it while he stood below, apparently awestruck. She pulled herself expertly through the opening and then looked down at him and said, "Well, come on if you're coming," and he began to climb the ladder, awkwardly bringing the suitcase with him.

"We won't need the Bible," she observed.

"You never can tell," he said, panting. After he had got into the loft, he was a few seconds catching his breath. She had sat down in a pile of straw. A wide sheath of sunlight, filled with dust particles, slanted over her. She lay back against a bale, her face turned away, looking out the front opening of the barn where hay was thrown from a wagon into the loft. The two pink-speckled hillsides lay back against a dark ridge of woods. The sky was cloudless and cold blue. The boy dropped down by her side and put one arm under her and the other over her and began methodically kissing her face, making little noises like a fish. He did not remove his hat but it was pushed far enough back not to interfere. When her glasses got in his way, he took them off of her and slipped them into his pocket.

The girl at first did not return any of the kisses but presently she began to and after she had put several on his cheek, she reached his lips and remained there, kissing him again and again as if she were trying to draw all the breath out of him. His breath was clear and sweet like a child's and the kisses were sticky like a child's. He mumbled about loving her and about knowing when he first seen her that he loved her, but the mumbling was like the sleepy fretting of a child being put to sleep by his mother. Her mind, throughout this, never stopped or lost itself for a second to her feelings. "You ain't said you loved me none," he whispered finally, pulling back from her. "You got to say that."

She looked away from him off into the hollow sky and then down at a black ridge and then down farther into what appeared to be two green swelling lakes. She didn't realize he had taken her glasses but this landscape could not seem exceptional to her for she seldom paid any close attention to her surroundings.

"You got to say it," he repeated. "You got to say you love me."

She was always careful how she committed herself. "In a sense," she began, "if you use the word loosely, you might say that. But it's not a word I use. I don't have illusions. I'm one of those people who see *through* to nothing."

The boy was frowning. "You got to say it. I said it and you got to say it," he said.

The girl looked at him almost tenderly. "You poor baby," she murmured. "it's just as well you don't understand," and she pulled him by the neck, face-down, against her. "We are all damned," she said, "but some of us have taken off our blindfolds and see that there's nothing to see. It's a kind of salvation."

The boy's astonished eyes looked blankly through the ends of her hair. "Okay," he almost whined, "but do you love me or don'tcher?"

"Yes," she said and added, "in a sense. But I must tell you something. There mustn't be anything dishonest between us." She lifted his head and looked him in the eye. "I am thirty years old," she said. "I have a number of degrees."

The boy's look was irritated but dogged. "I don't care," he said. "I don't care a thing about what all you done. I just want to know if you love me or don'tcher?" and he caught her to him and wildly planted her face with kisses until she said, "Yes, yes."

"Okay then," he said, letting her go. "Prove it."

She smiled, looking dreamily out on the shifty landscape. She had seduced him without even making up her mind to try. "How?" she asked, feeling that he should be delayed a little.

He leaned over and put his lips to her ear. "Show me where your wooden leg joins on," he whispered.

The girl uttered a sharp little cry and her face instantly drained of color. The obscenity of the suggestion was not what shocked her. As a child she had sometimes been subject to feelings of shame but education had removed the last traces of that as a good surgeon scrapes for cancer; she would no more have felt it over what he was asking than she would have believed in his Bible. But she was as sensitive about the artificial leg as a peacock about his tail. No one ever touched it but her. She took care of it as someone else would his soul, in private and almost with her own eyes turned away. "No," she said.

"I known it," he muttered, sitting up. "You're just playing me for a sucker."

"Oh no no!" she cried. "It joins on at the knee. Only at the knee. Why do you want to see it?"

The boy gave her a long penetrating look. "Because," he said, "it's what makes you different. You ain't like anybody else."

She sat staring at him. There was nothing about her face or her round freezing-blue eyes to indicate that this had moved her; but she felt as if her heart had stopped and left her mind to pump her blood. She decided that for the first time in her life she was face to face with real innocence. This boy, with an instinct that came from beyond wisdom, had touched the truth about her. When after a minute, she said in a hoarse high voice, "All right," it was like surrendering to him completely. It was like losing her own life and finding it again, miraculously, in his.

Very gently he began to roll the slack leg up. The artificial limb, in a white sock and brown flat shoe, was bound in a heavy material like canvas and ended in an ugly jointure where it was attached to the stump. The boy's face and his voice were entirely reverent as he uncovered it and said, "Now show me how to take it off and on."

She took it off for him and put it back on again and then he took it off himself, handling it as tenderly as if it were a real one. "See!" he said with a delighted child's face. "Now I can do it myself!"

"Put it back on," she said. She was thinking that she would run away with him and that every night he would take the leg off and every morning put it back on again. "Put it back on," she said.

"Not yet," he murmured, setting it on its foot out of her reach. "Leave it off for a while. You got me instead."

She gave a little cry of alarm but he pushed her down and began to kiss her again. Without the leg she felt entirely dependent on him. Her brain seemed to have stopped thinking altogether and to be about some other function that it was not very good at. Different expressions raced back and forth over her face. Every now and then the boy, his eyes like two steel spikes, would glance behind him where the leg stood. Finally she pushed him off and said, "Put it back on me now."

"Wait," he said. He leaned the other way and pulled the valise toward him and opened it. It had a pale blue spotted lining and there were only two Bibles in it. He took one of these out and opened the cover of it. It was hollow and contained a pocket flask of whiskey, a pack of cards, and a small blue box with printing on it. He laid these out in front of her one at a time in an evenly-spaced row, like one presenting offerings at the shrine of a goddess. He put the blue box in her hand. THIS PRODUCT TO BE USED ONLY FOR THE PREVENTION OF DISEASE, she read, and dropped it. The boy was unscrewing the top of the flask. He stopped and pointed, with a smile, to the deck of cards. It was not an ordinary deck but one with an obscene picture on the back of each card. "Take a swig," he said, offering her the bottle first. He held it in front of her, but like one mermerized, she did not move.

Her voice when she spoke had an almost pleading sound. "Aren't you," she murmured, "aren't you just good country people?"

The boy cocked his head. He looked as if he were just beginning to understand that she might be trying to insult him. "Yeah," he said, curling his lip slightly, "but it ain't held me back none. I'm as good as you any day in the week."

"Give me my leg," she said.

He pushed it farther away with his foot. "Come on now, let's begin to have us a good time," he said coaxingly. "We ain't got to know one another good yet."

Good Country People

"Give me my leg!" she screamed and tried to lunge for it but he pushed her down easily.

"What's the matter with you all of a sudden?" he asked, frowning as he screwed the top on the flask and put it quickly back inside the Bible. "You just a while ago said you didn't believe in nothing. I thought you was some girl!"

Her face was almost purple. "You're a Christian!" she hissed. "You're a fine Christian! You're just like them all—say one thing and do another. You're a perfect Christian, you're . . ."

The boy's mouth was set angrily. "I hope you don't think," he said in a lofty indignant tone, "that I believe in that crap! I may sell Bibles but I know which end is up and I wasn't born yesterday and I know where I'm going!"

"Give me my leg!" she screeched. He jumped up so quickly that she barely saw him sweep the cards and the blue box back into the Bible and throw the Bible into the valise. She saw him grab the leg and then she saw it for an instant slanted forlornly across the inside of the suitcase with a Bible at either side of its opposite ends. He slammed the lid shut and snatched up the valise and swung it down the hole and then stepped through himself.

When all of him had passed but his head, he turned and regarded her with a look that no longer had any admiration in it. "I've gotten a lot of interesting things," he said. "One time I got a woman's glass eye this way. And you needn't to think you'll catch me because Pointer ain't really my name. I use a different name at every house I call at and don't stay nowhere long. And I'll tell you another thing, Hulga," he said, using the name as if he didn't think much of it, "You ain't so smart. I been believing in nothing ever since I was born!" and then the toast-colored hat disappeared down the hole and the girl was left, sitting on the straw in the dusty sunlight. When she turned her churning face toward the opening, she saw his blue figure struggling successfully over the green speckled lake.

Mrs. Hopewell and Mrs. Freeman, who were in the back pasture, digging up onions, saw him emerge a little later from the woods and head across the meadow toward the highway. "Why, that looks like that nice dull young man that tried to sell me a Bible yesterday," Mrs. Hopewell said, squinting. "He must have been selling them to the Negroes back in there. He was so simple," she said, "but I guess the world would be better off if we were all that simple."

Mrs. Freeman's gaze drove forward and just touched him before he disappeared under the hill. Then she returned her attention to the evil-smelling onion shoot she was lifting from the ground. "Some can't be that simple," she said, "I know I never could."

The Balek Scales

Heinrich Böll

Where my grandfather came from, most of the people lived by working in the flax sheds. For five generations they had been breathing in the dust which rose from the crushed flax stalks, letting themselves be killed off by slow degrees, a race of long-suffering, cheerful people who ate goat cheese, potatoes, and now and then a rabbit; in the evening they would sit at home spinning and knitting; they sang, drank mint tea and were happy. During the day they would carry the flax stalks to the antiquated machines, with no protection from the dust and at the mercy of the heat which came pouring out of the drying kilns. Each cottage contained only one bed, standing against the wall like a closet and reserved for the parents, while the children slept all round the room on benches. In the morning the room would be filled with the odor of thin soup; on Sundays there was stew, and on feast days the children's faces would light up with pleasure as they watched the black acorn coffee turning paler and paler from the milk their smiling mother poured into their coffee mugs.

The parents went off early to the flax sheds, the housework was left to the children: they would sweep the room, tidy up, wash the dishes and peel the potatoes, precious pale-yellow fruit whose thin peel had to be produced afterwards to dispel any suspicion of extravagance or carelessness.

From *18 Stories* by Heinrich Böll. Translated by Leila Vennewitz. Copyright © 1966 by Heinrich Böll. Used with permission of McGraw-Hill Book Company.

The Balek Scales

As soon as the children were out of school they had to go off into the woods and, depending on the season, gather mushrooms and herbs: woodruff and thyme, caraway, mint and foxglove, and in summer, when they had brought in the hay from their meager fields, they gathered hayflowers. A kilo of hayflowers was worth one pfennig, and they were sold by the apothecaries in town for twenty pfennigs a kilo to highly strung ladies. The mushrooms were highly prized: they fetched twenty pfennigs a kilo and were sold in the shops in town for one mark twenty. The children would crawl deep into the green darkness of the forest during the autumn when dampness drove the mushrooms out of the soil, and almost every family had its own places where it gathered mushrooms, places which were handed down in whispers from generation to generation.

The woods belonged to the Baleks, as well as the flax sheds, and in my grandfather's village the Baleks had a chateau, and the wife of the head of the family had a little room next to the dairy where mushrooms, herbs and hayflowers were weighed and paid for. There on the table stood the great Balek scales, an old-fashioned, ornate bronze-gilt contraption, which my grandfather's grandparents had already faced when they were children, their grubby hands holding their little baskets of mushrooms, their paper bags of hayflowers, breathlessly watching the number of weights Frau Balek had to throw on the scale before the swinging pointer came to rest exactly over the black line, that thin line of justice which had to be redrawn every year. Then Frau Balek would take the big book covered in brown leather, write down the weight, and pay out the money, pfennigs or tenpfennig pieces and very, very occasionally, a mark. And when my grandfather was a child there was a big glass jar of lemon drops standing there, the kind that cost one mark a kilo, and when Frau Balek —whichever one happened to be presiding over the little room—was in a good mood, she would put her hand into this jar and give each child a lemon drop, and the children's faces would light up with pleasure, the way they used to when on feast days their mother poured milk into their coffee mugs, milk that made the coffee turn paler and paler until it was as pale as the flaxen pigtails of the little girls.

One of the laws imposed by the Baleks on the village was: no one was permitted to have any scales in the house. The law was so ancient that nobody gave a thought as to when and how it had arisen, and it had to be obeyed, for anyone who broke it was dismissed from the flax sheds, he could not sell his mushrooms or his thyme or his hayflowers, and the power of the Baleks was so far-reaching that no one in the neighboring villages would give him work either, or buy his forest herbs. But since the days when my grandfather's parents had gone out as small children to gather mushrooms and sell them in order that they might season the meat of the rich people of Prague or be baked into game pies, it had never occurred to anyone to break this law: flour could be measured in cups, eggs could be counted, what they had spun could be measured by the yard, and besides, the old-fashioned bronze-gilt, ornate Balek scales did not look as if there was anything wrong with them, and five generations had entrusted the swinging black pointer with what they had gone out as eager children to gather from the woods.

True, there were some among these quiet people who flouted the law, poachers bent on making more money in one night than they could earn in a whole month in the flax sheds, but even these people apparently never thought of buying scales or making their own. My grandfather was the first person bold enough to test the justice of the Baleks, the family who lived in the chateau and drove two carriages, who always maintained one boy from the village while he studied theology at the seminary in Prague, the family with whom the priest played taroc every Wednesday, on whom the local reeve, in his carriage emblazoned with the Imperial coat-of-arms, made an annual New Year's Day call and on whom the Emperor conferred a title on the first day of the year 1900.

My grandfather was hard-working and smart: he crawled further into the woods than the children of his clan had crawled before him, he penetrated as far as the thicket where, according to legend, Bilgan the Giant was supposed to dwell, guarding a treasure. But my grandfather was not afraid of Bilgan: he worked his way deep into the thicket, even when he was quite little, and brought out great quantities of mushrooms; he even found truffles, for which Frau Balek paid thirty pfennigs a pound. Everything my grandfather took to the Baleks he entered on the back of a torn-off calendar page: every pound of mushrooms, every gram of thyme, and on the right-hand side, in his childish handwriting, he entered the amount he received for each item; he scrawled in every pfennig, from the age of seven to the age of twelve, and by the time he was twelve the year 1900 had arrived, and because the Baleks had been raised to the aristocracy by the Emperor, they gave every family in the village a quarter of a pound of real coffee, the Brazilian kind; there was also free beer and tobacco for the men, and at the chateau there was a great banquet; many carriages stood in the avenue of poplars leading from the entrance gates to the chateau.

But the day before the banquet the coffee was distributed in the little room which had housed the Balek scales for almost a hundred years, and the Balek family was now called Balek von Bilgan because, according to legend, Bilgan the Giant used to have a great castle on the site of the present Balek estate.

My grandfather often used to tell me how he went there after school to fetch the coffee for four families: the Cechs, the Weidlers, the Vohlas and his own, the Brüchers. It was the afternoon of New Year's Eve: there were the front rooms to be decorated, the baking to be done, and the families did not want to spare four boys and have each of them go all the way to the chateau to bring back a quarter of a pound of coffee.

And so my grandfather sat on the narrow wooden bench in the little room while Gertrud the maid counted out the wrapped four-ounce packages of coffee, four of them, and he looked at the scales and saw that the pound weight was still lying on the left-hand scale; Frau Balek von Bilgan was busy with preparations for the banquet. And when Gertrud was about to put her hand into the jar with the lemon drops to give my grandfather one, she discovered it was empty: it was refilled once a year, and held one kilo of the kind that cost a mark.

Gertrud laughed and said: "Wait here while I get the new lot," and my grandfather waited with the four four-ounce packages which had been wrapped and sealed in the factory, facing the scales on which someone had left the pound weight, and my grandfather took the four packages of coffee, put them on the empty scale, and his heart thudded as he watched the black finger of justice come to rest on the left of the black line: the scale with the pound weight stayed down, and the pound of coffee remained up in the air; his heart thudded more than if he had been lying behind a bush in the forest waiting for Bilgan the Giant, and he felt in his pocket for the pebbles he always carried with him so he could use his catapult to shoot the sparrows which pecked away at his mother's cabbage plants—he had to put three, four, five pebbles beside the packages of coffee before the scale with the pound weight rose and the pointer at last came to rest over the black line. My grandfather took the coffee from the scale, wrapped the five pebbles in his kerchief, and when Gertrud came back with the big kilo bag of lemon drops which had to last for another whole year in order to make the children's faces light up with pleasure, when Gertrud let the lemon drops rattle into the glass jar, the pale little fellow was still standing there, and nothing seemed to have changed. My grandfather only took three of the packages, then Gertrud looked in startled surprise at the white-faced child who threw the lemon drop onto the floor, ground it under his heel, and said: "I want to see Frau Balek."

"Balek von Bilgan, if you please," said Gertrud.

"All right, Frau Balek von Bilgan," but Gertrud only laughed at him, and he walked back to the village in the dark, took the Cechs, the Weidlers and the Vohlas their coffee, and said he had to go and see the priest.

Instead he went out into the dark night with his five pebbles in his kerchief. He had to walk a long way before he found someone who had scales, who was permitted to have them; no one in the villages of Blaugau and Bernau had any, he knew that, and he went straight through them till, after two hours' walking, he reached the little town of Dielheim where

Honig the apothecary lived. From Honig's house came the smell of fresh pancakes, and Honig's breath, when he opened the door to the half-frozen boy, already smelled of punch, there was a moist cigar between his narrow lips, and he clasped the boy's cold hands firmly for a moment, saying: "What's the matter, has your father's lung got worse?"

"No, I haven't come for medicine, I wanted . . ." My grandfather undid his kerchief, took out the five pebbles, held them out to Honig and said: "I wanted to have these weighed." He glanced anxiously into Honig's face, but when Honig said nothing and did not get angry, or even ask him anything, my grandfather said: "It is the amount that is short of justice," and now, as he went into the warm room, my grandfather realized how wet his feet were. The snow had soaked through his cheap shoes, and in the forest the branches had showered him with snow which was not melting, and he was tired and hungry and suddenly began to cry because he thought of the quantities of mushrooms, the herbs, the flowers, which had been weighed on the scales which were short five pebbles' worth of justice. And when Honig, shaking his head and holding the five pebbles, called his wife, my grandfather thought of the generations of his parents, his grandparents, who had all had to have their mushrooms, their flowers, weighed on the scales, and he was overwhelmed by a great wave of injustice, and began to sob louder than ever, and, without waiting to be asked, he sat down on a chair, ignoring the pancakes, the cup of hot coffee which nice plump Frau Honig put in front of him, and did not stop crying till Honig himself came out from the shop at the back and, rattling the pebbles in his hand, said in a low voice to his wife: "Fifty-five grams, exactly."

My grandfather walked the two hours home through the forest, got a beating at home, said nothing, not a single word, when he was asked about the coffee, spent the whole evening doing sums on the piece of paper on which he had written down everything he had sold to Frau Balek, and when midnight struck, and the cannon could be heard from the chateau, and the whole village rang with shouting and laughter and the noise of rattles, when the family kissed and embraced all round, he said into the New Year silence: "The Baleks owe me eighteen marks and thirty-two pfennigs." And again he thought of all the children there were in the village, of his brother Fritz who had gathered so many mushrooms, of his sister Ludmilla; he thought of the many hundreds of children who had all gathered mushrooms for the Baleks, and herbs and flowers, and this time he did not cry but told his parents and brothers and sisters of his discovery.

When the Baleks von Bilgan went to High Mass on New Year's Day, their new coat-of-arms—a giant crouching under a fir tree—already em-

The Balek Scales 269

blazoned in blue and gold on their carriage, they saw the hard, pale faces of the people all staring at them. They had expected garlands in the village, a song in their honor, cheers and hurrahs, but the village was completely deserted as they drove through it, and in church the pale faces of the people were turned toward them, mute and hostile, and when the priest mounted the pulpit to deliver his New Year's sermon he sensed the chill in those otherwise quiet and peaceful faces, and he stumbled painfully through his sermon and went back to the altar drenched in sweat. And as the Baleks von Bilgan left the church after Mass, they walked through a lane of mute, pale faces. But young Frau Balek von Bilgan stopped in front of the children's pews, sought out my grandfather's face, pale little Franz Brücher, and asked him, right there in the church: "Why didn't you take the coffee for your mother?" And my grandfather stood up and said: "Because you owe me as much money as five kilos of coffee would cost." And he pulled the five pebbles from his pocket, held them out to the young woman and said: "This much, fifty-five grams, is short in every pound of your justice"; and before the woman could say anything the men and women in the church lifted up their voices and sang: "The justice of this earth, O Lord, hath put Thee to death. . . ."

While the Baleks were at church, Wilhelm Vohla, the poacher, had broken into the little room, stolen the scales and the big fat leatherbound book in which had been entered every kilo of mushrooms, every kilo of hayflowers, everything bought by the Baleks in the village, and all afternoon of that New Year's Day the men of the village sat in my great-grandparents' front room and calculated, calculated one tenth of everything that had been bought—but when they had calculated many thousands of talers and had still not come to an end, the reeve's gendarmes arrived, made their way into my great-grandfather's front room, shooting and stabbing as they came, and removed the scales and the book by force. My grandfather's little sister Ludmilla lost her life, a few men were wounded, and one of the gendarmes was stabbed to death by Wilhelm Vohla the poacher.

Our village was not the only one to rebel: Blaugau and Bernau did too, and for almost a week no work was done in the flax sheds. But a great many gendarmes appeared, and the men and women were threatened with prison, and the Baleks forced the priest to display the scales publicly in the school and demonstrate that the finger of justice swung to and fro accurately. And the men and women went back to the flax sheds—but no one went to the school to watch the priest: he stood there all alone, helpless and forlorn with his weights, scales, and packages of coffee.

And the children went back to gathering mushrooms, to gathering thyme, flowers and foxglove, but every Sunday, as soon as the Baleks entered the church, the hymn was struck up: "The justice of this earth, O Lord, hath put Thee to death," until the reeve ordered it proclaimed in every village that the singing of this hymn was forbidden.

My grandfather's parents had to leave the village, and the new grave of their little daughter; they became basket weavers, but did not stay long anywhere because it pained them to see how everywhere the finger of justice swung falsely. They walked along behind their cart, which crept slowly over the country roads, taking their thin goat with them, and passers-by could sometimes hear a voice from the cart singing: "The justice of this earth, O Lord, hath put Thee to death." And those who wanted to listen could hear the tale of the Baleks von Bilgan, whose justice lacked a tenth part. But there were few who listened.

Tickets, Please

D. H. Lawrence

There is in the midlands a single-line tramway system which boldly leaves the county town and plunges off into the black, industrial countryside, up hill and down dale, through the long ugly villages of workmen's houses, over canals and railways, past churches perched high and nobly over the smoke and shadows, through stark, grimy, cold little market-places, tilting away in a rush past cinemas and shops down to the hollow where the collieries are, then up again, past a little rural church, under the ash trees, on in a rush to the terminus, the last little ugly place of industry, the cold little town that shivers on the edge of the wild, gloomy country beyond. There the green and creamy coloured tram-car seems to pause and purr with curious satisfaction. But in a few minutes—the clock on the turret of the Cooperative Wholesale Society's Shops gives the time—away it starts once more on the adventure. Again there are the reckless swoops downhill, bouncing the loops: again the chilly wait in the hill-top market-place: again the breathless slithering round the precipitous drop under the church: again the patient halts at the loops, waiting for the outcoming car: so on and on, for two long hours, till at last the city looms beyond the fat gas-works, the narrow factories draw near, we are in the sordid streets of the great town, once more we sidle to a standstill at our terminus, abashed by the great crimson and cream-

From *The Complete Short Stories of D. H. Lawrence,* Vol. 2. Copyright © 1922 by Thomas B. Seltzer, Inc., 1950, Frieda Lawrence. All rights reserved. Reprinted by permission of The Viking Press, Inc.

coloured city cars, but still perky, jaunty, somewhat daredevil, green as a jaunty sprig of parsley out of a black colliery garden.

To ride on these cars is always on adventure. Since we are in war-time, the drivers are men unfit for active service: cripples and hunchbacks. So they have the spirit of the devil in them. The ride becomes a steeple-chase. Hurray! we have leapt in a clear jump over the canal bridges—now for the four-lane corner. With a shriek and a trail of sparks we are clear again. To be sure, a tram often leaps the rails—but what matter! It sits in a ditch till other trams come to haul it out. It is quite common for a car, packed with one solid mass of living people, to come to a dead halt in the midst of unbroken blackness, the heart of nowhere on a dark night, and for the driver and the girl conductor to call, "All get off—car's on fire!" Instead, however, of rushing out in a panic, the passengers stolidly reply: "Get on—get on! We're not coming out. We're stopping where we are. Push on, George." So till flames actually appear.

The reason for this reluctance to dismount is that the nights are howlingly cold, black, and windswept, and a car is a haven of refuge. From village to village the miners travel, for a change of cinema, of girl, of pub. The trams are desperately packed. Who is going to risk himself in the black gulf outside, to wait perhaps an hour for another tram, then to see the forlon notice "Depot Only," because there is something wrong! Or to greet a unit of three bright cars all so tight with people that they sail past with a howl of derision. Trams that pass in the night.

This, the most dangerous tram-service in England, as the authorities themselves declare, with pride, is entirely conducted by girls, and driven by rash young men, a little crippled, or by delicate young men, who creep forward in terror. The girls are fearless young hussies. In their ugly blue uniform, skirts up to their knees, shapeless old peaked caps in their heads, they have all the *sang-froid* of an old noncommissioned officer. With a tram packed with howling colliers, roaring hymns downstairs and a sort of antiphony of obscenities upstairs, the lasses are perfectly at their ease. They pounce on the youths who try to evade their ticket-machine. They push off the men at the end of their distance. They are not going to be done in the eye—not they. They fear nobody—and everybody fears them.

"Hello, Annie!"

"Hello, Ted!"

"Oh, mind my corn, Miss Stone. It's my belief you've got a heart of stone, for you've trod on it again."

"You should keep it in your pocket," replies Miss Stone, and she goes sturdily upstairs in her high boots.

"Tickets please."

She is peremptory, suspicious, and ready to hit first. She can hold her own against ten thousand. The step of that tram-car is her Thermopylae.

Tickets, Please 273

Therefore, there is a certain wild romance aboard these cars—and in the sturdy bosom of Annie herself. The time for soft romance is in the morning, between ten o'clock and one, when things are rather slack: that is, except market-day and Saturday. Thus Annie has time to look about her. Then she often hops off her car and into a shop where she has spied something, while the driver chats in the main road. There is very good feeling between the girls and the drivers. Are they not companions in peril, shipments aboard this careering vessel of a tram-car, forever rocking on the waves of a stormy land.

Then, also, during the easy hours, the inspectors are most in evidence. For some reason, everybody employed in this tram-service is young: there are no grey heads. It would not do. Therefore the inspectors are of the right age, and one, the chief, is also good-looking. See him stand on a wet, gloomy morning, in his long oilskin, his peaked cap well down over his eyes, waiting to board a car. His face is ruddy, his small brown moustache is weathered, he has a faint impudent smile. Fairly tall and agile, even in his waterproof, he springs aboard a car and greets Annie.

"Hello, Annie! Keeping the wet out?"

"Trying to."

There are only two people in the car. Inspecting is soon over. Then for a long and impudent chat on the foot-board, a good, easy, twelve-mile chat.

The inspector's name is John Thomas Raynor—always called John Thomas, except sometimes, in malice, Coddy. His face sets in fury when he is addressed, from a distance, with this abbreviation. There is considerable scandal about John Thomas in half a dozen villages. He flirts with the girl conductors in the morning and walks out with them in the dark night, when they leave their tram-car at the depot. Of course, the girls quit the service frequently. Then he flirts and walks out with the newcomer: always providing she is sufficiently attractive, and that she will consent to walk. It is remarkable, however, that most of the girls are quite comely, they are all young, and this roving life aboard the car gives them a sailor's dash and recklessness. What matter how they behave when the ship is in port? To-morrow they will be aboard again.

Annie, however, was something of a Tartar, and her sharp tongue had kept John Thomas at arm's length for many months. Perhaps, therefore, she liked him all the more: for he always came up smiling, with impudence. She watched him vanquish one girl, then another. She could tell by the movement of his mouth and eyes, when he flirted with her in the morning, that he had been walking out with this lass, or the other, the night before. A fine cock-of-the-walk he was. She could sum him up pretty well.

In this subtle antagonism they knew each other like old friends, they were as shrewd with one another almost as man and wife. But Annie had always kept him sufficiently at arm's length. Besides, she had a boy of her own.

The Statutes fair, however, came in November, at Bestwood. It happened that Annie had the Monday night off. It was a drizzling ugly night, yet she dressed herself up and went to the fair ground. She was alone, but she expected soon to find a pal of some sort.

The roundabouts were veering round and grinding out their music, the side-shows were making as much commotion as possible. In the coconut shies there were no coconuts, but artificial wartime substitutes, which the lads declared were fastened into the irons. There was a sad decline in brilliance and luxury. None the less, the ground was muddy as ever, there was the same crush, the press of faces lighted up by the flares and the electric lights, the same smell of naphtha and a few fried potatoes, and of electricity.

Who should be the first to greet Miss Annie, on the show-ground but John Thomas. He had a black overcoat buttoned up to his chin, and a tweed cap pulled down over his brows, his face between was ruddy and smiling and handy as ever. She knew so well the way his mouth moved.

She was very glad to have a "boy." To be at the Statutes without a fellow was no fun. Instantly, like the gallant he was, he took her on the Dragons, grim-toothed, roundabout switchbacks. It was not nearly so exciting as a tram-car actually. But, then, to be seated in a shaking, green dragon, uplifted above the sea of bubble faces, careering in a rickety fashion in the lower heavens, whilst John Thomas leaned over her, his cigarette in his mouth, was after all the right style. She was a plump, quick, alive little creature. So she was quite excited and happy.

John Thomas made her stay on for the next round. And therefore she could hardly for shame repulse him when he put his arm round her and drew her a little nearer to him, in a very warm and cuddly manner. Besides, he was fairly discreet, he kept his movement as hidden as possible. She looked down and saw that his red, clean hand was out of sight of the crowd. And they knew each other so well. So they warmed up to the fair.

After the dragons they went on the horses. John Thomas paid each time, so she could but be complaisant. He, of course, sat astride on the outer horse—named "Black Bess"—and she sat sideways, towards him, on the inner horse—named "Wildfire." But of course John Thomas was not going to sit discreetly on "Black Bess," holding the brass bar. Round they spun and heaved, in the light. And round he swung on his wooden steed, flinging one leg across her mount, and perilously tipping up and down, across the space, half lying back, laughing at her. He was perfectly happy; she was afraid her hat was on one side, but she was excited.

He threw quoits on a table and won for her two large, pale blue hat-pins. And then, hearing the noise of the cinemas, announcing another performance, they climbed the boards and went in.

Of course, during these performances pitch darkness falls from time to time, when the machine goes wrong. Then there is a wild whooping, and a loud smacking of simulated kisses. In these moments John Thomas drew Annie towards him. After all, he had a wonderfully warm, cosy way of holding a girl with his arm, he seemed to make such a nice fit. And after all, it was pleasant to be so held: so very comforting and cosy and nice. He leaned over her and she felt his breath on her hair; she knew he wanted to kiss her on the lips. And after all, he was so warm and she fitted in to him so softly. After all, she wanted him to touch her lips.

But the light sprang up; she also started electrically, and put her hat straight. He left his arm lying nonchalantly behind her. Well, it was fun, it was exciting to be at the Statutes with John Thomas.

When the cinema was over they went for a walk across the dark, damp fields. He had all the arts of love-making. He was especially good at holding a girl, when he sat with her on a stile in the black, drizzling darkness. He seemed to be holding her in space, against his own warmth and gratification. And his kisses were soft and slow and searching.

So Annie walked out with John Thomas, though she kept her own boy dangling in the distance. Some of the tram-girls chose to be huffy. But there, you must take things as you find them, in this life.

There was no mistake about it, Annie liked John Thomas a good deal. She felt so rich and warm in herself whenever he was near. And John Thomas really liked Annie, more than usual. The soft, melting way in which she could flow into a fellow, as if she melted into his very bones, was something rare and good. He fully appreciated this.

But with a developing acquaintance there began a developing intimacy. Annie wanted to consider him a person, a man; she wanted to take an intelligent interest in him, and to have an intelligent response. She did not want a mere nocturnal presence, which was what he was so far. And she prided herself that he could not leave her.

Here she made a mistake. John Thomas intended to remain a nocturnal presence; he had no idea of becoming an all-round individual to her. When she started to take an intelligent interest in him and his life and his character, he sheered off. He hated intelligent interest. And he knew that the only way to stop it was to avoid it. The possessive female was aroused in Annie. So he left her.

It is no use saying she was not surprised. She was at first startled, thrown out of her count. For she had been so *very* sure of holding him. For a while she was staggered, and everything became uncertain to her. Then she wept with fury, indignation, desolation, and misery. Then she had a spasm of despair. And then, when he came, still impudently, on to her car, still familiar, but letting her see by the movement of his head that he had gone away to somebody else for the time being and was enjoying pastures new, then she determined to have her own back.

She had a very shrewd idea what girls John Thomas had taken out. She went to Nora Purdy. Nora was a tall, rather pale, but well-built girl, with beautiful yellow hair. She was rather secretive.

"Hey!" said Annie, accosting her; then softly, "Who's John Thomas on with now?"

"I don't know," said Nora.

"Why tha does," said Annie, ironically lapsing into dialect. "Tha knows as well as I do."

"Well, I do, then," said Nora. "It isn't me, so don't bother."

"It's Cissy Meakin, isn't it?"

"It is, for all I know."

"Hasn't he got a face on him!" said Annie. "I don't half like his cheek. I could knock him off the foot-board when he comes round at me."

"He'll get dropped on one of these days," said Nora.

"Ay, he will when somebody makes up their mind to drop it on him. I should like to see him taken down a peg or two, shouldn't you?"

"I shouldn't mind," said Nora.

"You've got a quite as much cause to as I have," said Annie. "But we'll drop on him one of these days, my girl. What? Don't you want to?"

"I don't mind," said Nora.

But as a matter of fact, Nora was much more vindictive than Annie.

One by one Annie went the round of the old flames. It so happened that Cissy Meakin left the tramway service in quite a short time. Her mother made her leave. Then John Thomas was on the *qui vive*. He cast his eyes over his old flock. And his eyes lighted on Annie. He thought she would be safe now. Besides, he liked her.

She arranged to walk home with him on Sunday night. It so happened that her car would be in the depot at half-past nine: the last car would come in at 10.15. So John Thomas was to wait for her there.

At the depot the girls had a little waiting-room of their own. It was quite rough, but cosy, with a fire and an oven and a mirror, and table and wooden chairs. The half dozen girls who knew John Thomas only too well had arranged to take service this Sunday afternoon. So, as the cars began to come in, early, the girls dropped into the waiting-room. And instead of hurrying off home, they sat around the fire and had a cup of tea. Outside was the darkness and lawlessness of wartime.

John Thomas came on the car after Annie, at about a quarter to ten. He poked his head easily into the girls' waiting-room.

"Prayer-meeting?" he asked.

"Ay," said Laura Sharp. "Ladies only."

"That's me!" said John Thomas. It was one of his favourite exclamations.

"Shut the door, boy," said Muriel Baggaley.

"On which side of me?" said John Thomas.

"Which tha likes," said Polly Birkin.

He had come in and closed the door behind him. The girls moved in their circle, to make a place for him near the fire. He took off his greatcoat and pushed back his hat.

"Who handles the teapot?" he said.

Nora Purdy silently poured him out a cup of tea.

"Want a bit o' my bread and drippin'?" said Muriel Baggaley to him.

"Ay, give us a bit."

And he began to eat his piece of bread.

"There's no place like home, girls," he said.

They all looked at him as he uttered this piece of impudence. He seemed to be sunning himself in the presence of so many damsels.

"Especially if you're not afraid to go home in the dark," said Laura Sharp.

"Me! By myself I am."

They sat till they heard the last tram come in. In a few minutes Emma Houselay entered.

"Come on, my old duck!" cried Polly Birkin.

"It *is* perishing," said Emma, holding her fingers to the fire.

"But—I'm afraid to, go home in, the dark," sang Laura Sharp, the tune having got into her mind.

"Who're you going with tonight, John Thomas?" asked Muriel Baggaley, coolly.

"Tonight?" said John Thomas. "Oh, I'm going home by myself tonight —all on my lonely-o."

"That's me!" said Nora Purdy, using his own ejaculation.

The girls laughed shrilly.

"Me as well, Nora," said John Thomas.

"Don't know what you mean," said Laura.

"Yes, I'm toddling," said he, rising and reaching for his overcoat.

"Nay," said Polly. "We're all here waiting for you."

"We've got to be up in good time in the morning," he said in the benevolent official manner.

They all laughed.

"Nay," said Muriel. "Don't leave us all lonely, John Thomas. Take one!"

"I'll take the lot, if you like," he responded gallantly.

"That you won't, either," said Muriel. "Two's company; seven's too much of a good thing."

"Nay—take one," said Laura. "Fair and square, all above board and say which."

"Ay," cried Annie, speaking for the first time. "Pick, John Thomas; let's hear thee."

"Nay," he said. "I'm going home quiet tonight. Feeling good, for once."

"Whereabouts?" said Annie. "Take a good un, then. But tha's got to take one of us!"

"Nay, how can I take one," he said, laughing uneasily. "I don't want to make enemies."

"You'd only make *one*," said Annie.

"The chosen *one*," added Laura.

"Oh, my! Who said girls!" exclaimed John Thomas, again turning, as if to escape. "Well—good-night."

"Nay, you've got to make your pick," said Muriel. "Turn your face to the wall and say which one touches you. Go on—we shall only just touch your back—one of us. Go on—turn your face to the wall, and don't look, and say which one touches you."

He was uneasy, mistrusting them. Yet he had not the courage to break away. They pushed him to a wall and stood him there with his face to it. Behind his back they all grimaced, tittering. He looked so comical. He looked around uneasily.

"Go on!" he cried.

"You're looking—you're looking!" they shouted.

He turned his head away. And suddenly, with a movement like a swift cat, Annie went forward and fetched him a box on the side of the head that set his cap flying, and himself staggering. He started round.

But at Annie's signal they all flew at him, slapping him, pinching him, pulling his hair, though more in fun than in spite or anger. He, however, saw red. His blue eyes flamed with strange fear as well as fury, and he butted through the girls to the door. It was locked. He wrenched at it. Roused, alert, the girls stood round and looked at him. He faced them, at bay. At that moment they were rather horrifying to him, as they stood in their short uniforms. He was distinctly afraid.

"Come on, John Thomas! Come on! Choose!" said Annie.

"What are you after? Open the door," he said.

"We sha'n't—not till you've chosen!" said Muriel.

"Chosen what?" he said.

"Chosen the one you're going to marry," she replied.

He hesitated a moment.

"Open the blasted door," he said, "and get back to your senses." He spoke with official authority.

"You've got to choose!" cried the girls.

"Come on!" cried Annie, looking him in the eye. "Come on! Come on!"

He went forward, rather vaguely. She had taken off her belt, and swinging it, she fetched him a sharp blow over the head with the buckle end. He sprang and seized her. But immediately the other girls rushed upon him, pulling and tearing and beating him. Their blood was now thoroughly up. He was their sport now. They were going to have their own back, out of him. Strange, wild creatures, they hung on him and rushed at him to bear him down. His tunic was torn right up the back, Nora had hold at the back of his collar, and was actually strangling him. Luckily the button burst. He struggled in a wild frenzy of fury and terror, almost mad terror. His tunic was simply torn off his back, his shirt-sleeves were torn away, his arms were naked. The girls rushed at him, clenched their hands on him and pulled at him: or they rushed at him and pushed him, butted him with all their might: or they struck him wild blows. He ducked and cringed and struck sideways. They became more intense.

At last he was down. They rushed on him, kneeling on him. He had neither breath nor strength to move. His face was bleeding with a long scratch, his brow was bruised.

Annie knelt on him, the other girls knelt and hung on to him. Their faces were flushed, their hair wild, their eyes were all glittering strangely. He lay at last quite still, with face averted, as an animal lies when it is defeated and at the mercy of the captor. Sometimes his eye glanced back at the wild faces of the girls. His breast rose heavily, his wrists were torn.

"Now, then, my fellow!" gasped Annie at length. "Now then—now——"

At the sound of her terrifying cold triumph, he suddenly started to struggle as an animal might, but the girls threw themselves upon him with unnatural strength and power, forcing him down.

"Yes—now, then!" gasped Annie at length.

And there was a dead silence, in which the thud of heart-beating was to be heard. It was a suspense of pure silence in every soul.

"Now you know where you are," said Annie.

The sight of his white, bare arm maddened the girls. He lay in a kind of trance of fear and antagonism. They felt themselves filled with supernatural strength.

Suddenly Polly started to laugh—to giggle wildly—helplessly—and Emma and Muriel joined in. But Annie and Nora and Laura remained the same, tense, watchful, with gleaming eyes. He winced away from these eyes.

"Yes," said Annie, in a curious low tone, secret and deadly. "Yes! You've got it now! You know what you've done, don't you? You know what you've done."

He made no sound nor sign, but lay with bright, averted eyes, and averted, bleeding face.

"You ought to be *killed,* that's what you ought," said Annie tensely. "You ought to be *killed.*" And there was a terrifying lust in her voice.

Polly was ceasing to laugh, and giving long-drawn Oh-h-hs and sighs as she came to herself.

"He's got to choose," she said vaguely.

"Oh, yes, he has," said Laura, with vindictive decision.

"Do you hear—do you hear?" said Annie. And with a sharp movement that made him wince, she turned his face to her.

"Do you hear?" she repeated, shaking him.

But he was quite dumb. She fetched him a sharp slap on the face. He started, and his eyes widened. Then his face darkened with defiance, after all.

"Do you hear?" she repeated.

He only looked at her with hostile eyes.

"Speak!" she said, putting her face devilishly near his.

"What?" he said, almost overcome.

"You've got to *choose!*" she cried, as if it were some terrible menace, and as if it hurt her that she could not exact more.

"What?" he said in fear.

"Choose your girl, Coddy. You've got to choose her now. And you'll get your neck broken if you play any more of your tricks, my boy. You're settled now."

There was a pause. Again he averted his face. He was cunning in his overthrow. He did not give in to them really—no, not if they tore him to bits.

"All right, then," he said, "I choose Annie." His voice was strange and full of malice. Annie let go of him as if he had been a hot coal.

"He's chosen Annie!" said the girls in chorus.

"Me!" cried Annie. She was still kneeling, but away from him. He was still lying prostrate, with averted face. The girls grouped uneasily around.

"Me!" repeated Annie, with a terrible bitter accent.

Then she got up, drawing away from him with strange disgust and bitterness.

"I wouldn't touch him," she said.

But her face quivered with a kind of agony, she seemed as if she would fall. The other girls turned aside. He remained lying on the floor, with his torn clothes and bleeding, averted face.

"Oh, if he's choosen—" said Polly.

"I don't want him—he can choose again," said Annie, with the same rather bitter hopelessness.

"Get up," said Polly, lifting his shoulder. "Get up."

He rose slowly, a strange, ragged, dazed creature. The girls eyed him from a distance, curiously, furtively, dangerously.

"Who wants him?" cried Laura roughly.

"Nobody," they answered with contempt. Yet each one of them waited for him to look at her, hoped he would look at her. All except Annie, and something was broken in her.

He, however, kept his face closed and averted from them all. There was a silence of the end. He picked up the torn pieces of his tunic, without knowing what to do with them. The girls stood about uneasily, flushed, panting, tidying their hair and their dress unconsciously, and watching him. He looked at none of them. He espied his cap in a corner and went and picked it up. He put it on his head, and one of the girls burst into a shrill, hysteric laugh at the sight he presented. He, however, took no heed but went straight to where his overcoat hung on a peg. The girls moved away from contact with him as if he had been an electric wire. He put on his coat and buttoned it down. Then he rolled his tunic-rags into a bundle, and stood before the locked door, dumbly.

"Open the door, somebody," said Laura.

"Annie's got the key," said one.

Annie silently offered the key to the girls. Nora unlocked the door.

"Tit for tat, old man," she said. "Show yourself a man, and don't bear a grudge."

But without a word or sign he had opened the door and gone, his face closed, his head dropped.

"That'll learn him," said Laura.

"Coddy!" said Nora.

"Shut up, for God's sake!" cried Annie fiercely, as if in torture.

"Well, I'm about ready to go, Polly. Look sharp!" said Muriel.

The girls were all anxious to be off. They were tidying themselves hurriedly, with mute, stupefied faces.

A Still Moment

Eudora Welty

Lorenzo Dow rode the Old Natchez Trace at top speed upon a race horse, and the cry of the itinerant Man of God, "I must have souls! And souls I must have!" rang in his own windy ears. He rode as if never to stop, toward his night's appointment.

It was the hour of sunset. All the souls that he had saved and all those he had not took dusky shapes in the mist that hung between the high banks, and seemed by their great number and density to block his way, and showed no signs of melting or changing back into mist, so that he feared his passage was to be difficult forever. The poor souls that were not saved were darker and more pitiful than those that were, and still there was not any of the radiance he would have hoped to see in such a congregation.

"Light up, in God's name!" he called, in the pain of his disappointment.

Then a whole swarm of fireflies instantly flickered all around him, up and down, back and forth, first one golden light and then another, flashing without any of the weariness that had held back the souls. These were the signs sent from God that he had not seen the accumulated radiance of saved souls because he was not able, and that his eyes were more able to see the fire flies of the Lord than His blessed souls.

Copyright © 1942, 1970, by Eudora Welty. Reprinted from her volume *The Wide Net and Other Stories* by permission of Harcourt Brace Jovanovich, Inc.

"Lord, give me the strength to see the angels when I am in Paradise," he said. "Do not let my eyes remain in this failing proportion to my loving heart always."

He gasped and held on. It was that day's complexity of horse-trading that had left him in the end with a Spanish race horse for which he was bound to send money in November from Georgia. Riding faster on the beast and still faster until he felt as if he were flying he sent thoughts of love with matching speed to his wife Peggy in Massachusetts. He found it effortless to love at a distance. He could look at the flowering trees and love Peggy in fullness, just as he could see his visions and love God. And Peggy, to whom he had not spoken until he could speak fateful words ("Would she accept of such an object as him?"), Peggy, the bride, with whom he had spent a few hours of time, showing of herself a small round handwriting, declared all in one letter, her first, that she felt the same as he, and that the fear was never of separation, but only of death.

Lorenzo well knew that it was Death that opened underfoot, that rippled by at night, that was the silence the birds did their singing in. He was close to death, closer than any animal or bird. On the back of one horse after another, winding them all, he was always riding toward it or away from it, and the Lord sent him directions with protection in His mind.

Just then he rode into a thicket of Indians taking aim with their new guns. One stepped out and took the horse by the bridle, it stopped at a touch, and the rest made a closing circle. The guns pointed.

"Incline!" The inner voice spoke sternly and with its customary lightning-quickness.

Lorenzo inclined all the way forward and put his head to the horse's silky mane, his body to its body, until a bullet meant for him would endanger the horse and make his death of no value. Prone he rode out through the circle of Indians, his obedience to the voice leaving him almost fearless, almost careless with joy.

But as he straightened and pressed ahead, care caught up with him again. Turning half-beast and half-divine, dividing himself like a heathen Centaur, he had escaped his death once more. But was it to be always by some metamorphosis of himself that he escaped, some humiliation of his faith, some admission to strength and argumentation and not frailty? Each time when he acted so it was at the command of an instinct that he took at once as the word of an angel, until too late, when he knew it was the word of the devil. He had roared like a tiger at Indians, he had submerged himself in water blowing the savage bubbles of the alligator, and they skirted him by. He had prostrated himself to appear dead, and deceived bears. But all the time God would have protected him in His own way, less hurried, more divine.

Even now he saw a serpent crossing the Trace, giving out knowing glances.

He cried, "I know you now!," and the serpent gave him one look out of which all the fire had been taken, and went away in two darts into the tangle.

He rode on, all expectation, and the voices in the throats of the wild beasts went, almost without his noticing when, into words. "Praise God," they said. "Deliver us from one another." Birds especially sang of divine love which was the one ceaseless protection. "Peace, in peace," were their words so many times when they spoke from the briars, in a courteous sort of inflection, and he turned his countenance toward all perched creatures with a benevolence striving to match their own.

He rode on past the little intersecting trails, letting himself be guided by voices and by lights. It was battlesounds he heard most, sending him on, sometimes ocean sounds, that long beat of waves that would make his heart pound and retreat as heavily as they, and he despaired again in his failure in Ireland when he took a voyage and persuaded with the Catholics with his back against the door, and then ran away to their cries of "Mind the white hat!" But when he heard singing it was not the militant and sharp sound of Wesley's hymns, but a soft, tireless and tender air that had no beginning and no end, and the softness of distance, and he had pleaded with the Lord to find out if all this meant that it was wicked, but no answer had come.

Soon night would descend, and a camp-meeting ground ahead would fill with its sinners like the sky with its stars. How he hungered for them! He looked in prescience with a longing of love over the throng that waited while the flames of the torches threw change, change, change over their faces. How could he bring them enough, if it were not divine love and sufficient warning of all that could threaten them? He rode on faster. He was a filler of appointments, and he filled more and more, until his journeys up and down creation were nothing but a shuttle, driving back and forth upon the rich expanse of his vision. He was homeless by his own choice, he must be everywhere at some time, and somewhere soon. There hastening in the wilderness on his flying horse he gave the night's torchlit crowd a premature benediction, he could not wait. He spread his arms out, one at a time for safety, and he wished, when they would all be gathered in by his tin horn blasts and the inspired words would go out over their heads, to brood above the entire and passionate life of the wide world, to become its rightful part.

He peered ahead. "Inhabitants of Time! The wilderness is your souls on earth!" he shouted ahead into the treetops. "Look about you, if you would view the conditions of your spirit, put here by the good Lord to show you and afright you. These wild places and these trails of awesome loneliness lie nowhere, nowhere, but in your heart."

A Still Moment

A dark man, who was James Murrell the outlaw, rode his horse out of a cane brake and began going along beside Lorenzo without looking at him. He had the alternately proud and aggrieved look of a man believing himself to be an instrument in the hands of a power, and when he was young he said at once to strangers that he was being used by Evil, or sometimes he stopped a traveler by shouting, "Stop! I'm the Devil!" He rode along now talking and drawing out his talk, by some deep control of the voice gradually slowing the speed of Lorenzo's horse down until both the horses were softly trotting. He would have wondered that nothing he said was heard, not knowing that Lorenzo listened only to voices of whose heavenly origin he was more certain.

Murrell riding along with his victim-to-be, Murrell riding, was Murrell talking. He told away at his long tales, with always a distance and a long length of time flowing through them, and all centered about a silent man. In each the silent man would have done a piece of evil, a robbery or a murder, in a place of long ago, and it was all made for the revelation in the end that the silent man was Murrell himself, and the long story had happened yesterday, and the place *here*—the Natchez Trace. It would only take one dawning look for the victim to see that all of this was another story and he himself had listened his way into it, and that he too was about to recede in time (to where the dread was forgotten) for some listener and to live for a listener in the long ago. Destroy the present!—that must have been the first thing that was whispered in Murrell's heart —the living moment and the man that lives in it must die before you can go on. It was his habit to bring the journey—which might even take days —to a close with a kind of ceremony. Turning his face at last into the face of the victim, for he had never seen him before now, he would tower up with the sudden height of a man no longer the tale teller but the speechless protagonist, silent at last, one degree nearer the hero. Then he would murder the man.

But it would always start over. This man going forward was going backward with talk. He saw nothing, observed no world at all. The two ends of his journey pulled at him always and held him in a nowhere, half asleep, smiling and witty, dangling his predicament. He was a murderer whose final stroke was over-long postponed, who had to bring himself through the greatest tedium to act, as if the whole wilderness, where he was born, were his impediment. But behind him and before him he kept in sight a victim, he saw a man fixed and stayed at the point of death— no matter how the man's eyes denied it, a victim, hands spreading to reach as if for the first time for life. Contempt! That is what Murrell gave that man.

Lorenzo might have understood, if he had not been in haste, that Murrell in laying hold of a man meant to solve his mystery of being. It was as if other men, all but himself, would lighten their hold on the secret, upon assault, and let it fly free at death. In his violence he was only treating of enigma. The violence shook his own body first, like a force gathering, and now he turned in the saddle.

Lorenzo's despair had to be kindled as well as his ecstasy, and could not come without that kindling. Before the awe-filled moment when the faces were turned up under the flares, as though an angel hand tipped their chins, he had no way of telling whether he would enter the sermon by sorrow or by joy. But at this moment the face of Murrell was turned toward him, turning at last, all solitary, in its full, and Lorenzo would have seized the man at once by his black coat and shaken him like prey for a lost soul, so instantly was he certain that the false fire was in his heart instead of the true fire. But Murrell, quick when he was quick, had put his own hand out, a restraining hand, and laid it on the wavelike flesh of the Spanish race horse, which quivered and shuddered at the touch.

They had come to a great live-oak tree at the edge of a low marsh-land. The burning sun hung low, like a head lowered on folded arms, and over the long reaches of violet trees the evening seemed still with thought. Lorenzo knew the place from having seen it among many in dreams, and he stopped readily and willingly. He drew rein, and Murrell drew rein, he dismounted and Murrell dismounted, he took a step, and Murrell was there too; and Lorenzo was not surprised at the closeness, how Murrell in his long dark coat and over it his dark face darkening still, stood beside him like a brother seeking light.

But in that moment instead of two men coming to stop by the great forked tree, there were three.

From far away, a student, Audubon, had been approaching lightly on the wilderness floor, disturbing nothing in his lightness. The long day of beauty had led him this certain distance. A flock of purple finches that he tried for the first moment to count went over his head. He made a spelling of the soft *pet* of the ivory-billed woodpecker. He told himself always: remember.

Coming upon the Trace, he looked at the high cedars, azure and still as distant smoke overhead, with their silver roots trailing down on either side like the veins of deepness in this place, and he noted some fact to his memory—this earth that wears but will not crumble or slide or turn to dust, they say it exists in one other spot in the world, Egypt—and then forgot it. He walked quietly. All life used this Trace, and he liked to see the animals move along it in direct, oblivious journeys, for they had begun it and made it, the buffalo and deer and the small running creatures before man ever knew where he wanted to go, and birds flew a great mirrored course above. Walking beneath them Audubon remembered how in the cities he had seen these very birds in his imagination, calling them up whenever he wished, even in the hard and glittering outer parlors where if an artist were humble enough to wait, some idle hand held up promised money. He walked lightly and he went as carefully as he had started at two that morning, crayon and paper, a gun, and a small bottle of spirits disposed about his body. *(Note: "The mocking birds so gentle that they would scarcely move out of the way.")* He looked with care; great abundance had ceased to startle him, and he could see things one by one. In Natchez they had told him of many strange and marvelous birds that were to be found here. Their descriptions had been exact, complete, and wildly varying, and he took them for inventions and believed that like all the worldly things that came out of Natchez, they would be disposed of and shamed by any man's excursion into the reality of Nature.

In the valley he appeared under the tree, a sure man, very sure and tender, as if the touch of all the earth rubbed upon him and the strains of the flowery swamp had made him so.

Lorenzo welcomed him and turned fond eyes upon him. To transmute a man into an angel was the hope that drove him all over the world and never let him flinch from a meeting or withhold good-byes for long. This hope insistently divided his life into only two parts, journey and rest. There could be no night and day and love and despair and longing and satisfaction to make partitions in the single ecstasy of this alternation. All things were speech.

"God created the world," said Lorenzo, "and it exists to give testimony. Life is the tongue: speak."

But instead of speech there happened a moment of deepest silence.

Audubon said nothing because he had gone without speaking a word for days. He did not regard his thoughts for the birds and animals as susceptible, in their first change, to words. His long playing on the flute was not in its origin a talking to himself. Rather than speak to order or describe, he would always draw a deer with a stroke across it to communicate his need of venison to an Indian. He had only found words when he discovered that there is much otherwise lost that can be noted down each item in its own day, and he wrote often now in a journal, not wanting anything to be lost the way it had been, all the past, and he would write about a day, "Only sorry that the Sun Sets."

Murrell, his cheated hand hiding the gun, could only continue to smile at Lorenzo, but he remembered in malice that he had disguised himself once as an Evangelist, and his final words to this victim would have been, "One of my disguises was what you are."

Then in Murrell, Audubon saw what he thought of as "acquired sorrow"—that cumbrousness and darkness from which the naked Indian, coming just as he was made from God's hand, was so lightly free. He noted the eyes—the dark kind that loved to look through chinks, and saw neither closeness nor distance, light nor shade, wonder nor familiarity. They were narrowed to contract the heart, narrowed to make an averting plan. Audubon knew the finest-drawn tendons of the body and the working of their power, for he had touched them, and he supposed then that in man the enlargement of the eye to see started a motion in the hands to make or do, and that the narrowing of the eye stopped the hand and contracted the heart. Now Murrell's eyes followed an ant on a blade of grass, up the blade and down, many times in the single moment. Audubon had examined the Cave-In Rock where one robber had lived his hiding life, and the air in the cave was the cavelike air that enclosed this man, the same odor, flinty and dark. O secret life, he thought—is it true that the secret is withdrawn from the true disclosure, that man is a cave man, and that the openness I see, the ways through forests, the rivers brimming light, the wide arches where the birds fly, are dreams of freedom? If my origin is withheld from me, is my end to be unknown too? Is the radiance I see closed into an interval between two darks, or can it not illuminate them both and discover at last, though it cannot be spoken, what was thought hidden and lost?

In that quiet moment a solitary snowy heron flew down not far away and began to feed beside the marsh water.

At the single streak of flight, the ears of the race horse lifted, and the eyes of both horses filled wih the soft lights of sunset, which in the next instant were reflected in the eyes of the men too as they all looked into the west toward the heron, and all eyes seemed infused with a sort of wildness.

Lorenzo gave the bird a triumphant look, such as a man may bestow upon his own vision, and thought, Nearness is near, lighted in a marshland, feeding at sunset. Praise God, His love has come visible.

Murrell, in suspicion pursuing all glances, blinking into a haze, saw only whiteness ensconced in darkness, as if it were a little luminous shell that drew in and held the eyesight. When he shaded his eyes, the brand "H.T." on his thumb thrust itself into his own vision, and he looked at the bird with the whole plan of the Mystic Rebellion darting from him as if in rays of the bright reflected light, and he stood looking proudly, leader as he was bound to become of the slaves, the brigands and outcasts of the entire Natchez country, with plans, dates, maps burning like a brand into his brain, and he saw himself proudly in a moment of prophecy going down rank after rank of successively bowing slaves to unroll and flaunt an awesome great picture of the Devil colored on a banner.

Audubon's eyes embraced the object in the distance and he could see it as carefully as if he held it in his hand. It was a snowy heron alone out of its flock. He watched it steadily, in his care noting the exact inevitable things. When it feeds it muddies the water with its foot. . . . It was as if each detail about the heron happened slowly in time, and only once. He felt again the old stab of wonder—what structure of life bridged the reptile's scale and the heron's feather? That knowledge too had been lost. He watched without moving. The bird was defenseless in the world except for the intensity of its life, and he wondered, how can heat of blood and speed of heart defend it? Then he thought, as always as if it were new and unbelievable, it has nothing in space or time to prevent its flight. And he waited, knowing that some birds will wait for a sense of their presence to travel to men before they will fly away from them.

Fixed in its pure white profile it stood in the precipitous moment, a plumicorn on its head, its breeding dress extended in rays, eating steadily the little water creatures. There was a little space between each man and the others, where they stood overwhelmed. No one could say the three had ever met, or that this moment of intersection had ever come in their lives, or its promise fulfilled. But before them the white heron rested in the grasses with the evening all around it, lighter and more serene that the evening, flight closed in its body, the circuit of its beauty closed, a bird seen and a bird still, its motion calm as if it were offered: Take my flight. . . .

What each of them wanted was simply *all.* To save all souls, to destroy all men, to see and to record all life that filled this world—all, all—but now a single frail yearning seemed to go out of the three of them for a moment and to stretch toward this one snowy, shy bird in the marshes. It was as if three whirlwinds had drawn together at some center, to find there feeding in peace a snowy heron. Its own slow spiral of flight could take it away in its own time, but for a little it held them still, it laid quiet over them, and they stood for a moment unburdened. . . .

Murrell wore no mask, for his face was that, a face that was aware while he was somnolent, a face that watched for him, and listened for him, alert and nearly brutal, the guard of a planner. He was quick without that he might be slow within, he staved off time, he wandered and plotted, and yet his whole desire mounted in him toward the end (was this the end— the sight of a bird feeding at dusk?), toward the instant of confession. His incessant deeds were thick in his heart now, and flinging himself to the ground he thought wearily, when all these trees are cut down, and the Trace lost, then my Conspiracy that is yet to spread itself will be disclosed, and all the stone-loaded bodies of murdered men will be pulled up, and all everywhere will know poor Murrell. His look pressed upon Lorenzo, who stared upward, and Audubon, who was taking out his gun, and his eyes squinted up to them in pleading, as if to say, "How soon may

I speak, and how soon will you pity me?" Then he looked back to the bird, and he thought if it would look at him a dread penetration would fill and gratify his heart.

Audubon in each act of life was aware of the mysterious origin he half-concealed and half-sought for. People along the way asked him in their kindness or their rudeness if it were true, that he was born a prince, and was the Lost Dauphin, and some said it was his secret, and some said that that was what he wished to find out before he died. But if it was his identity that he wished to discover, or if it was what a man had to seize beyond that, the way for him was by endless examination, by the care for every bird that flew in his path and every serpent that shone underfoot. Not one was enough; he looked deeper and deeper, on and on, as if for a particular beast or some legendary bird. Some men's eyes persisted in looking outward when they opened to look inward, and to their delight, there outflung was the astonishing world under the sky. When a man at last brought himself to face some mirror-surface he still saw the world looking back at him, and if he continued to look, to look closer and closer, what then? The gaze that looks outward must be trained without rest, to be indomitable. It must see as slowly as Murrell's ant in the grass, as exhaustively as Lorenzo's angel of God, and then, Audubon dreamed, with his mind going to his pointed brush, it must see like this, and he tightened his hand on the trigger of the gun and pulled it, and his eyes went closed. In memory the heron was all its solitude, its total beauty. All its whiteness could be seen from all sides at once, its pure feathers were as if counted and known and their array one upon the other would never be lost. But it was not from that memory that he could paint.

His opening eyes met Lorenzo's, close and flashing, and it was on seeing horror deep in them, like fires in abysses, that he recognized it for the first time. He had never seen horror in its purity and clarity until now, in bright blue eyes. He went and picked up the bird. He had thought it to be a female, just as one sees the moon as female; and so it was. He put it in his bag, and started away. But Lorenzo had already gone on, leaning a-tilt on the horse which went slowly.

Murrell was left behind, but he was proud of the dispersal, as if he had done it, as if he had always known that three men in simply being together and doing a thing can, by their obstinacy, take the pride out of one another. Each must go away alone, each send the others away alone. He himself had purposely kept to the wildest country in the world, and would have sought it out, the loneliest road. He looked about with satisfaction, and hid. Travelers were forever innocent, he believed: that was his faith. He lay in wait; his faith was in innocence and his knowledge was of ruin; and had these things been shaken? Now, what could possibly be outside his grasp? Churning all about him like a cloud about the sun was the great

A Still Moment 291

folding descent of this thought. Plans of deeds made his thoughts, and they rolled and mingled about his ears as if he heard a dark voice that rose up to overcome the wilderness voice, or was one with it. The night would soon come; and he had gone through the day.

Audubon, splattered and wet, turned back into the wilderness with the heron warm under his hand, his head still light in a kind of trance. It was undeniable, on some Sunday mornings, when he turned over and over his drawings they seemed beautiful to him, through what was dramatic in the conflict of life, or what was exact. What he would draw, and what he had seen, became for a moment one to him then. Yet soon enough, and it seemed to come in that same moment, like Lorenzo's horror and the gun's firing, he knew that even the sight of the heron which surely he alone had appreciated, had not been all his belonging, and that never could any vision, even any simple sight, belong to him or to any man. He knew that the best he could make would be, after it was apart from his hand, a dead thing and not a live thing, never the essence, only a sum of parts; and that it would always meet with a stranger's sight, and never be one with the beauty in any other man's head in the world. As he had seen the bird most purely at its moment of death, in some fatal way, in his care for looking outward, he saw his long labor most revealingly at the point where it met its limit. Still carefully, for he was trained to see well in the dark, he walked on into the deeper woods, noting all sights, all sounds, and was gentler than they as he went.

In the woods that echoed yet in his ears, Lorenzo riding slowly looked back. The hair rose on his head and his hands began to shake with cold, and suddenly it seemed to him that God Himself, just now, thought of the Idea of Separateness. For surely He had never thought of it before, when the little white heron was flying down to feed. He could understand God's giving Separateness first and then giving Love to follow and heal in its wonder; but God had reversed this, and given Love first and then Separateness, as though it did not matter to Him which came first. Perhaps it was that God never counted the moments of Time; Lorenzo did that, among his tasks of love. Time did not occur to God. Therefore— did He even know of it? How to explain Time and Separateness back to God. Who had never thought of them, Who could let the whole world come to grief in a scattering moment?

Lorenzo brought his cold hands together in a clasp and stared through the distance at the place where the bird had been as if he saw it still; as if nothing could really take away what had happened to him, the beautiful little vision of the feeding bird. Its beauty had been greater than he could account for. The sweat of rapture poured down from his forehead, and then he shouted into the marshes.

"Tempter!"

He whirled forward in the saddle and began to hurry the horse to its high speed. His camp ground was far away still, though even now they must be lighting the torches and gathering in the multitudes, so that at the appointed time he would duly appear in their midst, to deliver his address on the subject of "In that day when all hearts shall be disclosed."

Then the sun dropped below the trees, and the new moon, slender and white, hung shyly in the west.

Mr Andrews

E. M. Forster

The souls of the dead were ascending towards the Judgment Seat and the Gate of Heaven. The world soul pressed them on every side, just as the atmosphere presses upon rising bubbles, striving to vanquish them, to break their thin envelope of personality, to mingle their virtue with its own. But they resisted, remembering their glorious individual life on earth, and hoping for an individual life to come.

Among them ascended the soul of a Mr Andrews who, after a beneficent and honourable life, had recently deceased at his house in town. He knew himself to be kind, upright and religious, and though he approached his trial with all humility, he could not be doubtful of its result. God was not now a jealous God. He would not deny salvation merely because it was expected. A righteous soul may reasonably be conscious of its own righteousness and Mr Andrews was conscious of his.

'The way is long,' said a voice, 'but by pleasant converse the way becomes shorter. Might I travel in your company?'

'Willingly,' said Mr Andrews. He held out his hand, and the two souls floated upwards together.

'I was slain fighting the infidel,' said the other exultantly, 'and I go straight to those joys of which the Prophet speaks.'

'Are you not a Christian?' asked Mr Andrews gravely.

From *The Eternal Moment and Other Stories* by E. M. Forster, copyright, 1928, by Harcourt Brace Jovanovich, Inc.; copyright © 1956, by E. M. Forster. Reprinted by permission of the publisher.

'No, I am a Believer, But you are a Moslem, surely?'

'I am not,' said Mr Andrews. 'I am a Believer.'

The two souls floated upwards in silence, but did not release each other's hands. 'I am broad church,' he added gently. The word 'broad' quavered strangely amid the interspaces.

'Relate to me your career,' said the Turk at last.

'I was born of a decent middle-class family, and had my education at Winchester and Oxford. I thought of becoming a missionary, but was offered a post in the Board of Trade, which I accepted. At thirty-two I married, and had four children, two of whom have died. My wife survives me. If I had lived a little longer I should have been knighted.'

'Now I will relate my career. I was never sure of my father, and my mother does not signify. I grew up in the slums of Salonika. Then I joined a band and we plundered the villages of the infidel. I prospered and had three wives, all of whom survive me. Had I lived a little longer I should have had a band of my own.'

'A son of mine was killed travelling in Macedonia. Perhaps you killed him.'

'It is very possible.'

The two souls floated upward, hand in hand. Mr Andrews did not speak again, for he was filled with horror at the approaching tragedy. This man, so godless, so lawless, so cruel, so lustful, believed that he would be admitted into Heaven. And into what a heaven—a place full of the crude pleasures of a ruffian's life on earth! But Mr Andrews felt neither disgust nor moral indignation. He was only conscious of an immense pity, and his own virtues confronted him not at all. He longed to save the man whose hand he held more tightly, who, he thought, was now holding more tightly on to him. And when he reached the Gate of Heaven, instead of saying 'Can I enter?' as he had intended, he cried out, 'Cannot *he* enter?'

And at the same moment the Turk uttered the same cry. For the same spirit was working in each of them.

From the gateway a voice replied, 'Both can enter.' They were filled with joy and pressed forward together.

Then the voice said, 'In what clothes will you enter?'

'In my best clothes,' shouted the Turk, 'the ones I stole.' And he clad himself in a splendid turban and a waistcoat embroidered with silver, and baggy trousers, and a great belt in which were stuck pipes and pistols and knives.

'And in what clothes will you enter?' said the voice to Mr Andrews.

Mr Andrews thought of his best clothes, but he had no wish to wear them again. At last he remembered and said, 'Robes.'

'Of what colour and fashion?' asked the voice.

Mr Andrews had never thought about the matter much. He replied, in hesitating tones, 'White, I suppose, of some flowing soft material,' and he was immediately given a garment such as he had described. 'Do I wear it rightly?' he asked.

'Wear it as it pleases you,' replied the voice. 'What else do you desire?'

'A harp,' suggested Mr Andrews. 'A small one.'

A small gold harp was placed in his hand.

'And a palm—no, I cannot have a palm, for it is the reward of martyrdom; my life has been tranquil and happy.'

'You can have a palm if you desire it.'

But Mr Andrews refused the palm, and hurried in his white robes after the Turk, who had already entered Heaven. As he passed in at the open gate, a man, dressed like himself, passed out with gestures of despair.

'Why is he not happy?' he asked.

The voice did not replay.

'And who are all those figures, seated inside on thrones and mountains? Why are some of them terrible, and sad, and ugly?'

There was no answer. Mr Andrews entered, and then he saw that those seated figures were all the gods who were then being worshipped on the earth. A group of souls stood round each, singing his praises. But the gods paid no heed, for they were listening to the prayers of living men, which alone brought them nourishment. Sometimes a faith would grow weak, and then the god of that faith also drooped and dwindled and fainted for his daily portion of incense. And sometimes, owning to a revivalist movement, or to a great commemoration, or to some other cause, a faith would grow strong, and the god of that faith grow strong also. And, more frequently still, a faith would alter, so that the features of its god altered and became contradictory, and passed from ecstasy to respectability, or from mildness and universal love to the ferocity of battle. And at times a god would divide into two gods, or three, or more, each with his own ritual and precarious supply of prayer.

Mr Andrews saw Buddha, and Vishnu, and Allah, and Jehovah, and the Elohim. He saw little ugly determined gods who were worshipped by a few savages in the same way. He saw the vast shadowy outlines of the neo-Pagan Zeus. There were cruel gods, and coarse gods, and tortured gods, and, worse still, there were gods who were peevish, or deceitful, or vulgar. No aspiration of humanity was unfulfilled. There was even a intermediate state for those who wished it, and for the Christian Scientists a place where they could demonstrate that they had not died.

He did not play his harp for long, but hunted vainly for one of his dead friends. And though souls were continually entering Heaven, it still seemed curiously empty. Though he had all that he expected, he was conscious of no great happiness, no mystic contemplation of beauty, no mystic union with good. There was nothing to compare with that moment outside the gate, when he prayed that the Turk might enter and heard the Turk uttering the same prayer for him. And when at last he saw his companion, he hailed him with a cry of human joy.

The Turk was seated in thought, and round him, by sevens, sat the virgins who are promised in the Koran.

'Oh, my dear friend!' he called out. 'Come here and we will never be parted, and such as my pleasures are, they shall be yours also. Where are my other friends? Where are the men whom I love, or whom I have killed?' 'I, too, have only found you,' said Mr Andrews. He sat down by the Turk, and the virgins, who were all exactly alike, ogled them with coal black eyes.

'Though I have all that I expected,' said the Turk, 'I am conscious of no great happiness. There is nothing to compare with that moment outside the gate when I prayed that you might enter, and heard you uttering the same prayer for me. These virgins are as beautiful and good as I had fashioned, yet I could wish that they were better.'

As he wished, the forms of the virgins became more rounded, and their eyes grew larger and blacker than before. And Mr Andrews, by a wish similar in kind, increased the purity and softness of his garment and the glitter of his harp. For in that place their expectations were fulfilled, but not their hopes.

'I am going,' said Mr Andrews at last. 'We desire infinity and we cannot imagine it. How can we expect it to be granted? I have never imagined anything infinitely good or beautiful excepting in my dreams.'

'I am going with you,' said the other.

Together they sought the entrance gate, and the Turk parted with his virgins and his best clothes, and Mr Andrew cast away his robes and his harp.

'Can we depart?' they asked.

'You can both depart if you wish,' said the voice, 'but remember what lies outside.'

As soon as they passed the gate, they felt again the pressure of the world soul. For a moment they stood hand in hand resisting it. Then they suffered it to break in upon them, and they, and all the experience they had gained, and all the love and wisdom they had generated, passed into it, and made it better.

Sunday

Ted Hughes

Michael marched off to chapel beside his sister, rapping his Sunday shoes down on to the pavement to fetch the brisk, stinging echo off housewalls, wearing the detestable blue blazer with its meaningless badge as a uniform loaded with honours and privilege. In chapel he sat erect, arms folded, instead of curling down on to his spine like a prawn and sinking his chin between his collar-bones as under the steady pressure of a great hand, which was his usual attitude of worship. He sang the hymns and during the prayers thought exultantly of Top Wharf Pub, trying to remember what time those places opened.

All this zest, however, was no match for the sermon. The minister's voice soared among the beams, tireless, as if he were still rehearsing, and after ten minutes these organ-like modulations began to work Michael into a torment of impatience. The nerve-ends all over his body prickled and swarmed. He almost had to sink to his knees. Thoughts of shouting, 'Oh, well!'—one enormous sigh, or simply running out of chapel, brought a fine sweat on to his temples. Finally he closed his eyes and began to imagine a wolf galloping through a snow-filled, moonlit forest. Without fail this image was the first thing in his mind whenever he shut his eyes on these situations of constraint, in school, in waiting-rooms, with visitors. The wolf urged itself with all its strength through a land empty of everything but trees and snow. After a while he drifted to vaguer

"Sunday" from *WODWO* by Ted Hughes. Copyright © 1962 by Ted Hughes. By permission of Harper and Row, Publishers, Inc. and Faber and Faber Ltd.

things, a few moments of freedom before his impatience jerked him back to see how the sermon was doing. It was still soaring. He closed his eyes and the wolf was there again.

By the time the doors opened, letting light stream in, he felt stupefied. He edged out with the crowd. Then the eleven-o'clock Sunday sky struck him. He had forgotten it was so early in the day. But with the light and the outside world his mind returned in a rush. Leaving his sister deep in the chapel, buried in a pink and blue bouquet of her friends, and evading the minister who, having processed his congregation generally within, had darted round the side of the chapel to the porch and was now setting his personal seal, a crushing smile and a soft, supporting handclasp, on each member of the flock as they stumbled out, Michael took the three broad steps at a leap and dodged down the crowded path among the graves, like a person with an important dispatch.

But he was no sooner out through the gate than the stitches of his shoes seemed suddenly to tighten, and his damped hair tightened on his scalp. He slowed to a walk.

To the farthest skyline it was Sunday. The valley walls, throughout the week wet, hanging, uncomfortable woods and mud-hole farms, were today neat, remote, and irreproachably pretty, postcard pretty. The blue sky, the sparkling smokeless Sunday air, had disinfected them. Picnickers and chapel-hikers were already up there, sprinkled like confetti along the steep lanes and paths, creeping imperceptibly upward towards the brown line of the moors. Spotless, harmless, church-going slopes! Life, over the whole countryside, was suspended for the day.

Below him the town glittered in the clear air and sunlight. Throughout the week it resembled from this point a volcanic pit, bottomless in places, a jagged fissure into a sulphurous underworld, the smoke dragging off the chimneys of the mills and houserows like a tearing fleece. Now it lay as under shallow, slightly warm, clear water, with still streets and bright yards.

There was even something Sundayish about the pavements, something untouchably proper, though nothing had gone over them since grubby Saturday except more feet and darkness.

Superior to all this for once, and quite enjoying it again now he was on his way, Michael went down the hill into the town with strides that jammed his toes into the ends of his shoes. He turned into the Memorial Gardens, past prams, rockeries, forbidden grass, trees with labels, and over the ornamental canal bridge to the bowling greens that lay on the level between canal and river.

His father was there, on the farthest green, with two familiar figures—Harry Rutley, the pork butcher, and Mr. Stinson, a tall, sooty, lean man who held his head as if he were blind and spoke rarely, and then only as if phrasing his most private thoughts to himself. A man Michael preferred not to look at. Michael sat on a park bench behind their jack and tried to make himself obvious.

The paths were full of people. Last night this had been a parade of couples, foursomes, gangs and lonely ones—the electricity gathered off looms, sewing-machines and shop counters since Monday milling round the circuit and discharging up the sidepaths among the shrubbery in giggling darkness and shrieks. But now it was families, an after-chapel procession of rustlings and murmurings, lacy bosoms, tight blue pin-stripe suits and daisy-chains of children. Soon Michael was worn out, willing the bowls against their bias or against the crown of the green or to roll one foot farther and into the trough or to collide and fall in halves. He could see the Wesleyan Church clock at quarter past eleven and stared at it for what seemed like five minutes, convinced it had stopped.

He stood up as the three men came over to study the pattern of the bowls.

'Are we going now, Dad?'

'Just a minute, lad. Come and have a game.'

That meant at least another game whether he played or not. Another quarter of an hour! And to go and get out a pair of bowls was as good as agreeing to stay there playing till one.

'We might miss him.'

His father laughed. Only just remembering his promise, thought Michael.

'He'll not be there til well on. We shan't miss him.'

His father kicked his bowls together and Harry Rutley slewed the rubber mat into position.

'But will he be there sure?'

Sunday dinner was closer every minute. Then it was sleepy Sunday afternoon. Then Aunt-infested Sunday tea. His father laughed again.

'Billy Red'll be coming down today, won't he, Harry?'

Harry Rutley, pale, slow, round, weighed his jack. He had lost the tip of an ear at the Dardanelles and carried a fragment of his fifth rib on the end of his watch-chain. Now he narrowed his eyes, choosing a particular blade of grass on the far corner of the green.

'Billy Red? Every Sunday. Twelve on the dot.' He dipped his body to the underswing of his arm and came upright as the jack curled away across the green. 'I don't know how he does it.'

The jack had come to rest two feet from the far corner. There followed four more games. They played back to Michael, then across to the far right, then a short one down to the far left, then back to the near right. At last the green was too full, with nine or ten games interweaving and shouts of 'feet' every other minute and bowls bocking together in mid-green.

At quarter to twelve on the clock—Michael now sullen with the punishment he had undergone and the certainty that his day had been played away—the three men came off the green, put away their bowls, and turned down on to the canal bank towpath.

The valley became narrower and its sides steeper. Road, river and canal made their way as best they could, with only a twenty-yard strip of wasteland—a tangle of rank weeds, elderberry bushes and rubble, bleached debris of floods—separating river and canal. Along the far side of the river squeezed the road, rumbling from Monday to Saturday with swaying lorry-loads of cotton and wool and cloth. The valley wall on that side, draped with a network of stone-walled fields and precariously-clinging farms and woods, came down sheer out of the sky into the backyards of a crouched stone row of weavers' cottages whose front doorsteps were almost part of the road. The river ran noisily over pebbles. On the strip of land between river and canal stood Top Wharf Pub—its buildings tucked in under the bank of the canal so that the towpath ran level with the back bedroom windows. On this side the valley wall, with overshadowing woods, dived straight into the black, motionless canal as if it must be a mile deep. The water was quite shallow, however, with its collapsed banks and accumulation of mud, so shallow that in some places the rushes grew right across. For years it had brought nothing to Top Wharf Pub but a black greasy damp and rats.

They turned down off the towpath into the wide, cobbled yard in front of the pub.

'You sit here. Now what would you like to drink?'

Michael sat on the cracked, weather-scrubbed bench in the yard under the bar-room window and asked for ginger beer.

'And see if he's come yet. And see if they have any rats ready.'

He had begun to notice the heat and now leaned back against the wall to get the last slice of shade under the eaves. But in no time the sun had moved out over the yard. The valley sides funnelled its rays down as into a trap, dazzling the quartz-points of the worn cobbles, burning the colour off everything. The flies were going wild, swirling in the air, darting and basking on the cobbles—big, green-glossed blue-bottles that leapt on to his hand when he laid it along the hot bench.

In twos and threes men came over the hog-backed bridge leading from the road into the yard, or down off the towpath. Correct, leisurely and a little dazed from morning service, or in overalls that were torn and whitened from obscure Sabbath labours, all disappeared through the door. The hubbub inside thickened. Michael strained to catch some mention of Billy Red.

At last his father brought him his ginger beer and informed him that Billy Red had not arrived yet but everybody was expecting him and he shouldn't be long. They had some nice rats ready.

In spite of the heat, Michael suddenly did not feel like drinking. His whole body seemed to have become frailer and slightly faint, as with hunger. When he sipped, the liquid trickled with a cold, tasteless weight into his disinterested stomach.

He left the glass on the bench and went to the Gents. Afterwards he walked stealthily round the yard, looking in at the old stables and coach-house, the stony cave silences. Dust, cobwebs, rat droppings. Old timbers, old wheels, old harness. Barrels, and rusty stoves. He listened for rats. Walking back across the blinding, humming yard he smelt roast beef and heard the clattering of the pub kitchen and saw through the open window fat arms working over a stove. The whole world was at routine Sunday dinner. The potatoes were already steaming, people sitting about killing time and getting impatient and wishing that something would fall out of the blue and knowing that nothing would. The idea stifled him, he didn't want to think of it. He went quickly back to the bench and sat down, his heart beating as if he had run.

A car nosed over the little bridge and stopped at the far side of the yard, evidently not sure whether it was permitted to enter the yard at all. Out of it stepped a well-to-do young man and a young woman. The young man unbuttoned his pale tweed jacket, thrust his hands into his trouser pockets and came sauntering towards the pub door, the girl on her high heels followed beside him, patting her hair and looking round at the scenery as if she had just come up out of a dark pit. They stood at the door for a moment, improvising their final decisions about what she would drink, whether this was the right place, and whether she ought to come in. He was sure it was the right place, this was where they did it all right, and he motioned her to sit on the end of the bench beside Michael. Michael moved accommodatingly to the other end. She ignored him, however, and perched on the last ten inches of the bench, arrayed her wide-skirted, summery, blue-flowered frock over her knees, and busied herself with her mirror. The flies whirled around, inspecting this new thing of scents.

Suddenly there came a shout from the doorway of the pub, long drawn words: 'Here comes the man.'

Immediately several crowded to the doorway, glasses in their hands.

'Here he comes.'

'The Red Killer!'

'Poor little beggar. He looks as if he lives on rat meat.'

'Draw him a half, Gab.'

Over the bridge and into the yard shambled a five-foot, ragged figure. Scarecrowish, tawny to colourless, exhausted, this was Billy Red, the rat-catcher. As a sideline he kept hens, and he had something of the raw, flea-bitten look of a red hen, with his small, sunken features and gingery hair. From the look of his clothes you would think he slept on the hen-house floor, under the roosts. One hand in his pocket, his back at a half-bend, he drifted aimlessly to a stop. Then, to show that after all he had only come for a sit in the sun, he sat down beside Michael with a long sigh.

'It's a grand day,' he announced. His voice was not strong—lungless, a shaky wisp, full of hen-fluff and dust.

Michael peered closely and secretly at this wrinkled, neglected fifty-year-old face shrunk on its small skull. Among the four-day stubble and enlarged pores and deep folds it was hard to make out anything, but there were one or two marks that might have been old rat bites. He had a little withered mouth and kept moving the lips about as if he couldn't get them comfortable. After a sigh he would pause a minute, leaning forward, one elbow on his knees, then sigh again, changing his position, the other elbow now on the other knee, like a man too weary to rest.

'Here you are, Billy.'

A hand held a half-pint high at the pub door like a sign and with startling readiness Billy leapt to his feet and disappeared into the pub, gathering the half-pint on the way and saying:

'I've done a daft bloody thing. I've come down all this way wi'out brass.'

There was an obliging roar of laughter and Michael found himself looking at the girl's powdered profile. She was staring down at her neatly-covered toe as it twisted this way and that, presenting all its polished surfaces.

Things began to sound livelier inside—sharp, loud remarks kicking up bursts of laughter and showering exclamations. The young man came out, composed, serious, and handed the girl a long-stemmed clear glass with a cherry in it. He sat down between her and Michael, splaying his knees as he did so and lunging his face forward to meet his streamingly raised pint—one smooth, expert motion.

'He's in there now,' he said, wiping his mouth. 'They're getting him ready.'

The girl gazed into his face, tilting her glass till the cherry bobbed against her pursed red lips, opening her eyes wide.

Michael looked past her to the doorway. A new figure had appeared. He supposed this must be the landlord, Gab—an aproned hemisphere and round, red greasy face that screwed itself up to survey the opposite hillside.

'Right,' called the landlord. 'I'll get 'em.' Away he went, wiping his hands on his apron, then letting them swing wide of his girth like penguin flippers, towards the coach-house. Now everybody came out of the pub and Michael stood up, surprised to see how many had been crowded in there. They were shouting and laughing, pausing to browse their pints, circulating into scattered groups. Michael went over and stood beside his father who was one of an agitated four. He had to ask twice before he could make himself heard. Even to himself his voice sounded thinner than usual, empty, as if at bottom it wanted nothing so much as to dive into his stomach and hide there in absolute silence, letting events go their own way.

'How many is he going to do?'

'I think they've got two.' His father half turned down towards him. 'It's usually two or three.'

Nobody took any notice of Billy Red who was standing a little apart, his hands hanging down from the slight stoop that seemed more or less permanent with him, smiling absently at the noisy, hearty groups. He brightened and straightened as the last man out of the pub came across, balancing a brimming pint glass. Michael watched. The moment the pint touched those shrivelled lips the pale little eye set with a sudden strangled intentness. His long, skinny, unshaven throat writhed and the beer shrank away in the glass. In two or three seconds he lowered the glass empty, wiped his mouth on his sleeve and looked around. Then as nobody stepped foreward to offer him a fill-up he set the glass down to the cobbles and stood drying his hands on his jacket.

Michael's gaze shifted slightly, and he saw the girl. He recognized his own thoughts in her look of mesmerized incredulity. At her side the young man was watching too, but shrewdly, between steady drinks.

The sun seemed to have come to a stop directly above. Two or three men had taken their jackets off, with irrelevant, noisy clowning, a few sparring feints. Somebody suggested they all go and stand in the canal and Billy Red do his piece under water, and another laughed so hard at this that the beer came spurting from his nostrils. High up on the opposite slope Michael could see a line of Sunday walkers, moving slowly across the dazed grey of the fields. Their coats would be over their shoulders, their ties in their pockets, their shoes agony, the girls asking to be pushed—but if they stood quite still they would feel a breeze. In the cobbled yard the heat had begun to dance.

'Here we are.'

The landlord waddled into the middle of the yard holding up an oblong wire cage. He set it down with a clash on the cobbles.

'Two of the best.'

Everybody crowded round. Michael squeezed to the front and

crouched down beside the cage. There was a pause of admiration. Hunched in opposite corners of the cage, their heads low and drawn in their backs pressed to the wires so that the glossy black-tipped hairs bristled out, were two big brown rats. They sat quiet. A long pinkish-grey tail, thick at the root as his thumb, coiled out by Michael's foot. He touched the hairy tip of it gently with his forefinger.

'Watch out, lad!'

The rat snatched its tail in, leapt across the cage with a crash and gripping one of the zinc bars behind its curved yellow teeth, shook till the cage rattled. The other rat left its corner and began gliding to and fro along one side—a continuous low fluidity, sniffing up and down the bars. Then both rats stopped and sat up on their hind-legs, like persons coming out of a trance, suddenly recognizing people. Their noses quivered as they directed their set, grey-chinned, inquisitive expressions at one face after another.

The landlord had been loosening the nooses in the end of two long pieces of dirty string. He lifted the cage again.

'Catch a tail, Walt.'

The group pressed closer. A hand came out and roamed in readiness under the high-held cage floor. The rats moved uneasily. The landlord gave the cage a shake and the rats crashed. A long tail swung down between the wires. The hand grabbed and pulled.

'Hold it.'

The landlord slipped the noose over the tail, down to the very butt, and pulled it tight. The caught rat, not quite convinced before but now understanding the whole situation, doubled round like a thing without bones, and bit and shook the bars and forced its nose out between them to get at the string that held its buttocks tight to the cage side.

'Just you hold that string, Walt. So's it can't get away when we open up.'

Now the the landlord lifted the cage again, while Walt held his string tight. The other rat, watching the operation on its companion, had bunched up in a corner, sitting on its tail.

'Clever little beggar. You know what I'm after, don't you?'

The landlord gave the cage a shake, but the rat clung on, its pink feet gripping the wires of the cage floor like hands. He shook the cage violently.

'Move, you stubborn little beggar,' demanded the landlord. He went on shaking the cage with sharp, jerking movements.

Then the rat startled everybody. Squeezing still farther into its corner, it opened its mouth wide and began to scream—a harsh, ripping, wavering scream travelling out over the yard like some thin, metallic, dazzling substance that decomposed instantly. As one scream died the rat started another, its mouth wide. Michael had never thought a rat could make so much noise. As it went on at full intensity, his stomach began to twist and flex like a thick muscle. For a moment he was so worried by these sensations that he stopped looking at the rat. The landlord kept on shaking the cage and the scream shook in the air, but the rat clung on, still sitting on its tail.

'Give him a poke, Gab, stubborn little beggar!'

The landlord held the cage still, reached into his top pocket and produced a pencil. At this moment, Michael saw the girl, extricating herself from the press, pushing out backwards. The ring of rapt faces and still legs closed again. The rat was hurtling round the cage, still screaming, leaping over the other, attacking the wires first at this side then at that. All at once it crouched in a corner, silent. A hand came out and grabbed the loop of tail. The other noose was there ready. The landlord set the cage down.

Now the circle relaxed and everyone looked down at the two rats flattened on the cage bottom, their tails waving foolishly outside the wires.

'Well then, Billy,' said the landlord. 'How are they?'

Billy Red nodded and grinned.

'Them's grand,' he said. 'Grand.' His little rustling voice made Michael want to cough.

'Right. Stand back.'

Everybody backed obediently, leaving the cage, Walt with his foot on one taut string and the landlord with his foot on the other in the middle of an arena six or seven yards across. Michael saw the young man on the far side, his glass still half full in his hand. The girl was nowhere to be seen.

Billy Red peeled his coat off, exposing an old shirt, army issue, most of the left arm missing. He pulled his trousers up under his belt, spat on his hands, and took up a position which placed the cage door a couple of paces or so from his left side and slightly in front of him. He bent forward a little more than usual, his arms hanging like a wary wrestler's, his eye fixed on the cage.

'Eye like a bloody sparrow-hawk,' somebody murmured.

There was a silence. The landlord waited, kneeling now beside the cage. Nothing disturbed the dramatic moment but the distant, brainless church bells.

'This one first, Walt,' said the landlord. 'Ready, Billy?'

He pushed down the lever that raised the cage door and let his rat have its full five- or six-yard length of string. He had the end looped round his hand. Walt kept his rat on a tight string.

Everybody watched intently. The freed rat pulled its tail in delicately and sniffed at the noose round it, ignoring the wide-open door. Then the landlord reached to tap the cage and in a flash the rat vanished.

Michael lost sight of it. But he saw Billy Red spin half round and drop smack down on his hands and knees on the cobbles.

'He's got it!'

Billy Red's face was compressed in a snarl and as he snapped his head from side to side the dark, elongated body of the rat whipped around his neck. He had it by the shoulders. Michael's eyes fixed like cameras.

A dozen shakes, and Billy Red stopped, his head lowered. The rat hanging from his mouth was bunching and relaxing, bunching and relaxing. He waited. Everyone waited. Then the rat spasmed, fighting with all its paws, and Billy shook again wildly, the rat's tail flying like a lash. This time when he stopped the body hung down limply. The piece of string, still attached to the tail, trailed away across the cobbles.

Gently Billy took the rat from his mouth and laid it down. He stood up, spat a couple of times, and began to wipe his mouth, smiling shamefacedly. Everybody breathed out—an exclamation of marvelling disgust and admiration, and loud above the rest:

'Pint now, Billy?'

The landlord walked back into the pub and most of the audience followed him to refresh their glasses. Billy Red stood separate, still wiping his mouth with a scrap of snuff-coloured cloth.

Michael went over and bent to look at the dead rat. Its shoulders were wet-black with saliva, and the fur bitten. It lay on its left side, slightly curved, its feet folded, its eyes still round and bright in their alert, inquisitive expression. He touched its long, springy whiskers. A little drip of blood was puddling under its nose on the cobblestones. As he watched, a bluebottle alighted on its tail and sprang off again, then suddenly reappeared on its nose, inspecting the blood.

He walked over to the cage. Walt was standing there talking, his foot on the taut string. This rat crouched against the wires as if they afforded some protection. It made no sign of noticing Michael as he bent low over it. Its black beads stared outward fixedly, its hot brown flanks going in and out. There was a sparkle on its fur, and as he looked more closely, thinking it must be perspiration, he became aware of the heat again.

He stood up, a dull pain in his head. He put his hands to his scalp and pressed the scorch down into his skull, but that didn't seem to connect with the dull, thick pain.

"I'm off now, Dad,' he called.

'Already? Aren't you going to see this other one?'

'I think I'll go.' He set off across the yard.

'Finish your drink,' his father called after him.

Sunday

Sunday

He saw his glass almost full on the end of the white bench but walked past it and round the end of the pub and up on to the tow-path. The sycamore trees across the canal arched over black damp shade and the still water. High up, the valley slopes were silvered now, frizzled with the noon brightness. The earthen tow-path was like stone. Fifty yards along he passed the girl in the blue-flowered frock sauntering back towards the pub, pulling at the heads of the tall bank grasses.

'Have they finished yet?' she asked.

Michael shook his head. He found himself unable to speak. With all his strength he began to run.

The Organizer

Michael Thelwell

The river of that name cuts in half the town of Bogue Chitto, Mississippi. All of importance is east of the river—the jail, the drugstore and Western Union, the hotel, the Greyhound station and the Confederate memorial in the tree-shaded park. West of the river one comes to a paper mill, a cemetery, a junk yard, which merges with a garbage dump, and the Negro community.

Perched on a rise overlooking the dump and cemetery on one side and the Negro shacks on the other is the Freedom House. A low, unpainted concrete structure with a huge storefront window, it had been built for use as a roadhouse in expectation of a road that had turned out to be campaign oratory. When the road failed to materialize, the owner left the state feeling, with some justification, that he had been misled, and the building remained unused until the present tenants moved in.

It is reported that when Sheriff John Sydney Hollowell was told of the new arrivals he said, "Wal, they sho' chose a mighty good place—ain't nothin' but trash nohow, an' mighty subjeck to needin' buryin'."

This sally was savored, chuckled over and repeated, rapidly making its rounds out of the jail house, to the bench sitters in the park, the loungers in the general store, to be taken home and repeated over the supper table.

Reprinted by permission of Scholastic Magazines, Inc. from *Story/The Yearbook of Discovery/1968*, edited by Whit and Hallie Burnett, © Copyright 1968 by Scholastic Magazines, Inc.

The Organizer 309

Thus by ten o'clock that same night it had filtered up by way of the kitchen to the tenants of the Freedom House.

"That peckerwood is a comical son-of-bitch, ain't he?" Travis Peacock asked, and the thought came to him that perhaps the first thing to be done was to board up the big storefront window. Either he forgot or changed his mind, for when the other members of his project arrived they painted "BOGUE CHITTO COMMUNITY CENTER, FREEDOM NOW" on the glass in huge black letters. Two weeks later, while everyone was at a mass meeting in the Baptist Church, someone demolished the window with three loads of buckshot. Peacock boarded it up.

Time passed.

Peacock lay on his back in the darkness listening to the clock on the town hall strike eleven. He turned on his side, then sat up and unsnapped the straps of his overalls. "Too damn tight, no wonder I can't sleep," he muttered, reached under the cot for the pint bottle that Mama Jean had slipped to him at the café that afternoon, laughing and cautioning him, "Now doan go gittin' yore head all tore up, honey."

He had no intention of getting his head "tore up," but the fiery stump likker was a comfort. He jerked to a sitting position, listening. It was just the creaking, rusty Dr. Pepper sign moaning as the wind came up. He made a note to fix the sign tomorrow: "Damn thing run me crazy soon."

He lit a cigarette and sat in the darkness listening to the squeaking sign and shaking. He had never before spent a night alone in the Freedom House. Maybe I do need that rest up North, he thought. At the last staff meeting when Truman had hinted at it he had gotten mad. "Look, if you don't like the way I'm running the project come out and say so, man." And Truman had muttered something about "owing it to the movement to take care of our health." Maybe he did need that rest.

He thought of going down to Mama Jean's or the Hightowers' and spending the night there. He pulled on his boots to go, then changed his mind. The first rule for an organizer, and maybe the hardest, was never to let the community know that you were afraid. He couldn't go, even though the people had all tried to get him to stay in the community that night. That afternoon when he was in the café Mama Jean had suggested that he stay in her son's room.

"Shoot, now, honey," she beamed, "yo' doan want to be catchin' yo' death o' cold up theah on thet cold concrete by yo'se'f."

Raf Jones had chimed in, "Yeah man, we gon' drink us some stump juice, tell some lies, and play some Georgia Skin tonight." But he had declined. And Old Mrs. Ruffin had met him and repeated her urging to come stay a few nights at her place. But that was above the call of duty.

A standing joke on the project was that the two places in Bogue Chitto to avoid were, "Buddy Hollowell's jail, and Ol' Miz Ruffin's kitchen. She a nice ol' lady, but she the worse cook in Mississippi. Man, that ol' lady burn Kool-aid."

As the afternoon progressed and he received two more invitations, he realized that the community was worried. They knew that the other three staff members were in Atlanta for a meeting and they didn't want him spending a night alone in the office.

By his watch it was nearly midnight. He took a drink and lit another cigarette. Maybe they'd skip tonight. He was tempted to take the phone off the hook. "Hell no," he muttered, "I ain't going to give them that satisfaction." But what did it mean if the phone didn't ring? At least when they on the phone you know they ain't sneaking around outside with a can of kerosene.

He got off the cot and went into the front room, the "office." It was the big public part of the building with a couple of desks, a table, chairs, mimeo machine and a few old typewriters, and in one section a blackboard where small meetings and literacy classes were held. He sat at a desk with the phone, staring at the boarded-up window.

"Ring, you son-ovva-bitch, ring. You kept me up, now ring." He calmed himself down by reading the posters. A black fist holding a broken chain. "Freedom." Goddamn you, ring. Another poster, "Pearl River County Voters' League: One Man One Vote." Would it be a man or a woman this time? It was five after midnight. They were late. That was unusual.

Maybe they wouldn't call tonight. They always seemed to know what was happening. Maybe they thought that everyone was gone to Atlanta. Suppose they thought that and came to wreck the office? Peacock was still, listening. He was certain that he heard the sounds of movement outside. He went into the storeroom, tripped over a box of old clothes and swore. He came back with the shotgun just as the phone rang, piercingly loud. He dropped the gun and jumped for the phone.

"Pearl River County Voters' League, can we help you?" His voice is steady and that gives him some satisfaction.

There is a low laugh coming over the receiver. "Heh, heh, heh."

"Hello, you are late tonight," Travis says.

"Nigger," the voice asks, "you alone up theah, ain'tchu?"

It's a man's voice. Good. The women are hysterical and foulmouthed.

"You alone up theah?" The voice persists. Travis' nervousness has become anger. He starts to say, "No Charlie, I ain't alone, yo' Momma's here with me." But restrains himself.

"I'm not alone, there are three of us here." He says and laughs, yeah me, Jesus and mah shotgun.

"Ah know you alone. Thet pointy-head nigger an' the Jew-boy gone to Atlanta. Heh, heh."

"If you think so, come up and find out." Peacock invited in an even voice. "Why don't you do that?" There was a pause.

"We comin' direckly, boy, an' you can sell the shithouse, cause hit's going to be yore ass." Peacock doesn't answer. He stands holding the phone listening to the hoarse breathing from the other end. "Heh, heh. Nigger, yo' subjeck to bein' blowed up." Click. The phone goes dead and Peacock, shaking violently, stands listening to his own breathing.

Somehow that final click is the most terrifying part. As long as you can feel that there is a human being on the other end, despite the obscenity and the threats, you have some contact. Peacock broke the shotgun and loaded it. The phone rings. Briefly he debates not answering it but he knows he has to. With Ray and Mac on the road, he has to; they could be in trouble. He picks up the phone.

"Hello." That demented chuckling.

"Knowed yo' wasn't sleepin', Nigger. Ain't nevah goin' sleep no mo'."

"If I don't, neither will you, brother."

"Boy, yo' subjeck to bein' blowed up." Click.

Well, hope that's over for the night. But it isn't. They're going to take turns calling. He went to get what was left of the bottle wishing he could remove the phone from the hook. They must rotate the telephone duty, everyone volunteering to give up a night's sleep on a regular basis. Damn.

Peacock began to regret his decision not to go to the meeting. It would have been nice to see everyone again and find how things were on other projects. In Alabama, things looked pretty mean. But so were things here. That was one of the reasons he had stayed. As project director he thought that he should stay with the community in case some crisis broke. Where did his responsibility end?

Sitting there waiting for the phone to ring, he began to leaf idly through the progress report that he had sent to the meeting. He had done a damn good organizing job. The community was together, and had really strong local leadership, whose skill and competence were increasing rapidly.

Morale was high. They had formed a voters' organization and elected Jesse Lee Hightower chairman. He was a good man with real leadership potential for the entire state. And every act of intimidation seemed to increase his determination and that of the community. After the deacon board of the New Hope Baptist Church had been informed that the insurance of the church would not be renewed, they had met and voted to continue to hold meetings there. A week later the church was a total loss. The Sheriff attributed its destruction to a mysterious and very active arsonist called Faulty Wiring who had been wreaking havoc with other Negro churches in the state.

Then Mama Jean's café came under fire. She had been publicly displaying posters and announcements. The merchants in town cut off her credit, and refused to sell her supplies for cash. She had been selling beer and wine for fifteen years with the approval of three sheriffs, although the county was allegedly dry. Now she was charged with the illegal sale of alcohol and a hearing scheduled for the purpose of cancelling her license.

When the news reached Peacock he had been worried. The huge, loud, tough-talking woman was a leader and a symbol in the community—it was Mama Jean and Jesse who had been the first to go across the river to try to register to vote—Mama Jean wearing her floppy, terrible flowered hat, gloves and long black coat in the summer heat. They had been met by the Sheriff and three deputies.

"This office is closed till four o'clock."

"We come to register, Sheriff Hollowell."

"This office is closed."

"Why, thass all right, honey." Mama Jean's gold teeth were flashing. "Usses done waited a hunnerd yeahs, be plumb easy to wait till fo' o'clock." And she swept into the hall, marched to the only chair available and composed herself to wait. Hollowell and his deputies, obviously not prepared for that, had remained muttering veiled threats and caressing their guns. All knew the office would not open that afternoon.

Without her and the Hightowers, Peacock could never have gotten started in the community. If she broke, the community would crumble overnight. So he had been very worried when he ran to her café that afternoon. He was somewhat surprised to find her behind the bar laughing and joking.

"Mama Jean, what are you going to do?"

"Whut ah'm gon' do? Do 'bout whut, honey?" She was looking at him as though surprised at the question.

"Didn't they cut your credit? I heard . . ."

"Oh shush now, take mo'n thet li'l bitty ol' sto'keeper to stop Mama Jean. Jes' doan yo' fret yo'se'f none, heah. Ah be keepin' on keepin' on like ah always done." And she had. No more was heard about the illegal sale of liquor, and twice a week she got into Jesse Lee's pickup truck and drove into Louisiana to buy supplies. She claimed it was much cheaper.

Then the town council tripled the tax assessment on her café. Peacock got her a lawyer, and she was challenging the assessment, even threatening to file a damage suit.

"Damn," Peacock muttered, "if that lady was thirty years younger I swear I'd ask her to marry me." Thinking of Mama Jean cheered him.

The Organizer

Some of the people in that poverty-stricken, hard-pressed community were so great, like the Hightowers and the Joneses, he felt warm with pride and love; it was as if he had returned to a home he had never known, but always missed.

He had lived with the Hightowers at first, while he met the people and learned the community. He felt closer to them than to his natural family who now seemed to him shadowy figures leading barren and futile lives in their Northern suburb.

He thought of Miss Vickie, Jesse's wife, a small fragile appearing woman always hovering around her burly husband, expressing her support by small, thoughtful acts. And the two kids, Richie and Fannie Lou who was extremely bright and curious beneath her shyness. Peacock loaned her books and had long talks with her, constantly being surprised at the range and breadth of her curiosity. The Negro school only went to the ninth grade, and she had long surpassed her teachers. She had finally quit, and was now a full-time volunteer, doing the typing and running the office.

His favorite was eight-year-old Richie, like his father a leader and a born organizer. He had created an organization to blanket the community with leaflets. Then he had badgered and begged until Miss Vickie bought him a denim jacket and overalls "like Travis'." A hell of an organizer he will be when he grows up, Peacock reflected.

Peacock noticed that his bottle was almost empty. He could feel the effects of the liquor, particularly potent after his recent tension.

"Hell, no wonder, you sittin' here getting so sentimental. A sixteen-year-old girl has a crush on you, her kid brother thinks you are Jesus, and your leader complex runs away again." But he felt easier now and tired. He went into the back room and stretched out on the cot, feeling his limbs relax as he gave in to exhaustion. But his mind wouldn't turn off.

He was in that half-way zone between sleep and wakefulness in which thoughts disguise themselves as dreams, when he heard the sound. That is, he sensed it, a kind of silent, dull reverberation, that reached his mind before the sound came to him—the heavy, somehow ponderous boom of dynamite. Silence, then a yapping, howling chorus as every dog in town began to bark.

Peacock froze on the cot. *Oh God. Oh God. Let it be a church, not anyone's house.*

He wanted to pull on his boots but was paralyzed. His stomach felt empty and weak. He retched and puked up all the hot acid liquor. His fear returned and he began to shake violently. Somebody's dead. They killed someone. Mama Jean. I don't want to know. I can't go. He sat there smelling his vomit, until he heard the pounding on the door. "Travis, ho, Travis!"

He stumbled into the front room, going for the door. Then he returned for the shotgun. His voice came as a hoarse whisper and it took two efforts to make himself audible. "Who is it?"

"Us, Raf Jones and Sweezy. We alone."

Peacock knew the men. They had both been fired from the paper mill after attempting to register. When there was money in the project he gave them subsistence, other times they helped Mama Jean in the café in return for meals. He opened the door. Jones and Sweezy were carrying rifles. They didn't know what had happened, either, having been outside the Freedom House when they heard the noise.

In a few moments they were running down the hill, past the edge of the cemetery towards the town and the café. Peacock was sure that the nightriders had tried for the café, but when, panting and gasping, they reached there, they found it intact. So was the little church that was now being used for meetings. Where was the explosion? A car turned into the road, going fast and raising a cloud of dust. The headlights picked them out, and they dived into the ditch. The car roared past.

"Hit's the Sher'f," Raf said. "Trouble taken place fo' sho'." They set out running in the car's dust. It passed two side roads, then turned. Peacock had no doubt where it was headed now.

"Good God Almighty." He half moaned, half shouted and stopped. The two men ran on without him, then stopped and turned.

"Yo' awright?"

Peacock nodded and waved them on. His eyes and nose were filled with dust. His chest heaved. He coughed. Whatever had happened wouldn't change before he got there. He even had a momentary urge to turn back, to run somewhere and hide, certain that something terrible and irrevocable had happened. He stood bent double in the road, clutching his sides, coughing, eyes streaming water, no longer gut-scared but filled with dread. He couldn't go on.

Wait, maybe no one had been hurt. A house can be rebuilt. He personally would go North to raise the money. He would gouge it out cent by cent from his family and their affluent and secure neighbors. If it was only the house! Then he was running again. He could smell burnt powder now. It seemed like the entire town was crowded in the road before him. He recognized faces, people, everyone was talking.

"Wha' happen? Wha' happen?"

"Whole family daid?"

"Two white fellers in a car."

Pushing his way through the crowd, Peacock realized that he was still carrying the shotgun. He didn't know what to do with it. The people would be looking to him, and if he had a gun. . . . Besides it'd be in every lousy newspaper in the country that the local representative of the organization had arrived on the scene carrying a weapon.

He pushed his way to the front of the crowd, no one called his name. Was it his imagination or were they stepping away from him? Oh God, were they blaming him?

The Sheriff's car was right in front of the house, its searchlight beaming into the living room. The front of the house was a shambles, porch completely gone, the front wall torn away. A pair of deputies stood facing the crowd carrying tear-gas guns, cumbersome, futuristic looking weapons that seemed to belong in a Flash Gordon kit. "Y'awl keep on back now. Sheriff's orduhs."

Clutching the shotgun, Peacock darted out of the crowd toward the house. One deputy turned to face him.

"Wheah yew going?"

"I'm kin," Peacock said without stopping. The deputy turned back to the crowd which had surged forward.

Peacock ran around the house and came up to the back door. The smell of burnt powder lingered strong. At the kitchen door he stopped, looking in; the kitchen was filled with people. Mama Jean turned to the door and saw him.

"Oh Travis, Travis, honey. They done hit. They done kilt Jesse." The people gave a low moan of assent. It seemed to Travis that they were looking at him accusingly, the stranger who had brought death among them. Then Mama Jean was holding him. He clung to her without shame, comforting himself in her large, warm strength. He was sure now that there was hostility in the room. The people gathered there had kept aloof from the Voter's League, explaining that they had to avoid commitment so that they could keep their position flexible and talk with the white community. He recognized the school principal, the minister from the big Baptist church, and the undertaker. No one spoke. Then Mama Jean was leading him into the bedroom. "The fam'ly bin askin' fo' yo', Travis."

Their heads all turned to Peacock as they entered. Fanny Lou was holding Richie, their eyes big, black solemn pools in their young faces. Miss Vickie huddled on the bed, leaning forward, her back sharply curved, hunch-shouldered, clutching her clasped hands between her knees. Her face seemed set, polished from smooth black stone. When she turned her head to the door her eyes showed nothing.

"See, he come. He all right, nothing happen to him." Mama Jean's tone was soothing, meant to reassure them. But for one second Peacock heard only a reproach for his safety and survival. *You must say something. You have to tell these folks something.*

From the next room he heard a low wailing hum. They were half humming, half singing one of those slow, dirge-like songs that was their response in times when no other response was possible. *"Shiine on Mee, Oh, shiiine on Meee..."*

Peacock crossed to Miss Vickie. His limbs felt heavy, as though he were moving through some heavy liquid medium, but his footsteps sounded loud. He bent and took her hands. They were limp at first, then they imprisoned his in a quick fierce grip. He was looking into her eyes for some sign of warmth, life, recognition, but most of all for some sign of absolution, forgiveness.

Jumbled phrases crowded through his mind. Trite, traditional words, phrases that were supposed to bear comfort, to move, to stir, to strengthen, and ultimately to justify and make right. But the will of which God? Whose God, that this man, this husband . . . *I am not to blame. I didn't do it.* Silently Peacock looked at her. She returned his look blankly. Then she pitched forward and her head rested on his arms.

"We will do everything . . . we must keep on . . . brave and good man . . . do what he would want us to do . . . death not in vain."

Which voice was that spewing out tired political phrases we hear too often. It couldn't have been me, please it was someone else. What hard hands she has. "Miss Vickie, I'm sorry," Peacock said, "I'm sorry."

"Hush chile. T'aint yore fault." Mama Jean's deep voice cracked. "T'aint none of us heah fault, cept we shoulda moved long time ago. Hit's a long time they been killin' us, little by little . . ."

"Ahmen," Miss Vickie said. Richie started to cry. Peacock picked him up, surprised at how light he was. The boy threw his skinny arms around Peacock's neck and buried his wet cheeks in his neck. Hugging him tightly, Travis felt his own tears starting for the first time.

"Who is comforting who?" he asked himself

There was a soft knock on the door, and the elderly unctuous minister clad in his black suit glided in from the kitchen.

"Miz Hightower, hit's the Sher'f come to talk to you." Miss Vickie sat up, a mixture of emotions crossing her face.

"Thet 'Buddy' Hollowell have no shame. Effen he did . . ." Mama Jean began as Sheriff Hollowell strode into the room, accompanied by a man in a business suit. "Seems like some folks doan even knock fo' they come bustin' into folks' houses," Mama Jean snorted.

The Sheriff stood in the center of the room. He ran his glance over the group, fingering his jowl. He was a big, solid man, heavy-boned, thick-waisted and with enormous red hands. He was wearing his khaki uniform and a planter's Stetson. He stared at the floor just in front of Miss Vickie, and his jaw moved slowly and steadily.

"Ah just come to get a statement from the widow." His voice must have sounded subdued and apologetic in his own ears for he paused briefly and continued in a louder voice. "So theah ain't no need fer anyone else to be saying nothin'." Mama Jean snorted. Then there was dead silence in the room. Rev. Battel who had been standing in the doorway made a sidling self-effacing motion and was frozen by a glare from Mama Jean.

"Well, which a yew is the widow?" the Sheriff asked.

"Ah'm Mrs. Hightower," Miss Vickie said and pulled herself up erect. She looked at the official with an expression of quiet, intense contempt that seemed to be almost physical, coming from a depth of outrage and grief beyond her will. Peacock would swear that Miss Vickie had no knowledge of what was in her eyes. His own spirit shrank within him.

"Sheriff Hollowell," he said softly, "there's been a death in this house."

The second man flushed and removed his hat. The Sheriff gave no sign of having seen or heard anything. "Yew have another room where ah can git yore statement?" He could have been addressing anyone in the room.

"We used to." Miss Vickie said. "Anythang need to be said kin be said right here. These my husband's family and friends."

Hollowell produced a notebook and flipped his Stetson back on his head. The second man was also holding a pad. "Wal, whut happened?" Again there was a pause.

" 'What happened? What happened,' Jesus God Almighty." The words flashed through Peacock's mind, and he only realized that he had spoken when Hollowell said "Ah'm not gon' tell yew to shut up again, boy."

Miss Vickie's voice was calm and low, without inflection or emphasis. "Ah wuz sleepin' an' then ah woke up. Heard like a car drive up in the road going slow like. Hit drive past three times like they was lookin' fo' something. Ah see that Jesse Lee wun't in the bed. Ah listen fo' a spell an' didn' heah nothin' so I call out an' he answer from the front.

" 'Hit's allright, go to sleep.' But ah knew hit wuz somethin' wrong and ah started to get up . . . Then, then like the room light up an' ah feel this hot win' an' the noise an' hit was nothin' but smoke and ah heah mah daughter scream . . ." Her voice broke off and she began to sob softly. The two children began to sob too. Mama Jean turned and stared at the wall.

"Is this necessary, Sheriff?" Peacock asked.

"Boy, yew not from round heah are yew?"

"You know who I am," Peacock said. Miss Vickie began to speak.

"An' thass all. Evrah thang wuz like yo' see hit now, only the children wuz cryin' and Jesse Lee was lyin' on the floor in the front room. Ah nevah seen no car."

"Jes' one thang more, Miz Hightower." Hollowell's voice was almost gentle. "Yew know any reason fo' anyone to dew a thang lak' this?"

Peacock stared at the Sheriff incredulously.

"Same reason he got arrest three time for drunk drivin' when evrahbody know he nevah did drink." Mama Jean said.

"Ah doan know why some folks do whut they do," Miss Vickie said.

"Wal, ah'l sho let yew know soon as ah find out anything." Hollowell snapped his book. "Mighty sorry myself. Only one thang more, this gentleman heah, be wanting to ask yew a few questions." His companion seemed uncomfortable, his Adam's apple bobbing jerkily in his thin neck. His cheek twitched and he passed a hand quickly over his thinning hair. "I think I've got all I need," he began. Hollowell looked at him. "Well maybe just one thing. I'm from the Associated Press in New Orleans, happened to be passing through." He darted a quick look at the Sheriff, and spoke more rapidly. "I want you to know how sorry I am. This is a terrible, terrible thing. I want you to know that you have the sympathy of every decent person in the state, Mrs. Hightower. I hope . . . I'm sure that whoever did this will be found and punished. I was wondering if there is anything that you would like to say, any kind of personal statement . . ."

"Why can't you leave the family in peace?" Peacock was on his feet. "What more statement do you want, isn't what happened statement enough? For God's sake, what more do you want?" But Peacock's anger was not at the timid little man, but at what he knew was to come for the family—an ordeal that would be as painful as the night before them and in its own way more obscene than the brute fact of death. He was lashing out at that future and the role that he could neither escape nor resolve.

"Now ah've warned yew." The Sheriff was advancing toward him.

"Mist'r Hollowell, come quick before something happen." A deputy was standing in the door. "Hit's the niggers, yew bettah come." The deputy disappeared, followed by Hollowell and the reporter.

"Preacher," the Sheriff called over his shoulder, "maybe yew better come on." The old man followed silently, and then Peacock heard the crowd. Waves of boos and shouts came in spurts, and in between shouted angry words:

"Thet sho' doan sound good. Them folks is mad. Them peoples is afixin' to turn this town out an' ah swears thet in mah heart ah doan blame 'em."

"Ain't that the truth," Peacock said, "but I'd blame myself. You know the Safety Patrol is coming, and maybe even the Army. Them peckerwoods will shoot us down like dogs. And we gotta do something. The only people can stop them is right here in this room." He looked at Miss Vickie. She rocked back and forth and wouldn't look at him. He thought for a while that she hadn't heard. Then she spoke very softly.

"Travis, ah jes' doan know no mo'. Seems like either they gits kilt tonight or one by one nex' week. Maybe this is what hit had to come to. Ah jes' ain't straight in mah own min'."

Peacock sat down silently on the bed, his head bowed. He understood how she felt. He too longed for the swift liberating relief of wild, mindless, purging violence, ending maybe in death. But survival, what of that? Suppose he was one of the survivors. It was a nightmare that had hovered in the back of his consciousness ever since he had joined the movement —yet he saw himself limping away from the burning town, away from the dead and maimed, people to whom he had come to singing songs of freedom and rewarded with death and ashes. The organizer is always responsible. That was the second rule.

"Miss Vickie. You know how much I loved Jesse, more than my natural father. I ain't got to tell you how I feel, but you know Jesse would feel this way too. If you won't come with me to speak to the folks, lemme give them a word from you." Miss Vickie did not answer immediately. There was a new frenzy of shouting outside, louder, more hysterical than before. Peacock couldn't wait for an answer, and Mama Jean followed him as he ran out into the shouting. . . .

"Look at them peckerwoods. Look at them. See who them guns pointing at. We din' kill nobody. We din' bomb no house. Hit wuzn't us, but who the guns pointing at? Why ain't they go find the killers? Why? 'Cause they knows who they is, they brothahs an' they cousins, thass who!"

Peacock recognized Raf Jones. Himself and Sweezy and some of the younger men were grouped in front of the police car. They were armed. "Look at thet Raf, fixin' to get hisse'f kilt too." Mama Jean muttered. "Yo' right Travis, now whut is we gon' do?" They walked over to the car. Hollowell began to talk through a bull horn, his flat, nasal voice magnified and echoing through the night.

"Awright, awright. This is Sher'f Hollowell. That's enough, ah want yew to cleah these streets." Angry shouts from the crowd. "Yew good collud folks of this town know me."

"Yo' damn right we does." Raf shouted back.

"Yew know me, and ah know most of yew. Ah know yew're good, decent folk that don't want no trouble. An' this town din' have no trouble till them agitators pull in heah to disrup' and destroy whut we had. Now a man was kilt heah tonight. Ah wanna ask yew, yew all sensible folk, ah wanna ask yew. Was theah any trouble fore these trouble-makers started hangin' round heah?"

"Allus bin trouble," Raf screamed. "Allus bin killin's." The crowd roared agreement.

"An' ah want to tell yew, ah have mah own feelin's bout who done this terrible thang heah tonight. Ah tell yew, yew got evrah right to be mad. Why, hit could'a jes' as easy bin a white man got blowed up. Yew're decent folk, ah know thet. Ah know hit wasn't none o' yew did this thang. We got a good town heah. But ah want to ask yew this. Dew yew *know* anythang 'bout these outsiders yew bin harboring? What dew yew know bout them? Tell me, dew yew thank thet these race mixahs an' agitators mean this town any good? Wheah dew they come from? Right now ah only see one ov 'em. Where's the othah two raht now? Ah want yew to go home an' thank 'bout thet. Yew will git the true answers, you cain't plant corn an' hit come up cotton. Y'awl go on home now an' thank 'bout whut ah said."

The crowd was silent, shuffling sullenly. No one left. "Ah want yew to go now. Ah've called the Safety Patrol barracks an' troopers is on the way. In ten minutes they be heah. Anyone still heah goes to jail. Yew heah me?" Silence.

"Awright, awright. Ah got someone heah yew all know. He is one of yew, a fine collud gentleman. He got somethin' to say, then he goin' lead yew in prayer, an' that'll be awl. Step up heah, Preacher Battel." Before the old man could move Mama Jean stepped in front of him, one hand on her hip, the other wagging in his face. Peacock heard her saying, ". . . Swear 'fo' Gawd, effen yo' git up now an' start in to Tommin' fo' thet cracker, ah'm gon' run ye outta town myse'f. Yo' heah me, Charlie Battel, ah'm sick an' tard of being' sick an' tard of yo' selling the folks out." Battel backed away before her fury. Hollowell came over fingering his gun.

"An' as fo' yo' Bo Hollowell, the onliest true thang yo' say wuz thet we knows yo'. An' ah knows yo' pappy befo' yo'. Yo' wuz none o' yo' any good. No mo' good than a rattlesnake. Whoa now, Bo Hollowell, yo' lay a han' to me an' hit's yo' las' living ack. Me 'n' Travis gon' git the folks to go home, but hit's gon' be our way. We gon' do hit cause we doan want no mo' peoples kilt, an' thass whut you fixing to do. But if hit's mo' dying tonight, t'aint only black folks gon' die."

She turned her back on him and marched over to the car, walking past an immobilized Hollowell as though he were not present. The passionate power of the fat, middle-aged woman was awesome even to Peacock, against whom it was not directed. He followed her automatically.

"Gi'mme a han' up," she demanded. She balanced herself on the fender of the car, holding Travis' shoulder for support. Silently she surveyed the crowd, her broad chest heaving, hair unkempt and standing out on her head. "Lookaheah. Hit's me, Mama Jean, an' ah ain't got much to say. But yo' all hear that rattlesnake talking 'bout outside agitators. Yo' all knowed he wuz talking 'bout Travis. Wal, maybe he is a agitator. But yo' seen the agitator in yo' white folks' washing machine. Yo' know what hit do, hit git the dirt out. Thass right, an' thass what Travis gon' do now. Listen to him, he got a message from Miss Vickie. An' he gon' git out all the dirt thet Hollowell bin asayin'." She jumped down. "Go on, son, talk some sense to the folks. Ah'm jes' too mean mad mese'f, but yo' kin tell them lak hit is."

Hollowell stepped up. "Don't look like ah got much choice." He drew his pistol from its holster. "So yew say yore piece, but remember ah'l be raht heah behind yew. Yew git them to go home now. Say one wrong word . . ." He waved his pistol suggestively.

The Organizer

Travis climbed onto the bonnet of the car and waved his arms for silence. The skin of his back crawled, sensitive to the slightest pressure of his shirt and waiting for the first probing touch of Hollowell's bullet. He closed his eyes and waited for the crowd's attention.

"Friends. Friends, you got to be quiet now, cause I ain't got no bull horn like Hollowell, an' I want you to hear every word." That's right, keep your voice low so they have to calm down to hear. "You all can see that house right there, least what the crackers left of it. There's a lady inside there, a black lady. And her husband's dead. They killed her husband an' she grievin'. You know she grievin'. Seem like thass all we black folk know to do, is grieve. We always grievin', it seem like." Peacock shook his head and bowed his head as though in grief or deep thought. A woman gave a low scream, "Jesus, Jesus," and began to sob, deep, animal, racking sounds that carried into the crowd. Peacock waitned, head bowed, until he heard a few more muffled sobs from the crowd.

"Yes, some o' us cryin'. Thass all right, let the good sister cry, she got reason. Will ease huh troubled heart. Lady inside thet bombed-out, burned-out house cryin' too. She cryin' right now but while her soul cry for the dead, her min' is on the livin'. She thinking 'bout you. That's the kind of lady she is. She say to tell you the time for weeping is almost over. Soon be over. She say she cryin' for her man tonight, an' she don't want to cry for her brothers and sisters tomorrow. She say they already kill one, don't give them a chance to kill no more. She say to go home peacefully."

"Why?" Raf shouted, "so they kin git the rest o' us when we lyin' up in the bed? Ah say, GIT ON WIT THE KILLIN'!" There was a roar from the people, but Peacock judged that it came mainly from Raf's little group. Raf, shut up, please. Every time you say something like that, I can just feel that cracker's finger jerking. He had to find something to divert the people. "Miss Vickie, say to go home, it's what Jesse Lee would want." A deep murmur of rejection came back.

"Jesse Lee was a fighter!" Raf yelled. This was greeted with cheers.

"Lookaheah," Travis said, raising his voice and adopting the accent of the folk. "Lookaheah, y'awl heard the Sheriff." I sure hope Hollowell doesn't loose his cool. I got to do this now. A small muscle in his back kept twitching. "Yeah, ah'm talkin' 'bout Bo Hollowell, that ugly ol' lard-ass, big belly, Bo Hollowell." Peacock held his breath. No sound came from behind him. There was scattered laughter in the crowd.

"Yeah," Peacock continued, "Look at him. Ain't he the sorriest, pitifullest thang yo' evah saw? Ain't he now? Looka him. See him standing there holdin' thet gun. He scared. Yo' heard him say he called fo' the troopers. Wal, he did. Yo' know he did, cause he scared as hell. Hit's too many angry black folk heah fo' him. He scared. Look at him." Peacock turned and pointed. Hollowell was standing in front of his deputies. His

Stetson was pulled down to hide his eyes, but Peacock could see the spreading black stain under his arms, and his heavy jaw grinding as he shook with barely controlled fury. But there were cheers and laughter in the crowd now.

"He scared lak a girl," Peacock shouted and forced himself to laugh. "Why ol' bad-assed Bo Hollowell standin' theah shaking jes' lak a dawg tryin' to shit a peach stone." That cracked the people up, real laughter, vindictive and punitive to the lawman, but full, deep and thereapeutic to the crowd.

"Yessuh, lak a dawg tryin' to shit a peachstone," Peacock repeated, and the people hooted. Jesse, I know you understand, Peacock apologized. I got to do this. He waved for silence and got it. His voice was soft now.

"But looka heah, very close now. Sho' he scared. But he scared jes' lak them peckerwoods whut blowed up this house. An' yo' knows whoevah done it ain't even folks. They scared, they sick. Thass right. Whenevah peckerwoods git scared, niggers git kilt. Ahuh, thass lak hit is, whenevah white folks git scared, black folks git kilt. Yo watch 'at ol' big belly Bo. He scared right enough to kill me right heah." Peacock was sweating in the night breeze. I have to do it just right, one word too much and he' goin' break, he warned himself.

"See," he said, "an' when them othah crackers git heah, they goin' be scared too. They gon' start whuppin' heads an shootin' folks lak we wuz rabbits."

"Thass right."

"He right."

"Tell the truth."

"See. An' they's a lot of women an' chillun, beautiful black chillun out heah. What's gon' happen to them? Now yo' men got yo' guns. An' thass good. If Jesse Lee hada had his'n he might be alive this minute. So we gotta be ready. But whoevah stay heah now, bettah be ready to die. Thass right, *be ready to die.*"

"We dyin' right now," Raf shouted.

"That wuz true. An' hit still is. But not no mo'. Hit's a new day comin'. Hit's gotta come. A new day. Thass whut scared them peckerwoods, why they kill Jesse Lee. 'Cause Jesse was a free man. He didn't take no mess. Y'awl know that? An' he was tryin' to git y'awl to come with him. That's what scare them folks. He was a free man. His min' was free. He was not afraid."

"Tell it."

"Right. Thass right."

"Yes, brothahs an' sistuhs, thass whut scare 'em. Black folks wuz fixin' to be free. Ahuh. See, an' ol' Bo knew thet. Them peckerwoods is mighty tricky. Yo' gotta study 'em, they *awful* tricky."

"Yes Jesus, they sho' is."

"So now, lookaheah very careful now. Inside that house is this black lady, an' she mournin' fo' her husband. An' she say, Go home. She say, Go home, cause she love yo', an' she cain't stan' no mo' grievin'. Then out heah, yo' got Bo Hollowell an' his gun. He say, Go home, too. Now why would he say that? 'Cause he scared? Thass part of hit. But mostly, yo' know why he say thet, 'cause he know we sick an' tard. He know we sick an' tard o' bein' whupped." Peacock was now chanting in the sing-song cadence of the ecstatic sermon with the full participation of the people.

"Sick an tard o' being starved."

"Oh yes, oh yes."

"Sick an' tard o' being worked to death."

"Oh yes, yes Jesus."

"Sick an' tard o' bein' cheated."

"Jesus Gawd, yes."

"Sick an' tard o' bein' kilt."

"Yeah, mah brothahs an' sistuhs, that cracker know we sick an' tard, thet we sick an' tard o' *bein' sick an' tard."*

"Tell it, tell it."

"Yeah, that cracker sure do know thet so long as we live, *we gon' be free.* He know that if he say go home, yo' gon' stay. An' yo' know somethin', even though he scared, he mad too. An' cause he scared he want yo' to go home. An' cause he mad, he kinda hope yo' gon' stay. An' yo' know why? Yo' know why that cracker, yeah look at him, yo' know why he want yo' to stay? SO HE CAN KILL SOME MO' BLACK FOLKS. Thass right. Evrahone heah know he bin sayin' he gon' come down heah an' clean the niggers out. Yo' know he say thet evrah time he get drunk."

"Thass right."

"The gospel truth."

"Yo' right, man."

Peacock waved his hands for silence. He spoke softly and clearly now as though he were revealing a great secret. He tried to inject into his voice certitude and calm authority. Yet he was tired and the slowness of his speech was not entirely for effect. His dripping body was lethargic, relaxed, and a peacefulness crept over him. For the first time he did not care about Hollowell's gun at his back.

"So whut we gon' do, mah brothers? We are going to go home like Miss Vickie say do. We going to trick ol' Bo Hollowell this time. No more black folk going to die tonight. We men with the guns going to get the women and kids home. We going to get them there safe. And then we going to stay there. When those troopers come, there ain't going to be no folks standing around for them to beat on, all right? And we are going to stay home so that if any more bomb-toting crackers come we can defend our children an' our homes, all right?"

The crowd shouted assent.

"But that's only tonight. We aren't going to let Jesse Lee Hightower jes' die like that, are we? No. Uhuh. Tomorrow night we going come back to a meeting. Tomorrow night at eight o'clock, we all going to come to a meeting an' plan and decide just what we going to do."

"Yes, we is!" the crowd roared.

"An' we going to do it all together. Us folks gotta stick together. And you know where the meeting is going to be tomorrow night? In Rev. Battel's church, that's where. Rev'ren' say he done seen the light, an' out of respect fo' Jesse Lee, he gon' let us have the church."

Peacock listened to the cries of surprise and approval from the people. They all knew that Battel had kept himself and his church apart from the activities of the movement. Glancing bchidn he could see Mama Jean rocking with mirth at a thoroughly unhappy looking Preacher Battle.

"All right, so we going home now. Raf an' Sweezy, will you get everything all straight so that folks get home safe? But before we do that, one more thing. Rev'ren' Battel will give us a prayer. An' we not going pray for no forgiveness, we going to pray for justice, an' for the soul of our brother."

Battel stepped forward. "Let us bow our haids an' ask the Almighty . . ." he intoned.

"Wait," Peacock shouted. Battel stopped. Bowed heads were raised. Peacock pointed to Hollowell and his deputies. "Folks, I didn't mean to interrupt the prayer. But remember what happened here tonight. A man is dead, murdered. And I know that Sheriff Hollowell and his men don't mean no disrespect. But I believe we should ask them to remove their hats. Even if *they* don't believe in prayer."

The crowd stood stock still for a moment, a low murmur growing and thickening. The officers made no move. Peacock could not see Hollowell's face which was shaded by the brim of the Stetson.

"Jesse Lee Hightower is one black man they had to respeck in life," Mama Jean boomed, "an they bettah respeck him in death too."

Slowly the crowd was closing the distance between itself and the lawmen. It had become very quiet, the only sound that Peacock heard was the soft hum of feet on the dusty road. The people were no longer the diffuse crowd, but had become a single unit.

The click of Hollowell's pistol cocking was sharp and clear. Peacock cursed himself; it had been such a close thing and now he had torn it.

"Take them off, take off the damned hats!" He thought that he had screamed, but apparently there had been no sound. The deputy on the left took a half pace backward. Hollowell's lips moved stiffly. "Hope the bastard's praying," Peacock murmured, but he was sure that Hollowell was only threatening the deputy. But the man's nerve had broken. Peacock saw his hand moving, stealthily, unbearably slowly in the direction of his head. It sneaked up, tremulously, then, faster than a striking rattler, streaking up to snatch the hat from the head.... The other deputy looked at Hollowell, then at the crowd. He made his choice. Hollowell was the last. Peacock did not see it happen. But the Sheriff's hat was suddenly cradled against his leg. The crowd let out a great moaning sigh, and Battel resumed the prayer in a quavering voice. Peacock felt an arm on his shoulder. He slumped onto Mama Jean's shoulder putting his arm around her neck and they stood watching the people disperse.

"Yo' done jes' great, Travis, hit was beautiful. But yo' know them crackers jes' ain't gon' take the way yo' done them tonight. Careful how yo' walk. Like ef that Hollowell should stop yo' on the road by yo'se'f ..." Her voice trailed off.

"I know, Mama Jean." Peacock squeezed her shoulder. "An' I'm gonna be watching him. But ain't nothing he can do for the next few weeks." And that's the truth, Peacock reflected. Come tomorrow this town is going to be so full of newsmen and TV cameras that everyone is going to be careful as hell.

"Yeah, but yo' know he ain't nevah gon' forget. He *cain't.*"

"Surprised to hear you talking like that, Mamma Jean. Way you light into him an' Battel, jes' like a duck on a June bug. Don't you know you gettin' a little old to be doing folks like that?"

"Who ol'?" She growled. "Long as ah keeps mah strength ah ain't nevah gon' be too ol'. Ef they want to stop me, they gon' have to kill me. An' ah ain't sho' but whut the ones thet gits kilt ain't the lucky ones. Whut 'bout those thet lef'?" She looked toward the broken house.

Yes, Peacock thought, what about them? Us? He watched the police car drive slowly down the road behind the last group. What about them? He wondered if the family in the house had heard him. Jesse wasn't four hours dead, and already he had cheapened and manipulated that fact. He had abstracted their grief and his own, used it, waved it in front of the crowd like a matador's cape and this was only the beginning.

Inside the house, Mama Jean took charge, bustling around collecting whatever she felt the family would need next morning. She was taking them to spend the night at her place. They still sat in the bedroom, as though they had not changed position during the time Peacock had been away. Looking at his watch, Peacock discovered that the incident outside had taken less than forty minutes. He looked up to meet Fannie Lou's eyes, big and dark with grief, staring at him. What was she thinking? Of her father? Or of him, the stranger who had come to live with them like the big brother she never had? How did they feel now? Miss Vickie used to call him her son, to introduce him to visitors that way. And he had felt closer to this family than to the family he never saw and rarely thought about. But there was nothing he could say. Everything that came to him sounded weak and inadequate, incapable of expressing the burden of his feeling. Unless he could find new words that would come fresh and living from his heart, that had never been said before, he could not say anything.

When Raf and the men came back they left for the café, Peacock walking between the mother and daughter and holding a sleepy Richie. He felt Fannie Lou's light touch on his arm.

"Travis, yo' gon' stay?" Peacock looked at her uncomprehendingly. She bit her lower lip and said quickly, "I mean tonight at Mama Jean's." Her eyes filled with tears.

"I'll be back later, but I have to go to the office first." But he knew she wasn't asking about tonight. They knew that he came from another world, and one that must seem to them far more attractive, to which he could return.

He had not told them his reason for wanting to go back to the office. He had to call the national office with a report of the evening's events and he did not want them to hear him reporting and describing their loss to unknown people.

Before he had begged and pleaded to be put on the organizing staff he had worked on the public relations staff in the national office. He had written hundreds of coldly factual reports of burnings, bombings, and murders. And the "statements," how many of those had he written, carefully worded, expressing rage, but disciplined controlled rage, phrases of grief balanced by grim determination, outrage balanced by dignity, moral indignation balanced by political demands. Every time it was the same, yet behind those phrases, the anger and the sorrow and the fear were real. So we become shapers of horror, artists of grief, giving form and shape and articulation to emotion, the same emotion, doing it so often that finally there is nothing left of that emotion but the form.

He reached the Freedom House and placed the call. Before it was completed Raf called through the door. Peacock let him and his companions in.

"The womens said we wuz to come stay with yo'." Raf explained. "We got some mens watching the café." Peacock watched them file into the office, gaunt men roughly dressed in overalls and Army surplus boots, as he was. One of them, an older man with balding gray hair and a creased face came up to him. Peacock did not know him. The man took his hand in a horny calloused grip.

The Organizer

"Ah knows ah ain't bin to the meetin's. Ah call myse'f keepin' outta trouble. Ah says them Freedom folk, they mean to do good, but they ain't from roun' heah, somethin' happen they be gone an' lef' us'ns in the mess. Ah wuz 'fraid, ah ain't shame to say hit. But ah seen yo' wit the laws tonight an' ah says, let the fur fly wit' the hide. Ef thet young feller kin do, ah kin do too. Ah's heah to do whatevah is to be did." Peacock was like an evangelist suffering from doubt in the face of a convert. He had heard those words before. Each time it had been a new and moving experience to see a man throwing off his burden of fear and hesitance and finding the courage to step forward. But this time the responsibility seemed too much. What was the man expecting? Reassurance, praise? The phone temporarily rescued him.

The connection was a bad one, and it was as though his voice and not another's, echoed hollowly back into his ear. "June 16th, Bogue Chitto, Miss. . . ." Peacock was staring into Richie's shock-glazed eyes. ". . . A Negro civil rights leader was killed in the blast that destroyed his home. His wife and two children were unharmed . . ." Peacock saw Miss Vickie's rigid sleepwalker's face . . . "Resentment is high in the Negro community. A crowd formed in front of the house, but the local representative of the Nonviolent Council persuaded the crowd to disperse peacefully . . ." The voice went on and on. Raf and the other men were watching him as though he had stepped into a new identity that they did not recognize.

"No," Peacock said, "I have no statement."

"But we should have something from the local movement. You are project director."

"Look, if you want a political statement, write it, that's your job. All I can say is I'm sorry." Peacock hung up the phone and sat cradling his head in his arms. He knew the office would call back. Tomorrow the networks would be in town, so would politicians, leaders of various organizations. For a few days the eyes of the country would be focused on the town and everyone would want to be included. He wanted no part of it. The secret fear of every organizer had become reality for him. How do you cope with the death of one of the people you work with?

The phone rang again. Peacock knew before he answered it that it would be Truman. Big, shaggy, imperturbable, bear-like Truman. He was the chairman and was always scrambling to keep the organization afloat, to keep the cars running, the rent paid. Before he had become administrator, he had worked in the field. He would be calling with a program to "respond" to the bombing.

"Hey, Travis, how you doing, you all right?"

"Yeah, Truman, I'm all right."

"Look, in the next couple days you are going to need help. Would you like me to come down?"

That was a normal question, but Peacock suddenly felt a need to lash out. "What do you want to come for, the publicity? To be in all the pictures, to project the organization?"

"I know you are upset, man, but I think you should apologize."

"I'm sorry, man. You know I don't mean that." No, he couldn't afford to mean it because it was too close. God, they were forcing us to be just like them. Then Truman started outlining the program. Peacock listened silently. Then he interrupted. "Stop, Truman, stop. You want to stage a circus. I can't ask the family to subject themselves to that."

"Look, Travis, I know how upset you must be. But we have to do it. Where is the money to come from to build back the house, to educate the kids? We've gotta launch a national appeal and the family must be there."

"Yes, I'm upset. If I hadna come here . . ."

"He might still have been killed. He was organizing before you came."

"But it was me who told him to go register. I went to that courthouse with him, not you."

"Travis, I know it's tough, but it's what happens in this kind of a struggle. We've got to live with it. You got to keep telling yourself that we don't ask anyone to do anything that we don't do ourselves. You gotta remember that. You or Ray or Mac could have been in that house."

"For God's sake, Truman, don't lobby me. I know the line."

"Listen. . . . You say you want to respect the family's privacy. So do I. But what's your responsibility? The only way to stop these bombings is to make them public. Yeah, we gotta exploit it. Yeah, we gotta have the family crying on national TV. The cat's dead and nothing can undo that, but we have a responsibility to use his death against the people that killed him."

"I don't want to argue politics. That's not the issue," Peacock said.

"Travis, how can you say that? It is already an issue. And we, whether we like it or not, have to take it from there."

Peacock agreed with Truman but he could no longer respond to that category of practical, pragmatic realities.

"Besides," Truman was saying, "even if we wanted to keep everything simple and pure we can't. If you think that the other organizations won't be in town tomorrow morning, then you are crazy. You call it a circus; well, it's going to be one with or without us. Just came over the wires that Williams is calling for a hero's burial in Arlington, a mourning train to Washington, all under the auspices of *his* organization. We can sit aside and refuse to participate or get in there and fight . . ."

"Yeah," Peacock said, "fight for the corpse. Fight for the corpse and raise some money?"

"Yeah, Peacock. That too." Truman was angry now. "You know how many folks been fired that we are carrying on the payroll? When those people off your project got arrested two weeks ago, where did you call to get the thousand dollars bond? You know people only send us money when they feel guilty. And that's the same as saying when someone gets killed. What the hell do you expect us to do?"

"It's true, but it's not right. Man, all I can see now is that little house blown to hell. And that lady just sitting and staring . . . Man, I just don't know."

"Look, I know what you're going through, but if you feel that you can't organize in the situation right now, I understand that. If you want to go someplace for a while . . ."

Peacock saw what was coming. He would go off to "rest" someplace, and someone else would come in. Someone who, without his guilts and hesitations, could milk the situation for the most mileage. He was furious precisely because something in him wanted to leap at the chance. "You really think I would do that? Run away now? Screw you, Truman!"

"It may be wrong. In fact it is . . ." Peacock heard a weary sigh, ". . . but man, I don't see how else we can operate. Get some sleep, man. Tomorrow you will feel different about what has to be done when the vultures sweep down. You decide then how to operate."

"Thank you," Peacock said.

"One last thing, man. Maybe I shouldn't even say this but . . . ask yourself this question. Suppose it was you who had got it, what would you want us to do? What would you expect us to do? Then ask yourself if Jesse Lee Hightower was a lesser man than you. Freedom."

"Freedom," Peacock said and hung up.

Peacock crossed over to the door, opened it and stood looking down on the sleeping town. Later today it would be overrun. Camera crews, reporters, photographers, dignitaries. Across the country guilty and shocked people would be writing to Congressmen. Some would reach for checkbooks. And the checks would go to the first name they read in the papers, the first face they recognized on the screen. Some labor leader would announce a Hightower relief fund and kick it off with a munificent contribution. Others would follow, even unions which somehow managed to have no black members. And the churches would send collections. Some conscience-striken soul would make the rounds of his suburban community where no black folk lived. The resulting check would somehow reflect that fact. In Washington, Jesse Lee's fate would be officially deplored and an investigation ordered. And in the middle of all this, the meaningful thing would be to try to get enough to keep going for another six months. He was known and trusted by the family and the community. They would be asking his advice on every proposal, at every development. He could stage-manage the entire proceedings for maximum effect, package the pain and the loss to ensure the greatest "exposure."

They were talking about a hero's burial. Well, he had seen the last one. He remembered the fight about which organization had priority, whose leaders would have the right to walk on the right of the bier where the cameras were set up. He remembered the night before the funeral. The "hero" lay in state, his coffin set up in the center of the room draped with a wrinkled American flag smelling of moth balls. At a table by the door an old woman sat selling memberships, buttons and pamphlets to the people who filed in. Outside, proselytes of all kinds sold or gave away their particular version of the truth. The people bought their memberships and filed past that rumpled, dingy flag.

Somehow a man's life should be reflected in the final ceremony at his death. Jesse had been a simple man, and honest. That had been his way in the world and that was how he should go out. Peacock turned and walked back into the room.

"Travis, Travis, Whut happen?" Raf sprang to his feet and was peering at him anxiously.

"I . . . I'm all right, what's the matter?"

"Wal," Raf said, "effen yo' seen yore own face jes' now hit would set yo' back, too. Yo' bettah take a taste." Peacock drank deeply, the hot liquor bringing tears to his eyes.

"We wuz jes' figurin'," Raf said, "whut is we gon' do now, Travis? Ah mean the movement heah in Bogue Chitto?"

Peacock sat down and shook his head. He passed his hands over his face, massaging his eyes. He shook his head again. But when he looked up the men were still looking at him questioningly.

"Well," Peacock said, "be a lot happening real quick during the next few days. Here's what I think . . . We got to start with that meeting tomorrow . . ." Peacock talked, the men listened, nodding from time to time. He kept looking at his watch. when morning came he had to go back to be with the family. Funny he hadn't thought of it before, but Miss Vickie had a great face. Be great on a poster or on TV. . . .

Venus, Cupid, Folly and Time

Peter Taylor

Their house alone would not have made you think there was anything so awfully wrong with Mr. Dorset or his old-maid sister. But certain things about the way both of them dressed had, for a long time, annoyed and disturbed everyone. We used to see them together at the grocery store, for instance, or even in one of the big department stores downtown, wearing their bedroom slippers. Looking more closely we would sometimes see the cuff of a pajama top or the hem of a hitched up nightgown showing from underneath their ordinary daytime clothes. Such slovenliness in one's neighbors is so unpleasant that even husbands and wives in West Vesey Place, which was the street where the Dorsets lived, had got so they didn't like to joke about it with each other. Were the Dorsets, poor old things, losing their minds? If so, what was to be done about it? Some neighbors got so they would not even admit to themselves what they saw. And a child coming home with an ugly report on the Dorsets was apt to be told that it was time he learned to curb his imagination.

Mr. Dorset wore tweed caps and sleeveless sweaters. Usually he had his sweater stuffed down inside his trousers with his shirt tails. To the women and young girls in West Vesey Place this was extremely distasteful. It made them feel as though Mr. Dorset had just come from the bathroom and had got his sweater inside his trousers by mistake. There was, in fact, nothing about Mr. Dorset that was not offensive to the women. Even the

Reprinted with the permission of Farrar, Straus, and Giroux, Inc. from *The Collected Stories of Peter Taylor,* copyright © 1958, 1969 by Peter Taylor.

old touring car he drove was regarded by most of them as a disgrace to the neighborhood. Parked out in front of his house, as it usually was, it seemed a worse violation of West Vesey's zoning than the house itself. And worst of all was seeing Mr. Dorset wash the car.

Mr. Dorset washed his own car! He washed it not back in the alley or in his driveway but out there in the street of West Vesey Place. This would usually be on the day of one of the parties which he and his sister liked to give for young people or on a day when they were going to make deliveries of the paper flowers or the home-grown figs which they sold to their friends. Mr. Dorset would appear in the street carrying two buckets of warm water and wearing a pair of skin-tight coveralls. The skin-tight coveralls, of khaki material but faded almost to flesh color, were still more offensive to the women and young girls than his way of wearing his sweaters. With sponges and chamois cloths and a large scrub brush (for use on the canvas top) the old fellow would fall to and scrub away, gently at first on the canvas top and more vigorously as he progressed to the hood and body, just as though the car were something alive. Neighbor children felt that he went after the headlights exactly as if he were scrubbing the poor car's ears. There was an element of brutality in the way he did it and yet an element of tenderness too. An old lady visiting in the neighborhood once said that it was like the cleansing of a sacrificial animal. I suppose it was some such feeling as this that made all women want to turn away their eyes whenever the spectacle of Mr. Dorset washing his car presented itself.

As for Mr. Dorset's sister, her behavior was in its way just as offensive as his. To the men and boys in the neighborhood it was she who seemed quite beyond the pale. She would come out on her front terrace at midday clad in a faded flannel bathrobe and with her dyed black hair all undone and hanging down her back like the hair of an Indian squaw. To us whose wives and mothers did not even come downstairs in their negligees, this was very unsettling. It was hard to excuse it even on the grounds that the Dorsets were too old and lonely and hard-pressed to care about appearances any more.

Moreover, there was a boy who had gone to Miss Dorset's house one morning in the early fall to collect for his paper route and saw this very Miss Louisa Dorset pushing a carpet sweeper about one of the downstairs rooms without a stitch of clothes on. He saw her through one of the little lancet windows that opened on the front loggia of the house, and he watched her for quite a long while. She was cleaning the house in preparation for a party they were giving for young people that night, and the boy said that when she finally got hot and tired she dropped down in an easy chair and crossed her spindly, blue-veined old legs and sat there completely naked, with her legs crossed and shaking one scrawny little foot, just as unconcerned as if she didn't care that somebody was likely to walk in on her at any moment. After a little bit the boy saw her get up again and go and lean across a table to arrange some paper flowers in a vase. Fortunately he was a nice boy, though he lived only on the edge of the West Vesey Place neighborhood, and he went away without ringing the doorbell or collecting for his paper that week. But he could not resist telling his friends about what he had seen. He said it was a sight he would never forget! And she an old lady more than sixty years old who, had she not been so foolish and self-willed, might have had a house full of servants to push that carpet sweeper for her!

This foolish pair of old people had given up almost everything in life for each other's sake. And it was not at all necessary. When they were young they could have come into a decent inheritance, or now that they were old they might have been provided for by a host of rich relatives. It was only a matter of their being a little tolerant—or even civil—toward their kinspeople. But this was something that old Mr. Dorset and his sister could never consent to do. Almost all their lives they had spoken of their father's kin as "Mama's in-laws" and of their mother's kin as "Papa's in-laws." Their family name was Dorset, not on one side but on both sides. Their parents had been distant cousins. As a matter of fact, the Dorset family in the city of Chatham had once been so large and was so long established there that it would have been hard to estimate how distant the kinship might be. But still it was something that the old couple never liked to have mentioned. Most of their mother's close kin had, by the time I am speaking of, moved off to California, and most of their father's people lived somewhere up east. But Miss Dorset and her old bachelor brother found any contact, correspondence, even an exchange of Christmas cards with these in-laws intolerable. It was a case, so they said, of the in-laws respecting the value of the dollar above all else, whereas they, Miss Louisa and Mr. Alfred Dorset, placed importance on other things.

They lived in a dilapidated and curiously mutilated house on a street which, except for their own house, was the most splendid street in the entire city. Their house was one that you or I would have been ashamed to live in—even in the lean years of the early thirties. In order to reduce taxes the Dorsets had had the third story of the house torn away, leaving an ugly, flat-topped effect without any trim or ornamentation. Also they had had the south wing pulled down and had sealed the scars not with matching brick but with a speckled stucco that looked raw and naked. All this the old couple did in violation of the strict zoning laws of West Vesey Place, and for doing so they would most certainly have been prosecuted except that they were the Dorsets and except that this was during the depression when zoning laws weren't easy to enforce in a city like Chatham.

To the young people whom she and her brother entertained at their house once each year Miss Louisa Dorset like to say: "We have given up everything for each other. Our only income is from our paper flowers and our figs." The old lady, though without showing any great skill or talent for it, made paper flowers. During the winter months her brother took her in that fifteen-year-old touring car of theirs, with its steering wheel on the wrong side and with isinglass side curtains that were never taken down, to deliver these flowers to her customers. The flowers looked more like sprays of tinted potato chips than like any real flowers. Nobody could possibly have wanted to buy them except that she charged next to nothing for them and except that to people with children it seemed important to be on the Dorsets' list of worthwhile people. Nobody could really have wanted Mr. Dorset's figs either. He cultivated a dozen little bushes along the back wall of their house, covering them in the wintertime with some odd-looking boxes which he had had constructed for the purpose. The bushes were very productive, but the figs they produced were dried-up little things without much taste. During the summer months he and his sister went about in their car, with the side curtains still up, delivering the figs to the same customers who bought the paper flowers. The money they made could hardly have paid for the gas it took to run the car. It was a great waste and it was very foolish of them.

And yet, despite everything, this foolish pair of old people, this same Miss Louisa and Mr. Alfred Dorset, had become social arbiters of a kind in our city. They had attained this position entirely through their fondness for giving an annual dancing party for young people. To *young* people—to *very* young people—the Dorsets' hearts went out. I don't mean to suggest that their hearts went out to orphans or to the children of the poor, for they were not foolish in that way. The guests at their little dancing parties were the thirteen and fourteen year-olds from families like the one they had long ago set themselves against, young people from the very houses to which, in season, they delivered their figs and their paper flowers. And when the night of one of their parties came round, it was in fact the custom for Mr. Alfred to go in the same old car and fetch all the invited guests to his house. His sister might explain to reluctant parents that this saved the children the embarrassment of being taken to their first dance by mommy and daddy. But the parents knew well enough that for twenty years the Dorsets had permitted no adult person, besides themselves, to put foot inside their house.

At those little dancing parties which the Dorsets gave, peculiar things went on—unsettling things to the boys and girls who had been fetched round in the old car. Sensible parents wished to keep their children away. Yet what could they do? For a Chatham girl to have to explain, a few years later, why she never went to a party at the Dorsets' was like having to explain why she had never been a debutante. For a boy it was like having to explain why he had not gone up east to school or even why his father hadn't belonged to the Chatham Racquet Club. If when you were thirteen or fourteen you got invited to the Dorsets' house, you went; it was the way of letting people know from the outset who you were. In a busy, modern city like Chatham you cannot afford to let people forget who you are—not for a moment, not at any age. Even the Dorsets knew that.

Many a little girl, after one of those evenings at the Dorsets', was heard to cry out in her sleep. When waked, or half waked, her only explanation might be: "It was just the fragrance from the paper flowers." Or: "I dreamed I could really smell the paper flowers." Many a boy was observed by his parents to seem "different" afterward. He became "secretive." The parents of the generation that had to attend those parties never pretended to understand what went on at the Dorsets' house. And even to those of us who were in that unlucky generation it seemed we were half a lifetime learning what really took place during our one evening under the Dorsets' roof. Before our turn to go ever came round we had for years been hearing about what it was like from older boys and girls. Afterward, we continued to hear about it from those who followed us. And, looking back on it, nothing about the one evening when you were actually there ever seemed quite so real as the glimpses and snatches which you got from those people before and after you—the secondhand impressions of the Dorsets' behavior, of things they said, of looks that passed between them.

Since Miss Dorset kept no servants she always opened her own door. I suspect that for the guests at her parties the sight of her opening her door, in her astonishing attire, came as the most violent shock of the whole evening. On these occasions she and her brother got themselves up as we had never seen them before and never would again. The old lady invariably wore a modish white evening gown, a garment perfectly fitted to her spare and scrawny figure and cut in such high fashion that it must necessarily have been new that year. And never to be worn but that one night! Her hair, long and thick and newly dyed for the occasion, would be swept upward and forward in a billowy mass which was topped by a corsage of yellow and coral paper flowers. Her cheeks and lips would be darkly rouged. On her long bony arms and her bare shoulders she would have applied some kind of sun-tan powder. Whatever else you had been led to expect of the evening, no one had ever warned you sufficiently about the radical change to be noted in her appearance—or in that of her brother, either. By the end of the party Miss Louisa might look as dowdy as ever, and Mr. Alfred a little worse than usual. But at the outset, when the party was assembling in their drawing room, even Mr. Alfred appeared resplendent in a nattily tailored tuxedo, with exactly the shirt, the collar, and the tie which fashion prescribed that year. His gray hair was nicely trimmed, his puffy old face freshly shaven. He was powdered with the same dark powder that his sister used. One felt even that his cheeks had been lightly touched with rouge.

A strange perfume pervaded the atmosphere of the house. The moment you set foot inside, this awful fragrance engulfed you. It was like a mixture of spicy incense and sweet attar of roses. And always, too, there was the profusion of paper flowers. The flowers were everywhere—on every cabinet and console, every inlaid table and carved chest, on every high, marble mantel piece, on the book shelves. In the entrance hall special tiers must have been set up to hold the flowers, because they were there in overpowering masses. They were in such abundance that it seemed hardly possible that Miss Dorset could have made them all. She must have spent weeks and weeks preparing them, even months, perhaps even the whole year between parties. When she went about delivering them to her customers, in the months following, they were apt to be somewhat faded and dusty; but on the night of the party the colors of the flowers seemed even more impressive and more unlikely than their number. They were fuchsia, they were chartreuse, they were coral, aquamarine, brown, they were even black.

Everywhere in the Dorsets' house too were certain curious illuminations and lighting effects. The source of the light was usually hidden and its purpose was never obvious at once. The lighting was a subtler element than either the perfume or the paper flowers, and ultimately it was more disconcerting. A shaft of lavender light would catch a young visitor's eye and lead it, seemingly without purpose, in among the flowers. Then just beyond the point where the strength of the light would begin to diminish, the eye would discover something. In a small aperture in the mass of flowrs, or sometimes in a larger grotto-like opening, there would be a piece of sculpture—in the hall a plaster replica of Rodin's *The Kiss,* in the library an antique plaque of Leda and the Swan. Or just above the flowers would be hung a picture, usually a black and white print but sometimes a reproduction in color. On the landing of the stairway leading down to the basement ballroom was the only picture that one was likely to learn the title of at the time. It was a tiny color print of Bronzino's *Venus, Cupid, Folly and Time.* This picture was not even framed. It was simply tacked on the wall, and it had obviously been torn—rather carelessly, perhaps hurriedly—from a book or magazine. The title and the name of the painter were printed in the white margin underneath.

About these works of art most of us had been warned by older boys and girls; and we stood in painful dread of that moment when Miss Dorset or her brother might catch us staring at any one of their pictures or sculptures. We had been warned, time and again, that during the course of the evening moments would come when she or he would reach out and touch the other's elbow and indicate, with a nod or just the trace of a smile, some guest whose glance had strayed among the flowers.

To some extent the dread which all of us felt of that evening at the Dorsets' cast a shadow over the whole of our childhood. Yet for nearly twenty years the Dorsets continued to give their annual party. And even the most sensible of parents were not willing to keep their children away.

But a thing happened finally which could almost have been predicted. Young people, even in West Vesey Place, will not submit forever to the prudent counsel of their parents. Or some of them won't. There was a boy named Ned Meriwether and his sister Emily Meriwether, who lived with their parents in West Vesey Place just one block away from the Dorsets' house. In November Ned and Emily were invited to the Dorsets' party, and because they dreaded it they decided to play a trick on everyone concerned—even on themselves, as it turned out . . . They got up a plan for smuggling an uninvited guest into the Dorsets' party.

The parents of this Emily and Ned sensed that their children were concealing something from them and suspected that the two were up to mischief of some kind. But they managed to deceive themselves with the thought that it was only natural for young people—"mere children"—to be nervous about going to the Dorsets' house. And so instead of questioning them during the last hour before they left for the party, these sensible parents tried to do everything in their power to calm their two children. The boy and the girl, seeing that this was the case, took advantage of it.

"You must not go down to the front door with us when we leave," the daughter insisted to her mother. And she persuaded both Mr. and Mrs. Meriwether that after she and her brother were dressed for the party they should all wait together in the upstairs sitting room until Mr. Dorset came to fetch the two young people in his car.

When, at eight'clock, the lights of the automobile appeared in the street below, the brother and sister were still upstairs—watching from the bay window of the family sitting room. They kissed Mother and Daddy goodbye and then they flew down the stairs and across the wide, carpeted entrance hall to a certain dark recess where a boy named Tom Bascomb was hidden. This boy was the uninvited guest whom Ned and Emily were going to smuggle into the party. They had left the front door unlatched for Tom, and from the upstairs window just a few minutes ago they had watched him come across their front lawn. Now in the little recess of the hall there was a quick exchange of overcoats and hats between Ned Meriwether and Tom Bascomb; for it was a feature of the plan that Tom should attend the party as Ned and that Ned should go as the uninvited guest.

In the darkness of the recess Ned fidgeted and dropped Tom Bascomb's coat on the floor. But the boy, Tom Bascomb, did not fidget. He stepped out into the light of the hall and began methodically getting into the overcoat which he would wear tonight. He was not a boy who lived in the West Vesey Place neighborhood (he was in fact the very boy who had once watched Miss Dorset cleaning house without any clothes on), and he did not share Emily's and Ned's nervous excitement about the evening. The sound of Mr. Dorset's footsteps outside did not disturb him. When both Ned and Emily stood frozen by that sound, he continued buttoning the unfamiliar coat and even amused himself by stretching forth one arm to observe how high the sleeve came on his wrist.

The doorbell rang, and from his dark corner Ned Meriwether whispered to his sister and to Tom: "Don't worry. I'll be at the Dorsets' in plenty of time."

Tom Bascomb only shrugged his shoulders at this reassurance. Presently when he looked at Emily's flushed face and saw her batting her eye like a nervous monkey, a crooked smile played upon his lips. Then, at a sign from Emily, Tom followed her to the entrance door and permitted her to introduce him to old Mr. Dorset as her brother.

From the window of the upstairs sitting room the Meriwether parents watched Mr. Dorset and this boy and this girl walking across the lawn toward Mr. Dorset's peculiar-looking car. A light shone bravely and protectively from above the entrance of the house, and in its rays the parents were able to detect the strange angle at which Brother was carrying his head tonight and how his new fedora already seemed too small for him. They even noticed that he seemed a bit taller tonight.

"I hope it's all right," said the mother.

"What do you mean 'all right'?" the father asked petulantly.

"I mean—" the mother began, and then she hesitated. She did not want to mention that the boy out there did not look like their own Ned. It would have seemed to give away her feelings too much. "I mean that I wonder if I should have put sister in that long dress at this age and let her wear my cape. I'm afraid the cape is really inappropriate. She's still young for that sort of thing."

"Oh," said the father, "I thought you meant something else."

"Whatever else did you think I meant, Edwin?" the mother said suddenly breathless.

"I thought you meant the business we've discussed before," he said although this was of course not what he had thought she meant. He had thought she meant that the boy out there did not look like their Ned. To him it had seemed even that the boy's step was different from Ned's. "The Dorsets' parties," he said, "are not very nice affairs to be sending your children off to, Muriel. That's all I thought you meant."

"But we *can't* keep them away," the mother said defensively.

"Oh, it's just that they are growing up faster than we realize," said the father, glancing at his wife out of the corner of his eye.

By this time Mr. Dorset's car had pulled out of sight, and from downstairs Muriel Meriwether thought she heard another door closing. "What was that?" she said, putting one hand on her husband's.

"Don't be so jumpy," her husband said irritably, snatching away his hand. "It's the servants closing up in the kitchen."

Both of them knew that the servants had closed up in the kitchen long before this. Both of them had heard quite distinctly the sound of the side door closing as Ned went out. But they went on talking and deceiving themselves in this fashion during most of that evening.

Even before she opened the door to Mr. Dorset, little Emily Meriwether had known that there would be no difficulty about passing Tom Bascomb off as her brother. In the first place, she knew that without his spectacles Mr. Dorset could hardly see his hand before his face and knew that owing to some silly pride he had he never put on his spectacles except when he was behind the wheel of his automobile. This much was common knowledge. In the second place, Emily knew from experience that neither he nor his sister ever made any real pretense of knowing one child in their general acquaintance from another. And so, standing in the doorway and speaking almost in a whisper, Emily had merely to introduce first herself and then her pretended brother to Mr. Dorset. After that the three of them walked in silence from her father's house to the waiting car.

Emily was wearing her mother's second-best evening wrap, a white lapin cape which, on Emily, swept the ground. As she walked between the boy and the man, the touch of the cape's soft silk lining on her bare arms and on her shoulders spoke to her silently of a strange girl she had seen in her looking glass upstairs tonight. And with her every step toward the car the skirt of her long taffeta gown whispered her own name to her: *Emily . . . Emily.* She heard it distinctly, and yet the name sounded unfamiliar. Once during this unreal walk from house to car she glanced at the mysterious boy, Tom Bascomb, longing to ask him—if only with her eyes —for some reassurance that she was really she. But Tom Bascomb was absorbed in his own irrelevant observations. With his head tilted back he was gazing upward at the nondescript winter sky where, among drifting clouds, a few pale stars were shedding their dull light alike on West Vesey

Place and on the rest of the world. Emily drew her wrap tightly about her, and when presently Mr. Dorset held open the door to the back seat of his car she shut her eyes and plunged into the pitch-blackness of the car's interior.

Tom Bascomb was a year older than Ned Meriwether and he was nearly two years older than Emily. He had been Ned's friend first. He and Ned had played baseball together on Saturdays before Emily ever set eyes on him. Yet according to Tom Bascomb himself, with whom several of us older boys talked just a few weeks after the night he went to the Dorsets, Emily always insisted that it was she who had known him first. On what she based this false claim Tom could not say. And on the two or three other occasions when we got Tom to talk about that night, he kept saying that he didn't understand what it was that had made Emily and Ned quarrel over which of them knew him first and knew him better.

We could have told him what it was, I think. But we didn't. It would have been too hard to say to him that at one time or another all of us in West Vesey had had our Tom Bascombs. Tom lived with his parents in an apartment house on a wide thoroughfare known as Division Boulevard, and his only real connection with West Vesey Place was that that street was included in his paper route. During the early morning hours he rode his bicycle along West Vesey and along other quiet streets like it, carefully aiming a neatly rolled paper at the dark loggia, at the colonnaded porch, or at the ornamented doorway of each of the palazzos and châteaux and manor houses that glowered at him in the dawn. He was well thought of as a paper boy. If by mistake one of his papers went astray and lit on an upstairs balcony or on the roof of a porch, Tom would always take more careful aim and throw another. Even if the paper only went into the shrubbery, Tom got off his bicycle and fished it out. He wasn't the kind of boy to whom it would have occurred that the old fogies and the rich kids in West Vesey could very well get out and scramble for their own papers.

Actually a party at the Dorsets' house was more a grand tour of the house than a real party. There was a half hour spent over very light refreshments (fruit jello, English tea biscuits, lime punch). There was another half hour ostensibly given to general dancing in the basement ballroom (to the accompaniment of victrola music). But mainly there was the tour. As the party passed through the house, stopping sometimes to sit down in the principal rooms, the host and hostess provided entertainment in the form of an almost continuous dialogue between themselves. This dialogue was famous and was full of interest, being all about how much the Dorsets had given up for each other's sake and about how much higher the tone of Chatham society used to be than it was nowadays. They would invariably speak of their parents, who had died within a year of each other when Miss Louisa and Mr. Alfred were still in their teens; they even spoke of their wicked in-laws. When their parents died, the wicked in-laws had first tried to make them sell the house, then had tried to separate them and send them away to boarding schools, and had ended by trying to marry them off to "just anyone." Their two grandfathers had still been alive in those days and each had had a hand in the machinations, after the failure of which each grandfather had disinherited them. Mr. Alfred and Miss Louisa spoke also of how, a few years later, a procession of "young nobodies" had come of their own accord trying to steal the two of them away from each other. Both he and she would scowl at the very recollection of those "just anybodies" and those "nobodies," those "would-be suitors" who always turned out to be misguided fortune-hunters and had to be driven away.

The Dorsets' dialogue usually began in the living room the moment Mr. Dorset returned with his last collection of guests. (He sometimes had to make five or six trips in the car.) There, as in other rooms afterward, they were likely to begin with a reference to the room itself or perhaps to some piece of furniture in the room. For instance, the extraordinary length of the drawing room—or reception room, as the Dorsets called it—would lead them to speak of an even longer room which they had had torn away from the house. "It grieved us, we wept," Miss Dorset would say, "to have Mama's French drawing room torn away from us."

"But we tore it away from ourselves," her brother would add, "as we tore away our in-laws—because we could not afford them." Both of them spoke in a fine declamatory style, but they frequently interrupted themselves with a sad little laugh which expressed something quite different from what they were saying and which seemed to serve them as an aside not meant to our ears.

"That was one of our greatest sacrifices," Miss Dorset would say, referring still to her mother's French drawing room.

And her brother would say: "But we knew the day had passed in Chatham for entertainments worthy of that room."

"It was the room which Mama and Papa loved best, but we gave it up because we knew, from our upbringing, which things to give up."

From this they might go on the anecdotes about their childhood. Sometimes their parents had left them for months or even a whole year at a time with only the housekeeper or with trusted servants to see after them. "You could trust servants then," they explained. And: "In those days parents could do that sort of thing, because in those days there was a responsible body of people within which your young people could always find proper companionship."

In the library, to which the party always moved from the drawing room, Mr. Dorset was fond of exhibiting snapshots of the house taken before the south wing was pulled down. As the pictures were passed around, the dialogue continued. It was often there that they told the story of how the in-laws had tried to force them to sell the house. "For the sake of economy!" Mr. Dorset would exclaim, adding an ironic "Ha ha!"

His sister would repeat the exclamation, "For the sake of economy!" and also the ironic "Ha ha!"

"As though money—" he would begin.

"As though money ever took the place," his sister would come in, "of living with your own kind."

"Or of being well born," said Mr. Dorset.

After the billiard room, where everyone who wanted it was permitted one turn with the only cue that there seemed to be in the house, and after the dining room, where it was promised refreshments would be served later, the guests would be taken down to the ballroom—purportedly for dancing. Instead of everyone's being urged to dance, however, once they were assembled in the ballroom, Miss Dorset would announce that she and her brother understood the timidity which young people felt about dancing and that all that she and he intended to do was to set the party a good example . . . It was only Miss Louisa and Mr. Alfred who danced. For perhaps thirty minutes, in a room without light excepting that from a few weak bulbs concealed among the flowers, the old couple danced; and they danced with such grace and there was such perfect harmony in all their movements that the guests stood about in stunned silence, as if hypnotized. The Dorsets waltzed, they two-stepped, they even fox-trotted, stopping only long enough between dances for Mr. Dorset, amid general applause, to change the victrola record.

But it was when their dance was ended that all the effects of the Dorsets' careful grooming that night would have vanished. And, alas, they made no effort to restore themselves. During the remainder of the evening Mr. Dorset went about with his bow tie hanging limply on his damp shirtfront, a gold collar button shining above it. A strand of gray hair, which normally covered his bald spot on top, now would have fallen on the wrong side of his part and hung like fringe about his ear. On his face and neck the thick layer of powder was streaked with perspiration. Miss Dorset was usually in an even more disheveled state, depending somewhat upon the fashion of her dress that year. But always her powder was streaked, her lipstick entirely gone, her hair falling down on all sides, and her corsage dangling somewhere about the nape of her neck. In this condition they led the party upstairs again, not stopping until they had reached the second floor of the house.

On the second floor we—the guests—were shown the rooms which the Dorsets' parents had once occupied (the Dorsets' own rooms were never shown). We saw, in glass museum cases along the hallway, the dresses and suits and hats and even the shoes which Miss Louisa and Mr. Alfred had worn to parties when they were very young. And now the dialogue, which had been left off while the Dorsets danced, was resumed. "Ah, the happy time," one of them would say, "was when we were *your* age!" And then, exhorting us to be happy and gay while we were still safe in the bosom of our own kind and before the world came crowding in on us with its ugly demands, the Dorsets would recall the happiness they had known when they were very young. This was their *pièce de résistance*. With many a wink and blush and giggle and shake of the forefinger—and of course standing before the whole party—they each would remind the other of his or her naughty behavior in some old-fashioned parlor game or of certain silly little flirtations which they had long ago caught each other in.

They were on their way downstairs again now, and by the time they had finished with this favorite subject they would be downstairs. They would be in the dark, flower-bedecked downstairs hall and just before entering the dining room for the promised refreshments: the fruit jello, the English tea biscuits, the lime punch.

And now for a moment Mr. Dorset bars the way to the dining room and prevents his sister from opening the closed door. "Now, my good friends," he says, "let us eat, drink and be merry!"

"For the night is yet young," says his sister.

"Tonight you must be gay and carefree," Mr. Dorset enjoins.

"Because in this house we are all friends," Miss Dorset says. "We are all young, we all love one another."

"And love can make us all young forever," her brother says.

"Remember!"

"Remember this evening always, sweet young people!"

"Remember!"

"Remember what our life is like here!"

And now Miss Dorset, with one hand on the knob of the great door which she is about to throw open, leans a little toward the guests and whispers hoarsely: "This is what it is like to be young forever!"

Ned Meriwether was waiting behind a big japonica shrub near the sidewalk when, about twenty minutes after he had last seen Emily, the queer old touring car drew up in front of the Dorsets' house. During the interval, the car had gone from the Meriwether house to gather a number of other guests, and so it was not only Emily and Tom who alighted on the sidewalk before the Dorsets' house. The group was just large enough to make it easy for Ned to slip out from his dark hiding place and join them without being noticed by Mr. Dorset. And now the group was escorted rather unceremoniously up to the door of the house, and Mr. Dorset departed to fetch more guests.

They were received at the door by Miss Dorset. Her eyesight was no doubt better than her brother's, but still there was really no danger of her detecting an uninvited guest. Those of us who had gone to that house in the years just before Ned and Emily came along, could remember that during a whole evening, when their house was full of young people, the Dorsets made no introductions and made no effort to distinguish which of their guests was which. They did not even make a count of heads. Perhaps they did vaguely recognize some of the faces, because sometimes when they had come delivering figs or paper flowers to a house they had of necessity encountered a young child there, and always they smiled sweetly at it, asked its age, and calculated on their old fingers how many years must pass before the child would be eligible for an invitation. Yet at those moments something in the way they had held up their fingers and in the way they had gazed *at* the little face instead of into it had revealed their lack of interest in the individual child. And later when the child was finally old enough to receive their invitation he found it was still no different with the Dorsets. Even in their own house it was evidently to the young people as a group that the Dorsets' hearts went out; while they had the boys and girls under their roof they herded them about like so many little thoroughbred calves. Even when Miss Dorset opened the front door she did so exactly as though she were opening a gate. She pulled it open very slowly, standing half behind it to keep out of harm's way. And the children, all huddled together, surged in.

How meticulously this Ned and Emily Meriwether must have laid their plans for that evening! And the whole business might have come out all right if only they could have foreseen the effect which one part of their plan—rather a last minute embellishment of it—would produce upon Ned himself. Barely ten minutes after they entered the house Ned was watching Tom as he took his seat on the piano bench beside Emily. Ned probably watched Tom closely, because certainly he knew what the next move was going to be. The moment Miss Louisa Dorset's back was turned Tom Bascomb slipped his arm gently about Emily's little waist and commenced kissing her all over her pretty face. It was almost as if he were kissing away tears.

This spectacle on the piano bench, and others like it which followed, had been an inspiration of the last day or so before the party. Or so Ned and Emily maintained afterward when defending themselves to their parents. But no matter when it was conceived, a part of their plan it was, and Ned must have believed himself fully prepared for it. Probably he expected to join in the round of giggling which it produced from the other guests. But now that the time had come—it is easy to imagine—the boy Ned Meriwether found himself not quite able to join in the fun. He watched with the others, but he was not quite infected by their laughter.

He stood a little apart, and possibly he was hoping that Emily and Tom would not notice his failure to appreciate the success of their comedy. He was no doubt baffled by his own feelings, by the failure of his own enthusiasm, and by a growing desire to withdraw himself from the plot and from the party itself.

It is easy to imagine Ned's uneasiness and confusion that night. And I believe the account which I have given of Emily's impressions and her delicate little sensations while on the way to the party has the ring of truth about it, though actually the account was supplied by girls who knew her only slightly, who were not at the party, who could not possibly have seen her afterward. It may, after all, represent only what other girls imagined she would have felt. As for the account of how Mr. and Mrs. Meriwether spent the evening, it is their very own. And they did not hesitate to give it to anyone who would listen.

It was a long time, though, before many of us had a clear picture of the main events of the evening. We heard very soon that the parties for the young people were to be no more, that there had been a wild scramble and chase through the Dorsets' house, and that it had ended by the Dorsets locking some boy—whether Ned or Tom was not easy to determine at first—in a queer sort of bathroom in which the plumbing had been disconnected, and even the fixtures removed, I believe. (Later I learned that there was nothing literally sinister about the bathroom itself. By having the pipes disconnected to this, and perhaps other bathrooms, the Dorsets had obtained further reductions in their taxes.) But a clear picture of the whole evening wasn't to be had—not without considerable searching. For one thing, the Meriwether parents immediately, within a week after the party, packed their son and daughter off to boarding schools. Accounts from the other children were contradictory and vague—perversely so, it seemed. Parents reported to each other that the little girls had nightmares which were worse even than those which their older sisters had had. And the boys were secretive and elusive, even with us older boys when we questioned them about what had gone on.

One sketchy account of events leading up to the chase, however, did go the rounds almost at once. Ned must have written it back to some older boy in a letter, because it contained information which no one but Ned could have had. The account went like this: When Mr. Dorset returned from his last round-up of guests, he came hurrying into the drawing room where the others were waiting and said in a voice trembling with excitement: "Now, let us all be seated, my young friends, and let us warm ourselves with some good talk."

At that moment everyone who was not already seated made a dash for a place on one of the divans or love seats or even in one of the broad window seats. (There were no individual chairs in the room.) Everyone made a dash, that is, except Ned. Ned did not move. He remained standing beside a little table rubbing his fingers over its polished surface. And from this moment he was clearly an object of suspicion in the eyes of his host and hostess. Soon the party moved from the drawing room to the library, but in whatever room they stopped Ned managed to isolate himself from the rest. He would sit or stand looking down at his hands until once again an explosion of giggles filled the room. Then he would look up just in time to see Tom Bascomb's cheek against Emily's or his arm about her waist.

For nearly two hours Ned didn't speak a word to anyone. He endured the Dorsets' dialogue, the paper flowers, the perfumed air, the works of art. Whenever a burst of giggling forced him to raise his eyes he would look up at Tom and Emily and then turn his eyes away. Before looking down at his hands again he would let his eyes travel slowly about the room until they came to rest on the figures of the two Dorsets. That, it seems, was how he happened to discover that the Dorsets understood, or thought they understood, what the giggles meant. In the great mirror mounted over the library mantel he saw them exchanging half-suppressed smiles. Their smiles lasted precisely as long as the giggling continued, and then, in the mirror, Ned saw their faces change and grow solemn when their eyes—their identical, tiny, dull, amber-colored eyes—focused upon himself.

From the library the party continued on the regular tour of the house. At last when they had been to the ballroom and watched the Dorsets dance, had been upstairs to gaze upon the faded party clothes in the museum cases, they descended into the downstairs hall and were just before being turned into the dining room. The guests had already heard the Dorsets teasing each other about the silly little flirtations and about their naughtiness in parlor games when they were young and listened to their exhortations to be gay and happy and carefree. Then just when Miss Dorset leaned toward them and whispered, "This is what it is like to be young forever," there rose a chorus of laughter, breathless and shrill, yet loud and intensely penetrating.

Ned Meriwether, standing on the bottom step of the stairway, lifted his eyes and looked over the heads of the party to see Tom and Emily half hidden in a bower of paper flowers and caught directly in a ray of mauve light. The two had squeezed themselves into a little niche there and stood squarely in front of the Rodin statuary. Tom had one arm placed about Emily's shoulders and he was kissing her lightly first on the lobe of one ear and then on the tip of her nose. Emily stood as rigid and pale as the plaster sculpture behind her and with just the faintest smile on her lips. Ned looked at the two of them and then turned his glance at once on the Dorsets.

He found Miss Louisa and Mr. Alfred gazing quite openly at Tom and Emily and frankly grinning at the spectacle. It was more than Ned could endure. "Don't you *know?*" he fairly wailed, as if in great physical pain. "Can't you *tell?* Can't you see who they *are?* They're *brother* and *sister!*"

From the other guests came one concerted gasp. And then an instant later, mistaking Ned's outcry to be something he had planned all along and probably intended—as they imagined—for the very cream of the jest, the whole company burst once again into laughter—not a chorus of laughter this time but a volley of loud guffaws from the boys, and from the girls a cacophony of separately articulated shrieks and trills.

None of the guests present that night could—or would—give a satisfactory account of what happened next. Everyone insisted that he had not even looked at the Dorsets, that he, or she, didn't know how Miss Louisa and Mr. Alfred reacted at first. Yet this was precisely what those of us who had gone there in the past *had* to know. And when finally we did manage to get an account of it, we knew that it was a very truthful and accurate one. Because we got it, of course, from Tom Bascomb.

Since Ned's outburst came after the dancing exhibition, the Dorsets were in their most disheveled state. Miss Louisa's hair was fallen half over her face, and that lone limp strand of Mr. Alfred's was dangling about his left ear. Like that, they stood at the doorway to the dining room grinning at Tom Bascomb's antics. And when Tom Bascomb, hearing Ned's wail, whirled about, the grins were still on the Dorsets' faces even though the guffaws and the shrieks of laughter were now silenced. Tom said that for several moments they continued to wear their grins like masks and that you couldn't really tell how they were taking it all until presently Miss Louisa's face, still wearing the grin, began turning all the queer colors of her paper flowers. Then the grin vanished from her lips and her mouth fell open and every bit of color went out of her face. She took a step backward and leaned against the doorjamb with her mouth still open and her eyes closed. If she hadn't been on her feet, Tom said he would have thought she was dead. Her brother didn't look at her, but his own grin had vanished just as hers did, and his face, all drawn and wrinkled, momentarily turned a dull copperish green.

Presently, though, he too went white, not white in faintness but in anger. His little brown eyes now shone like rosin. And he took several steps toward Ned Meriwether. "What we know is that you are not one of us," he croaked. "We have perceived that from the beginning! We don't know how you got here or who you are. But the important question is, What are you doing here among these nice children?"

The question seemed to restore life to Miss Louisa. Her amber eyes popped wide open. She stepped away from the door and began pinning up her hair which had fallen down on her shoulders, and at the same time addressing the guests who were huddled together in the center of the hall. "Who is he, children? He is an intruder, that we know. If you know who he is, you must tell us."

"Who *am* I? Why, I am Tom Bascomb!" shouted Ned, still from the bottom step of the stairway. "I am Tom Bascomb, your paper boy!"

Then he turned and fled up the stairs toward the second floor. In a moment Mr. Dorset was after him.

To the real Tom Bascomb it had seemed that Ned honestly believed what he had been saying; and his own first impulse was to shout a denial. But being a level-headed boy and seeing how bad things were, Tom went instead to Miss Dorset and whispered to her that Tom Bascomb was a pretty tough guy and that she had better let *him* call the police for her. She told him where the telephone was in the side hall, and he started away.

But Miss Dorset changed her mind. She ran after Tom telling him not to call. Some of the guests mistook this for the beginning of another chase. Before the old lady could overtake Tom, however, Ned himself had appeared in the doorway toward which she and Tom were moving. He had come down the back stairway and he was calling out to Emily, "We're going *home*, Sis!"

A cheer went up from the whole party. Maybe it was this that caused Ned to lose his head, or maybe it was simply the sight of Miss Dorset rushing at him that did it. At any rate, the next moment he was running up the front stairs again, this time with Miss Dorset in pursuit.

When Tom returned from the telephone, all was quiet in the hall. The guests—everybody except Emily—had moved to the foot of the stairs and they were looking up and listening. From upstairs Tom could hear Ned saying, "All right. All right. All right." The old couple had cornered him.

Emily was still standing in the little niche among the flowers. And it is the image of Emily Meriwether standing among the paper flowers that tantalizes me whenever I think or hear someone speak of that evening. That, more than anything else, can make me wish that I had been there. I shall never cease to wonder what kind of thoughts were in her head to make her seem so oblivious to all that was going on while she stood there, and, for that matter, what had been in her mind all evening while she endured Tom Bascomb's caresses. When, in years since, I have had reason to wonder what some girl or woman is thinking—some Emily grown older—my mind nearly always returns to the image of that girl among the paper flowers. Tom said that when he returned from the telephone she looked very solemn and pale still but that her mind didn't seem to be on any of the present excitement. Immediately he went to her and said, "Your dad is on his way over, Emily." For it was the Meriwether parents he had telephoned, of course, and not the police.

It seemed to Tom that so far as he was concerned the party was now over. There was nothing more he could do. Mr. Dorset was upstairs guarding the door to the strange little room in which Ned was locked up. Miss Dorset was serving lime punch to the other guests in the dining room, all the while listening with one ear for the arrival of the police whom Tom pretended he had called. When the doorbell finally rang and Miss Dorset hurried to answer it, Tom slipped quietly out through the pantry and through the kitchen and left the house by the back door as the Meriwether parents entered by the front.

There was no difficulty in getting Edwin and Muriel Meriwether, the children's parents, to talk about what happened after they arrived that night. Both of them were sensible and clearheaded people, and they were not so conservative as some of our other neighbors in West Vesey. Being fond of gossip of any kind and fond of reasonably funny stories on themselves, they told how their children had deceived them earlier in the evening and how they had deceived themselves later. They tended to blame themselves more than the children for what had happened. They tried to protect the children from any harm or embarrassment that might result from it by sending them off to boarding school. In their talk they never referred directly to Tom's reprehensible conduct or to the possible motives that the children might have had for getting up their plan. They tried to spare their children and they tried to spare Tom, but fortunately it didn't occur to them to try to spare the poor old Dorsets.

When Miss Louisa opened the door, Mr. Meriwether said, "I'm Edwin Meriwether, Miss Dorset. I've come for my son, Ned."

"And for your daughter Emily, I hope," his wife whispered to him.

"And for my daughter Emily."

Before Miss Dorset could answer him Edwin Meriwether spied Mr. Dorset descending the stairs. With his wife, Muriel, sticking close to his side Edwin now strode over to the foot of the stairs. "Mr. Dorset," he began, "my son Ned—"

From behind them, Edwin and Muriel now heard Miss Dorset saying, "All the invited guests are gathered in the dining room." From where they were standing the two parents could see into the dining room. Suddenly they turned and hurried in there. Mr. Dorset and his sister of course followed them.

Muriel Meriwether went directly to Emily who was standing in a group of girls. "Emily, where is your brother?"

Emily said nothing, but one of the boys answered: "I think they've got him locked up upstairs somewhere."

"Oh, no!" said Miss Louisa, a hairpin in her mouth—for she was still rather absent-mindedly working at her hair. "It is an intruder that my brother has upstairs."

Mr. Dorset began speaking in a confidential tone to Edwin. "My dear neighbor," he said, "our paper boy saw fit to intrude himself upon our company tonight. But we recognized him as an outsider from the start."

Muriel Meriwether asked: "Where *is* the paper boy? Where is the paper boy, Emily?"

Again one of the boys volunteered: "He went out through the back door, Mrs. Meriwether."

The eyes of Mr. Alfred and Miss Louisa searched the room for Tom. Finally their eyes met and they smiled coyly. "*All* the children are being mischievous tonight," said Miss Louisa, and it was quite as though she had said, "all *we* children." Then, still smiling, she said, "Your tie has come undone, Brother. Mr. and Mrs. Meriwether will hardly know what to think."

Mr. Alfred fumbled for a moment with his tie but soon gave it up. Now with a bashful glance at the Meriwether parents, and giving a nod in the direction of the children, he actually said, "I'm afraid we've all decided to play a trick on Mr. and Mrs. Meriwether."

Miss Louisa said to Emily: "We've hidden our brother somewhere, haven't we?"

Emily's mother said firmly: "Emily, tell me where Ned is."

"He's upstairs, Mother," said Emily in a whisper.

Emily's father said: "I wish you to take me to the boy upstairs, Mr. Dorset."

The coy, bashful expressions vanished from the two Dorsets' faces. Their eyes were little dark pools of incredulity, growing narrower by the second. And both of them were now trying to put their hair in order. "Why, *we* know nice children when we see them," Miss Louisa said peevishly. There was a pleading quality in her voice, too. "We knew from the beginning that the boy upstairs didn't belong amongst us," she said. "Dear neighbors, it isn't just the money, you know." All at once she sounded like a little girl about to burst into tears.

"It isn't just the money?" Edwin Meriwether repeated.

"Miss Dorset," said Muriel with new gentleness in her tone, as though she had just sensed that she was talking to a little girl, "there has been some kind of mistake—a misunderstanding."

Mr. Alfred Dorset said: "Oh, we wouldn't make a mistake of that kind! People *are* different. It isn't something you can put your finger on, but it isn't the money."

"I don't know what you're talking about," Edwin said, exasperated. "But I'm going upstairs and find that boy." He left the room with Mr.

Dorset following him with quick little steps—steps like those of a small boy trying to keep up with a man.

Miss Louisa now sat down in one of the high-backed dining chairs which were lined up along the oak wainscot. She was trembling, and Muriel came and stood beside her. Neither of them spoke, and in almost no time Edwin Meriwether came downstairs again with Ned. Miss Louisa looked at Ned, and tears came into her eyes. "Where is my brother?" she asked accusingly, as though she thought possibly Ned and his father had locked Mr. Dorset in the bathroom.

"I believe he has retired," said Edwin. "He left us and disappeared into one of the rooms upstairs."

"Then I must go up to him," said Miss Louisa. For a moment she seemed unable to rise. At last she pushed herself up from a chair and walked from the room with the slow, steady gait of a somnambulist. Muriel Meriwether followed her into the hall and as she watched the old woman ascending the steps, leaning heavily on the rail, her impulse was to go and offer to assist her. But something made her turn back into the dining room. Perhaps she imagined that her daughter Emily might need her now.

The Dorsets did not reappear that night. After Miss Louisa went upstairs, Muriel promptly got on the telephone and called the parents of some of the other boys and girls. Within a quarter of an hour half a dozen parents had arrived. It was the first time in many years that any adult had set foot inside the Dorset house. It was the first time that any parent had ever inhaled the perfumed air or seen the masses of paper flowers and the illuminations and the statuary. In the guise of holding consultations over whether or not they should put out the lights and lock up the house the parents lingered much longer than was necessary before taking the young people home. Some of them even tasted the lime punch. But in the presence of their children they made no comment on what had happened and gave no indication of what their own impressions were: not even their impressions of the punch. At last it was decided that two of the men should see to putting out the lights everywhere on the first floor and down in the ballroom. They were a long time in finding the switches for the indirect lighting. In most cases they simply resorted to unscrewing the bulbs. Meanwhile the children went to the large cloak closet behind the stairway and got their wraps. When Ned and Emily Meriwether rejoined their parents at the front door to leave the house, Ned was wearing his own overcoat and held his own fedora in his hand.

Miss Louisa and Mr. Alfred Dorset lived on for nearly ten years after that night, but they gave up selling their figs and paper flowers and of course they never entertained young people again. I often wonder if growing up in Chatham can ever have seemed quite the same since. Some of the terror must have gone out of it. Half the dread of coming of age must have vanished with the dread of the Dorsets' parties.

After that night, their old car would sometimes be observed creeping about town, but it was never parked in front of their house any more. It stood usually at the side entrance where the Dorsets could climb in and out of it without being seen. They began keeping a servant too—mainly to run their errands for them, I imagine. Sometimes it would be a man, sometimes a woman, never the same one for more than a few months at a time. Both of the Dorsets died during the Second World War while many of us who had gone to their parties were away from Chatham. But the story went round—and I am inclined to believe it—that after they were dead and the house was sold, Tom Bascomb's coat and hat were found still hanging in the cloak closet behind the stairs.

Tom himself was a pilot in the war and was a considerable hero. He was such a success and made such a name for himself that he never came back to Chatham to live. He found bigger opportunities elsewhere I suppose, and I don't suppose he ever felt the ties to Chatham that people with Ned's kind of upbringing do. Ned was in the war too, of course. He was in the navy and after the war he did return to Chatham to live, though actually it was not until then that he spent much time here since his parents bundled him off to boarding school. Emily came home and made her debut just two or three years before the war, but she was already engaged to some boy in the East; she never comes back any more except to bring her children to see their grandparents for a few days during Christmas or at Easter.

I understand that Emily and Ned are pretty indifferent to each other's existence nowadays. I have been told this by Ned Meriwether's own wife. Ned's wife maintains that the night Ned and Emily went to the Dorsets' party marked the beginning of this indifference, that it marked the end of their childhood intimacy and the beginning of a shyness, a reserve, even an animosity between them that was destined to be a sorrow forever to the two sensible parents who had sat in the upstairs sitting room that night waiting until the telephone call came from Tom Bascomb.

Ned's wife is a girl he met while he was in the navy. She was a Wave, and her background isn't the same as his. Apparently she isn't too happy with life in what she refers to as "Chatham proper." She and Ned have recently moved out into a suburban development, which she doesn't like either and which she refers to as "greater Chatham." She asked me at a party one night how Chatham got its name (she was just making conversation and appealing to my interest in such things) and when I told her that it was named for the Earl of Chatham and pointed out that the city is located in Pitt County she burst out laughing. "How very elegant," she said. "Why has nobody ever told me that before?" But what interests me most about her is that after a few drinks she likes to talk about Ned and Emily and Tom Bascomb and the Dorsets. Tom Bascomb has become a kind of hero—and I don't mean a wartime hero—in her eyes, though of course not having grown up in Chatham she has never seen him in her life. But she is a clever girl, and there are times when she will say to me, "Tell me about Chatham. Tell me about the Dorsets." And I try to tell her. I tell her to remember that Chatham looks upon itself as a rather old city. I tell her to remember that it was one of the first English-speaking settlements west of the Alleghenies and that by the end of the American Revolution, when veterans began pouring westward over the Wilderness Road or down the Ohio River, Chatham was often referred to as a thriving village. Then she tells me that I am being dull, because it is hard for her to concentrate on any aspect of the story that doesn't center around Tom Bascomb and that night at the Dorsets'.

But I make her listen. Or at least one time I did. The Dorset family, I insisted on saying, was in Chatham even in those earliest times right after the Revolution, but they had come here under somewhat different circumstances from those of the other early settlers. How could that really matter, Ned's wife asked, after a hundred and fifty years? How could distinctions between the first settlers matter after the Irish had come to Chatham, after the Germans, after the Italians? Well, in West Vesey Place it could matter. It had to. If the distinction was false, it mattered all the more and it was all the more necessary to make it.

But let me interject here that Chatham is located in a state about whose history most Chatham citizens—not newcomers like Ned's wife, but old-timers—have little interest and less knowledge. Most of us, for instance, are never even quite sure whether during the 1860's our state did secede or didn't secede. As for the city itself, some of us hold that it is geographically Northern and culturally Southern. Others say the reverse is true. We are all apt to want to feel misplaced in Chatham, and so we are not content merely to say that it is a border city. How you stand on this important question is apt to depend entirely on whether your family is one of those with a good Southern name or one that had its origin in New England, because those are the two main categories of old society families in Chatham.

But truly—I told Ned's wife—the Dorset family was never in either of those categories. The first Dorset had come, with his family and his possessions and even a little capital, direct from a city in the English Midlands to Chatham. The Dorsets came not as pioneers, but paying their way all the way. They had not bothered to stop for a generation or two to put down roots in Pennsylvania or Virginia or Massachusetts. And this was the distinction which some people wished always to make. Apparently those early Dorsets who cared no more for putting down roots in the soil of the New World than they had cared for whatever they had left behind in the Old. They were an obscure mercantile family who came to invest in a new western city. Within two generations the business—no, the industry!—which they established made them rich beyond any dreams they could have had in the beginning. For half a century they were looked upon, if any family ever was, as our first family.

And then the Dorsets left Chatham—practically all of them except the one old bachelor and the one old maid—left it just as they had come, not caring much about what they were leaving or where they were going. They were city people, and they were Americans. They knew that what they had in Chatham they could buy more of in other places. For them Chatham was an investment that had paid off. They went to live in Santa Barbara and Laguna Beach, in Newport and on Long Island. And the truth which it was so hard for the rest of us to admit was that, despite our families of Massachusetts and Virginia, we were all more like the Dorsets —those Dorsets who left Chatham—than we were *un*like them. Their spirit was just a little closer to being the very essence of Chatham than ours was. The obvious difference was that we had to stay on here and pretend that our life had a meaning which it did not. And if it was only by a sort of chance that Miss Louisa and Mr. Alfred played the role of social arbiters among the young people for a number of years, still no one could honestly question their divine right to do so.

"It may have been their right," Ned's wife said at this point, "but just think what might have happened."

"It's not a matter of what might have happened," I said. "It is a matter of what did happen. Otherwise, what have you and I been talking about?"

"Otherwise," she said with an irrepressible shudder, "I would not be forever getting you off in a corner at these parties to talk about my husband and my husband's sister and how it is they care so little for each other's company nowadays?"

And I could think of nothing to say to that except that probably we had now pretty well covered our subject.

Barn Burning

William Faulkner

   The store in which the Justice of the Peace's court was sitting smelled of cheese. The boy, crouched on his nail keg at the back of the crowded room, knew he smelled cheese, and more: from where he sat he could see the ranked shelves close-packed with the solid, squat, dynamic shapes of tin cans whose labels his stomach read, not from the lettering which meant nothing to his mind but from the scarlet devils and the silver curve of fish—this, the cheese which he knew he smelled and the hermetic meat which his intestines believed he smelled coming in intermittent gusts momentary and brief between the other constant one, the smell and sense just a little of fear because mostly of despair and grief, the old fierce pull of blood. He could not see the table where the Justice sat and before which his father and his father's enemy (*our enemy* he thought in that despair; *ourn! mine and hisn both! He's my father!*) stood, but he could hear them, the two of them that is, because his father had said no word yet:
   "But what proof have you, Mr. Harris?"
   "I told you. The hog got into my corn. I caught it up and sent it back to him. He had no fence that would hold it. I told him so, warned him. The next time I put the hog in my pen. When he came to get it I gave him enough wire to patch up his pen. The next time I put the hog up and

Copyright 1939 © and renewed 1967 by Estelle Faulkner and Jill Faulkner Summers. Reprinted from *Collected Stories of William Faulkner*, by permission of Random House, Inc.

kept it. I rode down to his house and saw the wire I gave him still rolled onto the spool in his yard. I told him he could have the hog when he paid me a dollar pound fee. That evening a nigger came with the dollar and got the hog. He was a strange nigger. He said, 'He say to tell you wood and hay kin burn.' I said, 'What?' 'That whut he say to tell you,' the nigger said. 'Wood and hay kin burn,' That night my barn burned. I got the stock out but I lost the barn."

"Where is the nigger? Have you got him?"

"He was a strange nigger, I tell you. I don't know what became of him."

"But that's not proof. Don't you see that's not proof?"

"Get that boy up here. He knows." For a moment the boy thought too that the man meant his older brother until Harris said, "Not him. The little one. The boy," and, crouching, small for his age, small and wiry like his father, in patched and faded jeans even too small for him, with straight, uncombed, brown hair and eyes gray and wild as storm scud, he saw the men between himself and the table part and become a lane of grim faces, at the end of which he saw the justice, a shabby, collarless, graying man in spectacles, beckoning him. He felt no floor under his bare feet; he seemed to walk beneath the palpable weight of the grim turning faces. His father, stiff in his black Sunday coat donned not for the trial but for the moving, did not even look at him. *He aims for me to lie,* he thought, again with that frantic grief and despair. *And I will have to do hit.*

"What's your name, boy?" the Justice said.

"Colonel Sartoris Snopes," the boy whispered.

"Hey?" the Justice said. "Talk louder. Colonel Sartoris? I reckon anybody named for Colonel Sartoris in this country can't help but tell the truth, can they?" The boy said nothing. *Enemy! Enemy!* he thought; for a moment he could not even see, could not see that the Justice's face was kindly nor discern that his voice was troubled when he spoke to the man named Harris: "Do you want me to question this boy?" But he could hear, and during those subsequent long seconds while there was absolutely no sound in the crowded little room save that of quiet and intent breathing it was as if he had swung outward at the end of a grape vine, over a ravine, and at the top of the swing had been caught in a prolonged instant of mesmerized gravity, weightless in time.

"No!" Harris said violently, explosively. "Damnation! Send him out of here!" Now time, the fluid world, rushed beneath him again, the voices coming to him again through the smell of cheese and sealed meat, the fear and despair and the old grief of blood:

"This case is closed. I can't find against you, Snopes, but I can give you advice. Leave this country and don't come back to it."

His father spoke for the first time, his voice cold and harsh, level, without emphasis: "I aim to. I don't figure to stay in a country among

Barn Burning 357

people who...." he said something unprintable and vile, addressed to no one.

"That'll do," the Justice said. "Take your wagon and get out of this country before dark. Case dismissed."

His father turned, and he followed the stiff black coat, the wiry figure walking a little stiffly from where a Confederate provost's man's musket ball had taken him in the heel on a stolen horse thirty years ago, followed the two backs now, since his older brother had appeared from somewhere in the crowd, no taller than the father but thicker, chewing tobacco steadily, between the two lines of grim-faced men and out of the store and across the worn gallery and down the sagging steps and among the dogs and half-grown boys in the mild May dust, where as he passed a voice hissed:

"Barn burner!"

Again he could not see, whirling; there was a face in a red haze, moonlike, bigger than the full moon, the owner of it half again his size, he leaping in the red haze toward the face, feeling no blow, feeling no shock when his head struck the earth, scrabbling up and leaping again, feeling no blow this time either and tasting no blood, scrabbling up to see the other boy in full flight and himself already leaping into pursuit as his father's hand jerked him back, the harsh, cold voice speaking above him: "Go get in the wagon."

It stood in a grove of locusts and mulberries across the road. His two hulking sisters in their Sunday dresses and his mother and her sister in calico and sunbonnets were already in it, sitting on and among the sorry residue of the dozen and more movings which even the boy could remember—the battered stove, the broken beds and chairs, the clock inlaid with mother-of-pearl, which would not run, stopped at some fourteen minutes past two o'clock of a dead and forgotten day and time, which had been his mother's dowry. She was crying, though when she saw him she drew her sleeve across her face and began to descend from the wagon. "Get back," the father said.

"He's hurt. I got to get some water and wash his...."

"Get back in the wagon," his father said. He got in too, over the tailgate. His father mounted to the seat where the older brother already sat and struck the gaunt mules two savage blows with the peeled willow, but without heat. It was not even sadistic; it was exactly that same quality which in later years would cause his descendants to over-run the engine before putting a motor car into motion, striking and reining back in the same movement. The wagon went on, the store with its quiet crowd of grimly watching men dropped behind; a curve in the road hid it. *Forever* he thought. *Maybe he's done satisfied now, now that he has* . . . stopping himself, not to say it aloud even to himself. His mother's hand touched his shoulder.

"Does hit hurt?" she said.

"Naw," he said. "Hit don't hurt. Lemme be."

"Can't you wipe some of the blood off before hit dries?"

"I'll wash tonight," he said, "Lemme be, I tell you."

The wagon went on. He did not know where they were going. None of them ever did or ever asked, because it was always somewhere, always a house of sorts waiting for them a day or two days or even three days away. Likely his father had already arranged to make a crop on another farm before he. . . . Again he had to stop himself. He (the father) always did. There was something about his wolflike independence and even courage when the advantage was at least neutral which impressed strangers, as if they got from his latent ravening ferocity not so much a sense of dependability as a feeling that his ferocious conviction in the rightness of his own actions would be of advantage to all whose interest lay with his.

That night they camped, in a grove of oaks and beeches where a spring ran. The nights were still cool and they had a fire against it, of a rail lifted from a nearby fence and cut into lengths—a small fire, neat, niggard almost, a shrewd fire; such fires were his father's habit and custom always, even in freezing weather. Older, the boy might have remarked this and wondered why not a big one; why should not a man who had not only seen the waste and extravagance of war, but who had in his blood an inherent voracious prodigality with material not his own, have burned everything in sight? Then he might have gone a step farther and thought that that was the reason: that niggard blaze was the living fruit of nights passed during those four years in the woods hiding from all men, blue or gray, with his strings of horses (captured horses, he called them). And older still, he might have divined the true reason: that the element of fire spoke to some deep mainspring of his father's being, as the element of steel or of powder spoke to other men, as the one weapon for the preservation of integrity, else breath were not worth the breathing, and hence to be regarded with respect and used with discretion.

But he did not think this now and he had seen those same niggard blazes all his life. He merely ate his supper beside it and was already half asleep over his iron plate when his father called him, and once more he followed the stiff back, the stiff and ruthless limp, up the slope and on to the starlit road where, turning, he could see his father against the stars but without face or depth—a shape black, flat, and bloodless as though cut from tin in the iron folds of the frockcoat which had not been made for him, the voice harsh like tin and without heat like tin:

"You were fixing to tell them. You would have told him." He didn't answer. His father struck him with the flat of his hand on the side of the head, hard but without heat, exactly as he had struck the two mules at the

store, exactly as he would strike either of them with any stick in order to kill a horse fly, his voice still without heat or anger: "You're getting to be a man. You got to learn. You got to learn to stick to your own blood or you ain't going to have any blood to stick to you. Do you think either of them, any man there this morning, would? Don't you know all they wanted was a chance to get at me because they knew I had them beat? Eh?" Later, twenty years later, he was to tell himself, "If I had said they wanted only truth, justice, he would have hit me again." But now he said nothing. He was not crying. He just stood there. "Answer me," his father said.

"Yes," he whispered. His father turned.

"Get on to bed. We'll be there tomorrow."

Tomorrow they were there. In the early afternoon the wagon stopped before a paintless two-room house identical almost with the dozen others it had stopped before even in the boy's ten years, and again, as on the other dozen occasions, his mother and aunt got down and began to unload the wagon, although his two sisters and his father and brother had not moved.

"Likely hit ain't fitten for hawgs," one of the sisters said.

"Nevertheless, fit it will and you'll hog it and like it," his father said. "Get out of them chairs and help your Ma unload."

The two sisters got down, big, bovine, in a flutter of cheap ribbons; one of them drew from the jumbled wagon bed a battered lantern, the other a worn broom. His father handed the reins to the older son and began to climb stiffly over the wheel. "When they get unloaded, take the team to the barn and feed them." Then he said, and at first the boy thought he was still speaking to his brother: "Come with me."

"Me?" he said.

"Yes," his father said. "You."

"Abner," his mother said. His father paused and looked back—the harsh level stare beneath the shaggy, graying, irascible brows.

"I reckon I'll have a word with the man that aims to begin tomorrow owning me body and soul for the next eight months."

They went back up the road. A week ago—or before last night, that is—he would have asked where they were going, but not now. His father had struck him before last night but never before had he paused afterward to explain why; it was as if the blow and the following calm, outrageous voice still rang, repercussed, divulging nothing to him save the terrible handicap of being young, the light weight of his few years, just heavy enough to prevent his soaring free of the world as it seemed to be ordered but not heavy enough to keep him footed solid in it, to resist it and try to change the course of its events.

Presently he could see the grove of oaks and cedars and the other flowering trees and shrubs where the house would be, though not the house yet. They walked beside a fence massed with honeysuckle and Cherokee roses and came to a gate swinging open between two brick pillars, and now, beyond a sweep of drive, he saw the house for the first time and at that instant he forgot his father and the terror and despair both, and even when he remembered his father again (who had not stopped) the terror and despair did not return. Because, for all the twelve movings, they had sojurned until now in a poor country, a land of small farms and fields and houses, and he had never seen a house like this before. *Hit's big as a courthouse* he thought quietly, with a surge of peace and joy whose reason he could not have thought into words, being too young for that: *They are safe from him. People whose lives are a part of this peace and dignity are beyond his touch, he no more to them than a buzzing wasp: capable of stinging for a little moment but that's all; the spell of this peace and dignity rendering even the barns and stables and cribs which belong to it impervious to the puny flames he might contrive* ... this, the peace and joy, ebbing for an instant as he looked again at the stiff black back, the stiff and implacable limp of the figure which was not dwarfed by the house, for the reason that it had never looked big anywhere and which now, against the serene columned backdrop, had more than ever that impervious quality of something cut ruthlessly from tin, depthless, as though, sidewise to the sun, it would cast no shadow. Watching him, the boy remarked the absolutely undeviating course which his father held and saw the stiff foot come squarely down in a pile of fresh droppings where a horse had stood in the drive and which his father could have avoided by a simple change of stride. But it ebbed only for a moment, though he could not have thought this into words either, walking on in the spell of the house, which he could even want but without envy, without sorrow, certainly never with that ravening and jealous rage which unknown to him walked in the ironlike black coat before him: *Maybe he will feel it too. Maybe it will even change him now from what maybe he couldn't help but be.*

They crossed the portico. Now he could hear his father's stiff foot as it came down on the boards with clocklike finality, a sound out of all proportion to the displacement of the body it bore and which was not dwarfed either by the white door before it, as though it had attained to a sort of vicious and ravening minimum not to be dwarfed by anything —the flat, wide, black hat, the formal coat of broadcloth which had once been black but which has now that friction-glazed greenish cast of the bodies of old house flies, the lifted sleeve which was too large, the lifted hand like a curled claw. The door opened so promptly that the boy knew the Negro must have been watching them all the time, an old man with neat grizzled hair, in a linen jacket, who stood barring the door with his body, saying, "Wipe yo foots, white man, fo you come in here. Major ain't home nohow."

"Get out of my way, nigger," his father said, without heat too, flinging the door back and the Negro also and entering, his hat still on his head. And now the boy saw the prints of the stiff foot on the doorjamb and saw them appear on the pale rug behind the machine-like deliberation of the foot which seemed to bear (or transmit) twice the weight which the body compassed. The Negro was shouting "Miss Lula! Miss Lula!" somewhere behind them, then the boy, deluged as though by a warm wave by a suave turn of carpeted stair and a pendant glitter of chandeliers and a mute gleam of gold frames, heard the swift feet and saw her too, a lady—perhaps he had never seen her like before either—in a gray, smooth gown with lace at the throat and an apron tied at the waist and the sleeves turned back, wiping cake or biscuit dough from her hands with a towel as she came up the hall, looking not at his father at all but at the tracks on the blond rug with an expression of incredulous amazement.

"I tried," the Negro cried. "I tole him to . . ."

"Will you please go away?" she said in a shaking voice. "Major de Spain is not at home. Will you please go away?"

His father had not spoken again. He did not speak again. He did not even look at her. He just stood stiff in the center of the rug, in his hat, the shaggy iron-gray brows twitching slightly above the pebble-colored eyes as he appeared to examine the house with brief deliberation. Then with the same deliberation he turned; the boy watched him pivot on the good leg and saw the stiff foot drag round the arc of the turning, leaving a final long and fading smear. His father never looked at it, he never once looked down at the rug. The Negro held the door. It closed behind them, upon the hysteric and indistinguishable woman-wail. His father stopped at the top of the steps and scraped his boot clean on the edge of it. At the gate he stopped again. He stood for a moment, planted stiffly on the stiff foot, looking back at the house. "Pretty and white, ain't it?" he said. "That's sweat. Nigger sweat. Maybe it ain't white enough yet to suit him. Maybe he wants to mix some white sweat with it."

Two hours later the boy was chopping wood behind the house within which his mother and aunt and the two sisters (the mother and aunt, not the two girls, he knew that; even at this distance and muffled by walls and flat loud voices of the two girls emanated an incorrigible idle inertia) were setting up the stove to prepare a meal, when he heard the hooves and saw the linen-clad man on a fine sorrel mare, whom he recognized even before he saw the rolled rug in front of the Negro youth following on a fat bay carriage horse—a suffused, angry face vanishing, still at full gallop, beyond the corner of the house where his father and brother were sitting in the two tilted chairs; and a moment later, almost before he could have put the axe down, he heard the hooves again and watched the sorrel mare go back out of the yard, already galloping again. Then his father began to shout one of the sisters' names, who presently emerged backward from the kitchen door dragging the rolled rug along the ground by one end while the other sister walked behind it.

"If you ain't going to tote, go on and set up the wash pot," the first said.

"You, Sarty!" the second shouted. "Set up the wash pot!" His father appeared at the door, framed against that shabbiness, as he had been against that other bland perfection, impervious to either, the mother's anxious face at his shoulder.

"Go on," the father said, "Pick it up." The two sisters stooped, broad, lethargic; stooping, they presented an incredible expanse of pale cloth and a flutter of tawdry ribbons.

"If I thought enough of a rug to have to git hit all the way from France I wouldn't keep hit where folks coming in would have to tromp on hit," the first said. They raised the rug.

"Abner," the mother said. "Let me do it."

"You go back and git dinner," his father said, "I'll tend to this."

From the woodpile through the rest of the afternoon the boy watched them, the rug spread flat in the dust beside the bubbling wash pot, the two sisters stooping over it with that profound and lethargic reluctance, while the father stood over them in turn, implacable and grim, driving them though never raising his voice again. He could smell the harsh homemade lye they were using; he saw his mother come to the door once and look toward them with an expression not anxious now but very like despair; he saw his father turn, and he fell to with the axe and saw from the corner of his eye his father raise from the ground a flattish fragment of field stone and examine it and return to the pot, and this time his mother actually spoke: "Abner. Abner. Please don't. Please, Abner."

Then he was done too. It was dusk; the whippoorwills had already begun. He could smell coffee from the room where they would presently eat the cold food remaining from the mid-afternoon meal, though when he entered the house he realized they were having coffee again probably because there was a fire on the hearth, before which the rug now lay spread over the backs of two chairs. The tracks of his father's foot were gone. Where they had been were now long, water-cloudy scoriations resembling the sporadic course of a lilliputian mowing machine.

It still hung there while they ate the cold food and then went to bed, scattered without order or claim up and down the two rooms, his mother in one bed, where his father would later lie, the older brother in the other, himself, the aunt, and the two sisters on pallets on the floor. But his father was not in bed yet. The last thing the boy remembered was the depthless, harsh silhouette of the hat and coat bending over the rug and it seemed to him that he had not even closed his eyes when the silhouette was standing over him, the fire almost dead behind it, the stiff foot prodding him awake. "Catch up the mule," his father said.

When he returned with the mule his father was standing in the black door, the rolled rug over his shoulder. "Ain't you going to ride?" he said.

"No. Give me your foot."

He bent his knee into his father's hand, the wiry, surprising power flowed smoothly, rising, he rising with it, on to the mule's bare back (they had owned a saddle once; the boy could remember it though not when or where) and with the same effortlessness his father swung the rug up in front of him. Now in the starlight they retraced the afternoon's path, up the dusty road rife with honeysuckle, through the gate and up the black tunnel of the drive to the lightless house, where he sat on the mule and felt the rough warp of the rug drag across his thighs and vanish.

"Don't you want me to help?" he whispered. His father did not answer and now he heard again that stiff foot striking the hollow portico with that wooden and clocklike deliberation, that outrageous overstatement of the weight it carried. The rug, hunched, not flung (the boy could tell that even in the darkness) from his father's shoulder struck the angle of wall and floor with a sound unbelievably loud, thunderous, then the foot again, unhurried and enormous; a light came on in the house and the boy sat, tense, breathing steadily and quietly and just a little fast, though the foot itself did not increase its beat at all, descending the steps now; now the boy could see him.

"Don't you want to ride now?" he whispered. "We kin both ride now," the light within the house altering now, flaring up and sinking. *He's coming down the stairs now,* he thought. He had already ridden the mule up beside the horse block; presently his father was up behind him and he doubled the reins over and slashed the mule across the neck, but before the animal could begin to trot the hard, thin arm came round him, the hard, knotted hand jerking the mule back to a walk.

In the first red rays of the sun they were in the lot, putting plow gear on the mules. This time the sorrel mare was in the lot before he heard it at all, the rider collarless and even bareheaded, trembling, speaking in a shaking voice as the woman in the house had done, his father merely looking up once before stooping again to the hame he was buckling, so that the man on the mare spoke to his stooping back:

"You must realize you have ruined that rug. Wasn't there anybody here, any of your women . . ." he ceased, shaking, the boy watching him, the older brother leaning now in the stable door, chewing, blinking slowly and steadily at nothing apparently. "It cost a hundred dollars. But you never had a hundred dollars. You never will. So I'm going to charge you twenty bushels of corn against the crop. I'll add it in your contract and when you come to the commissary you can sign it. That won't keep Mrs. de Spain quiet but maybe it will teach you to wipe your feet off before you enter her house again."

Then he was gone. The boy looked at his father, who still had not spoken or even looked up again, who was now adjusting the loggerhead in the hame.

"Pap," he said. His father looked at him—the inscrutable face, the shaggy brows beneath which the gray eyes glinted coldly. Suddenly the boy went toward him, fast, stopping as suddenly. "You done the best you could!" he cried. "If he wanted hit done different why didn't he wait and tell you how? He won't git no twenty bushels! He won't git none! We'll gether hit and hide hit! I kin watch . . ."

"Did you put the cutter back in that straight stock like I told you?"

"No, sir," he said.

"Then go do it."

That was Wednesday. During the rest of that week he worked steadily, at what was within his scope and some which was beyond it, with an industry that did not need to be driven nor even commanded twice; he had this from his mother, with the difference that some at least of what he did he liked to do, such as splitting wood with the half-size axe which his mother and aunt had earned, or saved money somehow, to present him with at Christmas. In company with the two older women (and on one afternoon, even one of the sisters), he built pens for the shoat and the cow which were a part of his father's contract with the landlord, and one afternoon, his father being absent, gone somewhere on one of the mules, he went to the field.

They were running a middle buster now, his brother holding the plow straight while he handled the reins, and walking beside the straining mule, the rich black soil shearing cool and damp against his bare ankles, he thought *Maybe this is the end of it. Maybe even that twenty bushels that seems hard to have to pay for just a rug will be a cheap price for him to stop forever and always from being what he used to be;* thinking, dreaming now, so that his brother had to speak sharply to him to mind the mule: *Maybe he even won't collect the twenty bushels. Maybe it will all add up and balance and vanish—corn, rug, fire; the terror and grief, the being pulled two ways like between two teams of horses—gone, done with for ever and ever.*

Then it was Saturday; he looked up from beneath the mule he was harnessing and saw his father in the black coat and hat. "Not that," his father said. "The wagon gear." And then, two hours later, sitting in the wagon bed behind his father and brother on the seat, the wagon accomplished a final curve, and he saw the weathered paintless store with its tattered tobacco- and patent-medicine posters and the tethered wagons and saddle animals below the gallery. He mounted the gnawed steps behind his father and brother, and there again was the lane of quiet, watching faces for the three of them to walk through. He saw the man in spectacles sitting at the plank table and he did not need to be told this was a Justice of the Peace; he sent one glare of fierce, exultant, partisan defiance at the man in collar and cravat now, whom he had seen but twice before in his life, and that on a galloping horse, who now wore on his face an expression not of rage but of amazed, unbelief which the boy could not have known was at the incredible circumstance of being sued by one of his own tenants, and came and stood against his father and cried at the Justice: "He ain't done it! He ain't burnt. . . ."

"Go back to the wagon," his father said.

"Burnt?" the Justice said. "Do I understand this rug was burned too?"

"Does anybody here claim it was?" his father said. "Go back to the wagon." But he did not, he merely retreated to the rear of the room, crowded as that other had been, but not to sit down this time, instead, to stand pressing among the motionless bodies, listening to the voices:

"And you claim twenty bushels of corn is too high for the damage you did to the rug?"

"He brought the rug to me and said he wanted the tracks washed out of it. I washed the tracks out and took the rug back to him."

"But you didn't carry the rug back to him in the same condition it was in before you made the tracks on it."

His father did not answer, and now for perhaps half a minute there was no sound at all save that of breathing, the faint, steady suspiration of complete and intent listening.

"You decline to answer that, Mr. Snopes?" Again his father did not answer. "I'm going to find against you, Mr. Snopes. I'm going to find that you were responsible for the injury to Major de Spain's rug and hold you liable for it. But twenty bushels of corn seems a little high for a man in your circumstances to have to pay. Major de Spain claims it cost a hundred dollars. October corn will be worth about fifty cents. I figure that if Major de Spain can stand a ninety-five dollar loss on something he paid cash for, you can stand a five-dollar loss you haven't earned yet. I hold you in damages to Major de Spain to the amount of ten bushels of corn over and above your contract with him, to be paid to him out of your crop at gathering time. Court adjourned."

It had taken no time hardly, the morning was but half begun. He thought they would return home and perhaps back to the field, since they were late, far behind all other farmers. But instead his father passed on behind the wagon, merely indicating with his hand for the older brother to follow with it, and crossed the road toward the blacksmith shop opposite, pressing on after his father, overtaking him, speaking, whispering up at the harsh, calm face beneath the weathered hat. "He won't git no ten bushels neither. He won't git one. We'll . . ." until his father glanced for an instant down at him, the face absolutely calm, the grizzled eyebrows tangled above the cold eyes, the voice almost pleasant, almost gentle:

"You think so? Well, we'll wait till October anyway."

The matter of the wagon—the setting of a spoke or two and the tightening of the tires—did not take long either, the business of the tires accomplished by driving the wagon into the spring branch behind the shop and letting it stand there, the mules nuzzling into the water from time to time, and the boy on the seat with the idle reins, looking up the slope and through the sooty tunnel of the shed where the slow hammer rang and where his father sat on an upended cypress bolt, easily, either talking or listening, still sitting there when the boy brought the dripping wagon up out of the branch and halted it before the door.

"Take them on to the shade and hitch," his father said. He did so and returned. His father and the smith and a third man squatting on his heels inside the door were talking, about crops and animals; the boy, squatting too in the ammoniac dust and hoofparings and scales of rust, heard his father tell a long and unhurried story out of the time before the birth of the older brother even when he had been a professional horsetrader. And then his father came up beside him where he stood before a tattered last year's circus poster on the other side of the store, gazing rapt and quiet at the scarlet horses, the incredible poisings and convolutions of tulle and tights and the painted leers of comedians, and said, "It's time to eat."

But not at home. Squatting beside his brother against the front wall, he watched his father emerge from the store and produce from a paper sack a segment of cheese and divide it carefully and deliberately into three with his pocket knife and produce crackers from the same sack. They all three squatted on the gallery and ate, slowly, without talking; then in the store again, they drank from a tin dipper tepid water smelling of the cedar bucket and of living beech trees. And still they did not go home. It was a horse lot this time, a tall rail fence upon and along which men stood and sat and out of which one by one horses were led, to be walked and trotted and then cantered back and forth along the road while the slow swapping and buying went on and the sun began to slant westward, they—the three of them—watching and listening, the older brother with his muddy eyes and his steady, inevitable tobacco, the father commenting now and then on certain of the animals, to no one in particular.

It was after sundown when they reached home. They ate supper by lamplight, then, sitting on the doorstep, the boy watched the night fully accomplish, listening to the whippoorwills and the frogs, when he heard his mother's voice: "Abner! No! No! Oh, God. Oh, God. Abner!" and he rose, whirled, and saw the altered light through the door where a candle stub now burned in a bottle neck on the table and his father, still in the hat and coat, at once formal and burlesque as though dressed carefully for some shabby and ceremonial violence, emptying the reservoir of the lamp back into the five-gallon kerosene can from which it had been filled, while the mother tugged at his arm until he shifted the lamp to the other hand and flung her back, not savagely or viciously, just hard, into the wall, her hands flung out against the wall for balance, her mouth open and in her face the same quality of hopeless despair as had been in her voice. Then his father saw him standing in the door. "Go to the barn and get that can of oil we were oiling the wagon with," he said. The boy did not move. Then he could speak.

"What ...," he cried. "What are you. ..."

"Go get that oil," his father said. "Go."

Then he was moving, running, outside the house, toward the stable: this the old habit, the old blood which he had not been permitted to choose for himself, which had been bequeathed him willy nilly and which had run for so long (and who knew where, battening on what of outrage and savagery and lust) before it came to him. *I could keep on,* he thought. *I could run on and on and never look back, never need to see his face again. Only I can't. I can't,* the rusted can in his hand now, the liquid sploshing in it as he ran back to the house and into it, into the sound of his mother's weeping in the next room, and handed the can to his father.

"Ain't you going to even send a nigger?" he cried. "At least you sent a nigger before!"

This time his father didn't strike him. The hand came even faster than the blow had, the same hand which had set the can on the table with almost excruciating care flashing from the can toward him too quick for him to follow it, gripping him by the back of his shirt and on to tiptoe before he had seen it quit the can, the face stooping at him in breathless and frozen ferocity, the cold, dead voice speaking over him to the older brother who leaned against the table, chewing with that steady, curious, sidewise motion of cows:

"Empty the can into the big one and go on. I'll catch up with you."

"Better tie him up to the bedpost," the brother said.

"Do like I told you," the father said. Then the boy was moving, his bunched shirt and the hard, bony hand between his shoulderblades, his toes just touching the floor, across the room and into the other one, past the sisters sitting with spread heavy thighs in the two chairs over the cold hearth, and to where his mother and aunt sat side by side on the bed, the aunt's arms about his mother's shoulders.

"Hold him," the father said. The aunt made a startled movement. "Not you," the father said. "Lennie. Take hold of him. I want to see you do it." His mother took him by the wrist. "You'll hold him better than that. If he gets loose don't you know what he is going to do? He will go up yonder." He jerked his head toward the road. "Maybe I'd better tie him."

"I'll hold him," his mother whispered.

"See you do then." Then his father was gone, the stiff foot heavy and measured upon the boards, ceasing at last.

Then he began to struggle. His mother caught him in both arms, he jerking and wrenching at them. He would be stronger in the end, he knew that. But he had no time to wait for it. "Lemme go!" he cried. "I don't want to have to hit you!"

"Let him go!" the aunt said. "If he don't go, before God, I am going up there myself!"

"Don't you see I can't?" his mother cried. "Sarty! Sarty! No! No! Help me, Lizzie!"

Then he was free. His aunt grasped at him but it was too late. He whirled, running, his mother stumbled forward on to her knees behind him, crying to the nearer sister: "Catch him, Net! Catch him!" But that was too late too, the sister (the sisters were twins, born at the same time, yet either of them now gave the impression of being, encompassing as much living meat and volume and weight as any other two of the family) not yet having begun to rise from the chair, her head, face, alone merely turned, presenting to him in the flying instant an astonishing expanse of young female features untroubled by any surprise even, wearing only an expression of bovine interest. Then he was out of the room, out of the house, in the mild dust of the starlit road and the heavy rifeness of honeysuckle, the pale ribbon unspooling with terrific slowness under his running feet, reaching the gate at last and turning in, running, his heart and lungs drumming, on up the drive toward the lighted house, the lighted door. He did not knock, he burst in, sobbing for breath, incapable for the moment of speech; he saw the astonished face of the Negro in the linen jacket without knowing when the Negro had appeared.

"De Spain!" he cried, panted "Where's . . ." then he saw the white man too emerging from a white door down the hall. "Barn!" he cried. "Barn!"

"What?" the white man said. "Barn?"

"Yes!" the boy cried. "Barn!"

"Catch him!" the white man shouted.

But it was too late this time too. The Negro grasped his shirt, but the entire sleeve, rotten with washing, carried away, and he was out that door too and in the drive again, and had actually never ceased to run even while he was screaming into the white man's face.

Behind him the white man was shouting, "My horse! Fetch my horse!" and he thought for an instant of cutting across the park and climbing the fence into the road, but he did not know the park nor how high the vine-massed fence might be and he dared not risk it. So he ran on down the drive, blood and breath roaring; presently he was in the road again though he could not see it. He could not hear either: the galloping mare was almost upon him before he heard her, and even then he held his course, as if the very urgency of his wild grief and need must in a moment more find him wings, waiting until the ultimate instant to hurl himself aside and into the weed-choked roadside ditch as the horse thundered past and on, for an instant in furious silhouette against the stars, the tranquil early summer night sky which, even before the shape of the horse and rider vanished, stained abruptly and violently upward: a long, swirling roar incredible and soundless, blotting the stars, and he springing up and into the road again, running again, knowing it was too late yet still running even after he heard the shot and, an instant later, two shots, pausing now without knowing he had ceased to run, crying "Pap! Pap!" running again before he knew he had begun to run, stumbling, tripping over something and scrabbling up again without ceasing to run, looking backward over his shoulder at the glare as he got up, running on among the invisible trees, panting, sobbing, "Father! Father!"

At midnight he was sitting on the crest of a hill. He did not know it was midnight and he did not know how far he had come. But there was no glare behind him now and he sat now, his back toward what he had called home for four days anyhow, his face toward the dark woods which he would enter when breath was strong again, small, shaking steadily in the chill darkness, hugging himself into the remainder of his thin, rotten shirt, the grief and despair now no longer terror and fear but just grief and despair. *Father. My father,* he thought. "He was brave!" he cried suddenly, aloud but not loud, no more than a whisper: "He was! He was in the war! He was in Colonel Sartoris' cav'ry!" not knowing that his father had gone to that war a private in the fine old European sense, wearing no uniform, admitting the authority of and giving fidelity to no man or army or flag, going to war as Malbrouck himself did: for booty —it meant nothing and less than nothing to him if it were enemy booty or his own.

The slow constellations wheeled on. It would be dawn and then sun-up after a while and he would be hungry. But that would be tomorrow and now he was only cold, and walking would cure that. His breathing was easier now and he decided to get up and go on, and then he found that he had been asleep because he knew it was almost dawn, the night almost over. He could tell that from the whippoorwills. They were everywhere now among the dark trees below him, constant and inflectioned and ceaseless, so that, as the instant for giving over to the day birds drew nearer and nearer, there was no interval at all between them. He got up. He was a little stiff, but walking would cure that too as it would the cold, and soon there would be the sun. He went on down the hill, toward the dark woods within which the liquid silver voices of the birds called unceasing—the rapid and urgent beating of the urgent and quiring heart of the late spring night. He did not look back.

Love: Three Pages from a Sportsman's Book

Guy de Maupassant

I have just read among the general news in one of the papers a drama of passion. He killed her and then he killed himself, so he must have loved her. What matters He or She? Their love alone matters to me, and it does not interest me because it moves me or astonishes me or because it softens me or makes me think, but because it recalls to my mind a remembrance of my youth, a strange recollection of a hunting adventure where Love appeared to me, as the Cross appeared to the early Christians, in the midst of the heavens.

I was born with all the instincts and the senses of primitive man, tempered by the arguments and the restraints of a civilized being. I am passionately fond of shooting, yet the sight of the wounded animal, of the blood on its feathers and on my hands, affects my heart so as almost to make it stop.

That year the cold weather set in suddenly toward the end of autumn, and I was invited by one of my cousins, Karl de Rauville, to go with him and shoot ducks on the marshes at daybreak.

My cousin was a jolly fellow of forty with red hair, very stout and bearded, a country gentleman, an amiable semibrute of a happy disposition and endowed with that Gallic wit which makes even mediocrity agreeable. He lived in a house, half farmhouse, half chateau, situated in a broad valley through which a river ran. The hills right and left were covered with woods, old manorial woods where magnificent trees still

From *Boule De Suif.* New York: Bigelow, Smith and Company, 1909.

remained and where the rarest feathered game in that part of France was to be found. Eagles were shot there occasionally, and birds of passage, such as rarely venture into our overpopulated part of the country, invariably lighted amid these giant oaks as if they knew or recognized some little corner of a primeval forest which had remained there to serve them as a shelter during these short nocturnal halts.

In the valley there were large meadows watered by trenches and separated by hedges; then, further on, the river, which up to that point had been kept between banks, expanded into a vast marsh. That marsh was the best shooting ground I ever saw. It was my cousin's chief care, and he kept it as a preserve. Through the rushes that covered it, and made it rustling and rough, narrow passages had been cut, through which the flat-bottomed boats, impelled and steered by poles, passed along silently over dead water, brushing up against the reeds and making the swift fish take refuge in the weeds and the wild fowl, with their pointed black heads, dive suddenly.

I am passionately fond of the water: of the sea, though it is too vast, too full of movement, impossible to hold; of the rivers which are so beautiful but which pass on and flee away; and above all of the marshes, where the whole unknown existence of aquatic animals palpitates. The marsh is an entire world in itself on the world of earth—a different world which has its own life, its settled inhabitants and its passing travelers, its voices, its noises and above all its mystery. Nothing is more impressive, nothing more disquieting, more terrifying occasionally, than a fen. Why should a vague terror hang over these low plains covered with water? Is it the low rustling of the rushes, the strange will-o'-the-wisp lights, the silence which prevails on calm nights, the still mists which hang over the surface like a shroud; or is it the almost inaudible splashing, so slight and so gentle, yet sometimes more terrifying than the cannons of men or the thunders of the skies, which make these marshes resemble countries one has dreamed of, terrible countries holding an unknown and dangerous secret?

No, something else belongs to it—another mystery, perhaps the mystery of the creation itself! For was it not in stagnant and muddy water, amid the heavy humidity of moist land under the heat of the sun, that the first germ of life pulsated and expanded to the day?

I arrived at my cousin's in the evening. It was freezing hard enough to split the stones.

During dinner, in the large room whose sideboards, walls and ceiling were covered with stuffed birds with wings extended or perched on branches to which they were nailed—hawks, herons, owls, nightjars, buzzards, tercels, vultures, falcons—my cousin, who, dressed in a sealskin jacket, himself resembled some strange animal from a cold country, told me what preparations he had made for that same night.

Love: Three Pages from a Sportsman's Book

We were to start at half-past three in the morning so as to arrive at the place which he had chosen for our watching place at about half-past four. On that spot a hut had been built of lumps of ice so as to shelter us somewhat from the trying wind which precedes daybreak, a wind so cold as to tear the flesh like a saw, cut it like the blade of a knife, prick it like a poisoned sting, twist it like a pair of pincers, and burn it like fire.

My cousin rubbed his hands. "I have never known such a frost," he said; "it is already twelve degrees below zero at six o'clock in the evening."

I threw myself onto my bed immediately after we had finished our meal and went to sleep by the light of a bright fire burning in the grate.

At three o'clock he woke me. In my turn I put on a sheepskin and found my cousin Karl covered with a bearskin. After having each swallowed two cups of scalding coffee, followed by glasses of liqueur brandy, we started, accompanied by a gamekeeper and our dogs, Plongeon and Pierrot.

From the first moment that I got outside I felt chilled to the very marrow. It was one of those nights on which the earth seems dead with cold. The frozen air becomes resisting and palpable, such pain does it cause; no breath of wind moves it, it is fixed and motionless; it bites you, pierces through you, dries you, kills the trees, the plants, the insects, the small birds themselves, who fall from the branches onto the hard ground and become stiff themselves under the grip of the cold.

The moon, which was in her last quarter and was inclining all to one side, seemed fainting in the midst of space, so weak that she was unable to wane, forced to stay up yonder, seized and paralyzed by the severity of the weather. She shed a cold mournful light over the world, that dying and wan light which she gives us every month at the end of her period.

Karl and I walked side by side, our backs bent, our hands in our pockets and our guns under our arms. Our boots, which were wrapped in wool so that we might be able to walk without slipping on the frozen river, made no sound, and I looked at the white vapor which our dogs' breath made.

We were soon on the edge of the marsh and entered one of the lanes of dry rushes which ran through the low forest.

Our elbows, which touched the long ribbonlike leaves, left a slight noise behind us, and I was seized, as I had never been before, by the powerful and singular emotion which marshes cause in me. This one was dead, dead from cold, since we were walking on it in the middle of its population of dried rushes.

Suddenly, at the turn of one of the lanes, I perceived the ice hut which had been constructed to shelter us. I went in, and as we had nearly an hour to wait before the wandering birds would awake I rolled myself up in my rug in order to try and get warm. Then, lying on my back, I began to look at the misshapen moon, which had four horns through the vaguely transparent walls of this polar house. But the frost of the frozen marshes, the cold of these walls, the cold from the firmament penetrated me so terribly that I began to cough. My cousin Karl became uneasy.

"No matter if we do not kill much today," he said. "I do not want you to catch cold; we will light a fire." And he told the gamekeeper to cut some rushes.

We made a pile in the middle of our hut, which had a hole in the middle of the roof to let out the smoke, and when the red flames rose up to the clear crystal blocks, they began to melt, gently, imperceptibly, as if they were sweating. Karl, who had remained outside, called out to me: "Come and look here!" I went out of the hut and remained struck with astonishment. Our hut, in the shape of a cone, looked like an enormous diamond with a heart of fire which had been suddenly planted there in the midst of the frozen water of the marsh. And inside we saw two fantistic forms, those of our dogs, who were warming themselves at the fire.

But a peculiar cry, a lost, a wandering cry, passed over our heads, and the light from our hearth showed us the wild birds. Nothing moves one so much as the first clamor of a life which one does not see, which passes through the somber air so quickly and so far off, just before the first streak of a winter's day appears on the horizon. It seems to me, at this glacial hour of dawn, as if that passing cry which is carried away by the wings of a bird is the sigh of a soul from the world!

"Put out the fire," said Karl; "it is getting daylight."

The sky was, in fact, beginning to grow pale, and the flights of ducks made long rapid streaks which were soon obliterated on the sky.

A stream of light burst out into the night; Karl had fired, and the two dogs ran forward.

And then nearly every minute now he, now I, aimed rapidly as soon as the shadow of a flying flock appeared above the rushes. And Pierrot and Plongeon, out of breath but happy, retrieved the bleeding birds whose eyes still, occasionally, looked at us.

The sun had risen, and it was a bright day with a blue sky, and we were thinking of taking our departure, when two birds with extended necks and outstretched wings glided rapidly over our heads. I fired, and one of them fell almost at my feet. It was a teal with a silver breast, and then, in the blue space above me, I heard a voice, the voice of a bird. It was a short, repeated heart-rending lament; and the bird, the little animal that had been spared, began to turn round in the blue sky over our heads, looking at its dead companion which I was holding in my hand.

Karl was on his knees, his gun to his shoulder, watching it eagerly until it should be within shot. "You have killed the duck," he said, "and the drake will not fly away."

He certainly did not fly away; he circled over our heads continually and continued his cries. Never have any groans of suffering pained me so much as that desolate appeal, as that lamentable reproach of this poor bird which was lost in space.

Occasionally he took flight under the menace of the gun which followed his movements and seemed ready to continue his flight alone, but as he could not make up his mind to this he returned to find his mate.

"Leave her on the ground," Karl said to me; "he will come within shot by and by." And he did indeed come near us, careless of danger, infatuated by his animal love, by his affection for his mate which I had just killed.

Karl fired, and it was as if somebody had cut the string which held the bird suspended. I saw something black descend, and I heard the noise of a fall among the rushes. And Pierrot brought it to me.

I put them—they were already cold—into the same gamebag, and I returned to Paris the same evening.

Wakefield

Nathaniel Hawthorne

In some old magazine or newspaper I recollect a story, told as truth, of a man—let us call him Wakefield—who absented himself for a long time from his wife. The fact, thus abstractedly stated, is not very uncommon, nor—without a proper distinction of circumstances—to be condemned either as naughty or nonsensical. Howbeit, this, though far from the most aggravated, is perhaps the strangest, instance on record, of marital delinquency; and, moreover, as remarkable a freak as may be found in the whole list of human oddities. The wedded couple lived in London. The man, under pretence of going a journey, took lodgings in the next street to his own house, and there, unheard of by his wife or friends, and without the shadow of a reason for such self-banishment, dwelt upwards of twenty years. During that period, he beheld his home every day, and frequently the forlorn Mrs. Wakefield. And after so great a gap in his matrimonial felicity—when his death was reckoned certain, his estate settled, his name dismissed from memory, and his wife, long, long ago, resigned to her autumnal widowhood—he entered the door one evening, quietly, as from a day's absence, and became a loving spouse till death.

This outline is all that I remember. But the incident, though of the purest originality, unexampled, and probably never to be repeated, is one, I think, which appeals to the generous sympathies of mankind. We know, each for himself, that none of us would perpetrate such a folly, yet

From *Twice-Told Tales,* published in 1837.

feel as if some other might. To my own contemplations, at least, it has often recurred, always exciting wonder, but with a sense that the story must be true, and a conception of its hero's character. Whenever any subject so forcibly affects the mind, time is well spent in thinking of it. If the reader choose, let him do his own meditation; or if he prefer to ramble with me through the twenty years of Wakefield's vagary, I bid him welcome; trusting that there will be a pervading spirit and a moral, even should we fail to find them, done up neatly, and condensed into the final sentence. Thought has always its efficacy, and every striking incident its moral.

What sort of a man was Wakefield? We are free to shape out our own idea, and call it by his name. He was now in the meridian of life; his matrimonial affections, never violent, were sobered into a calm, habitual sentiment; of all husbands, he was likely to be the most constant, because a certain sluggishness would keep his heart at rest, wherever it might be placed. He was intellectual, but not actively so; his mind occupied itself in long and lazy musings, that ended to no purpose, or had not vigor to attain it; his thoughts were seldom so energetic as to seize hold of words. Imagination, in the proper meaning of the term, made no part of Wakefield's gifts. With a cold but not depraved nor wandering heart, and a mind never feverish with riotous thoughts, nor perplexed with originality, who could have anticipated that our friend would entitle himself to a foremost place among the doers of eccentric deeds? Had his acquaintances been asked, who was the man in London the surest to perform nothing to-day which should be remembered on the morrow, they would have thought of Wakefield. Only the wife of his bosom might have hesitated. She, without having analyzed his character, was partly aware of a quiet selfishness, that had rusted into his inactive mind; of a peculiar sort of vanity, the most uneasy attribute about him; of a disposition to craft, which had seldom produced more positive effects than the keeping of petty secrets, hardly worth revealing; and, lastly, of what she called a little strangeness, sometimes, in the good man. This latter quality is indefinable, and perhaps nonexistent.

Let us now imagine Wakefield bidding adieu to his wife. It is the dusk of an October evening. His equipment is a drab greatcoat, a hat covered with an oilcloth, top-boots, an umbrella in one hand and a small portmanteau in the other. He has informed Mrs. Wakefield that he is to take the night coach into the country. She would fain inquire the length of his journey, its object, and the probable time of his return; but, indulgent to his harmless love of mystery, interrogates him only by a look. He tells her not to expect him positively by the return coach, nor to be alarmed should he tarry three or four days; but, at all events, to look for him at supper on Friday evening. Wakefield himself, be it considered, has no suspicion of what is before him. He holds out his hand, she gives her own, and meets his parting kiss in the matter-of-course way of a ten years' matrimony; and forth goes the middle-aged Mr. Wakefield, almost resolved to perplex his good lady by a whole week's absence. After the door has closed behind him, she perceives it thrust partly open, and a vision of her husband's face, through the aperture, smiling on her, and gone in a moment. For the time, this little incident is dismissed without a thought. But, long afterwards, when she has been more years a widow than a wife, that smile recurs, and flickers across all her reminiscences of Wakefield's visage. In her many musings, she surrounds the original smile with a multitude of fantasies, which make it strange and awful: as, for instance, if she imagines him in a coffin, that parting look is frozen on his pale features; or, if she dreams of him in heaven, still his blessed spirit wears a quiet and crafty smile. Yet, for its sake, when all others have given him up for dead, she sometimes doubts whether she is a widow.

But our business is with the husband. We must hurry after him along the street, ere he lose his individuality, and melt into the great mass of London life. It would be vain searching for him there. Let us follow close at his heels, therefore, until, after several superfluous turns and doublings, we find him comfortably established by the fireside of a small apartment, previously bespoken. He is in the next street to his own, and at his journey's end. He can scarcely trust his good fortune, in having got thither unperceived—recollecting that, at one time, he was delayed by the throng, in the very focus of a lighted lantern; and, again, there were footsteps that seemed to tread behind his own, distinct from the multitudinous tramp around him; and, anon, he heard a voice shouting afar, and fancied that it called his name. Doubtless, a dozen busybodies had been watching him, and told his wife the whole affair. Poor Wakefield! Little knowest thou thine own insignificance in this great world! No mortal eye but mine has traced thee. Go quietly to thy bed, foolish man; and, on the morrow, if thou wilt be wise, get thee home to good Mrs. Wakefield, and tell her the truth. Remove not thyself, even for a little week, from thy place in her chaste bosom. Were she, for a single moment, to deem thee dead, or lost, or lastingly divided from her, thou wouldst be woefully conscious of a change in thy true wife forever after. It is perilous to make a chasm in human affections; not that they gape so long and wide—but so quickly close again!

Almost repenting of his frolic, or whatever it may be termed, Wakefield lies down betimes, and starting from his first nap, spreads forth his arms into the wide and solitary waste of the unaccustomed bed. "No,"—thinks he, gathering the bedclothes about him,—"I will not sleep alone another night."

In the morning he rises earlier than usual, and sets himself to consider what he really means to do. Such are his loose and rambling modes of thought that he has taken this very singular step with the consciousness of a purpose, indeed, but without being able to define it sufficiently for his own contemplation. The vagueness of the project, and the convulsive effort with which he plunges into the execution of it, are equally characteristic of a feeble-minded man. Wakefield sifts his ideas, however, as minutely as he may, and finds himself curious to know the progress of matters at home—how his exemplary wife will endure her widowhood of a week, and, briefly, how the little sphere of creatures and circumstances, in which he was a central object, will be affected by his removal. A morbid vanity, therefore, lies nearest the bottom of the affair. But, how is he to attain his ends? Not, certainly, by keeping close in this comfortable lodging, where, though he slept and awoke in the next street to his home, he is as effectually abroad as if the stage-coach had been whirling him away all night. Yet, should he reappear, the whole project is knocked in the head. His poor brains being hopelessly puzzled with this dilemma, he at length ventures out partly resolving to cross the head of the street, and send one hasty glance towards his forsaken domicile. Habit—for he is a man of habits—takes him by the hand, and guides him, wholly unaware, to his own door, where, just at the critical moment, he is aroused by the scraping of his foot upon the step. Wakefield! whither are you going?

At that instant his fate was turning on the pivot. Little dreaming of the doom to which his first backward step devotes him, he hurries away, breathless with agitation hitherto unfelt, and hardly dares turn his head at the distant corner. Can it be that nobody caught sight of him? Will not the whole household—the decent Mrs. Wakefield, the smart maid servant, and the dirty little footboy—raise a hue and cry, through London streets, in pursuit of their fugitive lord and master? Wonderful escape! He gathers courage to pause and look homeward but is perplexed with a sense of change about the familiar edifice, such as affects us all, when, after a separation of months or years, we again see some hill or lake, or work of art, with which we were friends of old. In ordinary cases, this indescribable impression is caused by the comparison and contrast between our imperfect reminiscences and the reality. In Wakefield, the magic of a single night has wrought a similar transformation, because, in that brief period, a great moral change has been effected. But this is a secret from himself. Before leaving the spot, he catches a far and momentary glimpse of his wife, passing athwart the front window, with her face turned towards the head of the street. The crafty nincompoop takes to his heels, scared with the idea that, among a thousand such atoms of mortality, her eye must have detected him. Right glad is his heart, though his brain be somewhat dizzy, when he finds himself by the coal fire of his lodgings.

So much for the commencement of this long whimwham. After the initial conception, and the stirring up of the man's sluggish temperament to put it in practice, the whole matter evolves itself in a natural train. We may suppose him, as the result of deep deliberation, buying a new wig, of reddish hair, and selecting sundry garments, in a fashion unlike his customary suit of brown, from a Jew's old-clothes bag. It is accomplished. Wakefield is another man. The new system being now established, a retrograde movement to the old would be almost as difficult as the step that placed him in his unparalleled position. Furthermore, he is rendered obstinate by a sulkiness occasionally incident to his temper, and brought on at present by the inadequate sensation which he conceives to have been produced in the bosom of Mrs. Wakefield. He will not go back until she be frightened half to death. Well; twice or thrice has she passed before his sight, each time with a heavier step, a paler cheek, and more anxious brow; and in the third week of his nonappearance he detects a portent of evil entering the house, in the guise of an apothecary. Next day the knocker is muffled. Towards nightfall comes the chariot of a physician, and deposits its big-wigged and solemn burden at Wakefield's door, whence, after a quarter of an hour's visit, he emerges, perchance the herald of a funeral. Dear woman! Will she die? By this time, Wakefield is excited to something like energy of feeling, but still lingers away from his wife's bedside, pleading with his conscience that she must not be disturbed at such a juncture. If aught else restrains him, he does not know it. In the course of a few weeks she gradually recovers; the crisis is over; her heart is sad, perhaps, but quiet; and, let him return soon or late, it will never be feverish for him again. Such ideas glimmer through the mist of Wakefield's mind, and render him indistinctly conscious that an almost impassable gulf divides his hired apartment from his former home. "It is but in the next street!" he sometimes says. Fool! it is in another world. Hitherto, he has put off his return from one particular day to another; henceforward, he leaves the precise time undetermined. Not to-morrow —probably next week—pretty soon. Poor man! The dead have nearly as much chance of revisiting their earthly homes as the self-banished Wakefield.

Would that I had a folio to write, instead of an article of a dozen pages! Then might I exemplify how an influence beyond our control lays its strong hand on every deed which we do, and weaves its consequences into an iron tissue of necessity. Wakefield is spell-bound. We must leave him, for ten years or so, to haunt around his house, without once crossing the threshold, and to be faithful to his wife, with all the affection of which his heart is capable, while he is slowly fading out of hers. Long since, it must be remarked, he had lost the perception of singularity in his conduct.

Now for a scene! Amid the throng of a London street we distinguish a man, now waxing elderly, with few characteristics to attract careless observers, yet bearing, in his whole aspect, the handwriting of no common fate, for such as have the skill to read it. He is meagre; his low and narrow forehead is deeply wrinkled; his eyes, small and lustreless, sometimes wander apprehensively about him, but oftener seem to look inward. He bends his head, and moves with an indescribable obliquity of gait, as if unwilling to display his full front to the world. Watch him long enough to see what we have described, and you will allow that circumstances—which often produce remarkable men from nature's ordinary handiwork—have produced one such here. Next, leaving him to sidle along the footwalk, cast your eyes in the opposite direction, where a portly female, considerably in the wane of life, with a prayer-book in her hand, is proceeding to yonder church. She has the placid mien of settled widowhood. Her regrets have either died away, or have become so essential to her heart, that they would be poorly exchanged for joy. Just as the lean man and well-conditioned woman are passing, a slight obstruction occurs, and brings these two figures directly in contact. Their hands touch; the pressure of the crowd forces her bosom against his shoulder; they stand, face to face, staring into each other's eyes. After a ten years' separation, thus Wakefield meets his wife!

The throng eddies away, and carries them asunder. The sober widow, resuming her former pace, proceeds to church, but pauses in the portal, and throws a perplexed glance along the street. She passes in, however, opening her prayer-book as she goes. And the man! with so wild a face that busy and selfish London stands to gaze after him, he hurries to his lodgings, bolts the door, and throws himself upon the bed. The latent feelings of years break out; his feeble mind acquires a brief energy from their strength; all the miserable strangeness of his life is revealed to him at a glance: and he cries out, passionately, "Wakefield! Wakefield! You are mad!"

Perhaps he was so. The singularity of his situation must have so moulded him to himself, that, considered in regard to his fellow-creatures and the business of life, he could not be said to possess his right mind. He had contrived, or rather he had happened, to dissever himself from the world—to vanish—to give up his place and privileges with living men, without being admitted among the dead. The life of a hermit is nowise parallel to his. He was in the bustle of the city, as of old; but the crowd swept by and saw him not; he was, we may figuratively say, always beside his wife and at his hearth, yet must never feel the warmth of the one nor the affection of the other. It was Wakefield's unprecedented fate to retain his original share of human sympathies, and to be still involved in human interests, while he had lost his reciprocal influence on them. It would be a most curious speculation to trace out the effect of such circumstances on his heart and intellect, separately, and in unison. Yet, changed as he was, he would seldom be conscious of it, but deem himself the same man as ever; glimpses of the truth, indeed, would come, but only for the moment; and still he would keep saying, "I shall soon go back!"—nor reflect that he had been saying so for twenty years.

I conceive, also, that these twenty years would appear, in the retrospect, scarcely longer than the week to which Wakefield had at first limited his absence. He would look on the affair as no more than an interlude in the main business of his life. When, after a little while more, he should deem it time to reënter his parlor, his wife would clap her hands for joy, on beholding the middle-aged Mr. Wakefield. Alas, what a mistake! Would Time but await the close of our favorite follies, we should be young men, all of us, and till Doomsday.

One evening, in the twentieth year since he vanished, Wakefield is taking his customary walk towards the dwelling which he still calls his own. It is a gusty night of autumn, with frequent showers that patter down upon the pavement, and are gone before a man can put up his umbrella. Pausing near the house, Wakefield discerns, through the parlor windows of the second floor, the red glow and the glimmer and fitful flash of a comfortable fire. On the ceiling appears a grotesque shadow of good Mrs. Wakefield. The cap, the nose and chin, and the broad waist, form an admirable caricature, which dances, moreover, with the up-flickering and down-sinking blaze, almost too merrily for the shade of an elderly widow. At this instant a shower chances to fall, and is driven, by the unmannerly gust, full into Wakefield's face and bosom. He is quite penetrated with its autumnal chill. Shall he stand, wet and shivering here, when his own hearth has a good fire to warm him, and his own wife will run to fetch the gray coat and small-clothes, which, doubtless, she has kept carefully in the closet of their bed chamber? No! Wakefield is no such fool. He ascends the steps—heavily!—for twenty years have stiffened his legs since he came down—but he knows it not. Stay, Wakefield! Would you go to the sole home that is left you? Then step into your grave! The door opens. As he passes in, we have a parting glimpse of his visage, and recognize the crafty smile, which was the precursor of the little joke that he has ever since been playing off at his wife's expense. How unmercifully has he quizzed the poor woman! Well, a good night's rest to Wakefield!

This happy event—supposing it to be such—could only have occurred at an unpremeditated moment. We will not follow our friend across the threshold. He has left us much food for thought, a portion of which shall lend its wisdom to a moral, and be shaped into a figure. Amid the seeming confusion of our mysterious world, individuals are so nicely adjusted to a system, and systems to one another and to a whole, that, by stepping aside for a moment, a man exposes himself to a fearful risk of losing his place forever. Like Wakefield, he may become, as it were, the Outcast of the Universe.

Shadow Play

Nahid Rachlin

Pari is wearing a tight, red dress and black patent leather shoes that make a clunk-clunk sound on the cobble-stoned sidewalks. She has a robust beauty and she holds her head slightly upward to avoid men's glances at her. They look at her with desire, contempt or disapproval. Everyone knows her in this small Iranian town. The judge's pretty daughter. From the smile on her face I know she likes the attention.

She does not forget me, her little sister, holding on to her hand.

"I saw you today at school playing ping-pong. You were so good," she says. Or, "When you're older you're going to draw attention to yourself. You have such large eyes. . . ." Her tone is intense and dramatic.

We pass the mouth of a bazaar, crowded with vendors selling roasted corn, fresh pecans, toy camels, plastic handbags and dried locusts. A line of shops lit brightly with gas lamps, selling fabrics, jewelry, metal pitchers and pots and pans. A movie house playing an American movie, "A Duel in the Sun." Here Pari pauses and examines the photographs on the billboard. "Look at her pose here. Look at the way she smiles," she says about Jennifer Jones. She would stand there longer but a young man, wearing a folded handkerchief in his breast pocket, is staring at her, winking. Other men join in and begin to whistle or wink.

We walk through narrower, darker streets, streets full of dust, donkey's dung and dried spittle. We walk fast, my heart pounding with fear. Hands may come out of doorways and pull us in.

Copyright © Nahid Rachlin. Reprinted by permission.

Shadow Play

Across the street from our house, horsecarts have lined up, resting. Palm trees glisten with gold-red dates. The balcony of our house protrudes into the street, almost touching the top of the palms.

Our house is too large, full of rooms, hallways, and defunct doors. Termites have made holes in the doors and the walls bear the finger marks of many years.

"I wish I didn't have to go in," I say.

"I wish you and I were living alone. Then we would do whatever we wanted."

Inside, my mother is standing by a round pool, arguing with our old servant, Ali, about the quality of the fish he has just purchased.

"I told you not to buy anything from that old man." Two large fish lie in a basket, deadly dead beside the green frogs jumping in and out of the pool, the bats flapping frantically under the canopy.

Ali is half deaf and almost blind in one eye. He responds with the opacity of his damaged senses, "Yes, yes."

Pari and I try to walk past them without being seen. But my mother turns around as we come behind her. "I told you not to stay out so late," she says, addressing Pari. "Streets are full of lecherous men. And look at that short dress you're wearing." Her voice is shrill.

I hide behind Pari as I hear my father's distinct footsteps coming down the stairs. He is thunder about to fall.

We put our pillows together that night and talk.

"What do you want to be when you're older?" Pari asks.

"I don't know."

"You won't just get married, I know that."

"How about you?"

"Maybe I'll become an actress." In the dark I feel a nervousness in her eyes. "But maybe not. Maybe I'll just get married."

2

Her features are settled. Her gestures now are deliberate, her clothes in subdued colors, showing the weight of her experience. She has had a marriage, a miscarriage, and a divorce. She has lain in bed bleeding from an obscure disease. She has bled from her nose and gums.

She managed to divorce her husband by overlooking her *Mehrich,* a sum he would pay her if he had divorced her.

"He was a perfectly good man, young and rich. You just threw it away," my mother says.

"He once burnt my arm with his cigarette. He threw a hot iron at me."

"She's scatter-brained, irresponsible, stubborn," my father says, pacing rapidly, his dark, pock-marked face irate. "Letting him have all that money. Who ever heard of such a thing?"

Later he says, "And now she wants to be an actress, a whore. Of course I will disown her."

We have left the small town and live in Tehran. I wait in the stark anteroom of a theatrical agency while Pari walks into another room with a director. She looks around furtively before going in as though afraid my father would come out of the wall. Someone will find out about her secret plans and would drag her away.

The door between us is shut. The voices behind the door are fragmented and hushed. Outside a fine rain is falling in incessant, tiny drops.

Then the door opens and the two of them appear in the doorway. They do not seem to see me. He is stocky and his eyes are red. He whispers something to her. She begins to walk away and he waves at her.

I follow her outside. "What happened?" I ask.

She vaguely shakes her head. Does she hear me?

Muddy water flows in the gutters on the street. Cypresses and live oaks are damp and drooping. We buy hot, steaming beets and eat them quietly as we walk, ignoring the laboring men sucking at cooked entrails and whistling at us, ignoring the rain which still falls gently like dew.

At the curve of the street, we stop at a shop, selling photographs of actors. Pari buys a few pictures to add to others in an album she keeps. Her cheeks begin to take on color. There is a pulse on her face, beating. Then she bends over with sudden laughter. "It was a mistake—going to that man," she says. "But there will be other ads."

3

Airplanes up, down, gliding. People coming and going. Some crying, some laughing. Women hidden in tent-like *chadors* or wearing chic Western clothes. Indians in turbans, Arabs in jallabas. Americans and Europeans in smiling faces. My mother and father sit on a sofa along with other elderly people and children. The air is brazen with voices and loudspeakers.

"I knew you'd leave one day," Pari says. Her face is brittle, on the verge of laughter, tears.

"You could have too."

"School bores me," she says.

"You two were inseparable," my mother's voice comes from far away.

"Let her go, she's ugly," my father says and he chuckles at his own joke.

"Remember that noon when we sat on the shore," Pari says. "It was hot and my nose began to bleed."

"There was something else too."

She puts a forefinger on her temple, thinking.

"Someone was playing the flute somewhere. An Arab man was going up and down an arch over the bridge. People were watching him, or leaning over the railing looking at the water." Her eyes look backward, forward, into a narrow passage. "A man drowned a dog in the river. 'Dirty animal,' he said and his hands were shaking. He began to run."

"What a memory to bring up at this time."

A voice announces take off time. We touch; we kiss.

I stand in a line. The air reeks from an open bathroom and the ceiling is leaking.

"Once I leave this ruined country, I'll never step into it again," says a moustached man to a man beside him.

"Don't degrade your own country," says the other.

I am flat clay between two walls. It seems someone is pressing the two ends of the line together.

Where is Pari?

I walk into an open space. The sun is still there on slender cypresses, the edge of the clouds, distant houses. A patch of it clings to the ground and to my hesitant steps. The plane waits patiently, a sandpiper pecking at gold.

Behind me people are faceless figures of dreams. Hand waves are chilly winds. Windows, gaps in time.

4

Her letters are sparse and have none of her vitality. She does not talk even in my dreams.

We are walking over a chain of hills. Cacti with pale red and purple flowers spring up here and there. Behind us is a vast desert and before us a sea. We walk up and down, up and down the hills. Pari is wearing black and her face is chalk white.

"What should we do?" I ask. "We can't go on like this."

She walks ahead of me, her body strangely elongated, her head full of strands of gray.

"Is that you?" I ask.

She walks on languidly. There is a stain on the back of her dress. On the top of a hill she stops. She stretches her hand above her head and dives into the sea.

I lean and look down. A seagull dives into the water.

My mother writes that Pari is sick with dysentery. It has suddenly popped up.

Would you know she is working in a nursery school.

Would you know a man wants to marry her badly.

Pari's second husband has taken her to another town and she writes to no one.

5

The curtains are drawn and the air is blue. It is very quiet so that I can hear my father's footsteps brushing against dried leaves.

"Why is she so quiet, so pale," my mother says, pointing to Pari as if this is the first time she has noticed her. She sips her tea. "I made it too strong." She takes the last gulp and begins to fan herself by swaying the palm of her hand.

Pari sits propped up in bed and does not look at her.

They say she has visions at night. Of a demon locking her up in a room, of a powerful man forcing her to do things. She screams and throws things out of the window. Fear has pushed her face out of shape.

"Look at the way she just stares," her husband says, walking into the room. He blinks. He smiles, a yellow glow.

"I didn't expect her to be like this," my mother says.

I hold Pari's hand in mine. It is puffy and cold like a rubbery thing. Our childhood sits beside us. Too far to touch. Secrets, silences are a sharp diamond. A noose around my neck is tied to the dead weight in her.

Who is to blame? Who, me?

My father walks round and round in the courtyard, endlessly, like a victim.

"Remember how we used to talk," I say, leaning over her. "Remember that time in the public bath—how late we stayed and talked? We almost collapsed from the heat."

Tiny smiles twinkle in her eyes. She moves her head imperceptibly towards me.

I watch her husband leave the room.

"You have such a nice husband," my mother tells her. "Any other man would have thrown you out by now."

Certainly she has a nice, understanding husband.

Certainly her house is beautiful with its abundance of rugs, miniatures, blue vases, and lush flowers.

Her eyes are focused on me—dark, deep hollows.

"I hear Esther Williams has become very fat," she says. "Tell me is she fat?"

The Loneliness of the Long-Distance Runner

Alan Sillitoe

As soon as I got to Borstal* they made me a long-distance cross-country runner. I suppose they thought I was just the build for it because I was long and skinny for my age (and still am) and in any case I didn't mind it much, to tell you the truth, because running had always been made much of in our family, especially running away from the police. I've always been a good runner, quick and with a big stride as well, the only trouble being that no matter how fast I run, and I did a very fair lick even though I do say so myself, it didn't stop me getting caught by the cops after that bakery job.

You might think it a bit rare, having long-distance cross-country runners in Borstal, thinking that the first thing a long-distance cross-country runner would do when they set him loose at them fields and woods would be to run as far away from the place as he could get on a bellyful of Borstal slumgullion—but you're wrong, and I'll tell you why. The first thing is that them bastards over us aren't as daft as they most of the time look, and for another thing I'm not so daft as I would look if I tried to make a break for it on my long-distance running, because to abscond and then get caught is nothing but a mug's game, and I'm not falling for it. Cunning is what counts in this life, and even that you've got to use in the slyest way you can; I'm telling you straight: they're cunning, and I'm cunning.

From The Loneliness of the Long Distance Runner, by Alan Sillitoe. Copyright © 1959 by Alan Sillitoe. Reprinted by permission of Alfred A. Knopf. Inc.
*School in England for delinquent boys

If only 'them' and 'us' had the same ideas we'd get on like a house on fire, but they don't see eye to eye with us and we don't see eye to eye with them, so that's how it stands and how it will always stand. The one fact is that all of us are cunning, and because of this there's no love lost between us. So the thing is that they know I won't try to get away from them: they sit there like spiders in that crumbly manor house, perched like jumped-up jackdaws on the roof, watching out over the drives and fields like German generals from the tops of tanks. And even when I jog-trot on behind a wood and they can't see me anymore they know my sweeping-brush head will bob along that hedge-top in an hour's time and that I'll report to the bloke on the gate. Because when on a raw and frosty morning I get up at five o'clock and stand shivering my belly off on the stone floor and all the rest still have another hour to snooze before the bells go, I slink downstairs through all the corridors to the big outside door with a permit running-card in my fist, I feel like the first and last man in the world, both at once, if you can believe what I'm trying to say. I feel like the first man because I've hardly got a stitch on and am sent against the frozen fields in a shimmy and shorts—even the first poor bastard dropped on to the earth in midwinter knew how to make a suit of leaves, or how to skin a pterodactyl for a topcoat. But there I am, frozen stiff, with nothing to get me warm except a couple of hours' long-distance running before breakfast, not even a slice of bread-and-sheepdip. They're training me up fine for the big sports day when all the pig-faced snotty-nosed dukes and ladies—who can't add two and two together and would mess themselves like loonies if they didn't have slavies to beck-and-call—come and make speeches to us about sports being just the thing to get us leading an honest life and keep our itching finger-ends off them shop locks and safe handles and hairgrips to open gas meters. They give us a bit of blue ribbon and a cup for a prize after we've shagged ourselves out running or jumping, like race horses, only we don't get so well looked-after as race horses, that's the only thing.

So there I am, standing in the doorway in shimmy and shorts, not even a dry crust in my guts, looking out at frosty flowers on the ground. I suppose you think this is enough to make me cry? Not likely. Just because I feel like the first bloke in the world wouldn't make me bawl. It makes me feel fifty times better than when I'm cooped up in that dormitory with three hundred others. No, it's sometimes when I stand there feeling like the *last* man in the world that I don't feel so good. I feel like the last man in the world because I think that all those three hundred sleepers behind me are dead. They sleep so well I think that every scruffy head's kicked the bucket in the night and I'm the only one left, and when I look out into the bushes and frozen ponds I have the feeling that it's going to get colder and colder until everything I can see, meaning my red arms as well, is going to be covered with a thousand miles of ice, all the earth, right up to the sky and over every bit of land and sea. So I try to kick this feeling out and act like I'm the first man on earth. And that makes me feel good, so as soon as I'm steamed up enough to get this feeling in me, I take a flying leap out of the doorway, and off I trot.

I'm in Essex. It's supposed to be a good Borstal, at least that's what the governor said to me when I got here from Nottingham. "We want to trust you while you are in this establishment," he said, smoothing out his newspaper with lily-white workless hands, while I read the big words upside down: *Daily Telegraph.* "If you play ball with us, we'll play ball with you." (Honest to God, you'd have thought it was going to be one long tennis match.) "We want hard honest work and we want good athletics," he said as well. "And if you give us both these things you can be sure we'll do right by you and send you back into the world an honest man." Well, I could have died laughing, especially when straight after this I hear the barking sergeant-major's voice calling me and two others to attention and marching us off like we was Grenadier Guards. And when the governor kept saying how 'we' wanted you to do this, and 'we' wanted you to do that, I kept looking round for the other blokes, wondering how many of them there was. Of course, I knew there were thousands of them, but as far as I knew only one was in the room. And there *are* thousands of them, all over the poxeaten country, in shops, offices, railway stations, cars, houses, pubs—In-law blokes like you and them, all on the watch for Out-law blokes like me and us—and waiting to 'phone for the coppers as soon as we make a false move. And it'll always be there, I'll tell you that now, because I haven't finished making all my false moves yet, and I dare say I won't until I kick the bucket. If the In-laws are hoping to stop me making false moves they're wasting their time. They might as well stand me up against a wall and let fly with a dozen rifles. That's the only way they'll stop me, and a few million others. Because I've been doing a lot of thinking since coming here. They can spy on us all day to see if we're pulling our puddings and if we're working good or doing our 'athletics' but they can't make an X-ray of our guts to find out what we're telling ourselves. I've been asking myself all sorts of questions, and thinking about my life up to now. And I like doing all this. It's a treat. It passes the time away and don't make Borstal seem half so bad as the boys in our street used to say it was. And this long-distance running lark is the best of all, because it makes me think so good that I learn things even better than when I'm on my bed at night. And apart from that, what with thinking so much while I'm running I'm getting to be one of the best runners in the Borstal. I can go my five miles round better than anybody else I know.

So as soon as I tell myself I'm the first man ever to be dropped into the world, and as soon as I take that first flying leap out into the frosty grass of an early morning when even birds haven't the heart to whistle,

I get to thinking, and that's what I like. I go my rounds in a dream, turning at lane or footpath corners without knowing I'm turning, leaping brooks without knowing they're there, and shouting good morning to the early cow-milker without seeing him. It's a treat, being a long-distance runner, out in the world by yourself with not a soul to make you bad-tempered or tell you what to do or that there's a shop to break and enter a bit back from the next street. Sometimes I think that I've never been so free as during that couple of hours when I'm trotting up the path out of the gates and turning by that bare-faced, big-bellied oak tree at the lane end. Everything's dead, but good, because it's dead before coming alive, not dead after being alive. That's how I look at it. Mind you, I often feel frozen stiff at first. I can't feel my hands or feet or flesh at all, like I'm a ghost who wouldn't know the earth was under him if he didn't see it now and again through the mist. But even though some people would call this frost-pain suffering if they wrote about it to their mams in a letter, I don't, because I know that in half an hour I'm going to be warm, that by the time I get to the main road and am turning on to the wheatfield footpath by the bus stop I'm going to feel as hot as a potbellied stove and as happy as a dog with a tin tail.

It's a good life, I'm saying to myself, if you don't give in to coppers and Borstal-bosses and the rest of them bastard-faced In-laws. Trot-trot-trot. Puff-puff-puff. Slap-slap-slap go my feet on the hard soil. Swish-swish-swish as my arms and side catch the bare branches of a bush. For I'm seventeen now, and when they let me out of this—if I don't make a break and see that things turn out otherwise—they'll try to get me in the army, and what's the difference between the army and this place I'm in now? They can't kid me, the bastards. I've seen the barracks near where I live, and if there weren't swaddies on guard outside with rifles you wouldn't know the difference between their high walls and the place I'm in now. Even though the swaddies come out at odd times a week for a pint of ale, so what? Don't I come out three mornings a week on my long-distance running, which is fifty times better than boozing. When they first said that I was to do my long-distance running without a guard pedalling beside me on a bike I couldn't believe it; but they called it a progressive and modern place, though they can't kid me because I know it's just like any other Borstal, going by the stories I've heard, except that they let me trot about like this. Borstal's Borstal no matter what they do; but anyway I moaned about it being a bit thick sending me out so early to run five miles on an empty stomach, until they talked me round to thinking it wasn't so bad—which I knew all the time—until they called me a good sport and patted me on the back when I said I'd do it and that I'd try to win them the Borstal Blue Ribbon Prize Cup For Long Distance Cross Country

Running (All England). And now the governor talks to me when he comes on his rounds, almost as he'd talk to his prize race horse, if he had one.

"All right, Smith?" he asks.

"Yes, sir," I answer.

He flicks his grey moustache: "How's the running coming along?"

"I've set myself to trot round the grounds after dinner just to keep my hand in, sir," I tell him.

The pot-bellied pop-eyed bastard gets pleased at this: "Good show. I know you'll get us that cup," he says.

And I swear under my breath: "Like boggery, I will." No, I won't get them that cup, even though the stupid tash-twitching bastard has all his hopes in me. Because what does his barmy hope mean? I ask myself. Trot-trot-trot, slap-slap-slap, over the stream and into the wood where it's almost dark and frosty-dew twigs sting my legs. It don't mean a bloody thing to me, only to him, and it means as much to him as it would mean to me if I picked up the racing paper and put my bet on a hoss I didn't know, had never seen, and didn't care a sod if I ever did see. That's what it means to him. And I'll lose that race, because I'm not a race horse at all, and I'll let him know it when I'm about to get out—if I don't sling my hook even before the race. By Christ I will. I'm a human being and I've got thoughts and secrets and bloody life inside me that he doesn't know is there, and he'll never know what's there because he's stupid. I suppose you'll laugh at this, me saying the governor's a stupid bastard when I know hardly how to write and he can read and write and add-up like a professor. But what I say is true right enough. He's stupid, and I'm not, because I can see further into the likes of him than he can see into the likes of me. Admitted, we're both cunning, but I'm more cunning and I'll win in the end even if I die in gaol at eighty-two, because I'll have more fun and fire out of my life than he'll ever get out of his. He's read a thousand books I suppose, and for all I know he might even have written a few, but I know for a dead cert, as sure as I'm sitting here, that what I'm scribbling down is worth a million to what he could ever scribble down. I don't care what anybody says, but that's the truth and can't be denied. I know when he talks to me and I look into his army mug that I'm alive and he's dead. He's as dead as a doornail. If he ran ten yards he'd drop dead. If he got ten yards into what goes on in my guts he'd drop dead as well—with surprise. At the moment it's dead blokes like him as have the whip-hand over blokes like me, and I'm almost dead sure it'll always be like that, but even so, by Christ, I'd rather be like I am—always on the run and breaking into shops for a packet of fags and a jar of jam —than have the whip-hand over somebody else and be dead from the toe nails up. Maybe as soon as you get the whip-hand over somebody you do go dead. By God, to say that last sentence has needed a few hundred miles of long-distance running. I could no more have said that at first than I could have took a million-pound note from my back pocket. But it's true, you know, now I think of it again, and has always been true, and always will be true, and I'm surer of it every time I see the governor open that door and say Goodmorning lads.

As I run and see my smoky breath going out into the air as if I had ten cigars stuck in different parts of my body I think more on the little speech the governor made when I first came. Honesty. Be honest. I laughed so much one morning I went ten minutes down in my timing because I had to stop and get rid of the stitch in my side. The governor was so worried when I got back late that he sent me to the doctor's for an X-ray and heart check. Be honest. It's like saying: Be dead, like me, and then you'll have no more pain of leaving your nice slummy house for Borstal or prison. Be honest and settle down in a cosy six pounds a week job. Well, even with all this long-distance running I haven't yet been able to decide what he means by this, although I'm just about beginning to—and I don't like what it means. Because after all my thinking I found that it adds up to something that can't be true about me, being born and brought up as I was. Because another thing people like the governor will never understand is that I *am* honest, that I've never been anything else but honest, and that I'll always be honest. Sounds funny. But it's true because I know what honest means according to me and he only knows what it means according to him. I think my honesty is the only sort in the world, and he thinks his is the only sort in the world as well. That's why this dirty great walled-up and fenced-up manor house in the middle of nowhere has been used to coop-up blokes like me. And if I had the whip-hand I wouldn't even bother to build a place like this to put all the cops, governors, posh whores, penpushers, army officers, Members of Parliament in; no, I'd stick them up against a wall and let them have it, like they'd have done with blokes like us years ago, that is, if they'd ever known what it means to be honest, which they don't and never will so help me God Almighty.

I was nearly eighteen months in Borstal before I thought about getting out. I can't tell you much about what it was like there because I haven't got the hang of describing buildings or saying how many crumby chairs and slatted windows make a room. Neither can I do much complaining, because to tell you the truth I didn't suffer in Borstal at all. I gave the same answer a pal of mine gave when someone asked him how much he hated it in the army. "I didn't hate it," he said. "They fed me, gave me a suit, and pocket-money, which was a bloody sight more than I ever got before, unless I worked myself to death for it, and most of the time they wouldn't let me work but sent me to the dole office twice a week." Well, that's more or less what I say. Borstal didn't hurt me in that respect, so since I've got no complaints I don't have to describe what they gave us to eat, what the dorms were like, or how they treated us. But in another way Borstal does something to me. No, it doesn't get my back up, because it's always been up, right from when I was born. What it does do is show me what they've been trying to frighten me with. They've got other things as well, like prison and, in the end, the rope. It's like me rushing up to thump a man and snatch the coat off his back when, suddenly, I pull up because he whips out a knife and lifts it to stick me like a pig if I come too close. That knife is Borstal, clink, the rope. But once you've seen the knife you learn a bit of unarmed combat. You have to, because you'll never get that sort of knife in your own hands, and this unarmed combat doesn't amount to much. Still, there it is, and you keep on rushing up to this man, knife or not, hoping to get one of your hands on his wrist and the other on his elbow both at the same time, and press back until he drops the knife.

You see, by sending me to Borstal they've shown me the knife, and from now on I know something I didn't know before: that it's war between me and them. I always knew this, naturally, because I was in Remand Homes as well and the boys there told me a lot about their brothers in Borstal, but it was only touch and go then, like kittens, like boxing-gloves, like dobbie. But now that they've shown me the knife, whether I ever pinch another thing in my life again or not, I know who my enemies are and what war is. They can drop all the atom bombs they like for all I care: I'll never call it war and wear a soldier's uniform, because I'm in a different sort of war, that they think is child's play. The war they think is war is suicide, and those that go and get killed in war should be put in the clink for attempted suicide because that's the feeling in blokes' minds when they rush to join up or let themselves be called up. I know, because I've thought how good it would be sometimes to do myself in and the easiest way to do it, it occurred to me, was to hope for a big war so's I could join up and get killed. But I got past that when I knew I already was in a war of my own, that I was born into one, that I grew up hearing the sound of 'old soldiers' who'd been over the top at Dartmoor, half-killed at Lincoln, trapped in no-man's-land at Borstal, that sounded louder than any Jerry bombs. Government wars aren't my wars; they've got nowt to do with me, because my own war's all that I'll ever be bothered about. I remember when I was fourteen and I went out into the country with three of my cousins, all about the same age, who later went to different Borstals, and then to different regiments, from which they soon deserted, and then to different gaols where they still are as far as I know. But anyway, we were all kids then, and wanted to go out to the woods for a change, to get away from the roads of stinking hot tar one summer. We climbed over fences and went through fields, scrumping a few sour apples on our way, until we saw the wood about a mile off. Up Colliers' Pad we heard another lot of kids talking in high-school voices behind a hedge. We crept up on them and peeped through the brambles, and saw they were eating a picnic, a real posh spread out of baskets and flasks and towels. There must have been about seven of them, lads and girls sent out by their mams and dads for the afternoon. So we went on our bellies through the hedge like crocodiles and surrounded them, and then dashed into the middle, scattering the fire and batting their tabs and snatching up all there was to eat, then running off over Cherry Orchard fields into the wood, with a man chasing us who'd come up while we were ransacking their picnic. We got away all right, and had a good feed into the bargain, because we'd been clambed to death and couldn't wait long enough to get our chops ripping into them thin lettuce and ham sandwiches and creamy cakes.

Well, I'll always feel during every bit of my life like those daft kids should have felt before we broke them up. But they never dreamed that what happened was going to happen, just like the governor of this Borstal who spouts to us about honesty and all that wappy stuff don't know a bloody thing, while I know every minute of my life that a big boot is always likely to smash any nice picnic I might be barmy and dishonest enough to make for myself. I admit that there've been times when I've thought of telling the governor all this so as to put him on guard, but when I've got as close as seeing him I've changed my mind, thinking to let him either find out for himself or go through the same mill as I've gone through. I'm not hard-hearted (in fact I've helped a few blokes in my time with the odd quid, lie, fag, or shelter from the rain when they've been on the run) but I'm boggered if I'm going to risk being put in the cells just for trying to give the governor a bit of advice he don't deserve. If my heart's soft I know the sort of people I'm going to save it for. And any advice I'd give the governor wouldn't do him the least bit of good; it'd only trip him up sooner than if he wasn't told at all, which I suppose is what I want to happen. But for the time being I'll let things go on as they are, which is something else I've learned in the last year or two. (It's a good job I can only think of these things as fast as I can write with this stub of pencil that's clutched in my paw, otherwise I'd have dropped the whole thing weeks ago.)

By the time I'm half-way through my morning course, when after a frost-bitten dawn I can see a phlegmy bit of sunlight hanging from the bare twigs of beech and sycamore, and when I've measured my half-way mark by the short-cut scrimmage down the steep bush-covered bank and into the sunken lane, when still there's not a soul in sight and not a sound except the neighing of a piebald foal in a cottage stable that I can't see, I get to thinking **the deepest and daftest** of all. The governor would have a fit if he could see me sliding down the bank because I could break my neck or ankle, but I can't not do it because it's the only risk I take and the only excitement I ever get, flying flatout like one of them pterodactyls from the 'Lost World' I once heard on the wireless, crazy like a cut-balled cockerel, scratching myself to bits and almost letting myself go but not quite. It's the most wonderful minute because there's not one thought or word or picture or anything in my head while I'm going down. I'm empty, as empty as I was before I was born, and I don't let myself go, I suppose, because whatever it is that's farthest down inside me don't want me to die or hurt myself bad. And it's daft to think deep, you know, because it gets you nowhere, though deep is what I am when I've passed this half-way mark because the long-distance run of an early morning makes me think that every run like this is a life—a little life, I know—but a life as full of misery and happiness and things happening as you can ever get really around yourself—and I remember that after a lot of these runs I thought that it didn't need much know-how to tell how a life was going to end once it had got well started. But as usual I was wrong, caught first by the cops and then by my own bad brain, I could never trust myself to fly scot-free over these traps, was always tripped up sooner or later no matter how many I got over to the good without even knowing it. Looking back I suppose them big trees put their branches to their snouts and gave each other the wink, and there I was whizzing down the bank and not seeing a bloody thing.

II

I don't say to myself: "You shouldn't have done the job and then you'd have stayed away from Borstal"; no, what I ram into my runner-brain is that my luck had no right to scram just when I was on my way to making the coppers think I hadn't done the job after all. The time was autumn and the night foggy enough to set me and my mate Mike roaming the streets when we should have been rooted in front of the telly or stuck into a plush posh seat at the pictures, but I was restless after six weeks away from any sort of work, and well you might ask me why I'd been bone-idle for so long because normally I sweated my thin guts out on a milling-machine with the rest of them, but you see, my dad died from cancer of the throat, and mam collected a cool five hundred insurance and benefits from the factory where he'd worked, "for your bereavement," they said, or words like that.

Now I believe, and my mam must have thought the same, that a wad of crisp blue-black fivers ain't a sight of good to a living soul unless they're flying out of your hand into some shopkeeper's till, and the shopkeeper is passing you tip-top things in exchange over the counter, so as soon as she got the money, mam took me and my five brothers and sisters out to town and got us dolled-up in new clothes. Then she ordered a twenty-one-inch telly, a new carpet because the old one was covered with blood from dad's dying and wouldn't wash out, and took a taxi home with bags of grub and a new fur coat. And do you know—you wain't believe me when I tell you—she'd still near three hundred left in her bulging handbag the next day, so how could any of us go to work after that? Poor old dad, he didn't get a look in, and he was the one who'd done the suffering and dying for such a lot of lolly.

Night after night we sat in front of the telly with a ham sandwich in one hand, a bar of chocolate in the other, and a bottle of lemonade between our boots, while mam was with some fancy-man upstairs on the new bed she'd ordered, and I'd never known a family as happy as ours was in that couple of months when we'd got all the money we needed. And when the dough ran out I didn't think about anything much, but just roamed the streets—looking for another job, I told mam—hoping I suppose to get my hands on another five hundred nicker so's the nice life we'd got used to could go on and on for ever. Because it's surprising how quick you can get used to a different life. To begin with, the adverts on the telly had shown us how much more there was in the world to buy than we'd ever dreamed of when we'd looked into shop windows but hadn't seen all there was to see because we didn't have the money to buy it with anyway. And the telly made all these things seem twenty times better than we'd ever thought they were. Even adverts at the cinema were cool and tame, because now we were seeing them in private at home. We used to cock our noses up at things in shops that didn't move, but suddenly we saw their real value because they jumped and glittered around the screen and had some pasty-faced tart going head over heels to get her nail-polished grabbers on to them or her lipstick lips over them, not like the crumby adverts you saw on posters or in newspapers as dead as doornails; these were flickering around loose, half-open packets and tins, making you think that all you had to do was finish opening them before they were yours, like seeing an unlocked safe through a shop window with the man gone away for a cup of tea without thinking to guard his lolly. The films they showed were good as well, in that way, because we couldn't get our eyes unglued from the cops chasing the robbers who had satchel-bags crammed with cash and looked like getting away to spend it—until the last moment. I always hoped they would end up free to blow the lot, and could never stop wanting to put my hand out, smash into the screen (it only looked a bit of rag-screen like at the pictures) and get the copper in a half-nelson so's he'd stop following the bloke with the money-bags. Even when he'd knocked off a couple of bank clerks I hoped he wouldn't get nabbed. In fact then I wished more than ever he wouldn't because it meant the hot-chair if he did, and I wouldn't wish that on anybody no matter what they'd done, because I'd read in a book where the hot-chair worn't a quick death at all, but that you just sat there scorching to death until you were dead. And it was when these cops were chasing the crooks that we played some good tricks with the telly, because when one of them opened his big gob to spout about getting their man I'd turn the sound down and see his mouth move like a goldfish or mackerel or a minnow mimicking what they were supposed to be acting—it was so funny the whole family nearly went into fits on the brand-new carpet that hadn't yet found its way to the bedroom. It was the best of all though when we did it to some Tory telling us about how good his government was going to be if we kept on voting for them—their slack chops rolling, opening and bumbling, hands lifting to twitch moustaches and touching their button-holes to make sure the flower hadn't wilted, so that you could see they didn't mean a word they said, especially with not a murmur coming out because we'd cut off the sound. When the governor of the Borstal first talked to me I was reminded of those times so much that I nearly killed myself trying not to laugh. Yes, we played so many good stunts on the box of tricks that mam used to call us the Telly Boys, we got so clever at it.

My pal Mike got let off with probation because it was his first job—anyway the first they ever knew about—and because they said he would never have done it if it hadn't been for me talking him into it. They said I was a menace to honest lads like Mike—hands in his pockets so that they looked stone-empty, head bent forward as if looking for half-crowns to fill 'em with, a ripped jersey on and his hair falling into his eyes so that he could go up to women and ask them for a shilling because he was hungry—and that I was the brains behind the job, the guiding light when it came to making up anybody's mind, but I swear to God I worn't owt like that because really I ain't got no more brains than a gnat after hiding the money in the place I did. And I—being cranky like I am—got sent to Borstal because to tell you the honest truth I'd been to Remand Homes before—though that's another story and I suppose if ever I tell it it'll be just as boring as this one is. I was glad though that Mike got away with it, and I only hope he always will, not like silly bastard me.

So on this foggy night we tore ourselves away from the telly and slammed the front door behind us, setting off up our wide street like slow tugs on a river that'd broken their hooters, for we didn't know where the housefronts began what with the perishing cold mist all around. I was snatched to death without an overcoat: mam had forgotten to buy me one in the scrummage of shopping, and by the time I thought to remind her of it the dough was all gone. So we whistled 'The Teddy Boys Picnic' to keep us warm, and I told myself that I'd get a coat soon if it was the last thing I did. Mike said he thought the same about himself, adding that he'd also get some brand-new glasses with gold rims, to wear instead of the wire frames they'd given him at the school clinic years ago. He didn't twig it was foggy at first and cleaned his glasses every time I pulled him back from a lamp-post or car, but when he saw the lights on Alfreton Road looking like octopus eyes he put them in his pocket and didn't wear them again until we did the job. We hadn't got two ha-pennies between us, and though we weren't hungry we wished we'd got a bob or two when we passed the fish and chip shops because the delicious sniffs of salt and vinegar and frying fat made our mouths water. I don't mind telling you we walked the town from one end to the other and if our eyes worn't glued to the ground looking for lost wallets and watches they was swivelling around house windows and shop doors in case we saw something easy and worth nipping into.

Neither of us said as much as this to each other, but I know for a fact that that was what we was thinking. What I don't know—and as sure as I sit here I know I'll never know—is which of us was the first bastard to latch his peepers on to that baker's backyard. Oh yes, it's all right me telling myself it was me, but the truth is that I've never known whether it was Mike or not, because I do know that I didn't see the open window until he stabbed me in the ribs and pointed it out. "See it?" he said.

"Yes," I told him, "so let's get cracking."

"But what about the wall though?" he whispered, looking a bit closer.

"On your shoulders," I chipped in.

His eyes were already up there: "Will you be able to reach?" It was the only time he ever showed any life.

"Leave it to me," I said, ever-ready. "I can reach anywhere from your hamhock shoulders."

Mike was a nipper compared to me, but underneath the scruffy draughtboard jersey he wore were muscles as hard as iron, and you wouldn't think to see him walking down the street with glasses on and hands in pockets that he'd harm a fly, but I never liked to get on the wrong side of him in a fight because he's the sort that don't say a word for weeks on end—sits plugged in front of the telly, or reads a cowboy book, or just sleeps—when suddenly BIFF—half kills somebody for almost nothing at all, such as beating him in a race for the last Football Post on a Saturday night, pushing in before him at a bus stop, or bumping into him when he was day-dreaming about Dolly-on-the-Tub next door. I saw him set on a bloke once for no more than fixing him in a funny way with his eyes, and it turned out that the bloke was cockeyed but nobody knew it because he'd just that day come to live in our street. At other times none of these things would matter a bit, and I suppose the only reason why I was pals with him was because I didn't say much from one month's end to another either.

He put his hands up in the air like he was being covered with a Gatling-Gun, and moved to the wall like he was going to be mowed down, and I climbed up him like he was a stile or a step-ladder, and there he stood, the palms of his upshot maulers flat and turned out so's I could step on 'em like they was the adjustable jack-spanner under a car, not a sound of a breath nor the shiver of a flinch coming from him. I lost no time in any case, took my coat from between my teeth, chucked it up to the glass-topped wall (where the glass worn't too sharp because the jags had been worn down by years of accidental stones) and was sitting astraddle before I knew where I was. Then down the other side, with my legs rammed up into my throat when I hit the ground, the crack coming about as hard as when you fall after a high parachute drop, that one of my mates told me was like jumping off a twelve-foot wall, which this must have been. Then I picked up my bits and pieces and opened the gate for Mike, who was still grinning and full of life because the hardest part of the job was already done. "I came, I broke, I entered," like that clever-dick Borstal song.

I didn't think about anything at all, as usual, because I never do when I'm busy, when I'm draining pipes, looting sacks, yaling locks, lifting latches, forcing my bony hands and lanky legs into making something move, hardly feeling my lungs going in-whiff and out-whaff, not realizing whether my mouth is clamped tight or gaping, whether I'm hungry, itching from scabies, or whether my flies are open and flashing dirty words like muck and spit into the late-night final fog. And when I don't know anything about all this then how can I honest-to-God say I think of anything at such times? When I'm wondering what's the best way to get a window open or how to force a door, how can I be thinking or have anything on my mind? That's what the four-eyed white-smocked bloke with the note-book couldn't understand when he asked me questions for days and days after I got to Borstal; and I couldn't explain it to him then like I'm writing it down now; and even if I'd been able to maybe he still wouldn't have caught on because I don't know whether I can understand it myself even at this moment, though I'm doing my best you can bet.

So before I knew where I was I was inside the baker's office watching Mike picking up that cash box after he'd struck a match to see where it was, wearing a tailor-made fifty-shilling grin on his square crew-cut nut as his paws closed over the box like he'd squash it to nothing. "Out," he suddenly said, shaking it so's it rattled. "Let's scram."

"Maybe there's some more," I said, pulling half a dozen drawers out of a rollertop desk.

"No," he said, like he'd already been twenty years in the game, "this is the lot," patting his tin box, "this is it."

I pulled out another few drawers, full of bills, books and letters. "How do you know, you loony sod?"

He barged past me like a bull at a gate. "Because I do."

Right or wrong, we'd both got to stick together and do the same thing. I looked at an ever-loving babe of a brand-new typewriter, but knew it was too traceable, so blew it a kiss, and went out after him. "Hang on," I said, pulling the door to, "we're in no hurry."

"Not much we aren't," he says over his shoulder.

"We've got months to splash the lolly," I whispered as we crossed the yard, "only don't let that gate creak too much or you'll have the narks tuning-in."

"You think I'm barmy?" he said, creaking the gate so that the whole street heard.

I don't know about Mike, but now I started to think, of how we'd get back safe through the streets with that money-box up my jumper. Because he'd clapped it into my hand as soon as we'd got to the main road, which might have meant that he'd started thinking as well, which only goes to show how you don't know what's in anybody else's mind unless you think about things yourself. But as far as my thinking went at that moment it wasn't up to much, only a bit of fright that wouldn't budge not even with a hot blow-lamp, about what we'd say if a copper asked us where we were off to with that hump in my guts.

"What is it?" he'd ask, and I'd say: "A growth." "What do you mean, a growth, my lad?" he'd say back, narky like. I'd cough and clutch myself like I was in the most tripe-twisting pain in the world, and screw my eyes up like I was on my way to the hospital, and Mike would take my arm like he was the best pal I'd got. "Cancer," I'd manage to say to Narker, which would make his slow punch-drunk brain suspect a thing or two. "A lad of your age?" So I'd groan again, and hope to make him feel a real bully of a bastard, which would be impossible, but anyway: "It's in the family. Dad died of it last month, and I'll die of it next month by the feel of it." "What, did he have it in the guts?" "No, in the throat. But it's got me in the stomach." Groan and cough. "Well, you shouldn't be out like this if you've got cancer, you should be in the hospital." I'd get ratty now: "That's where I'm trying to go if only you'd let me and stop asking so many questions. Aren't I, Mike?" Grunt from Mike as he unslung his cosh. Then just in time the copper would tell us to get on our way, kind and considerate all of a sudden, saying that the outpatient department of the hospital closes at twelve, so hadn't he better call us a taxi? He would if we liked, he says, and he'd pay for it as well. But we tell him not to bother, that he's a good bloke even if he is a copper, that we know a short cut anyway. Then just as we're turning a corner he gets it into his big batchy head that we're going the opposite way to the hospital, and calls us back. So we'd start to run ... if you can call all that thinking.

Up in my room Mike rips open that money-box with a hammer and chisel, and before we know where we are we've got seventy-eight pounds fifteen and fourpence ha'penny *each* lying all over my bed like tea spread out on Christmas Day: cake and trifle, salad and sandwiches, jam tarts and bars of chocolate: all shared and shared alike between Mike and me because we believed in equal work and equal pay, just like the comrades my dad was in until he couldn't do a stroke anymore and had no breath left to argue with. I thought of how good it was that blokes like that poor baker didn't stash all his cash in one of the big marble-fronted banks that take up every corner of the town, how lucky for us that he didn't trust them no matter how many millions of tons of concrete or how many iron bars and boxes they were made of, or how many coppers kept their blue pop-eyed peepers glued onto them, how smashing it was that he believed in money-boxes when so many shopkeepers thought it old-fashioned and tried to be modern by using a bank, which wouldn't give a couple of sincere, honest, hardworking, conscientious blokes like Mike and me a chance.

Now you'd think, and I'd think, and anybody with a bit of imagination would think, that we'd done as clean a job as could ever be done, that, with the baker's shop being at least a mile from where we lived, and with not a soul having seen us, and what with the fog and the fact that we weren't more than five minutes in the place, that the coppers should never have been able to trace us. But then, you'd be wrong, I'd be wrong, and everybody else would be wrong, no matter how much imagination was diced out between us.

Even so, Mike and I didn't splash the money about, because that would have made people think straightaway that we'd latched on to something that didn't belong to us. Which wouldn't do at all, because even in a street like ours there are people who love to do a good turn for the coppers, though I never know why they do. Some people are so mean-gutted that even if they've only got tuppence more than you and they think you're the sort that would take it if you have half the chance, they'd get you put inside if they saw you ripping lead out of a lavatory, even if it weren't their lavatory—just to keep their tuppence out of their reach. And so we didn't do anything to let on about how rich we were, nothing like going down town and coming back dressed in brand-new Teddy boy suits and carrying a set of skiffle-drums like another pal of ours who'd done a factory office about six months before. No, we took the odd bobs and pennies out and folded the notes into bundles and stuffed them up the drainpipe outside the door in the backyard. "Nobody'll ever think of looking for it there," I said to Mike. "We'll keep it doggo for a week or two, then take a few quid a week out till it's all gone. We might be thieving bastards, but we're not green."

Some days later a plain-clothes dick knocked at the door. And asked for me. I was still in bed, at eleven o'clock, and had to unroll myself from the comfortable black sheets when I heard mam calling me. "A man to see you," she said. "Hurry up, or he'll be gone."

I could hear her keeping him at the back door, nattering about how fine it had been but how it looked like rain since early this morning—and he didn't answer her except to snap out a snotty yes or no. I scrambled into my trousers and wondered why he'd come—knowing it was a copper because 'a man to see you' always meant just that in our house—and if I'd had any idea that one had gone to Mike's house as well at the same time I'd have twigged it to be because of that hundred and fifty quid's worth of paper stuffed up the drainpipe outside the back door about ten inches away from that plain-clothed copper's boot, where mam still talked to him thinking she was doing me a favour, and I wishing to God she'd ask him in, though on second thoughts realizing that that would seem more suspicious than keeping him outside, because they know we hate their guts and smell a rat if they think we're trying to be nice to them. Mam wasn't born yesterday, I thought, thumping my way down the creaking stairs.

I'd seen him before: Borstal Bernard in nicky-hat, Remand Home Ronald in rowing-boat boots. Probation Pete in a pit-prop mackintosh, three-months clink in collar and tie (all this out of a Borstal skiffle-ballad that my new mate made up, and I'd tell you it in full but it doesn't belong in this story), a 'tec who'd never had as much in his pockets as that drainpipe had up its jackses. He was like Hitler in the face, right down to the paint-brush tash, except that being six-foot tall made him seem worse. But I straightened my shoulders to look into his illiterate blue eyes—like I always do with any copper.

Then he started asking me questions, and my mother from behind said: "He's never left that television set for the last three months, so you've got nowt on him, mate. You might as well look for somebody else, because you're wasting the rates you get out of my rent and the income tax that comes out of my pay-packet standing there like that"—which was a laugh because she'd never paid either to my knowledge, and never would, I hoped.

"Well, you know where Papplewick Street is, don't you?" the copper asked me, taking no notice of mam.

"Ain't it off Alfreton Road?" I asked him back, helpful and bright.

"You know there's a baker's half-way down on the left-hand side, don't you?"

"Ain't it next door to a pub, then?" I wanted to know.

He answered me sharp: "No, it bloody well ain't." Coppers always lose their tempers as quick as this, and more often than not they gain nothing by it. "Then I don't know it," I told him, saved by the bell.

He slid his big boot round and round on the doorstep. "Where were you last Friday night?" Back in the ring, but this was worse than a boxing match.

I didn't like him trying to accuse me of something he wasn't sure I'd done. "Was I at the baker's you mentioned? Or in the pub next door?"

"You'll get five years in Borstal if you don't give me a straight answer," he said, unbuttoning his mac even though it was cold where he was standing.

"I was glued to the telly, like mam says," I swore blind. But he went on and on with his looney questions: "Have you got a television?"

The things he asked wouldn't have taken in a kid of two, and what else could I say to the last one except: "Has the aerial fell down? Or would you like to come in and see it?"

He was liking me even less for saying that. "We know you weren't listening to the television set last Friday, and so do you, don't you?"

"P'raps not, but I was *looking* at it, because sometimes we turn the sound down for a bit of fun." I could hear mam laughing from the kitchen, and I hoped Mike's mam was doing the same if the cops had gone to him as well.

"We know you weren't in the house," he said, starting up again, cranking himself with the handle. They always say 'We' 'We', never 'I' 'I'—as if they feel braver and righter knowing there's a lot of them against only one.

"I've got witnesses," I said to him. "Mam for one. Her fancy-man, for two. Ain't that enough? I can get you a dozen more, or thirteen altogether, if it was a baker's that got robbed."

"I don't want no lies," he said, not catching on about the baker's dozen. Where do they scrape cops up from anyway? "All I want is to get from you where you put that money."

Don't get mad, I kept saying to myself, don't get mad—hearing mam setting out cups and saucers and putting the pan on the stove for bacon. I stood back and waved him inside like I was a butler. "Come and search the house. If you've got a warrant."

"Listen, my lad," he said, like the dirty bullying jumped-up bastard he was, "I don't want too much of your lip, because if we get you down to the Guildhall you'll get a few bruises and black-eyes for your trouble." And I knew he wasn't kidding either, because I'd heard about all them sort of tricks. I hoped one day though that him and all his pals would be the ones to get the black-eyes and kicks; you never knew. It might come sooner than anybody thinks, like in Hungary. "Tell me where the money is, and I'll get you off with probation."

"What money?" I asked him, because I'd heard that one before as well.

"You know what money."

"Do I look as though I'd know owt about money?" I said, pushing my fist through a hole in my shirt.

"The money that was pinched, that you know all about," he said. "You can't trick me, so it's no use trying."

"Was it three-and-eightpence ha'penny?" I asked.

"You thieving young bastard. We'll teach you to steal money that doesn't belong to you."

I turned my head around: "Mam," I called out, "get my lawyer on the blower, will you?"

"Clever, aren't you?" he said in a very unfriendly way, "but we won't rest until we clear all this up."

"Look," I pleaded, as if about to sob my socks off because he'd got me wrong, "it's all very well us talking like this, it's like a game almost, but I wish you'd tell me what it's all about, because honest-to-God I've just got out of bed and here you are at the door talking about me having pinched a lot of money, money that I don't know anything about."

He swung around now as if he'd trapped me, though I couldn't see why he might think so. "Who said anything about money? I didn't. What made you bring money into this little talk we're having?"

"It's you," I answered, thinking he was going barmy, and about to start foaming at the chops, "you've got money on the brain, like all policemen. Baker's shops as well."

He screwed his face up. "I want an answer from you: where's that money?"

But I was getting fed-up with all this. "I'll do a deal."

Judging by his flash-bulb face he thought he was suddenly onto a good thing. "What sort of a deal?"

So I told him: "I'll give you all the money I've got, one and fourpence ha'penny, if you stop this third-degree and let me go in and get my breakfast. Honest, I'm clambed to death. I ain't had a bite since yesterday. Can't you hear my guts rollin'?"

His jaw dropped, but on he went, pumping me for another half hour. A routine check-up, as they say on the pictures. But I knew I was winning on points.

Then he left, but came back in the afternoon to search the house. He didn't find a thing, not a French farthing. He asked me questions again and I didn't tell him anything except lies, lies, lies, because I can go on doing that forever without batting an eyelid. He'd got nothing on me and we both of us knew it, otherwise I'd have been down at the Guildhall in no time, but he kept on keeping on because I'd been in a Remand Home for a high-wall job before; and Mike was put through the same mill because all the local cops knew he was my best pal.

When it got dark me and Mike were in our parlour with a low light on and the telly off, Mike taking it easy in the rocking chair and me slouched out on the settee, both of us puffing a packet of Woods. With the door bolted and curtains drawn we talked about the dough we'd crammed up the drainpipe. Mike thought we should take it out and both of us do a bunk to Skegness or Cleethorpes for a good time in the arcades, living like lords in a boarding house near the pier, then at least we'd both have had a big beano before getting sent down.

"Listen, you daft bleeder," I said, "we aren't going to get caught at all, *and* we'll have a good time, later." We were so clever we didn't even go out to the pictures, though we wanted to.

In the morning old Hitler-face questioned me again, with one of his pals this time, and the next day they came, trying hard as they could to get something out of me, but I didn't budge an inch. I know I'm showing off when I say this, but in me he'd met his match, and I'd never give in to questions no matter how long it was kept up. They searched the house a couple of times as well, which made me think they thought they really had something to go by, but I know now that they hadn't, and that it was all buckshee speculation. They turned the house upside down and inside out like an old sock, went fron top to bottom and front to back but naturally didn't find a thing. The copper even poked his face up the front-room chimney (that hadn't been used or swept for years) and came down looking like Al Jolson so that he had to swill himself clean at the scullery sink. They kept tapping and pottering around the big aspidistra plant that grandma had left to mam, lifting it up from the table to look under the cloth, putting it aside so's they could move the table and get at the boards under the rug—but the big headed stupid ignorant bastards never once thought of emptying soil out of the plant pot, where they'd have found the crumpled-up money-box that we'd buried the night we did the job. I suppose it's still there, now I think about it, and I suppose mam wonders now and again why the plant don't prosper like it used to —as if it could with a fistful of thick black tin lapped around its guts.

The last time he knocked at our door was one wet morning at five minutes to nine and I was sleep-logged in my crumby bed as usual. Mam had gone to work that day so I shouted for him to hold on a bit, and then went down to see who it was. There he stood, six-feet tall and sopping wet, and for the first time in my life I did a spiteful thing I'll never forgive myself for: I didn't ask him to come in out of the rain, because I wanted him to get double pneumonia and die. I suppose he could have pushed by me and come in if he'd wanted, but maybe he'd got used to asking questions on the doorstep and didn't want to be put off by changing his ground even though it was raining. Not that I don't like being spiteful because of any barmy principle I've got, but this bit of spite, as it turned out, did me no good at all. I should have treated him as a brother I hadn't seen for twenty years and dragged him in for a cup of tea and a fag, told him about the picture I hadn't seen the night before, asked him how his wife was after her operation and whether they'd shaved her moustache off to make it, and then sent him happy and satisfied out by the front door. But no, I thought, let's see what he's got to say for himself now.

He stood a little to the side of the door, either because it was less wet there, or because he wanted to see me from a different angle, perhaps having found it monotonous to watch a bloke's face always telling lies from the same side. "You've been identified," he said, twitching raindrops from his tash. "A woman saw you and your mate yesterday and she swears blind you are the same chaps she saw going into that bakery."

I was dead sure he was still bluffing, because Mike and I hadn't even seen each other the day before, but I looked worried. "She's a menace then to innocent people, whoever she is, because the only bakery I've been in lately is the one up our street to get some cut-bread on tick for mam."

He didn't bite on this. "So now I want to know where the money is" —as if I hadn't answered him at all.

"I think mam took it to work this morning to get herself some tea in the canteen." Rain was splashing down so hard I thought he'd get washed away if he didn't come inside. But I wasn't much bothered, and went on: "I remember I put it in the telly-vase last night—it was my only one-and-three and I was saving it for a packet of tips this morning—and I nearly had a jibbering black fit just now when I saw it had gone. I was reckoning on it for getting me through today because I don't think life's worth living without a fag, do you?"

I was getting into my stride and began to feel good, twigging that this would be my last pack of lies, and that if I kept it up for long enough this time I'd have the bastards beat: Mike and me would be off to the coast in a few weeks time having the fun of our lives, playing at penny football and latching on to a couple of tarts that would give us all they were good for. "And this weather's no good for picking-up fag-ends in the street," I said, "because they'd be sopping wet. Course, I know you could dry 'em out near the fire, but it don't taste the same you know, all said and done. Rainwater does summat to 'em that don't bear thinkin' about: it turns 'em back into hoss-tods without the taste though."

I began to wonder, at the back of my brainless eyes, why old copperlugs didn't pull me up sharp and say he hadn't got time to listen to all this, but he wasn't looking at me anymore, and all my thoughts about Skegness went bursting to smithereens in my sludgy loaf. I could have dropped into the earth when I saw what he'd fixed his eyes on.

He was looking at *it,* an ever-loving fiver, and I could only jabber: "The one thing is to have some real fags because new hoss-tods is always better than stuff that's been rained on and dried, and I know how you feel about not being able to find money because one-and-three's one-and-three in anybody's pocket, and naturally if I see it knocking around I'll get you on the blower tomorrow straightaway and tell you where you can find it."

I thought I'd go down in a fit: three green-backs as well had been washed down by the water, and more were following, lying flat at first after their fall, then getting tilted at the corners by wind and rainspots as if they were alive and wanted to get back into the dry snug drainpipe out of the terrible weather, and you can't imagine how I wished they'd be able to. Old Hitler-face didn't know what to make of it but just kept staring down and down, and I thought I'd better keep on talking, though I knew it wasn't much good now.

"It's a fact, I know, that money's hard to come by and half-crowns don't get found on bus seats or in dustbins, and I didn't see any in bed last night because I'd 'ave known about it, wouldn't I? You can't sleep with things like that in the bed because they're too hard, and anyway at first they're. ..." It took Hitler-boy a long time to catch on; they were beginning to spread over the yard a bit, reinforced by the third colour of a ten-bob note, before his hand clamped itself onto my shoulder.

III

The pop-eyed potbellied governor said to a pop-eyed potbellied Member of Parliament who sat next to his pop-eyed potbellied whore of a wife that I was his only hope for getting the Borstal Blue Ribbon Prize Cup For Long Distance Cross Country Running (All England), which I was, and it set me laughing to myself inside, and I didn't say a word to any potbellied pop-eyed bastard that might give them real hope, though I knew the governor anyway took my quietness to mean he'd got that cup already stuck on the bookshelf in his office among the few other mildewed trophies.

"He might take up running in a sort of professional way when he gets out," and it wasn't until he'd said this and I'd heard it with my own flap-tabs that I realized it might be possible to do such a thing, run for money, trot for wages on piece work at a bob a puff rising bit by bit to a guinea a gasp and retiring through old age at thirty-two because of lace-curtain lungs, a football heart, and legs like varicose beanstalks. But I'd have a wife and car and get my grinning long-distance clock in the papers and have a smashing secretary to answer piles of letters sent by tarts who'd mob me when they saw who I was as I pushed my way into Woolworth's for a packet of razor blades and a cup of tea. It was something to think about all right, and sure enough the governor knew he'd got me when he said, turning to me as if I would at any rate have to be consulted about it all: "How does this matter strike you, then, Smith, my lad?"

A line of potbellied pop-eyes gleamed at me and a row of goldfish mouths opened and wiggled gold teeth at me, so I gave them the answer they wanted because I'd hold my trump card until later. "It'd suit me fine, sir," I said.

"Good lad. Good show. Right spirit. Splendid."

"Well," the governor said, "get that cup for us today and I'll do all I can for you. I'll get you trained so that you whack every man in the Free World." And I had a picture in my brain of me running and beating everybody in the world, leaving them all behind until only I was trot-trotting across a big wide moor alone, doing a marvelous speed as I ripped between boulders and reed-clumps, when suddenly: CRACK! CRACK!—bullets that can go faster than any man running, coming from a copper's rifle planted in a tree, winged me and split my gizzard in spite of my perfect running, and down I fell.

The potbellies expected me to say something else. "Thank you, sir," I said.

Told to go, I trotted down the pavilion steps, out onto the field because the big cross-country was about to begin and the two entries from Gunthorpe had fixed themselves early at the starting line and were ready to move off like white kangaroos. The sports ground looked a treat: with big tea-tents all round and flags flying and seats for families—empty because no mam or dad had known what opening day meant—and boys still running heats for the hundred yards, and lords and ladies walking from stall to stall, and the Borstal Boys Brass Band in blue uniforms; and up on the stands the brown jackets of Hucknall as well as our own grey blazers, and then the Gunthorpe lot with shirt sleeves rolled. The blue sky was full of sunshine and it couldn't have been a better day, and all of the big show was like something out of Ivanhoe that we'd seen on the pictures a few days before.

"Come on, Smith," Roach the sports master called to me, "we don't want you to be late for the big race, eh? Although I dare say that you'd catch them up if you were." The others cat-called and grunted at this, but I took no notice and placed myself between Gunthorpe and one of the Aylesham trusties, dropped on my knees and plucked a few grass blades to suck on the way round. So the big race it was, for them, watching from the grandstand under a fluttering Union Jack, a race for the governor, that he had been waiting for, and I hoped he and all the rest of his pop-eyed gang were busy placing big bets on me, hundred to one to win, all the money they had in their pockets, all the wages they were going to get for the next five years, and the more they placed the happier I'd be. Because here was a dead cert going to die on the big name they'd built for him, going to go down dying with laughter whether it choked him or not. My knees felt the cool soil pressing into them, and out of my eye's corner I saw Roach lift his hand. The Gunthorpe boy twitched before the signal was given; somebody cheered too soon; Medway bent forward; then the gun went, and I was away.

We went once around the field and then along a half-mile drive of elms, being cheered all the way, and I seemed to feel I was in the lead as we went out by the gate and into the lane, though I wasn't interested enough to find out. The five-mile course was marked by splashes of whitewash gleaming on gateposts and trunks and stiles and stones, and a boy with a waterbottle and bandage-box stood every half-mile waiting for those that dropped out or fainted. Over the first stile, without trying, I was still nearly in the lead but one; and if any of you want tips about running, never be in a hurry, and never let any of the other runners know you are in a hurry even if you are. You can always overtake on long-distance running without letting the others smell the hurry in you; and when you've used your craft like this to reach the two or three up front then you can do a big dash later that puts everybody else's hurry in the shade because you've not had to make haste up till then. I ran to a steady jog-trot rhythm, and soon it was so smooth that I forgot I was running, and I was hardly able to know that my legs were lifting and falling and my arms going in and out, and my lungs didn't seem to be working at all, and my heart stopped that wicked thumping I always get at the beginning of a run. Because you see I never race at all; I just run, and somehow I know that if I forget I'm racing and only jog-trot along until I don't know I'm running I always win the race. For when my eyes recognize that I'm getting near the end of the course—by seeing a stile or cottage corner —I put on a spurt, and such a fast big spurt it is because I feel that up till then I haven't been running and that I've used up no energy at all. And I've been able to do this because I've been thinking; and I wonder if I'm the only one in the running business with this system of forgetting that I'm running because I'm too busy thinking; and I wonder if any of the other lads are onto the same lark, though I know for a fact that they aren't. Off like the wind along the cobbled footpath and rutted lane, smoother than the flat grass track on the field and better for thinking because it's not too smooth, and I was in my element that afternoon knowing that nobody could beat me at running but intending to beat myself before the day was over. For when the governor talked to me of being honest when I first came in he didn't know what the word meant or he wouldn't have had me here in this race, trotting along in shimmy and shorts and sunshine. He'd have had me where I'd have had him if I'd been in his place: in a quarry breaking rocks until he broke his back. At least old Hitler-face the plain-clothes dick was honester than the governor, because he at any rate had had it in for me and I for him, and when my case was coming up in court a copper knocked at our front door at four o'clock in the morning and got my mother out of bed when she was paralytic tired, reminding her she had to be in court at dead on half past nine. It was the finest bit of spite I've ever heard of, but I would call it honest, the same as my mam's words were honest when she really told that copper what she thought of him and called him all the dirty names she'd ever heard of, which took her half an hour and woke the terrace up.

I trotted on along the edge of a field bordered by the sunken lane, smelling green grass and honeysuckle, and I felt as though I came from a long line of whippets trained to run on two legs, only I couldn't see a toy rabbit in front and there wasn't a collier's cosh behind to make me keep up the pace. I passed the Gunthorpe runner whose shimmy was already black with sweat and I could just see the corner of the fenced-up copse in front where the only man I had to pass to win the race was going all out to gain the half-way mark. Then he turned into a tongue of trees and bushes where I couldn't see him anymore, and I couldn't see anybody, and I knew what the loneliness of the long-distance runner running across country felt like, realizing that as far as I was concerned this feeling was the only honesty and realness there was in the world and I knowing it would be no different ever, no matter what I felt at odd times, and no matter what anybody else tried to tell me. The runner behind me must have been a long way off because it was so quiet, and there was even less noise and movement than there had been at five o'clock of a frosty winter morning. It was hard to understand, and all I knew was that you had to run, run, run, without knowing why you were running, but on you went through fields you didn't understand and into woods that made you afraid, over hills without knowing you'd been up and down, and shooting across streams that would have cut the heart out of you had you fallen into them. And the winning post was no end to it, even though crowds might be cheering you in, because on you had to go before you got your breath back, and the only time you stopped really was when you tripped over a tree trunk and broke your neck or fell into a disused well and stayed dead in the darkness forever. So I thought: they aren't going to get me on this racing lark, this running and trying to win, this jog-trotting for a bit of blue ribbon, because it's not the way to go on at all, though they swear blind that it is. You should think about nobody and go your own way, not on a course marked out for you by people holding mugs of water and bottles of iodine in case you fall and cut yourself so that they can pick you up—even if you want to stay where you are—and get you moving again.

On I went, out of the wood, passing the man leading without knowing I was going to do so. Flip-flap, flip-flap, jog-trot, jog-trot, crunchslap-crunchslap, across the middle of a broad field again, rhythmically running in my greyhound effortless fashion, knowing I had won the race though it wasn't half over, won it if I wanted it, could go on for ten or fifteen or twenty miles if I had to and drop dead at the finish of it, which would be the same, in the end, as living an honest life like the governor wanted me to. It amounted to: win the race and be honest, and on trot-trotting I went, having the time of my life, loving my progress because it did me good and set me thinking which by now I liked to do, but not caring at all when I remembered that I had to win this race as well as run it. One of the two, I had to win the race or run it, and I knew I could do both because my legs had carried me well in front—now coming to the short cut down the bramble bank and over the sunken road—and would carry me further because they seemed made of electric cable and easily alive to keep on slapping at those ruts and roots, but I'm not going to win because the only way I'd see I came in first would be if winning meant that I was going to escape the coppers after doing the biggest bank job of my life, but winning means the exact opposite, no matter how they try to kill or kid me, means running right into their white-gloved wall-barred hands and grinning mugs and staying there for the rest of my natural long life of stone-breaking anyway, but stone-breaking in the way I want to do it and not in the way they tell me.

Another honest thought that comes is that I could swing left at the next hedge of the field, and under its cover beat my slow retreat away from the sports ground winning post. I could do three or six or a dozen miles across the turf like this and cut a few main roads behind me so's they'd never know which one I'd taken; and maybe on the last one when it got dark I could thumb a lorry-lift and get a free ride north with somebody who might not give me away. But no, I said I wasn't daft didn't I? I won't pull out with only six months left, and besides there's nothing I want to dodge and run away from; I only want a bit of my own back on the In-laws and Potbellies by letting them sit up there on their big posh seats and watch me lose this race, though as sure as God made me I know that when I do lose I'll get the dirtiest crap and kitchen jobs in the months to go before my time is up. I won't be worth a threpp'ny-bit to anybody here, which will be all the thanks I get for being honest in the only way I know. For when the governor told me to be honest it was meant to be in his way not mine, and if I kept on being honest in the way he wanted and won my race for him he'd see I got the cushiest six months still left to run; but in my own way, well, it's not allowed, and if I find a way of doing it such as I've got now then I'll get what-for in every mean trick he can set his mind to. And if you look at it in my way, who can blame him? For this is war—and ain't I said so?—and when I hit him in the only place he knows he'll be sure to get his own back on me for not collaring that cup when his heart's been set for ages on seeing himself standing up at the end of the afternoon to clap me on the back as I take the cup from Lord Earwig or some such chinless wonder with a name like that. And so I'll hit him where it hurts a lot, and he'll do all he can to get his own back, tit for tat, though I'll enjoy it most because I'm hitting first, and because I planned it longer. I don't know why I think these thoughts are better than any I've ever had, but I do, and I don't care why. I suppose it took me a long time to get going on all this because I've had no time and peace in all my bandit life, and now my thoughts are coming pal and the only trouble is I often can't stop, even when my brain feels as if it's got cramp, frostbite and creeping paralysis all rolled into one and I have to give it a rest by slap-dashing down through the brambles of the sunken lane. And all this is another uppercut I'm getting in first at people like the governor, to show how—if I can—his races are never won even though some bloke always comes unknowingly in first, how in the end the governor is going to be doomed while blokes like me will take the pickings of his roasted bones and dance like maniacs around his Borstal's ruins. And so this story's like the race and once again I won't bring off a winner to suit the governor; no, I'm being honest like he told me to, without him knowing what he means, though I don't suppose he'll ever come in with a story of his own, even if he reads this one of mine and knows who I'm talking about.

I've just come up out of the sunken lane, kneed and elbowed, thumped and bramble-scratched, and the race is two-thirds over, and a voice is going like a wireless in my mind saying that when you've had enough of feeling good like the first man on earth of a frosty morning, and you've known how it is to be taken bad like the last man on earth on a summer's afternoon, then you get at last to being like the only man on earth and don't give a bogger about either good or bad, but just trot on with your slippers slapping the good dry soil that at least would never do you a bad turn. Now the words are like coming from a crystal-set that's broken down, and something's happening inside the shell-case of my guts that bothers me and I don't know why or what to blame it on, a grinding near my ticker as though a bag of rusty screws is loose inside me and I shake them up every time I trot forward. Now and again I break my rhythm to feel my left shoulderblade by swinging a right hand across my chest as if to rub the knife away that has somehow got stuck there. But I know it's nothing to bother about, that more likely it's caused by too much thinking that now and again I take for worry. For sometimes I'm the greatest worrier in the world I think (as you twigged I'll bet from me having got this story out) which is funny anyway because my mam don't know the meaning of the word so I don't take after her; though dad had a hard time of worry all his life up to when he filled his bedroom with hot blood and kicked the bucket that morning when nobody was in the house. I'll never forget it, straight I won't, because I was the one that found him and I often wished I hadn't. Back from a session on the fruit-machines at the fish-and-chip shop, jingling my three-lemon loot to a nail-dead house, as soon as I got in I knew something was wrong, stood leaning my head against the cold mirror above the mantelpiece trying not to open my eyes and see my stone-cold clock—because I knew I'd gone as white as a piece of chalk since coming in as if I'd been got at by a Dracula-vampire and even my penny-pocket winnings kept quite on purpose.

Gunthorpe nearly caught me up. Birds were singing from the briar hedge, and a couple of thrushies flew like lightning into some thorny bushes. Corn had grown high in the next field and would be cut down soon with scythes and mowers; but I never wanted to notice much while running in case it put me off my stroke, so by the haystack I decided to leave it all behind and put on such a spurt, in spite of nails in my guts, that before long I'd left both Gunthorpe and the birds a good way off; I wasn't far now from going into that last mile and a half like a knife through margarine, but the quietness I suddenly trotted into between two pickets was like opening my eyes underwater and looking at the pebbles on a stream bottom, reminding me again of going back that morning to the house in which my old man had croaked, which is funny because I hadn't thought about it at all since it happened and even then I didn't brood much on it. I wonder why? I suppose that since I started to think on these long-distance runs I'm liable to have anything crop up and pester at my tripes and innards, and now that I see my bloody dad behind each grassblade in my barmy runner-brain I'm not so sure I like to think and that it's such a good thing after all. I choke my phlegm and keep on running anyway and curse the Borstal-builders and their athletics—flappity-flap, slop-slop, crunchslap-crunchslap-crunchslap—who've maybe got their own back on me from the bright beginning by sliding magic-lantern slides into my head that never stood a chance before. Only if I take whatever comes like this in my runner's stride can I keep on keeping on like my old self and beat them back; and now I've thought on this far I know I'll win, in the crunchslap end. So anyway after a bit I went upstairs one step at a time not thinking anything about how I should find dad and what I'd do when I did. But now I'm making up for it by going over the rotten life mam led him ever since I can remember, knocking-on with different men even when he was alive and fit and she not caring whether he knew it or not, and most of the time he wasn't so blind as she thought and cursed and roared and threatened to punch her tab, and I had to stand up to stop him even though I knew she deserved it. What a life for all of us. Well, I'm not grumbling, because if I did I might just as well win this bleeding race, which I'm not going to do, though if I don't lose speed I'll win it before I know where I am, and then where would I be?

Now I can hear the sportsground noise and music as I head back for the flags and the lead-in drive, the fresh new feel of underfoot gravel going against the iron muscles of my legs. I'm nowhere near puffed despite that bag of nails that rattles as much as ever, and I can still give a big last leap like gale-force wind if I want to, but everything is under control and I know now that there ain't another long-distance cross-country running runner in England to touch my speed and style. Our doddering bastard of governor, our half-dead gangrened gaffer is hollow like an empty petrol drum, and he wants me and my running life to give him glory, to put in him blood and throbbing veins he never had, wants his potbellied pals to be his witnesses as I gasp and stagger up to his winning post so's he can say: "My Borstal gets that cup, you see. I win my bet, because it pays to be honest and try to gain the prizes I offer to my lads, and they know it, have known it all along. They'll always be honest now, because I made them so." And his pals will think: "He trains his lads to live right, after all; he deserves a medal but we'll get him made a Sir"—and at this very moment as the birds come back to whistling I can tell myself I'll never care a sod what any of the chinless spineless In-laws think or say. They've seen me and they're cheering now and loudspeakers set around the field like elephant's ears are spreading out the big news that I'm well in the lead, and can't do anything else but stay there. But I'm still thinking of the Out-law death my dad died, telling the doctors to scat from the house when they wanted him to finish up in hospital (like a bleeding guinea-pig, he raved at them). He got up in bed to throw them out and even followed them down the stairs in his shirt though he was no more than skin and stick. They tried to tell him he'd want some drugs but he didn't fall for it, and only took the painkiller that mam and I got from a herb-seller in the next street. It's not till now that I know what guts he had, and when I went into the room that morning he was lying on his stomach with the clothes thrown back, looking like a skinned rabbit, his grey head resting just on the edge of the bed, and on the floor must have been all the blood he'd had in his body, right from his toe-nails up, for nearly all of the lino and carpet was covered in it, thin and pink.

And down the drive I went, carrying a heart blocked up like Boulder Dam across my arteries, the nail-bag clamped down tighter and tighter as though in a woodwork vice, yet with my feet like birdwings and arms like talons ready to fly across the field except that I didn't want to give anybody that much of a show, or win the race by accident. I smell the hot dry day now as I run towards the end, passing a mountain-heap of grass emptied from cans hooked onto the fronts of lawnmowers pushed by my pals; I rip a piece of tree-bark with my fingers and stuff it in my mouth, chewing wood and dust and maybe maggots as I run until I'm nearly sick, yet swallowing what I can of it just the same because a little birdie whistled to me that I've got to go on living for at least a bloody sight longer yet but that for six months I'm not going to smell that grass or taste that dusty bark or trot this lovely path. I hate to have to say this but something bloody-well made me cry, and crying is a thing I haven't bloody-well done since I was a kid of two or three. Because I'm slowing down now for Gunthorpe to catch me up, and I'm doing it in a place just where the drive turns in to the sportsfield—where they can see what I'm doing, especially the governor and his gang from the grandstand, and I'm going so slow I'm almost marking time. Those on the nearest seats haven't caught on yet to what's happening and are still cheering like mad ready for when I make that mark, and I keep on wondering when the bleeding hell Gunthorpe behind me is going to nip by onto the field because I can't hold this up all day, and I think Oh Christ it's just my rotten luck that Gunthorpe's dropped out and that I'll be here for half an hour before the next bloke comes up, but even so, I say, I won't budge, I won't go for that last hundred yards if I have to sit down cross-legged on the grass and have the governor and his chinless wonders pick me up and carry me there, which is against their rules so you can bet they'd never do it because they're not clever enough to break the rules—like I would be in their place—even though they are their own. No, I'll show him what honesty means if it's the last thing I do, though I'm sure he'll never understand because if he and all them like him did it'd mean they'd be on my side which is impossible. By God I'll stick this out like my dad stuck out his pain and kicked them doctors down the stairs: if he had guts for that then I've got guts for this and here I stay waiting for Gunthorpe or Aylesham to bash that turf and go right slap-up against that bit of clothes-line stretched across the winning post. As for me, the only time I'll hit that clothes-line will be when I'm dead and a comfortable coffin's been got ready on the other side. Until then I'm a long-distance runner, crossing country all on my own no matter how bad it feels.

The Essex boys were shouting themselves blue in the face telling me to get a move on, waving their arms, standing up and making as if to run at that rope themselves because they were only a few yards to the side of it. You cranky lot, I thought, stuck at that winning post, and yet I knew they didn't mean what they were shouting, were really on my side and always would be, not able to keep their maulers to themselves, in and out of cop-shops and clink. And there they were now having the time of their lives letting themselves go in cheering me which made the governor think they were heart and soul on his side when he wouldn't have thought any such thing if he'd had a grain of sense. And I could hear the lords and ladies now from the grandstand, and could see them standing up to wave me in: "Run!" they were shouting in their posh voices. "Run!" But I was deaf, daft and blind, and stood where I was, still tasting the bark in my mouth and still blubbing like a baby, blubbing now out of gladness that I'd got them beat at last.

Because I heard a roar and saw the Gunthorpe gang throwing their coats up in the air and I felt the pat-pat of feet on the drive behind me getting closer and closer and suddenly a smell of sweat and a pair of lungs on their last gasp passed me by and went swinging on towards that rope, all shagged out and rocking from side to side, grunting like a Zulu that didn't know any better, like the ghost of me at ninety when I'm heading for that fat upholstered coffin. I could have cheered him myself: "Go on, go on, get cracking. Knot yourself up on that piece of tape." But he was already there, and so I went on, trot-trotting after him until I got to the rope, and collapsed, with a murderous sounding roar going up through my ears while I was still on the wrong side of it.

It's about time to stop; though don't think I'm not still running, because I am, one way or another. The governor at Borstal proved me right; he didn't respect my honesty at all; not that I expected him to, or tried to explain it to him, but if he's supposed to be educated then he should have more or less twigged it. He got his own back right enough, or thought he did, because he had me carting dustbins about every morning from the big full-working kitchen to the garden-bottoms where I had to empty them; and in the afternoon I spread out slops over spuds and carrots growing in the allotments. In the evenings I scrubbed floors, miles and miles of them. But it wasn't a bad life for six months, which was another thing he could never understand and would have made it grimmer if he could, and it was worth it when I look back on it, considering all the thinking I did, and the fact that the boys caught onto me losing the race on purpose and never had enough good words to say about me, or curses to throw out (to themselves) at the governor.

The work didn't break me; if anything it made me stronger in many ways, and the governor knew, when I left, that his spite had got him nowhere. For since leaving Borstal they tried to get me in the army, but I didn't pass the medical and I'll tell you why. No sooner was I out, after that final run and six-months hard, that I went down with pleurisy, which means as far as I'm concerned that I lost the governor's race all right, and won my own twice over, because I know for certain that if I hadn't raced my race I wouldn't have got this pleurisy, which keeps me out of khaki but doesn't stop me doing the sort of work my itchy fingers want to do.

I'm out now and the heat's switched on again, but the rats haven't got me for the last big thing I pulled. I counted six hundred and twenty-eight pounds and am still living off it because I did the job all on my own, and after it I had the peace to write all this, and it'll be money enough to keep me going until I finish my plans for doing an even bigger snatch, something up my sleeve I wouldn't tell to a living soul. I worked out my systems and hiding-places while pushing scrubbing-brushes around them Borstal floors, planned my outward life of innocence and honest work, yet at the same time grew perfect in the razor-edges of my craft for what I knew I had to do once free; and what I'll do again if netted by the poaching coppers.

In the meantime (as they say in one or two books I've read since, useless though because all of them ended on a winning post and didn't teach me a thing) I'm going to give this story to a pal of mine and tell him that if I do get captured again by the coppers he can try and get it put into a book or something, because I'd like to see the governor's face when he reads it, if he does, which I don't suppose he will; even if he did read it though I don't think he'd know what it was all about. And if I don't get caught the bloke I give this story to will never give me away; he's lived in our terrace for as long as I can remember, and he's my pal. That I do know.

The Unworthy Friend

Jorges Luis Borges

Our image of the city is always slightly out of date. Cafés have degenerated into barrooms; old arched entranceways with their grilled inner gates, once giving us a glimpse of patios and of overhanging grapevines, are now dingy corridors that lead abruptly to an elevator. For years, in this way, I thought that in a certain block of Talchuano Street I might still find the Buenos Aires Bookstore. But one morning I discovered its place had been taken by an antique shop, and I was told that don Santiago Fischbein, its owner, had died. Fischbein had been a heavyset, rather overweight man, whose features I now remember less than our long talks. In a quiet but firm way he had always been against Zionism, which he held would turn the Jew into a man like anyone else—tied down to a single tradition and a single homeland, and no longer enriched by strife and complexities. He'd been at work, he once told me, putting together a comprehensive anthology of the writings of Baruch Spinoza, freed of all that Euclidean apparatus, which, while lending to its strange system an illusory rigor, bogs the reader down. He would not sell me, but let me look at, a rare copy of Rosenroth's *Kabbala Denudata*. At home I still have a few books on the Kabbalah by Ginsburg and by Waite which bear the seal of Fischbein's shop.

From the book *Doctor Brodie's Report* by Jorge Luis Borges. Translated by Norman Thomas di Giovanni in collaboration with the author. Copyright © 1970, 1971, 1972 by Emece Editores, S. A., and Norman Thomas di Giovanni. Published by E. P. Dutton and Co., Inc. and used with their permission.

The Unworthy Friend

One afternoon, when the two of us were alone, he confided a story to me about his early life, and I feel I can now set it down. As may be expected, I will alter one or two details. Here is what Fischbein said.

I'm going to tell you something I've never told anyone before. Ana—my wife—doesn't know a word about this, nor do any of my closest friends. These things took place so many years ago now that I sometimes feel they might have happened to another person. Maybe you can make some use of this as a story—which, of course, you'll dress up with daggers. I wonder if I've already told you I was born in the Province of Entre Ríos. I can't say we were Jewish gauchos—there never were any Jewish gauchos. We were shopkeepers and farmers. Anyway, I was born in Urdinarrain, a town I can hardly remember anymore. I was very young when my parents moved to Buenos Aires to open up a shop. A few blocks away from where we lived was the Maldonado, and beyond that ditch were open lots.

Carlyle says that men need heroes to worship. Argentine schoolbooks tried getting me to worship San Martín, but in him I found little more than a soldier who'd fought his battles in other countries and who's now only a bronze statue and the name of a square. Chance, however—unfortunately enough for the two of us—provided me with another kind of hero. This is probably the first time you've ever heard of him. His name was Francisco Ferrari.

Our neighborhood may not have been as tough as the Stockyards or the waterfront, but it had its share of hoodlums who hung out in the old saloons. Ferrari's particular hangout was a place at the corner of Triunvirato and Thames. It was there the thing happened that brought me under his spell. I'd been sent around to the saloon to buy a small package of maté, when in walked a stranger with long hair and a moustache, and ordered a shot of gin. Ferrari said to him, mildly, "By the way, didn't we see each other night before last dancing at Juliana's? Where are you from?"

"From San Cristóbal," the other man said.

"My advice," Ferrari said, still gently, "is that you might find it healthier to keep away from here. This neighborhood's full of people on the lookout for trouble."

On the spot, the man from San Cristóbal turned tail—moustache and all. Maybe he was just as much a man as Ferrari was, but he knew others of the gang were around.

From that afternoon on, Francisco Ferrari was the hero my fifteen years were in search of. He was dark and stood straight and tall—good-looking in the style of the day. He always wore black. One day, a second episode brought us together. I was on the street with my mother and aunt, when we ran into a bunch of young toughs and one of them said loudly to the others:

"Old stuff. Let them by."

I didn't know what to do. At that moment, Ferrari stepped in. He had just left his house. He looked the ringleader straight in the eye and said, "If you're out for fun, why not try having some with me?"

He kept staring them up and down, one after the other, and there wasn't a word out of any of them. They knew all about him. Ferrari shrugged his shoulders, tipped his hat, and went on his way. But before starting off, he said to me, "If you have nothing else to do, drop in at the saloon later on."

I was tongue-tied. "There's a gentleman who demands respect for ladies," my Aunt Sarah pronounced.

Coming to my rescue, my mother said, "I'd say more a hoodlum who wants no competition."

I don't really know how to explain this now. I've worked my way up, I own this shop—which I love—and I know my books; I enjoy friendships like ours, I have my wife and children, I belong to the Socialist Party, I'm a good Argentine and a good Jew. People look up to me. As you can see, I'm almost bald; in those days I was just a poor redheaded Jew-boy, living in a down-and-out neighborhood. Like all young men, of course, I tried hard to be the same as everyone else. Still, I was sneered at. To shake off the Jacob, I called myself Santiago, but just the same there was the Fischbein. We all begin taking on the idea others have of us. Feeling people despised me, I despised myself as well. At that time, and above all in that neighborhood, you had to be tough. I knew I was a coward. Women scared the daylights out of me, I was deeply ashamed of my inexperience with them, and I had no friends my own age.

That night I didn't go around to the saloon. How I wish I never had! But the feeling grew on me that Ferrari's invitation was something of an order, so the next Saturday, after dinner, I finally walked into the place.

Ferrari sat at the head of one of the tables. I knew all the other men by sight. There were six or seven of them. Ferrari was the eldest, except for an old man who spoke little and wearily and whose name is the only one I have not forgotten—don Eliseo Amaro. The mark of a slash crossed his broad, flabby face. I found out afterward he'd spent some time in jail.

Ferrari sat me down at his left, making don Eliseo change places for me. I felt a bit uneasy, afraid Ferrari would mention what had happened on the street a few days before. But nothing of the kind took place. They talked of women, cards, elections, of a street singer who was about to show up but never did, of neighborhood affairs. At first, they seemed unwilling to accept me, then later—because it was what Ferrari wanted—they loosened up. In spite of their names, which for the most part were

Italian, every one of them thought of himself (and thought of each other) as Argentine and even gaucho. Some of them owned or drove teams or were butchers at the slaughter yards, and having to deal with animals made them a lot like farm hands. My suspicion is that their one desire was to have played the outlaw Juan Moreira. They ended up calling me the Sheeny, but they didn't mean it in a bad way. It was from them that I learned to smoke and do other things.

In a brothel on Junín Street, somebody asked me whether I wasn't a friend of Francisco Ferrari's. I told him I wasn't, feeling that to have answered yes would have been bragging.

One night the police came into the saloon and frisked us. Two of the gang were taken into custody, but Ferrari was left alone. A couple of weeks later the same thing happened all over again; this second time they rounded up Ferrari, too. Under his belt he was carrying a knife. What happened was that he must have had a falling out with the political boss of our ward.

As I look back on Ferrari today, I see him as an unlucky young man who was filled with illusions and in the end was betrayed; but at the time, to me he was a god.

Friendship is no less a mystery than love or any other aspect of this confusion we call life. There have been times when I've felt the only thing without mystery is happiness, because happiness is an end in itself. The plain fact is that, for all his brass, Francisco Ferrari, the tough guy, wanted to be friends with someone as pitiful as me. I was sure he'd made a mistake, I was sure I was unworthy of his friendship, and I did my best to keep clear of him. But he wouldn't let me. My anxiety over this was made even worse by my mother's disapproval. She just couldn't get used to the company I kept and went around aping, and referred to them as trash and scum. The point of what I'm telling you is my relationship with Ferrari, not the sordid facts, which I no longer feel sorry about. As long as any trace of remorse remains, guilt remains.

One night, the old man, who had again taken up his usual place beside Ferrari, was whispering back and forth in Ferrari's ear. They were up to something. From the other end of the table, I thought I made out the name of Weidemann, a man who owned a textile mill out on the edge of the neighborhood. Soon after, without any explanation, I was told to take a stroll around Weidemann's factory and to have a good look at the gates. It was beginning to get dark when I crossed the Maldonado and cut through the freight yards. I remember the houses, which grew fewer and farther between a clump of willows, and the empty lots. Weidemann's was new, but it was lonely and somehow looked like a ruin; in my memory, its red brick gets mixed up with the sunset. The mill was surrounded by a tall fence. In addition to the front entrance, there were two big doors out back opening into the south side of the building.

I have to admit it took me some time to figure out what you've probably guessed already. I brought back my report, which was confirmed by one of the others, who had a sister working in the place. Then the plan was laid out. For the gang not to have shown up at the saloon on a Saturday night would have attracted attention, so Ferrari set the robbery for the following Friday. I was the one they picked for lookout. Meanwhile, it was best that we shouldn't be seen together. When we were alone in the street —just Ferrari and myself—I asked him, "Are you sure you can trust me?"

"Yes," he answered. "I know you'll handle yourself like a man."

That night and the following nights I slept well. Then, on Wednesday, I told my mother I was going downtown to see a new cowboy picture. I put on my best clothes and started out for Moreno Street. The trip on the streetcar was a long one. At police headquarters I was kept waiting, but finally one of the desk sergeants—a certain Eald or Alt—saw me. I told him I'd come about a confidential matter and he said I could speak without fear. I let him in one the gang's plan. What surprised me was that Ferrari's name meant nothing to him; but it was something else again when I mentioned don Eliseo.

"Ah," he said. "He used to be one of the old Móntevideo gang."

He called in another man, who came from my part of town, and the two of them talked things over. The second officer asked me, with a certain scorn in his voice, "Have you come here with this information because you think of yourself as a good citizen?"

I knew he would never understand, but I answered, "Yes, sir. I'm a good Argentine."

They told me to go through with my job exactly as Ferrari had ordered, but not to whistle when I saw the police arrive. As I was leaving, one of them warned me:

"Better be careful. You know what happens to stoolies."

Policemen are just like kids when it comes to using slang. I answered him, "I wish they would lay their hands on me—maybe that's the best thing that could happen."

From early in the morning that Friday, I had the feeling of relief that the day had come, and at the same time I felt the guilt of not feeling guilty. The hours seemed to drag. All day I barely ate a mouthful. At ten that night we met a couple of blocks away from the factory. When one of the gang didn't show up, don Eliseo remarked that someone always turned yellow. I knew when it was over he'd be the one they'd blame.

It looked like it was about to pour. At first, I was scared someone else would be named to stand watch with me, but when it came time I was left alone near one of the back doors. After a while, the police, together with a superior officer, put in their appearance. They came on foot, having left their horses some distance off. Ferrari had forced one of the two doors and the police were able to slip in without a sound. Then four shots rang out, deafening me. I imagined that there on the inside, in all that dark, they were slaughtering each other. At that point the police led a few of the men out in handcuffs. Then two more policemen came out, dragging the bodies of Francisco Ferrari and don Eliseo Amaro. In the official report it was stated that they had resisted arrest and had been the first to open fire. I knew the whole thing was a lie because I'd never once seen any of the gang carrying guns. They'd just been shot down; the police had used the occasion to settle an old score. A few days later, I heard that Ferrari had tried to escape but had been stopped by a single bullet. As was to be expected, the newspapers made the hero of him he had never been except maybe in my eyes.

As for me, they rounded me up with the others and a short time later set me free.

The Gardener

Rudyard Kipling

Every one in the village knew that Helen Turrell did her duty by all her world, and by none more honourably than by her only brother's unfortunate child. The village knew, too, that George Turrell had tried his family severely since early youth, and were not surprised to be told that, after many fresh starts given and thrown away, he, an Inspector of Indian Police, had entangled himself with the daughter of a retired noncommissioned officer, and had died of a fall from a horse a few weeks before his child was born. Mercifully, George's father and mother were both dead, and though Helen, thirty-five and independent, might well have washed her hands of the whole disgraceful affair, she most nobly took charge, though she was, at the time, under threat of lung trouble which had driven her to the South of France. She arranged for the passage of the child and a nurse from Bombay, met them at Marseilles, nursed the baby through an attack of infantile dysentery due to the carelessness of the nurse, whom she had had to dismiss, and at last, thin and worn but triumphant, brought the boy late in the autumn, wholly restored, to her Hampshire home.

All these details were public property, for Helen was as open as the day, and held that scandals are only increased by hushing them up. She admitted that George had always been rather a black sheep, but things might have been much worse if the mother had insisted on her right to keep the

"The Gardener" from the book *Debits and Credits* by Rudyard Kipling. Copyright © 1926 by Rudyard Kipling. Reprinted by permission of Doubleday and Company, Inc.

boy. Luckily, it seemed that people of that class would do almost anything for money, and, as George had always turned to her in his scrapes, she felt herself justified—her friends agreed with her—in cutting the whole noncommissioned officer connection, and giving the child every advantage. A christening, by the Rector, under the name of Michael, was the first step. So far as she knew herself, she was not, she said, a child-lover, but, for all his faults, she had been very fond of George, and she pointed out that little Michael had his father's mouth to a line; which made something to build upon.

As a matter of fact, it was the Turrell forehead, broad, low, and well-shaped, with the widely-spaced eyes beneath it, that Michael had most faithfully reproduced. His mouth was somewhat better cut than the family type. But Helen, who would concede nothing good to his mother's side, vowed he was a Turrell all over, and, there being no one to contradict, the likeness was established.

In a few years Michael took his place, as accepted as Helen had always been—fearless, philosophical, and fairly good-looking. At six, he wished to know why he could not call her "Mummy," as other boys called their mothers. She explained that she was only his auntie, and that aunties were not quite the same as mummies, but that, if it gave him pleasure, he might call her "Mummy" at bedtime, for a pet-name between themselves.

Michael kept his secret most loyally, but Helen, as usual, explained the fact to her friends; which when Michael heard, he raged.

"Why did you tell? *Why* did you tell?" came at the end of the storm.

"Because it's always best to tell the truth," Helen answered, her arm around him as he shook in his cot.

"All right, but when the troof's ugly I don't think it's nice."

"Don't you, dear?"

"No, I don't, and"—she felt the small body stiffen—"now you've told, I won't call you 'Mummy' any more—not even at bedtimes."

"But isn't that rather unkind?" said Helen, softly.

"I don't care! I don't care! You've hurted me in my insides and I'll hurt you back. I'll hurt you as long as I live!"

"Don't, oh, don't talk like that, dear! You don't know what—"

"I will! And when I'm dead I'll hurt you worse!"

"Thank goodness, I shall be dead long before you, darling."

"Huh! Emma says, 'Never know your luck.' " (Michael had been talking to Helen's elderly, flat-faced maid.) "Lots of little boys die quite soon. So'll I. *Then* you'll see!"

Helen caught her breath and moved towards the door, but the wail of "Mummy! Mummy!" drew her back again, and the two wept together.

At ten years old, after two terms at a prep school, something or somebody gave him the idea that his civil status was not quite regular. He attacked Helen on the subject, breaking down her stammered defences with the family directness.

"Don't believe a word of it," he said, cheerily, at the end. "People wouldn't have talked like they did if my people had been married. But don't you bother, Auntie. I've found out all about my sort in English Hist'ry and the Shakespeare bits. There was William the Conqueror to begin with, and—oh, heaps more, and they all got on first-rate. 'Twon't make any difference to you, my being *that*—will it?"

"As if anything could—" she began.

"All right. We won't talk about it any more if it makes you cry." he never mentioned the thing again of his own will, but when, two years later, he skilfully managed to have measles in the holidays, as his temperature went up to the appointed one hundred and four he muttered of nothing else, till Helen's voice, piercing at last his delirium, reached him with assurance that nothing on earth or beyond could make any difference between them.

The terms at his public school and the wonderful Christmas, Easter, and summer holidays followed each other, variegated and glorious as jewels on a string; and as jewels Helen treasured them. In due time Michael developed his own interests, which ran their courses and gave way to others; but his interest in Helen was constant and increasing throughout. She repaid it with all that she had of affection or could command of counsel and money; and since Michael was no fool, the war took him just before what was like to have been a most promising career.

He was to have gone up to Oxford, with a scholarship, in October. At the end of August he was on the edge of joining the first holocaust of public-school boys who threw themselves into the Line; but the captain of his O.T.C., where he had been sergeant for nearly a year, headed him off and steered him directly to a commission in a battalion so new that half of it still wore the old Army red, and the other half was breeding meningitis through living overcrowdedly in damp tents. Helen had been shocked at the idea of direct enlistment.

"But it's in the family," Michael laughed.

"You don't mean to tell me that you believed that old story all this time?" said Helen. (Emma, her maid, had been dead now several years.) "I gave you my word of honour—and I give it again—that—that it's all right. It is indeed."

"Oh, *that* doesn't worry me. It never did," he replied valiantly. "What I meant was, I should have got into the show earlier if I'd enlisted—like my grandfather."

"Don't talk like that! Are you afraid of its ending so soon, then?"

"No such luck. You know what K. says."

The Gardener

"Yes. But my banker told me last Monday it couldn't *possibly* last beyond Christmas—for financial reasons."

" 'Hope he's right, but our Colonel—and he's a Regular—says it's going to be a long job."

Michael's battalion was fortunate in that, by some chance which meant several "leaves," it was used for coast-defence among shallow trenches on the Norfolk coast; thence sent north to watch the mouth of a Scotch estuary, and, lastly, held for weeks on a baseless rumour of distant service. But, the very day that Michael was to have met Helen for four whole hours at a railway-junction up the line, it was hurled out, to help make good the wastage of Loos, and he had only just time to send her a wire of farewell.

In France luck again helped the battalion. It was put down near the Salient, where it led a meritorious and unexacting life, while the Somme was being manufactured; and enjoyed the peace of the Armentières and Laventie sectors when that battle began. Finding that it had sound views on protecting its own flanks and could dig, a prudent Commander stole it out of its own Division, under pretence of helping to lay telegraphs, and use it round Ypres at large.

A month later, and just after Michael had written Helen that there was nothing special doing and therefore no need to worry, a shell-splinter dropping out of a wet dawn killed him at once. The next shell uprooted and laid down over the body what had been the foundation of a barn wall, so neatly that none but an expert would have guessed that anything unpleasant had happened.

By this time the village was old in experience of war, and, English fashion, had evolved a ritual to meet it. When the postmistress handed her seven-year-old daughter the official telegram to take to Miss Turrell, she observed to the Rector's gardener: "It's Miss Helen's turn now." he replied, thinking of his own son: "Well, he's lasted longer than some." The child herself came to the front-door weeping aloud, because Master Michael had often given her sweets. Helen, presently, found herself pulling down the house-blinds one after one with great care, and saying earnestly to each: "Missing *always* means dead." Then she took her place in the dreary procession that was impelled to go through an inevitable series of unprofitable emotions. The Rector, of course, preached hope and prophesied word, very soon, from a prison camp. Several friends, too, told her perfectly truthful tales, but always about other women, to whom, after months and months of silence, their missing had been miraculously restored. Other people urged her to communicate with infallible Secretaries of organisations who could communicate with benevolent neutrals, who could extract accurate information from the most secretive of Hun prison commandants. Helen did and wrote and signed everything that was suggested or put before her.

Once, on one of Michael's leaves, he had taken her over a munition factory, where she saw the progress of a shell from blank-iron to the all but finished article. It struck her at the time that the wretched thing was never left alone for a single second; and "I'm being manufactured into a bereaved next-of-kin," she told herself, as she prepared her documents.

In due course, when all the organisations had deeply or sincerely regretted their inability to trace, etc., something gave way within her and all sensation—save of thankfulness for the release—came to an end in blessed passivity. Michael had died and her world had stood still and she had been one with the full shock of that arrest. Now she was standing still and the world was going forward, but it did not concern her—in no way or relation did it touch her. She knew this by the ease with which she could slip Michael's name into talk and incline her head to the proper angle, at the proper murmur of sympathy.

In the blessed realisation of that relief, the Armistice with all its bells broke over her and passed unheeded. At the end of another year she had overcome her physical loathing of the living and returned young, so that she could take them by the hand and almost sincerely wish them well. She had no interest in any aftermath, national or personal, of the War, but, moving at an immense distance, she sat on various relief committees and held strong views—she heard herself delivering them—about the site of the proposed village War Memorial.

Then there came to her, as next of kin, an official intimation, backed by a page of a letter to her in indelible pencil, a silver identity-disc, and a watch, to the effect that the body of Lieutenant Michael Turrell had been found, identified, and re-interred in Hagenzeele Third Military Cemetery—the letter of the row and the grave's number in that row duly given.

So Helen found herself moved on to another process of the manufacture—to a world full of exultant or broken relatives, now strong in the certainty that there was an altar upon earth where they might lay their love. These soon told her, and by means of time-tables made clear, how easy it was and how little it interfered with life's affairs to go and see one's grave.

"*So* different," as the Rector's wife said, "if he'd been killed in Mesopotamia, or even Gallipoli."

The agony of being waked up to some sort of second life drove Helen across the Channel, where, in a new world of abbreviated titles, she learnt that Hagenzeele Third could be comfortably reached by an afternoon train which fitted in with the morning boat, and that there was a comfortable little hotel not three kilometers from Hagenzeele itself, where one could spend quite a comfortable night and see one's grave next morning. All this she had from a Central Authority who lived in a board and tarpaper shed on the skirts of a razed city full of whirling lime-dust and blown papers.

"By the way," said he, "you know your grave, of course?"

"Yes, thank you," said Helen, and showed its row and number typed on Michael's own little typewriter. The officer would have checked it, out of one of his many books; but a large Lancashire woman thrust between them and bade him tell her where she might find her son, who had been corporal in the A.S.C. His proper name, she sobbed, was Anderson, but, coming of respectable folk, he had of course enlisted under the name of Smith; and had been killed at Dickiebush, in early 'Fifteen. She had not his number nor did she know which of his two Christian names he might have used with his alias; but her Cook's tourist ticket expired at the end of Easter week, and if by then she could not find her child she should go mad. Whereupon she fell forward on Helen's breast; but the officer's wife came out quickly from a little bedroom behind the office, and the three of them lifted the woman on to the cot.

"They are often like this," said the officer's wife, loosening the right bonnet-strings. "Yesterday she said he'd been killed at Hooge. Are you sure you know your grave? It makes such a difference."

"Yes, thank you," said Helen, and hurried out before the woman on the bed should begin to lament again.

Tea in a crowded mauve and blue striped wooden structure, with a false front, carried her still further into the nightmare. She paid her bill beside a stolid, plain-featured Englishwoman, who, hearing her inquire about the train to Hagenzeele, volunteered to come with her.

"I'm going to Hagenzeele myself," she explained. "Not to Hagenzeele Third; mine is Sugar Factory, but they call it La Rosière now. It's just south of Hagenzeele Three. Have you got your room at the hotel there?"

"Oh yes, thank you. I've wired."

"That's better. Sometimes the place is quite full, and at others there's hardly a soul. But they've put bathrooms into the old Lion d'Or—that's the hotel on the west side of Sugar Factory—and it draws off a lot of people, luckily."

"It's all new to me. This is the first time I've been over."

"Indeed! This is my ninth time since the Armistice. Not on my own account. *I* haven't lost any one, thank God—but, like every one else, I've a lot of friends at home who have. Coming over as often as I do, I find it helps them to have some one just look at the—the place and tell them about it afterwards. And one can take photos for them, too. I get quite a list of commissions to execute." She laughed nervously and tapped her slung Kodak. "There are two or three to see at Sugar Factory this time, and plenty of others in the cemeteries all about. My system is to save them up, and arrange them, you know. And when I've got enough commissions for one area to make it worth while, I pop over and execute them. It *does* comfort people."

"I suppose so," Helen answered, shivering as they entered the little train.

"Of course it does. (Isn't it lucky we've got window-seats?) It must do or they wouldn't ask one to do it, would they? I've a list of quite twelve or fifteen commissions here"—she tapped the Kodak again—"I must sort them out to-night. Oh, I forgot to ask you. What's yours?"

"My nephew," said Helen. "But I was very fond of him."

"Ah yes! I sometimes wonder whether *they* know after death? What do you think?"

"Oh, I don't—I haven't dared to think much about that sort of thing," said Helen, almost lifting her hands to keep her off.

"Perhaps that's better," the woman answered. "The sense of loss must be enough, I expect. Well, I won't worry you any more."

Helen was grateful, but when they reached the hotel Mrs. Scarsworth (they had exchanged names) insisted on dining at the same table with her, and after the meal, in the little, hideous salon full of low-voiced relatives, took Helen through her "commissions" with biographies of the dead, where she happened to know them, and sketches of their next of kin. Helen endured till nearly half-past nine, ere she fled to her room.

Almost at once there was a knock at her door and Mrs. Scarsworth entered; her hands, holding the dreadful list, clasped before her.

"Yes—yes—*I* know," she began. "You're sick of me, but I want to tell you something. You—you aren't married are you? Then perhaps you won't.... But it doesn't matter. I've *got* to tell some one. I can't go on any longer like this."

"But please—" Mrs. Scarsworth had backed against the shut door, and her mouth worked dryly.

"In a minute," she said. "You—you know about these graves of mine I was telling you about downstars, just now? They really *are* commissions. At least several of them are." Her eyes wandered round the room. "What extraordinary wall-papers they have in Belgium, don't you think? ... Yes. I swear they are commissions. But there's *one,* d'you see, and—and he was more to me than anything else in the world. Do you understand?"

Helen nodded.

"More than any one else. And, of course, he oughtn't to have been. He ought to have been nothing to me. But he *was*. He *is*. That's why I do the commissions, you see. That's all."

"But why do you tell me?" Helen asked desperately.

"Because I'm *so* tired of lying. Tired of lying—always lying—year in and year out. When I don't tell lies I've got to act 'em and I've got to think 'em always. *You* don't know what that means. He was everything to me that he oughtn't to have been—the one real thing—the only thing that ever happened to me in all my life; and I've had to pretend he wasn't. I've had to watch every word I said, and think out what lie I'd tell next, for years and years!"

"How many years?" Helen asked.

"Six years and four months before, and two and three-quarters after. I've gone to him eight times, since. To-morrow'll make the ninth, and—and I can't—I *can't* go to him again with nobody in the world knowing. I want to be honest with some one before I go. Do you understand? It doesn't matter about *me*. I was never truthful, even as a girl. But it isn't worthy of *him*. So—so I—I had to tell you. I can't keep it up any longer. Oh, I can't!"

She lifted her joined hands almost to the level of her mouth, and brought them down sharply, still joined, to full arms' length below her waist. Helen reached forward, caught them, bowed her head over them, and murmured: "Oh, my dear! My dear!" Mrs. Scarsworth stepped back, her face all mottled.

"My God!" said she. "Is *that* how you take it?"

Helen could not speak, the woman went out; but it was a long while before Helen was able to sleep.

Next morning, Mrs. Scarsworth left early on her round of commissions, and Helen walked alone to Hagenzeele Third. The place was still in the making, and stood some five or six feet above the metalled road, which it flanked for hundreds of yards. Culverts across a deep ditch served for entrances through the unfinished boundary wall. She climbed a few wooden-faced earthen steps and then met the entire crowded level of the thing in one held breath. She did not know that Hagenzeele Third counted twenty-one thousand dead already. All she saw was a merciless sea of black crosses, bearing little strips of stamped tin at all angles across their faces. She could distinguish no order or arrangement in their mass; nothing but a waist-high wilderness as of weeds stricken dead, rushing at her. She went forward, moved to the left and the right hopelessly, wondering by what guidance she should ever come to her own. A great distance away there was a line of whiteness. It proved to be a block of some two or three hundred graves whose headstones had already been set, whose flowers were planted out, and whose new-sown grass showed green. Here she could see clear-cut letters at the ends of the rows, and, referring to her slip, realised that it was not here she must look.

A man knelt behind a line of headstones—evidently a gardener, for he was firming a young plant in the soft earth. She went towards him, her paper in her hand. He rose at her approach and without prelude or salutation asked: "Who are you looking for?"

"Lieutenant Michael Turrell—my nephew," said Helen slowly and word for word, as she had many thousands of times in her life.

The man lifted his eyes and looked at her with infinite compassion before he turned from the fresh-sown grass towards the naked black crosses.

"Come with me," he said, "and I will show you where your son lies."

When Helen left the Cemetery she turned for a last look. In the distance she saw the man bending over his young plants; and she went away, supposing him to be the gardener.

Glossary of Terms

ACTION What happens in the story. In the *Poetics* Aristotle says that any literary form that tells a story involves the imitation of human action (*praxis*). The term action may be most useful for pointing to the general movement of the story before the writer has superimposed all the refinements of PLOT.

ALLEGORY A literary work in which the characters and events stand for a set of ideas or moral qualities or abstractions. Allegorical stories are seldom concerned with realistic plots or complex characterization, but with illustrating doctrines or theses.

ALLUSION A reference in a story, poem, or play to a generally well-known person, place, event, or situation outside the literary work. Allusions to memorable, influential ideas and people of the past expand and enrich the meaning of the work. The main sources of literary allusions are history, literature, the Bible, and mythology.

ANTAGONIST The character in opposition to the **PROTAGONIST** or central character. *Agon,* as in ant*agon*ist and prot*agon*ist, is a Greek word meaning "public performance" or "contest."

ATMOSPHERE The mood of a story; the general feeling created by all the details of plot, character, setting, and diction. Atmosphere sets up expectations in the reader as to whether the story will end happily, sadly, or frighteningly. A horror story depends for much of its effect on the creation of a "spooky," eerie atmosphere. Atmosphere should be distinguished from **TONE,** which refers to the author's attitude toward his subject and toward his audience.

CHARACTER A person in a story. Character also denotes the beliefs, habits of mind, moral choices, and **MOTIVATION** which distinguish one fictional person from another. For a fuller discussion, see the chapter entitled "CHARACTER."

CONFLICT In a story or drama, an encounter between opposing forces which creates interest and suspense in the reader or viewer. The simplest conflict to recognize—and one frequently used—is between the "good guy" and the "bad guy." In addition to conflict between characters, there may be conflict between characters and their environment or circumstances; and a character may be at war with himself, feeling an internal struggle between conflicting ideas, thoughts, or feelings.

CONNOTATION The cluster of meanings implied or suggested by a word, as distinguished from its literal or denotative meaning. The connotations of a word often carry powerful emotional charges. The word "snake" has a literal meaning; however, as Stephen Crane demonstrates in his story "The Snake," the word also connotes fear, danger, hatred, enemy, evil. Crane's story can be seen as an illustration of the connotations associated with "snake." See **DENOTATION.**

435

DENOTATION The literal, dictionary meaning of a word. Scientific writing depends for much of its precision on careful use of the denotative meaning of words. Imaginative literature depends for much of its emotional and aesthetic effectiveness on the connotative meaning of words. The word "brother" literally means "male sibling," but it may connote love and friendship for one person, hate and envy for another. See **CONNOTATION.**

DENOUEMENT A French word denoting an "untying"; that part of the plot in which conflicts are finally resolved.

DICTION The words used by an author; his vocabulary in a particular story. In "The Facts in the Case of M. Valdemar" Poe uses a great many technical, medical words; his diction is also Latinate and formal.

DIDACTIC Designed to teach or instruct the reader. Parables, fables, and allegories are didactic; their "moral" themes determine the characters and the plots. **PROPAGANDA** is a kind of didactic work which seeks to convince the reader to take action; propaganda may oversimplify characters and events in order to make its message clear. There is a strong propagandistic impulse in Michael Thelwell's story "The Organizer." Thelwell wants his reader to despise the bigotry and immorality of Southern white people, so he makes all of them "bad," while making all the Black characters generous, kind, loving.

EPISODE One incident in a longer story containing several incidents.

EPISODIC A literary term used to describe a work in which the connections between one episode and the next are weak and loose instead of controlled or artfully arranged to form a constructed plot.

EXPOSITION That information about characters and events necessary for the reader to understand the developing action.

FABLE A simple story or tale designed to illustrate some maxim about human nature, often by having animals talk and act like human beings.

FIGURATIVE LANGUAGE Language which uses figures of speech to create special effects and to extend its meanings beyond its mere denotation. The two most common figures of speech are **SIMILE** and **METAPHOR.** Simile is a comparison between two things, using the words *"like"* or *"as"* to link the two: "The tornado, like a huge top, spun recklessly through the town." Metaphor shows an identification between two things, not a comparison: "The huge top spun recklessly through the town." When figures of speech are fresh and lively, they create vivid pictorial effects and suggest analogies or comparisons which show that seemingly unlike things have similarities.

FLASHBACK A passage in a story which breaks the chronological sequence by presenting an event or episode that happened earlier.

FOIL Usually a minor character whom the story writer contrasts with a major character (most often the protagonist), thus "setting off" qualities of personality, and clarifying the story's theme. In Joyce's "A Little Cloud," for example,

Glossary of Terms

Gallaher is a foil to Little Chandler; Gallaher's presence heightens Chandler's sense of failure and desperation.

FORESHADOWING Clues or hints that prepare the reader for some future event or action. See the discussion of Hardy's "The Three Strangers," for an illustration of how one writer uses foreshadowing to achieve his desired effects.

GENRE A French word used to refer to a literary species or form such as tragedy, comedy, epic, lyric, novel, or short story.

IMAGE An aspect of **DICTION** whereby words and phrases suggest concrete, physical, or descriptive details such as sounds, odors, colors and tactile sensations. Language which presents a sense experience.

IMAGERY A pattern of figurative language which supports and expands the theme of a literary work. In "The Snake" Stephen Crane compares the meeting of man and reptile, two natural enemies, to war:

> And so he cried his cry, an incredibly swift jangle of tiny bells, as burdened with pathos as the hammering upon quaint cymbals by the *Chinese at war*. . . .
>
> This was *another detail of a war* that had begun evidently when first there were men and snakes.
>
> This *attack* . . . was despairing, but it was nevertheless impetuous, gallant, ferocious, of the same quality as the *charge of the lone chief* when the walls of white faces close in upon him in the mountains.
>
> The last muscular quivers of the snake were causing the rattles to still sound their treble cry, the shrill, *ringing war chant* and hymn of the grave of the thing that faces foes. . . . [Emphasis added.]

This war imagery invests the death encounter with more significance than the mere killing of a snake would ordinarily have.

INTERIOR MONOLOGUE The artistic rendering of thoughts, fragments of thought, and interruptions, just as they occur in the mind of a character. For the purposes of the nonspecialist, interior monologue may be considered very much like stream of consciousness.

IRONY A term referring to contrasts or discrepancies between what seems to be and what actually is, between what is said and what is meant, between expectations and outcomes. Most people are familiar with "verbal irony," used by a speaker who deliberately says one thing but means something else. "Situation irony" points to a situation in which expectation is not fulfilled in the apparently fitting way. "Dramatic irony" refers to a situation in a story or drama in which there are ramifications to what a character or narrator says and does that are not apparent to that character or narrator. The reader or audience knows, however, at least at the conclusion of the work. (See Kipling's "The Gardener" for many sentences which take on added ironic significance in the light of what one knows at the end of the story.)

MOTIVATION The reason a character has for doing what he does. One might well discuss whether Hawthorne's character, Wakefield, was motivated toward his strange escape by the tedium of his daily existence, or whether he was simply mad.

NARRATIVE TECHNIQUE
Methods of presenting a story. Theorists of modern fiction suggest that there are two basic techniques for presenting a story—through **NARRATIVE SUMMARY** or through **SCENE**. Narrative summary *tells* the reader *what happened* and is a kind of reporting; scene, like drama, *shows* the reader *what is happening* through dialogue and action. Summary allows the writer to roam freely over his material, to probe deeply into the mind and feelings of his characters, to condense large chunks of time and action, to analyze and even judge motivations and actions. The chief advantages of the scenic method are its sense of immediacy and objectivity. No narrator stands between the reader and the situation; thus the reader seems close to the action, as if he were experiencing it first hand. The scenic method also permits the reader to use his imagination and intellect to discover the meaning of events and talk. Most stories rely on a careful mixture of both techniques. (See our discussion of Joyce Carol Oates's "Where Are You Going, Where Have You Been.")

PERSONA The character or voice assumed by the writer of a story for the telling of that story. In the novel *The Catcher in the Rye* the author has assumed the persona of an overly sensitive adolescent prep school boy who purports to be telling his adventures to a psychiatrist. The teller of Julio Cortazar's "End of the Game" was a participant in the strange games that she relates. See the discussion, too, of Baldwin's "Going to Meet the Man."

PLOT The interplay and sequence of events in a story artfully arranged so that the author may attain the desired aesthetic or artistic effect. A case history or a chronologically accurate rendering of events would seldom make for a plotted story. A plot, as we explain in the chapter devoted to that term, implies causality.

POINT OF VIEW The aspect or perspective from which any teller sees what he is relating. Edouard Roditi's story, "The Vampires of Istanbul" is written from *many* points of view—each letter writer having his own perception of the situation in Istanbul.

The point of view may be *omniscient,* in which case the teller knows everything, including what the characters think; or it may be *partial* or *limited,* in which case characters' thoughts, for example, may be hidden from the narrator.

There are many more very technical distinctions regarding point of view, for tellers may range in reliability from complete omniscience and truthfulness to total blindness or even intentional duplicity (*wanting* to mislead the reader).

PROPAGANDA   See **DIDACTIC**.

PROTAGONIST   The central character in a drama or story. He or she is frequently in conflict with another main character, an *antagonist*.

REALISM   In the most general sense, a not very useful term to designate the degree to which a story is "true to life." The term is not very helpful because, whereas some stories seem real in the manner in which they focus on both pleasant and unpleasant minutiae of the commonplace (for example, Hughes' "Sunday"), others, though wild and fantastical in the tale they tell, nonetheless have a great deal of psychological or "inner" truth or realism (for example, the stories of Poe or of Cortazar).

SCENE   A more or less self-contained unit or segment of the action in a story or play. The suicide of the young lieutenant in Mishima's "Patriotism" is one scene in that story.

See **NARRATIVE TECHNIQUES** for a discussion of the **SCENE** method of story telling.

SENTIMENTALISM   The representation (or eliciting) of emotion in excess of the amount of emotion warranted by the objective situation. Good writers of our time let readers infer the nature of a character or his emotions from his words and actions. They don't bully the reader with sentimental renderings. For the opposite of sentimentalism, see the one sentence description of Michael Turrell's death in Kipling's story "The Gardener" (p.429). (If one needs a term for Kipling's "opposite of sentimentalism" one might call it "sardonic understatement.")

SETTING   The place where the story occurs. The opening setting for Hardy's "The Three Strangers" is in a lonely cottage on a grassy down. Often the setting furthers the mood, and even the meaning, of the story. The loneliness of Hardy's setting heightens the fugitive's solitary plight. The orderliness and the decorum of the setting for Mishima's story heightens the sense we are given of the ritualistic and religious significance of the sacrifice of the two protagonists.

STOCK CHARACTERS   Characters of one dimension, literary clichés, without the complexities and ambiguities that we know people have in real life. The "good cowboy" and the "bad Indian" of the old style Western pictures were stock characters. Humphrey Bogart created for himself a role which he repeated so often that it became a stock character—the "tough guy with the soft heart." Other stock characters: the prostitute with the heart of gold, the dumb blonde, the tough first sergeant who will go through hell for his men.

STREAM OF CONSCIOUSNESS   An attempt to render the thoughts of a character just as they occur in his mind, with all the strange jumps and lapses that characterize actual thinking processes. James Joyce and William Faulkner are recognized masters of this narrative device, though its use can be found as early as the eighteenth century in England.

STRUCTURE The "shape" of a story and the arrangement of its elements. Part of the structure of "Goldilocks and the Three Bears" is that the same thing happens three times: first the largest, then the middle-sized, then the littlest bear asks "Who has been sleeping in my bed?" A second part of the structure of that tale is the increasing tension, the fact that with each bear's question, the suspense rises and we approach a climax or resolution. The structure of that nursery tale then includes the repetition of the same element three times, all in a pattern of rising action or increased tension.

STYLE The effect attained by an author through the purposeful selection of words (diction) and sentence structures (syntax).

The first sentence of a Hemingway novel reads, "Robert Cohn was once middleweight boxing champion of Princeton" (Ernest Hemingway, *The Sun Also Rises.* © 1926 Charles Scribner's Sons). This is a simple declarative sentence in the active voice, having a tangible subject and a copulative verb. Except that the verb is in the past tense, there is not a single element in the sentence that is not perfectly clear, present, and straightforward. Nothing in the sentence is subordinate or contingent on anything else. It is almost as simple as saying "This is a plow."

"The Prince had always liked his London, when it had come to him; he was one of the modern Romans who find by the Thames a more convincing image of the truth of the ancient state than any they have left by the Tiber" (Henry James, *The Golden Bowl.* © 1937 Charles Scribner's Sons). So reads the first sentence of a novel by Henry James.

In contrast to the Hemingway sentence, the one by James, with its subordinate structures ("when it had come to him"), its eliptical reference ("liked *his* London"), its neat balance on either side of the semicolon, the second clause obliquely (that is, in an indirect and difficult way) shedding some light on the first clause, and its abstract concepts ("convincing image of the truth ... ") is an infinitely complex and intricate one. We may say that James's style is complex, involved, indirect, difficult, tentative, etc. Of Hemingway's style, we may say it is simple and direct.

These are merely a few of the elements of style. Everything, from punctuation to spelling to sentence structure, contributes to an author's style.

SYMBOL A word or phrase or image (sign) that stands for a larger idea. We have divided symbols into three types: *natural symbols, conventional symbols,* and *private symbols.* A *natural symbol* is a word or image that suggests its larger meaning to the reader without the reader having to be instructed in that meaning. The image of a journey, to stand for life, may be a natural symbol. A *conventional symbol* is an image that has, by tradition and by certain people in the course of time and in a limited space, been assigned a meaning beyond itself. The cross or the star of David could be considered conventional symbols. Finally, a *private symbol* is one that one author, or perhaps a small group of writers or artists, has made his own conventional symbol. The scissors in Kafka's story "Jackals and Arabs" is a private symbol.

Glossary of Terms

THEME The controlling idea that informs the work. It must not be confused with the "moral," or the "message." Nor is it the "meaning," precisely. Rather, theme helps to establish meaning. Theme is what the story signifies. Unfortunately "theme" is so difficult to define that one must resort to illustration. The theme of the Book of Ruth has something to do with lovingness, decorum, consideration (but it is not "be good to outcast kinfolk"!) The theme of Mishima's story "Patriotism" is largely given in the title itself.

One cannot really draw a moral from Mishima's story, but one may say it is pervaded by feelings of custom, ritual, rightness, nobility, and—as we have suggested in the text—a slight note of hysteria. Its theme must have something to do with control, tradition, ritual, love, and patriotism.

TONE A term referring to an author's *attitude toward* his subject or audience. The tone helps to define the attitude toward his subject. We use the term "tone" frequently, as in the expression "tone of voice," and we may well imagine a "friendly" tone, a "harsh" tone. By the selection of incidents an author chooses to focus on, or to omit, an author helps establish his tone. Such a tone might be contemptuous or admiring of his subject, and likewise, it might be contemptuous or admiring (or any number of other attitudes) of his audience. We have spoken of the tone of "civilized consideration" achieved in the Book of Ruth, a story which, if told with another attitude, could be a sordid story of the horrors of famine.

VERSIMILITUDE A term which, when used in a literary context, means trueness to life. However, the concept is an elusive one for all the reasons that the term "Realism" (Glossary) is an unsatisfactory one too. A horrendous and implausible story by Edgar Allen Poe may have a good deal of versimilitude in the depiction of the thought processes of the character who is in the implausible situation.